BASIC VOCABULARY

英文字彙王

基礎 單字 2000

Levels 1 & 2

序

　　本系列套書依據大學入學考試中心於 109 年 7 月頒布之「高中英文參考詞彙表」重新編修，將原先的單字依使用者文化背景、日常用語及教學層面高頻用字考量，去除詞頻低、口語型詞彙及部分縮寫字與專有名詞等，將單字以**使用頻率**適度排序，另增補學習必備、各類考試重要字詞，除自學外，也適用**學測**、**高中英語聽力測驗**、**全民英檢初級**、**新制多益普及**……等考試。

　　內容方面，每單元單字除提供 K.K. 音標、詞性、實用例句、中文解釋外，亦嚴選補充該單字重要的**片語**、**衍生字**、**近似字**、**反義字**、**比較用字**、**延伸用法**及**文法說明**等，讓讀者在日常英語閱讀、聆聽、口說、寫作能力養成上，都能靈活運用這些字詞。

　　音檔設計上，我們特請專業美籍老師朗讀單字及例句，且為了結合科技、響應環保，全書採用 "**QR Code**"，讀者可依使用習慣，自由選擇聆聽**分頁式音檔**或**一次完整下載音檔**，邊聽邊朗讀單字及例句，可大幅改善發音並增進口語能力。

　　本系列《英語字彙王》套書，依單字難易程度分為基礎單字 2000 (Levels 1 & 2)、核心單字 4000 (Levels 3 & 4)、進階單字 6000 (Levels 5 & 6) 三套書，方便讀者循序漸進規劃學習。祝各位學習成功！

使用說明

每 1 ～ 2 頁皆有 QR Code 可下載該頁音檔分段學習，另有一個單元一個完整音檔，皆可於小書名頁掃描 QR Code 下載。

單字背熟後，可在框內打勾。

 ◀)) 0412-0418

12　star [star] *n.* 恆星；明星 & *vi.* 主演 & *vt.* 由……主演

三 star, starred [stɑrd], starred

片 (1) a shooting star　流星
　　(2) a pop / movie star
　　　　流行 / 電影明星
　　(3) star in...　主演……

衍 superstar [ˋsupɚˏstar] *n.* 超級巨星

似 celebrity [səˋlɛbrətɪ] *n.* 名人 ⑤

▶ The Sun is the closest star to Earth.
　太陽是距離地球最近的恆星。

▶ When Reggie looked up, he saw a shooting star.
　雷吉往上看時，看到一顆流星。

▶ Hal's favorite movie star is Lily Collins.
　海爾最喜歡的影星是莉莉·柯林斯。

▶ Lady Gaga starred in *A Star is Born*.
　女神卡卡主演《一個巨星的誕生》。

補充單字的難度級數

與單字相關的重要片語、衍生字、近似字、反義字、比較用字、延伸用法及文法說明等補充。

代號說明

三 動詞三態

複 名詞的複數形

片 片語

衍 衍生字

似 近似字（含形音義）

比 多個近似字比較說明

反 反義字

用法 重要文法說明

延伸 相關補充

[美] 美式英語

[英] 英式英語

索　引

A	
ability	214 → 頁數
able	81
about	40
above	91
abroad	209
absence	379
absent	379
accept	245
accident	235

目　錄

Level ❶

Unit 01 → 1	Unit 11 → 97	Unit 21 → 180
Unit 02 → 11	Unit 12 → 107	Unit 22 → 188
Unit 03 → 21	Unit 13 → 116	Unit 23 → 197
Unit 04 → 30	Unit 14 → 124	Unit 24 → 206
Unit 05 → 38	Unit 15 → 133	Unit 25 → 214
Unit 06 → 48	Unit 16 → 142	
Unit 07 → 59	Unit 17 → 150	
Unit 08 → 69	Unit 18 → 159	
Unit 09 → 78	Unit 19 → 166	
Unit 10 → 88	Unit 20 → 173	

Level ❷

Unit 26 → 225	Unit 36 → 318	Unit 46 → 409
Unit 27 → 234	Unit 37 → 327	Unit 47 → 418
Unit 28 → 243	Unit 38 → 336	Unit 48 → 427
Unit 29 → 253	Unit 39 → 345	Unit 49 → 436
Unit 30 → 262	Unit 40 → 354	Unit 50 → 446
Unit 31 → 271	Unit 41 → 363	索　引 → 457
Unit 32 → 281	Unit 42 → 372	附　錄 → 476
Unit 33 → 290	Unit 43 → 381	
Unit 34 → 300	Unit 44 → 390	
Unit 35 → 309	Unit 45 → 400	

| Level ❶ |

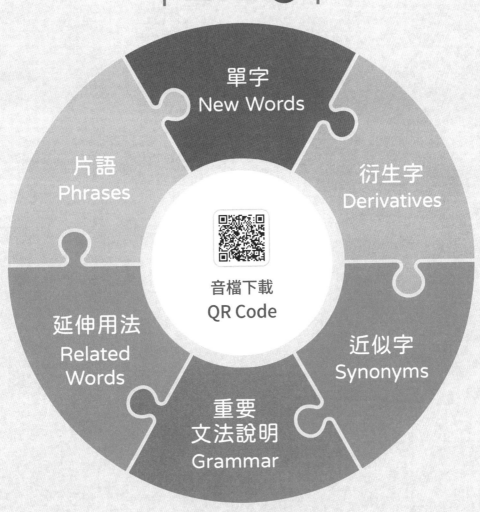

單字
New Words

衍生字
Derivatives

片語
Phrases

音檔下載
QR Code

近似字
Synonyms

延伸用法
Related
Words

重要
文法說明
Grammar

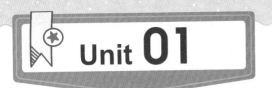

Unit 01

0101-0103

1　boy [bɔɪ] *n.* 男孩；兒子

片 (1) a young / little boy　小男孩
　(2) a mama's boy　媽寶

衍 boyhood [ˋbɔɪhʊd] *n.* (男性的) 童年

似 son [sʌn] *n.* 兒子 ①

▶ Karen thought the boy was rude for yelling at her.
凱倫覺得那位男孩對她大吼很無禮。

▶ When Raymond was a young boy, he wanted to be a doctor.
雷蒙小時候想要成為一名醫生。

▶ Ken is a mama's boy who can't make a decision on his own.
肯是一個無法自己做決定的媽寶。

---

girl [gɝl] *n.* 女孩；女兒

片 a young / little girl　小女孩

衍 girlhood [ˋgɝlhʊd] *n.* (女性的) 童年

似 daughter [ˋdɔtɚ] *n.* 女兒 ①

▶ At the age of 35, Arlene hates to be called a "girl."
亞琳 35 歲了，很討厭被稱作『女孩』。

▶ Lisa and Tom have four girls but no sons.
麗莎和湯姆有四名女兒，但沒有兒子。

2　man [mæn] *n.* (成年) 男子；人；人類 (此意不可數) & *vt.* 看管，操作

複 men [mɛn]

三 man, manned [mænd], manned

衍 mankind [ˋmænˏkaɪnd]
　n. 人類 (不可數) ③

似 (1) male [mel] *n.* 男子 & *a.* 男性的 ②
　(2) person [ˋpɝsn] *n.* 人 ①
　(3) human [ˋhjumən] *n.* 人 ②
　(4) human being　人，人類

用法 man 表『人類』時為總稱，僅用單數，且不加冠詞。

▶ Everyone agrees that Liam is a nice man.
大家都同意連恩是個好男人。

▶ It is every man's right to be free.
自由是每一個人的權利。

▶ Man is the cleverest creature on earth.
人類是地球上最聰明的生物。

▶ George was the only one who knew how to man the equipment.
喬治是唯一知道如何操作這個設備的人。

---

woman [ˋwʊmən] *n.* (成年) 女子

複 women [ˋwɪmɪn / ˋwɪmən]

似 female [ˋfimel] *n.* 女子 & *a.* 女性的 ②

▶ Robert thought Donna was the most beautiful woman he'd ever seen.
羅伯特認為唐娜是他所見過最美的女子。

3　go [go] *vi.* 走；去；從事 (活動)；離開；變成；進行 & *n.* 嘗試

三 go, went [wɛnt], gone [gɔn]

片 (1) go up / down (the) stairs
　　走上 / 下樓梯

　(2) go to + 地方　去某地

　(3) go on a trip / tour　去旅行

▶ Julia went down the stairs instead of taking the elevator.
茱麗亞走下樓梯，而沒有搭電梯。
*elevator [ˋɛləˏvetɚ] *n.* 電梯

▶ Roger went to the bakery to buy some bread.
羅傑去麵包店買些麵包。

(4) go for a walk / drive
去散步 / 開車兜風

(5) go well / badly
進行地很順利 / 不順利

(6) have a go (at + N/V-ing)
嘗試 (……)

用法 (1) go 表『從事』時，可以用 go + V-ing
表從事某活動，且大多是指戶外的
活動，例：
go hiking / surfing / skiing /
camping / shopping
去健行 / 衝浪 / 滑雪 / 露營 / 血拼

(2) go 作連綴動詞表『變成』時，其後
須加形容詞作主詞補語。
go + adj.　　變得……
go bad / sour　（食物）腐敗

▶ Owen likes to go camping on weekends.
歐文週末時喜歡去露營。

▶ James went on a long trip to Canada.
詹姆士去加拿大長途旅行。

▶ Lucy likes to go for a walk after dinner.
露西吃過晚餐後喜歡去散步。

▶ Derrick asked his wife if she was ready to go yet.
德瑞克問他太太是否準備好出發了。

▶ The milk has gone sour.
牛奶變酸了。

▶ Everything is going well here.
這裡一切都進行得很順利。

▶ I'll have a go at fixing the machine myself.
我想試試看自己修那臺機器。

4　bag [bæg] n. 袋子，提袋

片 (1) a shopping / plastic / paper
bag　購物袋 / 塑膠袋 / 紙袋

(2) a bag of apples　一袋蘋果

衍 handbag [ˋhænd͵bæg] n. 手提袋

▶ Josephine brought a shopping bag with her to the supermarket.
喬瑟芬帶了一個購物袋去超市。

▶ The heavy bottles fell through the bottom of the plastic bag.
沉重的瓶子從塑膠袋底部掉出來。

5　cake [kek] n. (一整個) 蛋糕

片 (1) a chocolate / strawberry cake
巧克力 / 草莓蛋糕

(2) a birthday / wedding cake
生日 / 結婚蛋糕

(3) a slice of cake　一片蛋糕

(4) make / bake a cake　做 / 烤蛋糕

(5) be a piece of cake
很簡單的事情

▶ Tony bought a big chocolate birthday cake for his girlfriend.
東尼買了一個巧克力口味的大生日蛋糕給他女友。

▶ Evelyn's mother taught her how to make a delicious cake.
艾芙琳的媽媽教她做美味的蛋糕。

▶ Most of the students thought the test was a piece of cake.
大部分學生覺得這個考試很簡單。

6　long [lɔŋ] a. (時間、距離、長度等) 長的 & adv. (時間) 長地；(時間) 整個地 & vi. 渴望

片 (1) long time no see　好久不見

(2) long to V　渴望做……

(3) long for sth　渴望得到某事物

▶ Josh saw a long movie yesterday.
喬許昨天看了一部很長的電影。

▶ Your hair is too long; you need to have it cut.
你頭髮太長，需要剪了。

衍 (1) long-term [`lɔŋ,tɝm] *a.* 長期的
(2) length [lɛŋθ] *n.* 長度 ②

▶ Their fight didn't last long—only ten minutes.
他們的爭吵沒有持續很久 —— 僅 10 分鐘而已。

▶ Sharon's baby cried all night long last night.
雪倫的寶寶昨晚哭了整晚。

▶ I long to have a chance to talk to Mandy.
= I long for a chance to talk to Mandy.
我渴望有機會跟曼蒂說話。

---

short [ʃɔrt]
a. (時間、距離、長度等) 短的；(身高)
矮的；缺乏的；縮寫的 & *adv.* 突然地

片 (1) be short of / on sth
　　某物短缺 / 不足
　(2) be short for...
　　是……的縮寫 / 簡稱
　(3) in short　簡言之，總之

衍 (1) shorts [ʃɔrts] *n.* 短褲 (恆用複數) ①
　(2) shortly [`ʃɔrtlɪ] *adv.* 不久，立刻 ③
　(3) shortage [`ʃɔrtɪdʒ] *n.* 短缺 ⑤

似 suddenly [`sʌdn̩lɪ] *adv.* 突然

▶ Winter is coming, and the days are getting shorter.
冬天來了，白晝越來越短。

▶ I'm too short to reach the top of the shelf.
我太矮了，碰不到架子最上層。

▶ Since Ben was a bit short on time, he had to hurry.
由於班的時間不多，他動作得快一點。

▶ "Info" is short for "information."
『info』是『information』的縮寫。

▶ The man stopped short and walked back.
這名男子突然停下來並往回走。

▶ In short, smoking does harm to your health.
簡言之，抽菸有害健康。

7　**city** [`sɪtɪ] *n.* 城市

反 country [`kʌntrɪ] *n.* 鄉村，鄉下 ①

▶ There are over three million people living in the city.
有超過 300 萬人住在這座城市。

8　**head** [hɛd] *n.* 頭；頭腦；領導人 & *vi.* 前往 & *vt.* 率領，主管

片 (1) nod /shake one's head
　　點 / 搖頭
　(2) in one's head　在某人腦中
　(3) the head of...　……的領導人
　(4) keep one's head　保持冷靜
　(5) lose one's head　失去冷靜
　(6) head for / toward + 地方
　　前往某地

▶ Trevor nodded his head while Bart talked to him.
崔佛在巴特和他說話時點頭。

▶ Robert has many thoughts in his head.
羅伯特腦中有很多想法。

▶ Who is the head of this department?
誰是這個部門的主管？

▶ Whatever happens, keep your head. Don't lose your head.
不管發生什麼事，你都得保持冷靜，別亂了方寸。

▶ Let's head for the beach this weekend.
我們這週末去海邊吧！

▶ Mr. Thomas heads a department of 55 people.
湯瑪斯先生管理一個有 55 個人的部門。

face [fes] *n.* 臉，面孔；人；(物體的) 表面 & *vt.* 面對；朝向

🔑 (1) a happy / sad / poker face
   開心的臉 / 難過的臉 / 撲克臉
   (2) lose face　　　　丟臉
   (3) in the face of...　面對……
   (4) be faced with...　面對……
   = face...

▶ Although Jane was sad, she tried to put on a happy face.
   儘管珍很難過，她仍裝出一個笑臉。
   ＊put on...　裝出……

▶ Kelly knew some of the faces at the party.
   凱莉認得派對上的一些面孔。

▶ The southern face of Grant's house gets the most sun.
   葛蘭特家的南面晒到最多太陽。

▶ David lost face when his friends found out he had lied.
   大衛在他朋友發現他說謊時感到很丟臉。

▶ What would you do in the face of such a problem?
   面臨這樣的問題時，你會怎麼辦？

▶ Stay calm when you face a problem.
= Stay calm when you're faced with a problem.
   面對問題時要保持冷靜。

▶ Please give me a room that faces the sea.
   請給我一個面海的房間。

9　book [bʊk] *n.* 書 & *vt.* & *vi.* 預訂

🔑 (1) hit the books　用功讀書
   (2) book a table / room　訂位 / 房
   (3) be fully booked (up)　預訂滿了
衍 (1) bookstore [ˈbʊkˌstɔr] *n.* 書店 ②
   (2) bookcase [ˈbʊkˌkes] *n.* 書櫃 ③

▶ I have to hit the books tonight, so I can't go to the movies with you.
   我今晚必須用功讀書，因此沒辦法跟你去看電影。

▶ I'd like to book a room for three nights, please.
   我想訂房住 3 晚。

▶ The restaurant was fully booked, so Tammy couldn't make a reservation.
   這間餐廳被訂滿了，所以譚美沒辦法訂位。
   ＊reservation [ˌrɛzəˈveʃən] *n.* 預訂

---

library [ˈlaɪˌbrɛrɪ] *n.* 圖書館

複 libraries [ˈlaɪˌbrɛrɪz]
🔑 (1) go to the library　去圖書館
   (2) a school library　學校圖書館

▶ Thomas went to the library to borrow some books.
   湯瑪斯去圖書館借了幾本書。

10　open [ˈopən] *a.* 打開的；營業的 & *vt.* & *vi.* 打開；營業；開始

🔑 be open to...　對……開放
似 (1) begin [bɪˈgɪn] *vt.* & *vi.* 開始 ①
   (2) start [stɑrt] *vt.* & *vi.* 開始 ①

▶ The window is wide open.
   這扇窗戶是敞開著的。

▶ The store is not open today.
   這家商店今天沒有營業。

▶ The library is open to the public.
   這座圖書館是對大眾開放的。

▶ It was hot in the room, so Jason opened a window.
房間裡很熱，所以傑森把一扇窗戶打開。

▶ That store opens at eight in the morning and closes at ten at night.
那家店早上 8 點營業，晚上 10 點打烊。

▶ The manager opened the meeting with a speech.
經理以一席話展開了會議。

---

close [klos] *a.* 接近的；親近的 & *adv.* 靠近地 & [kloz] *vt.* & *vi.* 關上；結束營業；結束 & *n.* 結束

🔒 (1) be close to...　接近 / 靠近……
(2) a close friend　親近的朋友
(3) come close to + N/V-ing
　　差一點……
(4) close with...　以……作為結尾
(5) come to a close　結束

似 (1) shut [ʃʌt] *vt.* & *vi.* 關上 ②
(2) end [ɛnd] *vt.* & *vi.* & *n.* 結束 ①

▶ Tina's home is close to a big park.
蒂娜的家鄰近一座大公園。

▶ Bill is a close friend of mine.
比爾是我一個很親近的朋友。

▶ We came close to winning the contest.
我們差一點就贏了這場比賽。

▶ It started to rain, so I closed all the windows.
開始下雨了，所以我關上所有的窗戶。

▶ They closed the store due to poor sales.
由於生意清淡，他們結束了那家店。

▶ The movie closed with the woman falling in love and moving to New York.
電影結尾時，那名女子墜入情網並搬到紐約。

▶ They left the gym before the close of the game.
比賽結束前，他們就離開了體育館。

11　also [ˈɔlso] *adv.* 也，而且

似 (1) too [tu] *adv.* 也，而且
(2) in addition　此外

▶ Sharon is a businesswoman and also a mother of three children.
= Sharon is a businesswoman and a mother of three children, too.
雪倫是女企業家，也是 3 個小孩的母親。
＊businesswoman [ˈbɪzɪnəsˌwʊmən] *n.* 女企業家

12　arm [ɑrm] *n.* 手臂 & *vt.* 使武裝

🔒 (1) with (one's) open arms
　　張開 (某人的) 雙臂歡迎
(2) arm sb with sth
　　為某人提供某武器裝備

▶ There is a cut on my arm.
我的手臂上有一道傷口。

▶ Mr. Johnson welcomed me with open arms.
強森先生張開雙臂歡迎我。

▶ The general armed his troops with sophisticated weapons.
這名將軍用精良的武器裝備他的部隊。
＊sophisticated [səˈfɪstəˌketɪd] *a.* 精密的

leg [lɛg] *n.* 腿；(桌、椅的) 腳
🔒 a table / chair leg　桌 / 椅腳
Ⓢ lag [læg] *vi.* 落後 & *n.* 時間差，間歇 ④

▶ Susan hurt her leg when she went jogging.
　蘇珊慢跑時傷到腿。
▶ We're going to throw that table away because one of the legs is broken.
　我們要丟掉那張桌子，因為其中一隻桌腳斷了。

knee [ni] *n.* 膝蓋 & *vt.* 用膝蓋撞
🔒 (1) sit on sb's knee(s)
　　坐在某人的膝蓋 / 腿上
　(2) get down on one's knees
　　跪下
　= fall to one's knees
Ⓔ kneel [nil] *vi.* 跪，跪下 ④

▶ As Harry gets older, he's having more problems with his knees.
　隨著哈利年歲漸增，他膝蓋的問題也變多了。
▶ The little girl sat on her dad's knee.
　小女孩坐在她爸爸的膝蓋上。
▶ The thief got down on his knees and begged the victim for forgiveness.
= The thief fell to his knees and begged the victim for forgiveness.
　小偷跪下來求受害者原諒。
▶ Sean accidentally kneed Rodney in the face.
　尚恩不小心用膝蓋撞到羅德尼的臉。
　*accidentally [ˌæksəˈdɛntḷɪ] *adv.* 無意間

13 nose [noz] *n.* 鼻子

🔒 (1) have a runny nose　流鼻水 / 涕
　(2) blow / wipe one's nose
　　擤 / 擦鼻涕
　(3) pick one's nose　挖鼻孔

▶ Do you have a runny nose?
　你流鼻水了嗎？
▶ The little boy wiped his nose with a handkerchief.
　小男孩用一條手帕擦鼻涕。
　*handkerchief [ˈhæŋkɚˌtʃɪf] *n.* 手帕
▶ The mother told her child not to pick his nose in public.
　這位媽媽告訴她的小孩不要在公眾場合挖鼻孔。

eye [aɪ] *n.* 眼睛
🔒 (1) have an eye for...
　　對……有眼光 / 鑑賞力
　(2) keep an eye on...
　　留意 / 照看……

▶ Louise felt sad, and there were tears in her eyes.
　露易絲很傷心，她的眼裡有淚水。
▶ Nancy always looks great because she has an eye for fashion.
　南希看起來總是很亮眼，因為她對時尚很有眼光。
▶ Trevor asked his brother to keep an eye on his backpack.
　崔佛請他弟弟幫忙留意他的背包。

ear [ɪr] *n.* 耳朵
🔒 be all ears　洗耳恭聽

▶ Some people wear hats in winter so their ears don't get cold.
　有些人會在冬天戴帽子，讓他們的耳朵不會受凍。

> Paul was all ears when Sherry talked about herself.
> 雪莉講述自己的事情時，保羅全神貫注地聽。

14　buy [baɪ] *vt.* & *vi.* & *n.* 購買 & *vt.* 相信

三 buy, bought [bɔt], bought

複 buys [baɪz]

片 (1) buy sb sth　買某物給某人
　 = buy sth for sb
　 (2) a good buy
　　　 值得入手 / 購買的東西

似 (1) purchase [ˋpɝtʃəs]
　　 vt. & *n.* 購買 ⑤
　 (2) believe [bəˋliv] *vt.* 相信 ①

> Lori bought her mother an expensive purse.
> = Lori bought an expensive purse for her mother.
> 蘿蕊買了一個昂貴的錢包給她媽媽。

> When housing prices fall, it is a good time to buy.
> 房價下跌時，就是購屋的好時機。

> The salesman told Sally that the stock was a good buy now.
> 業務告訴莎莉現在這支股票很值得入手。

> Tim didn't buy Charlie's excuse for being late.
> 提姆不相信查理遲到的藉口。

---

sell [sɛl] *vt.* & *vi.* 賣，銷售

三 sell, sold [sold], sold

片 sell sb sth　把某物賣給某人
　 = sell sth to sb

> Martin sold Jerry his old cellphone at a cheap price.
> = Martin sold his old cellphone to Jerry at a cheap price.
> 馬丁以便宜的價格把他的舊手機賣給傑瑞。

15　bad [bæd] *a.* 壞的，不好的；很差的；餿掉的

片 (1) be in a bad mood　心情不好
　 (2) be bad at + N/V-ing　不擅長……
　 (3) go bad　腐壞，餿掉

> The rain has had a very bad effect on the crops.
> 那場雨對農作物造成了不好的影響。

> Don't talk to Bill when he's in a bad mood.
> 別在比爾心情不好時跟他說話。

> Kevin is really bad at math.
> 凱文的數學真的很差。

> The milk will go bad if you leave it outside too long.
> 如果你把牛奶放在外面太久的話會壞掉。

16　duck [dʌk] *n.* 鴨子 & *vt.* & *vi.* (突然) 低頭 / 彎腰 (以躲避……)

片 duck down　低頭，彎腰

> Ducks were swimming peacefully in the pond.
> 鴨子在池塘裡悠閒地划著水。

> The tall man had to duck his head when he walked through the door.
> 那位高個兒的男子走過這扇門時得把頭低下來。

> I ducked down when Tom threw a ball at me.
> 湯姆朝我丟球時，我低頭閃開了。

chicken [ˈtʃɪkən]
n. 雞（可數）；雞肉（不可數）

H (1) chicken soup　雞湯
　 (2) fried chicken　炸雞
似 (1) hen [hɛn] *n.* 母雞 ①
　 (2) cock [kɑk] *n.* 公雞 ③

▶ The farmer owns many chickens and sells eggs to customers.
這位農場主人有很多雞，並販售雞蛋給顧客。

▶ Gordon hates pork and beef, but he eats a lot of chicken.
高登討厭豬肉和牛肉，不過他吃很多雞肉。

17　game [gem] *n.* 遊戲；比賽；（比賽中的）一局

H (1) a card / board / video game
　　　紙牌遊戲 / 桌遊 / 電玩
　 (2) a basketball / baseball game
　　　籃球 / 棒球比賽
似 match [mætʃ] *n.* 比賽 ②

▶ Poker is a card game that people around the world play.
撲克牌是一種全世界的人都會玩的紙牌遊戲。

▶ Ian and his friends watched the basketball game on TV.
伊恩和他的朋友看電視上的籃球比賽。

▶ Kathy's team was unhappy because they lost the first game.
凱西的隊伍不開心，因為他們輸了第一局。

18　enough [ɪˈnʌf] *adv.* 足夠地；很，十分 & *a.* 足夠的 & *pron.* 足夠，充分

H (1) be + adj. + enough to V
　　　夠……到能做……
　 (2) can't get enough of...
　　　（因喜愛而）對……永遠不嫌多

▶ Yesterday, it was hot enough to fry an egg on the street.
昨天的天氣夠熱到能在街上煎蛋了。

▶ Greg is rich, but strangely enough, he isn't happy.
葛瑞格很有錢，但很奇怪的是，他並不快樂。

▶ Tanya didn't have enough water on the hike, so she was thirsty.
譚雅健行沒有帶夠水，所以她很渴。

▶ Ron wants a job that pays him enough to live comfortably.
榮恩想要一份可以給他足夠所需而又能舒適生活的工作。

▶ Joy can't get enough of Hello Kitty items.
對喬伊來說，凱蒂貓的東西永遠不嫌多。

19　smile [smaɪl] *n.* & *vi.* 微笑

H (1) wear a smile　帶著笑容
　 = have a smile on sb's face
　 (2) give sb a smile　對某人微笑
　 (3) smile at...　對……微笑

▶ Claire always wears a smile.
= Claire always has a smile on her face.
克萊兒總是面帶微笑。

▶ The baby girl gave her nanny a smile.
= The baby girl smiled at her nanny.
小女嬰對她的保姆微笑。
＊nanny [ˈnænɪ] *n.* 保姆

laugh [læf] *vi.* & *n.* 笑

搭 (1) laugh at...　對……笑；取笑……
　　(2) laugh about...　因……而笑
　　(3) break into a laugh　突然大笑起來
　　= burst out laughing
　　= break / burst into laughter
衍 laughter [ˋlæftɚ] *n.* 笑聲 (不可數) ③

▶ Ginny laughed at the ridiculous story that Dan told her.
　金妮因丹告訴她的愚蠢故事而笑了出來。
▶ Don't laugh at Joe just because he is fat.
　不要因為喬很胖就取笑他。
▶ I'd like to know what you are laughing about.
　我想知道你因什麼事情而笑。
▶ After a short silence, Harry broke into a laugh.
= After a short silence, Harry burst out laughing.
= After a short silence, Harry burst into laughter.
　在沉默片刻後，哈利突然大笑起來。

cry [kraɪ] *vi.* 哭 & *vi.* & *vt.* & *n.* 喊叫

變 cry, cried [kraɪd], cried
搭 (1) cry over / about...　因……而哭
　　(2) make sb cry　使某人哭泣
　　(3) cry out for help　大聲求救
　　(4) let out a cry　發出叫聲
　　(5) a cry of pain / delight
　　　疼痛 / 開心地喊叫
似 shout [ʃaʊt] *vi.* & *n.* 喊叫 ①

▶ The baby is crying loudly because she's hungry.
　小嬰兒因肚子餓而哇哇大哭。
▶ It's no use crying over spilt milk.
　為了打翻的牛奶而哭沒有用 / 覆水難收。── 諺語。
▶ The sad movie made many people cry.
　這部悲傷的電影讓許多人哭了。
▶ The soldier cried out for help.
　那名士兵大聲求救。
▶ "I've found my purse!" cried Anna.
　安娜大叫說：『我找到手提包了！』
▶ Sandy let out a cry of pain when she was hit.
　珊蒂被打到時，發出疼痛的叫聲。

20　kid [kɪd] *n.* 小孩 (口語) & *vt.* & *vi.* 開玩笑

變 kid, kidded [ˋkɪdɪd], kidded
搭 kid sb　開某人的玩笑
似 child [tʃaɪld] *n.* 小孩 ①

▶ After her husband left, Addison raised her three kids alone.
　自從她先生離開後，艾蒂森獨自撫養 3 個孩子。
▶ I'm not kidding you! I really won the lottery!
　我沒有跟你開玩笑！我真的中樂透了！
　*lottery [ˋlɑtərɪ] *n.* 樂透
▶ Don't be so serious. I was just kidding.
　別那麼認真，我不過是在開玩笑。

baby [ˋbebɪ]
n. 嬰兒；(對另一半的稱呼) 寶貝

複 babies [ˋbebɪz]

▶ After she had a baby, Maggie took several months off work.
　梅姬生小孩後，工作請假了好幾個月。

片 (1) have a baby　生小孩
　　(2) be expecting a baby　懷孕
　　(3) a baby boy / girl　男／女嬰
似 infant [`ɪnfənt] *n.* 嬰兒 ④

▸ Wanda is expecting a baby, which is due in April.
汪達懷孕了，預產期在 4 月。
＊due [d(j)u] *a.* 預期的

21　pig [pɪg] *n.* 豬

延伸 (1) ham [hæm] *n.* 火腿 ①
　　(2) pork [pɔrk] *n.* 豬肉 ②
　　(3) bacon [`bekən] *n.* 培根 ③

▸ In fact, pigs are very clever and like to be clean.
事實上，豬很聰明，也愛乾淨。
＊clever [`klɛvɚ] *a.* 聰明的

22　body [`bɑdɪ] *n.* 身體

複 bodies [`bɑdɪz]
片 (1) body temperature　　體溫
　　(2) body language　　　肢體語言

▸ Harriet wasn't happy with her body, so she decided to lose weight.
哈莉特不滿意自己的身體，因此決定減重。
＊lose weight [wet]　減重

▸ Companies often take people's body temperature because of COVID-19.
由於新冠肺炎，各公司經常量大家的體溫。

23　dance [dæns] *n.* 舞蹈；跳舞；舞會 & *vi.* & *vt.* 跳舞

片 (1) a traditional / folk dance
　　　傳統／民俗舞蹈
　　(2) save a dance for sb　和某人跳舞
　　(3) ask sb to a dance　邀某人去舞會
衍 (1) dancer [`dænsɚ] *n.* 舞者 ②
　　(2) dancing [`dænsɪŋ] *n.* 跳舞
似 ball [bɔl] *n.* 舞會 ①

▸ There are many different dances, such as the twist.
有許多不同種類的舞蹈，例如扭扭舞。

▸ Quentin asked Lucy to save the last dance for him.
昆丁請露西和他跳最後一支舞。

▸ Gilbert asked Helen to the dance, but she told him no.
吉爾伯特邀海倫去舞會，但她拒絕了他。

▸ Fred doesn't like to dance, which bothers his girlfriend.
佛萊德不喜歡跳舞，這點讓他女友很困擾。
＊bother [`bɑðɚ] *vt.* 使苦惱

▸ Victor never learned how to dance the tango.
維克多從未學過如何跳探戈舞。
＊tango [`tæŋgo] *n.* 探戈舞

Unit 02

0201-0202

1 **hand** [hænd] *n.* 手 & *vt.* 遞給

片 (1) shake sb's hand　與某人握手
(2) give sb a hand (with sth)
　　幫助某人 (抬 / 拿某物)
(3) hand sb sth　把某物遞給某人
　= hand sth to sb
(4) hand in sth / hand sth in
　　交出某物
(5) hand down sth / hand sth
　　down　將某物傳承下來

似 (1) give [gɪv] *vt.* 給 ①
(2) pass [pæs] *vt.* 傳遞 ①

▶ Greg walked up to the manager and shook his hand.
　葛瑞格走向經理並和他握手。
▶ Give me a hand with this box, please.
　請幫我抬這個箱子。
▶ Please hand me the folder that's on the desk.
= Please hand the folder that's on the desk to me.
　請把桌上的文件夾遞給我。
▶ Hand in your paper after class.
= Turn in your paper after class.
　下課後把報告交出來。
▶ The gold necklace has been handed down in my family for generations.
　這條金項鍊已經在我家傳了好幾代。

finger [ˈfɪŋgɚ]
n. 手指 & *vt.* (用手指) 觸摸

片 (1) an index finger　食指
　= forefinger [ˈfɔrˌfɪŋgɚ]
(2) a middle finger　中指
(3) a ring finger　　無名指
(4) a little finger　　小指
(5) keep sb's fingers crossed
　　祈求好運
　= cross sb's fingers

延伸 (1) thumb [θʌm] *n.* 大拇指 ③
(2) nail [nel] *n.* 指甲 ②

▶ Denise nearly cut her finger with the sharp knife.
　狄妮絲的手指差點被這把銳利的刀子割到。
▶ Your ring finger is next to your little finger.
　無名指在你小指的旁邊。
▶ I have a test tomorrow, so keep your fingers crossed for me.
= I have a test tomorrow, so cross your fingers for me.
　我明天要考試，因此替我祈求好運吧。
▶ When Kathy gets nervous, she fingers her necklace.
　凱西緊張時會用手指摸她的項鍊。

2 **foot** [fʊt] *n.* (一隻) 腳；英尺 & *vt.* 支付 (帳單、費用等)

複 feet [fit]
(foot 意思為『英尺』時，複數形寫為
foot 或 feet 皆可，亦可縮寫為 ft)

片 (1) a left / right foot　左 / 右腳
(2) on foot　　走路，步行
(3) foot a bill　　付款

似 pay [pe] *vt.* & *vi.* 付款 ①

▶ Harry's shoes are too small for his feet, so they are uncomfortable.
　哈利的鞋子對他的腳來說太小了，所以穿起來很不舒服。
▶ It takes Vicky 20 minutes to get to school on foot.
　薇琪走路去學校要花 20 分鐘。
▶ The dining table was about eight feet in length.
　這張餐桌的長度大約是 8 英尺。
▶ The boss said he would foot the bill for the staff party.
　老闆說他會替員工派對付款。

toe [to] *n.* 腳趾

(1) a big / little toe　腳拇指 / 小腳趾
(2) step on sb's toes
　　踩到某人的腳趾

▶ Wendy kept stepping on Nick's toes when they danced together.
溫蒂和尼克一起跳舞時，不斷踩到尼克的腳趾。

3　tea [ti] *n.* 茶(飲)；茶葉

(1) a cup of tea　一杯茶
(2) black / green / milk tea
　　紅 / 綠 / 奶茶
(3) be not sb's cup of tea
　　不是某人的菜，不是某人所喜歡的

衍 (1) teapot [ˈtiˌpɑt] *n.* 茶壺 ②
(2) teacup [ˈtiˌkʌp] *n.* 茶杯

▶ Monica read the newspaper while drinking a cup of tea.
莫妮卡邊讀報紙邊喝一杯茶。

▶ Charlene prefers green tea over coffee.
夏琳喜歡綠茶勝過咖啡。

▶ Romantic movies aren't Tom's cup of tea; he prefers action movies.
愛情電影非湯姆所好，他比較喜歡動作片。
＊romantic [roˈmæntɪk] *a.* 浪漫的

4　cow [kaʊ] *n.* 乳牛

(1) a herd of cows　一群牛
(2) milk a cow　擠牛奶

延伸 (1) bull [bʊl] *n.* 公牛 ②
(2) calf [kæf] *n.* 小牛

▶ A herd of cows is eating grass over there.
那裡有一群牛正在吃草。

▶ Can you teach me how to milk a cow?
你能否教我如何擠牛奶？

---

rabbit [ˈræbɪt] *n.* 兔子

延伸 bunny [ˈbʌnɪ] *n.* 小兔子

▶ My brother feeds his rabbits three times a day.
我哥哥一天餵兔子 3 次。

---

elephant [ˈɛləfənt] *n.* 大象

▶ The largest animal on land is the elephant.
大象是陸地上最大的動物。

5　shoe [ʃu] *n.* (一隻) 鞋子

(1) a pair of shoes　一雙鞋子
(2) running shoes　跑步鞋
(3) wear shoes　穿著鞋子
(4) put one's shoes on　穿上鞋子
(5) take off one's shoes　脫下鞋子

▶ When Bill is not working, he likes to wear running shoes.
比爾沒上班時喜歡穿跑步鞋。

▶ Trevor put his shoes on and went to the store.
崔佛穿上鞋子並前往商店。

▶ In Japan, people usually take off their shoes before entering their homes.
在日本，大家通常會在進家裡前把鞋子脫掉。

6　bed [bɛd] *n.* 床

(1) a single / double bed
　　單 / 雙人床
(2) go to bed　去睡覺

▶ Robert found his missing shoe under his bed.
羅伯特在床底下找到他不見的鞋子。

衍 **bedroom** [ˋbɛd͵rʊm]
n. 臥室，房間 ①

似 **bad** [bæd] *a.* 不好的 ①

用法 in bed 和 on the bed 皆表『在床上』，然而 in bed 指的是在床上蓋著毛毯、棉被的狀態；on the bed 則是沒有蓋毛毯、棉被的狀態。

▶ Sam went to bed late last night and is tired today.
山姆昨晚很晚才去睡覺，所以今天很累。

▶ Willa lay in bed with a cold yesterday.
薇拉昨天因感冒躺在床上。

▶ Eric laid his shirt on the bed instead of hanging it up.
艾瑞克把他的襯衫放在床上，而不是掛起來。

---

7 want [wɑnt] *vt.* 想要 & *n.* 需求（常用複數）；缺乏

片 (1) want to V   想要做……
   (2) want sb to V   想要某人做……
   (3) wants and needs   需求
   (4) for (the) want of...
       因為沒有 / 缺乏……

用法 want 作動詞時，不使用進行式：
I am wanting this hat. (✗)
應說：
→ I want this hat. (○)
我想要這頂帽子。

▶ What do you want to do tomorrow?
你明天要做什麼？

▶ Nelly wants her boyfriend to buy her a bouquet of flowers.
納莉想要她男友買一束花給她。
*bouquet [buˋke] *n.* 一束（花）

▶ The hotel promises to look after all our wants and needs.
飯店承諾會照顧到我們所有的需求。
*look after...   照顧 / 看……

▶ This flower is dying for want of water.
這朵花因為缺水快枯死了。

---

8 hot [hɑt] *a.* 熱的；辛辣的；熱門的；暴躁易怒的

片 (1) a hot day   熱天
   (2) hot weather   熱天氣
   (3) a hot song / issue
       熱門歌曲 / 話題
   (4) have a hot temper   脾氣暴躁
似 (1) hat [hæt] *n.* 帽子 ①
   (2) spicy [ˋspaɪsɪ] *a.* 辛辣的 ⑤
   (3) popular [ˋpɑpjələ] *a.* 受歡迎的 ①

▶ The weather's been quite hot recently.
最近的天氣很熱。

▶ Most Korean dishes are hot.
大部分的韓式料理都很辣。

▶ Gal Gadot is one of the hottest actresses in Hollywood.
蓋兒‧加朵是好萊塢最炙手可熱的女演員之一。

▶ David has a hot temper, so nobody wants to work with him.
大衛脾氣暴躁，所以沒人想和他一起工作。

---

cold [kold]
a. 冷的 & *n.* (天氣) 冷，寒冷；感冒

片 (1) a cold day   冷天
   (2) cold weather   冷天氣
   (3) a cold drink   冷飲
   (4) in the cold   在冷天

▶ Patty put on a sweater because of the cold weather.
由於天氣冷，佩蒂把毛衣穿上了。

▶ The poor, wet dog stood all day in the cold.
這隻可憐又溼答答的狗在冷天站了整天。

(5) **catch / get a (bad) cold**
　　得（重）感冒
(6) **have (got) a cold** 感冒

▶ Sharon didn't go to work because she caught a bad cold.
雪倫得了重感冒，所以沒去上班。

似 (1) **cool** [kul] *a.* 涼快的 ①
(2) **chilly** [ˋtʃɪlɪ] *a.* 寒冷的 ③

▶ People should wear masks if they have a cold.
如果感冒了，應該要戴口罩。
*wear a mask　戴口罩

9　high [haɪ] *a.* 高的 & *adv.* (很) 高地 & *n.* 高峰

片 (1) **be high in...**
　　含有豐富／大量的……
　 = **be rich in...**
(2) **reach a new high** 創新高

▶ New York City has many high buildings.
紐約市有很多高樓。

▶ Guavas are high in Vitamin C.
= Guavas are rich in Vitamin C.
芭樂含有豐富的維生素 C。

衍 **highly** [ˋhaɪlɪ] *adv.* 非常；身居高位 ②

似 **tall** [tɔl] *a.* 高的 ①

用法 **high** 作形容詞表『高的』，一般用於形容事物上，若要形容人的身高很高，須用 tall。

▶ A bird is flying high in the sky.
有隻鳥在空中高飛。

▶ House prices in this area reached a new high this year.
這地區的房價今年創新高。

---

low [lo]
a. 低的；(音量、燈光等) 小的；(嗓音) 低沉的；消沉的 & *adv.* (很) 低地 & *n.* 低點

片 (1) **be low in...**　……的含量低
(2) **in low voices**　小聲地
(3) **a low / high voice**　聲音很低／高
(4) **be in a low mood**　心情低落
(5) **reach a new low**　創新低

衍 **lower** [ˋloɚ] *vt.* 降低 ②

似 (1) **short** [ʃɔrt] *a.* 矮的 ①
(2) **sad** [sæd] *a.* 難過的 ①
(3) **unhappy** [ʌnˋhæpɪ] *a.* 不開心的

反 **loud** [laʊd] *a.* 大聲的 ①

▶ The price of the watch is low.
這只手錶的價格很低。

▶ Fruits are usually low in protein.
水果的蛋白質含量通常很低。

▶ The children are talking in low voices.
孩子們正小聲地講話。

▶ Paul has a low voice and cannot sing the high notes.
保羅的聲音低沉，沒辦法唱高音。

▶ Jason was in a low mood because he failed the math test.
傑森數學考試不及格，所以心情低落。

▶ The worker bent low to check the machine.
這名工人低下身來去檢查機器。

▶ The pound has reached a new low against the dollar.
英鎊兌美元的匯率創新低。

10　stop [stɑp] *vt.* & *vi.* & *n.* 停止 & *vt.* 阻止 & *vi.* (短暫) 逗留 & *n.* 站牌

三 **stop, stopped** [stɑpt], **stopped**

▶ Gavin stopped to talk to me.
蓋文停下來跟我說話。

片 (1) stop to V
　　停下原本的動作並開始做……
(2) stop + V-ing
　　停止做（目前正在做的事）……
(3) come to a stop　停下來，中止
(4) stop sb from + N/V-ing
　　阻止某人做……
(5) stop by / in　順道拜訪
(6) a bus / train stop　公 / 火車站

反 (1) start [stɑrt] *vt.* & *vi.* 開始 ①
(2) begin [bɪˋgɪn] *vt.* & *vi.* 開始 ①
(3) continue [kənˋtɪnju]
　　vt. & *vi.* 繼續 ②

▶ Abby stopped playing the guitar a long time ago.
艾比很久以前就不再彈吉他了。

▶ If you push the red button, the escalator will stop right away.
如果你按下那顆紅色按鈕，手扶梯會馬上停下。

▶ The bus came to a stop because of the accident.
公車因為那起事故而停下來了。

▶ The heavy rain stopped us from going camping.
那場大雨使我們不能去露營。

▶ We stopped for a picnic after walking for two hours.
我們走了兩小時後，停下來野餐。

▶ Stop by and see me when you have a chance.
= Stop in and see me when you have a chance.
有機會時，順道來看我。

▶ Get off at the next bus stop if you want to go to the mall.
要去購物中心的話，你就要在下一個公車站下車。

---

11 **movie** [ˋmuvɪ] *n.* 電影，影片；電影院（恆用複數）〔美〕

片 (1) a movie star / theater
　　電影明星 / 電影院
(2) go to (see) a movie　去看電影
(3) go to the movies　去看電影
(4) be at the movies　在電影院

似 cinema [ˋsɪnəmə] *n.* 電影院〔英〕③

▶ Let's go to a movie tonight! What would you like to see?
我們今晚去看電影吧！你想要看什麼呢？

▶ Adam prefers to go to the movies on his own.
亞當偏好自己去看電影。

▶ Jessica always buys popcorn when she's at the movies.
潔西卡在電影院時總會買爆米花。

---

film [fɪlm]
n. 電影，影片；底片 & *vt.* & *vi.* 拍攝
（成電影）

片 (1) make / shoot a film　拍電影
　= make / shoot a movie
(2) a roll of film　一捲底片

▶ The team is making a film in Italy.
= The team is shooting a film in Italy.
= The team is filming in Italy.
這個團隊正在義大利拍電影。

▶ I'd like to buy two rolls of film.
我想買 2 捲底片。

▶ The TV ad was filmed in the Sahara Desert.
這部電視廣告是在撒哈拉沙漠拍攝的。

---

12 **milk** [mɪlk] *n.* 牛奶（不可數）& *vt.* 擠奶

片 (1) a glass / bottle of milk
　　一杯 / 瓶牛奶

▶ I'd like to add some milk to my coffee.
我想在咖啡裡加點牛奶。

(2) milk shake　奶昔
(3) milk a cow / goat
　　擠牛奶 / 山羊奶

▶ My uncle showed me how to milk a cow by hand.
我叔叔示範如何用手擠牛奶給我看。

---

cheese [tʃiz] *n.* 起司

🔑 (1) a piece / slice of cheese
　　一塊 / 片起司
(2) a big cheese
　　大人物，重量級人物
= a big wheel / shot

▶ Cheese is an important part of the Western diet.
起司是西方飲食中重要的一環。

▶ A big cheese from our British division is coming in today.
今天英國分部有位重要人物要來。

---

butter [ˋbʌtɚ]

n. 奶油 & *vt.* 塗奶油於……

🔑 (1) spread butter on sth
　　在某物上塗奶油
(2) bread and butter
　　奶油麵包；生計
(3) peanut butter　花生醬

▶ I helped my little brother spread butter on his toast.
= I helped my little brother butter his toast.
我幫弟弟把奶油塗在吐司上。

▶ Who brings home the bread and butter?
誰負責家中的生計？

13　important [ɪmˋpɔrtṇt] *a.* 重要的

🔑 (1) be important to sb
　　對某人來說很重要
(2) It is important (for sb) to V
　　（某人）做……是很重要的

衍 importance [ɪmˋpɔrtṇs] *n.* 重要性 ②

反 unimportant [ˏʌnɪmˋpɔrtṇt]
　　a. 不重要的

▶ What the teacher has just said is really important.
老師剛才所說的話真的很重要。

▶ You are so important to me. Don't ever forget that.
你對我來說很重要，千萬別忘了這點。

▶ It is important for you to pay attention in class.
你把注意力集中在課堂上很重要。

14　reason [ˋrizṇ] *n.* 原因，理由 & *vt.* & *vi.* 推論，推理

🔑 (1) a reason for sth　某事的理由
(2) a reason + 疑問詞 why 引導的名
　　詞子句　……的理由
(3) for some / no reason
　　不知怎地 / 沒有原因地
(4) reason + (that)...　推論 / 理……
(5) reason with sb
　　說服某人，和某人講理

▶ I don't know the reason for my girlfriend's anger.
= I don't know the reason why my girlfriend is angry.
我不知道我女友生氣的原因。

▶ For some reason, Mr. Brown didn't arrive as scheduled.
不知怎地，布朗先生沒有依約前來。

▶ They reasoned that the boss wouldn't accept the idea.
他們推想老闆不會接受這個主意。

▶ It's important for children to learn to reason.
孩童學習推理是很重要的。

衍 (1) reasonable [ˈriznəbl̩]
　　　a. 合理的 ③
　　(2) reasonably [ˈriznəblɪ]
　　　adv. 合理地

▶ Jack tried to reason with the man, but in vain.
　傑克試圖和那名男子講理，但徒勞無功。
　*in vain [ven]　徒勞無功

15　story [ˈstɔrɪ] *n.* 故事；新聞報導；（建築物的）層

複 stories [ˈstɔrɪz]
片 (1) a story about / of...
　　　有關……的故事
　　(2) a true story　真實故事
　　(3) tell / read sb a story
　　　告訴某人一個故事 / 唸故事給某人聽
　　(4) To make a long story short, ...
　　　長話短說，……
　　(5) a news / main / cover story
　　　新聞報導 / 主要報導 / 封面故事
似 (1) tale [tel] *n.* 故事 ②
　　(2) report [rɪˈpɔrt] *n.* 報導 ①

▶ This TV series is based on a true story.
　這部電視影集是根據一則真實故事。

▶ Every night, Jim tells his son a story.
　吉姆每晚都唸故事給兒子聽。

▶ To make a long story short, you should change your study habits.
　長話短說，你應該改變你的讀書習慣。

▶ I read a news story about the fires in Australia.
　我看了有關澳洲大火的新聞報導。

▶ It is a building of ten stories.
= It is a ten-story building.
　那是棟 10 層樓高的建築物。

16　hard [hɑrd] *a.* 硬的；難的 & *adv.* 努力地；猛烈地

片 It is hard to V　做……很困難
衍 hardship [ˈhɑrdʃɪp] *n.* 困苦 ④
似 difficult [ˈdɪfɪˌkəlt] *a.* 難的 ①
反 (1) soft [sɔft] *a.* 軟的 ②
　　(2) easy [ˈizɪ] *a.* 簡單的 ①

▶ This bed is too hard. I like a soft one.
　這張床太硬了。我喜歡軟床。

▶ It's hard to talk Jack into going out with us.
　要說服傑克跟我們外出很困難。

▶ John studied hard and passed the test.
　約翰用功讀書，通過了考試。

▶ It's raining hard now.
　雨現在下得很大。

17　boss [bɔs] *n.* 老闆，上司 & *vt.* 使喚，發號施令

複 bosses [ˈbɔsɪz]
片 boss sb around　使喚某人
衍 bossy [ˈbɔsɪ] *a.* 愛指揮別人的

▶ My boss is in a meeting right now. Could you leave a message?
　我老闆正在開會。您可以留言嗎？

▶ Stop bossing me around! I've got my own things to do.
　別再使喚我了！我有自己的事情要做。

18　make [mek] *vt.* 做，製作；使得；趕到，到達

三 make, made [med], made

▶ Jason made a coffee table out of wood.
　傑森用木頭做了一張咖啡桌。

囝 (1) be made of...
　由……製成 (用於可辨認原材料時)
　(2) be made from
　由……製成 (用於無法辨認原材料時)
　(3) make it to + 地方
　(成功) 趕到某地

衍 maker [ˈmekɚ] *n.* 製作者

用法 (1) make 作使役動詞時，用法為：
　make + 受詞 + 原形動詞
　(2) make 不作使役動詞，但表『使得 /
　成為……』之意時，用法為：
　make + 受詞 + 形容詞 / 名詞 (作受
　詞補語)

▶ Emma's bag was made of plastic.
　艾瑪的背包是由塑膠製成的。
▶ Everybody knows that paper is made from wood.
　每個人都知道紙是由木頭製成。
▶ The wind made the curtains move back and forth.
　風使得窗簾前後擺動。
▶ Rick made Tori angry by being late for their date.
　瑞克約會遲到讓托莉很生氣。
▶ Sam made it to the airport in time to catch his flight.
　山姆及時趕到機場搭上飛機。
　*in time　及時

19　sea [si] *n.* 海

囝 (1) by the sea　在海邊
　(2) by sea　搭船

似 ocean [ˈoʃən] *n.* 海洋 ②

▶ Adam sat by the sea to watch the sunset.
　亞當坐在海邊觀賞日落。
▶ We traveled to Green Island by sea.
　我們搭船去綠島。

---

ship [ʃɪp]
n. (大) 船 & *vt.* & *vi.* (用船、飛機或卡車等) 運送

三 ship, shipped [ʃɪpt], shipped

囝 (1) a cruise ship　郵輪
　(2) by ship　搭船；由海運

衍 shipment [ˈʃɪpmənt] *n.* 運輸

▶ The goods were carried from Asia to Europe by ship.
　這些貨物經由海運從亞洲運往歐洲。
▶ We ship our products to many countries around the world.
　我們將產品運送到全球許多國家。

---

boat [bot] *n.* (小) 船

囝 (1) by boat　乘船
　(2) be in the same boat　處境相同

▶ We could only cross the river by boat.
　我們只能坐小船渡河。
▶ Stop complaining! We're all in the same boat.
　別再抱怨了！我們的處境都一樣。

20　sky [skaɪ] *n.* 天空

複 skies [skaɪz]

囝 (1) in the sky　在天空
　(2) pie in the sky
　不太可能實現的想法 / 計畫
　= castles in the air

▶ The sun shone brightly in the sky on the hot summer's day.
　太陽在炎熱的夏天高掛空中閃耀。
▶ Eddie's dream of opening a business seems like pie in the sky.
　艾迪開業的夢想似乎不太可能實現。

21 **sun** [sʌn] *n.* 太陽（前面加定冠詞 the，字首可大寫）；陽光 & *vt.* & *vi.* 晒太陽，做日光浴

目 sun, sunned [sʌnd], sunned

片 (1) in the sun　在陽光下
　 (2) sun oneself
　　　某人晒太陽 / 做日光浴

衍 (1) sunshine [ˋsʌnˏʃaɪn] *n.* 陽光
　 (2) sunbath [ˋsʌnˏbæθ] *n.* 日光浴

似 sunbathe [ˋsʌnˏbeð]
　　 vi. 晒太陽，做日光浴

▶ It was so cloudy that the sun could not be seen.
　烏雲密布，以致於看不到太陽。

▶ Roland's skin hurt from being in the sun all day.
　羅蘭的皮膚因為在陽光下晒了整天而疼痛。

▶ Belinda sunned herself on the beach this afternoon.
　貝琳達今天下午在海灘晒太陽。

▶ After sunning for a couple of days, Ramona had a great tan.
　做了幾天的日光浴，雷蒙娜晒了一身漂亮的古銅膚色。
　*tan [tæn] *n.* 古銅膚色

moon [mun]
n. 月亮（前面加定冠詞 the，字首可大寫）

片 a full / half moon　滿 / 半月

▶ Humans first landed on the moon in July, 1969.
　人類在 1969 年 7 月首次登陸月球。

22 **crazy** [ˋkrezɪ] *a.* 瘋狂的；荒唐愚蠢的；著迷的

片 (1) make / drive sb crazy
　　　讓某人抓狂
　 (2) be crazy to V　做……很荒唐
　 (3) be crazy about...　對……很著迷

似 (1) mad [mæd] *a.* 瘋的 ①
　 (2) insane [ɪnˋsen]
　　　 a. 瘋狂的；荒唐的 ⑤

▶ Turn that music down! It's driving me crazy!
　把音樂關掉！它讓我快抓狂了！

▶ You'd be crazy to turn down an opportunity like this.
　你拒絕像這樣的機會真是荒唐。
　*turn down sth　拒絕某事物

▶ I'm crazy about chocolate ice cream.
　我好喜歡巧克力冰淇淋。

23 **bean** [bin] *n.* 豆子

片 (1) a green bean　四季豆
　 (2) a coffee bean　咖啡豆
　 (3) spill the beans　洩密

▶ I hate to eat beans.
　我討厭吃豆子。

▶ Don't tell Annie any secrets; she always spills the beans.
　別告訴安妮任何祕密，她總是會洩密。

24 **doll** [dɑl] *n.* 玩偶，洋娃娃

▶ Alice loves to play with her dolls.
　艾莉絲喜歡玩她的玩偶。

25 letter [ˈlɛtɚ] *n.* 信；字母

H write / send / receive a letter
寫 / 寄 / 收信

似 (1) latter [ˈlætɚ] *a.* 後面的 ②
(2) later [ˈletɚ] *adv.* 稍後 ①

▸ Because of email, fewer and fewer people write letters these days.
由於有電子郵件，現在越來越少人寫信了。

▸ Gary couldn't tell if the letter was an "a" or an "o."
蓋瑞分不出來這個字母是 "a" 還是 "o"。

26 belt [bɛlt] *n.* 腰帶，皮帶

H (1) wear a belt 繫腰 / 皮帶
(2) a seat belt 安全帶

▸ These pants are too big. I need to wear a belt.
這條褲子太大了。我得繫皮帶。

▸ You should always fasten your seat belt while in a car.
在車裡你應該要繫好安全帶。
＊fasten [ˈfæsn̩] *vt.* 繫緊

Unit 03

0301-0303

1　dog [dɔg] *n.* 狗

田 (1) a pet dog　寵物狗
　 (2) walk a / sb's dog　遛狗
　 = take a / sb's dog for a walk

▶ Suzie enjoys playing with her dog in the park.
　蘇西喜歡和她的狗在公園一起玩。

▶ Billy walks his dog every day after school.
= Billy takes his dog for a walk every day after school.
　比利每天放學後都會去遛狗。

---

cat [kæt] *n.* 貓

田 (1) a pet cat　寵物貓
　 (2) have a cat　養貓

▶ Some people prefer to have cats as pets.
　有些人比較喜歡養貓作寵物。

2　big [bɪg] *a.* 大的；年長的；重要的

田 (1) a big sister / brother
　　 姊姊 / 哥哥
　 (2) a big day / decision
　　 重要的日子 / 決定

似 (1) large [lɑrdʒ] *a.* 大的 ①
　 (2) old [old] *a.* 老的 ①
　 (3) important [ɪmˈpɔrtn̩t]
　　 a. 重要的 ①

▶ John's room is not as big as his older brother's.
　約翰的房間不如他哥哥的房間大。

▶ Ashley is chatting with her big sister.
　艾希莉在和她姊姊聊天。

▶ Buying a home and getting married are big decisions.
　買房子和結婚是重要的決定。

---

small [smɔl]
a. 小的；年幼的；不重要的 & *adv.* 小地 &
n. (尺寸) 小號

似 (1) little [ˈlɪtl̩] *a.* 小的 ①
　 (2) tiny [ˈtaɪnɪ] *a.* 極小的 ②
　 (3) minor [ˈmaɪnɚ] *a.* 不重要的 ②
　 (4) unimportant [ˌʌnɪmˈpɔrtn̩t]
　　 a. 不重要的

延伸 (1) medium [ˈmidɪəm]
　　 n. (尺寸) 中號 ①
　 (2) large [lɑrdʒ] *n.* (尺寸) 大號 ①

▶ The car is really small; only two people can fit in it.
　這輛車真的很小，只有 2 個人能坐進去。

▶ When he was small, Ted lived in France for a while.
　泰德年幼時曾在法國住了一陣子。

▶ It was just a small mistake, so it was easily fixed.
　這只是個小錯誤，可以很輕易地解決。

▶ Karl wrote small because there wasn't much space on the paper.
　由於紙上沒有太多空位，卡爾字寫得很小。

▶ Jackson lost a lot of weight and now he wears smalls.
　傑克森減了很多重量，現在穿得下小號尺寸了。

3　love [lʌv] *n.* & *vt.* & *vi.* 愛，喜愛

田 (1) sb's love for...　某人對……的喜愛
　 (2) fall in love with sb
　　 愛上某人，與某人相戀

▶ Vicky's love for her husband grew over the years.
　多年來，薇琪對老公的愛越來越深。

(3) love at first sight 一見鍾情
(4) love to V 喜愛做……
= love + V-ing
衍 (1) lovely [ˈlʌvlɪ] *a.* 可愛的 ①
(2) lover [ˈlʌvɚ] *n.* 愛人 ③
反 hate [het] *n. & vt.* 厭惡 ①

▶ Jasper fell in love with Clara two years ago.
　賈斯柏 2 年前與克萊拉相戀。
▶ When Jack met Rose, it was love at first sight.
　傑克遇見蘿絲時,對她一見鍾情。
▶ Daniel loves this song so much that he sings it all the time.
　丹尼爾太愛這首歌了,所以一直在唱。
▶ Janice loves to read novels in bed before going to sleep.
= Janice loves reading novels in bed before going to sleep.
　珍妮絲睡前很愛窩在床上看小說。

4　pen [pɛn] *n.* (用墨水的) 筆 & *vt.* 寫

三 pen, penned [pɛnd], penned
片 pen a letter / novel / poem
　寫信 / 小說 / 詩
似 write [raɪt] *vt. & vi.* 寫 ①

▶ Ginny couldn't find a pen, so she wrote in pencil.
　金妮找不到筆,所以用鉛筆來寫。
▶ It had been a long time since Jim penned a letter.
　吉姆已好久沒寫信了。

---

pencil [ˈpɛnsḷ] *n.* 鉛筆

▶ Tom likes to use a pencil to draw.
　湯姆喜歡用鉛筆畫畫。

---

eraser [ɪˈresɚ] *n.* 橡皮擦〔美〕
衍 erase [ɪˈres] *vt.* 擦掉 ③
似 rubber [ˈrʌbɚ] *n.* 橡皮擦〔英〕②

▶ Harper erased the wrong answer with an eraser.
　哈珀用橡皮擦把錯誤的答案擦掉。

5　fruit [frut] *n.* 水果

片 (1) fruit and vegetables 蔬果
(2) the fruit(s) of sth
　某事的結 / 成果
用法 fruit 若泛指所有水果時,視為集合名詞,不可數;若指特定一種或是幾種水果時,則視為可數名詞。

▶ It's important that you eat fruit and vegetables every day.
　每天吃蔬果是很重要的。
▶ Grandpa grew different kinds of fruits in his yard.
　爺爺在他的院子裡種了不同種類的水果。
▶ This book is the fruit of the author's ten years' work.
　這本書是該作者 10 年耕耘的成果。

---

apple [ˈæpḷ] *n.* 蘋果
片 the apple of one's eye
　某人的心肝寶貝,某人最珍視的人

▶ The apple that Sophie ate tasted juicy and delicious.
　蘇菲吃的那顆蘋果多汁又美味。
▶ Lucy's son was truly the apple of her eye.
　露西的兒子是她最珍視的人。

banana [bəˈnænə] *n.* 香蕉
片 a bunch of bananas　一串香蕉

▶ There's a bunch of bananas on the dining table.
餐桌上有一串香蕉。

---

6 bicycle [ˈbaɪsɪkl̩] *n.* 腳踏車，自行車 (= bike [baɪk])

片 (1) ride a bicycle　騎腳踏車
　　= ride a bike
　　(2) by bicycle　騎腳踏車
　　= by bike

▶ Wendy's father taught her how to ride a bicycle.
溫蒂的爸爸教她如何騎腳踏車。

▶ Stephen goes to school by bicycle every day.
史蒂芬每天騎腳踏車去上課。

---

7 say [se] *vt.* 說，講；(肯定地) 表明／表達

三 say, said [sɛd], said
片 (1) hard to say　難斷言，很難說
　　(2) It is said that...　據說……

▶ Gordon finds it difficult to say how he feels.
高登覺得很難把他的感受說出來。

▶ It's hard to say whether it will rain tomorrow.
很難斷言明天會不會下雨。

▶ It is said that dogs are more loyal than cats.
據說狗狗比貓咪更忠心。
*loyal [ˈlɔɪəl] *a.* 忠誠的

---

8 only [ˈonlɪ] *adv.* 只，僅 & *a.* 唯一的 & *conj.* 可是，但是

似 (1) just [dʒʌst] *adv.* 只，僅 ①
　　(2) simply [ˈsɪmplɪ] *adv.* 僅僅 ②
　　(3) sole [sol] *a.* 唯一的 ⑤
　　(4) but [bʌt] *conj.* 可是，但是 ①

▶ Only 10 people came to the party, but 50 were invited.
來參加派對的人只有 10 個，但邀請了 50 個人。

▶ The only student in the class that knew the answer was Peter.
彼得是班上唯一一個知道答案的學生。

▶ Randy wanted to ask Sally out, only he was too shy.
藍迪想要約莎莉出去，但他太害羞了。

---

9 tree [tri] *n.* 樹 (木)

片 an apple / oak [ok] tree
蘋果／橡樹

▶ There were many large oak trees in Mason's backyard.
梅森家的後院有很多大橡樹。

---

10 bee [bi] *n.* 蜜蜂

片 a swarm [swɔrm] of bees
一群蜜蜂
似 honeybee [ˈhʌnɪˌbi] *n.* 蜜蜂
延伸 (1) bumblebee [ˈbʌmbl̩ˌbi]
　　n. 大黃蜂
　　(2) wasp [wɑsp] *n.* 黃蜂

▶ Ian got scared when he saw some bees flying near his head.
伊恩看到有些蜜蜂在他頭附近飛時嚇壞了。

honey [ˈhʌnɪ]

n. 蜂蜜 (不可數)；親愛的 (稱呼)

衍 honeycomb [ˈhʌnɪˌkom] *n.* 蜂巢
= beehive [ˈbiˌhaɪv]

似 (1) darling [ˈdɑrlɪŋ] *n.* 親愛的 ③
　　(2) sweetheart [ˈswitˌhɑrt] *n.* 甜心

▶ Life is not all milk and honey.
人生不完全像蜂蜜一樣甜 / 人生有苦有樂。── 諺語

▶ "Honey, have a nice day!" Mom said as she waved me goodbye.
媽媽對我揮手道別時說：『寶貝，祝你今天愉快！』

11　car [kɑr] *n.* 汽車

用 (1) get in / into a car　上車
　　(2) get out of a car　下車
　　(3) by car　開車

▶ Oscar waited for the cars to pass by before crossing the street.
奧斯卡等車子都開過了才穿過街道。

▶ Anderson got in the car and drove home.
安德森上車後開車回家。

▶ Fred usually goes to work by car, but today he didn't.
佛萊德通常開車去上班，但今天沒有。

---

bus [bʌs] *n.* 公車；巴士

複 buses / busses [ˈbʌsɪz]

用 (1) on a bus　在公車 / 巴士上
　　(2) get on / off a bus
　　　　上 / 下公車 / 巴士
　　(3) wait for a bus　等公車 / 巴士
　　(4) by bus　搭公車 / 巴士

▶ Helena couldn't get a seat on the bus because it was crowded.
海蓮娜在公車上沒有位子坐，因為人太多了。

▶ Bert got off the bus and went to school.
伯特下公車後走到學校。

▶ I saw Phoebe waiting for the bus yesterday.
我昨天看到菲比在等公車。

▶ Carla would rather travel by car than by bus.
卡拉寧可開車旅行，也不要搭巴士。

12　desk [dɛsk] *n.* 桌子 (尤指附抽屜的書桌、辦公桌等)

用 a wooden desk　木桌
　*wooden [ˈwʊdn̩] *a.* 木 (製) 的

▶ This wooden desk is quite beautiful.
這張木桌相當漂亮。

---

table [ˈtebl̩] *n.* 桌子

用 (1) a dinner / dining table　餐桌
　　(2) on a table　在桌上
　　(3) book / reserve a table (for + 人
　　　　數)　預訂 (若干人的) 桌位

▶ Kathy cooked some food and put it on the table.
凱西煮了些食物，然後把它們放在桌上。

▶ Gail booked a table for four at this French restaurant.
蓋兒在這間法式餐廳訂了 4 人的桌位。

---

chair [tʃɛr]

n. 椅子；主席 & *vt.* 主持 (會議)

用 (1) a folding / beach chair
　　　　折疊 / 沙灘椅

▶ Evelyn sat on a chair on the balcony and enjoyed the beautiful view.
艾芙琳坐在陽臺的椅子上享受美景。

(2) sit on a chair　坐椅子
(3) pull up a chair　拉椅子過來
(4) chair a meeting　主持會議
衍 chairperson [ˋtʃɛr͵pɝsn̩] *n.* 主席 ⑥
似 be in charge of...　負責管理……

▶ Ralph told his friend to pull up a chair next to him.
拉爾夫叫他朋友把旁邊的椅子拉過來。
▶ Charlie asked the chair if he could say a few things.
查理問主席他是否可以說幾件事情。
▶ The manager was sick, so Andy was asked to chair the meeting.
經理生病了，所以請安迪來主持會議。

13　rain [ren] *n.* 雨；雨季 (恆用複數，前面加定冠詞 the) & *vi.* 下雨

用 (1) the rain falls (heavily / lightly)　下 (大 / 小) 雨
(2) heavy / light / pouring rain　大雨 / 小雨 / 滂沱大雨
(3) when it rains, it pours　禍不單行
衍 (1) rainbow [ˋren͵bo] *n.* 彩虹 ①
(2) raincoat [ˋren͵kot] *n.* 雨衣 ②
(3) rainfall [ˋren͵fɔl] *n.* 降雨量 ④
似 rein [ren] *n.* 韁繩

▶ Taipei is a good city, but it gets a lot of rain.
臺北是個好城市，但很常下雨。
▶ Jackie wears a raincoat because the rain is falling heavily.
因為下大雨，潔琪穿著雨衣。
▶ The cat sat outside the house in the pouring rain.
這隻貓咪在滂沱大雨中坐在房子外面。
▶ Don't take a trip to Thailand when the rains come.
別在雨季來臨時到泰國旅遊。
▶ Charlie wonders when it will stop raining.
查理想知道什麼時候會停止下雨。
▶ Hank lost his wallet and then his keys; when it rains, it pours.
漢克弄丟了他的錢包跟鑰匙，真是禍不單行。

14　next [nɛkst] *a.* 下一個的，緊接著的 & *adv.* 接下來，然後；下次

用 (1) (the) next day / week / month / Monday　隔天 / 週 / 月 / 週一
(2) (the) next time　下次
(3) next to...　在……旁邊；僅次於……
似 following [ˋfɑləwɪŋ] *a.* 接著的 ②

▶ The students will go on a school trip next Friday.
學生下週五會去校外教學。
▶ Gary didn't know what to do next, so he asked his boss.
蓋瑞不知道接下來要做什麼，所以他請教了老闆。
▶ You can return this book when we next see each other.
你可以在我們下次碰面時再還我這本書。
▶ Roberta's high school is next to a museum.
蘿貝塔的高中就在一間博物館旁邊。
▶ Next to basketball, Chad likes playing baseball the most.
查德最喜歡打籃球，其次是棒球。

15 door [dɔr] n. 門；門口

(1) open / close a door
開 / 關門

(2) knock on / answer a door
敲 / 應門

(1) doorway [ˈdɔrˌwe] n. 門口 ⑤

(2) doorstep [ˈdɔrˌstɛp] n. 門階

▶ Ron forgot to close the door when he came into the house.
榮恩進到家裡後忘了關門。

▶ Lucy knocked on the door, but no one was home.
露西敲了敲門，但沒人在家。

▶ Mike could see a big cat through the open door.
麥克從敞開的門口看見一隻大貓。

gate [get] n. (尤指金屬製或木製的) 大門，柵門；登機門

a front / back / main gate
前 / 後 / 主門

▶ The main gate was locked, so Ian couldn't get in the building.
主門被鎖住了，所以伊恩沒辦法進到建築物裡。
＊lock [lɑk] vt. 鎖，鎖上

▶ When the gate opened, the people walked onto the plane.
登機門開放後，大家開始登機。

window [ˈwɪndo] n. 窗戶

(1) open / close a window
開 / 關窗

(2) gaze / stare / look out of a window 看向窗外，往窗外看

▶ Joe opened a window to let some air in.
喬打開窗戶讓一些空氣進來。

▶ Bobby gazed out of the window and watched the snow fall.
巴比看著窗外的雪落下。

16 cup [kʌp] n. (尤指附有手柄，用來喝茶、咖啡的) 杯子

(1) cap [kæp] n. 帽子 ①

(2) mug [mʌg] n. 馬克杯 ②

▶ Stewart dropped the cup on the floor, and it broke.
史都華把杯子掉在地板上摔破了。

17 old [old] a. 年老的；……歲的；老舊的；從前的

be + 數字 + year(s) old   若干歲

(1) elderly [ˈɛldɚlɪ] a. 年老的 ③

(2) former [ˈfɔrmɚ] a. 從前的 ②

(3) previous [ˈprivɪəs] a. 從前的 ③

可以用『數字-year-old』表『若干歲的』，惟須注意的是，此為形容詞，須置名詞前，且用法中的 year 不加 s，例：a two-year-old girl   2 歲的女孩

▶ The old man can no longer walk very well.
這名老先生已經無法好好走路了。

▶ In two weeks, Rita will be 21 years old.
瑞塔再過 2 週就滿 21 歲了。

▶ Steven's car is pretty old, but it still works fine.
史蒂芬的車相當老舊了，但仍能正常運作。

▶ Glen saw an old boss of his on the street yesterday.
葛倫昨天在街上看見以前的老闆。

young [jʌŋ] a. 幼小的；年輕的 & n. 年輕人 (前面加定冠詞 the)

▶ When she was young, Jennifer wanted to become a singer.
珍妮佛小時候想成為一名歌手。

H young at heart 心態年輕
衍 (1) youngster [ˈjʌŋstɚ] n. 年輕人 ③
(2) youth [juθ]
n. 青春 (不可數)；青年 (可數) ②
(3) youthful [ˈjuθfəl]
a. 年輕 (人) 的 ④

▶ Brian thought the colorful shirt looked too young for him.
布萊恩覺得這件鮮豔的襯衫在他身上看起來太過年輕。

▶ Benjamin is almost 75, but he is still young at heart.
班傑明年近 75，但仍保有一顆年輕的心。

▶ Dancing is not only for the young; older people can do it, too.
跳舞不只是年輕人做的活動，年長者也跳舞。

---

new [n(j)u] a. 新的；不熟悉的
H be new to sb 對某人來說很陌生
衍 (1) news [n(j)uz] n. 新聞 (不可數) ①
(2) newly [ˈn(j)ulɪ] adv. 最近

▶ Abby went to the store to buy some new clothes.
艾比去店裡買些新衣服。

▶ The job was still new to Ryan, so he made some mistakes.
萊恩對這份工作仍很生疏，所以會犯一些錯。

---

18 cute [kjut] a. 可愛的

衍 cuteness [ˈkjutnəs] n. 可愛

▶ Glenda saw a cute dress and bought it.
葛蘭達看到一件可愛的洋裝並買了下來。

---

19 hen [hɛn] n. 母雞

延伸 (1) chicken [ˈtʃɪkən] n. 雞 (肉) ①
(2) rooster [ˈrustɚ] n. 公雞 ②
(3) chick [tʃɪk] n. 小雞

▶ The hen is surrounded by many chicks.
這隻母雞被許多隻小雞圍繞。
*surround [səˈraʊnd] vt. 圍繞

---

egg [ɛg] n. (可食用的) 蛋；卵
H (1) egg white / yolk [jok]
蛋白 / 黃
(2) lay an egg 下蛋

▶ Larry eats eggs for breakfast every day before going to work.
賴瑞每天去上班前，都會吃蛋當早餐。

▶ Sharon looked in the nest and saw five eggs.
雪倫往鳥巢內看，看到了 5 顆蛋。

▶ When the hens lay eggs, the farmer takes them away.
母雞下蛋後，農夫就會把蛋拿走。

---

20 insect [ˈɪnsɛkt] n. 昆蟲

延伸 (1) bug [bʌg] n. 小蟲子 ①
(2) worm [wɝm] n. 蟲 ②

▶ Spiders feed on small insects.
蜘蛛捕食小昆蟲維生。
*feed on... 以……為食

---

21 busy [ˈbɪzɪ] a. 忙碌的

H (1) be busy with sth 忙於某事
(2) be busy + V-ing 忙著做……

▶ George is too busy to talk to anyone now.
喬治現在很忙，沒有辦法跟其他人講話。

▶ Paul is busy with his work at the office.
保羅在辦公室忙於他的工作。

▶ Tammy was busy doing her homework in her room.
譚美在她房間忙著寫功課。

22　now [nau] *adv.* 現在，目前；馬上，立刻 & *n.* 現在

日 (1) right now
馬上，立刻 (= right away)；現在，
就是此刻
(2) by now　到現在，到目前
(3) from now on　從現在開始

衍 nowadays [ˋnauəˌdez] *adv.* 現今 ④

似 at present　現在，目前
= at the present time
= at the moment

▶ David now works at a big company in the US.
大衛現在在美國的一間大公司上班。

▶ Mrs. Rand told the students to stop talking now!
蘭德老師要學生們立刻停止說話！

▶ Hal knew that he had to go to school right now.
= Hal knew that he had to go to school right away.
海爾知道他得馬上去上學。

▶ By now, Debbie should know how to read, but she doesn't.
黛比到現在應該要知道如何閱讀，但她並不知道。

▶ Julie said that from now on she would study harder.
茱麗說從此刻起她會用功念書。

23　get [gɛt] *vt.* 收到，得到；買到；拿來；感染上；使得；理解 & *vi.* 到達；變得

三 get, got [gɑt], got / gotten [ˋgɑtn̩]

日 (1) get sb sth　買 / 拿某物給某人
= get sth for sb
(2) get a cold (from sb)
（被某人傳染）感冒
(3) get sb/sth + adj.
使某人 / 某事物……
(4) get home　回到家
(5) get to + 地方　到達某地

似 (1) receive [rɪˋsiv] *vt.* 收到 ②
(2) buy [baɪ] *vt.* & *vi.* 買 ①
(3) bring [brɪŋ] *vt.* 拿來 ①
(4) understand [ˌʌndɚˋstænd]
vt. 理解 ①
(5) arrive [əˋraɪv] *vi.* 到達 ①
(6) become [bɪˋkʌm] *vi.* 變得 ①

▶ Nancy got a lot of great gifts for her birthday.
南希收到一大堆很棒的生日禮物。

▶ Jay got a new scooter the day before yesterday.
傑伊前天買了一輛新摩托車。
＊the day before yesterday　前天

▶ Wendy got her friend a cup of tea.
= Wendy got a cup of tea for her friend.
溫蒂拿了一杯茶給她朋友。

▶ Tommy thinks he got a cold from his sister.
湯米認為自己被姊姊傳染感冒。

▶ Sean got his mother mad because he didn't clean his room.
尚恩因為沒有清理房間，讓他媽媽氣炸了。

▶ Mickey told a joke, but no one got it.
米奇講了一則笑話，但沒有人聽得懂。

▶ Melvin gets home from the office at 7:30 p.m. every day.
梅爾文每天晚上 7 點半下班到家。

用法 (1) get 作及物動詞，表『理解』之意時，時態上不可使用現在進行式。

(2) get 表『變得』之意時，是作連綴動詞，因此需在 get 後加上形容詞。
get + adj.　變得……

▶ Dan got to the department store five minutes after it closed.

丹到百貨公司時，已經打烊五分鐘了。

▶ After walking for 45 minutes, Jack got a bit tired.

走了 45 分鐘後，傑克變得有點累了。

0401-0404

1 family [ˈfæməlɪ] *n.* 家，家庭；子女 ☐

目 families [ˈfæməlɪz]

円 (1) a family member 家庭成員
(2) raise a family 養家，養小孩
(3) start a family 成家，生小孩

衍 (1) familiar [fəˈmɪljɚ] *a.* 熟悉的 ③
(2) familiarity [fə͵mɪlɪˈærətɪ]
n. 熟悉 ⑥

▶ Clark is the youngest member of his family.
克萊克是他家中最年輕的成員。

▶ It can be hard to raise a family in today's world.
在現在的世界，養小孩可能會是一件難事。

▶ Todd and Marie decided to get married and start a family.
陶德和瑪莉決定結婚生小孩。

---

father [ˈfɑðɚ] *n.* 父親，爸爸 ☐

似 (1) dad [dæd] *n.* 爸爸
(2) daddy [ˈdædɪ] *n.* 爹地

▶ Randolph's father is a doctor in a big hospital.
藍道夫的爸爸是一間大醫院的醫生。

---

mother [ˈmʌðɚ] *n.* 母親，媽媽 ☐

似 (1) mom [mɑm] *n.* 媽媽
(2) mommy [ˈmɑmɪ] *n.* 媽咪

▶ Tina gave her mother a nice present for her birthday.
蒂娜送她媽媽一個很棒的生日禮物。

---

sister [ˈsɪstɚ] *n.* 姊姊；妹妹 ☐

円 (1) a big / an older sister 姊姊
(2) a little / younger sister 妹妹

衍 sis [sɪs] *n.* 姊姊；妹妹

▶ Gloria's sister wants to be a singer in the future.
葛洛莉雅的姊姊 / 妹妹未來想當歌手。

---

brother [ˈbrʌðɚ] *n.* 哥哥；弟弟 ☐

円 (1) a big / an older brother 哥哥
(2) a little / younger brother 弟弟

衍 bro [bro] *n.* 兄弟

▶ Mike has one older brother and two younger brothers.
麥克有一個哥哥、兩個弟弟。

---

grandfather [ˈgrænd͵fɑðɚ]
n. 爺爺；外公 ☐

衍 grandpa [ˈgrændpa] *n.* 爺爺；外公

▶ Simon became a grandfather when his daughter had a son.
賽門的女兒生兒子後，他成了外公。

---

grandmother [ˈgrænd͵mʌðɚ]
n. 奶奶；外婆 ☐

衍 grandma [ˈgrændma] *n.* 奶奶；外婆

▶ Lisa's grandmother is over 80, but she is still healthy.
麗莎的奶奶超過 80 歲了，但仍很健康。

---

uncle [ˈʌŋkḷ] *n.* 叔叔；伯父；舅舅 ☐

▶ Liz has an uncle in Iceland that she has never met.
麗茲有一個從未見過的叔叔在冰島。

aunt [ænt] *n.* 阿姨；姑姑

衍 **auntie** [ˈænti] *n.* 阿姨；姑姑

▶ Marnie's aunt owns a small restaurant.
瑪妮的阿姨擁有一間小餐館。

2　come [kʌm] *vi.* 來，過來

目 come, came [kem], come

片 (1) **come to a party / wedding**
來參加派對 / 婚禮

(2) **come to V**　過來做……

(3) **come with sb**　和某人一起來

(4) **come back**　回來

(5) **come from + 地方**　來自某地

(6) **come across sb/sth**
偶遇某人 / 偶然發現某物

(7) **come up with sth**
想出 (計畫、點子等)

▶ Aria came to the party and brought some cake.
艾瑞亞來參加派對，也帶了些蛋糕。

▶ Veronica came to discuss the project with us.
薇洛妮卡過來和我們討論這項企畫。

▶ Terry's friend came with him to his home after school.
放學後，泰瑞的朋友和他一起到家裡來。

▶ Dennis liked the restaurant so much that he came back many times.
丹尼斯很喜歡這間餐廳，所以他再訪好幾次了。

▶ Helen comes from a small town in the south of France.
海倫來自南法的一個小鎮。

▶ Monica came across a pretty dress while she was shopping.
莫妮卡逛街時偶然發現一件漂亮的洋裝。

▶ Harold came up with a good idea for his school essay.
哈洛德想出一個好點子來寫學校的作文。

3　television [ˈtɛləˌvɪʒən] *n.* 電視機 (= TV，可數)；電視節目 (= TV，不可數)

片 (1) **turn on / off the television**
開 / 關電視
= **turn on / off the TV**

(2) **watch television**　看電視
= **watch TV**

(3) **a television program**　電視節目
= **a TV program**

▶ Susan turned off the television and went to bed.
蘇珊關掉電視去睡覺。

▶ Raymond likes to watch television on the weekends.
雷蒙德週末時喜歡看電視。

▶ Shelley is waiting for her favorite television program to start.
雪莉在等她最喜歡的電視節目開播。

4　food [fud] *n.* 食物

片 (1) **fast food**　速食

(2) **food for thought**
心靈雞湯，發人深省的事情

用法 food 一般視為集合名詞，不可數，但若指特定一種或是幾種食物時，則視為可數名詞。

▶ Jerry eats a lot of food, but he is still slim.
傑瑞吃一大堆食物，但他還是很瘦。

▶ Olive thinks that it's fine to eat fast food sometimes.
奧莉芙覺得偶爾吃速食是沒問題的。

▶ The comments from Ron's teacher were food for thought.
榮恩的老師給他的評語啟發他思考。

5 o'clock [əˋklɑk] *adv.* ……點（整）

片 數字 + o'clock　幾點整

▸ At six o'clock, Peter finished his job and went home.
彼得在 6 點時做完工作回家。

clock [klɑk] *n.* 時鐘

片 around the clock　全天地

衍 clockwise [ˋklɑk,waɪz] *a.* 順時針的 & *adv.* 順時針地 ⑥

▸ The clock on the wall has been broken for a while.
牆上的時鐘壞掉一陣子了。

▸ The convenience store is open around the clock.
這間便利商店全天都有營業。

6 hour [aʊr] *n.* 小時

衍 hourly [ˋaʊrlɪ] *a.* 每小時的 & *adv.* 每小時地 ③

▸ Mike and Judy played tennis for two hours.
麥克和茱蒂打了 2 小時的網球。

minute [ˋmɪnɪt] *n.* 分（鐘）；片刻；會議記錄（此意恆用複數）

片 (1) wait a minute　等等，等一下
= hold on a minute
(2) take / do the minutes　做會議紀錄

▸ After running for 50 minutes, Dianne stopped to take a rest.
黛安跑了 50 分鐘後停下來休息。

▸ Tony said he could only talk to Phil for a minute.
東尼說他只能跟菲爾講一下話而已。

▸ Please wait a minute. I'll take your order soon.
請稍等一下。我晚點會來幫您點餐。

▸ We don't know who took the minutes of the last meeting.
我們不清楚上次做會議紀錄的人是誰。

7 else [ɛls] *adv.* 其他，另外

片 or else　否則，要不然；要不，要麼

衍 elsewhere [ˋɛls,(h)wɛr] *adv.* 在別處 ④

用法 else 用於 any-、every-、no-、some- 開頭的詞，以及疑問詞之後，惟須注意的是 else 不用於 which 後。

▸ Rita said she didn't want anything else to eat.
瑞塔說她不想吃其他任何東西。

▸ Lily knew she should study or else she would fail the test.
莉莉知道她該讀書，要不然可能會考不及格。

▸ Ben either forgot about the meeting or else he is late.
班要麼是忘了這場會議，要麼就是他遲到了。

8 nice [naɪs] *a.* 愉快的，美好的；好的，不錯的；友善的

片 have a nice time / day
有一段美好的時光 / 有美好的一天

▸ Grant had a nice time visiting his friends.
葛蘭特拜訪好友度過一段美好的時光。

▸ The sofa looked nice, so Patty bought it.
這張沙發看起來還不錯，所以派蒂買了下來。

似 (1) lovely [ˈlʌvlɪ] *a.* 美好的 ①
(2) pleasant [ˈplɛzn̩t] *a.* 愉快的 ②
(3) enjoyable [ɪnˈdʒɔɪəbl̩]
  a. 愉快的 ③
(4) friendly [ˈfrɛndlɪ] *a.* 友善的 ①

▶ Freddy is a nice guy, so he has lots of friends.
弗萊迪很友善，所以他有很多朋友。

---

9 **road** [rod] *n.* 路

片 (1) a paved / dirt road
  柏油路 / 土砂道
(2) along the road　　沿路
(3) hit the road　　出發

▶ Kirk turned right and drove onto a dirt road.
柯克右轉並開上土砂道。

▶ Larry was traveling fast along the road before the accident.
車禍前，賴瑞沿路飛快行駛。

▶ Miranda said it was time to hit the road.
米蘭達說是時候出發了。

---

street [strit] *n.* 街

片 (1) across the street　　在對街
(2) cross the street　　過街，穿越街道
(3) walk down the street　　走過街道

▶ Ronald lives across the street from a big museum.
羅納德住在一間大博物館的對街。

▶ Ellen crossed the street to go to the supermarket.
艾倫穿越街道去超市。

▶ Bart walked down the street while singing a song.
巴特邊唱歌邊走過街道。

---

10 **computer** [kəmˈpjutɚ] *n.* 電腦

延伸 (1) laptop [ˈlæptɑp] *n.* 筆記型電腦
(2) desktop [ˈdɛsktɑp] *n.* 桌上型電腦

▶ Computers have made life much easier.
電腦使生活方便多了。

---

11 **student** [ˈst(j)udənt] *n.* 學生

似 pupil [ˈpjupl̩] *n.* 小學生 ②

▶ All students should do their homework carefully.
所有學生都應仔細做功課。

---

teacher [ˈtitʃɚ] *n.* 教師

▶ Mrs. Simpson works as a math teacher.
辛普森女士的工作是一名數學老師。

---

teach [titʃ] *vt. & vi.* 教，教導
三 teach, taught [tɔt], taught
片 (1) teach sb about sth
  教某人某事物
(2) teach sb (how) to V
  教某人做⋯⋯

▶ Grant teaches his students about science.
葛蘭特教他的學生自然科學。

▶ Carleen's father taught her how to drive a car.
卡琳的爸爸教她如何開車。

▶ Glenda went to college to learn how to teach.
葛蘭達上大學學習如何教書。

12 star [star] *n.* 恆星；明星 & *vi.* 主演 & *vt.* 由……主演

- star, starred [stɑrd], starred
- (1) a shooting star　流星
  (2) a pop / movie star
　　　流行 / 電影明星
  (3) star in...　主演……
- superstar [ˈsupɚˌstɑr] *n.* 超級巨星
- celebrity [səˈlɛbrətɪ] *n.* 名人 ⑤

▶ The Sun is the closest star to Earth.
　太陽是距離地球最近的恆星。

▶ When Reggie looked up, he saw a shooting star.
　雷吉往上看時，看到一顆流星。

▶ Hal's favorite movie star is Lily Collins.
　海爾最喜歡的影星是莉莉・柯林斯。

▶ Lady Gaga starred in *A Star is Born*.
　女神卡卡主演《一個巨星的誕生》。

▶ The TV show stars some famous actors.
　這檔電視節目由一些知名演員主演。

13 hundred [ˈhʌndrəd] *n.* 一百 & *a.* 一百的

- hundreds of...　很多 / 數百個……
- 用法 以『數字 + hundred』表『幾百』時，無論前面的數字為多少，hundred 一律不加 s，例：
  one / two / three / four hundred
  一 / 兩 / 三 / 四百

▶ About one hundred could fit into the large room.
　這間大房間可以容納大約 1 百人。

▶ Nancy has hundreds of friends on Facebook.
　南希的臉書好友有上百位。

▶ More than a hundred people attended the event.
　超過 1 百人參加這場活動。

thousand [ˈθaʊzənd]
n. 一千 & *a.* 一千的

- thousands of...　很多 / 數千個……
- 用法 以『數字 + thousand』表『幾千』時，無論前面的數字為多少，thousand 一律不加 s，例：
  one / two / three / four thousand
  一 / 兩 / 三 / 四千

▶ One thousand applied, but only 20 people were hired.
　有 1 千人應徵，但只有 20 人被錄用。

▶ Craig has gone swimming thousands of times.
　克雷格去游泳好多次了。

▶ On his trip, Carl flew over one thousand kilometers.
　卡爾的旅途飛了 1 千多公里。

14 box [bɑks] *n.* 箱子，盒子 & *vt.* 把……裝箱 (= box up)

- boxes [ˈbɑksɪz]
- a box of...　一箱的……

▶ Brenda put her old clothes into a large box.
　布蘭達把她的舊衣服放進一個大箱子裡。

▶ Rita bought three boxes of cookies at the store.
　麗塔在店裡買了 3 箱的餅乾。

▶ Clare asked the salesperson to box up the shirt for her.
　克萊兒請店員幫她把襯衫裝進箱內。

15 bird [bɝd] *n.* 鳥

H kill two birds with one stone
一石二鳥，一舉兩得

▶ Tracy keeps a bird in a cage as a pet.
崔西養一隻鳥在籠子裡當作寵物。

▶ Chloe killed two birds with one stone by exercising while working.
克蘿伊邊運動邊工作，真是一舉兩得。

16 again [əˈɡɛn] *adv.* 又，再

H (1) once again　　再次，再度
(2) again and again　一再，再三
(3) all over again　　從頭再來

▶ Frank played tennis yesterday and then again today.
法蘭克昨天打網球，今天又打了一次。

▶ Julie said it was nice to see me again.
茱麗說能再見到我真好。

▶ Once again, Rick's team was beaten by the stronger team.
瑞克的隊伍又再次被那個較強勁的隊伍打敗了。

▶ Millie's mother told her again and again to clean her room.
米莉的媽媽再三叫她清理自己的房間。

▶ Harry had to do his assignment all over again.
哈利得重新再做他的功課。

17 thing [θɪŋ] *n.* 物，東西；事情

H (1) first thing (in the morning)
(一大早) 首要 / 馬上做的事情
(2) for one thing, ... for another, ...
首先 / 一方面……，再者 / 另一方面……

▶ Jeff took some things out of his bag.
傑夫從袋子裡拿出一些東西。

▶ Doing the laundry is one thing that Eric hates.
洗衣服是一件艾瑞克討厭做的事情。

▶ Vicky had a few things to do before going home.
維琪回家前還有幾件事情得做。

▶ Pete sent Wendy an email first thing in the morning.
彼特一早就馬上寄電子郵件給溫蒂。

▶ For one thing, milk is good for your bones; for another, it's rich in protein.
一方面，牛奶對骨骼有益；另一方面，它富含蛋白質。
*protein [ˈprotiɪn] *n.* 蛋白質

18 money [ˈmʌnɪ] *n.* 金錢 (不可數)

H (1) save money　　　存錢；省錢
(2) make / earn money　賺錢
(3) Money doesn't grow on trees.
錢得來不易。

▶ Erica's house cost a lot of money to buy.
艾瑞卡的家花了很多錢買。

延伸 (1) change [tʃendʒ]
n. 零錢；硬幣（皆不可數）①
(2) coin [kɔɪn] n. 硬幣 ②
(3) bill [bɪl]
n. 鈔票〔美〕（= note [not]〔英〕）②

▶ Ron saves money by riding a bike to school.
榮恩騎腳踏車去上學來省錢。

▶ Charlie made some money by investing.
查理透過投資賺了點錢。
＊invest [ɪnˋvɛst] vi. 投資

▶ Oscar always says, "Money doesn't grow on trees, so you should use it wisely."
奧斯卡總是說：『錢得來不易，你應該要明智用錢。』

19 place [ples] n. 地方，場所；家；名次 & vt. 放置，擺放

片 (1) sb's place 某人的家
(2) first / second / third place
第一／二／三名
(3) take place 發生；舉辦
(4) place importance on sth
強調／重視某事
(5) placed an order (for sth)
下訂（某物）

衍 (1) replace [rɪˋples] vt. 取代 ③
(2) placement [ˋplesmənt]
n. 放置 ⑤

▶ Shirley thinks Sydney is the nicest place to live.
雪莉認為雪梨是最棒的居住地。

▶ Ted went to Jim's place to play games.
泰德去吉姆的家玩遊戲。

▶ David didn't win, but he came in second place.
大衛沒有獲勝，但他拿了第二名。

▶ The meeting will take place on Thursday afternoon.
這場會議會在週四下午舉辦。

▶ Rodney placed his elbows on the table.
羅德尼把他的手肘放在桌上。

▶ Trina places a lot of importance on fashion.
崔娜很看重時尚。

▶ Wayne placed an order for a hamburger at the counter.
韋恩在櫃臺點了一份漢堡。

20 color [ˋkʌlɚ] n. 顏色；色彩 & vt. 染色 & vt. & vi. 上色，著色

衍 colorful [ˋkʌlɚfəl]
a. 富有色彩的；生動的 ③

▶ Janet's favorite colors are pink and purple.
珍妮特最喜歡的顏色是粉色和紫色。

▶ Diana painted the walls yellow to give the room color.
黛安娜把牆漆成黃色，來增添房間的色彩。

▶ Veronica colors her hair to hide the gray.
維洛妮卡染髮來遮住灰白髮。

▶ The girl drew a picture and then colored it in.
這位女孩畫了一張圖，然後替它上色。

▶ Cindy can spend hours just coloring.
辛蒂可以花好幾個小時只著色。

blue [blu] a. 憂鬱的；藍色的 & n. 藍色
片 (1) feel blue 感到憂鬱

▶ When winter comes, some people easily feel blue because of the gloomy weather.
冬天來臨時，有些人容易因為陰沉的天氣而感到憂鬱。

(2) dark / light blue　深 / 淺藍色

(3) out of the blue
突然地，出乎意料地

衍 blues [bluz]
n. 憂鬱 (前面須加定冠詞 the)；藍調音樂
(皆不可數)

似 (1) gloomy [ˋglumɪ] a. 憂鬱的 ⑤

(2) depressed [dɪˋprɛst]
a. 感到沮喪的

▶ My girlfriend is a Canadian with blonde hair and blue eyes.
我女友是加拿大人，有金黃色的頭髮和湛藍的雙眼。

▶ Eileen thinks that light blue is the most beautiful color.
艾琳覺得淺藍色是最漂亮的顏色。

▶ We were having dinner when Peter appeared out of the blue.
我們正在吃晚餐，此時彼得突然出現了。

---

red [rɛd] a. 紅色的 & n. 紅色

片 (1) a red envelope　紅包

(2) dark / bright red　深 / 亮紅色

(3) go / turn red
(因尷尬、生氣) 臉通紅的，漲紅的

▶ Troy got a red envelope with some money in it.
特洛伊拿到一個裝了點錢的紅包袋。

▶ Phil turned red when the boss found his mistake.
老闆發現菲爾出錯時，他的臉都紅了。

▶ Betty likes to use red to paint with.
貝蒂喜歡用紅色來畫畫。

---

yellow [ˋjɛlo]
a. 黃色的 & n. 黃色 & vi. & vt. (使) 變黃

▶ Monica didn't want to buy the yellow car.
莫妮卡不想買那輛黃色的車。

▶ Samantha chose yellow for her bedroom walls.
莎曼珊選了黃色做她房間牆壁的顏色。

▶ Over time, the photograph began to yellow.
照片隨著時間過去變黃了。

▶ The sun yellowed the papers by the window.
太陽染黃了窗邊的文件。

---

green [grin]
a. 綠色的；環保的 & n. 綠色；草地 & vt.
綠化

片 (1) green energy　綠色能源

(2) a green issue　環保議題

(3) be green with envy
感到嫉妒，眼紅

似 grass [græs]
n. 草地 (前須置定冠詞 the) ①

▶ Fanny wore a green dress to the party.
芬妮穿了一件綠色的洋裝出席派對。

▶ Chuck bought an electric scooter because it uses green energy.
查克買了一臺電動摩托車，因為它使用綠能。

▶ Because his friend is rich, Steve is green with envy.
史蒂夫嫉妒他朋友很有錢。

▶ The green of the grass made Nicole feel happy.
草地綠油油的顏色讓妮可感到快樂。

▶ Many children played on the green near the library.
許多小朋友在圖書館旁的草地上玩耍。

▶ To green the town, many trees were planted.
種植了許多樹木以綠化這座城鎮。

Unit 05

0501-0505

---

1 for [fɔr] *prep.* 給；為了；因為；贊成 & *conj.* 因為

反 **against** [əˈgɛnst] *prep.* 反對 ②

比 for 與 because 皆可表『因為』，惟 for 可作對等連接詞，連接兩個對等的子句，使用時不置句首；because 是從屬連接詞，其所引導的子句可置於句首或主要子句之後。

▸ Lucas wrote a song for his wife.
盧卡斯寫了一首歌給他太太。

▸ Those people are fighting for their freedom.
那些人是為了他們的自由而戰。

▸ For some reason, Nora decided not to study abroad.
基於某些原因，諾拉決定不出國念書。

▸ Are you for or against the proposal?
你是贊成或反對本提案？

▸ Jerry decided to stop for lunch first, for he was feeling hungry.
傑瑞決定先停下來吃午餐，因為他肚子餓了。

---

because [bɪˈkʌz] *conj.* 因為

片 because of + N/V-ing　因為……
　= due to + N/V-ing
　= as a result of + N/V-ing
　= thanks to + N/V-ing

▸ I like Jeremy because he is polite.
= Because Jeremy is polite, I like him.
因為傑洛米有禮貌，所以我喜歡他。

▸ Because of COVID-19, we couldn't travel abroad.
由於新冠肺炎，我們無法出國旅行。

---

2 will [wɪl] *aux.* 將要 (縮寫為 'll) & *n.* 意志；意願；遺囑

片 (1) against one's will
　　 違背某人的意願
　(2) at will　隨意地，任意地
　(3) make a will　立遺囑

衍 **willing** [ˈwɪlɪŋ] *a.* 有意願的 ②

用法 will 作助動詞用於未來式，其過去式為 would [wʊd]，於過去的時間點認為未來會發生時使用；will 的否定形式 will not 亦可縮寫為 won't。

▸ I will arrive in New York tomorrow morning.
= I'll arrive in New York tomorrow morning.
明早我將會抵達紐約。

▸ Nobody can question Stanley's will to win.
沒有人可以質疑史坦利的求勝意志。

▸ You can't just ignore the rules at will.
你不能隨意忽略這些規定。

▸ The man made his final will a month before he died.
這名男子在去世前一個月立下最後的遺囑。

---

3 can [kæn] *aux.* 能，可以 & *n.* 金屬罐〔美〕& *vt.* 裝 (食物) 於罐頭內

三 can, canned [kænd], canned

片 a can of...　一罐……

衍 **canned** [kænd] *a.* 裝成罐頭的
　 canned food　罐頭食物

▸ Can you speak French?
你會說法文嗎？

▸ You can't talk loudly in the library.
= You cannot talk loudly in the library.
在圖書館內不能大聲喧嘩。

38

似 tin [tɪn] *n.* 金屬罐〔英〕⑤

用法 can 作助動詞時，其過去式為 could [kʊd]；can 的否定形式為 cannot 或亦可縮寫為 can't。

▶ Matthew drank ten cans of soda at the party.
馬修在派對上喝了 10 罐汽水。

▶ My mother always cans fruit at the end of the summer.
每年夏末，我母親總是把水果製成罐頭。

---

4 **time** [taɪm] *n.* 時間；次數，回 & *vt.* 選定時間

片 (1) have time　　　　有時間
　　(2) take one's time　　某人慢慢來
　　(3) for the time being　暫時
　　(4) in no time　　　　很快地
　　(5) on time　　　　　準時
　　(6) in time　　　　　及時
　　(7) from time to time　偶爾
　　＝ at times
　　＝ sometimes
　　＝ on occasion
　　＝ occasionally
　　(8) time sth to V
　　　　把 (某活動) 安排在……的時候
衍 (1) timing [ˈtaɪmɪŋ] *n.* 時機
　　(2) overtime [ˈovɚˌtaɪm] *n.* 加班

▶ Time passes quickly when you're having fun.
玩樂時，時間過得特別快。

▶ Nate goes to the gym three times a week.
奈特一週上健身房 3 次。

▶ John didn't have time to prepare for the test.
約翰沒有時間來準備考試。

▶ Take your time with the meal; there's no rush.
你可以慢慢用餐，不用急。

▶ I'm afraid that you have to share your room for the time being.
恐怕你得暫時跟別人合住一間房。

▶ Luke finished the job in no time and left.
路克很快地把工作做完就離開了。

▶ The train arrived at the station on time.
火車準時到站。

▶ Will you be here in time for the concert?
你來得及趕來聽這場演唱會嗎？

▶ My parents come to Taipei to see me from time to time.
我父母偶爾會來臺北看我。

▶ Tom timed his visit to suit Judy's convenience.
湯姆選在茱蒂方便的時候去拜訪她。

---

5 **take** [tek] *vt.* 拿；帶……去；搭乘；花費，需要 (時間、精力等) & *n.* 看法

三 take, took [tʊk], taken [ˈtekən]
片 (1) take sb/sth to + 地方
　　　帶某人 / 某物去某地
　　(2) take a taxi / train / bus
　　　搭計程車 / 火車 / 公車
　　(3) It takes sb + 時間 + to V
　　　某人花若干時間做……
　　(4) a take on...　對……的看法
　　(5) give and take
　　　互相讓步，有所取捨

▶ Do you know who took my book?
你知道誰拿走我的書嗎？

▶ Eric took his children to the amusement park.
艾瑞克帶他的小孩到遊樂園。

▶ Grace takes a bus to work every day.
葛瑞絲每天搭公車去上班。

▶ It took me five hours to finish the book.
我花了 5 個小時看完那本書。

▶ What's your take on this issue?
你對這個議題的看法為何？

▶ We should all learn to give and take.
我們都應該學會互相讓步。

give [gɪv] *vt.* & *vi.* 給予；捐贈
▤ give, gave [gev], given [ˈgɪvən]
☷ (1) give sb sth　把某物拿給某人
　= give sth to sb
　(2) give to...　捐給……
　(3) give in to...　屈服於……

▶ Give me that book over there.
= Give that book over there to me.
把那邊那本書拿給我。

▶ Uncle Tom gave generously to the charity.
湯姆叔叔慷慨捐獻給那個慈善機構。

▶ Never give in to fate.
永不向命運低頭。

6　then [ðɛn] *adv.* 然後，接著；那時，當時；那麼 & *a.* 當時的

☷ (1) since then　從那時起
　(2) (every) now and then
　　有時，偶爾
　= sometimes
㊣ (1) next [nɛkst] *adv.* 然後，接著 ①
　(2) at that time　在當時
　(3) in that case　那樣的話

▶ Add the milk, and then stir the soup for five minutes.
加牛奶，接著攪拌湯 5 分鐘。

▶ Mr. Brown was a famous singer then.
布朗先生當時是位知名歌手。

▶ The whole system has changed since then.
從那時起整個系統就改變了。

▶ We still get together every now and then after all these years.
過了這些年，我們有時還會聚在一起。

▶ If you want to lose weight, then you have to eat less.
如果你想減肥，那麼就得少吃一點。

▶ In 1941, America's then president declared war on Japan.
1941 年，當時的美國總統向日本宣戰。

7　about [əˈbaʊt] *prep.* 有關 & *adv.* 大約；幾乎

☷ be about to V　即將做……
㊣ (1) regarding [rɪˈgardɪŋ]
　　prep. 有關 ④
　(2) concerning [kənˈsɝnɪŋ]
　　prep. 關於 ④
　(3) almost [ˈɔlmost] *adv.* 幾乎 ①

▶ This book is about music.
這是一本有關音樂的書。

▶ The bus will leave in about ten minutes.
公車大約再過 10 分鐘就要開走了。

▶ Ron was about ready to leave, but his wife wasn't.
榮恩幾乎準備好要出發了，但他太太還沒好。

▶ The principal is about to arrive.
校長快要到了。

8 **find** [faɪnd] *vt.* 發現，找到；認為 & *n.* 發現（物）

目 find, found [faʊnd], found

用 (1) find out... 找到……
　(2) find sb/sth + adj.
　　認為某人 / 某事物……

似 discover [dɪsˋkʌvɚ] *vt.* 發現，找到 ②

▶ The police still couldn't find enough evidence.
　警方還是無法找到足夠的證據。

▶ You have to find out the answer by yourself.
　你必須自己找出答案。

▶ Cory found the TV show interesting.
　柯瑞認為這檔電視節目很有趣。

▶ Harry's new home is great—it's a real find!
　哈利的新家真棒 —— 能找到這種住所真不錯！

9 **way** [we] *n.* 路；方向；方法；作風

用 (1) on the / one's way to + 地方
　　某人前往某地的途中
　(2) stand in the / one's way
　　擋住某人去路；阻礙某人
　(3) a way to V　做……的方法
　(4) in a way　在某一方面
　(5) in some / many ways
　　在一些 / 許多方面

似 (1) route [rut / raʊt] *n.* 路線 ④
　(2) direction [dəˋrɛkʃən] *n.* 方向 ②
　(3) method [ˋmɛθəd] *n.* 方法 ②

▶ I ran into Jenny on my way to the post office.
　我去郵局的途中遇見了珍妮。

▶ Keep on trying. Let nothing stand in your way.
　繼續努力。別讓任何困難阻礙你。

▶ Ted didn't know which way to go.
　泰德不知道要走哪邊。

▶ We tried to think of some ways to fix the problem.
　我們設法想出幾個辦法來解決這個問題。

▶ You need to get used to the way he talks.
　你得要習慣他的說話風格。

▶ What you said is right in a way.
　你所說的話就某方面而言是對的。

10 **even** [ˋivən] *adv.* 甚至 & *a.* 相等的；平坦的；偶數的 & *vt.* 使平等

用 (1) even if　即使 (視作連接詞)
　(2) even though　雖然 (視作連接詞)

衍 evenly [ˋivənlɪ]
　adv. 平等地；均勻地；平坦地

似 (1) equal [ˋikwəl] *a.* 相等的 ②
　(2) flat [flæt] *a.* 平坦的 ②
　(3) smooth [smuð] *a.* 平坦的 ②

反 (1) uneven [ʌnˋivən] *a.* 不平坦的
　(2) unequal [ʌnˋikwəl] *a.* 不相等的

▶ We're not friends; I don't even know his name.
　我們不是朋友，我甚至連他的名字都不知道。

▶ I'll give you the money even if you can't pay me back.
　即使你沒能力還錢，我還是會給你錢。

▶ Even though he is poor, she still loves him.
　雖然他窮，她仍愛他。

▶ Gordy thought he had an even chance of winning.
　高迪認為自己也有同等獲勝的機會。

▶ The floor was not even, and I almost fell.
　這地面不平，我差點跌倒。

▶ Even numbers can be divided exactly by 2.
　偶數可被 2 整除。

▶ With the goal, Ben evened the game at 3-3.
　班射門得分，讓比賽以 3-3 打平。

11 use [juz] *vt.* 使用 & [jus] *n.* 用處，用途

片 (1) use sth to V　用某物做……
　　(2) use A as B　用 A 作為 B
　　(3) be of (great) use　很有用
　　= be (very) useful
衍 (1) used [juzd] *a.* 二手的 ②
　　(2) user [ˋjuzɚ] *n.* 使用者 ②
　　(3) usage [ˋjusɪdʒ] *n.* 使用 ④

▶ You can use your smartphone to listen to podcasts.
你可以用智慧型手機來聽播客。

▶ Sharon uses her garage as an office.
雪倫把她的車庫當作辦公室來使用。

▶ I thought that his advice was of great use.
= I thought that his advice was very useful.
我認為他的忠告很有用。

useful [ˋjusfḷ] *a.* 有用的

片 be useful for...　對……有用
似 handy [ˋhændɪ] *a.* 有用的 ③

▶ This online map is very useful for driving.
這個線上地圖對開車非常有用。

useless [ˋjusləs] *a.* 沒有用的

片 It is useless to V　做……是沒有用的

▶ I think it's useless to try to fix this machine.
我認為修理這部機器是沒有用的。

12 like [laɪk] *vt.* 喜歡 & *n.* 相似的人或物；喜好 (此意常用複數) & *prep.* 像

片 (1) like + V-ing　喜歡做……
　　= like to V
　　(2) would like to V　想要做……
　　= feel like + V-ing
　　(3) and the like　等等，諸如此類
　　= and so on
　　(4) look like sb　長得像某人
反 dislike [dɪsˋlaɪk]
vt. 討厭 & *n.* 嫌惡 ③

▶ Tim likes playing soccer very much.
= Tim likes to play soccer very much.
提姆非常喜歡踢足球。

▶ I would like to see a movie tonight.
= I feel like seeing a movie tonight.
我今晚想去看場電影。

▶ At the zoo we saw pandas, tigers, lions, and the like.
在動物園，我們看到熊貓、老虎、獅子等等的動物。

▶ Everyone has his own likes and dislikes.
人各有好惡。

▶ Kate looks like her father.
凱特長得像她爸爸。

13 think [θɪŋk] *vt.* & *vi.* 認為；想，思考

三 think, thought [θɔt], thought
片 (1) think that...　認為……
　　(2) think about / of...　想……
衍 thinking [ˋθɪŋkɪŋ] *n.* 想法
似 believe [bəˋliv] *vt.* 認為 ①

▶ I think that this is an exceptional case.
我認為這是一個例外的情形。

▶ It was so noisy outside that I couldn't think.
外面太吵了，吵到我無法思考。

▶ Jessica is thinking about the story for her new novel.
潔西卡在想新小說的故事。

14　own [on] *a.* 自己的 & *pron.* 自己 & *vt.* 擁有

片 (1) of one's own　某人自己的
(2) on one's own　靠自己

衍 (1) owner [ˈonɚ] *n.* 擁有者 ②
(2) ownership [ˈonɚˌʃɪp]
　　n. 所有權 ③

似 (1) have [hæv] *vt.* 擁有 ①
(2) possess [pəˈzɛs] *vt.* 持有 ④

▶ You'll have to make up your own mind.
你必須自己拿定主意。

▶ Believe it or not, the guy has a plane of his own.
信不信由你，這傢伙有一架自己的飛機。

▶ From now on, you'll have to be on your own.
從今以後，你一切得靠自己了。

▶ They don't own the house—they rent it.
他們沒擁有這棟房子 —— 他們是用租的。

15　life [laɪf] *n.* 生命；人生；生活；生物（此意為集合名詞，不可數）

複 lives [laɪvz]

片 lead / live a(n) + adj. + life
過著……的生活

衍 (1) lifetime [ˈlaɪfˌtaɪm] *n.* 一生 ③
(2) lifestyle [ˈlaɪfˌstaɪl] *n.* 生活方式

▶ Joy thinks there is life on other planets.
喬伊認為其他星球上有生命。

▶ The flood claimed 20 lives.
洪水奪走了 20 條人命。

▶ Life is a long journey.
人生是一條漫長的旅程。

▶ Aunt Joyce leads a simple life in the country.
喬伊絲阿姨過著簡樸的鄉間生活。

▶ There is almost no life at all in that desert.
那個沙漠裡幾乎沒有生物。

16　live [lɪv] *vi.* 活著；居住；生活 & [laɪv] *a.* 活的；現場的

片 live a(n) + adj. + life
過著……的生活

衍 (1) lively [ˈlaɪvlɪ]
　　a. 有生氣的，生動的 ③
(2) living [ˈlɪvɪŋ] *a.* 活著的 & *n.* 生計

似 alive [əˈlaɪv] *a.* 活著的 ②

▶ People cannot live long without water.
沒有水的話，人活不了多久。

▶ Susan lives next door to me.
蘇珊住在我隔壁。

▶ Gail lives a happy life with her husband.
蓋兒和她老公過著快樂的生活。

▶ The cat was playing with a live mouse.
這隻貓正在玩一隻活生生的老鼠。

▶ We went to see a live band last night.
昨晚我們去看了現場樂團的表演。

17　just [dʒʌst] *adv.* 剛剛；正好；只是；非常 & *a.* 公正的

片 just a second / minute / moment
等一下，稍等一會

▶ I just saw Eric leave the office.
我剛才看到艾瑞克離開辦公室。

43

衍 justice [ˈdʒʌstɪs] *n.* 公平，正義 ②

似 (1) only [ˈonlɪ] *adv.* 只，僅僅 ①
　　(2) simply [ˈsɪmplɪ] *adv.* 只，僅僅 ②
　　(3) fair [fɛr] *a.* 公正的 ②

反 unjust [ʌnˈdʒʌst] *a.* 不公平的

▶ Amanda came just as I was leaving.
　我正好要離開時，亞曼達就來了。

▶ I'm just looking; I don't want to buy anything today.
　我只是看一看，今天不想買東西。

▶ The weather is just marvelous.
　天氣真是非常棒。
　*marvelous [ˈmɑrvələs] *a.* 好極的

▶ Just a minute, I'll be right back.
　請等一下，我馬上就回來。

▶ We all think that the judge made a just decision.
　我們都認為這名法官做了一個公正的決定。

18　between [brˈtwin] *prep. & adv.* 在 (兩者、時間等) 之間 (地)

片 (1) between A and B
　　　在 A 與 B 之間
　　(2) in between
　　　在 (兩者、時間等) 之間 (地)

▶ The post office is between the bank and the grocery store.
　郵局位在銀行和雜貨店的中間。

▶ We have two meetings this afternoon, with a break in between.
　我們下午有 2 場會議，中間會休息一次。

19　still [stɪl] *adv.* 仍然，還；更加 (加強比較級) & *a.* 靜止不動的

用法 still 表『還』的意思時，僅用於肯定句。
若句中動詞為一般動詞，still 置一般動詞前；若為 be 動詞，則置 be 動詞後。

▶ I've eaten five hamburgers, but I'm still hungry.
　我已經吃了 5 個漢堡，但還是很餓。

▶ Although Kate got good grades, her parents asked her to study still harder.
　雖然凱特成績很好，她父母叫她還要更努力。

▶ Keep still while I take your picture.
　我幫你拍照時，請保持不動。

20　another [əˈnʌðɚ] *a.* 再 / 另一 & *pron.* 再 / 另一個

片 one another　互相
= each other

▶ Ted ordered another drink for himself.
　泰德為自己再點了一杯飲料。

▶ I just watched a film, and I'll probably watch another.
　我剛看完一部電影，有可能會再看一部。

▶ They gave one another presents at Christmas.
　他們在聖誕節期間彼此互送禮物。

21　work [wɜk] *vt. & vi.* 工作 & *vi.* 運轉，運行；有效 & *n.* 工作 (不可數)；作品

片 (1) work for... 替……工作
 (2) work out sth / work sth out
　　解決某事
 (3) look for work　找工作
 ＝ look for a job

▸ My grandmother used to work for a publisher.
　我奶奶曾替一間出版社工作。

▸ The machine doesn't work.
　這機器故障了無法運作。

▸ I'm glad this method works!
　我很高興這個方法行得通！

▸ They teamed up and worked out the problem.
　他們合作解決了這個問題。

▸ Vanessa is looking for work now.
　凡妮莎正在找工作。

▸ The artist's works are on display at the gallery.
　這名藝術家的作品正在藝廊展出。

worker [ˋwɜkɚ] *n.* 工人；員工

▸ There are thousands of workers in the factory.
　工廠裡有數千名工人。

coworker [ˋko͵wɜkɚ]
n. 同事 (＝ co-worker)

似 colleague [ˋkɑlig] *n.* 同事 ④

▸ Terry gets along well with his coworkers.
　泰瑞跟同事們處得很好。

22　well [wɛl] *adv.* 很好地 & *a.* (身體) 健康的 & *n.* 井

片 an oil well　油井
似 healthy [ˋhɛlθɪ] *a.* 健康的 ①

▸ If you do your duties well, you'll be rewarded.
　如果好好盡你的職責，你就會得到獎賞。

▸ I don't feel well today, so I'll call in sick.
　我今天身體不舒服，所以我會打電話請病假。

▸ The oil well has gone dry, so we'll have to find another one.
　這座油井枯竭了，我們必須找另一座。

23　how [haʊ] *adv.* 如何；多麼地

片 How come ＋ S ＋ V?　為什麼……？

▸ How did Martin do on the test last week?
　馬丁上週的考試成績如何？

▸ How well the girl sings!
　這女孩唱得多麼好聽啊！

▸ How come the little boy is crying?
　小男孩為什麼在哭？

24　great [gret] *a.* (數量、規模) 大的；偉大的；很棒的 & *n.* 偉人 (常用複數)

片 be one of the all-time greats
有史以來最偉大的人之一

似 (1) large [lɑrdʒ] *a.* 大的 ①
(2) wonderful [ˈwʌndəˌfəl]
　　a. 很棒的 ①
(3) fabulous [ˈfæbjələs] *a.* 很棒的 ⑤

▶ A great fire burned down the house.
大火燒毀了那棟房子。

▶ Gandhi was a great man.
甘地是個偉大的人物。

▶ Peter just came up with a great idea.
彼得剛剛想出一個很棒的點子。

▶ Chopin is one of the all-time greats in music.
蕭邦是有史以來最偉大的音樂家之一。

25　thank [θæŋk] *vt.* & *n.* 感謝 (作名詞時，恆用複數)

片 thank sb for + N/V-ing
因……感謝某人

衍 thankful [ˈθæŋkfəl] *a.* 感謝的 ③

▶ Mark thanked his friends for helping him move.
馬克感謝他的朋友幫他搬家。

▶ Tina bought Ellie a meal to show her thanks.
蒂娜請艾麗吃一頓飯以表達感激。

sorry [ˈsɔrɪ] *a.* 抱歉的；難過的

片 (1) be / feel sorry about...
對……感到抱歉；
對……感到很難過
(2) be sorry that...
對……感到抱歉；
對……感到很難過
(3) be sorry to see / hear...
看 / 聽到……很難過

▶ Nancy felt sorry about forgetting Bob's birthday.
南希很抱歉忘了鮑伯的生日。

▶ Ricky was sorry that he broke Vicky's toy.
瑞奇對摔壞薇琪的玩具感到抱歉。

▶ Kelly was sorry to hear Tony's dog died.
凱莉聽到東尼的狗去世很難過。

26　eat [it] *vt.* & *vi.* 吃

三 eat, ate [et], eaten [ˈitn̩]
片 eat out / in　外出用餐 / 在家吃飯

▶ Dean ate breakfast quickly and then left home.
狄恩快速吃了早餐後離開家裡。

▶ Barbara told her kids it was time to eat.
芭芭拉告訴她小孩吃飯的時間到了。

▶ Ian doesn't eat out often because it's expensive.
伊恩不常外出用餐，因為費用昂貴。

drink [drɪŋk] *vt.* & *vi.* 喝 & *n.* 飲料
三 drink, drank [dræŋk],
　drunk [drʌŋk]

▶ Greg drank a lot of water on the hot day.
葛瑞格在那個大熱天喝了很多水。

▶ Wayne didn't want anything to drink.
韋恩不想喝任何東西。

▶ Jolene's favorite drink is orange juice with ice.
喬琳最喜歡的飲料是加冰塊的柳橙汁。

27　all [ɔl] *a.* 整個的；全部的 & *adv.* 完全地 & *pron.* 所有 & *n.* 所有一切

片 (1) all alone　獨自一人
　 (2) not... at all　一點也不

▸ Riley was so hungry he ate all the pizza.
雷利太餓了，所以他吃了一整個披薩。

▸ All Minnie's teachers think that she is smart.
米妮的老師都認為她很聰明。

▸ Freda watched TV all alone in her living room.
芙蕾達自己一人在客廳看電視。

▸ Noah doesn't like carrots at all.
諾亞一點都不喜歡紅蘿蔔。

▸ All Paul had in his pocket was a dollar.
保羅口袋裡所有的東西僅是 1 美元。

28　become [bɪˋkʌm] *vi.* 變得；成為

三 become, became [bɪˋkem],
become
片 become + adj.　變得……

▸ Gloria decided to exercise and become healthy.
葛洛利亞決定要運動變得健康。

▸ Oscar became an actor after graduating from college.
奧斯卡從大學畢業後成為一名演員。

29　tell [tɛl] *vt.* 講，告訴；辨別

三 tell, told [told], told
片 (1) tell sb (that)...　告訴某人……
　 (2) tell (sb) about...
　　　告訴 (某人) 有關……
似 tale [tel] *n.* 故事 ②

▸ Roy told his mom he wanted to be a doctor.
洛伊告訴他媽媽他想成為一名醫生。

▸ Clark told his daughter about her grandfather.
克萊克告訴他女兒有關她爺爺的事。

▸ Sally could tell that her boss was mad.
莎莉看得出來她的老闆很火大。

30　ask [æsk] *vt.* & *vi.* 詢問；請求 & *vt.* 邀請

片 (1) ask sb to V　請 / 要某人做……
　 (2) ask for help　尋求協助
　 (3) ask sb out (on a date / to dinner)
　　　約某人出來 (約會 / 吃晚餐)
似 invite [ɪnˋvaɪt] *vt.* 邀請 ①

▸ Roger asked his teacher if he could go home early.
羅傑詢問老師他是否可以早點回家。

▸ Bobby asked his father to buy him a bike.
巴比請他爸爸買一臺腳踏車給他。

▸ Carmen asked for help from her coworker.
卡門向她的同事尋求協助。

▸ Willy finally asked Fiona out to dinner.
威利終於邀費歐娜共進晚餐。

Unit 06

0601-0604

---

1 **most** [most] *a.* 最多的；大多數的 & *adv.* 最 & *pron.* 最多；大多數

片 at most　最多

衍 mostly [ˋmostlɪ]
adv. 大部分地，主要地 ③

用法 (1) most 作形容詞，表『最多的』時，其前要加 the；表『大多數的』時，則不加 the。
(2) most 作最高級副詞，表『最』，修飾句中的副詞、動詞時，不一定要加 the；但修飾名詞時，則須加 the。

▶ The player who scores the most points is the winner.
得到最多分的選手是贏家。

▶ Most people find it hard to stop smoking.
大多數人認為戒菸很難。

▶ Lilly is the most beautiful girl I've ever seen.
莉莉是我見過最漂亮的女生。

▶ It will take 40 minutes at most to get to the airport.
最多只要花 40 分鐘就可以到機場。

▶ Most of what Grace told you was true.
葛瑞絲告訴你的事情大多數是真的。

---

least [list]
a. 最少的 & *adv.* 最少地 & *pron.* 最少

片 at least　至少

用法 (1) least 作形容詞，表『最少的』時，其前要加 the。
(2) least 作最高級副詞，表『最少地』，修飾句中的副詞、動詞時，不一定要加 the；但修飾名詞時，則須加 the。

▶ Terry has the least workload of us all.
泰瑞的工作量在我們當中是最少的。

▶ This is the least interesting event I've ever attended.
這是我所參加過最無聊的活動了。

▶ At least five hundred people showed up for the rally.
至少有 500 人出席該集會。
*rally [ˋrælɪ] *n.* 集會

---

2 **front** [frʌnt] *n.* 前面 & *a.* 前面的

片 (1) the front of...　……的前面 / 方
(2) in the front of...
在 (某物內部) 的前面 / 方
(3) in front of...
在 (某物外部) 的前方

▶ Maria walked to the front of the stage and took a bow.
瑪麗亞走到舞臺前方鞠躬。

▶ I'd like to sit in the front of the theater.
我想坐在電影院的前排。

▶ There was a long lineup in front of the stand.
攤位前方有一條很長的排隊隊伍。
*lineup [ˋlaɪnˌʌp] *n.* 隊伍

▶ The front tire of Linda's bicycle was flat.
琳達腳踏車的前輪沒氣了。

---

back [bæk]
n. 背部；背面 & *a.* 後面的 & *adv.* 向後；回原處 & *vt.* & *vi.* (使) 後退

▶ I hate people who speak ill of me behind my back.
我討厭在背後說我壞話的人。

▶ The baseball hit Jack on the back of his head.
棒球打到傑克頭的後部。

48

片 (1) behind sb's back　在某人背後
(2) the back of...
　　在……的背面 / 後部
(3) back and forth　來回地
(4) go back (to + 地點)　回去 (某地)
(5) go back home　回家

▸ Rebecca keeps her phone in her back pocket.
蕾貝卡把電話放在後面的口袋。

▸ The security guard walked back and forth in front of the bank.
警衛在銀行前面來回走動。

▸ Victor never went back to that restaurant.
維克多再也沒有回去那間餐廳。

▸ Dylan doesn't know how to back his car into the garage.
狄倫不知道要怎麼倒車入庫。

3　show [ʃo] vt. 給……看；顯示；展出 & vt. & vi. 放映 & n. 節目，表演

三 show, showed [ʃod], shown [ʃon] / showed
片 (1) show up　出現
　　= appear
(2) a TV / talk show
　　電視節目 / 脫口秀
似 (1) display [dɪˋsple] vt. 展出 ②
(2) exhibit [ɪgˋzɪbɪt]
　　vt. 顯示，現出；展示 ④

▸ Can you show me your favorite photo?
可以給我看你最喜歡的照片嗎？

▸ A study shows that staying up all night to study isn't a great idea.
一項研究顯示，通宵念書並不是個好主意。

▸ The gallery shows the work of local artists.
這間藝廊展出當地藝術家的成果作品。

▸ Jack didn't show up on time.
傑克沒有準時出現。

▸ All the theaters are showing the new James Bond movie.
所有電影院都在放映《007》系列的新電影。

▸ The talk show I saw on TV last night was fantastic.
我昨晚在電視看到的脫口秀很精采。

4　house [haʊs] n. 房子 & [haʊz] vt. 供給住所，收容

衍 (1) housekeeper [ˋhaʊsˌkipɚ]
　　n. 管家 ③
(2) housework [ˋhaʊsˌwɝk]
　　n. 家事 (不可數) ④
(3) household [ˋhaʊsˌhold]
　　n. 戶，家庭 ④

▸ My grandmother's house is old and shabby.
我奶奶的房子已經老舊不堪了。
＊shabby [ˋʃæbɪ] a. 破爛的

▸ We need a bigger place to house those stray dogs.
我們需要大一點的地方來收留那些流浪狗。

housewife [ˋhaʊsˌwaɪf]
n. 家庭主婦

複 housewives [ˋhaʊsˌwaɪvz]

▸ Holly has been a housewife since she got married.
荷莉婚後就成了家庭主婦。

5 call [kɔl] vt. & vi. 打電話；喊叫 & vt. 稱呼；叫來；召開 & n. 一通電話；呼叫

片 (1) call sb (up) / call (up) sb
　　打電話給某人
　 = give sb a call
　(2) call a meeting　召開會議
　(3) call sth off / call off sth
　　取消……
　(4) a call for help　求救聲
似 name [nem] vt. 給……命名 ①

▶ Call me whenever you need help.
= Call me up whenever you need help.
= Give me a call whenever you need help.
　任何時候需要幫忙都可以打電話給我。

▶ My mom called me, but I didn't hear her.
　我媽在叫我，可是我沒聽見。

▶ When Max was little, his parents called him Maxie.
　麥可斯的父母在他小時候叫他麥西。

▶ Janine called the waiter over to order another drink.
　珍寧叫服務生過來再點另一杯飲料。

▶ The boss called a meeting to discuss the issue.
　老闆召開會議來討論這個議題。

▶ The game was called off because of rain.
　這場比賽因雨取消。

▶ When I was walking along the river, I heard a call for help.
　我沿河散步時，聽見了求救聲。

6 leave [liv] vt. & vi. 離開 & vt. 留下；使處於 (某種狀態) & n. 休假 (不可數)

三 leave, left [lɛft], left
片 (1) leave sb/sth + adj.
　　讓某人 / 某事物處於 (某種狀態)
　(2) leave for + 地方　動身前往某地
　 = set off for + 地方
　 = head to / for + 地方
　 = depart for + 地方
　(3) sick / annual leave　病 / 年假
　(4) take leave　請假

▶ As soon as Molly left the room, her baby cried.
　茉莉一離開房間，她的小寶寶就哭了。

▶ I left my cellphone in the office.
　我把手機留在辦公室裡了。

▶ Ian left the door open, so that I could come in.
　伊恩讓門開著，這樣我才能進來。

▶ John left for Hong Kong yesterday.
　約翰昨天動身前往香港。

▶ I'll take leave to attend my sister's wedding.
　我會請假去參加妹妹的婚禮。

7 school [skul] n. 學校；魚群 & vt. 教育，訓練

片 (1) before / after school
　　上學前 / 放學後
　(2) a school of fish / whales
　　一群魚 / 鯨魚

▶ We enjoy playing basketball after school.
　我們喜歡在放學後打籃球。

▶ We saw a school of fish in the river.
　我們看到河中有一群魚。

▶ Tony schooled his son in the rules of grammar.
　東尼教他兒子文法規則。

course [kɔrs]
n. 課程；路線；過程；一道菜 & *vi.* (大量) 流動

月 (1) in the course of...
　　　　在……的過程中
　　= during...
　　(2) the first / main course
　　　　第一道菜 / 主菜
　　(3) course down　流下

似 (1) class [klæs] *n.* 課堂 ①
　　(2) route [rut / raʊt] *n.* 路線 ④
　　(3) dish [dɪʃ] *n.* 一道菜 ①

▶ Next month I'm taking a writing course.
　下個月我要修一門寫作課。
▶ The course takes the runners through the woods.
　這條路線會帶跑者們穿越樹林。
▶ They'll find time to read in the course of their travels.
　他們在旅途中會找時間閱讀。
▶ The main course is steak.
　主菜是牛排。
▶ Tammy's tears coursed down her cheeks.
　譚美的眼淚滾落她的雙頰。

8　while [(h)waɪl] *conj.* 當；而；雖然 & *n.* 一段時間 (只用單數) & *vt.* 消磨

月 (1) (for) a while　　一會兒
　　(2) once in a while　偶爾
　　= sometimes
　　(3) while sth away / while away
　　　　sth　消磨 (時間等)

衍 (1) meanwhile [ˈminˌ(h)waɪl]
　　　　adv. 同時 ③
　　(2) awhile [əˈ(h)waɪl]
　　　　adv. 片刻，一會兒 ⑥

▶ While we were having dinner, the phone rang.
　我們在吃晚餐時，電話響了。
▶ Linda likes singing, while Peter enjoys dancing.
　琳達喜歡唱歌，而彼得喜歡跳舞。
▶ While Vivian's thin, she can eat a lot.
　雖然薇薇安很瘦，但她可以吃很多。
▶ I'll stay here for a while.
　我將在這裡停留一會兒。
▶ Aaron whiled his weekend away playing Nintendo Switch games.
　艾倫週末玩任天堂的 Switch 遊戲消磨時間。

9　part [pɑrt] *n.* 部分；零件；角色 & *vt.* & *vi.* (使) 分開

月 (1) get / play a part of...
　　　　獲得 / 扮演……的角色
　　(2) play a... part / role in...
　　　　在……扮演……的角色
　　(3) take part in...　參與……
　　= participate in...

衍 (1) partial [ˈpɑrʃəl]
　　　　a. 部分的；偏心的 ④
　　(2) partly [ˈpɑrtlɪ] *adv.* 部分地 ⑤

似 (1) role [rol] *n.* 角色 ②
　　(2) separate [ˈsɛpəˌret]
　　　　vt. & *vi.* (使) 分開 ②

▶ I don't like the first part of the novel.
　我不喜歡這本小說的第一部分。
▶ The part you want is quite hard to get.
　你要的那種零件很難取得。
▶ Sophie played the part of Cinderella.
　蘇菲扮演灰姑娘的角色。
▶ Gandhi played an important role in India's liberation from the UK.
　甘地在印度脫離英國獨立的過程中扮演重要的角色。
▶ How many students took part in the speech contest?
　這次演講比賽有多少學生參加？
▶ The clouds parted, and the sun began to shine.
　雲朵散開，陽光開始閃耀。

10 end [ɛnd] *n.* 末端；結尾 & *vt.* & *vi.* (使) 結束

(1) at the end of...
在……的末端 / 結尾
(2) end up + V-ing 到頭來做……

衍 (1) ending [ˋɛndɪŋ] *n.* (故事) 結局 ②
(2) endless [ˋɛndləs] *a.* 無盡的

似 (1) stop [stɑp] *vt.* & *vi.* 停止 ①
(2) finish [ˋfɪnɪʃ] *vt.* & *vi.* 結束 ①

▶ At the end of the concert, everybody stood up.
大家在演唱會的尾聲站了起來。

▶ The end of the movie was the best part.
這部電影的結局是最棒的部分。

▶ They decided to end their relationship.
他們決定結束關係。

▶ It seems that my schoolwork will never end.
我的功課似乎永遠做不完。

▶ I knew you would end up borrowing money from me.
我就知道你最後還是會跟我借錢。

---

start [stɑrt] *vt.* & *vi.* & *n.* 開始

(1) start to V 開始做……
= start + V-ing
(2) get off to a good / poor start
開頭很 / 不順利

▶ Renee started to exercise three days ago.
= Renee started exercising three days ago.
芮妮 3 天前開始做運動。

▶ The meeting will start in five minutes.
會議將在 5 分鐘後開始。

▶ The school play got off to a poor start.
學校演出的開頭不太順利。

---

begin [bɪˋgɪn] *vi.* & *vt.* 開始

三 begin, began [bɪˋgæn], begun [bɪˋgʌn]

begin + V-ing 開始做……
= begin to V

衍 (1) beginner [bɪˋgɪnɚ] *n.* 初學者 ②
(2) beginning [bɪˋgɪnɪŋ] *n.* 開始

▶ The movie began an hour ago.
電影 1 小時前開演。

▶ I began studying English right after I entered junior high school.
= I began to study English right after I entered junior high school.
我一上國中就開始學英文。

---

11 feel [fil] *vi.* & *vt.* 感覺，感受到 & *vt.* 觸摸 & *n.* 觸覺；感受

三 feel, felt [fɛlt], felt

feel like + V-ing 想要做……
= would like to V
= want to V

衍 feeling [ˋfilɪŋ]
n. (感官、情緒的) 感覺 ②

似 touch [tʌtʃ] *vt.* & *vi.* 觸摸 & *n.* 觸覺 ①

▶ I feel encouraged when I hear those words.
聽到這些話時，我感到備受鼓舞。

▶ I felt her hand in the darkness.
在黑暗中我碰到她的手。

▶ Do you feel like going to the movies tonight?
你今晚想看電影嗎？

▶ Natalie loves the feel of soft wool on her skin.
娜塔莉喜愛羊毛在她肌膚上柔軟的觸感。

▶ The new restaurant has a Mediterranean feel to it.
這間新開的餐廳充滿地中海風情。
＊Mediterranean [ˌmɛdətəˈrenɪən] a. 地中海的

12 number [ˈnʌmbɚ] n. 號碼，數字；數量 & vt. 給……編號

片 (1) the number of + 複數名詞
……的數量 (其後使用單數形動詞)

(2) a number of + 複數名詞
幾個…… (其後使用複數形動詞)

衍 (1) numerous [ˈn(j)umərəs]
a. 為數眾多的 ④

(2) outnumber [ˌaʊtˈnʌmbɚ]
vt. (數量上) 勝過 ⑥

▶ May I have your phone number?
我可以問你的電話號碼嗎？

▶ The number of car accidents fell last year.
去年車禍的數目減少了。

▶ A number of kids are playing in the park.
幾個小朋友正在公園玩耍。

▶ It took us four days to number all the books.
我們花了 4 天的時間將全部的書編號。

13 follow [ˈfalo] vt. 跟隨；順著；遵從；理解

衍 (1) following [ˈfaloɪŋ]
a. 接著的；下述的 ②

(2) follower [ˈfaloɚ]
n. 追隨者，擁護者 ③

似 (1) obey [əˈbe] vt. 遵從 ②

(2) understand [ˌʌndɚˈstænd]
vt. 理解 ①

▶ I followed the teacher into the classroom.
我跟著老師進入教室。

▶ Follow the sign, and you'll find the restroom.
順著指標走，你就會找到洗手間。

▶ Please follow these instructions.
請遵從這些指示。

▶ I just can't follow her explanation.
我就是聽不懂她的解釋。

14 turn [tɝn] vi. & vt. (使) 轉動 / 向；(使) 變成 & n. 順次，輪到的機會

片 (1) turn around　轉身 / 向
(2) turn right / left　右 / 左轉
(3) turn into...　變成……
(4) turn A into B　把 A 變成 B
= change A into B
(5) It's sb's turn to V
輪到某人做……

▶ I turned around and saw Vincent standing by the door.
我轉身看到文森站在門邊。

▶ Turn right at the next intersection.
在下個十字路口右轉。

▶ Leaves turn yellow in autumn.
秋天時，樹葉會變黃。

▶ Suddenly, the frog turned into a prince.
突然，那隻青蛙變成了王子。

▶ The witch turned the prince into a beast.
巫婆把王子變成了一頭野獸。

▶ It's your turn to wash the dishes.
輪到你洗碗盤了。

15 problem [ˈprɑbləm] n. 問題；困難

匙 (1) solve / face a problem
  解決 / 面對問題
  (2) have problems / difficulty +
  V-ing 做……很難
  = have a hard time + V-ing

▶ Let's try our best to solve the problem.
  我們盡全力來解決這個問題吧！
▶ I have problems communicating with that stubborn guy.
  我很難和那固執的傢伙溝通。

question [ˈkwɛstʃən]
n. 問題；懷疑 (不可數) & vt. 質問；質疑

匙 (1) have / ask / answer a question
  有 / 問 / 回答問題
  (2) There is no question about /
  of... ……是無庸置疑的

衍 questionnaire [ˌkwɛstʃənˈɛr]
  n. 問卷 ⑤

似 doubt [daʊt] n. & vt. 懷疑 ②

▶ If you have any questions, please raise your hands.
  如果你們有任何問題，請舉手。
▶ There is no question about the CEO's ability.
  執行長的能力是不用懷疑的。
▶ The police questioned Robert for nearly four hours.
  警方訊問羅伯特將近 4 小時。
▶ Danny felt bad when his boss questioned his honesty.
  丹尼的老闆質疑他的誠實時，他覺得很難受。

16 hold [hold] vt. 握 / 抓住；舉行 & n. 握，抓

三 hold, held [hɛld], held
匙 (1) hold a meeting / wedding
  舉行會議 / 舉辦婚禮
  (2) hold on 等一下，稍後
  (3) take / catch hold of...
  握 / 抓住……

似 holder [ˈholdɚ] n. 保持者；持有人 ③

▶ Paul held his new baby gently in his arms.
  保羅輕柔地把他剛出生的寶寶摟在懷裡。
▶ We'll be holding a meeting at noon today.
  今天中午我們要舉行會議。
▶ Hold on while I grab my jacket.
  等一下，我拿件外套。
▶ The worker took hold of the rope and pulled it hard.
  工人握住繩子猛力一拉。

17 fact [fækt] n. 事實

匙 as a matter of fact 事實上
  = in fact
似 truth [truθ] n. 事實 ②
反 lie [laɪ] n. 謊話 ①

▶ What you see is not always fact.
  你看到的不一定是事實。
▶ As a matter of fact, I don't believe Ray at all.
  事實上，我根本就不相信雷伊。

18 keep [kip] vt. 保留；飼養 & vt. & vi. (使) 保持 & vi. 繼續 & n. 生計

三 keep, kept [kɛpt], kept
匙 (1) keep + adj. 保持……
  (2) keep (on) + V-ing 繼續做……

▶ You may keep the change.
  零錢你留著吧。
▶ The old man keeps cows and sheep on his farm.
  這名老人在他的農場飼養牛和羊群。

(3) keep up with... 跟上……
(4) earn sb's keep
　謀生計，賺生活費

衍 keeper [ˈkipɚ] *n.* 保管者；飼養員 ②

似 (1) stay [ste] *vi.* 仍保持是 ①
　(2) remain [rɪˈmen] *vi.* 仍保持是 ③

▶ Keep quiet when you are in the hospital.
　在醫院裡要保持安靜。
▶ Keep on working hard, and you'll be successful some day.
　繼續努力，那麼有朝一日你就會成功。
▶ Don't walk so fast. I can't keep up with you.
　別走那麼快，我跟不上你。
▶ I got a part-time job so I could earn my keep.
　我有一份兼職工作，以讓我能賺取生活費。

19　put [put] *vt.* 放置

三 三態同形
片 (1) put down...
　　把……放下；寫下……
　(2) put up with... 容忍……
似 place [ples] *vt.* 放置 ①

▶ You should put the book on the bookshelf.
　你應該把書放在書架上。
▶ Put down your address before leaving.
= Write down your address before leaving.
　寫下你的住址之後再離開。
▶ I can't put up with Alan's rudeness anymore.
　我受不了艾倫的粗魯了。

20　bring [brɪŋ] *vt.* 帶來；引起

三 bring, brought [brɔt], brought
片 (1) bring sb sth　帶某物給某人
　= bring sth to sb
　(2) bring sb up / bring up sb
　　養育某人長大
似 cause [kɔz] *vt.* 引起 ②

▶ Nick brought his wife a bunch of roses.
= Nick brought a bunch of roses to his wife.
　尼克帶了一束玫瑰花給他太太。
▶ The medicine brought great relief to the patient.
　這種藥讓病人的狀況大大緩解。
▶ John was brought up in the country.
　約翰是在鄉下長大的。

21　group [grup] *n.* 組，群；團體 & *vt.* 分組，分類

片 a group of... 一群……

▶ A small group of students lined up at the bus stop.
　一小群學生在公車站牌前排隊。
▶ Jessy joined a group for foreign students on campus.
　潔西參加了學校裡給外籍學生加入的團體。
▶ Pamela's clothes are grouped by color.
　潘蜜拉的衣服按顏色分類。

22　case [kes] *n.* 案件；案例；箱，盒 & *vt.* 把……裝入箱中

片 (1) in that case　那樣的話
　(2) (just) in case　萬一，以防

▶ The police are still looking into the case.
　警方仍在調查這件案子。

(3) in case of + N　萬一……
= in the event of + N
(4) a phone case　手機殼

▶ It was a case of love at first sight.
這就是一見鍾情的例子。

▶ In that case, I have nothing else to say.
那樣的話，我沒有其他要說的了。

▶ You should take a sweater, in case it gets cold.
你應該帶件毛衣，以防天氣變冷。

▶ In case of emergency, call this number.
萬一有緊急事件，請打這個號碼。

▶ The rich woman cased the expensive jewelry in a leather box.
這名有錢的女子把昂貴珠寶裝入一個皮革製的箱子裡。

23　point [pɔɪnt] *n.* 點；觀點；重點；分數 & *vi.* 指向 & *vt.* 用……對準

片 (1) sb's point of view　某人的觀點
(2) get / come to the point
(3) point at...　指向……
(4) point A at B　把 A 對準 B
(5) point sth out / point out sth
指出某事
衍 (1) pointless [ˋpɔɪntləs] *a.* 無意義的
(2) viewpoint [ˋvju͵pɔɪnt] *n.* 觀點 ⑤

▶ Harry drew a line between the two points.
哈利在 2 個點之間畫一條線。

▶ I'm just trying to explain my point of view.
我正試著解釋我的看法。

▶ Eileen talked for ten minutes before she got to the point.
艾琳講了 10 分鐘才講到重點。

▶ The team lost the game by only a few points.
那個隊伍只以幾分之差輸了這場比賽。

▶ The little boy pointed at the toy he wanted.
小男孩指著他想要的玩具。

▶ I pointed my camera at the movie star.
我把照相機對準這個電影明星。

▶ The teacher pointed out two grammar mistakes in my essay.
老師指出我文章中的 2 個文法錯誤。

---

line [laɪn]
n. 線；隊伍〔美〕 & *vi.* 排成一列

片 (1) stand / cut in line　排 / 插隊
(2) line up　排隊
似 queue [kju] *n.* 隊伍 & *vi.* 排隊〔英〕
queue up　排隊

▶ Please stand behind the yellow line.
請站在黃線後。

▶ Some people were standing in line at the hotdog stand.
有些人在熱狗攤排隊。

▶ Cafés and restaurants line the busy street.
繁忙的街道上有一排咖啡廳和餐廳。

▶ All of the students are lining up to receive their awards.
所有的學生正排隊等著領獎。

24 area [ˈɛrɪə] *n.* 地區；領域，範圍

- 片 an area code （電話）區碼
- 似 (1) region [ˈridʒən] *n.* 地區 ②
- (2) field [fild] *n.* 領域，範圍 ②

▶ The hurricane caused a lot of damage in many areas of this country.
颶風重創這個國家的許多地區。

▶ Frank is an expert in the area of marketing.
法蘭克是行銷領域的專家。

25 let [lɛt] *vt.* 讓，允許

- 三 三態同形
- 片 (1) let sb + 原形動詞　讓某人做……
- (2) let's + 原形動詞　讓我們做……
- = let us + 原形動詞
- (3) let alone...
  更別說……（用於否定句中）

▶ Mia's parents won't let her go out after 10 p.m.
晚上 10 點後，米雅的爸媽就不讓她出門。

▶ Let's go picnicking this afternoon!
我們今天下午去野餐吧！

▶ Ben can't afford a car, let alone a house.
班買不起車子，更別說買房子。

26 side [saɪd] *n.* 面，邊；身邊，旁邊；(對立團體中的) 一方

- 片 take sides (with...)
  表明支持 (某一方)
- 衍 (1) inside [ɪnˈsaɪd] *n.* 裡面 ①
- (2) outside [aʊtˈsaɪd] *n.* 外面 ①

▶ There is a lake on the other side of the park.
公園的另一邊有座湖。

▶ The scared little girl would not leave her mom's side.
受驚嚇的小女孩不願離開她媽媽身邊。

▶ George took sides with Linda in the argument.
喬治在這次爭論中支持琳達。

27 try [traɪ] *vt. & vi.* 設法，試圖 & *vt. & n.* 嘗試 (作名詞時，常用單數)

- 三 try, tried [traɪd], tried
- 片 (1) try to V　　設法 / 試圖做……
- (2) try + V-ing　嘗試……
- (3) try sth on / try on sth
  試穿 / 戴 (衣服、帽子等)
- 似 attempt [əˈtɛmpt]
  vt. 試圖 & *n.* 嘗試 ②

▶ I know you're busy, but try to come.
我知道你很忙，但試著來看看。

▶ I tried shutting the computer, but it didn't work.
我試過將電腦關機，但沒有效。

▶ Can I try on these shoes?
我可以試穿一下這雙鞋子嗎？

▶ You made several mistakes, but it was a good try.
雖然你犯了幾個錯，但是個好的嘗試。

28 water [ˈwɑtɚ] *n.* 水 (不可數) & *vt.* 澆 / 餵水 & *vi.* 流口水

- 片 a glass of water　一杯水
- 衍 (1) waterfall [ˈwɑtɚˌfɔl] *n.* 瀑布 ③
- (2) waterproof [ˈwɑtɚˌpruf]
  a. 防水的 ⑥

▶ Just give me a glass of water.
給我一杯水就可以了。

▶ Jenny waters her garden every day.
珍妮每天替她的花園澆水。

▶ My mouth watered when I saw the food.
我看到那些食物時，便流口水了。

 **0629**

29 **move** [muv] *vt. & vi.* (使) 移動 & *vt.* 感動 & *vi.* 搬家 & *n.* 動作，行動

片 (1) move sb to tears
　　使某人感動落淚
　= make sb cry
　(2) move to + 地方　搬到某地
　(3) the first / next move
　　第 / 下一步

衍 (1) moving [ˈmuvɪŋ]
　　可移動的；感動的
　(2) remove [rɪˈmuv] *vt.* 移開 ②

▶ Please move the desk to the other room.
　請把這張書桌移到另一間房間去。

▶ The turtle began to move slowly.
　這隻烏龜開始慢慢地移動。

▶ The movie moved us to tears.
　這部電影使我們感動得落淚。

▶ Next week we are moving to a new apartment.
　下星期我們就要搬到新公寓。

▶ We are still discussing the next move.
　我們還在討論下一步怎麼做。

---

movement [ˈmuvmənt]
n. 移動；(社會或政治的) 運動

▶ There was no sign of movement in the woods.
　樹林裡一點動靜都沒有。

▶ The Civil Rights Movement brought great changes to the US in all aspects.
　民權運動對美國各方面都造成很大的改變。

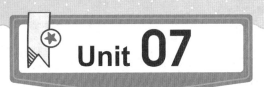

1　stand [stænd] *vi.* 站立 & *vt.* 忍受 & *n.* 立場，主張；攤位

- stand, stood [stʊd], stood
- (1) stand up　　　　站起來
  (2) stand for...　　　代表 / 象徵……
  (3) stand by sb　　　支持某人
  (4) stand up for...　支持……
  (5) take a stand on sth
  　　表明對某事的立場
- outstanding [aʊtˋstændɪŋ]
  a. 傑出的 ④
- (1) put up with...　忍受……
  (2) tolerate [ˋtɑləˌret] *vt.* 容忍 ④
  (3) attitude [ˋætət(j)ud] *n.* 態度 ③

- ▶ Don't stand on that chair. It might break.
  別站在椅子上。它可能會斷掉。
- ▶ Dennis stood up to shake his boss' hand.
  丹尼斯站起來和老闆握手。
- ▶ I just can't stand Teddy's bad temper.
  我就是無法忍受泰迪的壞脾氣。
- ▶ To most people, roses stand for love.
  對大部分的人來說，玫瑰花象徵愛情。
- ▶ Whatever happens, I will stand by you.
  不論發生什麼事，我都會支持你。
- ▶ Jerry stood up for my proposal at the meeting.
  傑瑞在會議中支持我的提案。
- ▶ The prime minister took a stand on animal rights.
  總理就動物權益表明立場。
- ▶ Kelly bought some ice cream from the stand.
  凱莉在那個攤位買了些冰淇淋。

---

sit [sɪt] *vi.* 坐，坐下
- sit, sat [sæt], sat
- sit down　坐下
  = take a seat
- seat [sit] *n.* 座位 ①

- ▶ Arnold was sitting next to his best friend.
  阿諾坐在他最要好的朋友旁。
- ▶ As soon as I arrived home, I sat down.
  我一回到家就坐下。

---

bear [bɛr]
vt. 忍受；生 (小孩)；結 (果實) & *n.* 熊
- bear, bore [bɔr], borne [bɔrn]
- a black / polar / teddy bear
  黑 / 北極 / 泰迪熊
- (1) put up with...　忍受……
  (2) tolerate [ˋtɑləˌret] *vt.* 容忍 ④
- borne 是動詞 bear 的過去分詞，而 born (出生的) 則是形容詞。

- ▶ I can't bear all of that noise.
- = I can't put up with all of that noise.
  我無法忍受那些噪音。
- ▶ Bella bore her first child at the age of 30.
  貝拉 30 歲時生了第一胎。
- ▶ The apple tree will bear fruit this year.
  這棵蘋果樹今年會結果。
- ▶ They say there are bears in the mountains.
  據說山中有熊出沒。

2　since [sɪns] *conj.* 自從；因為 & *prep.* 自從 & *adv.* 此後

- ▶ It has been raining since I left for work this morning.
  從早上我去上班後，雨就一直下個不停。

用法 since 表『自從』時，可作連接詞，其所引導的副詞子句須使用過去式；作介詞時，其所引導的介詞片語則須為過去的時間點，而主要子句的時態應採『現在完成式』或『現在完成進行式』。

▶ Since there is no more work, we can all go home.
由於沒工作要做了，我們全都可以回家。

▶ We haven't seen each other since last year.
我們從去年起就沒見過面了。

▶ Luke moved to Belgium three years ago, and I haven't seen him since.
路克 3 年前搬去比利時，自那之後我便沒再見過他了。

---

3 run [rʌn] *vi. & n.* 跑，奔跑 & *vi.* (機器) 運作 & *vt.* 經營

≡ run, ran [ræn], run

衍 runner [ˋrʌnɚ] *n.* 跑步者 ②

片 (1) run away (from...)
(從……) 逃走
(2) go for a run　去跑步
(3) run into...
與……不期而遇；撞上……
(4) run out of sth　用盡某物

似 (1) operate [ˋɑpəˏret]
vi. 運作 & *vt.* 經營 ②
(2) manage [ˋmænɪdʒ] *vt.* 經營 ②

▶ Tessa ran down the road to meet her friend.
泰莎跑到路上去見她的朋友。

▶ Little Billy ran away from the big dog.
小比利逃離那隻大狗。

▶ I'm going for a run after work.
我下班後要去跑步。

▶ The copier isn't running properly.
這部影印機運作不正常。

▶ The young couple runs a restaurant in Taipei.
這對年輕夫婦在臺北經營一家餐廳。

▶ Terry ran into his ex-wife on the street.
泰瑞在街上偶遇前妻。

▶ Our car was running out of gas.
我們的車子快沒汽油了。

---

4 need [nid] *vt.* 需要；必須 & *n.* 需要；必需品 (此意常用複數) & *aux.* 需要〔英〕

片 (1) need to V　需要 / 必須做……
(2) sth needs + V-ing　某物需要
以……方法處理
= sth needs to be + p.p.
(3) be in need of sth　需要某物
(4) basic / daily needs
基本需求 / 日需品

衍 needy [ˋnidɪ] *a.* 貧窮的 ④

用法 need 作助動詞的用法，在英式英語中較常見，且多用於否定句構中，例：
need not V　不必做……
= needn't V

▶ Jackson needs help with his homework.
傑克森的家庭作業需要協助。

▶ Your car needs washing.
= Your car needs to be washed.
你的車需要洗了。

▶ Sally's hair is in need of a cut.
莎莉的頭髮需要剪一下了。

▶ Housing and food are basic needs.
吃住是基本需求。

▶ It's only a short test; you needn't worry.
這只是個簡短的考試，你不必擔心。

5　order [ˈɔrdɚ] vt. & n. 命令；訂購；點菜 & n. 順序；秩序

片 (1) order sb to V　命令某人做……

(2) cancel an order　取消訂單

(3) take sb's order　接受某人的點餐

(4) in order of importance / difficulty　按重要性／難度的順序

(5) keep sth in order　把某事物整理得井然有序

(6) in order to V　為了做……

(7) be out of order　（機器）故障

衍 (1) disorder [dɪsˈɔrdɚ]　n. 無秩序，雜亂 & vt. 使混亂 ④

(2) orderly [ˈɔrdɚlɪ] a. 井然有序的 ⑥

似 (1) demand [dɪˈmænd]　vt. & n. 要求 ④

(2) sequence [ˈsikwəns] n. 順序 ⑤

▶ Don't order me to do this or that.
別命令我做這做那的。

▶ Everyone on this team should obey the leader's orders.
這隊伍裡的每個人都應聽從組長的命令。

▶ The shoes I ordered still haven't arrived yet.
我訂的鞋子還沒有送達。

▶ Carl told the manager he wanted to cancel his order.
卡爾告訴經理他想取消他的訂單。

▶ I'd like to order some cold drinks.
我想點一些冷飲。

▶ The waiter came to take my order.
服務生過來幫我點餐。

▶ We learned those words in order of importance.
我們是依重要性的順序來學那些字。

▶ Peter always keeps his room in order.
彼得總是把房間整理得井然有序。

▶ Fred leaves home at 7 a.m. in order to get to work on time.
為了能準時上班，佛萊德早上 7 點離開家裡。

▶ The telephone is out of order again!
這電話又壞了。

6　once [wʌns] adv. 一次；曾經 & conj. 一……就…… & n. 一次

片 (1) once and for all　斷然地，最後一次地

(2) once upon a time　（故事開頭）很久以前

▶ I went to Australia once, but that was a long time ago.
我去過澳洲一次，但那是好久以前的事了。

▶ John has quit smoking once and for all.
約翰徹底戒菸了。

▶ The Nobel Prize winner once lived here.
那位諾貝爾獎得主曾住在這裡。

▶ Once upon a time, here lived a beautiful elf.
很久以前，這裡住著一個漂亮的小精靈。
*elf [ɛlf] n. 小精靈

▶ Once I get back, I'll call you.
= As soon as I get back, I'll call you.
我一回來就會打電話給你。

7 **interest** [ˋɪnt(ə)rɪst] *vt.* 使……感興趣 & *n.* 興趣；愛好

🔗 have an / no interest in...
對……有 / 沒有興趣

💭 (1) attract [əˋtræk] *vt.* 吸引 ③
(2) hobby [ˋhɑbɪ] *n.* 愛好，嗜好 ①

▶ The novel interested me a lot. I want to read it again.
我對那本小說很感興趣。我想要再讀一遍。

▶ I have no interest in music. I love dancing.
我對音樂沒興趣，我喜歡跳舞。

▶ Playing computer games is Henry's main interest.
亨利最主要的嗜好是玩電腦遊戲。

interested [ˋɪnt(ə)rɪstɪd]
a. 感興趣的

🔗 be interested in + N/V-ing
對……感興趣

▶ I'm interested in the magazine you're reading.
我對你在看的那本雜誌有興趣。

interesting [ˋɪnt(ə)rɪstɪŋ]
a. (令人覺得) 有趣的

▶ I find this story quite interesting.
我覺得這個故事很有趣。

8 **room** [rum] *n.* 房間 (可數)；空間 (不可數) & *vi.* 租住

🔗 (1) make room for sth
為某物騰出空間
(2) room together　合租，一起租屋

衍 roommate [ˋrum,met] *n.* 室友

▶ The room was full of people.
這房間裡都是人。

▶ Can we make room for one more table?
我們可以騰出空間再放一張桌子嗎？

▶ We've been best friends since we roomed together after college.
自大學畢業一起租屋後，我們就一直是最好的朋友。

9 **hear** [hɪr] *vt.* & *vi.* 聽到；聽聞 (皆不用於進行式)

📋 hear, heard [hɜd], heard
🔗 (1) hear + 受詞 + V/V-ing
聽到……做……
(2) hear from sb　收到某人 (寄信、來電等) 的訊息
(3) hear of / about...
聽說有關……的事

▶ I heard someone knocking on the door.
我聽到有人在敲門。

▶ I haven't heard from you in a long time.
我好久沒收到你的消息了。

▶ Have you heard about Cole's promotion?
你有沒有聽說柯爾升遷了？

listen [ˋlɪsṇ] *vi.* 聆聽；聽從

🔗 listen to...　聆聽 / 聽從……

衍 listener [ˋlɪsṇɚ] *n.* 聽者 ②

比 hear 與 listen 均有『聽』的意思，惟 hear 指的是耳朵聽到聲音，listen 則是指用耳朵專注聆聽。

▶ I enjoy listening to music at night.
我喜歡在晚上聆聽音樂。

▶ This is serious—stop what you're doing and just listen!
這不是開玩笑 —— 停下你正在做的事，注意聽我說的！

10　set [sɛt] *vt.* 放置；設定；(電影等) 以……為背景 & *n.* 一組 / 套；場景

三 三態同形

用 (1) set the table　（在桌上）擺好碗筷
(2) set the alarm / clock
設鬧鐘 / 時鐘
(3) be set in...　以……為背景
(4) set up...　建立 / 安排 / 設定好……
(5) set out for＋地方　出發前往某地
(6) a set of...　一組 / 套……
(7) a movie set　電影場景

▶ Then, set the pan on the stove.
接著，將平底鍋放在爐子上。

▶ Set the table for dinner.
擺碗筷準備吃晚餐。

▶ Don't forget to set the alarm.
別忘了設鬧鐘。

▶ The film is set in Spain in the 1930s.
這部電影以 1930 年代的西班牙為背景。

▶ We set up a statue in memory of the hero.
我們建立一座雕像記念這位英雄。

▶ They set out for Seoul last night.
他們昨晚出發去首爾了。

▶ We bought a set of coffee cups.
我們買了一組咖啡杯。

▶ The director asked me to come to the movie set tomorrow.
導演請我明天到電影場景來。

11　several [ˈsɛvərəl] *a.* 幾個的，一些的 & *pron.* 幾個，一些

似 (1) some [sʌm]
a. 一些的 & *pron.* 一些 ①
(2) a few　一些

用法 several 後須接複數可數名詞。

▶ Several students missed the exam and had to do a make-up.
有幾個學生缺考，所以必須補考。

▶ Several of the cars were damaged in the accident.
有幾輛車在這起事故中毀壞了。

12　mean [min] *vt.* 意思是；意味；有意；對……很重要 & *a.* 卑鄙的，刻薄的

三 mean, meant [mɛnt], meant

用 (1) mean (that)...
意思是……；意味……
(2) mean to V　有意要做……
= intend to V
(3) mean a lot / nothing to sb
對某人意義重大 / 毫無意義

衍 (1) means [minz]
n. 方法，手段 (單複數同形) ②
(2) meaning [ˈminɪŋ]
n. 意思；意義 ②
(3) meaningful [ˈminɪŋfəl]
a. 有意義的 ③

▶ What does the word mean?
= What's the meaning of this word?
這個字是什麼意思？

▶ I don't mean that you are wrong.
我不是說你錯了。

▶ I meant to help Ryan, but he turned me down.
我有意要幫萊恩，但他拒絕了。

▶ Your support means a lot to me.
你的支持對我來說意義非凡。

▶ Edward is so mean that nobody wants to do business with him.
愛德華太卑鄙了，所以沒人想跟他做生意。

13 **name** [nem] *n.* 名字 & *vt.* 命名

- (1) first / last name　名字 / 姓氏
  (2) by the name of...　名叫……
  (3) name A + 名字 + after B
  　　依 B 之名將 A 取名為……
- call [kɔl] *vt.* 給……取名 ①

▶ I met a guy by the name of John Smith.
= I met a guy named John Smith.
= I met a guy called John Smith.
　我遇到一位名叫約翰・史密斯的人。

▶ We named him Henry after his grandfather.
= He is named Henry after his grandfather.
　我們以他祖父之名將他命名為亨利。

14 **power** [ˈpaʊɚ] *n.* 權力；力量；電力 & *vt.* 為……提供電力

- (1) wind / solar / nuclear power
  　　風 / 太陽 / 核能
  (2) a power plant　發電廠
  (3) a power failure　停電
- powerful [ˈpaʊɚfl̩] *a.* 強大的 ②
- authority [əˈθɔrətɪ] *n.* 權力 ④

▶ The poor king has no power in his country.
　這個可憐的國王在國內沒權力。

▶ This new machine uses solar power to operate.
　這臺新機器使用太陽能來運轉。

▶ We paid a visit to the power plant yesterday.
　我們昨天去參觀發電廠。

▶ The fan is powered by batteries.
　這臺電風扇是靠電池驅動的。

15 **possible** [ˈpɑsəbl̩] *a.* 可能的

- (1) be possible (for sb) to V
  　　（某人）做……是可能的
  (2) as + adj./adv. + as possible
  　　儘可能地……
- (1) possibility [ˌpɑsəˈbɪlətɪ]
  　　n. 可能性 ②
  (2) possibly [ˈpɑsəblɪ] *adv.* 可能

▶ It's possible to order a copy of the book online.
　從網路上訂一本這本書是可行的。

▶ Come here as soon as possible. I have something important to tell you.
　儘快過來，我有重要的事要告訴你。

impossible [ɪmˈpɑsəbl̩]
a. 不可能的

- be impossible (for sb) to V
  　（某人）做……是不可能的
- impossibility [ɪmˌpɑsəˈbɪlətɪ]
  　n. 不可能性

▶ It's impossible for Nick to get to work on time.
　要尼克準時上班是不可能的事。

16 **service** [ˈsɝvɪs] *n.* 服務 & *vt.* 保養維修

- be at one's service　為某人服務

▶ The best thing about the hotel was the service.
　這間飯店最棒的就是它的服務了。

衍 (1) serve [sɜv] *vt.* 服務；供應 (餐點) ②
(2) servant [ˈsɜvənt] *n.* 僕人 ②
(3) server [ˈsɜvɚ]
　　n. 伺服器；服務生 ⑤

▶ I'm glad to be at your service.
我很樂意為您服務。

▶ The car is being serviced and won't be ready until Friday.
車子正在保養，星期五前不會好。

17　matter [ˈmætɚ] *n.* 事情；麻煩 & *vi.* 重要，有關係

片 as a matter of fact　事實上
＝ in fact
似 (1) problem [ˈprɑbləm] *n.* 問題 ①
(2) trouble [ˈtrʌbḷ] *n.* 麻煩 ①

▶ We should take care of the matter now.
我們現在就應處理這件事情。

▶ What's the matter with Leo?
＝ What's the problem with Leo?
＝ What's wrong with Leo?
里歐發生什麼麻煩了嗎？

▶ Belle isn't my girlfriend. As a matter of fact, she is my wife.
貝兒不是我女朋友。事實上，她是我老婆。

▶ It doesn't matter when he'll come.
他何時來並不重要。

18　meet [mit] *vt.* & *vi.* (初次) 見面；碰面 & *vt.* 遇見；滿足，符合

三 meet, met [mɛt], met
片 meet sb's expectations
符合某人的期望
似 (1) encounter [ɪnˈkauntɚ]
　　vt. 偶遇 ④
(2) run / bump into sb
(偶然) 遇到某人

▶ Michael met Hannah in a dance class.
麥可在舞蹈課上初次見到漢娜。

▶ I'll meet you at the airport at 2 o'clock sharp.
2 點整我會在機場跟你碰面。

▶ I met Rachel in the park this morning.
我今早在公園碰到瑞秋。

▶ This restaurant failed to meet its customers' expectations.
這間餐廳未能符合顧客的期望。

---

meeting [ˈmitɪŋ] *n.* 會議
似 conference [ˈkɑnfərəns] *n.* 會議 ④

▶ I missed the meeting because of the traffic jam.
因為塞車，我錯過了會議。
*a traffic jam　塞車，交通堵塞

19　appear [əˈpɪr] *vi.* 出現；似乎

片 (1) appear (to be) + adj.
似乎是……

▶ Andy didn't appear until five minutes ago.
安迪直到 5 分鐘前才出現。

0719-0725

(2) It appears that...　似乎……
= It seems that...

衍 appearance [əˈpɪrəns] *n.* 外表 ②

似 (1) show up　出現
(2) seem [sim] *vi.* 似乎 ②

▶ The painting appears to be a fake.
這幅畫似乎是假的。

▶ It appears to me that something is wrong with the plane's engine.
我感覺飛機的引擎似乎有點問題。

20　act [ækt] *vt.* & *vi.* 演 & *vi.* 採取行動；舉止 & *n.* 行為；(戲劇的) 幕

片 act the part of...　扮演……的角色

衍 (1) active [ˈæktɪv] *a.* 活躍的 ②
(2) acting [ˈæktɪŋ] *n.* 表演 & *a.* 代理的

似 (1) behave [brˈhev]
vi. 表現，行為舉止 ②
(2) deed [did] *n.* 行為 (可數) ③
(3) behavior [brˈhevjɚ]
n. 行為 (不可數) ④

▶ Emma Watson acted the part of Hermione in the Harry Potter movie series.
艾瑪‧華森在《哈利波特》系列電影裡飾演妙麗一角。

▶ When Ben saw the drowning boy, he was quick to act.
班看到那名溺水的男孩時，快速採取行動。
*drowning [ˈdraʊnɪŋ] *a.* 溺水的

▶ David has been acting strangely recently.
大衛最近的行徑很奇怪。

▶ You must admit that it was a brave act.
你必須承認那是勇敢的行為。

▶ The play has five acts, each of which is divided into six scenes.
該劇共有 5 幕，每一幕分成 6 場。

---

action [ˈækʃən] *n.* 行動

片 take action　採取行動

▶ Let's take action before it is too late.
我們採取行動以免太遲。

---

actor [ˈæktɚ] *n.* (男) 演員

▶ Brad's father used to be a famous actor.
布萊德的父親曾是位知名演員。

---

actress [ˈæktrɪs] *n.* 女演員

複 actresses [ˈæktrɪsɪz]

▶ That young actress is popular with teenagers.
那名年輕的女演員很受青少年歡迎。

21　believe [bəˈliv] *vt.* & *vi.* 相信 & *vt.* 認為

片 (1) believe (that)...　相信 / 認為……
(2) believe in...
相信……(的存在)；信仰……

衍 belief [bəˈlif] *n.* 信念 ②

反 disbelieve [ˌdɪsbəˈliv]
vt. & *vi.* 不信

▶ Do you believe that he is telling the truth?
你相信他在說實話嗎？

▶ Michael doesn't believe in Santa Claus.
麥可不相信有聖誕老公公。

▶ John believes that he will be president one day.
約翰認為他有一天會成為總統。

22　mind [maɪnd] *n.* 頭腦 & *vt.* & *vi.* 介意

片 (1) in sb's mind　在某人腦海 / 心中

▶ Eddie is the coolest guy in my mind.
艾迪是我心中最酷的男人。

(2) on sb's mind　令某人煩惱/心
(3) have one's mind set on +
N/V-ing
心意已決要做……
(4) mind (sb) + V-ing
介意（某人）做……

▶ You don't look happy. What's on your mind?
你不太高興的樣子。什麼讓你煩心？

▶ Sophie has her mind set on becoming an actress.
蘇菲決心要成為一名演員。

▶ Would you mind if I opened the window?
你介意我把窗戶打開嗎？

▶ I don't mind driving if you want to take a rest.
如果你想休息的話，我不介意開車。

23　reach [ritʃ] *vt.* 到達；達到 & *vt.* & *vi.* 伸手拿 & *n.* 伸手可及的範圍

🅷 (1) reach + 地點　到達某地
　 = arrive at / in + 地點
(2) reach for sth　伸手拿某物
(3) out of sb's reach　某人碰不到
(4) within sb's reach　某人碰得到

▶ By the time we reached the station, the train had already gone.
等到我們到達火車站時，火車已經開走了。

▶ I can't believe the temperature reached 40 degrees today.
我真不敢相信今天溫度高達 40 度。

▶ Ezra reached for his wallet.
以斯拉伸手拿皮夾。

▶ Knives and forks should be put out of children's reach.
刀叉應該放在孩童伸手拿不到的地方。

24　lead [lid] *vt.* & *vi.* 帶領；領先；帶（路）& *n.* 領先

🇪 lead, led [lɛd], led
🅷 (1) lead to...　導致……
　 = result in...
　 = contribute to...
　 = give rise to...
　 = bring about...
(2) take the lead
名列前茅，一馬當先

▶ Gareth led his team to success in the competition.
加瑞斯帶領他的隊伍在比賽中獲勝。

▶ Our team is now leading by ten points.
我們的隊伍現在以 10 分領先。

▶ Our teacher led us into the language laboratory.
老師帶著我們進入語言教室。

▶ The driver's carelessness led to the accident.
駕駛員的粗心導致這起意外。

▶ The home team took the lead from the beginning.
地主隊從一開始即取得領先。

---

leader [ˈlidɚ] *n.* 領袖，領導者
🇫 leadership [ˈlidɚʃɪp] *n.* 領導能力 ②

▶ The leader of the group has many years of experience.
這個團體的領導人擁有多年的經驗。

25　carry [ˈkærɪ] *vt.* & *vi.* 攜帶，提

🇪 carry, carried [ˈkærɪd], carried

▶ Can you help me carry this bag to my house?
你能幫我把這個袋子提到我家裡去嗎？

(1) carry on + N/V-ing　繼續做……
　= go on + N/V-ing
　= keep on + N/V-ing
　= continue + N/V-ing
(2) carry out sth
　　執行某事；完成某事

▸ If you carry on eating like that, you're going to gain a lot of weight.
如果你照那樣繼續吃下去，會變胖很多。

▸ To carry out the plan, we need at least another $50,000.
為了要執行這個計畫，我們至少需要再追加 5 萬美元。

---

26 **pay** [pe] *n.* 薪水，待遇 & *vt.* & *vi.* 付（款）；值得，有好處

pay, paid [ped], paid

(1) pay a bill　付帳
(2) pay for sth　付某事物的款項
(3) It pays to V　做……是值得的

(1) salary [ˈsælərɪ]
　　n. (按月發放的) 薪水 ③
(2) wage [wedʒ]
　　n. (按時發放的) 工資 ③

▸ I don't like the job, but the pay is good.
我不喜歡這份工作，不過待遇卻挺不錯的。

▸ Thomas has already paid the bill.
湯瑪斯已經付帳了。

▸ Let me pay for the meal.
這頓飯讓我來付錢。

▸ It pays to study English.
學英文是值得的。

---

payment [ˈpemənt] *n.* 支付，付款

▸ They only accept payment in cash.
他們只接受現金付款。

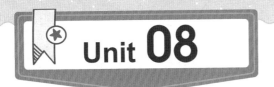

Unit 08

0801-0804

1 perhaps [pɚˋhæps] *adv.* 也許，可能 (= maybe)

▶ Perhaps I'll call on you tonight.
也許今晚我會去看你。
*call on sb　拜訪某人

maybe [ˋmebi] *adv.* 也許 (= perhaps)

比 perhaps 與 maybe 均表『也許，可能』，但 perhaps 是比 maybe 稍微正式一點的說法。

▶ Maybe I can help you with the work.
也許我可以幫忙你做這項工作。

2 person [ˋpɝsn̩] *n.* 人

複 people [ˋpipl̩]
片 in person　親自地
= personally [ˋpɝsn̩lɪ]
衍 (1) personal [ˋpɝsn̩l]
　　a. 個人的，私人的 ②
　　(2) personality [ˌpɝsn̩ˋælətɪ]
　　n. 個性 ②

▶ Do you know who was the first person to land on the moon?
你知道第 1 個登陸月球的人是誰嗎？

▶ I'd like to speak with you in person about your son.
我想親自和你談談關於你兒子的事。

people [ˋpipl̩]
n. 人；人們，大家 (皆為複數) & *vt.* (人) 居住於

片 地方 + be peopled by / with...
　　……居住於某地

▶ There were too many people at the concert.
參加演唱會的人很多。

▶ Abigail cares what people think of her.
艾碧蓋兒很在意大家怎麼想她。

▶ The town is peopled by students from the nearby university.
附近大學的學生居住在這個城鎮。

3 church [tʃɝtʃ] *n.* 教堂 (可數)；禮拜儀式 (不可數)

複 churches [ˋtʃɝtʃɪz]
片 go to church　上教堂，做禮拜

▶ We go to church together every Sunday.
每個星期天我們都會一起上教堂。

4 play [ple] *vi.* & *vt.* 玩；參加 (遊戲、球類運動等)；演奏 (樂器、曲子等)；播放；扮演 (角色) & *n.* 戲劇

片 (1) play with...　　和……一起玩
　　(2) play house　　玩扮家家酒
　　(3) play + 球類運動　打某球類運動

▶ Little Vincent loves to play with his toy cars.
小文森喜歡玩他的玩具車。

0804-0810

(4) play the + 樂器名稱　彈奏某樂器
(5) play a(n) + adj. + role in...
　　在……方面扮演……的角色
衍 (1) playground [`ple͵graʊnd]
　　 n. 學校操場，遊樂場 ②
(2) playful [`plefl] *a.* 愛玩耍的 ③

▶ I enjoy playing house with my friends.
　我喜歡和朋友玩扮家家酒。
▶ Will you play basketball with us?
　你要和我們打籃球嗎？
▶ My sister plays the guitar very well.
　我姊姊很會彈吉他。
▶ The radio is playing classical music.
　收音機正在播放古典音樂。
▶ Hard work plays an important role in achieving success.
　努力在獲致成功方面扮演重要的角色。
▶ What do you think of the play you saw last night?
　昨晚看的那齣戲，你覺得怎麼樣？

player [`pleɚ]
n. 選手，球員；演奏者；播放機
片 a CD player　CD 播放機

▶ Every player must follow the rules.
　每位選手都必須遵守規則。
▶ Yo-Yo Ma is an excellent cello player.
　馬友友是一位優秀的大提琴演奏者。
　cello [`tʃɛlo] n. 大提琴

5　different [`dɪfərənt] *a.* 不同的

片 A is different from B (in...)
　A 與 B (在……方面) 不同
= A differs from B in...
衍 (1) difference [`dɪfərəns] *n.* 差別 ②
(2) differ [`dɪfɚ] *vi.* 不同 ④
反 similar [`sɪmələ] *a.* 相似的 ②

▶ May decided to try a different restaurant for lunch.
　梅決定試一間不同的餐廳吃午餐。
▶ Gina is very different from her sister in personality.
= Gina differs greatly from her sister in personality.
　吉娜與她妹妹在個性方面很不同。

6　pass [pæs] *vt. & vi.* 經過；通過 & *vt.* 傳遞 & *vi.* (時間) 流逝 & *n.* 通行證

片 (1) pass out　　　　昏倒
(2) pass away　　　去世，過世
(3) a boarding pass　登機證
衍 passage [`pæsɪdʒ]
　　 n. 通道；一段 (文字)；(時間) 消逝 ③
似 (1) hand [hænd] *vt.* 傳遞 ①
(2) go by　 (時間) 流逝

▶ I pass the church on my way to work every day.
　我每天上班的路上都會經過這座教堂。
▶ A train just passed right in front of me.
　有一班火車剛才就從我前方經過。
▶ My daughter just passed the driving test.
　我女兒剛通過駕照考試。
▶ Pass me the salt, please.
　請把鹽遞過來給我。
▶ Two years have passed without any word from him.
　2 年過去了，沒收到他的隻字片語。

▶ Sally passed out when she saw the big rat.
莎莉看到那隻大老鼠時昏倒了。

▶ My grandma passed away ten years ago.
我的奶奶 10 年前過世。

▶ Please show your boarding pass to the officer.
請把您的登機證給這位官員看。

7　grow [gro] *vt.* 種植 & *vi.* 生長；成長；變得

- grow, grew [gru], grown [gron]
- (1) grow + adj.　變得……
  (2) grow up　長大
- growth [groθ] *n.* 成長 ②
- (1) plant [plænt] *vt.* 種植 ①
  (2) sow [so] *vt.* & *vi.* 播種 ⑤
  (3) become [bɪˋkʌm] *vi.* 變成 ①

▶ The farmer grows all types of crops.
這位農夫什麼農作物都種。

▶ Carrots grow well in this soil.
紅蘿蔔在這種土壤裡生長得很好。

▶ Our sales have grown by 18% over the past two years.
過去 2 年來，我們的業績成長了 18%。

▶ As time went by, Clara grew older and wiser.
隨著歲月流逝，克萊拉變老也更有智慧。

▶ Lawrence wants to be a pianist when he grows up.
勞倫斯長大後想做一名鋼琴家。

8　job [dʒɑb] *n.* 工作；職責，任務

- (1) a full-time / part-time job
  全 / 兼職工作
  (2) get / find a job　找到工作
  (3) be out of a job　失業
- jobless [ˋdʒɑbləs] *a.* 失業的
- work [wɝk] *n.* & *vi.* 工作 (不可數) ①

▶ Alex has got a job as a car salesman.
艾力克斯找到一份擔任汽車銷售員的工作。

▶ If you make another mistake, you're out of a job.
如果你再犯錯，就會沒有工作了。

▶ It is Nick's job to do the laundry.
尼克負責洗衣服。

9　whether [ˋ(h)wɛðɚ] *conj.* 是否 (引導名詞子句)；不論 (引導副詞子句)

- (1) whether to V　是否做……
  (2) whether... or...　不論……還是……
- if [ɪf] *conj.* 是否 ①
- whether 表『是否』時，其後可引導名詞子句，或接不定詞片語，若接不定詞片語，則此時不能以 if 代替 whether。

▶ Tell me whether Kyle will come.
= Tell me if Kyle will come.
告訴我凱爾是否會來。

▶ Carmen couldn't decide whether to buy the blue dress.
卡門無法決定是否買那件藍色洋裝。

▶ I don't mind whether we go to France or Spain.
不論我們去法國或西班牙，我都不介意。

10　add [æd] *vt.* & *vi.* 相加；增加，添加

- (1) add A to B　將 A 加進 B
  (2) add to sth　增添某事物

▶ If you add two and three, you get five.
2 加 3 等於 5。

衍 (1) addition [əˋdɪʃən]
  n. 加法；增加 ②
  (2) additional [əˋdɪʃənḷ] *a.* 額外的 ③

▶ Add some wood to the fire to keep the room warm.
加些木柴進火堆裡，讓房間保持溫暖。

▶ The fancy dress added to Wendy's charm.
這件漂亮的洋裝增添了溫蒂的魅力。

11 office [ˋɔfɪs] *n.* 辦公室；公職

片 take office　就職

衍 (1) official [əˋfɪʃəl] *a.* 官方的 ②
  (2) officially [əˋfɪʃəlɪ] *adv.* 官方地

▶ There is no one in the office now.
現在辦公室裡沒人。

▶ Mr. Smith took office as mayor of this city yesterday.
史密斯先生昨天就職為本市市長。

officer [ˋɔfəsɚ] *n.* 軍官；警官；官員
片 a police officer　警察，員警

▶ Emily's father is a police officer.
艾蜜莉的父親是警察。

12 yet [jɛt] *adv.* 還，尚未 & *conj.* 然而 (= but)

用法 yet 作副詞，表『還，尚未』時，須用於否定句或疑問句。

▶ Chris hasn't shown up yet.
克里斯還未現身。

▶ The hotel was luxurious yet affordable.
= The hotel was luxurious but affordable.
這間飯店很奢華，但價格還能負擔得起。
＊luxurious [lʌgˋʒʊrɪəs] *a.* 奢華的

13 almost [ˋɔl͵most] *adv.* 幾乎，差不多

似 nearly [ˋnɪrlɪ] *adv.* 幾乎 ②

▶ Liam will play almost any sport.
連恩幾乎會做任何一種運動。

14 happen [ˋhæpən] *vi.* (尤指未經計劃而) 發生；碰巧

片 (1) happen to sb/sth
  發生在某人 / 某事物上
  (2) happen to V　碰巧……

似 occur [əˋkɝ] *vi.* 發生 ②

▶ The accident happened at midnight last night.
這起意外事故發生在昨晚午夜。

▶ What happened to your left eye?
= What's the matter with your left eye?
你的左眼發生了什麼事？

▶ I happen to have $100 with me.
我碰巧身上有 100 元。

15 win [wɪn] *vi.* & *vt.* & *n.* 贏

三 win, won [wʌn], won

▶ Who do you think will win?
你認為誰會贏？

🔑 (1) win a game / race　贏得比賽
(2) win by + 分數　以若干分數獲勝

▸ We won the game by two points.
我們以 2 分之差贏得比賽。

衍 winner [ˋwɪnɚ] *n.* 贏家

▸ Our team has had only two wins so far.
我們球隊到目前為止只有 2 勝。

比 win、beat、defeat 均有『獲勝』之意，惟 win 之後的受詞是『比賽』或『獎品』，beat 和 defeat 則可接『人』或『隊伍』。

---

lose [luz]

vt. & vi. 輸掉 & *vt.* 丟失；失去

▸ The team played well but still lost the game.
這隊打得很好，卻還是輸了那場比賽。

三 lose, lost [lɔst], lost

▸ Adrian has lost his new phone.
亞德里安弄丟了他的新手機。

🔑 lose one's temper　發脾氣

▸ Jack has lost interest in his job.
傑克對工作失去了興趣。

衍 (1) loss [lɔs] *n.* 喪失 ②
(2) loser [ˋluzɚ] *n.* 輸家 ③
(3) lost [lɔst] *a.* 遺失的；迷途的

▸ Stay calm. Don't lose your temper.
保持冷靜，別發脾氣。

16　moment [ˋmomənt] *n.* 片刻；時刻，時候

🔑 (1) in a moment　很快，一會
(2) at the moment　現在，此刻

▸ I believe we'll get the truth in a moment.
我相信我們很快就會知道真相。

▸ What are you doing at the moment?
此刻你正在做什麼？

17　public [ˋpʌblɪk] *a.* 公共的；大眾的；公開的 & *n.* 公眾 (前面加定冠詞 the)

🔑 (1) public opinion　民意，公眾輿論
(2) sb's public image
某人的公眾形象
(3) in public　公開地，當眾

▸ We may not smoke in public places.
公共場所不可吸菸。

▸ Public opinion is in favor of the candidate.
民意支持這位候選人。
＊candidate [ˋkændə͵det] *n.* 候選人

衍 (1) publicity [pʌbˋlɪsətɪ] *n.* 知名度 ④
(2) publication [͵pʌblɪˋkeʃən]
n. 刊物 (可數)；發表，公布 (不可數)
④

▸ The actor's public image has been ruined by the incident.
這名演員的公眾形象被這起事件毀了。

反 private [ˋpraɪvɪt]
a. 私人的；私下的 ②

▸ The pool is open to the public from 7 a.m. to 9 p.m.
本游泳池對大眾開放的時間是從早上 7 點到晚上 9 點。

▸ The basketball star hasn't been seen in public for years.
這名籃球明星好幾年沒公開出現了。

18　age [edʒ] *n.* 年齡；時代，時期 & *vi. & vt.* (使) 老化

🔑 (1) at the age of + 數字　在若干歲時
(2) the Middle Ages　中世紀時期

▸ Steven left home at the age of 25.
史蒂芬在 25 歲時離家。

(3) for ages 很久
= for a long time

衍 aging [ˈedʒɪŋ]
　a. 逐漸年邁的 & n. 變老，老化

▶ We are living in a computer age.
　我們生活在電腦時代裡。

▶ Mark is an expert on the history of the Middle Ages.
　馬克是中世紀時期歷史的專家。

▶ I haven't seen Sam for ages.
　我好久都沒見到山姆了。

▶ Aiden is aging fast because of his busy work.
　艾登因為工作繁忙而老化得很快。

19　air [ɛr] n. 空氣

片 (1) in the air　空氣中
(2) be up in the air
　　尚未決定，懸而未決
(3) on (the) air　（廣播、電視）播出

▶ We couldn't live without air.
　沒有空氣我們就無法生存。

▶ There was a sense of excitement in the air.
　空氣中充斥著刺激感。

▶ The team's future is still up in the air.
　該隊的前途仍懸而未決。

▶ The program will soon be on the air.
　這節目很快就要播出。

---

airplane [ˈɛrˌplen]
n. 飛機 (= plane)

片 by airplane　搭飛機

似 aircraft [ˈɛrˌkræft]
　n. 飛機 (單複數同形) ②

▶ Matt is scared to travel by airplane.
= Matt is scared to travel by plane.
　麥特害怕搭飛機旅行。

---

airport [ˈɛrˌpɔrt] n. 機場

▶ How long will it take to get to the airport?
　到機場要多久？

20　far [fɑr] adv. 遙遠地；(程度) 更 (= much，修飾比較級) & a. 遙遠的

片 (1) be far from + adj./N/V-ing
　　遠不及……
(2) as far as sb can remember /
　　tell...
　　就某人能記得 / 理解的，……

用法 far 的形容詞、副詞比較級和最高級為
不規則變化：far, farther [ˈfɑrðə] /
further [ˈfɝðə], farthest [ˈfɑrðɪst] /
furthest [ˈfɝðɪst]。

▶ We no longer have to travel far to watch a movie.
　我們不必再跑很遠去看電影了。

▶ The new model is far better than the old one.
　新型號比起舊的還要好。

▶ What Elaine said was far from the truth.
　伊蓮所說的跟事實相差甚遠。

▶ As far as I can remember, Joan wasn't at the party.
　就我能記得的，瓊安不在派對上。

▶ I don't want to walk there—it's too far.
　我不想走到那邊 —— 太遠了。

near [nɪr]
a. 近的 & *adv.* 接近 & *prep.* 在……附近 & *vt.* & *vi.* 接近

🄗 draw near　即將來臨

衍 (1) nearly [ˋnɪrlɪ] *adv.* 幾乎 ②
　(2) nearby [ˋnɪrˏbaɪ]
　　a. 附近的 & *adv.* 在附近 ②

似 (1) close [klos] *a.* 近的 & *adv.* 接近 ①
　(2) approach [əˋprotʃ]
　　vt. & *vi.* 接近 ②

▶ My school is quite near.
我的學校很近。

▶ The Chinese Lunar New Year is drawing near.
農曆春節快到了。

▶ Daisy lives near the MRT station.
= Daisy lives close to the MRT station.
黛西住在捷運站附近。

▶ My dog won't go near water.
我的狗不會到水附近。

▶ The boat was nearing the beach.
那艘小船駛近海灘。

21　center [ˋsɛntɚ] *n.* 中心點，中央；(設施) 中心 & *vt.* 使置中 & *vi.* 集中於

🄗 (1) the center of...
　　……的中心點 / 中央
　(2) a shopping center　購物中心
　(3) center on...　集中於……
　　= focus on...

衍 central [ˋsɛntrəl] *a.* 中央的 ②

似 middle [ˋmɪdḷ] *n.* 中央 ①

▶ Wall Street has become the center of business in New York City.
華爾街已成為紐約市的商業中心。

▶ The shopping center is going to open next month.
這個購物中心將於下個月開幕。

▶ You should center the photo on the document.
你應該把文件上的照片置中擺放。

▶ Much of the debate centered on privacy issues.
大部分的辯論都集中於隱私權議題。

22　die [daɪ] *vi.* 死去

目 die, died [daɪd], died (現在分詞為 dying)

🄗 die of / from...　死於 (事故或疾病等)

似 (1) dye [daɪ] *vt.* 染色 ④
　(2) pass away　去世

▶ The girl died from head injuries.
這女孩死於腦部創傷。

▶ The poor young man died of lung cancer.
這個可憐的年輕人死於肺癌。

---

dead [dɛd]
a. 死亡的；失效的 & *adv.* 完全地

衍 deadly [ˋdɛdlɪ]
　a. 致命的 & *adv.* 非常 ⑤

似 completely [kəmˋplitlɪ] *adv.* 完全地

▶ My grandfather has been dead for over ten years.
我爺爺過世 10 多年了。

▶ I couldn't call you because my phone was dead.
我不能打給你是因為我的電話沒電了。

▶ You're dead right: That lecture was a waste of time.
你完全正確：這堂課根本是浪費時間。

---

death [dɛθ] *n.* 死亡

▶ The mayor's death made all the citizens sad.
市長的離世讓所有市民都感到很難過。

23 learn [lɜn] vi. & vt. 學習；得知

片 (1) learn from / about...
從……中學習 / 學習有關……
　(2) learn one's lesson　學到教訓
　(3) learn of...　得知……

衍 (1) learning [ˈlɜnɪŋ]
　　n. 學識 (不可數) ③
　(2) learned [ˈlɜnɪd] a. 學問淵博的 ④

▶ You should learn from your mistakes.
你應從錯誤中學習。

▶ Tom learned his lesson and will never lie again.
湯姆學到教訓，再也不會說謊了。

▶ Candice was shocked when she learned of her friend's marriage.
坎迪絲得知好友結婚的事時感到很震驚。

---

class [klæs]

n. 班級；課程；階級，等級 & vt. 把……
歸類

複 classes [ˈklæsɪz]

片 (1) cut / skip class　蹺課
　(2) first / business / economy class
頭等 / 商務 / 經濟艙
　(3) be classed as...　被歸類為……

衍 classmate [ˈklæsˌmet] n. 同學 ②

似 classify [ˈklæsəˌfaɪ] vt. 分類；歸類 ④

▶ There are twenty-eight students in our class.
我們班上有 28 名學生。

▶ We have got English class next.
我們下一堂是英文課。

▶ Joe never skips class.
喬從不蹺課。

▶ My boss prefers to fly in first class.
我老闆偏好搭頭等艙。

▶ Kurt is classed as a temporary worker.
柯特被歸類為臨時員工。

---

24 history [ˈhɪst(ə)rɪ] n. 歷史

片 make history　創造歷史

衍 (1) historical [hɪsˈtɔrɪkḷ]
　　a. 有關歷史的 ②
　(2) historic [hɪsˈtɔrɪk]
　　a. 歷史上著名的 ③
　(3) historian [hɪsˈtɔrɪən]
　　n. 歷史學家 ③

▶ My father teaches history in that school.
我父親在那所學校教歷史。

▶ Neil Armstrong made history by walking on the moon.
尼爾‧阿姆斯壯在月球上漫步創造了歷史。

---

25 across [əˈkrɔs] prep. 越過；在……對面 & adv. 橫越

片 across from...　在……對面

▶ Be careful when you walk across the street.
你過街時要小心。

▶ I live in a building across from the post office.
我住在郵局對面的一棟大樓裡。

▶ We have to swim across. There is no other way.
我們得游泳橫渡過去，沒別的方法了。

cross [krɔs]
vt. & vi. 越過;(使) 交叉 & *n.* 叉號;十字形;十字架

複 crosses [ˈkrɔsɪz]
衍 (1) crossing [ˈkrɔsɪŋ]
　　　 n. 斑馬線;十字路口 ⑥
　　(2) crossroads [ˈkrɔsˌrodz]
　　　 n. 十字路口 (恆用複數)
　　= intersection [ˌɪntɚˈsɛkʃən]
　　　 at the crossroads　在十字路口
　　= at the intersection

▶ Look both ways before you cross the street.
= Look both ways before you go across the street.
　過馬路前注意兩側。

▶ Highway 14 crosses highway 90 in this area.
　14 號公路和 90 號公路在這個區域交會。

▶ Mrs. Reynolds marked the wrong answers with a cross.
　雷諾斯老師在錯的答案上以叉號標記。

▶ Annie bought a necklace in the shape of a cross.
　安妮買了一條十字形的項鍊。

▶ The girl is wearing a silver cross around her neck.
　這名女孩脖子上戴了一個銀質的十字架。

26　real [ˈrɪəl] *a.* 真正的;真實的

片 for real　真正的;真實的
衍 (1) reality [rɪˈælətɪ] *n.* 現實 ②
　　(2) realize [ˈrɪəˌlaɪz] *vt.* 實現 ②
　　(3) realistic [ˌrɪəˈlɪstɪk] *a.* 現實的 ④
似 true [tru] *a.* 真的;真實的 ②
反 (1) false [fɔls] *a.* 假的 ②
　　(2) unreal [ʌnˈril] *a.* 不真實的

▶ A real friend will give you a hand when you are down.
　真正的朋友會在你失意時伸出援手。

▶ The writer often writes about real people.
　這位作家時常描寫真實人物。

▶ I've just won the lottery! For real!
　我剛中樂透了!是真的!

---

really [ˈrɪəlɪ]
adv. 實際地;確實地;很,非常

似 truly [ˈtrulɪ] *adv.* 真正地

▶ I want to know what really happened.
　我要知道實際到底發生了什麼事。

▶ Tom is really a man you can count on.
　湯姆是你真正可以仰賴的人。

▶ The problem is really difficult to solve.
　這個問題非常難解決。

Unit 09

0901-0907

1 build [bɪld] *vt.* 建造；建立 (= build up)

- build, built [bɪlt], built
- building [ˋbɪldɪŋ] *n.* 建築物 ②

▶ My grandfather built this house all by himself.
我爺爺一手建造這棟房子。

▶ Peter built up the successful business on his own.
彼得獨自建立起這個成功的事業。

2 fall [fɔl] *vi.* 跌倒，落下 & *vi.* & *n.* 減少，降低 & *n.* 秋天 (= autumn [ˋɔtəm])

- fall, fell [fɛl], fallen [ˋfɔlən]
- fall down 跌倒
- decrease [dɪˋkris]
  vt. & *vi.* 減少 & [ˋdikris] *n.* 減少 ③
- (1) rise [raɪz] *vi.* & *n.* 上升 ①
  (2) increase [ɪnˋkris]
  vt. & *vi.* 增加 & [ˋɪnkris] *n.* 增加 ②

▶ The old woman fell down and hurt her leg.
老婆婆跌倒，傷了腿。

▶ The temperature has been falling for the past week.
過去一週氣溫持續下降。

▶ There has been a fall in house prices.
房價已下跌了。

▶ Last fall, I went to visit my aunt in Spain.
去年秋天，我到西班牙看我阿姨。

3 half [hæf] *a.* 一半的 & *n.* 一半 & *adv.* 一半地

- halves [hævz]
- cut / split sth in half 把某物對半切
- 『half (of) the + 名詞』的用法中 of 可省略，接複數可數名詞時，採複數形動詞；接單數可數名詞或不可數名詞時，採單數形動詞。

▶ Brett came to the office a half hour early.
布萊特提早半個小時到辦公室。

▶ Let's split the pizza in half.
我們把披薩切成兩半吧。

▶ Half of the work is finished.
工作已完成了一半。

▶ Natasha is half German and half Scottish.
娜塔莎是半個德國人和半個蘇格蘭人。

4 free [fri] *a.* 自由的；免費的；空閒的 & *adv.* 自由地；免費地 & *vt.* 釋放

- (1) be free to V
  自由做……；有空做……
  (2) free time 空閒時間
  (3) for free 免費
  = free of charge
  (4) be freed (from + 地點)
  (從某地) 被釋放

▶ When you've finished this task, you're free to go.
你做完這份工作後，就可以離開了。

▶ I didn't need to pay for the book because it was free.
我不用花錢買這本書，因為是免費的。

▶ If you are free, come visit us.
如果你有空，請來看我們。

▶ Kent likes to go surfing in his free time.
肯特閒暇時喜歡去衝浪。

衍 (1) freedom [ˈfridəm] *n.* 自由 ②
(2) freely [ˈfrilɪ] *adv.* 自由地
似 available [əˈveləbḷ] *a.* 有空的 ②

▶ Peggy let her dog run free in the park.
佩姬讓她的狗狗在公園自由奔跑。

▶ The elderly can get in the museum for free.
= The elderly can get in the museum free of charge.
年長者可以免費進入博物館。

▶ The prisoner was freed from jail last month.
這名囚犯上個月被釋放出獄了。

5　cost [kɔst] *n.* 費用；代價 & *vt.* 花費；使失去

三 三態同形
片 (1) at the cost of...　以……的代價
(2) sth cost sb + 金額
　　某物花某人若干金額
(3) cost sb sth　使某人失去某物
衍 costly [ˈkɔstlɪ] *a.* 昂貴的 ③
似 (1) price [praɪs] *n.* 價格 ①
(2) expense [ɪkˈspɛns] *n.* 費用 ②
比 cost 和 spend 的中文均可譯成『花費』，惟 cost 的主詞是事物，spend 的主詞則是人。

▶ We need to lower our transportation cost.
我們必須減少交通成本。

▶ Roger transformed the business at the cost of his health.
羅傑犧牲了健康來改變公司。

▶ How much does that book cost?
那本書花多少錢買的？

▶ That car cost me a fortune.
買那輛車花了我不少錢。

▶ The reporter's racist comments cost him his job.
這位記者種族歧視的言論讓他丟了工作。
*racist [ˈresɪst] *a.* 種族主義的

6　special [ˈspɛʃəl] *a.* 特別的

反 (1) usual [ˈjuʒuəl] *a.* 通常的 ②
(2) ordinary [ˈɔrdṇˌɛrɪ] *a.* 普通的 ②

▶ What's so special about this car?
這輛車有什麼特別之處？

▶ I'm doing nothing special for Thanksgiving this year.
今年感恩節我沒做什麼特別的事情。

7　husband [ˈhʌzbənd] *n.* 丈夫

▶ A good husband should always be loyal to his wife.
好丈夫應始終對妻子忠實。

---

wife [waɪf] *n.* 妻子
複 wives [waɪvz]

▶ My wife has been a great help to me.
我妻子一直給我很大的幫助。

---

child [tʃaɪld] *n.* 小孩，兒童
複 children [ˈtʃɪldrən]
片 an only child　獨生子 / 女
似 kid [kɪd] *n.* 孩童 ①

▶ My wife wants to have another child.
我太太想再有一個小孩。

▶ Vincent loves being an only child.
文森喜歡當獨生子。

8 remember [rɪˈmɛmbɚ] *vt.* 想起，記得

H (1) remember to V　記得要做⋯⋯
　(2) remember + V-ing
　　記得曾做⋯⋯

▶ I can't remember the woman's name.
我想不起這名女子的名字。

▶ Remember to close the door when you leave.
你走時記得要把門關上。

▶ I remember visiting this place before.
我記得曾到過這個地方。

forget [fɚˈgɛt] *vt.* 忘記

目 forget, forgot [fɚˈgɑt], forgot /
forgotten [fɚˈgɑtn̩]

H (1) forget to V　　忘了要做⋯⋯
　(2) forget + V-ing　忘了曾做⋯⋯

▶ Don't forget your promise.
別忘了你的承諾。

▶ My mother forgot to wake me up this morning.
我媽媽今早忘記叫我起床。

▶ I forgot watching this film.
我忘了曾看過這部影片。

9 level [ˈlɛvl̩] *n.* 程度，水準 & *a.* 平的 & *vt.* 弄平

H at... level　在⋯⋯的程度

▶ Tom's English is at the highest level in his class.
湯姆的英文程度是班上最好的。

▶ After you hang the picture, make sure it's level.
把畫掛上去後，要確定畫有放平。

▶ Betty asked the workers to level her garden.
貝蒂請工人們剷平她的花園。

10 ground [graʊnd] *n.* 地面 (前面加定冠詞 the)；(有特定用途的) 場地 & *vt.* 根據；使擱淺；使停飛；禁足

H be grounded in / on...
　以⋯⋯為根據
＝ be based on...

衍 (1) playground [ˈpleˌgraʊnd]
　　n. 操場 ②
　(2) underground [ˈʌndɚˌgraʊnd]
　　a. 地面下的 ②
　(3) background [ˈbækˌgraʊnd]
　　n. 背景 ③

似 floor [flɔr] *n.* 地面 ①

▶ Autumn is here, and the ground is covered with fallen leaves.
秋天到了，地上鋪滿了落葉。

▶ The lion returned to its hunting ground.
這隻獅子回到牠的狩獵場。

▶ Your report should not be grounded in imagination.
你的報告不該以想像為根據。

▶ The ship was grounded and the canal was blocked.
這艘船擱淺了，運河也被堵住了。
*canal [kəˈnæl] *n.* 運河

▶ All planes are grounded until the typhoon leaves.
所有飛機都得停飛，等到颱風離開才能起飛。

▶ The boy's parents grounded him for a week.
這名小男孩的父母罰他禁足一個星期。

11　cut [kʌt] vt. 切，割，剪；降低，削減 & n. 傷口

目 三態同形

片 (1) cut costs　減少開支，降低成本
　　(2) cut down (on sth)　減少 (某物)

似 reduce [rɪ`d(j)us] vt. 減少 ③

▶ Mom cut the apple with a sharp knife.
　媽媽用一把鋒利的刀切蘋果。

▶ The boss asked his workers to cut costs by half.
　老闆要求員工削減一半的開支。

▶ The doctor advised Leo to cut down on his drinking.
　醫生建議里歐減少飲酒。

▶ The homeless man has a long cut on his face.
　那個遊民的臉上有一條長長的傷口。

12　full [fʊl] a. 充滿的；完整的；飽的

片 be full of...　充滿……
　= be filled with...

衍 full-time [ˌfʊl`taɪm] a. 全職的

似 complete [kəm`plit] a. 完整的 ②

反 empty [`ɛmptɪ] a. 空的 ②

▶ My heart was full of warmth when he offered to help.
　當他主動提議幫忙時，我的心中充滿著溫馨的感覺。

▶ I was asked to write down my full name.
　我被要求寫下全名。

▶ I'm too full to eat anymore.
　我很飽，再也吃不下了。

fully [`fʊlɪ] adv. 充分地，完全地

▶ I fully understand what you mean.
　我完全了解你的意思。

13　able [`ebḷ] a. 有能力的，能夠

片 be able to V　有能力做……
　= be capable of + V-ing

衍 (1) ability [ə`bɪlətɪ] n. 能力 ①
　　(2) enable [ɪn`ebḷ] vt. 使能夠 ③

▶ I'm sure David is able to do it by himself.
= I'm sure David is capable of doing it by himself.
　我確定大衛有能力獨自做這件事。

unable [ʌn`ebḷ] a. 不能的

片 be unable to V　不能做……
　= be incapable of + V-ing

▶ Jennie was unable to conduct the research.
= Jennie was incapable of conducting the research.
　珍妮無法進行這份研究。

14　art [ɑrt] n. 藝術；藝術 (作) 品 (皆不可數)

片 (1) modern art　現代藝術
　　(2) the arts
　　　藝術 (含繪畫、舞蹈、音樂等的總稱)

衍 (1) artist [`ɑrtɪst] n. 藝術家 ②
　　(2) artistic [ɑr`tɪstɪk] a. 藝術的 ④

▶ I know nothing of modern art.
　我對現代藝術一無所知。

▶ The government is cutting funding for the arts.
　政府削減提供給藝術的資金。

▶ The exhibition features the art of Picasso.
　這場展覽展出畢卡索的藝術作品。

15 break [brek] *vt.* & *vi.* (使) 破碎；弄壞 & *vt.* 打破 (紀錄)；違反 & *vi.* 破曉 & *n.* 休息；裂口

目 break, broke [brok], broken [`brokən]

片 (1) break into pieces　　破成碎片
　 (2) break down
　　　(車輛) 拋錨；(機器) 故障；(情緒) 崩潰
　 (3) break into...　　　　闖入⋯⋯
　 (4) break a record　　　打破紀錄
　 (5) break the law / rule　違法 / 規
　 (6) take a break / rest　休息一下
　 (7) a lunch break　　　午休

衍 outbreak [`aut,brek] *n.* 爆發 ⑥

似 (1) shatter [`ʃætɚ]
　　　vi. & *vt.* (使) 粉碎 ⑤
　 (2) smash [smæʃ] *vt.* 使粉碎 ⑤

▶ Chad broke his mother's vase by accident.
　查德不小心打破他媽媽的花瓶。

▶ Wayne's heart broke into pieces when his wife left him.
　當韋恩的老婆離開他時，他的心碎了。

▶ The car broke down in the middle of nowhere.
　這輛車子在荒郊野外拋錨了。

▶ The thief broke into my house and stole a gold watch.
　小偷闖入我家偷走了一只金錶。

▶ He just broke the Olympic record for the men's 100-meter dash.
　他剛剛打破了男子 100 公尺短跑奧運紀錄。

▶ Christina would never break the school rules.
　克莉絲蒂娜絕不會違反校規。

▶ The day was breaking when they parted.
　他們分別時天正破曉。

▶ Let's take a break for ten minutes before we go back to work again.
　我們休息 10 分鐘再繼續工作。

▶ We found a break in the pipe.
　我們發現水管有一道裂痕。

16 land [lænd] *n.* 陸地 (不可數)；土地 (不可數)；國家 & *vi.* & *vt.* (使) 著陸

片 (1) a piece of land　　一塊地
　 (2) sb's native land　　某人的母國

衍 (1) landmark [`lænd,mɑrk] *n.* 地標 ④
　 (2) landscape [`lænd,skep] *n.* 風景 ④

反 take off　起飛

▶ The passengers were pleased to see the land.
　乘客很開心能看到陸地。

▶ This piece of land is used for farming.
　這塊地供農作用。

▶ He returned to his native land after a few years.
　幾年後，他回到了自己的母國。

▶ The plane was landing on the runway.
　那架飛機正降落在跑道上。

landing [`lændɪŋ] *n.* 降落，著陸

片 a safe / smooth landing
　安全 / 平穩降落

▶ We were all relieved to know that the plane made a safe landing.
　知道飛機安全著陸時，我們都鬆了一口氣。

17 quite [kwaɪt] *adv.* 相當

似 (1) pretty [ˋprɪtɪ] *adv.* 相當 ①
　　 (2) fairly [ˋfɛrlɪ] *adv.* 相當 ③

▶ Paul was quite sad after his dog died.
保羅的狗狗死了之後，他相當難過。

18 less [lɛs] *a.* 較少的 & *adv.* 較少地 & *prep.* 減去 & *pron.* 較少的量

片 (1) no less than... 至少……
　　 (2) much less 更別說 (與否定句並用)

用法 (1) less 作形容詞，用以修飾不可數名詞。
　　 (2) less 作比較副詞，用法為：
　　　　 less + adj./adv. + than + 比較對象
　　　　 比……還不……

▶ Ella spent less money than she expected.
艾拉花的錢比她預計的少。

▶ No less than 9 students passed the exam.
至少有 9 個學生通過這次的考試。

▶ Cindy is less energetic than other kids.
辛蒂跟其他孩子比起來較沒活力。

▶ Greg's version of events is less believable than yours.
葛瑞格對於事件的說法比你的還不可信。

▶ Ryan can barely cook meat, much less pasta.
雷恩不會煮肉，更別說煮義大利麵了。

▶ The cost for the hotel is $100, less the $20 deposit.
旅館的費用是 100 美元，再扣掉 20 美元的訂金。

▶ If you want to lose weight, you have to eat less and exercise more.
如果你想減肥，就得少吃多動。

19 draw [drɔ] *vt. & vi.* 畫 & *vt.* 吸引；拉 & *n.* 有吸引力的人 / 事 / 物；平局

三 draw, drew [dru], drawn [drɔn]
片 (1) draw (sb's) attention
　　　　 吸引 (某人的) 注意力
　　 (2) a big draw
　　　　 大家很喜歡的人 / 事 / 物
　　 (3) end in a draw 以平局告終
衍 drawing [ˋdrɔɪŋ] *n.* 描繪；素描 ②
似 (1) paint [pent] *vt. & vi.* 畫 ①
　　 (2) attract [əˋtrækt] *vt.* 吸引 ③
　　 (3) attraction [əˋtrækʃən]
　　　　 n. 吸引力；吸引人的事物 ④
　　 (4) tie [taɪ] *n.* 平手 ①

▶ I'm drawing a picture of a dog, not a pig.
我畫的是一隻狗，不是豬。

▶ I'd like to draw your attention to page ten.
我想請大家注意看第 10 頁。

▶ Paul drew a stool in the fireplace.
保羅拉了一張凳子到壁爐邊。

▶ This famous actress will be the big draw at the film festival.
這位知名女星會是這次影展的一大看頭。

▶ The soccer match ended in a draw.
這場足球賽打成平手。

20 walk [wɔk] *n. & vi. & vt.* 走，步行 & *vt.* 陪 (某人) 走路

片 (1) a ten-minute walk
　　　　 10 分鐘的腳程

▶ Let's take a walk after work.
我們下班後去散步吧。

(2) take a walk　散步
= go for a walk
(3) walk away (from sth)
（從某事中）脫身，離開
(4) walk sb home　陪某人走回家

▶ Walk faster, or we won't make it to the office on time.
走快一點，要不然我們無法準時趕到辦公室。

▶ Henry decided to walk away from the deal.
亨利決定從這場交易中脫身。

▶ Please let me walk you home.
請讓我陪你走路回家。

21　certain [ˋsɝtṇ] *a.* 某些 (= some)；確定的 (= sure) & *pron.* 一些 ☐

片 (1) certain + 複數名詞　　某些……
(2) a certain + 單數名詞　　某個……
(3) be certain (that)...　　確定……
(4) be certain of / about...　確定……
(5) know for certain / sure　確知
(6) certain of...　一些……
= some of...

衍 certainty [ˋsɝtṇtɪ] *n.* 確定 ⑤

似 sure [ʃʊr] *a.* 確信的 ①

▶ Certain answers are not correct.
某些答案有誤。

▶ A certain man called you yesterday.
昨天有某個人打電話找你。

▶ I'm certain that Miley will succeed.
= I'm certain of Miley's success.
我確信麥莉會成功。

▶ Nobody knows for certain when Michael is coming back.
沒有人確知邁可什麼時候會回來。

▶ Certain of the employees take long coffee breaks.
有些員工喝咖啡的休息時間很久。

---

uncertain [ʌnˋsɝtṇ] *a.* 不確定的 ☐

片 be uncertain of / about...
對……不確定

似 unsure [ˌʌnˋʃʊr] *a.* 不確信的

▶ I'm uncertain about what we should do next.
我不確定我們接下來該做什麼。

22　enter [ˋɛntɚ] *vt. & vi.* 進入；(電腦) 輸入；(報名) 參加 ☐

衍 (1) entrance [ˋɛntrəns] *n.* 入口 ②
(2) entry [ˋɛntrɪ] *n.* 進入；入口 ③

反 exit [ˋɛgzɪt / ˋɛksɪt]
vt. 離開 & *n.* 出口 ②

▶ Please enter the room through the back door.
請由後門進入屋裡。

▶ You must enter a password to start the system.
你必須輸入密碼以啟動系統。

▶ Tracy entered the beauty contest simply for fun.
崔希參加選美比賽單純只是為了好玩。

23　truly [ˋtrulɪ] *adv.* 真地，確實地 ☐

似 really [ˋrɪəlɪ] *adv.* 真地，確實地 ①

▶ Your opinion is truly important to me.
你的意見對我來說確實很重要。

24　voice [vɔɪs] *n.* (人的) 聲音 & *vt.* (用言語) 表達

🅗 in a low / loud voice　小 / 大聲地

🅑 sound 可用來表『任何聲音』,而 voice 則專指『人所發出來的聲音』。

▸ Jeff has a quiet voice; I can barely hear him.
傑夫的聲音很小,我幾乎聽不到他說話。

▸ Alex is so shy that he only talks in a low voice.
艾力克斯太害羞了,只敢小聲地說話。

▸ The workers voiced their complaints about the decision.
工人們對這項決議表示不滿。

---

sound [saʊnd]

n. 聲音 & *vi.* 聽起來 & *a.* 健全 / 康的;不錯的

🅗 (1) sound + adj.　聽起來……
　 (2) sound like + N　聽起來像……
　 (3) safe and sound　安然無恙

🅕 soundly [ˋsaʊndlɪ] *adv.* 充分地

▸ There was a weird sound coming from the kitchen.
廚房裡傳來一個奇怪的聲音。

▸ Your idea sounds good to me.
我覺得你的想法聽起來很好。

▸ That sounds like a good idea!
那聽起來是個好主意!

▸ A sound mind is in a sound body.
健全的精神寓於健康的身體。── 諺語

▸ Thank you for your sound idea.
謝謝你的好點子。

25　right [raɪt] *a.* 正確的;右邊的 & *adv.* 向右;正好;正確地 & *n.* 權利;右邊

🅗 (1) on sb's / the right side　在右邊
　 (2) turn right　右轉
　 = turn to the right
　 (3) have the right to V/N
　　　有……的權利

🅕 (1) right-hand [ˋraɪtˏhænd]
　　　a. 右手邊的
　 (2) righteous [ˋraɪtʃəs] *a.* 公正的

🅘 correct [kəˋrɛkt] *a.* 正確的 ①

▸ The theory has been proved right.
此理論經證明是正確的。

▸ The Opera House is on your right side.
歌劇院在你的右邊。

▸ Turn right at the next block, and you'll see the restaurant.
= Turn to the right at the next block, and you'll see the restaurant.
在下一個街區右轉,你就會看到那間餐廳了。

▸ I left my suitcase right here.
我的行李箱就放在這裡。

▸ Did I guess right?
我猜對了嗎?

▸ In certain countries, women don't have the right to vote.
在某些國家,女性沒有投票權。

0925-0928

wrong [rɔŋ] *a.* 錯誤的；不正當的；出問題的 & *adv.* 不對地 & *n.* 錯誤 & *vt.* 不公平對待

- (1) It is wrong (of sb) to V
  （某人）做……是不對的
- (2) (be) wrong with sth
  某物出問題 / 故障
- (3) go wrong　出問題
- (4) tell right from wrong　明辨是非

似 incorrect [ˌɪnkəˈrɛkt] *a.* 不正確的

▸ Most of the answers he wrote were wrong.
他寫的答案大部分是錯的。

▸ It's wrong to take something that isn't yours.
拿別人的東西是不對的。

▸ There's something wrong with Becky's phone.
貝琪的電話出了點問題。

▸ I just don't know where we went wrong.
我就是不知道我們到底哪裡出問題了。

▸ The boy is too young to tell right from wrong.
小男孩太小了，還不能明辨是非。

▸ Two wrongs do not make a right.
兩惡不成一善 / 勿以惡報惡。—— 諺語

▸ Jack decided to forgive those who have wronged him.
傑克決定原諒那些待他不公的人。

---

left [lɛft]
a. 左邊的 & *adv.* 向左 & *n.* 左邊

- turn left　向左轉
  = turn to the left
- 衍 left-hand [ˈlɛftˌhænd] *a.* 左手邊的

▸ They live on the left bank of the river.
他們住在河的左岸。

▸ Turn left at the next corner.
= Turn to the left at the next corner.
在下一個街角左轉。

26　behind [bɪˈhaɪnd] *adv.* 在後方；在原地 & *prep.* 在……之後

- (1) stay behind　留下來
- (2) fall behind　落後

▸ The bridesmaids entered the church, with the bride following behind.
伴娘們進入教堂，新娘跟在後方。

▸ Maureen stayed behind to help clean up.
莫琳留下來幫忙清理。

▸ Sherry fell behind with her schoolwork.
雪莉的功課落後了。

▸ There's a little girl standing behind you.
有一個小女孩站在你後方。

27　decide [dɪˈsaɪd] *vt.* 決定 & *vi.* 選定

- (1) decide that...　決定……
  = decide to V
  = make a decision to V
- (2) decide on...　選定……

▸ We've decided that we would change the plan.
= We've decided to change the plan.
= We've made a decision to change the plan.
我們已決定要改變計畫。

衍 (1) decision [dɪˋsɪʒən] *n.* 決定 ②
　(2) decisive [dɪˋsaɪsɪv]
　　a. 決定性的 ⑥

▶ Has the company decided on the color of the uniform?
公司已選定制服的顏色了嗎？

28　as [æz] *conj.* 因為；當……時；像 & *adv.* 一樣地 & *prep.* 作為

片 (1) as if...　好像／似乎……
　(2) as + adj./adv. + as + N
　　和……一樣……（第一個 as 為副詞，
　　第二個 as 為連接詞）

似 (1) because [bɪˋkɔz] *conj.* 因為 ①
　(2) when [(h)wɛn] *conj.* 當……時 ①
　(3) like [laɪk] *conj.* 像 ①

▶ I can't eat steak as I'm a vegetarian.
我不能吃牛排，因為我吃素。
＊vegetarian [ˏvɛdʒəˋtɛrɪən] *n.* 素食者

▶ Emma arrived just as Beth was leaving.
艾瑪抵達時，貝絲正要離開。

▶ The house looks exactly as it did when I was a child.
這棟房子看起來就像我小時候所看到的那樣。

▶ The man looked as if he was going to faint.
那名男子看起來好像要暈倒了。

▶ You are as smart as a genius.
你像天才一樣聰明。

▶ Brian has a job as a journalist.
布萊恩有份當記者的工作。
＊journalist [ˋdʒɝnəlɪst] *n.* 記者

Unit 10

1 **along** [əˋlɔŋ] *prep.* 沿著 & *adv.* 向前；一起

- (1) along with...
  和……一起；還有……
  (2) get along with sb　與某人相處
- alongside [əˏlɔŋˋsaɪd]
  prep. 沿著……旁邊 & *adv.* 靠邊地 ⑤

▶ They walked along the street and enjoyed the city view.
他們沿街而行，欣賞著城市風景。

▶ A group of children was walking along in a line, holding hands with their partners.
一群孩子和夥伴手牽著手，排成一列往前走。

▶ My camera was stolen, along with my cellphone.
我的相機連同手機一起被偷了。

▶ It's hard to get along with selfish people.
和自私的人相處是一件很難的事。

2 **lie** [laɪ] *vi.* 說謊 & *n.* 謊言

- lie, lied [laɪd], lied (現在分詞為 lying)
- (1) tell a lie　說謊
  (2) a white lie　善意的謊言
- liar [ˋlaɪɚ] *n.* 說謊者 ④

▶ I was punished for lying.
我因說謊而受罰。

▶ Jason was accused of telling a lie.
傑森被指責說謊。

＊accuse [əˋkjuz] *vt.* 指責

lie [laɪ] *vi.* 躺；位於；在於

- lie, lay [le], lain [len] (現在分詞為 lying)
- (1) lie down　躺下來
  (2) lie in...　在於……

▶ Oliver feels like lying in his bed all day.
奧利佛想躺在床上一整天。

▶ Debra was tired, so she lay down on the sofa.
黛珀拉感到疲憊，所以在沙發上躺下。

▶ My hometown lies on the west coast of Norway.
我的家鄉位於挪威的西海岸。

▶ The strength of the movie lies in its plot.
這部電影的優點在於它的情節。

3 **allow** [əˋlaʊ] *vt.* 允許，讓

- allow sb/sth to V
  允許某人／某事物……
- allowance [əˋlaʊəns] *n.* 零用錢 ④
- permit [pɚˋmɪt] *vt.* 允許 ③
- forbid [fɚˋbɪd] *vt.* 禁止 ④

▶ Talking is not allowed during the test.
考試期間不得交談。

▶ My parents wouldn't allow me to go out alone.
我爸媽不允許我一個人出門。

4 **sure** [ʃʊr] *a.* 確信的，肯定的；必定的 & *adv.* (用於強調) 的確

- (1) be sure (that)...　確信……
  (2) be sure of / about sth
  確信某事物

▶ I am sure (that) Taylor will succeed.
= I am sure of Taylor's success.
我確信泰勒會成功。

(3) be sure to V　必定／一定……

(4) make sure (that)...
　　確定／確保……

似 certain [ˈsɝtn̩] *a.* 確信的 ①

▶ When traveling to Paris, be sure to visit the Eiffel Tower.
到巴黎旅遊時，一定要去看看艾菲爾鐵塔。

▶ You'd better make sure (that) all the answers are correct.
你最好確認所有答案都是正確的。

▶ I sure am hungry! What about you?
我的確餓了！那你呢？

5　rise [raɪz] *n.* & *vi.* 上漲，增加 & *vi.* 升起　☐

目 rise, rose [roz], risen [ˈrɪzn̩]

片 (1) be on the rise　上升

(2) give rise to...　引起／導致……

= result in...

= contribute to...

= bring about...

(3) rise to fame　出名

反 fall [fɔl] *n.* & *vi.* 下降 ①

▶ Oil prices are on the rise.

= Oil prices are rising.
油價上漲中。

▶ The mayor's speech gave rise to a heated discussion.
市長的演說引發熱烈的討論。

▶ The sun rises in the east.
太陽從東方升起。

▶ The celebrity rose to fame overnight.
這個名人一夕成名。
*overnight [ˌovɚˈnaɪt] *adv.* 一夕之間

---

raise [rez]

vt. 舉起；增加；撫／飼養；募 (款) & *n.* 加薪　☐

片 (1) raise one's hand　某人舉手

(2) raise money　募款

(3) a pay raise　加薪

似 bring up sb　撫養某人長大

反 lower [ˈloɚ] *vt.* 放下 & *vi.* 降低 ②

▶ Raise your hand if you know the answer.
如果知道答案，請舉手。

▶ The landlord raised the rent by 5%.
房東將租金調漲了 5%。

▶ Irene was raised by her grandfather.
艾琳是由她爺爺撫養長大的。

▶ They raised money for the homeless.
他們為遊民募款。

▶ Ted would like to ask for a pay raise.
泰德想要求加薪。

6　soon [sun] *adv.* 不久，很快　☐

片 (1) as soon as...　一……就……

(2) sooner or later　遲早

= eventually [ɪˈvɛntʃʊəlɪ]

似 in a short time　很快

▶ Paul will be here very soon.
保羅很快就要來了。

▶ The boy cried as soon as he saw the stranger.
小男孩一看到那個陌生人就哭了。

▶ If you don't listen, you'll be sorry sooner or later.
你要是不聽的話，遲早會後悔的。

later [ˋletə] *adv.* 晚點地

片 (1) 時間 + later　若干時間後
(2) no later than + 時間
　　在某個時間點之前

▶ I don't have time now; I'll do it later.
我現在沒空,我晚點再做。

▶ The couple met in 2016 and got married three years later.
這對夫妻在 2016 年相遇,3 年後就結婚了。

▶ The article must be submitted no later than May 31st.
這篇文章得在 5 月 31 日前遞交。

7　strong [strɔŋ] *a.* 強壯 / 烈 / 勁的;堅固的;堅定的;(味道等) 濃的

片 (1) a strong feeling / desire
　　強烈的感覺 / 渴望
(2) a strong wind　強勁的風
(3) a strong point　長處,優點

衍 (1) strongly [ˋstrɔŋlɪ]
　　adv. 強烈地;堅固地
(2) strength [strɛŋθ] *n.* 力量 ③

似 powerful [ˋpauəfəl] *a.* 有力的 ②

▶ That man is strong because he exercises every day.
那名男子天天運動,所以身體很強壯。

▶ The wall is too strong to break.
這牆太堅固了,打不破。

▶ A man with a strong will is more likely to succeed.
意志堅強的人比較可能成功。

▶ My father likes strong coffee.
我爸爸喜歡濃咖啡。

---

weak [wik]
a. 虛弱的;能力弱的;薄弱的

片 (1) a weak point　弱點
(2) be weak in...　拙於……

衍 (1) weaken [ˋwikən] *vt. & vi.* 削弱 ③
(2) weakness [ˋwiknəs]
　　n. 軟弱 (不可數);弱點 (可數)

▶ I'm feeling tired and weak. I think I've got the flu.
我覺得又累又虛弱。我想我得了流感了。

▶ Jack is weak in English grammar.
傑克的英文文法不太好。

▶ The excuse was weak, and no one believed it.
這藉口太薄弱了,沒人相信。

8　clear [klɪr] *a.* 清澈的;晴朗的;清楚的 & *vt.* 清理 & *adv.* 清楚地

片 loud and clear　清楚明白地
似 clean [klin] *a.* 乾淨的 ①
反 (1) unclear [ʌnˋklɪr] *a.* 不清楚的
　　be unclear about...
　　對……不清楚
(2) vague [veg] *a.* 模糊的 ⑤

▶ The water is so clear that I can see fish swimming around.
水好清澈,我可以看到魚兒游來游去。

▶ The sky was clear after a thunderstorm.
大雷雨過後,天空晴朗無雲。
*thunderstorm [ˋθʌndəˏstɔrm] *n.* 大雷雨

▶ Ben has a clear plan for his future career.
班對未來的職業有明確的計畫。

▶ Clear the dishes from the table after you've finished.
你吃完以後,把桌上的碗盤收拾乾淨。

▶ I can hear your voice loud and clear.
我可以清楚地聽到你的聲音。

clearly [ˈklɪrlɪ] *adv.* 清楚地；明顯地

似 **obviously** [ˈɑbvɪəslɪ] *adv.* 明顯地

▶ Professor Lin has the ability to explain those ideas clearly.
林教授能夠將那些觀念解釋得清清楚楚。

▶ Clearly, your answer is wrong.
很明顯地，你的答案錯了。

---

9 cover [ˈkʌvɚ] *vt.* 覆蓋；涵蓋 & *vi.* 代替 & *n.* 蓋子；封面

片 (1) be covered with... 被……所覆蓋
　 (2) cover up sth / cover sth up
　　　 掩蓋某事物
　 (3) cover for sb　替某人代班

衍 (1) coverage [ˈkʌvɚrɪdʒ]
　　　 n. 覆蓋範圍；新聞報導 ⑤
　 (2) uncover [ʌnˈkʌvɚ] *vt.* 揭露 ⑤
　 (3) discover [dɪsˈkʌvɚ] *vt.* 發現 ②

似 include [ɪnˈklud] *vt.* 包括 ②

反 reveal [rɪˈvil] *vt.* 揭露 ③

▶ In winter, the mountain is covered with snow.
冬天時，整座山被白雪覆蓋。

▶ The police tried to cover up the truth.
警方企圖掩飾真相。

▶ The course covers a wide variety of topics.
本課程涵蓋各式各樣的主題。

▶ Rita covered for me while I went to the dentist.
我去看牙醫時，瑞塔幫我代班。

▶ I couldn't find the cover of the pot.
我找不到這個壺的蓋子。

▶ On the cover of the magazine is a movie star.
這本雜誌的封面是一位影星。

---

10 common [ˈkɑmən] *a.* 普通的；共同的 & *n.* 公用地

片 (1) common sense
　　　 道理，人之常情（不可數）
　 (2) have little / a lot / nothing in
　　　 common (with sb)
　　　 （與某人）有很少 / 許多 / 沒有共同點

似 ordinary [ˈɔrdn̩ˌɛrɪ] *a.* 普通的 ②

反 rare [rɛr] *a.* 罕見的 ②

▶ Earthquakes are common in this part of the world.
在地球的這一帶，地震可說是司空見慣。

▶ We had a common goal, so we decided to work together.
我們有共同的目標，所以決定要一起合作。

▶ Even though we are twins, we have very little in common with each other.
雖然我們是雙胞胎，彼此的共同點卻很少。

---

11 finally [ˈfaɪnlɪ] *adv.* 最後，終於 (= at last)

衍 final [ˈfaɪnl̩]
　 a. 最後的 & *n.* 期末考；決賽 ②

▶ It's the weekend, and I can finally relax.
週末到了，我終於可以放鬆了。

---

12 above [əˈbʌv] *prep.* 在……上面 & *adv.* 在上面；在上文 & *a.* 前述的

似 over [ˈovɚ] *prep.* 在……上面 ①

▶ I saw some birds flying above the tower.
我看見幾隻鳥兒在塔的上方翱翔。

▶ I see a bird above.
我看見上面有隻鳥。

▶ As I mentioned above, there have been a lot of changes lately.
如上所述，近來有許多改變。

▶ If you agree to the above rules, please sign here.
如果你同意上述規定，請在這裡簽名。

below [bəˋlo / brˋlo]
prep. 在……下面；低於 & *adv.* 在下面

(似) (1) under [ˋʌndɚ]
　　prep. 在……下面 & *adv.* 在下面 ①
(2) beneath [brˋniθ]
　　prep. 在……下面 & *adv.* 在下面 ③

▶ From the plane, we could see the city below us.
我們可以從飛機上看到在我們下方的城市。

▶ When the temperature is below zero, water will freeze.
溫度降至零下時，水會結凍。

▶ He heard singing from the room below.
他聽到樓下房間傳來的歌聲。

13　piece [pis] *n.* 一塊 / 片 / 件 / 張；(藝術、文學) 作品 & *vt.* 拼湊

(片) (1) a piece of...
　　一塊 / 片 / 件 / 張……
　　a piece of paper / furniture / advice
　　一張紙 / 一件傢俱 / 一則建議
(2) piece sth together / piece together sth　把某物拼湊在一起

▶ Dad bought a piece of land near my school.
爸爸在我學校附近買了一塊地。

▶ This wonderful piano piece is popular with many people.
這首美妙的鋼琴曲受很多人歡迎。

▶ The detective pieced together the events of the night.
偵探將那一晚發生的事件拼湊起來。

14　fill [fɪl] *vt.* & *vi.* (使) 充滿，裝滿 & *n.* 足夠 (不可數)

(片) (1) be filled with...　充滿……
　　= be full of...
(2) fill out / in sth　填寫 (表格)
(3) have had one's fill of + N/V-ing
　　已經受夠……

(反) empty [ˋɛmptɪ] *vt.* 清空 ②

▶ My heart was filled with joy when I saw my old friend again.
再次見到老友時，我的內心充滿喜悅。

▶ Fill out the form, and then give it back to me.
填好表格後，交還給我。

▶ I've had my fill of listening to this song.
我已經受夠聽這首歌了。

15　heart [hɑrt] *n.* 心，心臟；內心

(片) (1) sb's heart beats
　　某人的心臟跳動
(2) a kind / cold / broken heart
　　善良 / 冷血 / 受傷的心
(3) follow one's heart　隨心所欲
(4) at heart　內心
(5) from the bottom of one's heart
　　打從某人心底，由衷地

▶ My heart was beating fast with excitement.
因為興奮，我的心跳得好快。

▶ You should follow your heart and ask her out.
你應該跟隨自己的內心，邀她出去。

▶ Jay is serious in appearance but kind at heart.
傑伊外表嚴肅，但內心很和善。

衍 heartbeat [`hɑrt,bit] *n.* 心跳

▶ I thanked the man from the bottom of my heart.
我由衷地感謝這名男子。

16　nature [`netʃə] *n.* 大自然 (不可數，字首可大寫)；(事物的) 本質，性質；(人的) 天性

片 (1) the nature of sth
　　某事物的本質 / 性質
　　(2) sb's nature　某人的本 / 天性

衍 (1) natural [`nætʃərəl]
　　a. 自然的；天然的 ②
　　(2) naturally [`nætʃərəlɪ]
　　adv. 自然地；天然地

▶ I love nature, which is why I enjoy country life.
我熱愛大自然，這正是我喜歡鄉村生活的原因。

▶ Elaine explained the nature of this material.
伊蓮解釋了這個材料的性質。

▶ It is just part of John's nature to be friendly with people.
待人親切正是約翰的天性之一。

17　report [rɪ`pɔrt] *n.* & *vt.* & *vi.* 報導；報告

片 (1) a report on / of sth
　　有關某事物的報導 / 報告
　　(2) It is reported that...
　　據報導，……
　　(3) report to sb (on sth)
　　向某人報告 (某事)

衍 reporter [rɪ`pɔrtə] *n.* 記者 ①

▶ Zoey did a report on butterflies.
柔伊做了一篇有關蝴蝶的報導。

▶ It is reported that the flood claimed 20 lives.
據報導，此次洪水奪走了 20 條人命。
＊claim [klem] *vt.* 奪去 (性命)

▶ Report to me after you've finished the work.
你工作做完後向我報告。

18　drive [draɪv] *vt.* & *vi.* 開車 & *vt.* 迫使 & *n.* 駕車路程；幹勁 (此意不可數)

三 drive, drove [drov], driven
　　[`drɪvən]

片 (1) drive sb to + 地方
　　開車載某人到某地
　　(2) drive sb crazy　使某人抓狂

衍 driveway [`draɪv,we]
　　n. (私人) 車道 ⑤

延伸 drunk driving　酒駕

▶ I drive my son to school every day.
我每天開車送我兒子上學。

▶ My wife is just learning how to drive.
我太太才剛開始學開車。

▶ That noise is driving me crazy.
那噪音讓我抓狂。

▶ It's a one-hour drive to that restaurant.
到那間餐廳要 1 小時的車程。

▶ Rebecca is full of drive—she'll go far in life.
蕾貝卡充滿幹勁 —— 她會成功的。
＊go far　成功

---

driver [`draɪvə] *n.* 駕駛人

片 a taxi / bus / truck driver
計程車 / 公車 / 卡車司機

▶ My father is a taxi driver.
我父親是計程車司機。

19　either [`ˈiðɚ / ˈaɪðɚ`] *adv.* 也 (不) (與 not 並用) & *pron.* 兩者之一 & *conj.* 或者 & *a.* 兩者之一的

片 (1) not... either　也不……
　　(2) either... or...　不是……就是……

用法 (1) either 作代名詞時，用法為：
　　　either + 單數動詞
　　　either of + 複數名詞 + 複數動詞
　　(2) either... or... 為對等連接詞，若連接主詞時，動詞按最接近的主詞做變化。

▶ Josh can't sing, and he can't dance either.
　喬許不會唱歌，也不會跳舞。

▶ Ruby thinks either of the wedding dresses look perfect.
　露比認為兩件婚紗看起來都很完美。

▶ I'll have either the steak or the salmon.
　我要麼點牛排，要麼點鮭魚。

▶ Passengers crowded on either side of the platform.
　兩側月臺上擠滿了乘客。

20　except [`ɪkˈsɛpt`] *prep.* 除……之外 & *conj.* 只不過，要不是

片 except for...　除……之外

衍 (1) exception [`ɪkˈsɛpʃən`] *n.* 例外 ④
　　(2) exceptional [`ɪkˈsɛpʃən!`]
　　　a. 例外的 ⑤

用法 except 須與 all-、any-、every-、no- 開頭的字並用。

▶ No one can do it except Peter.
= No one can do it except for Peter.
　除了彼得以外，沒有人能做這件事。

▶ Everyone except Lisa will stay home.
　除了麗莎外，大家都會待在家裡。

▶ I'd buy the laptop, except it's too expensive.
　要不是太貴，我會買那臺筆電。

21　fire [`faɪr`] *n.* 火；火堆，篝火 & *vt.* 開除 & *vt.* & *vi.* 發射

片 (1) a forest fire　森林火災
　　(2) catch fire　著火
　　(3) make a fire　生火
　　(4) fire a shot at sth　朝……開槍

衍 (1) fireworks [`ˈfaɪr͵wɝks`]
　　　n. 煙火 (恆用複數) ③
　　(2) fireplace [`ˈfaɪr͵ples`] *n.* 壁爐 ④

似 lay off sb　解僱某人

▶ A forest fire broke out last night.
　昨晚發生了一場森林火災。

▶ Paper catches fire easily.
　紙張很容易著火。

▶ Let's make a fire to keep us warm.
　我們生火來保暖吧！

▶ Andrew was fired from his job last week.
　上星期安德魯被開除了。

▶ The hunter fired a shot at a tiger.
　獵人朝著老虎開了一槍。

22　stay [`ste`] *vi.* & *n.* 停留 & *vi.* 保持

片 (1) stay + adj.　保持……
　　(2) stay up　熬夜
　　(3) stay away (from sb/sth)
　　　遠離 (某人 / 某事物)

▶ Where did you stay while you were in Paris?
　你在巴黎時住哪？

▶ Jayden visited a lot of places during his stay in Kyoto.
　傑登在京都停留的期間造訪了許多地方。

似 remain [rɪˋmen] vi. 仍然 ③

▶ To stay healthy, you should exercise regularly.
要保持健康，你就應規律運動。

▶ Last night, I stayed up until one.
我昨晚熬夜到 1 點。

▶ Stay away from Owen. He's a bad guy.
離歐文遠一點，他不是善類。

23　space [spes] *n.* 空間 (不可數)；空位，空地；太空 (不可數) & *vt.* 留間隔

片 (1) space for sth　　　放某物的空間
　　(2) a parking space　　停車位
　　(3) outer space　　　　外太空
　　(4) space sth + 距離 + apart
　　　　以若干距離間隔開某物

衍 spacious [ˋspeʃəs] *a.* 寬敞的 ⑤

▶ I need some space for that piano.
我需要一些空間來放那架鋼琴。

▶ I couldn't find a parking space.
我找不到停車位。

▶ Do you believe there is life in outer space?
你相不相信外太空中有生物？

▶ The gardener spaced these plants ten inches apart.
園丁以 10 英寸的距離間隔開這些植物。

24　watch [wɑtʃ] *n.* 手錶 & *vt.* & *vi.* 觀看 & *vt.* 看顧；小心，留意

複 watches [ˋwɑtʃɪz]
片 (1) one's watch says...
　　　某人的手錶顯示……
　　(2) watch TV / a movie
　　　看電視 / 電影
　　(3) watch the traffic　注意交通
　　(4) watch out　　　　留神，注意
似 (1) look after　看管……
　　(2) mind [maɪnd] *vt.* 留意 ①
反 neglect [nɪˋglɛkt] *vt.* 忽視 ④

▶ My watch says it's 12:30 p.m. now.
我的錶顯示現在是中午 12 點 30 分。

▶ Lily watched an interesting movie this afternoon.
莉莉今天下午看了一部有趣的電影。

▶ Could you please watch my bag for a minute?
你可以幫我看著包包一會兒嗎？

▶ Watch the traffic while you cross the street.
過馬路時要注意交通。

▶ Watch out! That car almost hit you.
小心！那輛車差點撞到你。

---

see [si] *vt.* & *vi.* 看，看見 & *vt.* 明白；探望；和……交往

三 see, saw [sɔ], seen [sin]
片 (1) see a doctor / client
　　　看醫生 / 拜訪客戶
　　(2) see sb　和某人交往

▶ I could see you from across the street.
我可以從對街看到你。

▶ It was so foggy that Greg could barely see.
天氣太霧了，所以葛瑞格看不太清楚。

▶ I could see what Debra meant.
我能明白黛珀拉的意思。

▶ Henry saw the doctor this morning.
亨利今早去看醫生。

▶ Katie has been seeing her boyfriend for two years.
凱蒂和她男朋友交往 2 年了。

read [rid] *vt. & vi.* 讀，閱讀；讀出

目 read, read [rɛd], read [rɛd]

用 (1) read the newspaper　看報紙
　　(2) read sb sth　唸某物給某人聽
　　= read sth to sb

衍 reader [ˋridɚ] *n.* 讀者

▶ Jill reads the newspaper every morning.
吉兒每天早上都會看報紙。

▶ Jasper doesn't have time to read.
賈斯柏沒有時間閱讀。

▶ Ben read the whole class his story.
= Ben read his story to the whole class.
班唸他的故事給全班聽。

---

25 prepare [prɪˋpɛr] *vt. & vi.* 準備

用 (1) prepare breakfast / lunch /
　　dinner　準備早 / 午 / 晚餐
　　(2) prepare for...　為……做準備

衍 preparation [ˌprɛpəˋreʃən]
　　n. 準備 ③

▶ Mother is preparing breakfast.
媽媽正在準備早餐。

▶ Every student is preparing for the test.
每個學生都在準備考試。

---

26 friend [frɛnd] *n.* 朋友

用 (1) sb's best / close friend
　　某人最好 / 親近的朋友
　　(2) make friends (with sb)
　　（與某人）交朋友

衍 friendship [ˋfrɛndʃɪp] *n.* 友誼 ②

▶ Michael is one of my closest friends.
麥可是我最親近的朋友之一。

▶ Kevin makes friends very easily.
凱文很容易交朋友。

friendly [ˋfrɛndlɪ] *a.* 友善的

反 hostile [ˋhɑstaɪl] *a.* 不友善的 ⑤

▶ John's friendly attitude is the reason why we all like him so much.
約翰友善的態度是我們大家都很喜歡他的原因。

---

27 tip [tɪp] *n.* 尖端；小費；祕訣 & *vt. & vi.* (給) 小費

目 tip, tipped [tɪpt], tipped

用 (1) give sb a tip of + 金錢 + for...
　　給某人若干金額的小費以酬謝……
　　= tip sb + 金錢 + for...
　　(2) give sb a tip on sth
　　告訴某人做某事的祕訣 / 訣竅
　　(3) tip sb off / tip off sb
　　向某人通風報信

似 point [pɔɪnt] *n.* 尖端 ①

▶ The tip of the pencil needs to be sharpened.
鉛筆頭該削尖了。

▶ I gave the taxi driver a tip of five dollars for his service.
= I tipped the taxi driver five dollars for his service.
我給計程車司機 5 美元小費以感謝他的服務。

▶ Thank you for giving me some tips on how to ski.
謝謝你告訴我一些滑雪的祕訣。

▶ The informant tipped off the police about the robbery.
線民向警方密報這樁搶案。
*informant [ɪnˋfɔrmənt] *n.* 線民

Unit 11

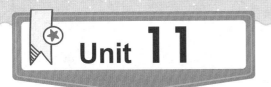
 1101-1102

1 hope [hop] *n. & vt. & vi.* 希望

片 (1) hope (that)... 希望……
(2) hope to V 希望做……
(3) hope for... 希望……

衍 (1) hopeful [ˋhopfəl] *a.* 充滿希望的 ③
(2) hopeless [ˋhopləs] *a.* 絕望的

▶ No matter what happens, never give up hope.
不管發生什麼事，千萬不要放棄希望。

▶ I hope (that) I will see you soon.
= I hope to see you soon.
我希望很快就可以見到你。

▶ The team is hoping for success in the final game.
這支隊伍期望在決賽中獲勝。

---

wish [wɪʃ]

n. 願望；祝福（用於信件文末）& *vt. & vi.*
希望；祝福；但願

複 wishes [ˋwɪʃɪz]

片 (1) make a wish 許願
(2) wish to V 希望做……
= hope to V
(3) wish sb sth
祝某人（快樂、幸運……）

用法 wish 作動詞表『但願』時，其後接
that 子句，形成假設語氣。與現在事
實相反時，that 子句使用過去式；與
過去事實相反時，that 子句使用過去
完成式。

▶ Make a wish on a falling star.
對流星許個願。

▶ With best wishes, Frank Foster.
把最誠摯的祝福獻給你，法蘭克·福斯特。（書信結尾用語）

▶ I wish to become a doctor one day.
= I hope to become a doctor one day.
我希望有朝一日能成為醫生。

▶ I wish you a Merry Christmas.
祝你聖誕快樂。

▶ I wish that my friend were here now.
= If only my friend were here now.
但願我的朋友此刻在這裡。

▶ I wish that John had been with us last night.
要是約翰昨晚與我們在一起就好了。

2 difficult [ˋdɪfəˌkʌlt] *a.* 困難的

片 be difficult (for sb) to V
（某人）很難做……

衍 difficulty [ˋdɪfəˌkʌltɪ] *n.* 困難 ②

似 (1) hard [hard] *a.* 困難的 ①
(2) tough [tʌf] *a.* 棘手的 ③

▶ It's very difficult for me to answer the question.
這個問題我很難回答。

▶ Tina finds it very difficult to get a job.
蒂娜發覺要找到一份工作很難。

---

simple [ˋsɪmpl̩] *a.* 簡單的；樸素的

衍 simply [ˋsɪmplɪ]
adv. 簡單地；樸素地；全然；僅僅 ②

似 (1) easy [ˋizɪ] *a.* 簡單的 ①
(2) plain [plen] *a.* 樸素的 ②

▶ It's a simple question; just answer "yes" or "no."
這是個簡單的問題，只要回答『是』或『不是』就好。

▶ Annie's wearing a simple dress.
安妮穿著一件樸素的洋裝。

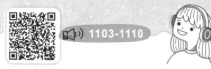

3　note [not] *n.* 筆記 (恆用複數)；便條 & *vt.* 注意

用 (1) take notes　抄筆記
　　(2) leave (sb) a note
　　　　（給某人）留便條
　　(3) take note of...　留意……
　　(4) note (that)...　注意到……

衍 (1) noted [`notɪd] *a.* 著名的
　　(2) notebook [`not͵bʊk] *n.* 筆記本 ②

▶ Tom never takes notes in class.
　湯姆上課時從來不抄筆記。
▶ Steve left a note on the refrigerator.
　史蒂夫在冰箱上留了一張便條。
▶ You should take note of Ned's behavior. He is a little bit weird today.
　你該注意奈德的言行。他今天有點怪。
▶ I noted that Sharon didn't feel well today.
　我注意到雪倫今天不太舒服。

4　earth [ɝθ] *n.* 地球 (字首可大寫)；土壤 (不可數)

用 (1) on earth　世界上
　　= in the world
　　(2) 疑問詞 + on earth... ?
　　　　到底……？
　　= 疑問詞 + in the world... ?

衍 (1) earthquake [`ɝθ͵kwek] *n.* 地震 ②
　　(2) earthworm [`ɝθ͵wɝm] *n.* 蚯蚓

似 soil [sɔɪl] *n.* 土壤 ②

▶ Everyone should do their part to protect the earth.
　每個人都應盡本分保護地球。
▶ We tried to cover the box with earth.
　我們設法用土將盒子埋起來。
▶ Who is the tallest man on earth?
　誰是世界上最高的人？
▶ What on earth is Gary doing?
　蓋瑞到底在做什麼？

5　floor [flɔr] *n.* 地板 (= ground)；樓層 & *vt.* 鋪地板

用 be floored with...
　地板以……鋪設而成

比 表『在第幾樓』用 floor 一字，表『幾層樓高』則用 story 一字。
　That's a five-floor building. (✕)
→ That's a five-story building. (○)
　那是一棟 5 層樓高的建築。

▶ Be careful! The floor is wet.
　小心！地板是濕的。
▶ I live on the fifth floor.
　我住在 5 樓。
▶ The room is floored with blue and white tiles.
　這房間的地板是以藍、白色的磁磚鋪設而成。

6　market [`markɪt] *n.* 市場 & *vt.* 行銷

用 (1) a night / flea market
　　　夜市 / 跳蚤市場
　　(2) be on the market　上市

衍 supermarket [`supɚ͵markɪt]
　n. 超市 ①

▶ This market is open every morning until noon.
　這個市場每天從早上營業到中午。
▶ This new product will soon be on the market.
　這個新產品很快就會上市。
▶ They wanted to market the product for people aged twenty to thirty.
　他們想要將這項產品銷售給 20 到 30 歲的人。

7　river [ˈrɪvɚ] *n.* 河

似 stream [strim] *n.* 小河，溪流 ②	▶ We went fishing in the nearby river. 我們在附近的那條河中釣魚。

8　lot [lɑt] *n.* 許多；一批 (貨)；一塊地

片 (1) a lot of...
　　很多的…… (之後可接複數可數名詞
　　或不可數名詞)
　＝ lots of...
　(2) a parking lot　停車場

▶ I have a lot of things to do.
　我有許多事情要做。
▶ Don't worry. I still have a lot of money left.
　別擔心。我還剩很多錢。
▶ This lot of books sells very well.
　這批書賣得很好。
▶ They asked the government to build more parking lots for local people.
　他們要求政府為當地居民多建一些停車場。

9　station [ˈsteʃən] *n.* 車站；局，所，隊；電 (視) 臺 & *vt.* 使駐紮，部署

片 (1) a bus / train / MRT station
　　公車 / 火車 / 捷運站
　(2) a gas station　加油站
　(3) a police / fire station
　　警察局 / 消防站
　(4) a TV / radio station
　　電視臺 / 廣播電臺

▶ That train stops at every station.
　那班火車每一站都停。
▶ The fire engines are kept at the fire station.
　這些消防車全停放在消防站。
▶ Security guards were stationed at every entrance.
　每個入口處都部署了警衛。

10　agree [əˈgri] *vi.* & *vt.* 贊成；同意

片 (1) agree to + N　贊成 (提案)
　(2) agree to V　同意做……
　(3) agree with sb (on sth)
　　(就某事) 同意某人
　(4) agree that...　同意……
衍 agreeable [əˈgriəbl] *a.* 令人愉悅的 ④
反 disagree [ˌdɪsəˈgri] *vi.* 意見不合 ②

▶ My parents didn't agree to our plan.
　我父母親不贊成我們的計畫。
▶ Tom finally agreed to go to the movies with us.
　湯姆最後總算同意和我們一起去看電影。
▶ I don't agree with you on this matter.
　有關這件事，我不同意你的看法。
▶ I agree that Hank should be given a second chance.
　我同意應該再給漢克一次機會。

agreement [əˈgrimənt]
n. 同意；協定
片 come to / reach an agreement
　達成協議

▶ After a long discussion, we finally came to an agreement on this issue.
　經過漫長的討論後，我們終於在這個議題上達成協議。

11 chance [tʃæns] *n.* 機會；可能性；偶然 & *vt.* 冒險 & *vi.* 碰巧

片 (1) have a chance to V
有機會做……

(2) have a good chance of...
有很高的可能性……

(3) by chance　　　偶然間

(4) take a chance　　冒險，碰運氣

(5) chance + N/V-ing　冒險做……

(6) chance to V　　　碰巧……
= happen to V

似 (1) opportunity [ˌɑpɚˈt(j)unətɪ]
n. 機會 ③

(2) likelihood [ˈlaɪklɪˌhʊd]
n. 可能性 ⑤

▶ I hope I have a chance to see Mary again.
我希望有機會再見瑪麗一面。

▶ You have a good chance of winning the contest.
你贏得比賽的可能性很大。

▶ I found the secret by chance.
我偶然間發現這個祕密。

▶ Do not take chances with your health.
健康不能碰運氣。

▶ Neil decided to chance going out without his cellphone.
尼爾決定冒險不帶手機出門。

▶ I chanced to be there when Jerome came.
= I happened to be there when Jerome came.
傑洛姆來的時候，我碰巧在那裡。

12 trouble [ˈtrʌbḷ] *n.* 麻煩；問題 & *vt.* 使煩惱；打擾

片 (1) ask for trouble　　自找麻煩

(2) get into trouble　　陷入麻煩

(3) be in trouble　　　有麻煩

(4) have trouble + V-ing
做……有困難
= have difficulty + V-ing
= have problems + V-ing
= have a hard time + V-ing

(5) trouble oneself with sth
某人為某事而煩惱

衍 troublesome [ˈtrʌbḷsəm]
a. 棘手的 ④

▶ You're just asking for trouble if you drink and drive.
如果你酒駕就是在自找麻煩。

▶ If you don't stop talking in class, you'll get into trouble.
你上課繼續講話的話，就有麻煩了。

▶ I'm having trouble starting my car.
我的車子很難發動。

▶ Don't trouble yourself with trifles.
不要為小事情煩惱。
＊trifle [ˈtraɪfḷ] *n.* 瑣事

▶ I'm sorry to trouble you, but could you tell me how to get to the park?
對不起打擾你，能不能告訴我公園怎麼去？

13 throw [θro] *vt.* & *vi.* & *n.* 扔，擲 & *vt.* 舉辦 (= hold)

三 throw, threw [θru], thrown
[θron]

片 (1) throw sth at sb
朝某人丟某物 (有傷害意味)

(2) throw sth to sb
扔某物給某人 (使某人接住)
= throw sb sth

▶ Sam threw a stone at me.
山姆朝我扔石頭。

▶ The bride threw the bouquet to her bridesmaids.
新娘把花束丟給她的伴娘們。
＊bridesmaid [ˈbraɪdzˌmed] *n.* 伴娘

▶ You need to throw away those stinky sneakers.
你應把那雙臭球鞋丟掉。

(3) throw sth away / throw away sth
將某物扔掉

(4) throw a party   舉行派對

▶ The baseball player was congratulated on his great throw.
這名棒球選手因出色的投球而受到祝賀。
*congratulate [kənˋgrætʃə͵let] vt. 道賀

▶ We threw a party for our son's birthday.
我們開派對為兒子慶生。

---

14 fight [faɪt] vi. & n. 爭吵；打架；奮戰 & n. 戰役

⊟ fight, fought [fɔt], fought

闬 (1) fight over...   為……吵架
    = have a fight over...
    (2) fight for...   為……奮戰
    (3) fight against...   抵抗……

衍 fighter [ˋfaɪtɚ] n. 鬥士；戰鬥機 ③

▶ My parents fought over money last night.
= My parents had a fight over money last night.
昨晚我爸媽為錢吵架。

▶ The teacher stopped the kids from fighting.
老師阻止孩子們打架。

▶ We should fight for freedom.
我們應為自由而戰。

▶ We have to work together to fight against crime.
我們必須團結一起對抗犯罪。

▶ I hope they can win the fight.
我希望他們能贏得這場戰役。

---

15 rest [rɛst] n. 休息；其餘 & vi. 休息；長眠

闬 (1) take / have a rest   休息一下
    = take a break
    (2) the rest of...
    其餘的……（動詞單複數視其後所接
    名詞而定）
    (3) rest in peace   安息

衍 restless [ˋrɛstləs] a. 浮躁的

▶ Let's take a rest before continuing our hike.
我們休息一下再繼續健行吧。

▶ The man spent the rest of his life in jail.
這名男子在獄中度過餘生。

▶ The rest of the money is to be given to Hanks.
其餘的錢要給漢克斯。

▶ I always rest for an hour after lunch.
我總是在午餐過後休息 1 小時。

▶ May the dead rest in peace!
願該死者安息！

---

16 wear [wɛr] vt. 穿 / 戴著；留 (頭髮，鬍子)；磨損

⊟ wear, wore [wɔr], worn [wɔrn]

延伸 be worn out   累壞了
= be tired out
= be exhausted

▶ I was worn out after all the work.
所有工作做完後，我累壞了。

▶ Who's that man wearing a blue cap?
戴著藍色棒球帽的那個男人是誰？

▶ Santa Claus wears a white beard.
聖誕老公公留著白鬍子。

▶ Jerry wears his hair long.
傑瑞留長髮。

▸ You've worn a hole in your sock.
你的襪子磨破了一個洞。

17 list [lɪst] n. 清單，名單 & vt. 將……列出

(1) a shopping list　　購物清單
(2) make a list　　　　列出清單
(3) a waiting list　　　候補名單

▸ Make a list of all the things you want to buy.
把你要買的所有東西列成清單。

▸ They forgot to put my name on the waiting list.
他們忘記把我加進候補名單裡了。

▸ List the names of all of your classmates on this paper.
把你班上所有同學的名字列在這張紙上。

18 cent [sɛnt] n. (美元) 一分錢

似 penny [ˋpɛnɪ] n. 一分錢；便士〔英〕③

▸ In the US, a quarter is a coin worth 25 cents.
在美國，一個 quarter 就是值 25 分錢的硬幣。

dollar [ˋdɑlɚ]
n. (美國等的貨幣單位) 元

似 buck [bʌk] n. 美元 (口語)

▸ The trip to New York cost me more than seven hundred dollars.
紐約之行花了我超過 700 美元。

19 north [nɔrθ] n. 北方 & a. 北方的 & adv. 朝北

in the north of...　在……的北部
衍 northern [ˋnɔrðɚn] a. 北方的 ②

▸ Taipei is in the north of Taiwan.
臺北在臺灣的北部。

▸ Jenny was born in North Africa.
珍妮在北非出生。

▸ Drive north for about three blocks, and then you'll see the store on your right.
向北開約 3 個街區，然後你會看到店在你的右邊。

south [saʊθ]
n. 南方 & a. 南方的 & adv. 朝南

(1) to the south of...
　在…… (境外) 的南方
(2) in the south of...
　在…… (境內) 的南方

衍 southern [ˋsʌðɚn] a. 南方的 ②

▸ Mexico is to the south of the US.
墨西哥在美國的南方。

▸ The village is on the south side of the mountain.
這個村莊位於山的南面。

▸ Birds usually fly south in the winter.
鳥類冬天時通常往南飛。

east [ist]
n. 東方 & a. 東方的 & adv. 朝東

衍 eastern [ˋistɚn] a. 東方的 ②

▸ The sun rises in the east.
太陽從東邊升起。

▸ We fell in love with the scenic views of the east coast.
我們愛上了東海岸的美麗景緻。

用法 **rise in the east** 從東方升起
不可寫成：rise from the east (✗)

▶ Go east, and you'll see the gas station on the left.
朝東走，你就可以在左手邊看到加油站。

---

west [wɛst]
n. 西方 & *a.* 西方的 & *adv.* 朝西

衍 **western** [ˈwɛstən]
a. 西方的 & *n.* 西部片 ②

用法 west 作名詞指『西方國家』時，應使用大寫的 West，即 in the West。

▶ The sun sets in the west.
太陽在西方落下。

▶ Please enter the building through the west door.
請由西側的門進入這棟大樓。

▶ According to the map, we're heading west.
根據地圖，我們正朝西走。

20　join [dʒɔɪn] *vt.* 連接；加入 & *vi.* 會合 & *n.* 接合處

片 **join sb in + V-ing**
和某人一起從事……

衍 **joint** [dʒɔɪnt] *a.* 聯合的 & *n.* 關節 ②

▶ The mechanic joined the two wires together.
這位技工將 2 條電線接起來。

▶ I joined the drama club last year.
我去年加入了戲劇社。

▶ Would you like to join us in going dancing tonight?
你今晚要跟我們一起去跳舞嗎？

▶ Do you know where the two rivers join?
你知道這兩條河在哪裡交會嗎？

▶ The vase has been fixed, but you can still see the join.
這個花瓶修好了，但仍可以看到接縫處。

21　price [praɪs] *n.* 價錢；代價 & *vt.* 標價（常用被動）

片 **pay a price for...** 為……付出代價
衍 (1) **priceless** [ˈpraɪsləs] *a.* 無價的 ⑥
　　(2) **unpriced** [ʌnˈpraɪst] *a.* 未標價的

▶ Nobody will buy it at that price.
沒有人會以那種價錢去買它。

▶ David paid a high price for his success.
大衛為他的成功付出了很高的代價。

▶ The tickets are priced at NT$250 each.
門票每張定價是新臺幣 250 元。

22　rule [rul] *n.* 規則 & *vt.* & *n.* 統治

片 (1) **break a rule** 違反規則
　　(2) **obey / follow a rule** 遵守規定
　　(3) **under... rule** 在……的統治下
　　(4) **make it a rule to V** 有……的習慣
　　(5) **As a rule, ...** 按慣例，……
衍 **ruling** [ˈrulɪŋ] *a.* 統治的
　　the ruling party 執政黨

▶ If you break the rules, you will be punished.
你如果違反規則就會被處罰。

▶ The king has ruled this kingdom for forty years.
國王統治這個國家 40 年了。

▶ Taiwan was under Japanese rule for fifty years.
臺灣被日本統治過 50 年。

▶ My father makes it a rule to get up early.
我爸爸有早起的習慣。

▶ As a rule, I get up at eight in the morning.
通常我都是早上 8 點起床。

....

ruler [ˈrulɚ] *n.* 尺；統治者
似 leader [ˈlidɚ] *n.* 領導者 ①

▶ Joe drew a straight line with a ruler.
喬用尺劃了條直線。

▶ The king is loved by his people as a kind and generous ruler.
身為一位仁慈又慷慨的統治者，這位國王受到人民愛戴。

23 ready [ˈrɛdɪ] *a.* 準備好的 & *vt.* 使準備好

目 ready, readied [ˈrɛdɪd], readied
月 (1) be ready to V
　　準備好……；隨時都會……
　(2) ready oneself to V
　　某人準備好做……
似 prepare [prɪˈpɛr] *vt.* & *vi.* 準備 ①

▶ Are you ready to go now?
你準備好要走了嗎？

▶ Mr. Smith is always ready to criticize others.
史密斯先生隨時都會批評別人。

▶ Joyce readied herself to perform on stage for the first time.
喬伊絲準備好第一次上臺表演。

24 fine [faɪn] *a.* 優良的，漂亮的；晴朗的；細微的 & *n.* & *vt.* 罰款 & *adv.* 令人滿意地

月 (1) a fine line between A and B
　　A 與 B 之間僅有一線之隔
　(2) get a + 金額 + for...
　　因……被罰若干金額
＝ be fined + 金額 + for...

▶ The store around the corner sells fine jewelry.
街角那家店販售高級珠寶。

▶ I don't want to work on such a fine day.
我不想在天氣這麼好的日子裡工作。

▶ There is a fine line between love and hate.
愛與恨只有一線之隔。

▶ Bill got a NT$6,000 fine for speeding.
＝ Bill was fined NT$6,000 for speeding.
比爾因超速被罰款新臺幣 6,000 元。

▶ Cassandra did fine on the exam.
卡珊卓考試考得很好。

25 kill [kɪl] *vt.* & *vi.* 殺死 & *n.* (動物) 捕殺

月 (1) kill time by + V-ing
　　藉……打發時間
　(2) move in for the kill
　　移動以捕食獵物
衍 killer [ˈkɪlɚ] *n.* 殺手

▶ Many people were killed in this accident.
這次意外有很多人喪生。

▶ We killed time by watching TV.
我們藉看電視來打發時間。

▶ The snake was moving in for the kill.
那隻蛇逼近以捕食獵物。

26 top [tɑp] *n.* 頂端；重要的地位 & *a.* 頂端的 & *vt.* 超越

目 top, topped [tɑpt], topped

片 (1) at the top of...

　　在……頂端；位居……的要職

　　(2) on top of...　除了……之外

　　= in addition to...

▶ We walked slowly to the top of the hill.
我們緩緩走向小山頂。

▶ Brian is at the top of his class.
布萊恩在班上名列前茅。

▶ On top of English, Johnny also speaks German.
除了英文外，強尼還會說德文。

▶ Tom lives on the top floor.
湯姆住在頂樓。

▶ William plans on topping John's home run record.
威廉計劃超越約翰的全壘打紀錄。

bottom [ˋbɑtəm]

n. 底部 & *a.* 最低的 & *vi.* 到達最低點

片 (1) the bottom of...

　　……的底部

　　(2) the bottom lip　下唇

　　(3) bottom out　到達最低點

▶ There's something on the bottom of my right shoe.
我右腳鞋底上有東西。

▶ When Beth is nervous, she bites her bottom lip.
貝絲緊張時，會咬她的下唇。

▶ House prices have bottomed out recently.
房價近期已經見底了。

27 size [saɪz] *n.* 尺寸 & *vt.* 按特定尺寸製作

片 (1) the size of...　……的尺寸

　　(2) A is the size of B

　　　A 的尺寸和 B 一樣

　　(3) come in... sizes　有……種尺寸

　　(4) size sth (up)　按尺寸製作某物

延伸 (1) king-size [ˋkɪŋ͵saɪz] *a.* 特大號的

　　(2) queen-size [ˋkwin͵saɪz] *a.* 大號的

▶ The little baby was the size of his father's hand.
這個小嬰兒的大小和他爸爸的手一樣大。

▶ This T-shirt comes in three sizes: small, medium, and large.
這件 T 恤有 3 種尺寸：小、中、大。

▶ Mrs. Jackson sized the dress up for the customer.
傑克森女士按這位顧客的尺寸製作洋裝。

28 spring [sprɪŋ] *n.* 春天；泉水；彈簧 & *vi.* 躍起；湧現

目 spring, sprang [spræŋ], sprung [sprʌŋ]

片 (1) a hot spring　溫泉

　　(2) spring to one's feet

　　　某人突然站起

　　(3) spring to mind　在腦海中湧現

似 (1) fountain [ˋfaʊntn̩] *n.* 噴泉 ③

　　(2) leap [lip] *vi.* 跳 ③

▶ Cherry trees blossom in early spring.
櫻花於初春時盛開。

▶ There used to be lots of hot springs in this area.
從前這地區有很多溫泉。

▶ The spring is rusty. We should replace it with a new one.
這個彈簧生鏽了，我們應換一個新的。
*rusty [ˋrʌstɪ] *a.* 生鏽的

▶ Tim sprang to his feet upon seeing the headline.
提姆一看到那則新聞標題便突然站了起來。

▶ The picture of a rainy day sprang to mind after I heard that song.

聽了那首歌後，一個雨天的畫面在我腦海裡湧現。

29 pot [pɑt] *n.* 鍋；壺；罐 & *vt.* 栽種 (植物) 於盆中

目 pot, potted [`pɑtɪd], potted

片 a pot of... 一鍋／壺／罐……

衍 pottery [`pɑtərɪ]
   n. 陶器 (集合名詞，不可數) ③

▶ What's in the pot on the stove?
爐上的鍋子裡有什麼東西？

▶ Catherine made a pot of tea for her guests.
凱瑟琳替她的客人沏了一壺茶。

▶ Henry sat in his garden, potting some plants.
亨利坐在花園內，把一些植物種入盆中。

Unit 12

1201-1204

1 plant [plænt] *n.* 植物；工廠 & *vt.* 種植

片 a power plant　發電廠

衍 plantation [ˌplænˈteʃən]
n. (熱帶地區種植橡膠、咖啡、甘蔗等)
大農場 ⑥

似 factory [ˈfæktərɪ] *n.* 工廠 ①

▶ This plant only grows in the tropics.
這種植物只生長在熱帶地區。
＊the tropics　熱帶 (地區)

▶ Nobody likes to live near a power plant.
沒人喜歡住在發電廠附近。

▶ I saw farmers planting seeds in the fields.
我看到農人在田裡播種。

2 dark [dɑrk] *a.* 昏暗的；(顏色) 深的 & *n.* 黑暗 (此意前面加定冠詞 the)

片 (1) in the dark　在黑暗中
(2) keep sb in the dark
　　把某人蒙在鼓裡

衍 (1) darkness [ˈdɑrknəs]
　　n. 黑暗；夜色
(2) darken [ˈdɑrkən] *vi.* & *vt.* 變暗

▶ By the time Sam got home, it was dark outside.
山姆回到家時，外面天色已暗。

▶ Larry wore a dark suit to attend the ceremony.
賴瑞穿著一襲深色西裝去參加典禮。

▶ We couldn't see each other in the dark.
在黑暗中我們看不見彼此。

▶ John kept everyone in the dark about the problem.
約翰隱瞞這個問題，讓所有人都蒙在鼓裡。

3 answer [ˈænsɚ] *vt.* & *n.* 回答 & *vt.* 回應 (電話、門鈴等) & *n.* 答案

片 (1) answer the door / phone
　　應門 / 接電話
(2) the answer to sth　某事物的答案

似 (1) reply [rɪˈplaɪ] *n.* & *vt.* & *vi.* 答覆 ②
(2) respond [rɪˈspɑnd] *vi.* 回答 ②
(3) response [rɪˈspɑns] *n.* 回答 ③

反 ask [æsk] *vt.* 詢問 ①

▶ The teacher asked Johnny to answer the question on the blackboard.
老師叫強尼回答黑板上的問題。

▶ I won't take no for an answer.
我不接受拒絕這個回答 / 你非答應不可。

▶ I rang the doorbell, but no one answered the door.
我按了門鈴，但是沒有人應門。

▶ I have the answer to this question.
我知道這個問題的答案。

4 foreign [ˈfɔrɪn] *a.* 外國的；陌生的

片 be foreign to...　對⋯⋯很陌生

反 (1) domestic [dəˈmɛstɪk] *a.* 國內的 ②
(2) native [ˈnetɪv] *a.* 本土的 ③

▶ We have a foreign visitor today.
我們今天會有一位外賓來訪。

▶ The idea of democracy is foreign to the country's citizens.
這個國家的人民對民主的想法很陌生。
＊democracy [dɪˈmɑkrəsɪ] *n.* 民主

foreigner [ˋfɔrɪnɚ] *n.* 外國人

▶ We have many foreigners in our town.
我們鎮上有很多外國人。

---

5 save [sev] *vt.* 拯救 & *vt.* & *vi.* 節省；儲存

□ (1) save sb from...
救某人使免於……
(2) save time 節省時間
(3) save money for a rainy day
存錢以備不時之需
衍 saving [ˋsevɪŋ]
n. 節省（費用）；存款（恆用複數）③

▶ The boy was saved from drowning.
這男孩被人救起才免於溺水。

▶ We travel by plane to save time.
我們搭飛機旅行來省時。

▶ You should save money for a rainy day.
你應存錢以備不時之需。

---

heat [hit]
n. 熱（不可數）；溫度 & *vt.* 使變熱

□ (1) a low / medium / high heat
小 / 中 / 大火
(2) heat up sth 加熱某物
衍 (1) heater [ˋhitɚ] *n.* 暖氣機③
(2) heated [ˋhitɪd] *a.* 激烈的

▶ If you can't stand the heat, get out of the kitchen.
你若受不了熱，就離開廚房吧。

▶ You should cook the fish over a medium heat.
你應該以中火煮這條魚。

▶ We heat our house during the cold season.
我們在寒冷的季節裡開暖氣溫暖整間房子。

▶ We heated up some soup for lunch.
我們把一些湯加熱當午餐。

---

6 animal [ˋænəml̩] *n.* 動物

▶ Animals are not allowed in this restaurant.
這間餐廳不准帶動物進入。

---

zoo [zu] *n.* 動物園

▶ At the zoo, you can see many different kinds of animals.
在動物園裡你可以看到許多種不同的動物。

---

7 monkey [ˋmʌŋkɪ] *n.* 猴子

▶ There are many monkeys in India.
印度有很多猴子。

---

8 train [tren] *n.* 火車 & *vt.* 訓練

□ (1) by train 搭火車
(2) get on / off the train
上 / 下火車
衍 trained [trend] *a.* 經過訓練的

▶ We prefer traveling by train.
我們比較喜歡搭火車旅行。

▶ These dogs are trained to help the blind.
這些狗兒是訓練來幫助盲人的。

training [ˈtrenɪŋ] *n.* 訓練 (不可數)

▶ Training for the job will take about two months.
那項工作的訓練期將耗時約 2 個月。

---

9 pull [pʊl] *vt. & vi. & n.* 拉，拖

🔑 pull the door open　把門拉開

▶ Pull the door, and it should open easily.
拉開門，應該很容易就打開了。

▶ I felt a pull on my T-shirt, so I turned around to see what it was.
我感到 T 恤被拉扯，所以就轉過去看看是什麼東西。

---

push [pʊʃ]
vt. & vi. 推；按；*vt.* 強迫 & *n.* 推

🔑 (1) push the door open　把門推開
(2) push sb to V　強迫某人做……
(3) give it a push　推一下

▶ The robber pushed the door open.
搶匪把門推開。

▶ Push the red button to close the door.
按紅色的按鈕關門。

▶ Don't push your child to do something he doesn't want to do.
別逼你的孩子做他不想做的事。

▶ If the door is stuck, just give it a push.
如果門卡住了，就推一下。

---

10 married [ˈmærɪd] *a.* 已婚的

衍 (1) marry [ˈmærɪ]
vi. & vt. 結婚，嫁，娶 ②
(2) marriage [ˈmærɪdʒ] *n.* 婚姻 ②

▶ Everybody knows that Frank is married.
每個人都知道法蘭克結婚了。

---

11 farm [fɑrm] *n.* 農場 & *vi. & vt.* 耕種；養殖

🔑 on the farm　在農場上

▶ Angela was brought up on the farm.
安琪拉是在農場長大的。

▶ My uncle farms for a living.
我叔叔種田維生。

▶ Aaron has farmed fish for nearly thirty years.
艾倫養殖魚類已近 30 年。

---

farmer [ˈfɑrmɚ] *n.* 農夫

▶ The farmers worked the land until the sun went down.
農夫們在田裡幹活，直到日落。

---

12 wide [waɪd] *a.* 寬的；廣泛的 & *adv.* 張大地；十分地

🔑 (1) a wide variety of...
各式各樣的……

▶ The room was only five feet wide.
= The room was only five feet in width.
這個房間只有 5 英尺寬。

(2) (be) wide open　張得大大的
(3) be wide awake　十分清醒
衍 (1) widely [ˋwaɪdlɪ] *adv.* 廣泛地
(2) width [wɪdθ] *n.* 寬度 ②
(3) widen [ˋwaɪdn̩]
　　　vt. & *vi.* (使) 變寬 ③
似 broad [brɔd] *a.* 寬闊的 ②
反 narrow [ˋnæro] *a.* 狹窄的 ②

▸ Tim likes to read a wide variety of books in his free time.
提姆有空時喜歡廣泛閱讀各類書籍。

▸ The actor stood with his mouth wide open.
那名演員站著，嘴巴張得大大的。

▸ Sophie couldn't fall asleep and was wide awake all night.
蘇菲睡不著，整晚十分清醒。

13 sale [sel] *n.* 銷售 (量)；拍賣

片 (1) 店家 + have a sale　舉行拍賣
(2) 物品 + be on sale
　　　販售某物；某物特價
(3) 物品 + be for sale　販售某物
衍 salesperson [ˋselz͵pɝsn̩] 銷售員 ②
反 purchase [ˋpɝtʃəs] *n.* 購買 ⑤

▸ Sales of computers were up last year.
去年電腦的銷售量上升。

▸ This department store is having a sale on clothes.
這間百貨公司正舉行衣服大拍賣。

▸ Ken will buy the laptop when it is on sale.
肯等到筆電特價時就會買。

▸ I'm sorry—this apartment is not for sale.
我很抱歉，但這間公寓沒要出售。

14 easy [ˋizɪ] *a.* 容易的；安逸的；從容的 & *adv.* 從容地

片 take it easy　放輕鬆
衍 (1) ease [iz] *n.* 舒適 ②
(2) easily [ˋizɪlɪ] *adv.* 容易地
反 (1) difficult [ˋdɪfə͵kʌlt] *a.* 困難的 ①
(2) hard [hard] *a.* 困難的 ①
(3) uneasy [ʌnˋizɪ] *a.* 不安的

▸ The copier is very easy to operate.
這部影印機操作很容易。

▸ Terry is leading an easy life.
泰瑞過著安逸的生活。

▸ Take it easy. It's not that serious.
放輕鬆。沒那麼嚴重。

15 hair [hɛr] *n.* (人的) 頭髮；(人或動物的) 毛髮

片 have one's hair cut　理髮
衍 (1) haircut [ˋhɛr͵kʌt] *n.* 理髮 ②
(2) hairdresser [ˋhɛr͵drɛsɚ]
　　　n. 美髮師 ③

▸ You need to have your hair cut; it's too long.
你需要理髮了；它太長了。

▸ Why are there dog hairs all over the sofa?
為什麼沙發上都是狗毛？

16 finish [ˋfɪnɪʃ] *vt.* & *vi.* 完成 & *vi.* & *n.* 結束

片 (1) finish + N/V-ing　完成……
(2) come to a finish　結束
　= come to an end

▸ I have finished my homework.
= I have finished doing my homework.
= I'm finished with my homework.
我做完功課了。(第三句的 finished 是形容詞)

110

衍 finished [ˈfɪnɪʃt] *a.* 完成的
似 end [ɛnd] *vt. & vi. & n.* 結束 ①

▶ I think the meeting will soon finish.
我想這場會議很快就會結束。

▶ The race has come to a finish.
比賽已經結束了。

17　deal [dil] *vt. & vi. & n.* 交易，買賣

三 deal, dealt [dɛlt], dealt
片 (1) deal in...　從事……的買賣
(2) deal with...
　與……交易；處理……
(3) a great deal of + 不可數名詞
　大量的……
(4) It's a deal.　成交／一言為定。
衍 dealer [ˈdilɚ] *n.* 業者 ③

▶ David's father deals in used cars.
大衛的父親從事中古車買賣。

▶ This week, I have a lot of work to deal with.
這個星期我有很多工作要處理。

▶ We shook hands after the deal was done.
交易完成後我們握了握手。

▶ William lost a great deal of money buying lottery tickets.
威廉買彩券損失了很多錢。

18　poor [pʊr] *a.* 貧窮的；可憐的；差勁的

衍 (1) poorly [ˈpʊrlɪ]
　adv. 差勁地，糟糕地
(2) poverty [ˈpɑvɚtɪ] *n.* 貧窮 ③

▶ Hank was born into a poor family.
漢克出身貧窮的家庭。

▶ The poor old man has no one to rely upon.
這名可憐的老先生沒人可依靠。

▶ Tony's English is so poor that I can hardly understand him.
東尼的英文真爛，我幾乎聽不懂他的話。

19　practice [ˈpræktɪs] *n. & vi. & vt.* 練習 & *vt. & n.* (慣例) 實行

片 (1) practice + V-ing　練習……
(2) put sth into practice　實行某事
衍 (1) practical [ˈpræktɪkl̩] *a.* 實際的 ③
(2) practitioner [prækˈtɪʃənɚ]
　n. 執業醫生／律師 ⑤

▶ Practice makes perfect.
練習造就完美／熟能生巧。—— 諺語

▶ Our team practices every day.
我們的球隊每天都練習。

▶ Melinda practices playing the piano three hours a day.
梅琳達每天練習彈鋼琴 3 個小時。

▶ The Japanese practice the custom of removing their shoes upon entering a temple.
日本人奉行進寺廟必須脫鞋的習慣。

▶ I want to put my idea into practice as soon as possible.
我想要將我的理念儘早付諸實行。

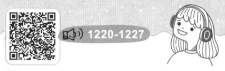
20 **trip** [trɪp] *n.* 旅行 & *vt.* & *vi.* (使) 絆倒

- trip, tripped [trɪpt], tripped
- (1) take a trip to + 地方　到某地旅行
  (2) trip over sth　被某物絆倒
- (1) tour [tur] *n.* 旅行②
  (2) travel ['trævl] *n.* 旅行②
  (3) journey ['dʒɝnɪ] *n.* 旅行③
  (4) stumble ['stʌmbl] *vi.* 絆倒⑤

▶ My family and I took a trip to Japan a few years ago.
我和家人幾年前到日本走了一趟。

▶ The boy was tripped by a stone and fell down.
小男孩被石頭絆倒，跌到地上。

▶ Kevin tripped over a cable and hurt his toe yesterday.
凱文昨天被電線絆倒，撞傷了他的腳趾。

21 **date** [det] *n.* 日期；約會；約會對象 & *vt.* & *vi.* 約會 & *vt.* 寫上日期 & *vi.* 始於 (某時期)

- (1) be out of / up to date
  過時的 / 最新的
  (2) go out on a date (with sb)
  （與某人）約會
  (3) date sb　與某人約會
  (4) date from + 特定時間點
  自……起，追溯自……

▶ What's the date of the next show?
下一場表演的日期是幾號？

▶ Your hairstyle is out of date.
你的髮型過時了。

▶ I went out on a date with Rebecca last night.
我昨晚與蕾貝卡約會。

▶ The handsome guy over there is my sister's date.
那邊那位英俊的男人是我妹妹的約會對象。

▶ Jack's dating an American model.
傑克現在正與一位美籍模特兒約會。

▶ The letter is dated March 28th.
這封信上寫的日期是 3 月 28 日。

▶ The museum dates from the 19th century.
這座博物館的歷史可追溯自 19 世紀。

22 **police** [pə'lis] *n.* 警方 (集合名詞，視為複數) & *vt.* 維持……的治安

- call the police　報警
- (1) policeman [pə'lismən] *n.* 警察②
  (2) cop [kɑp] *n.* 警察，條子 (口語)②

▶ Did you call the police when the accident happened?
意外發生時，你有報警嗎？

▶ The officers policed the streets where the march was taking place.
警方在舉行示威遊行的街道上維持秩序。
*march [mɑrtʃ] *n.* 示威遊行

23 **home** [hom] *n.* 家；故鄉 & *adv.* 在家；到家 & *a.* 家裡的；家用的 & *vi.* 回家

- (1) the home of sth　某物的故鄉；
  某事的發源地
  (2) be / feel at home　感到自在
  (3) go home　回家

▶ Sophie's home is located in Hsinchu city.
蘇菲的家位在新竹市。

▶ Spain is the home of the Spanish eagle.
西班牙是西班牙帝鵰的故鄉。

(4) **on one's way home**
某人回家的路上

(5) **a home address** 住家地址

衍 (1) **homesick** [ˈhomˌsɪk] *a.* 思鄉的 ③

(2) **hometown** [ˈhomtaun]
n. 故鄉 ③

▶ Thank you for making me feel right at home.
謝謝你讓我感覺就像在家一樣自在。

▶ Nick can't wait to leave work and go home.
尼克等不及要下班回家了。

▶ Ernie stopped for a drink on his way home.
爾尼回家路上去小酌一杯。

▶ Please send this to my home address.
請把這個東西寄到我家地址。

▶ Hannah misses her mom's home cooking.
漢娜想念她媽媽的自家料理。

---

24 talk [tɔk] *vi.* 講話 & *n.* 談話；演講

片 (1) **talk about sth** 談論某事
(2) **talk to sb** 和某人談話
(3) **talk sb into + N/V-ing**
說服某人做……
(4) **give a talk on...**
發表關於……的演講

似 **speech** [spitʃ] *n.* 演講 ②

▶ We spent the evening talking about politics.
我們花了一個晚上談論政治。

▶ I talked to a very interesting man at the party.
我在派對上和一個很有趣的男子交談。

▶ Albert talked me into going skydiving.
艾爾伯特說服我去跳傘。

▶ The two friends made up after a long talk.
兩位朋友經過長談後和好了。

▶ Mr. Johnson will give a talk on environmental protection.
強森先生將會發表關於環保的演說。

---

25 same [sem] *a.* 相同的 & *pron.* 同樣的人 / 事 / 物 & *adv.* 同樣地

似 **alike** [əˈlaɪk] *adv.* 相同地 ②

用法 same 作形容詞、代詞或副詞時，其前均須置 the；same 作形容詞時，在口語中有時會省略 the。

▶ Ariana eats in the same restaurant every day.
亞莉安娜每天都去同一間餐廳吃飯。

▶ Chris had a Coke, and I had the same.
克里斯點了一瓶可樂，我也點了一樣的。

▶ Those two birds look the same to me.
我覺得那 2 隻鳥看起來長得一樣。

---

26 cookie [ˈkuki] *n.* (甜) 餅乾〔美〕

似 **biscuit** [ˈbɪskɪt] *n.* 餅乾〔英〕②

▶ Freya dunked a cookie in the glass of milk.
芙蕾亞把餅乾泡進一杯牛奶裡。
＊dunk [dʌŋk] *vt.* 泡，浸

---

27 truck [trʌk] *n.* 卡車

▶ Jamie's dad drives a truck.
傑米的爸爸開卡車。

28 hospital [ˈhɑspɪtl̩] *n.* 醫院

(1) in the hospital　　在醫院
(2) go to the hospital　去醫院

延伸 clinic [ˈklɪnɪk] *n.* 診所 ③

▶ Amy works as a nurse in the hospital.
　艾咪在醫院當護士。

▶ I have to go to the hospital for my results.
　我得去醫院看我的報告結果。

29 plan [plæn] *n.* 計畫 & *vt.* & *vi.* 計劃

(1) have a plan for...　有……的計畫
(2) plan to V　　　　　計劃做……
(3) plan on + V-ing　　計劃……

▶ The manager has a plan for dealing with the problem.
　經理有處理這個問題的計畫。

▶ Jessica and Sam are planning their wedding.
　潔西卡和山姆正在籌劃他們的婚禮。

▶ Do you plan to go to university?
　你有打算去上大學嗎？

▶ I plan on traveling the world.
　我計劃要環遊世界。

idea [aɪˈdiə]
n. 想法，點子；了解，明白

(1) the idea of...　……的想法
(2) the idea behind sth
　　某事物背後的想法
(3) give sb an idea of...
　　讓某人知道……
(4) have no idea　不知道

▶ It was Barbara's idea to book this hotel.
　訂這間飯店是芭芭拉的想法。

▶ Lenny hates the idea of being a boss.
　藍尼不想當老闆。

▶ Rita couldn't understand the idea behind the experiment.
　瑞塔不明白這個實驗背後的想法。

▶ Could you give me an idea of what to write about?
　你可以告訴我要寫什麼好嗎？

▶ I have no idea where I can park my car.
　我不知道能把車子停在哪裡。

30 radio [ˈredɪ͵o] *n.* 收音機；廣播節目；無線電 & *vi.* & *vt.* 用無線電傳送

(1) turn on / up the radio
　　打開收音機
(2) turn off / down the radio
　　關掉收音機
(3) the news on the radio
　　廣播新聞
(4) radio for...　用無線電……

▶ Please turn down the radio—I can't concentrate.
　請把收音機關掉 —— 我無法專心。
　*concentrate [ˈkɑnsɛn͵tret] *vi.* 專心

▶ Hugh listens to the news on the radio every day.
　休每天都收聽廣播新聞。

▶ The message was sent over the radio.
　訊息透過無線電傳送。

▶ The police officers radioed for assistance.
　警察透過無線電求助。

31 pool [pul] *n.* 游泳池；撞球 (不可數) & *vt.* 集結 (資金、資源等)

H (1) a swimming pool　游泳池
(2) play pool　打撞球

▶ Tina swam ten lengths of the hotel pool.
蒂娜在飯店的游泳池游了 10 趟。
＊length [lɛŋθ] *n.* 泳池的長度

▶ James likes playing pool in his free time.
詹姆士閒暇時喜歡打撞球。

▶ The roommates pooled their money and bought a new TV.
室友們一起集資買新電視。

1301-1307

---

1 **heavy** [ˈhɛvɪ] *a.* (重量) 重的；大量的

- (1) a heavy heart   心情沉重
- (2) heavy traffic   交通擁擠
- (3) heavy rain / snow   大雨／雪
- 衍 heavily [ˈhɛvəlɪ] *adv.* 大量地
- 反 light [laɪt] *a.* 輕的 ①

▶ Help me lift this heavy box.
幫我擡這個重箱子。

▶ Frank left with a heavy heart.
法蘭克帶著沉重的心情離開了。

▶ The traffic was really heavy this morning.
今天早上交通流量真的很大。

---

2 **ride** [raɪd] *n.* 乘坐；遊樂設施 & *vt.* & *vi.* 騎；乘坐

- 三 ride, rode [rod], ridden [ˈrɪdn̩]
- (1) go for a ride   開車兜風
- (2) give sb a ride to + 地方
    載某人到某地
- 衍 rider [ˈraɪdɚ] *n.* 騎馬者；騎車者

▶ Let's go for a ride in my new car!
我們坐我的新車去兜風吧！

▶ Could you give me a ride to the supermarket?
你可不可以載我一程到超市？

▶ I love the rides and the food at amusement parks.
我喜歡遊樂園的設施還有食物。

▶ Clara doesn't allow her 18-year-old son to ride a scooter.
克萊拉不讓她 18 歲的兒子騎摩托車。

▶ They rode the train from Taipei to Kaohsiung.
他們從臺北搭火車到高雄。

---

3 **page** [pedʒ] *n.* 頁，面；網頁

- 片 a web / home page   網／首頁

▶ Open your books to page 40, please.
請把你們的書翻到第 40 頁。

▶ The words on the web page were too small to read.
網頁上的字太小了，很難閱讀。

---

4 **help** [hɛlp] *vt.* & *vi.* & *n.* 幫助 & *n.* 有助益的人／事／物

- (1) help sb (to) V   幫助某人做……
   = assist sb in + V-ing
- (2) cannot help + V-ing   忍不住……
   = cannot help but V
- (3) be a great help (to sb)
    （對某人）非常有幫助
   = be of great help (to sb)
- 衍 helper [ˈhɛlpɚ] *n.* 幫手
- 似 assist [əˈsɪst] *vt.* & *vi.* 幫助 ③

▶ I helped Mom do the dishes after dinner.
晚餐後我幫老媽洗碗筷。

▶ David looked so funny that I couldn't help laughing.
= David looked so funny that I couldn't help but laugh.
大衛看起來好滑稽，我不禁笑了出來。

▶ Your advice was a great help.
= Your advice was of great help.
你的建議非常有幫助。

helpful [`ˋhɛlpfəl `]
a. 有助益的，有用的；樂於助人的

(似) (1) useful [`ˋjusfḷ`] *a.* 有用的 ①
　 (2) handy [`ˋhændɪ`] *a.* 有用的 ③

(反) helpless [`ˋhɛlpləs`] *a.* 無用的；無助的

▶ You may find this book helpful.
你會發現這本書很有用。

▶ Emily's a pleasant and helpful girl.
艾蜜莉是個人見人愛且樂於助人的女孩。

5　shape [`ʃep`] *n.* 形狀；(健康) 狀態 (不可數) & *vt.* 塑造 (形狀、型態等)

(片) (1) in the shape of...
　　　呈現……的形狀
　 (2) be in good / bad shape
　　　身體很好 / 差
　 (3) be in shape　　　身體健康
　 (4) be out of shape　身體不好
　 (5) shape A into B　把 A 製成 B 形狀

(似) (1) form [`fɔrm`] *n.* 形狀 ②
　 (2) condition [`kənˋdɪʃən`]
　　　n. (健康) 狀態 ②

▶ I bought a cake in the shape of a star.
我買了一個星形的蛋糕。

▶ Though he is eighty, my grandfather is still in good shape.
我爺爺已 80 歲，但他身體仍然很硬朗。

▶ Kane shaped the clay into the form of a dog.
坎恩把泥土捏成狗的模樣。

▶ Going to college will really help me shape my future.
上大學對我塑造未來很有幫助。

6　store [`stɔr`] *n.* 商店 (= shop)；儲存 (量) & *vt.* 儲存

(片) (1) a department / grocery store
　　　百貨公司 / 雜貨店
　 (2) a store of sth　某物的儲存量

(衍) storage [`ˋstɔrɪdʒ`] *n.* 貯藏 ⑤

▶ I went to the store to buy some milk.
我到商店去買些牛奶。

▶ We've got a large store of food in the cellar.
我們有很多食物儲存在地窖中。
＊cellar [`ˋsɛlɚ`] *n.* 地窖

▶ This flash disk stores a lot of information.
這個隨身碟儲存了許多資料。

---

shop [`ʃɑp`] *n.* 商店 (= store) & *vi.* 購買

(三) shop, shopped [`ʃɑpt`], shopped

(片) (1) shop at + 地點　在某地購物
　 (2) shop for...　買……

(衍) shopper [`ˋʃɑpɚ`] *n.* 購物者

▶ The flower shop is around the corner.
那家花店就在轉角處。

▶ Mike often shops at the store near his home.
麥克經常在他家附近的商店購物。

▶ Suzie likes to shop for clothes with her friends.
蘇琪喜歡和朋友一起買衣服。

7　hit [`hɪt`] *vt.* 打，擊；碰撞；侵襲，使遭受 & *n.* 打，擊；成功的人 / 事 / 物

(三) 三態同形

(片) (1) hit sb on the + 部位
　　　打中某人某部位

▶ The ball hit me on the head.
＝ The ball hit my head.
這球打中我的頭。

(2) a big / smash hit
極為成功的人 / 事 / 物

(3) a hit song / movie
熱門歌曲 / 電影

▶ Be careful! You almost hit that man.
小心！你幾乎要撞到那個人。

▶ A typhoon hit the small island last night.
昨晚颱風侵襲這座小島。

▶ The man was killed by a hit to the head.
這名男子因腦部的一擊而喪命。

▶ Ricky's song was a big hit in Japan.
瑞奇的歌在日本紅極一時。

---

8 total [ˋtotl] *n.* 總數 & *a.* 全部的；完全的 & *vt.* 合計為，加總為

片 (1) a total of + 數字　總共……
= 數字 + in total

(2) total (up) sth　加總某物

似 (1) entire [ɪnˋtaɪr] *a.* 全部的 ②

(2) complete [kəmˋplit]
a. 全部的；完全的 ②

反 partial [ˋpɑrʃəl] *a.* 部分的 ④

▶ A total of seven players left the team.
= Seven players left the team in total.
總共有 7 名選手離開球隊。

▶ The total number was over two thousand.
總數超過 2 千。

▶ The old man was a total stranger to me.
我完全不認識這位老先生。

▶ The company's losses totaled $105 million last year.
這家公司去年總計虧損了 1 億 5 百萬元。

▶ I totaled up the scores with a calculator.
我用計算機加總分數。

---

totally [ˋtotḷɪ] *adv.* 完全，徹底

似 completely [kəmˋplitḷɪ] *adv.* 完全

▶ Jenny has totally changed her appearance.
珍妮完全改變了她的外表。

---

9 slow [slo] *a.* (動作、鐘錶) 慢的 & *adv.* 慢地 (= slowly) & *vi.* & *vt.* (使) 變慢

片 (1) 時間 + slow　慢了若干時間

(2) slow (...) down / up
(使……) 放慢速度

衍 slowly [ˋsloɪ] *adv.* 慢慢地

反 (1) speed up　加速

(2) accelerate [əkˋsɛlə‚ret]
vt. & *vi.* (使) 加速 ⑤

▶ Patty reads at a slow speed because she is young.
因為佩蒂還小，所以閱讀速度很慢。

▶ My watch is ten minutes slow.
我的錶慢了 10 分鐘。

▶ Drive slower so that we can enjoy the view.
請開慢一點，這樣我們才能欣賞風景。

▶ Slow down, or you'll get a ticket.
放慢速度，否則你會被開罰單。

▶ The driver slowed the bus down near the station.
快到車站時，駕駛放慢了公車的速度。

---

fast [fæst] *a.* 快速的 & *adv.* 快速地

似 rapid [ˋræpɪd] *a.* 快的，迅速的 ②

▶ Bruce prefers not to drive fast cars.
布魯斯傾向不開快車。

▸ Wow, that was a fast journey!
哇，那真是一趟快速的旅程！

▸ Vernon completed the task as fast as he could.
維儂儘快完成了這份工作。

quick [kwɪk] *a.* 快速的；反應快的 & *adv.* 快速地（= quickly）

衍 quickly [ˋkwɪklɪ] *adv.* 快速地

▸ The train is very quick and convenient.
火車既快速又方便。

▸ The boy is quick and understands things very easily.
這男孩反應伶俐，事情很容易就懂了。

▸ Jason runs as quick as a horse.
傑森跑得跟馬一樣快。

---

10 hill [hɪl] *n.* 小山，山丘

衍 hilltop [ˋhɪlˌtɑp] *n.* 山頂

▸ The hills are filled with butterflies of all shapes and colors.
山丘裡盡是各式各樣色彩繽紛的蝴蝶。

---

mountain [ˋmaʊntn̩] *n.* (高) 山
片 mountain climbing　登山

▸ Mountain climbing is one of my favorite pastimes.
登山是我最喜愛的消遣之一。
＊pastime [ˋpæsˌtaɪm] *n.* 消遣

---

11 news [n(j)uz] *n.* 新聞；消息 (皆不可數)

片 (1) a piece of news
　　 一件新聞 / 消息
(2) the news　(電視) 新聞節目
(3) the good / bad / latest news
　　 好 / 壞 / 最新消息

▸ Ted likes to watch the news at 6 p.m.
泰德喜歡看晚間 6 點的新聞。

▸ Peter burst out crying when he heard the bad news.
彼得聽到這個壞消息時號啕大哭。

---

newspaper [ˋn(j)uzˌpepɚ] *n.* 報紙；報社 (= paper)

▸ The *Daily Mail* is a popular newspaper in the UK.
《每日郵報》是英國的熱門報紙。

▸ Paul has got a job at the newspaper.
保羅有一份在報社的工作。

---

12 care [kɛr] *vi.* 關心，在意；想要 & *n.* 照顧，照料；小心 (皆不可數)

片 (1) care about...　關心……
(2) care for sth/sb
　　 想要某物 / 照顧某人
(3) take care of...　照顧……
(4) leave A in the care of B
　　 將 A 託給 B 照料
(5) with care　小心
= carefully

▸ I really care about you.
我真的關心你。

▸ Would you care for some pudding?
你想要來點布丁嗎？

▸ I'm looking for a babysitter to care for my son.
= I'm looking for a babysitter to take care of my son.
我正在找一位保姆來照顧我兒子。

▶ We left the baby in the care of my mother when we went on vacation.
我們去度假時，將小寶寶託給我媽媽照料。

▶ Please clean that vase with care.
請小心清理那個花瓶。

careful [ˈkɛrfəl] *a.* 小心的
🅗 (1) be careful with sth　小心某物
　　(2) be careful about...　對⋯⋯小心
🅦 carefully [ˈkɛrfəlɪ] *adv.* 小心地

▶ Be careful with that vase. It may break.
小心那花瓶。它容易破。

▶ Be careful about what you say and do.
說話行事要謹慎／謹言慎行。—— 諺語

careless [ˈkɛrləs] *a.* 粗心的

▶ The careless man caused the car accident.
那名粗心的男子造成這起車禍。

13　race [res] *n.* 競賽；種族 & *vt.* & *vi.* 與⋯⋯競賽 & *vi.* 快速移動

🅗 race against time　跟時間賽跑
🅦 (1) racial [ˈreʃəl] *a.* 種族的 ③
　　(2) racism [ˈresɪzəm] *n.* 種族主義 ⑤

▶ Jeff's son came in last place in the running race.
傑夫的兒子在賽跑中得最後一名。

▶ The college welcomes students of all races.
這所大學歡迎各種族的學生。

▶ We are racing against time to finish our work.
我們正在跟時間賽跑，要趕快完成工作。

▶ Michael raced home after he got his mother's call.
邁可在接到母親的電話後，火速趕回家。

14　health [hɛlθ] *n.* 健康（不可數）

🅗 be in good / poor health
健康很好／差

▶ Chris is in good health because he exercises regularly.
克里斯規律運動，所以很健康。

healthy [ˈhɛlθɪ] *a.* 健康的
🅗 stay healthy　保持健康
🅦 healthful [ˈhɛlθfəl] *a.* 有益健康的 ⑥

▶ Tofu is a healthy food.
豆腐是健康食品。

▶ Rona stays healthy by eating fruit and vegetables.
羅娜吃蔬果保持健康。

15　past [pæst] *a.* 以往的；（時間）剛過去的 & *n.* 過去 & *prep.* 經過；超過 & *adv.* 經過

🅗 in the past
在過去（與過去式或過去進行式並用）
延伸 (1) at present　現在，目前（與現在式或現在進行式並用）

▶ I'm quite busy at present.
我目前很忙。

▶ Based on her past performance, we think she can handle the work.
根據她以往的表現，我們認為她可以勝任這份工作。

▶ It has been raining for the past few weeks.
= It has been raining for the last few weeks.
最近這幾週都在下雨。

(2) in the future　在未來（與未來式或未來進行式並用）

▶ What will you be doing in the future?
你未來要做什麼？

▶ Jake was a policeman in the past.
杰克過去是個警察。

▶ Judy walked past several shops without stopping.
茱蒂走過幾間商店都沒停下來。

▶ It's ten past five.
現在是 5 點 10 分。

▶ The celebrity drove past slowly and waved to all of her fans.
這位名人將車緩緩駛過，向她所有的粉絲揮手致意。

16 king [kɪŋ] *n.* 國王

田 the king of...　……之王

衍 kingdom [ˋkɪŋdəm] *n.* 王國 ③

▶ The king made the poor girl his queen.
國王娶這位窮姑娘為后。

▶ Just as the lion is the king of beasts, so the eagle is the king of birds.
正如獅子是百獸之王，老鷹也是百鳥之王。

queen [kwin] *n.* 王后；女王

▶ Queen Elizabeth I never married in her lifetime.
伊莉莎白女王一世一生都沒有結婚。

17 feed [fid] *vt.* 餵食 & *vi.* 以……為食 & *n.* 飼料 (不可數)

目 feed, fed [fɛd], fed

田 feed on...　（動物）以……為食

比 live on...　（人）以……為食

▶ Don't forget to feed the baby.
別忘了要餵小寶寶。

▶ Cattle feed on grass.
牛以草為食。

▶ We need to get some feed for the horse.
我們得去買一些飼料給馬吃。

18 belong [bɪˋlɔŋ] *vi.* 屬於

田 belong to...
屬於……；是……的成員

衍 belongings [bəˋlɔŋɪŋz]
n. 所有物 (恆用複數) ⑤

▶ All the things you see here belong to me.
你在這兒所看到的東西都屬於我。

19 block [blɑk] *n.* (木、石) 塊；街區 & *vt.* 阻擋，封鎖；堵塞

田 (1) a block of...　一塊……
(2) block sth up / block up sth
使某物堵住

▶ Steve is so strong that he can carry a block of rock.
史提夫非常強壯，可以搬運一塊石塊。

衍 blockage [ˈblɑkɪdʒ] *n.* 障礙物；堵塞
- ► The store is only two blocks from here.
  那家店離這裡只有 2 個街區。
- ► The police blocked the entrance to the building.
  警方封鎖了大樓的入口。
- ► Nick's nose is blocked up because of the cold.
  尼克感冒所以鼻子塞住了。

20 park [pɑrk] *n.* 公園 & *vt.* & *vi.* 停車

H (1) a national park　國家公園
(2) a theme park　主題樂園
(3) an amusement park　遊樂園

- ► The park near my house is full of trees.
  我家附近的公園長滿了樹。
- ► You can't park your car next to a red line.
  你不可以把車停在紅線旁。
- ► It's illegal to park here.
  把車停在這裡是違法的。

parking [ˈpɑrkɪŋ] *n.* 停車 (不可數)
H a parking lot / space　停車場 / 位

- ► It's hard to find a parking space in downtown Chicago.
  在芝加哥市區很難找到停車位。

21 deep [dip] *a.* 深的 & *adv.* 深地

衍 (1) deeply [ˈdiplɪ] *adv.* 深深地
(2) depth [dɛpθ] *n.* 深度 ②
(3) deepen [ˈdipən]
　vt. & *vi.* (使) 變深 ③
反 shallow [ˈʃælo] *a.* 淺的 ③

- ► The swimming pool is 25 meters long and 4 meters deep.
  游泳池長 25 公尺，深 4 公尺。
- ► The swimmer went deep into the ocean.
  泳者潛入大海深處。

22 please [pliz] *vt.* & *vi.* (使) 開心，取悅 & *vi.* 喜歡

H do as / whatever one pleases
　隨某人想怎麼做
衍 (1) pleasure [ˈplɛʒɚ] *n.* 樂趣 ①
(2) pleasant [ˈplɛznt] *a.* 愉悅的 ②

- ► You can't please everyone.
  你無法討好每個人。
- ► You can do whatever you please with your money.
  隨你高興怎麼花錢就怎麼花。

pleased [plizd]
a. 感到高興的；感到滿意的
H (1) be pleased (that)...　很高興……
(2) be pleased with...　對……很滿意

- ► I'm very pleased (that) you've given up smoking.
  我非常高興你戒菸了。
- ► The family was very pleased with the new house.
  這家人對新房子感到非常滿意。

pleasing [ˈplizɪŋ] *a.* 令人愉快的
似 (1) lovely [ˈlʌvlɪ] *a.* 令人愉快的 ①
(2) agreeable [əˈgriəbl̩]
　a. 令人愉快的 ④

- ► It was a pleasing spring day.
  那天是一個令人愉快的春天。

23　season [ˋsizn̩] *n.* 季節 & *vt.* 調味

片 (1) be in season　正值盛產季，當令
(2) be out of season
過了產季，不當令

▶ Of the four seasons, I love spring best.
4 個季節中，我最喜歡春天。

▶ Watermelons are in season now, while strawberries are out of season.
現在西瓜正當令，而草莓則過了產季。

▶ Mother seasoned the soup with a bit of salt.
媽媽在湯裡加了點鹽巴調味。

24　horse [hɔrs] *n.* 馬

片 ride a horse　騎馬
延伸 pony [ˋponɪ] *n.* 小馬

▶ I'd like to learn how to ride a horse.
我想學騎馬。

25　wave [wev] *n.* 波浪；揮手示意 / 道別 & *vt.* & *vi.* 揮 (手)，揮動

片 (1) give sb a wave
跟某人揮手示意 / 道別
= wave at / to sb
(2) make waves　興風作浪
衍 wavy [ˋwevɪ] *a.* 波浪的

▶ I like to see waves breaking on the rocks.
我喜歡看海浪打在岩石上。

▶ The girl gave her parents a wave when she saw them.
= The girl waved at her parents when she saw them.
這女孩看到父母時，向他們揮手。

▶ I hate people who like to make waves.
我討厭興風作浪的人。

▶ The fishermen waved their hats at us as we passed by in our boat.
當我們乘船經過時，漁民向我們揮帽致意。

▶ The wind made Joy's kite wave in the sky.
這陣風讓喬伊的風箏在空中晃動。

1 look [lʊk] *vi.* 看；看起來；找 & *n.* 看；表情

片 (1) look at... 盯著……看
(2) look + adj. 看起來……
(3) look for... 尋找……
(4) look forward to + N/V-ing
期待……
(5) look down upon / on sb
輕視某人
(6) look up to sb 尊敬某人
(7) have / take a look at...
瞧一瞧……
(8) give sb a(n) + adj. + look
以……的神情看著某人

似 watch [wɑtʃ] *vt.* & *vi.* 觀看 ①

▶ Mark enjoys looking at the stars in the sky.
馬克喜歡看著天上的星星。
▶ You look nervous. What's the matter?
你看起來很緊張，怎麼一回事？
▶ Steve looked for his phone for more than an hour.
史蒂夫找他的電話花了 1 個多小時。
▶ Shelly is looking forward to her birthday party.
雪莉很期待她的生日派對。
▶ Never look down upon other people.
永不輕視他人。
▶ Can I have a look at that?
我可以瞧一瞧那個東西嗎？
▶ Angela gave me an angry look.
安琪拉以生氣的神情看著我。

2 touch [tʌtʃ] *vt.* & *vi.* & *n.* 觸摸 & *vt.* 使感動 & *n.* 聯絡 (不可數)

複 touches [ˈtʌtʃɪz]
片 (1) keep in touch with sb
與某人保持聯絡
= keep in contact with sb
(2) get in touch with sb 與某人聯絡
衍 (1) touched [tʌtʃt] *a.* 受感動的
(2) touching [ˈtʌtʃɪŋ] *a.* 令人感動的
似 move [muv] *vt.* 使感動 ①

▶ Don't touch anything before the police come.
警方來之前，不要動任何東西。
▶ Kevin felt a light touch on his hand.
凱文覺得有人輕碰他的手。
▶ Mother Teresa's story has touched the hearts of people around the world.
德蕾莎修女的故事感動了全世界的人。
▶ Though John rarely sees Peter, they keep in touch with each other by email.
雖然約翰很少見到彼得，但他們仍藉電子郵件保持聯絡。
▶ Please get in touch with me as soon as possible.
請儘快跟我聯絡。

3 miss [mɪs] *vt.* 錯過；想念 & *n.* 未擊中

複 misses [ˈmɪsɪz]
衍 missing [ˈmɪsɪŋ] *a.* 找不到的 ③

▶ Dean missed the train by five minutes.
狄恩以 5 分鐘之差錯過火車。
▶ Annie missed her parents badly when she was abroad.
安妮在國外時很想念爸媽。
▶ Bobby's first shot was a miss, but he went on to score two baskets.
巴比第一次投籃沒進，但他接著投進 2 球得分。

4 ball [bɔl] *n.* 球；舞會 & *vt.* 把……做成球形 (= ball up)

片 a tennis / soccer ball　網 / 足球

延伸 (1) basketball [ˈbæskɪt͵bɔl]
　　　　n. 籃球 ①
　　 (2) volleyball [ˈvɑlɪ͵bɔl] *n.* 排球 ③

▶ Bruce passed the ball to Jacob.
　布魯斯把球傳給雅各。

▶ We had a great time at the ball.
　我們在舞會上玩得很開心。

▶ Jake balled up his clothes and threw them in the laundry basket.
　傑克把他的衣服揉成一團，扔進洗衣籃裡。

5 mouth [maʊθ] *n.* 嘴巴 & *vt.* 用嘴型示意

片 have / be a big mouth
　是大嘴巴 (不能守密)

衍 mouthful [ˈmaʊθfəl]
　n. 滿口 / 一口 (的分量)

▶ Danny has a big mouth, so don't tell him any secrets.
　丹尼是個大嘴巴，因此不要把任何祕密告訴他。

▶ Darren mouthed the answer to the question to his classmate.
　達倫用嘴型把那一題的答案告訴他同學。

---

lip [lɪp] *n.* 嘴唇 (因有兩片，故常用複數)

片 sb's lips are sealed　某人口風很緊

衍 lipstick [ˈlɪp͵stɪk] *n.* 口紅 ④

▶ When Tommy bit his lip, it hurt a lot.
　湯米咬嘴唇時感到很痛。

▶ Maria told Bob that her lips were sealed.
　瑪麗亞告訴鮑伯她的口風很緊。

6 inside [ɪnˈsaɪd / ˈɪnsaɪd] *n.* 內部 & *adv.* 在內部 & *prep.* 在……內部 & *a.* 內部的

片 inside out　裡面翻到外面地

衍 insider [ɪnˈsaɪdɚ] *n.* 局內人

▶ The door is locked from the inside.
　這扇門從裡面被反鎖了。

▶ Don't stay inside too long. Get out and exercise for a while.
　別在裡面待太久。出去運動一下。

▶ Sam didn't notice that he was wearing his T-shirt inside out.
　山姆沒發現他把 T 恤裡外穿反了。

▶ Eddie was locked alone inside the haunted house.
　艾迪一個人被關在鬼屋裡。

▶ Monica put her credit card in the inside pocket of her bag.
　莫妮卡把信用卡放到她包包裡面的內袋。

---

outside [aʊtˈsaɪd / ˈaʊtsaɪd]
n. 外面 & *adv.* 在外面 & *prep.* 在……外面
& *a.* 外面的

▶ The outside of the fruit is red and shiny.
　這水果的外皮又紅又亮。

▶ The boys were playing baseball outside.
　男孩們正在外面打棒球。

衍 outsider [aʊtˈsaɪdə] *n.* 局外人 ⑤

▶ The fans stood outside the theater, waiting for the star to arrive.
粉絲們站在電影院外，等待明星來臨。

▶ Remember to turn off the outside lights before going to bed.
睡覺前記得要關掉外面的燈。

7　bridge [brɪdʒ] *n.* 橋 & *vt.* 縮小差異

片 (1) build / cross a bridge　造／過橋
(2) bridge the gap between A and
　　B　縮小 A 與 B 間的差異

▶ On his way home, Kyle has to cross a bridge.
凱爾回家的路上必須過橋。

▶ Our company will bridge the gap between dairy farmers and supermarkets.
我們公司將會彌合酪農業者與超市間的差異。

8　inch [ɪntʃ] *n.* 英寸

複 inches [ˈɪntʃɪz]
片 by inches　以些微之差

▶ One inch is equal to 2.54 centimeters.
一英寸相當於 2.54 公分。

▶ The big truck missed the cow by inches.
那輛大卡車差一點撞到一頭乳牛。

9　sight [saɪt] *n.* 視力 (= eyesight)；看見；名勝 (常用複數) & *vt.* 看見，發現

片 (1) at the sight of...　一看見……
(2) see the sights of + 地點
　　欣賞某地的名勝
衍 (1) sightseeing [ˈsaɪtˌsiɪŋ] *n.* 觀光 ④
(2) eyesight [ˈaɪˌsaɪt]
　　n. 視力 (不可數) ⑥

▶ My grandmother's sight is still very good.
我祖母的視力仍舊非常好。

▶ The children ran away at the sight of the black bear.
孩子們一看到黑熊拔腿就跑。

▶ We enjoyed seeing the sights of Kyoto.
我們欣賞了京都的名勝。

▶ The sailor sighted another ship in the distance.
這名水手看到遠方有另一艘船。

10　rock [rɑk] *n.* 岩石 & *vt.* & *vi.* (使) 搖晃

衍 rocky [ˈrɑkɪ] *a.* 多岩石的 ②

▶ During the earthquake, several large rocks fell onto the road.
地震時數塊巨石掉到路上。

▶ The mother rocked the baby to sleep.
這位媽媽搖著嬰兒，哄他入睡。

▶ The hammock rocked back and forth as the wind blew.
風吹時，吊床前後搖動。
＊hammock [ˈhæmək] *n.* 吊床

shake [ʃek] *vi.* 發抖 & *vi.* & *vt.* (尤指較大力的) 搖晃 & *n.* 搖動

▣ shake, shook [ʃʊk], shaken ['ʃekən]

☐ (1) shake with fear　害怕得發抖
(2) a shake of the / one's head
　　某人搖頭
(3) milk shake　奶昔

▸ The first time Zack stood on the podium as a teacher, he shook with fear.
查克第一次站在講臺上當老師時，害怕得直發抖。
＊podium ['podɪəm] *n.* 講臺

▸ Shake the juice before drinking it.
把果汁搖一搖再飲用。

▸ Owen said "no" with a shake of the head.
歐文搖了一下頭說『不』。

11　**fresh** [frɛʃ] *a.* 新鮮的；清新的

☐ (1) fresh fruit / vegetables
　　新鮮的水果 / 蔬菜
(2) fresh air　清新的空氣

衍 refresh [rɪ'frɛʃ] *vt.* 使提振精神 ⑥

▸ These cookies are fresh. I just baked them.
這些餅乾很新鮮，我才剛烤好。

▸ George enjoys the fresh air in the country.
喬治喜歡鄉下的清新空氣。

12　**paint** [pent] *vt.* & *vi.* 粉刷，上油漆；畫畫 & *n.* 顏料；油漆 (不可數)

衍 (1) painting ['pentɪŋ] *n.* 畫作 ②
(2) painter ['pentɚ] *n.* 畫家 ③

似 color ['kʌlɚ] *vt.* 上色，著色 ①

▸ Jessica would like to paint the room pink.
潔西卡想把房間漆成粉紅色。

▸ Children at this age love to paint.
這年紀的小孩喜歡畫畫。

▸ Jeff bought his daughter a box of paints.
傑夫買了一盒顏料給女兒。

▸ Ron used blue paint to paint the walls.
榮恩用藍色的油漆來粉刷牆壁。

13　**neck** [nɛk] *n.* 頸部，脖子

☐ (1) neck and neck
　　並駕齊驅，旗鼓相當
(2) a pain in the neck
　　討厭的人 / 事 / 物

衍 (1) necklace ['nɛkləs] *n.* 項鍊 ②
(2) necktie ['nɛk͵taɪ] *n.* 領帶 ③

▸ Gwen has a pearl necklace around her neck.
小關脖子上有一串珍珠項鍊。

▸ So far, the two main parties are still neck and neck.
到目前為止，這兩大黨還是不分上下。

▸ Stop being a pain in the neck!
別做個討厭鬼！

---

shoulder ['ʃoldɚ]
n. (單一邊的) 肩膀 & *vt.* 肩負，承擔

☐ (1) shrug one's shoulders
　　某人聳肩

▸ Frank just shrugged his shoulders and said nothing.
法蘭克只是聳聳肩，一句話也沒說。

▸ They walked shoulder to shoulder.
他們並肩而行。

(2) shoulder to shoulder　肩並肩地
(3) give sb the cold shoulder
　　冷淡待某人
(4) shoulder a burden /
　　responsibility of...
　　肩負起……的重擔 / 責任

▶ Audrey gave Marcus the cold shoulder when he asked her out.
馬可斯約奧黛莉出去時，她給他吃閉門羹。

▶ Bob is willing to shoulder the burden of raising the children.
鮑伯願意肩負起養育孩子的重擔。

---

14 bank [bæŋk] *n.* 銀行；(河) 岸，堤 & *vi.* 存錢於 (某固定銀行)

(1) a bank account / clerk
　　銀行帳戶 / 行員
(2) the bank of the river　河岸
衍 banker [ˈbæŋkɚ] *n.* 銀行家 ③

▶ Mark went to the bank to open an account.
馬克到銀行開戶。

▶ Kelly likes to take a walk along the bank of the river.
凱莉喜歡沿著河岸散步。

▶ Sarah usually banks at the one nearest her company.
莎拉通常把錢存在離她公司最近的那家銀行。

---

15 garden [ˈgɑrdn̩] *n.* 花 / 菜園 & *vi.* 從事園藝

衍 (1) gardener [ˈgɑrdənɚ] *n.* 園丁 ②
　　(2) gardening [ˈgɑrdnɪŋ] *n.* 園藝

▶ We grow vegetables in the garden.
我們在菜園種了蔬菜。

▶ Paul likes to garden in his spare time.
保羅在閒暇之餘喜歡從事園藝。

---

16 oil [ɔɪl] *n.* (食用) 油；石油 (不可數) & *vt.* 給 (機器等) 上油

(1) olive / vegetable oil
　　橄欖 / 植物油
(2) oil prices　(石) 油價
(3) burn the midnight oil　熬夜
似 petroleum [pəˈtrolɪəm]
　　n. 石油 (不可數) ⑥

▶ Vegetable oil is good for your health.
植物油對你的健康有益。

▶ Oil prices have been going up recently.
油價最近一直上漲。

▶ Ron burned the midnight oil studying last night.
榮恩昨晚熬夜讀書。

▶ The workman oiled the machine so that it would stop sticking.
那名工人給機器上油，這樣它就不會一直卡住。

---

17 fly [flaɪ] *vi.* 飛 & *vi.* & *vt.* (搭飛機) 飛行；駕駛 (飛機) & *n.* 蒼蠅

三 fly, flew [flu], flown [flon]
複 flies [flaɪz]
(1) fly a plane / kite
　　開飛機 / 放風箏
(2) fly to + 地點　(搭飛機) 飛到某地

▶ Johnny saw a plane flying across the sky.
強尼看到一架飛機飛過天空。

▶ Denise needs to fly to Boston for work.
狄妮絲需要搭飛機到波士頓工作。

▶ Can you fly the plane?
你會開飛機嗎？

衍 flight [flaɪt] *n.* 飛行；班機 ②

▶ Shut the door, or flies will fly in.
把門關上，否則蒼蠅會飛進來。

---

18 wind [wɪnd] *n.* 風 & [waɪnd] *vt.* 上發條 (= wind up)；纏繞 & *vi.* (道路、河流) 蜿蜒

三 wind, wound [waʊnd], wound

片 (1) a gust of wind　　一陣風
　　(2) wind (up) a clock　將時鐘上發條
　　(3) wind up (sth)　　結束 (某事)

衍 (1) windy [ˋwɪndɪ] *a.* 風大的 ②
　　(2) winding [ˋwaɪndɪŋ] *a.* 彎曲的
　　　　a winding road　蜿蜒的路

▶ The wind is blowing hard.
風颳得很厲害。

▶ Rick forgot to wind the clock, so the alarm didn't ring this morning.
瑞克忘了將鬧鐘上發條，所以今早鬧鐘沒有響。

▶ Wind the rope around your hand and hold on as tight as you can.
把繩子纏在手上，使盡全力握緊。

▶ The road winds up the mountain like a snake.
道路像蛇一般蜿蜒上山。

▶ Lauren might wind up her business this year.
蘿倫可能會在今年結束她的事業。

---

19 bright [braɪt] *a.* 明亮的；聰明的；鮮豔的；開朗的 & *adv.* 明亮地

片 look on the bright side of life /
　things　對人生 / 事物保持樂觀態度

衍 (1) brightly [ˋbraɪtlɪ] *adv.* 明亮地
　　(2) brighten [ˋbraɪtn̩]
　　　　vt. & *vi.* (使) 發亮
　　(3) brightness [ˋbraɪtnəs] *n.* 明亮

▶ The moon was very bright last night.
昨晚的月亮真明亮。

▶ Thank you for such a bright idea.
謝謝你提供我這麼一個聰明的點子。

▶ Mandy likes to wear bright colors.
曼蒂喜歡穿鮮豔的衣服。

▶ You should try to look on the bright side of things.
你該設法以樂觀的態度看待事物。

---

20 check [tʃɛk] *vt.* & *vi.* 檢查，核對；確認 & *n.* 帳單 (= bill)；支票；檢查

片 (1) check in / out　辦理住 / 退房手續
　　(2) give sth a (quick) check
　　　　(快速) 檢查一下某事物

衍 (1) checkup [ˋtʃɛkˌʌp] *n.* 身體檢查 ⑥
　　　　a physical checkup　體檢
　　(2) checkbook [ˋtʃɛkˌbʊk] *n.* 支票簿

似 (1) examine [ɪgˋzæmɪn]
　　　　vt. & *vi.* 檢查 ②
　　(2) examination [ɪgˌzæməˋneʃən]
　　　　n. 檢查 ②

▶ They are checking Zion's record.
他們正在核對席恩的紀錄。

▶ Tammy checked her wallet and found it was empty.
譚美確認了一下她的錢包，發現裡面是空的。

▶ You need to check in at the hotel first.
你得先在飯店辦理住房手續。

▶ The waitress gave me the check for dinner.
女服務生把晚餐的帳單交給我。

▶ This is a check for $65,000.
這是一張 6 萬 5 千美元的支票。

▶ Raymond gave the report a quick check for mistakes.
雷蒙德快速檢查這份報告是否有誤。

21 sharp [ʃɑrp] *a.* 銳利的；敏銳的；(疼痛) 劇烈的 & *adv.* (時間) 整

片 時間 + sharp　幾點整
= 時間 + exactly

衍 (1) sharply [ˋʃɑrplɪ]
　　adv. 突然地；嚴厲地
(2) sharpen [ˋʃɑrpn̩] *vt.* 削尖 ⑥

似 exactly [ɪgˋzæktlɪ] *adv.* 正好地

反 dull [dʌl] *a.* 鈍的；(疼痛) 隱約的 ②

▶ Be careful with that knife because it's very sharp.
小心那把刀，因為它很利。

▶ Jenny is very sharp and can answer all the questions right away.
珍妮很機靈，可以馬上回答所有問題。

▶ When the policeman was shot, he felt a sharp pain in his arm.
那名員警中彈時，手臂傳來一陣劇烈的痛。

▶ Meet me at the corner at three o'clock sharp.
= Meet me at the corner at three o'clock exactly.
3 點整在轉角處等我。

22 worry [ˋwɝɪ] *n.* 令人憂慮的事 (可數)；憂慮 (不可數) & *vi.* & *vt.* (使) 擔憂

複 worries [ˋwɝɪz]

三 worry, worried [ˋwɝɪd], worried

片 (1) worry about sb/sth
　　擔心某人 / 某事物
= be worried about sb/sth
(2) worry that...　擔心……
= be worried that...

衍 (1) worried [ˋwɝɪd]
　　a. 感到煩惱的，擔心的
(2) worrisome [ˋwɝɪsəm]
　　a. 令人擔憂的

▶ Money has been a big worry for Harry since he lost his job.
自哈利失業後，他就一直煩惱錢的問題。

▶ While on vacation, we were free from worry.
度假期間，我們完全沒有憂慮。

▶ The mother worried about her son's health.
= The mother was worried about her son's health.
這位母親很擔心她兒子的健康。

▶ Evan worries that they can't finish the work on time.
= Evan is worried that they can't finish the work on time.
艾凡擔心他們無法如期完成工作。

23 roll [rol] *vt.* & *vi.* (使) 滾動；捲 (起) & *n.* 一捲；名冊

片 (1) roll up one's sleeves
　　某人捲起袖子
(2) roll down　　　　滾下去
(3) a roll of sth　　　一捲某物
(4) call / take the roll　點名

▶ Paul rolled the ball to his little sister.
保羅把球滾到妹妹那邊。

▶ Ian rolled up his sleeves and started to work.
伊恩捲起袖子，開始工作。

▶ The ball rolled down into the pond.
球滾下去，掉進池塘裡。

▶ Mother bought a roll of tape in the store.
媽媽在店裡買了一捲膠帶。

▶ Gather all the men here. I want to call the roll.
將全體弟兄集合起來。我要點名。

24 camp [kæmp] n. 營地；營隊 & vi. 露營

片 (1) an enemy camp　　敵營
　　(2) a summer camp　　夏令營
　　(3) go camping　　　　去露營

衍 campfire [ˈkæmpˌfaɪr] n. 營火

▶ The enemy camp is only five miles away.
敵營只有 5 英里遠。

▶ Luke has decided to go to a summer camp where he can learn outdoor skills.
路克已決定參加夏令營，在那兒他可以學到戶外技能。

▶ We went camping in the mountains last week.
上星期我們去山中露營。

25 excited [ɪkˈsaɪtɪd] a. 感到興奮的

片 be excited over / about...
因……感到興奮

衍 (1) excite [ɪkˈsaɪt] vt. 使興奮 ②
　　(2) excitement [ɪkˈsaɪtmənt]
　　　 n. 興奮 ②

似 (1) delighted [dɪˈlaɪtɪd]
　　　 a. 感到高興的
　　(2) thrilled [θrɪld] a. 極愉快的

▶ The excited crowd cheered when the player hit a home run.
興奮的群眾在球員擊出全壘打時歡呼。

▶ Luna was excited over the good news that she had passed the exam.
露娜聽到自己考及格的好消息時很興奮。

exciting [ɪkˈsaɪtɪŋ]
a. 令人興奮的，刺激的

▶ Sandy believes vacationing in Peru will be a very exciting experience.
珊蒂覺得去祕魯度假會是個很刺激的經驗。
＊vacation [vəˈkeʃən] vi. 度假

26 late [let] a. 延遲的；晚的 & adv. 延遲地；晚地

片 (1) be late for work / school
　　　上班 / 上學遲到
　　(2) in one's late twenties / thirties
　　　快 30 / 40 歲

衍 (1) later [ˈletɚ]
　　　 a. 較晚的 & adv. 較晚地 ①
　　(2) lately [ˈletlɪ] adv. 最近 ③

反 early [ˈɝlɪ] a. 早的 & adv. 早 ①

▶ Nick apologized for being late for work again.
尼克為上班再度遲到一事道歉。

▶ David didn't retire until he was in his late seventies.
大衛一直快 80 歲才退休。

▶ The train arrived ten minutes late.
火車晚了 10 分鐘抵達。

▶ The sun started to shine late in the day.
今天晚點時陽光才開始閃耀。

27 always [ˈɔlwez] adv. 總是；永遠

片 as always　　如往常一樣

▶ Katie always takes the MRT home.
凱蒂總是搭捷運回家。

131

似 (1) at all times　總是
(2) forever [fə`ɛvə] *adv.* 永遠 ③

▶ John told Becky that he would love her always.
約翰告訴貝琪他會永遠愛她。

▶ You were a wonderful host, as always.
你如往常一樣是很棒的主辦人。

usually [`juʒʊəlɪ] *adv.* 通常
衍 usual [`juʒʊəl] *a.* 通常的 ②

▶ I usually exercise for half an hour before I go to work.
我通常上班前會先運動半小時。

often [`ɔfən] *adv.* 經常，時常
似 frequently [`frikwəntlɪ] *adv.* 經常地

▶ Jake often goes to France at this time of year.
杰克時常在一年的這個時刻去法國。

sometimes [`sʌm,taɪmz]
adv. 有時，偶爾
似 occasionally [ə`keʒənlɪ] *adv.* 偶爾

▶ We all need a good cry sometimes.
我們偶爾都需要好好的哭一場。
＊a good cry　好好的哭一場

never [`nɛvə] *adv.* 從未；絕不

▶ I've never seen that man in my life.
我一生中從未看過那名男子。

▶ I'll never go to that restaurant again!
我絕不會再去那間餐廳了！

28 paper [`pepə] *n.* 紙 (不可數)；文件；報紙 (= newspaper) & *vt.* 在……上貼壁紙

片 (1) a piece / sheet of paper　一張紙
(2) tissue / recycled paper
面紙 / 回收紙

▶ Pass me a pen and some paper.
遞給我一支筆和一些紙。

▶ Adam went through his grandfather's personal papers.
亞當仔細查看他爺爺的個人文件。
＊go through sth　仔細查看某物

▶ The story is on the front of today's paper.
這篇報導登在今日報紙的頭版。
＊on the front of...　在……的頭版 / 封面

▶ Susie wants to paper the living room.
蘇西想替客廳貼上壁紙。

Unit 15

1501-1505

1　strange [strendʒ] *a.* 陌生的；奇怪的

- 片 be strange to sb　對某人而言很陌生
- 衍 stranger [ˋstrendʒɚ] *n.* 陌生人 ②
- 似 (1) unfamiliar [ˌʌnfəˋmɪljɚ] *a.* 不熟悉的
  - (2) odd [ɑd] *a.* 奇怪的 ③

▶ The place was all strange to the boy, and he lost his way.
　這地方對那男孩而言是全然陌生的，所以他迷路了。

▶ After trying the soup, Paul had a strange look on his face.
　嘗過湯後，保羅的臉上出現奇怪的表情。

2　notice [ˋnotɪs] *vt.* 注意到 & *n.* 注意 (不可數)；通知 (不可數)；公告

- 片 (1) notice (that)...　注意到……
  - (2) take notice (of...)　注意 (……)
  - = take note (of...)
  - (3) without notice　無通知
- 衍 (1) noticeable [ˋnotɪsəbḷ] *a.* 顯著的 ⑤
  - (2) notify [ˋnotəˌfaɪ] *vt.* 通知 ⑤

▶ The woman was so busy shopping that she didn't notice her child walking away.
　那名婦女忙著購物，以致沒注意到小孩走開了。

▶ Take notice of every word I'm going to say.
　注意我將要說的每個字。

▶ Our landlord has raised the rent without notice.
　我們的房東沒有通知就提高租金。

▶ You should go and read the notice on the wall.
　你應該去看看牆上的公告。

3　rich [rɪtʃ] *a.* 有錢的，富裕的；豐富的

- 片 (1) the rich　有錢人
  - = the rich people
  - (2) be rich in...　富含……
  - = be high in...
- 反 (1) poor [pʊr] *a.* 貧窮的 ①
  - (2) low [lo] *a.* (量) 少的 ①

▶ Though Michael is rich, he is thrifty.
　雖然麥可很有錢，但他很節儉。
　＊thrifty [ˋθrɪftɪ] *a.* 節儉的

▶ Avocados are rich in vitamin C.
= Avocados are high in vitamin C.
　酪梨含有豐富的維他命 C。

4　beach [bitʃ] *n.* 海灘 & *vt.* 將 (船) 拖上岸

- 複 beaches [ˋbitʃɪz]
- 片 (1) on the beach　在海灘上
  - (2) at the beach　在海邊

▶ I like to play on the beach in summer.
　夏天時我喜歡在海灘上玩。

▶ The inexperienced captain beached the ship on the shore.
　這位沒有經驗的船長把船拖上岸。

5　key [ki] *n.* 鑰匙；關鍵 & *a.* 重要的，關鍵的 & *vt.* 用鍵盤輸入 (訊息)

- 複 keys [kiz]
- 三 key, keyed [kid], keyed

▶ Melissa searched in her purse for her car keys.
　梅麗莎在她的手提包內找車鑰匙。

133

片 (1) the key to sth
　　某物的鑰匙；某事物的關鍵
　(2) key sth in / key in sth
　　用鍵盤輸入某訊息
似 crucial [ˈkruʃəl] *a.* 決定性的 ⑤

▸ Hard work is the key to success.
　努力是成功的關鍵。
▸ After talking with his parents, Tom made a key decision.
　湯姆和爸媽討論過後，做了一個重要的決定。
▸ Key in your PIN and press "Enter."
　輸入你的 PIN 碼後按『輸入』鍵。

6　middle [ˈmɪdl̩] *n.* 中間 & *a.* 中間的 ☐

片 (1) in the middle of...　在……中間
　(2) middle class　　　中產階級
衍 middle-aged [ˈmɪdl̩ˌedʒd] *a.* 中年的

▸ Scott fell asleep in the middle of the meeting.
　史考特在開會中途睡著了。
▸ Benson is a man of middle height.
　班森是個中等身高的男人。

7　pair [pɛr] *n.* 一雙，一對 ☐

片 (1) a pair of + 複數名詞
　　一雙 / 對……
　(2) in pairs　兩個兩個地，成對地

▸ I just bought two new pairs of shoes.
　我剛剛買了 2 雙新鞋。
▸ The teacher asked us to practice in pairs.
　老師要我們 2 人一組做練習。

8　surprise [səˈpraɪz] *n.* 驚訝 (不可數)；意料之外的事 & *vt.* 使吃驚 ☐

片 (1) To sb's surprise, ...
　　令某人驚訝的是，……
　(2) catch / take sb by surprise
　　使某人措手不及
　(3) come as a surprise (to sb)
　　(某人) 意料之外
似 shock [ʃɑk] *n.* & *vt.* 震驚 ②

▸ To my surprise, the lazy student did quite well on the test.
　令我驚訝的是，那個懶惰的學生考試考得挺好的。
▸ The difficult question caught the student by surprise.
　這個困難的問題讓該學生不知所措。
▸ The announcement of Sophie's marriage came as a surprise.
　蘇菲宣布要結婚的消息讓人驚訝。
▸ I decided to surprise my mom with flowers.
　我決定送花，讓我媽媽驚喜。

---

surprised [səˈpraɪzd]
a. 感到驚訝的

片 (1) be surprised at...
　　對……感到驚訝
　(2) be surprised to V　做……很吃驚

▸ I was surprised at the news.
　我對那消息感到驚訝。
▸ James was surprised to learn that he'd passed the test.
　詹姆士得知自己通過考試很驚訝。

---

surprising [səˈpraɪzɪŋ]
a. 令人驚訝的

▸ The patient made a surprising recovery.
　這名病患的復原情況令人驚訝。

9　quiet [ˈkwaɪət] *a.* 安靜的 & *vt.* 使安靜 & *n.* 安靜 (不可數)

片 (1) Be quiet!　安靜！
(2) peace and quiet　寧靜

衍 quietly [ˈkwaɪətlɪ]
adv. 靜靜地，悄悄地

似 silent [ˈsaɪlənt] *a.* 寂靜無聲的 ②

▶ I couldn't hear Eddie because he spoke in a quiet voice.
我聽不到艾迪在說什麼，因為他的聲音很小。

▶ The teacher struggled to quiet her students.
老師努力讓她的學生安靜下來。

▶ June is heading to the country for some peace and quiet.
茱恩正前往鄉下尋求一些寧靜的空間。

10　count [kaʊnt] *vt.* & *vi.* & *n.* 計數 & *vi.* 重要

片 (1) count down (sth)　倒數 (某事)
(2) a quick count　快速計算
(3) count on...　依賴……
= depend on...
= rely on...

衍 (1) countable [ˈkaʊntəbḷ]
a. 可數的 ③
(2) countless [ˈkaʊntləs] *a.* 無數的
(3) countdown [ˈkaʊntˌdaʊn]
n. 倒數計時

▶ Don't count your chickens before they are hatched.
雞孵出來之前先別數 / 如意算盤不要打得太早。── 諺語

▶ We counted down from ten to one to welcome the new year.
我們從 10 倒數到 1 來迎接新年。

▶ The teacher did a quick count and realized one student was missing.
這名老師快速點了一下，發現少一個學生。

▶ Every dollar counts.
每一塊錢都重要。

▶ We can count on Ivy for help.
我們可以依賴艾薇的幫忙。

11　dozen [ˈdʌzṇ] *n.* 一打；許多 (恆用複數)

複 dozen / dozens [ˈdʌzṇs]
片 dozens of...　很多……
用法 dozen 作『一打』解時，單複數同形；
作『許多』解時，恆用複數 dozens。

▶ I bought a dozen eggs in the supermarket.
我在超市買了一打蛋。

▶ I've been to Europe dozens of times.
我去過歐洲好多次了。

12　cloud [klaʊd] *n.* 雲 & *vt.* 遮蔽，使變暗

衍 cloudy [ˈklaʊdɪ] *a.* 多雲的 ②

▶ The clouds are gray, and it looks like rain.
雲灰灰的，看起來要下雨的樣子。

▶ The heavy mist in the mountains has clouded my vision.
山區裡的濃霧遮蔽了我的視線。

13　light [laɪt] *n.* 光線 (不可數)；燈 & *a.* 輕的；(顏色) 淺的；輕鬆的 & *vt.* 點燃；照亮 & *adv.* 輕便地

三 light, lighted / lit [lɪt], lighted / lit

▶ Light came into the room.
光線照進房裡。

 **1513-1518**

片 (1) turn on / off the light　開 / 關燈	▶ Turn off the light before you leave the room.
(2) light sth up / light up sth	離開房間前把燈關掉。
照亮某物	
(3) travel light　輕便地旅行	▶ The box isn't heavy; it's light.
衍 (1) lightly [ˈlaɪtlɪ] adv. 輕輕地	這箱子不重，很輕。
(2) lighten [ˈlaɪtn̩] vt. 減輕 ⑥	▶ My favorite color is light blue.
似 (1) brightness [ˈbraɪtnəs] n. 明亮	我最喜歡的顏色是淺藍色。
(2) lamp [læmp] n. 燈 ①	▶ When you go sightseeing, you should wear light and comfortable shoes.
反 (1) darkness [ˈdɑrknəs] n. 黑暗	觀光時應穿著輕便、舒服的鞋子。
(2) dark [dɑrk] a. (顏色) 深的 ①	▶ I'll light some candles to make it more romantic.
	我會點一些蠟燭來讓氣氛更加浪漫。
	▶ Fireworks lit up the night sky over the city.
	煙火照亮了該座城市的夜空。
	▶ Pete thinks it is best to always travel light.
	彼特覺得輕便旅行始終是最好的方式。

14　gray [gre] n. 灰色 & a. (天氣) 昏暗的；灰色的 & vi. 變灰 (= grey〔英〕) ☐

片 go / turn gray　變灰白	▶ Dalton is always dressed in gray.
	達爾頓總是穿著灰色的衣服。
	▶ It was another gray January day.
	又是一個一月陰暗的一天。
	▶ My dad's hair is turning gray.
	= My dad's hair is graying.
	我爸的頭髮已漸漸變得灰白。

black [blæk]	▶ Jessica walked in, wearing a black dress.
a. 黑色的；漆黑的 & n. 黑色	潔西卡穿著一件黑洋裝走進來。
片 black coffee　黑咖啡	▶ The night was black, with no moon or stars.
延伸 blackout [ˈblækˌaʊt] n. 停電	那晚漆黑，看不見月亮或星星。
	▶ Jamie wants his bedroom painted in black.
	傑米想把臥室漆成黑色。

white [(h)waɪt]	▶ Sam spilled ketchup on his white T-shirt.
a. 白色的；(面色) 蒼白的 & n. 白色	山姆灑了一些番茄醬在他的白色 T 恤上。
似 pale [pel] a. 蒼白的 ②	▶ Edward's face turned white when he answered the phone.
延伸 snow-white [ˈsnoˈwaɪt] a. 雪白的	愛德華接到電話後臉色變得蒼白。
	▶ The bride is traditionally in white.
	傳統上，新娘都會穿著白色禮服。

15 beautiful [ˈbjutəf!̣] a. 美麗的；美好的

衍 (1) beauty [ˈbjutɪ] n. 美 ②
(2) beautify [ˈbjutəˌfaɪ] vt. 美化 ⑥
似 pleasant [ˈplɛzn̩t] a. 美好的 ②

▶ Has anyone told you that you have beautiful eyes?
有人告訴過你，你有一雙美麗的眼睛嗎？

▶ We went hiking on a beautiful sunny day.
我們在一個美好的晴天去健行。

pretty [ˈprɪtɪ] a. 漂亮的 & adv. 相當地

似 (1) quite [kwaɪt] adv. 相當地 ①
(2) fairly [ˈfɛrlɪ] adv. 相當地 ③

▶ Rebecca is a pretty girl.
蕾貝卡是位美女。

▶ It's pretty hot today. Let's turn on the air conditioning.
= It's quite hot today. Let's turn on the air conditioning.
今天挺熱的。我們把空調打開吧。

16 band [bænd] n. 帶子，細繩；樂隊

片 (1) a rubber band 橡皮筋
(2) a rock / jazz band
搖滾 / 爵士樂隊
(3) a live band 現場樂隊

▶ Sophie likes to tie her hair back in a band.
蘇菲喜歡用髮圈把頭髮往後紮。

▶ My brother started a band with some of his classmates.
我哥哥和幾個同學組了一支樂團。

17 knife [naɪf] n. 刀子 & vt. 用刀砍

複 knives [naɪvz]

▶ That knife is very sharp, so you should be careful when using it.
那把刀子很利，因此使用時要小心。

▶ In the movie, the villain knifed the victim in the back.
電影中，這名壞蛋用刀砍了受害者的背。

fork [fɔrk] n. 叉子；(馬路) 分岔口

片 a knife and fork
一副刀叉 (fork 前面不加 a)

▶ We have to use knives and forks when eating beef steak.
吃牛排時我們必須使用刀叉。

▶ You should turn right at the fork in the road.
你應該在那條路的分岔口右轉。

18 shout [ʃaʊt] vi. 大吼，大叫 & n. 喊叫 (聲)

片 (1) shout at sb 對某人大吼
(2) give a shout 大叫一聲

▶ Stop shouting at me. I haven't done anything wrong.
別對我大吼大叫，我又沒做錯事。

▶ Jenny gave a shout when she saw him.
珍妮看到他時大叫了一聲。

19 warm [wɔrm] *a.* (溫度、衣物等) 溫暖的；熱情的 & *vt.* & *vi.* (使) 暖和

片 warm up　變暖；暖身

衍 warmth [wɔrmθ] *n.* 溫暖 ③

延伸 warm-up　暖身運動

▶ You should do your warm-ups before you exercise.
你運動前要做暖身運動。

▶ It was warm yesterday, but it is cold today.
昨天天氣暖和，今天卻冷了起來。

▶ My best friend gave me a warm hug.
我的摯友給我一個熱情的擁抱。

▶ Alicia warmed her hands in front of the campfire.
艾莉西亞把手放在營火前取暖。

▶ You should warm up before swimming.
游泳前應該先熱身。

cool [kul] *a.* 涼爽的；冷靜的；酷的 & *vi.* 冷靜下來 & *n.* 冷靜

片 (1) stay cool　保持冷靜
(2) cool down　冷靜下來
(3) keep / maintain one's cool　某人保持冷靜
(4) lose one's cool　某人失去理智

衍 coolness [ˈkulnəs] *n.* 涼爽

似 calm [kɑm] *a.* 冷靜的 & *vt.* & *vi.* (使) 冷靜 & *n.* 冷靜 ②

▶ It's cool in September in Korea.
韓國 9 月的天氣很涼爽。

▶ The clerk stayed cool even when the woman yelled at him.
即使那個女人衝著他咆哮，那名店員仍然保持冷靜。

▶ Wow! That shirt is really cool. Where did you get it?
哇塞！那件襯衫真酷。你在哪兒買的？

▶ Diana had an argument with her husband and went for a walk to cool down.
黛安娜和先生吵架，因此去散步讓自己冷靜下來。

▶ Mira always tries to keep her cool when facing difficulties.
米拉面對困難時，總是試著保持冷靜。

20 dry [draɪ] *a.* 乾燥的；枯燥無味的 & *vt.* 使乾燥

三 dry, dried [draɪd], dried

片 run dry　乾涸

衍 dryer [ˈdraɪɚ] *n.* 烘乾機 (= drier) ②

反 wet [wɛt] *a.* 濕的 ①

延伸 dry-clean [ˈdraɪˌklin] *vt.* & *vi.* 乾洗 (衣物)

▶ The lake ran dry last year.
那座湖去年乾涸了。

▶ The book was so dry that I couldn't finish reading it.
那本書太枯燥了，因此我根本沒辦法讀完。

▶ Dry your hair after you wash it, or you'll catch a cold.
洗頭之後要把頭髮弄乾，否則會著涼的。

21 taste [test] *n.* 味道；一口；品味 (不可數) & *vi.* 嚐起來 & *vt.* 品嚐；體驗

片 (1) have a taste of...　嚐一口……
(2) have good / bad / similar taste in...　對……的品味很好 / 差 / 相似
(3) taste + adj.　嚐起來……
(4) taste of + N　嚐起來……

▶ This fruit has a slightly bitter taste.
= This fruit tastes slightly bitter.
這種水果嚐起來有一點苦。

▶ Would you like to have a taste of this fruitcake?
你想要嚐一口這個水果蛋糕嗎？

似 (1) flavor [ˋflevɚ] *n.* 味道 ③
(2) experience [ɪkˋspɪrɪəns]
　　vt. 體驗 ①

▶ We have similar taste in clothes.
　我們對衣服的品味相似。

▶ The tea tastes of lemon.
　這茶嚐起來有檸檬味。

▶ Taste the soup, and tell me if it is too salty.
　嚐嚐這道湯，告訴我會不會太鹹。

▶ If you have tasted success once, you can certainly do it again.
　如果你曾嚐過一次成功的滋味，你一定能再做到。

22　chocolate [ˋtʃɑklət] *n.* 巧克力

片 a bar of chocolate　一條巧克力

▶ I like ice cream with chocolate sauce.
　我喜歡冰淇淋淋上巧克力醬。

23　glass [glæs] *n.* 玻璃 (不可數)；玻璃杯 (可數)

片 (1) a piece of glass　一塊 / 片玻璃
(2) a glass bottle / vase
　玻璃瓶 / 花瓶

▶ Coke tastes better out of a glass bottle.
　用玻璃瓶喝可樂比較好喝。

▶ The waiter brought two wine glasses to the table.
　服務生拿了兩個紅酒杯到桌上。

glasses [ˋglæsɪz] *n.* 眼鏡 (恆用複數)
片 (1) wear glasses　　戴眼鏡
(2) a pair of glasses　一副眼鏡

▶ Tammy has to wear glasses while driving.
　譚美開車時需要戴眼鏡。

▶ That new pair of glasses really suits you!
　那副新眼鏡真的很適合你！

24　little [ˋlɪtl̩] *a.* 小的；幼小的；不重要的；不多的 & *adv.* 不多地 & *n.* 一點

片 (1) a little (+ 不可數名詞)
　　一點 (……)
(2) a little (bit)　一點
　= a bit
似 (1) small [smɔl] *a.* 小的 ①
(2) young [jʌn] *a.* 幼小的 ①
用法 little 作形容詞，表『不多的』時，其後接不可數名詞。

▶ Santorini is a little island in southeastern Europe.
　聖托里尼是歐洲東南部的一座小島。

▶ Vincent is such a cute little boy!
　文森真是個可愛的小男孩！

▶ Brad knows every little detail of the movie.
　布萊德知道這部電影的每一個小細節。

▶ I'm not going to that restaurant—there's so little choice.
　我不會再去那間餐廳了，因為選擇不多。

▶ The singer's music is little known outside of Canada.
　這名歌手的音樂在加拿大以外的地方較不為人知。

▶ We understand little of the event.
　我們對這件事情知道得不多。

▶ I want a little sugar, please.
請給我一點糖。

▶ I was a little bit annoyed at what Ken said.
我對肯說的話感到有點惱怒。

few [f ju] *a.* 很少的，幾乎沒有的 & *pron.* 極少數

片 a few (+ 複數名詞)　一些 (……)

用法 few 作形容詞，表『很少的』時，其後接複數名詞。

▶ Todd has been very busy for the past few weeks.
陶德過去幾週一直非常忙碌。

▶ I have only invited a few people.
我只邀請了一些人。

▶ Simon knew few of the people at the party.
賽門在派對上認識的人不多。

---

25 sing [sɪŋ] *vi.* & *vt.* 唱歌

三 sing, sang [sæŋ], sung [sʌŋ]

片 sing along (to...)　跟著一起唱 (……)

▶ Laura and her husband love to sing.
蘿拉和她先生喜愛唱歌。

▶ Bruno Mars sang "Leave the Door Open" at the concert.
火星人布魯諾在演唱會上唱〈Leave the Door Open〉。

▶ Everyone should sing along to the national anthem.
大家應該要跟著一起唱國歌。
＊anthem [ˈænθəm] *n.* 國歌

---

singer [ˈsɪŋɚ] *n.* 歌手

片 a pop singer　流行歌手

▶ Taylor Swift is Sophie's favorite singer.
泰勒‧絲薇芙特是蘇菲最喜歡的歌手。

---

song [sɔŋ] *n.* 歌曲

▶ I know all the words to this song.
我知道這首歌所有的歌詞。

---

26 tall [tɔl] *a.* 高的；身高為……

比 tall 和 high 皆有『高的』之意，形容『人』很高的時候，用 tall 而不用 high。

▶ Fred's new girlfriend is very tall.
佛萊德的新女友非常高。

▶ Tom Cruise is 1.7 meters tall.
湯姆‧克魯斯身高 1.7 公尺。

---

height [haɪt] *n.* 高度

片 高度 + in height　高度為……

衍 (1) high [haɪ]
　　a. 高的 & *adv.* 高地 & *n.* 高峰 ①
　(2) highly [ˈhaɪlɪ] *adv.* 極，非常 ②

▶ The height of the tree is about two meters.
這棵樹的高度約為 2 公尺。

▶ I'm six feet in height.
= My height is six feet.
= I'm six feet tall.
我身高 6 英尺。

27 planet [ˈplænɪt] *n.* 行星

延伸 (1) star [stɑr] *n.* 恆星 ①
(2) satellite [ˈsætl̩ˌaɪt] *n.* 人造衛星 ④

▶ The Earth is a planet, while the Sun is a star.
地球是行星，而太陽是恆星。

1 guess [gɛs] *n.* & *vt.* 猜測

片 (1) make a guess　猜一猜
　(2) sb guess that...　某人猜……
　= sb's guess is that...

▶ I don't know the answer, but I'll make a guess at it.
　我不知道答案，但我會猜一猜。

▶ I guess that Tom and Jenny have fallen in love.
= My guess is that Tom and Jenny have fallen in love.
　我猜湯姆和珍妮相戀了。

2 lake [lek] *n.* 湖

衍 (1) lakeside [ˈlekˌsaɪd] *n.* 湖邊
　(2) lakelet [ˈleklət] *n.* 小湖

▶ Please don't fish or swim in the lake.
　請勿在湖中釣魚或游泳。

pond [pɑnd] *n.* 池塘
片 a big fish in a small pond
　小地方的大人物

▶ In his hometown, Ted is a big fish in a small pond.
　泰德在他的家鄉可是赫赫有名的大人物。

3 clean [klin] *a.* 乾淨的；光明正大的，清白的 & *vt.* 清潔，弄乾淨 & *adv.* 徹底地 & *n.* 清潔

片 clean (sth) up / clean up (sth)
　(將某物)清理乾淨
衍 (1) cleanly [ˈklinlɪ] *adv.* 乾淨地
　　do thing cleanly　做事乾淨利落
　(2) cleaner [ˈklinɚ]
　　n. 清潔工；清潔劑 ③

▶ Your room must always be kept clean.
　你的房間必須隨時保持乾淨。

▶ "I want a good and clean fight," said the coach.
　這位教練說：『我要一場精采、光明正大的比賽。』

▶ I often help Mom clean the table and do the dishes after dinner.
　晚餐後，我常幫媽媽收拾桌子，清洗碗盤。

▶ Clean up your room, John. It's a mess.
　約翰，把你的房間整理乾淨。你房間很亂。

▶ Carey clean forgot to pick up her son from school.
　凱莉完全忘記要去學校接她兒子了。

▶ This bathroom needs a good clean.
　這間浴室需要好好打掃。

tidy [ˈtaɪdɪ] *a.* 整潔的 & *vt.* 使整潔
三 tidy, tidied [ˈtaɪdɪd], tidied
片 (1) keep... clean and tidy
　　將……保持得乾淨整潔
　(2) tidy (up)...　將……收拾／整理乾淨
反 (1) untidy [ʌnˈtaɪdɪ]
　　a. 凌亂的，不潔的
　(2) sloppy [ˈslɑpɪ] *a.* 邋遢的 ⑥

▶ This lazybones is sloppy and never seems to be able to keep his room clean and tidy.
　這個懶鬼很邋遢，似乎從沒辦法把他的房間保持乾淨整潔。
　＊lazybones [ˈlezɪˌbonz] *n.* 懶骨頭，懶鬼 (單複數同形)

▶ Tidy (up) your bedroom, Johnny. Dad is coming back.
　強尼，把你的房間整理乾淨。爸爸就要回來了。

4　jump [dʒʌmp] *vi. & n.* 跳

📵 (1) jump to one's feet
　　某人跳起來，一躍而起
　　(2) jump for joy　雀躍
📵 (1) hop [hɑp] *vt. & vi.* 跳 ②
　　(2) leap [lip] *vt. & vi.* 跳 ③

▸ I jumped to my feet when Eddie patted me on the back.
艾迪拍我的背時，我跳了起來。
▸ When Connie heard the good news, she jumped for joy.
康妮一聽到這個好消息就雀躍不已。
▸ Tom's jump was five centimeters farther than mine.
湯姆跳得比我遠 5 公分。

5　tool [tul] *n.* 工具

▸ The only tool you need is a hammer.
你需要的唯一工具就是榔頭。

6　safe [sef] *a.* 安全的 & *n.* 保險箱

📵 safe and sound　安然無恙地
📵 (1) safety [ˈsefti] *n.* 安全 ②
　　(2) safely [ˈsefli] *adv.* 安全地
📵 save [sev] *vt.* 拯救；節省；儲存 ①
📵 unsafe [ʌnˈsef] *a.* 不安全的

▸ I felt happy to learn that Ben had come back safe and sound.
知道班已經安然無恙地回來，我感到很高興。
▸ Please keep your valuables in the hotel safe.
請把貴重物品存放在旅館的保險箱裡。

dangerous [ˈdendʒərəs] *a.* 危險的

📵 (1) be dangerous for sb
　　對某人來說很危險
　　(2) be dangerous (for sb) to V
　　（某人）做……很危險
📵 danger [ˈdendʒɚ] *n.* 危險 ②
📵 (1) harmful [ˈhɑrmfəl] *a.* 有害的 ③
　　(2) risky [ˈrɪskɪ] *a.* 危險的 ⑤

▸ Drunk driving is always dangerous.
酒駕一向是很危險的。
▸ Staying outdoors when it is very cold is dangerous for an old person.
對年長者來說，天氣很冷的時候待在室外是很危險的。
▸ It is dangerous for you to accept rides from strangers.
你隨便搭陌生人的便車是很危險的。

7　hat [hæt] *n.* 帽子

📵 take off / put on a hat
　　脫下 / 戴上帽子

▸ Take off your hat when you enter the room.
進入室內時要脫帽。

cap [kæp] *n.* 帽子 (尤指棒球帽)；蓋子 & *vt.* 覆蓋 (常用被動)

📵 cap, capped [kæpt], capped
📵 (1) no cap　真的 (口語)
　　(2) be capped with...　被……覆蓋

▸ The man wearing a cap is my boyfriend.
戴棒球帽的那個人是我男友。
▸ Please put the cap back on the Coke bottle.
請把蓋子蓋回可樂瓶上。

▶ I slept for 15 hours last night, no cap!
我昨晚睡了 15 個小時,真的!

▶ The beautiful Austrian mountains were capped with snow.
美麗的奧地利山脈被白雪覆蓋。

8 sweet [swit] *a.* 甜的;甜美的;體貼的 & *n.* 甜食 (常用複數)

片 have a sweet tooth 愛吃甜食
= enjoy sweets

衍 sweeten [ˈswitən] *vt.* 使變甜

延伸 sweet-and-sour pork 糖醋肉

▶ Mary has a sweet tooth.
= Mary enjoys sweets.
瑪麗很愛吃甜食。

▶ I had a sweet dream last night.
我昨晚做了個美夢。

▶ How sweet of you to send me the card!
你送我卡片真貼心!

9 factory [ˈfæktərɪ] *n.* 工廠

似 plant [plænt] *n.* 工廠 ①

▶ The shoe factory closed down last year.
這家製鞋工廠去年關門了。

10 afraid [əˈfred] *a.* 害怕的;恐怕

片 (1) be afraid of... 害怕……
  = be scared of...
(2) be afraid to V 害怕做……
(3) be afraid that... 恐怕……

似 scared [skɛrd] *a.* 害怕的 ②

▶ I'm no longer afraid of the dark.
我不再怕黑了。

▶ I'm afraid to talk to that serious teacher.
我很怕跟那位嚴肅的老師說話。

▶ I'm afraid that it's going to rain pretty soon.
恐怕很快就會下雨。

11 hate [het] *vt.* 憎恨 & *n.* 恨意

片 hate + V-ing 討厭 / 厭惡做……
= hate to V

衍 hatred [ˈhetrɪd] *n.* 恨意 ④

反 love [lʌv] *vt.* & *vi.* 愛 ①

▶ I hate traveling alone.
= I hate to travel alone.
我討厭一個人旅行。

▶ Paul looked up at the bully with hate in his eyes.
保羅抬起頭來,用帶著恨意的眼神看著惡霸。

12 seat [sit] *n.* 座位 & *vt.* 使就座

片 (1) take / have a seat 坐下
  = be seated
  = sit down

▶ I'm sorry, but this seat is taken.
很抱歉,但這個位子有人坐了。

▶ Take a seat, please.
= Have a seat, please.
　請坐。

▶ I was seated by the window.
　我被安排坐在窗邊。

13　tie [taɪ] *n.* 領帶；關係 (常用複數)；平手 & *vt.* & *vi.* 綁；平手

目 tie, tied [taɪd], tied
片 (1) close / strong ties　關係緊密
　 (2) end in a tie　　　不分勝負
　 (3) tie the knot　　　結婚
　 (4) (be) tied with sb
　　　與某人打成平手
似 necktie [ˋnɛkˏtaɪ] *n.* 領帶 ③

▶ Peter always wears a shirt and tie to work.
　彼得總是穿著襯衫、打上領帶去上班。

▶ I have close ties with my relatives in England.
　我和在英格蘭的親戚關係很緊密。

▶ The basketball game ended in a tie.
　這場籃球比賽的結果不分勝負。

▶ Let me help you tie the rope around your waist.
　讓我幫忙你把繩子綁在腰上。

▶ I can't wait to see you two tie the knot.
　我等不及要看你們兩位步入禮堂。

▶ At the end of the game, we (were) tied with that team.
　比賽結束時，我們和那隊打成平手。

14　beside [bɪˋsaɪd] *prep.* 在……旁邊

片 be beside oneself with joy
　樂瘋了
似 (1) besides [bɪˋsaɪdz]
　　 adv. 此外 & *prep.* 除……之外 ③
　 (2) next to...　在……旁邊

▶ A little boy is standing beside the door.
　有個小男孩正站在門邊。

▶ I was beside myself with joy when I heard the good news.
　我聽到這好消息時樂瘋了。

15　row [ro] *vt.* & *vi.* 划 (船) & *n.* 排，列

片 in a row　成一列；連續

▶ Jenny rowed the boat to the shore.
　珍妮把船划到岸邊。

▶ Our seats were in the last row of the theater.
　我們的座位在戲院的最後一排。

▶ It has been raining here five days in a row.
　這裡連續下了 5 天雨。

16　blow [blo] *vt.* & *vi.* 吹；爆炸 & *n.* 吹動；痛打；打擊

目 blow, blew [blu], blown [blon]

▶ The girl blew out the candles on the cake.
　女孩把蛋糕上的蠟燭吹熄了。

🗁 (1) blow (...) out (將……) 吹熄
(2) blow up 爆炸
(3) blow up... 將……炸掉
(4) blow one's nose 擤鼻涕
(5) a blow of... 吹來一陣……
(6) a fatal blow 致命的一擊

▶ The helicopter blew up in the sky.
直升機在空中爆炸。

▶ The enemy soldiers blew up the building.
敵軍士兵炸掉該棟建築。

▶ I need a tissue to blow my nose.
我需要一張衛生紙來擤鼻涕。

▶ I felt a strong blow of wind from the window.
我感覺到窗戶吹來一陣強風。

▶ The man died from a heavy blow to his neck.
這名男子死於頸後的一記重擊。

▶ We gave the enemy a fatal blow and won the war.
我們給敵軍致命的一擊,贏得了這場戰役。

17 pocket [ˋpɑkɪt] *n.* 口袋 & *vt.* 把……裝進口袋

🗁 pocket money 零用錢
衍 pickpocket [ˋpɪkͺpɑkɪt] *n.* 扒手 ⑥

▶ Little Hank put the money into my pocket, but now it's gone.
小漢克把錢放在我的口袋裡,現在錢卻不見了。

▶ I am saving my pocket money to buy a computer.
我把零用錢省下來,打算買部電腦。

▶ Matt pocketed Sarah's phone when she wasn't looking.
麥特趁莎拉不注意時把她的手機放進口袋。

18 meat [mit] *n.* (食用的) 肉類 (不可數)

▶ Eating too much meat can cause heart problems.
食用太多肉類可能造成心臟問題。

▶ One man's meat is another man's poison.
一個人喜歡吃的肉是另一個人的毒藥 / 人各有所好。
—— 諺語

beef [bif] *n.* 牛肉 (不可數)
延伸 steak [stek] *n.* 牛排 ②

▶ My favorite food is beef noodles.
我最愛吃的食物就是牛肉麵。

19 lesson [ˋlɛsṇ] *n.* 課程;教訓

🗁 (1) teach sb a lesson 教訓某人
(2) learn one's lesson 學到教訓

▶ "Tomorrow's lesson will be about frogs," said the teacher.
老師說:『明天的課程要談的是青蛙。』

▶ We decided to teach the naughty boy a lesson.
我們決定要教訓那名頑皮的男孩。

▶ I hope you've learned your lesson and won't cheat again!
我希望你已經得到教訓不會再作弊了！

20　salt [sɔlt] *n.* 鹽巴 (不可數) & *vt.* 加鹽巴；用鹽醃製 & *a.* 含鹽的；用鹽醃製的

衍 salty [ˈsɔltɪ] *a.* 鹹的 ②

▶ I think you put too much salt in the soup.
我想你加太多鹽在湯裡了。

▶ Peter salted the tomatoes to improve their taste.
彼得幫番茄加鹽巴來改善味道。

▶ The cod was salted and dried to preserve it.
這條鱈魚用鹽醃製並且乾燥以利保存。
＊cod [kɑd] *n.* 鱈魚
　preserve [prɪˈzɝv] *vt.* 保存

▶ Edward went swimming in the salt lake.
艾德華在鹽湖裡游泳。

▶ Janine bought some salt beef at the market.
珍寧在市場買了些醃牛肉。

sugar [ˈʃʊgɚ] *n.* 糖 (不可數)

▶ Do you take sugar in your coffee?
您的咖啡要加糖嗎？

21　mistake [məˈstek] *n.* 錯誤 & *vt.* 誤認

三 mistake, mistook [məˈstʊk],
mistaken [məˈstekən]

片 (1) make a mistake　犯錯
　(2) mistake A for B　誤將 A 當成 B

▶ We all learn by making mistakes.
我們都是從犯錯中學習。

▶ Because of his long hair, I mistook the boy for a girl.
因為那男生留長髮，所以我把他誤認成女生。

22　seed [sid] *n.* 種子 & *vt.* 播種

片 seed A with B　在 A 上種 B

似 sow [so] *vt.* 播種 ⑤

▶ The farmers are sowing seeds in the fields.
農夫們正在田中播種。

▶ My grandpa seeded the land with grass.
我爺爺在這塊地上種草。

23　magic [ˈmædʒɪk] *n.* 魔術 & *a.* 魔術的

片 (1) as if by magic　像變魔術般
　(2) a magic trick　魔術把戲

衍 (1) magical [ˈmædʒɪkl̩]
　　 a. 有魔力的；美妙的 ③
　(2) magician [məˈdʒɪʃən]
　　 n. 魔術師 ③

▶ The little boy disappeared as if by magic.
那個小男孩像變魔術般消失不見了。

▶ Can you teach me some magic tricks?
你可以教我一些魔術把戲嗎？

24 know [no] *vt.* 知道；熟識；確定

目 know, knew [nju] , known [non]

月 As sb know, ... 如某人所知，……

▶ Talking clocks help blind people know the time.
會報時的時鐘幫助盲人知道時間。

▶ As everybody knows, the early bird catches the worm.
每個人都知道早起的鳥兒有蟲吃。

▶ Bobby knew his way around the town.
巴比很熟悉鎮上的路。

▶ I don't know which team will win for sure.
我不確定哪一隊會贏。

knowledge [ˈnɑlɪdʒ] *n.* 知識；了解

月 have a good knowledge of...
很懂……

= have a good understanding of...

衍 knowledgeable [ˈnɑlɪdʒəbḷ]
a. 很有知識的 ⑥

▶ Knowledge is power.
知識就是力量。—— 諺語

▶ John has a good knowledge of Chinese history.
約翰精通中國史。

25 supermarket [ˈsupəˌmɑrkɪt] *n.* 超市

似 market [ˈmɑrkɪt] *n.* 市場 ①

▶ Barbara goes to the supermarket every Friday night.
芭芭拉每週五晚上都會上超市。

26 Mr. [ˈmɪstə] *n.* 先生 (為 mister 的縮寫)

用法 Mr. 常在後加人名使用。

▶ "Do you have any change, mister?" asked the beggar.
乞丐問：『先生，您有零錢嗎？』

▶ Our teacher this year will be Mr. Johnson.
今年我們的老師是強森先生。

Mrs. [ˈmɪsɪz]
n. 夫人，太太 (對已婚女子使用)

▶ The letter should be addressed to Mrs. Cartwright.
這封信應該寄給卡特萊特夫人。
*address [əˈdrɛs] *vt.* 寄 (信) 給……

Ms. [mɪz]
n. 小姐 (對未婚或已婚女子皆可使用)

▶ I'd like to introduce you to Ms. Turner.
我想介紹透納小姐給你認識。

27 visit [ˈvɪzɪt] *vi. & vt. & n.* 拜訪；參觀

月 (1) pay sb a visit   拜訪某人
　 (2) pay a visit to + 地方   拜訪某地

▶ Rebecca is only visiting for a few days.
蕾貝卡只來拜訪幾天而已。

▶ We visited the national museum in that city.
我們參觀了那座城市裡的國家博物館。

▶ Alan paid his best friend a visit on Saturday.
亞倫禮拜六去拜訪他的摯友。

▶ Sam needs to pay a visit to the bank.
山姆需要去銀行一趟。

visitor [ˈvɪzɪtɚ] *n.* 訪客

片 a visitor to + 地方　造訪某地的人

似 (1) guest [gɛst] *n.* 客人，來賓 ②
(2) tourist [ˈtʊrɪst] *n.* 觀光客 ③

▶ There are many visitors to the museum on Sundays.
每逢週日便有許多遊客去參觀博物館。

28　type [taɪp] *n.* 類型 & *vt.* 打字

片 (1) be (not) sb's type
(不) 是某人喜歡的類型
(2) a blood type　血型

衍 (1) typical [ˈtɪpɪk!] *a.* 典型的 ②
(2) typing [ˈtaɪpɪŋ] *n.* 打字

似 (1) kind [kaɪnd] *n.* 種類 ①
(2) sort [sɔrt] *n.* 種類 ②

▶ Although he's a nice guy, Michael just isn't my type of man.
雖然他是個好人，但是麥可並不是我喜歡的男人類型。

▶ Please type this letter and send it to Mr. Blair.
請將這封信打字並寄給布萊爾先生。

Unit 17

1701-1703

1 first [fɜst] *a.* 第一的；最重要的 & *adv.* 最先地；最重要地；第一次地 & *n.* 第一個

片 (1) for the first time　第一次
(2) in the first place　一開始
(3) first of all　最重要的是，首先
(4) from the (very) first　從一開始

衍 firstly [ˈfɜstlɪ] *adv.* 首先地

▶ That was my first visit to London. I was so excited.
那是我第一次去倫敦玩。我超興奮的。

▶ I tried fish and chips for the first time.
我第一次試吃炸魚薯條。

▶ I didn't say anything about fighting with Andy in the first place.
一開始我對於跟安迪吵架這件事隻字未提。

▶ You will always be my first priority.
你永遠都是我的首要之務。
*priority [praɪˈɔrətɪ] *n.* 優先考慮的事

▶ I'm coming. Just let me park my car first.
我快到了。讓我先停好車。

▶ Safety comes first.
安全第一。

▶ First of all, you've made some spelling mistakes.
首先，你已經犯了一些拼字錯誤。

▶ The movie *Soul* was first released in 2020.
電影《靈魂急轉彎》於 2020 年首映。

▶ I've been worried about this project from the first.
我從一開始就很擔心這項企畫。

---

second [ˈsɛkənd]
a. 第二的；另一個的 & *adv.* 第二地 &
n. 秒；很短的時間

片 (1) be second to none
是首屈一指的
(2) a second opinion　其他的意見
(3) have second thoughts
有其他想法，改變心意
(4) on second thought
再次考慮〔美〕
= on second thoughts〔英〕
(5) in a second　一會兒後
= in a moment

衍 (1) secondary [ˈsɛkənˌdɛrɪ]
a. 第二的 ②

▶ I hope you'll give me a second chance.
我希望你會給我第二次機會。

▶ When it comes to singing, Peter is second to none.
說到唱歌，彼得是最棒的。

▶ The patient wanted to get a second opinion.
病患想再聽聽其他意見。

▶ Craig was going to buy the car, but he had second thoughts.
克雷格本來打算要買車，但他改變心意了。

▶ On second thought, I'll have the steak.
再次考慮後我決定要吃牛排。

▶ Judy came second in the race last time.
茱蒂上次賽跑得第二。

▶ There are sixty seconds in a minute.
1 分鐘有 60 秒。

(2) second-hand [ˈsɛkənˌhænd]
　　a. 二手的
　　second-hand smoke　二手菸
(3) secondly [ˈsɛkəndlɪ]
　　adv. 第二，其次

▶ I'll be back in a second.
我一會兒就回來。

third [θɝd] *a.* 第三的 & *n.* 三分之一
片 (1) the third time's the charm
　　第三次會成功
(2) a third of...　三分之一個……
衍 thirdly [ˈθɝdlɪ] *adv.* 第三地

▶ This is the third banana I've had today.
這是我今天吃的第三根香蕉。
▶ We've failed twice, but the third time's the charm.
我們已經失敗兩次了，但第三次會成功的。
▶ I ate a third of the pie.
我吃了三分之一塊派。

2　root [rut] *n.* 根；根源 & *vi.* 根植於……

片 (1) by the roots　　連根；從根本
(2) be rooted in...　根植於……
似 origin [ˈɔrədʒɪn] *n.* 來源 ②

▶ The big tree was pulled up by the roots.
那棵大樹被連根拔起。
▶ The love of money is the root of all evil.
金錢是萬惡的根源。—— 諺語
▶ Most prejudice is rooted in ignorance and fear.
大部分的偏見都根植於無知和恐懼。
＊ignorance [ˈɪgnərəns] *n.* 無知
　prejudice [ˈprɛdʒədɪs] *n.* 偏見

3　climb [klaɪm] *vt.* 爬 & *vi.* 爬；爬升，增加 & *n.* 攀爬；增加

片 (1) climb (up)...　　爬……
(2) go mountain / rock climbing
　　去登山 / 攀岩

▶ The monkey climbed the tree looking for bananas.
猴子爬樹找香蕉吃。
▶ Lisa helped her grandmother to climb up the stairs.
麗莎協助她奶奶爬上樓梯。
▶ Global temperatures have climbed steadily over the last few years.
過去幾年全球氣溫不斷上升。
＊steadily [ˈstɛdəlɪ] *adv.* 不斷地，穩定地
▶ Tori likes to go rock climbing on weekends.
托莉喜歡週末去攀岩。
▶ The climb to the top of the mountain was difficult.
攀登到山頂的過程是艱辛的。
▶ The pound continues its climb against the euro.
英鎊對歐元持續升值。
＊pound [paʊnd] *n.* 英鎊
　euro [ˈjuro] *n.* 歐元

4 gift [gɪft] *n.* 天賦；禮物

have a gift / talent for...
有⋯⋯的天賦

(衍) **gifted** [ˋgɪftɪd] *a.* 有天賦的 ④

(似) **talent** [ˋtælənt] *n.* 天賦 ③

▶ John has a gift for music.
約翰有音樂的天賦。

▶ Thank you for the birthday gift. I really like it.
謝謝你送我的生日禮物。我真的很喜歡。

---

present [ˋprɛzənt]
n. 禮物；目前 & *a.* 目前的；出席的 &
[prɪˋzɛnt] *vt.* 獻給，頒發；提出，發表；
介紹；上演

(1) **at present**　目前
(2) **present sb with sth**
將某物獻給某人
= **present sth to sb**

▶ I gave my wife a ruby ring as her birthday present.
我送我太太一枚紅寶石戒指當作生日禮物。

▶ Mr. Lai is away on business at present.
賴先生目前出差中。

▶ My present English teacher is from Seattle.
我目前的英文老師來自西雅圖。

▶ Now that the whole class is present, let's begin the lesson.
既然全班都在場，我們開始上課吧。

▶ A young girl presented the singer with flowers.
= A young girl presented flowers to the singer.
一名年輕小姐獻花給這位歌手。

▶ No good ideas were presented at the meeting.
這次會議上沒提出什麼好點子。

▶ Let me present Mr. White, one of today's greatest artists.
容我介紹懷特先生，他是當今最偉大的藝術家之一。

▶ The University Theater will present *Death of a Salesman* tonight.
大學劇場今晚將上演《推銷員之死》。

5 cook [kʊk] *n.* 做飯的人；廚師 & *vt.* 烹調

(衍) **cooker** [ˋkʊkɚ] *n.* 炊具 ③

(似) **chef** [ʃɛf] *n.* (餐廳) 大廚師 ⑤

▶ My dad is a really good cook.
我爸爸很會做飯。

▶ Too many cooks spoil the broth.
太多廚師會壞了羹湯 / 人多手雜。—— 諺語

▶ I'm not feeling well today. Could you please cook me something to eat?
我今天人不太舒服。你煮點東西給我吃好不好？

6 joy [dʒɔɪ] *n.* 歡樂

(衍) **joyful** [ˋdʒɔɪfl] *a.* 高興的 ③

▶ Seeing my daughter smile fills my heart with joy.
看見我女兒微笑讓我心中充滿歡喜。

7　ring [rɪŋ] *n.* 鈴聲；戒指；圓圈，環狀物 & *vi.* (鈴聲) 響起 ☐

目 ring, rang [ræŋ], rung [rʌŋ]

片 (1) give sb a ring / call
　　打電話給某人

　　(2) a diamond / wedding ring
　　鑽戒 / 結婚戒指

▶ There was a ring at the door, and then Jane walked in.
　門鈴響了一下，然後珍就走進來了。

▶ Give me a ring when you have time.
　有空打電話給我。

▶ Peter bought a diamond ring for his girlfriend.
　彼得買了一只鑽戒給他女友。

▶ The children formed a ring around the teacher.
　小朋友們繞著老師圍成一圈。

▶ The phone has just rung.
　電話剛剛響了。

8　sentence [ˈsɛntn̩s] *n.* 句子；判刑 & *vt.* 判刑 ☐

片 (1) receive a sentence　被判刑

　　(2) be sentenced to death / life
　　imprisonment
　　被判死刑 / 無期徒刑

　　(3) be sentenced to + 數字 + years
　　in prison / jail
　　被判若干年有期徒刑

▶ Your sentences should be short and meaningful.
　你的句子應該要簡短且有意義。

▶ Tom received a five-year prison sentence.
　湯姆被判坐牢 5 年。

▶ The criminal was sentenced to life imprisonment.
　該名罪犯被判終生監禁。

▶ The robber was sentenced to ten years in prison.
　該搶匪被判 10 年有期徒刑。

word [wɝd] *n.* 字詞；話語；消息 ☐

片 (1) word for / by word　逐字地

　　(2) without (saying) a word
　　不發一語地

　　(3) a man / woman of few words
　　話不多的男 / 女子

　　(4) have a word (with sb)
　　(和某人) 簡短交談 (以尋求 / 提供建
　　議)

▶ Rose knows that poem word for word.
　蘿絲知道那首詩的一字一句。

▶ The junior office worker stood there without saying a word.
　那名辦公室的新進人員不發一語地站在那。

▶ James is a man of few words.
　詹姆士是個沉默寡言的男子。

▶ Excuse me, Lauren. Can I have a word?
　蘿倫，不好意思。我可以和妳談談嗎？

9　noise [nɔɪz] *n.* 噪音 ☐

片 make noise　發出噪音

▶ Stop making noise! I'm studying.
　別再吵了！我在念書。

noisy [ˈnɔɪzɪ] *a.* 吵鬧的

似 loud [laʊd] *a.* 大聲的 ①

▶ The pub was crowded and noisy.
　這酒館又擠又吵。

10 coat [kot] *n.* 外套 & *vt.* 塗在……上，覆蓋……的表面

🅗 coat A with B　把 B 塗在 A 上
衍 overcoat [ˋovɚˏkot] *n.* 大衣 ④

▸ Hang up your coat after you take it off.
脫下外套後把它掛好。

▸ The painter coated the door with red paint.
油漆匠把紅漆塗在門上。

jacket [ˋdʒækɪt] *n.* 夾克；西裝上衣

▸ Tom looks very handsome in that leather jacket.
湯姆穿那件皮夾克很帥。

11 correct [kəˋrɛkt] *a.* 正確的 & *vt.* 糾正，修改

衍 (1) correctly [kəˋrɛktlɪ] *adv.* 正確地
　 (2) correction [kəˋrɛkʃən] *n.* 改正
似 (1) right [raɪt] *a.* 正確的 ①
　 (2) accurate [ˋækjərət] *a.* 正確的 ③

▸ There is no correct answer to this question.
這個問題並沒有正確的答案。

▸ Please correct me when I make mistakes.
我犯錯時請糾正我。

incorrect [ˏɪnkəˋrɛkt] *a.* 不正確的

似 wrong [rɔŋ] *a.* 錯誤的 ①

▸ The information proved to be incorrect.
這項訊息經證實是錯誤的。

12 send [sɛnd] *vt.* 郵寄；遞送；發送 (訊息、電子郵件等)；派遣

🔢 send, sent [sɛnt], sent
🅗 (1) send sb sth　寄送某物給某人
　 = send sth to sb
　 (2) send sth/sb in
　　 遞交某物／派遣某人

▸ Mr. Parker sent a copy of the contract.
派克先生寄來了合約的影本。

▸ Duncan sent his girlfriend a bunch of flowers.
= Duncan sent a bunch of flowers to his girlfriend.
鄧肯寄給他女友一束花。

▸ Vera sent in her university applications last month.
薇拉上個月遞送了大學申請表。

▸ Martin sent the email to the wrong person.
馬丁把電子郵件寄錯對象了。

▸ Michelle was sent to the company's Taipei office.
蜜雪兒被派到公司的臺北辦公處。

▸ The police were sent in to break up the riot.
警方被派送去平息暴動。

mail [mel]
n. 郵件 (集合名詞，不可數) & *vt.* 郵寄 (信)

🅗 by mail　藉由書信，用郵件的方式
衍 mailman [ˋmelˏmən] *n.* 郵差
　 = postman [ˋpostmən]
似 post [post] *n.* 郵件 & *vt.* 郵寄〔英〕②

▸ You can contact me by mail.
你可藉由書信跟我聯絡。

▸ Could you mail the letter for me?
可否請你替我寄這封信？

email [ˈiˌmel]
n. 電子郵件 & *vt.* 對……發送電子郵件

▶ I wrote an email to my friend in America.
我寫了一封電子郵件給我在美國的友人。

▶ Email me as soon as you get any news.
你一收到任何消息就發電子郵件給我。

13 camera [ˈkæmərə] *n.* 相機

🔑 a digital camera　數位相機

▶ Could you take a picture of me with my camera?
能不能麻煩您用我的相機為我照一張相？

photograph [ˈfotəˌgræf]
n. 照片 (= photo [ˈfoto]) & *vt.* 照相

🔑 take a photograph　拍照
衍 photography [fəˈtɑgrəfɪ] *n.* 攝影 ④
似 picture [ˈpɪktʃɚ] *n.* 照片；圖片 ①

▶ I took some photographs in front of the tower.
我在高塔前拍了幾張相片。

▶ We photographed a lot of beautiful scenery during our trip.
旅途中我們拍了很多美景的照片。

14 angry [ˈæŋgrɪ] *a.* 生氣的

🔑 (1) be angry with / at sb
生某人的氣
(2) be angry about / at sth
生某事物的氣
衍 angrily [ˈæŋgrɪlɪ] *adv.* 憤怒地

▶ Don't worry. I'm not angry with you.
別擔心。我沒生你的氣。

▶ Eddie was angry at the government's position.
艾迪對政府的立場感到憤怒。

mad [mæd] *a.* 生氣的；瘋狂的〔英〕

🔑 (1) be mad at / about...
對……生氣
(2) be mad about / for / on sb/sth
非常喜歡某人 / 某物〔英〕

▶ Melody is mad about the new rules at work.
美樂蒂對工作上的新規定感到憤怒。

▶ Nina is mad for that new pop star.
妮娜非常喜歡那位剛出道的流行歌手。

15 snake [snek] *n.* 蛇 & *vi.* & *vt.* 蜿蜒地展延

🔑 snake its way　彎彎曲曲地延伸
延伸 python [ˈpaɪθɑn] *n.* 蟒蛇

▶ I have been afraid of snakes since I was a little girl.
我從小就怕蛇。

▶ The famous road snakes along the coast.
那條知名的道路沿著海岸蜿蜒。

▶ The line of people snaked its way through the streets.
排隊人龍蜿蜒於街道中。

16 fat [fæt] *a.* 胖的 & *n.* 脂肪

衍 fatty [ˈfætɪ]
a. 脂肪多的 & *n.* 胖子（口語）

▶ Jenny used to be fat, but now she's thin.
珍妮以前很胖，不過現在很瘦。

反 thin [θɪn] *a.* 瘦的 ①

延伸 low-fat [ˌloˈfæt] *a.* 低脂的
a low-fat diet　低脂飲食

▶ Bears need to increase their fat before winter.
熊需要在冬天來臨之前增加牠們的脂肪。

---

slim [slɪm] *a.* 苗條的；微小的

片 have a slim chance of...
　……的機會微乎其微

似 (1) thin [θɪn] *a.* 瘦的 ①
　(2) skinny [ˈskɪnɪ]
　　a. 皮包骨的 (有時帶有負面意味) ③

▶ Jennifer stays slim by exercising regularly.
珍妮佛靠規律的運動維持苗條身材。

▶ The company has a slim chance of earning profits this year.
這家公司今年獲利的希望甚微。

17　am [ˌeˈɛm] *adv.* 上午 (= a.m. = A.M. = AM)

用法 a.m. 及 p.m. 通常用小寫，必須置於阿拉伯數字後，且不可與 o'clock 並用。
a.m. 10 (✕)
ten a.m. (✕)
10 o'clock a.m. (✕)
→ 10 a.m. (○)　上午 10 點

▶ The meeting will start at 10 am.
會議將於上午 10 點召開。

---

pm [ˌpiˈɛm]
adv. 下午 (= p.m. = P.M. = PM)

▶ It's 2:30 pm in New York right now.
紐約現在是下午 2 點 30 分。

18　bread [brɛd] *n.* 麵包 (集合名詞，不可數)

▶ Wendy baked some bread for her children.
溫蒂烤了些麵包給孩子吃。

19　fun [fʌn] *n.* 樂趣 (不可數) & *a.* 有趣的，愉快的

片 (1) have fun + V-ing　……很愉快
　= have a good time + V-ing
　(2) make fun of sb　取笑某人

▶ We had a lot of fun chatting last night.
我們昨晚聊天聊得很愉快。

▶ Don't make fun of John. He is so embarrassed.
不要取笑約翰。他很尷尬。

▶ This is a fun book to read.
這是一本讀起來很有趣的書。

---

funny [ˈfʌnɪ] *a.* 滑稽的；奇怪的

▶ The manager told a funny story, but no one laughed.
經理講了一個滑稽的故事，不過卻沒有人捧場。

▶ Do you think this soup tastes funny?
你覺得這湯喝起來怪怪的嗎？

20　tired [taɪrd] *a.* 感到疲倦的；感到厭煩的

片 (1) be tired from + N/V-ing
　　因……而勞累
　(2) be tired of + N/V-ing
　　對……感到厭煩
　= be bored with

衍 (1) tire [taɪr] *vt.* 使疲倦；使厭倦 &
　　n. 輪胎（= tyre〔英〕）②
　(2) tiresome [ˋtaɪrsəm]
　　a. 令人厭倦的 ⑥

▶ Michael was tired from working.
麥可因工作而疲累。

▶ We are tired of hearing Ben's complaints.
我們對聽班的抱怨感到厭煩了。

tiring [ˋtaɪrɪŋ] *a.* 令人疲倦的

▶ It has been a rather long and tiring day.
這真是個相當漫長又累人的一天。

21　bottle [ˋbɑtḷ] *n.* 瓶子 & *vt.* 將……裝入瓶中

片 a bottle of...　一瓶……

衍 bottleneck [ˋbɑtḷˏnɛk] *n.* 瓶頸；隘路

延伸 bottled water　瓶裝水

▶ There is a bottle of juice on the table.
桌上有一瓶果汁。

▶ Jim bottles fresh mountain spring water.
吉姆將新鮮的山泉水裝入瓶中。

22　brown [braʊn] *a.* 棕色的 & *n.* 棕色 & *vt.* (食物) 烹調至棕色

▶ Chelsea has big, beautiful brown eyes.
雀兒喜有一雙又大又漂亮的棕色眼睛。

▶ We've decided to paint the walls light brown.
我們決定把牆壁漆成淺咖啡色。

▶ The recipe says to brown the meat first.
食譜上說要先把肉煎到褐色。

23　coffee [ˋkɑfi] *n.* 咖啡

延伸 caffeine [kæˋfin] *n.* 咖啡因 ⑥

▶ Would you like to join me for a coffee?
你想跟我一起喝杯咖啡嗎？

24　bow [bo] *n.* 弓；蝴蝶結 & [baʊ] *vi.* 鞠躬 & *n.* 鞠躬；船首

片 (1) wear a bow
　　繫蝴蝶結；帶上蝴蝶領結
　(2) bow to...
　　向……鞠躬 / 低頭 / 讓步
　(3) take / give a bow　一鞠躬

▶ The tribesmen went hunting with bows and arrows.
這些部落的族人用弓箭打獵。

▶ The girl is wearing a big bow in her hair.
這個女孩繫了一個大蝴蝶結在頭髮上。

▶ Never bow to terrorism.
= Never yield to terrorism.
= Never surrender to terrorism.

千萬不要屈服於恐怖主義。

＊terrorism [`tɛrə,rɪzəm] *n.* 恐怖主義

▶ All the actors and actresses took a bow on the stage when the show was over.

表演結束時，所有演員都站在臺上一鞠躬。

▶ Three sailors stood on the bow of the boat.

船頭站了 3 名水手。

Unit 18

1801-1805

1　popcorn [ˈpɑpˌkɔrn] *n.* 爆米花（不可數）

🔲 a bag of popcorn 　一袋爆米花

▶ I love to eat popcorn while watching a movie.
我喜歡在看電影時吃爆米花。

2　holiday [ˈhɑləˌde] *n.* （法定）節日；假日〔英〕（= vacation〔美〕）

🔲 (1) a national holiday 　國定假日
(2) be on holiday 　在度假中〔英〕
= be on vacation〔美〕

▶ We don't have to go to work tomorrow because it's a national holiday.
我們明天不用上班，因為明天是國定假日。

▶ On holidays, I like to stay at home and listen to music.
每逢假日我喜歡待在家裡聽音樂。

3　smell [smɛl] *n.* 氣味 & *vt.* 聞到 & *vi.* 聞起來；散發異味

🔲 smell, smelled [smɛld] / smelt [smɛlt], smelled / smelt

🔲 smelly [ˈsmɛlɪ] *a.* 臭的

🔲 smell 為感官動詞，後加形容詞，表示『聞起來……』。其他感官動詞還有：look（看起來）、sound（聽起來）、taste（嚐起來）、feel（感覺起來）

▶ There is a bad smell in this room.
這房間有一股臭味。

▶ I smelled something burning in the kitchen.
我聞到廚房裡有燒焦的味道。

▶ Those flowers smell wonderful.
那些花聞起來很香。

▶ Your feet smell. Stay away from me.
你的腳好臭。離我遠一點。

4　ice [aɪs] *n.* 冰（不可數）

🔲 icy [ˈaɪsɪ] *a.* 冰的，結冰的 ③

▶ May I have some ice in my glass of water?
我能不能在這杯水裡加一些冰塊？

5　dish [dɪʃ] *n.* 碗盤；菜餚 & *vi.* & *vt.* 說八卦

🔲 dishes [ˈdɪʃɪz]
🔲 (1) do / wash the dishes 　洗碗盤
(2) dish on... 　八卦……
(3) dish the dirt (on sb) 　揭發（某人的）醜事

▶ It's your turn to do the dishes.
輪到你洗碗了。

▶ My favorite dish is my mother's spring rolls.
我最喜歡的一道菜是我媽媽做的春捲。

▶ The actor dished on his co-stars in the interview.
該演員在訪問中說出了與他合作的明星的八卦。

▶ Come on—dish the dirt on Sophie!
快一點 —— 跟我說蘇菲的八卦！

bowl [bol] *n.* 碗

🔲 a bowl of... 　一碗……

▶ I can eat five bowls of rice for a meal.
我一餐可以吃下 5 碗飯。

1805-1811

plate [plet] *n.* 盤子；牌子 & *vt.* 電鍍

(1) a license plate　車牌
(2) have a lot on one's plate
　　事情很多
(3) be plated with...　是鍍……的

▶ Did you put the fish on my plate?
　你在我的盤子上放了魚肉嗎？

▶ Helen took a peek at the car's license plate.
　海倫偷看了那輛車的車牌。
　*take a peek　偷看

▶ I have a lot on my plate right now, so I can't go to Canada with you.
　我現在很忙，所以無法和你一起去加拿大。

▶ The king's car is plated with gold.
　國王的座車是鍍金的。

6　dig [dɪg] *vt.* 挖掘 & *n.* 嘲諷，挖苦

dig, dug [dʌg], dug
take a dig at sb　嘲諷 / 挖苦某人

▶ Let's dig a hole and plant the tree.
　我們挖個洞把樹種下去。

▶ Nick took several digs at John in his best man speech.
　尼克在發表伴郎祝賀詞時數次挖苦約翰。

7　round [raʊnd] *n.* 回合；巡視 (此意恆用複數) & *a.* 圓的 & *prep.* & *adv.* 繞著〔英〕(= around〔美〕) & *vt.* 繞過

(1) in the first / second round
　　在第 1 / 2 回合
(2) make one's rounds　巡視
(3) round the bend　過 / 轉彎
延伸 a round-trip ticket　來回票

▶ Our team was eliminated in the first round.
　我們的隊伍在第 1 回合遭到淘汰。

▶ The doctor makes his rounds first thing every morning.
　這名醫生每天早上第一件事就是巡房。

▶ The lady has a round face and a double chin.
　那位女士有張圓臉及雙下巴。

▶ The Earth moves round the Sun.
= The Earth moves around the Sun.
　地球繞著太陽轉。

▶ When Sally called my name, I turned round.
　莎莉叫我時，我就轉身。

▶ The car rounded the bend at high speed.
　這臺車高速過彎。

8　dear [dɪr] *a.* 親愛的；珍貴的；昂貴的〔英〕(= expensive) & *n.* 親愛的 (親切友好的稱呼)；好人 & *adv.* 珍視地；昂貴地〔英〕

(1) be dear to sb　對某人來說很珍貴
(2) hold sth dear　珍惜某物
= value sth
= cherish sth

▶ My dear husband gave me this scarf.
　我親愛的老公送我這條圍巾。

▶ Friendship is very dear to me.
　友誼對我來說非常珍貴。

(3) cost sb dear
花某人很多錢；使某人付出代價

衍 dearly [ˈdɪrlɪ] adv. 昂貴地；非常

▶ The car is too dear for me. I can't afford it.
那輛車對我來說太貴了。我買不起。

▶ Can I help you with those bags, dear?
親愛的，要我幫你拿那些袋子嗎？

▶ Kevin helped me carry my shopping—he's such a dear.
凱文幫我拿購買的物品 —— 他真是個好人。

▶ I'll hold your love dear to my heart.
我會在心中珍惜你的愛。

▶ That one bad decision cost Harry dear.
那個錯誤的決定讓哈利得不償失。

---

9 bath [bæθ] n. 洗澡

片 take a bath   泡澡

衍 (1) bathroom [ˈbæθˌrum] n. 浴室 ①
(2) bathe [beθ]
    vt. 沐浴，使沈浸於…… ②
(3) bathtub [ˈbæθˌtʌb] n. 浴缸

▶ Daniel was taking a bath when Angela called him.
安琪拉打給丹尼爾時，他正在泡澡。

---

shower [ˈʃaʊɚ]
n. 淋浴；陣雨 & vi. (像陣雨般) 落下

片 (1) take a shower   淋浴
(2) a shower cap   浴帽
(3) shower gel   沐浴乳
(4) shower down   (像陣雨般) 落下

▶ I was taking a shower when the phone rang.
我正在淋浴時電話就響了。

▶ Take an umbrella with you in case of a shower.
帶把傘在身上以防陣雨。

▶ The building collapsed and ashes showered down from everywhere.
建築物倒塌，灰塵從四面八方落下。

---

10 fish [fɪʃ] n. 魚 & vt. 釣魚，捕魚

複 單複數同形
片 go fishing   去釣魚
衍 fisherman [ˈfɪʃɚmən] n. 漁夫 ②
用法 若要表示不同種類的魚，則可將 fish 寫為複數 fishes。

▶ Ted caught lots of fish today.
泰德今天捕到很多魚。

▶ We went fishing soon after the exam was over.
一考完試我們便釣魚去了。

---

11 kick [kɪk] vt. & n. 踢

片 give... a kick   踢……一下

▶ The soccer player kicked the ball into the goal.
那位足球選手把球踢進球門。
*goal [gol] n. 球門

▶ The naughty boy gave the dog a kick.
這個頑皮的男孩踢了這隻狗一下。

12 smoke [smok] *n.* 煙 (不可數) & *vi.* 抽菸;冒煙

片 quit smoking 戒菸

延伸 chain-smoker [`tʃɛn,smokɚ]
　　n. 菸癮很大的人

▶ During the fire, smoke filled the air.
　火災時煙霧瀰漫各處。

▶ There's no smoke without fire.
　無火不生煙 / 無風不起浪。── 諺語

▶ You should quit smoking as soon as possible.
　你應該儘快戒菸。

▶ A car is parked along the road. Its hood is up and the engine is smoking.
　有輛車停在路邊。它的引擎蓋開著,引擎正冒煙。

13 god [gɑd] *n.* 神

用法 god 若寫成大寫的 God,專指基督教的上帝,不加冠詞。

▶ Mars is the god of war in Roman mythology.
　在羅馬神話中,馬爾斯是戰神。
　＊mythology [mɪ`θɑlədʒɪ] *n.* 神話

goddess [`gɑdɪs] *n.* 女神

▶ Venus is called the goddess of love.
　維納斯被稱為愛神。

14 tail [tel] *n.* 尾巴;尾端 & *vt.* 跟蹤,尾隨

片 (1) wag a tail 搖尾巴
　(2) can't make head nor tail of sth
　　　完全無法了解某事

▶ The dog was chasing its own tail.
　那隻狗正在追自己的尾巴。

▶ I can't make head nor tail of this math problem.
　我實在搞不懂這道數學題。

▶ Johnny always tails his sister when she goes out on a date.
　每次他姊姊出去約會時,強尼都會跟蹤她。

15 sir [sɝ] *n.* 先生

反 madam [`mædəm] *n.* 女士 ⑥

▶ May I take your order now, sir?
　先生,我可以為您點餐了嗎?

16 stair [stɛr] *n.* (一階) 樓梯

衍 (1) staircase [`stɛr,kes] *n.* 樓梯
　(2) downstairs [,daun`stɛrz]
　　　adv. 在樓下 ②
　(3) upstairs [,ʌp`stɛrz] *adv.* 在樓上 ②

▶ Jimmy ran down the stairs to answer the phone.
= Jimmy ran downstairs to answer the phone.
　吉米跑下樓梯去接電話。

17　potato [pəˈteto] *n.* 馬鈴薯

複 potatoes [pəˈtetoz]
片 (1) a couch potato
　　成天坐在沙發上看電視的人
　　(2) small potatoes
　　小人物（常用複數形，不可數）
　　(3) potato chips　洋芋片

▶ My dad ordered a steak with a baked potato.
我爸點了一客牛排，搭配烤馬鈴薯。

▶ Don't be such a couch potato─get up and move!
別當懶骨頭 ── 起身動一動！

▶ The college graduate is only small potatoes in this company.
那位大學畢業生只是這家公司的小人物而已。

---

tomato [təˈmeto] *n.* 番茄
複 tomatoes [təˈmetoz]
延伸 ketchup [ˈkɛtʃʌp] *n.* 番茄醬 ②

▶ My grandfather grows his own tomatoes.
我爺爺自己種番茄。

18　dirty [ˈdɝtɪ] *a.* 髒的；卑鄙的，差勁的 & *vt.* 使變髒；貶低

三 dirty, dirtied [ˈdɝtɪd], dirtied
片 (1) play dirty tricks on sb
　　對某人耍花招
　　(2) give sb a dirty look
　　給某人白眼；瞪某人一眼
衍 dirt [dɝt] *n.* 泥土 ③
反 clean [klin] *a.* 乾淨的 ①

▶ My blue jeans are dirty and have to be washed.
我的牛仔褲很髒，需要洗了。

▶ Sam always played dirty tricks on Johnny when they were in high school.
高中時，山姆總是對強尼耍花招。

▶ Jenny gave me a dirty look after I commented on her weight.
我評論珍妮的體重後，她給了我一個白眼。

▶ Peter dirtied the cream rug with his shoes.
彼得的鞋子把奶油色地毯弄髒了。

▶ The prime minister's words dirtied the government's reputation.
該首相的話敗壞了政府的名聲。

19　map [mæp] *n.* 地圖 & *vt.* 繪製成地圖；詳細計劃

三 map, mapped [mæpt], mapped
片 (1) map... out　安排……
　　(2) map out a plan　擬定計畫
　　= draw up a plan

▶ Follow the map, and you'll find the post office.
按照地圖的指示，你就可以找到郵局。

▶ Some regions have not been mapped yet.
有些地區還沒被繪製成地圖。

▶ We're going to map out our road trip for next week.
我們要著手詳細計劃下星期的公路旅遊了。

20　mud [mʌd] *n.* (爛) 泥巴 (不可數)

衍 muddy [ˈmʌdɪ] *a.* 泥濘的 ④
似 soil [sɔɪl] *n.* 泥土 ②

▶ The car got stuck in the mud.
車子陷在爛泥裡動彈不得。

21 joke [dʒok] *n.* 玩笑 & *vi.* 開玩笑

片 (1) play a joke on sb　對某人開玩笑
(2) joke about sth　取笑某事

▶ I was only playing a joke on you. I wasn't serious.
我只是對你開個玩笑罷了。我不是認真的。

▶ Don't joke about Ben's poor English.
不要取笑班的破英文。

22 hurt [hɜt] *vt.* 傷害 & *vi.* 疼痛 & *n.* 傷，痛

三 三態同形
片 get hurt　受傷

▶ Many people got hurt in the accident.
這次意外有很多人受傷。

▶ My head is hurting badly.
我頭痛得要命。

▶ Johnny is trying to get over the hurt of being dumped.
強尼正設法克服被甩的傷痛。
＊dump [dʌmp] *vt.* 遺棄 (戀人)

23 music [ˈmjuzɪk] *n.* 音樂

片 (1) listen to music　聽音樂
(2) play music　演奏音樂
(3) be music to sb's ears
(話語) 令某人非常開心

▶ Phoebe likes to listen to music while she works.
菲比喜歡一邊聽音樂一邊工作。

▶ The guitarist will play music in the background.
吉他手將在後臺演奏音樂。

▶ The news of Tom's safe arrival was music to my ears.
湯姆平安抵達的消息讓我非常開心。

24 piano [pɪˈæno] *n.* 鋼琴

片 play the piano　彈鋼琴
衍 pianist [pɪˈænɪst] *n.* 鋼琴家 ⑥

▶ Rebecca started playing the piano at the age of 5.
蕾貝卡 5 歲時開始彈鋼琴。

violin [ˌvaɪəˈlɪn] *n.* 小提琴
片 play the violin　拉小提琴
衍 violinist [ˌvaɪəˈlɪnɪst] *n.* 小提琴手 ⑥

▶ Do you play the violin?
你會拉小提琴嗎？

drum [drʌm] *n.* 鼓
片 play the drums　打鼓
衍 drummer [ˈdrʌmɚ] *n.* 鼓手

▶ Peter is skilled in playing the drums.
彼得很會打鼓。

guitar [gɪˈtɑr] *n.* 吉他
片 play the guitar　彈吉他
衍 guitarist [gɪˈtɑrɪst] *n.* 吉他手

▶ I can't play the guitar, but I can play the piano.
我不會彈吉他，不過我會彈鋼琴。

25 **bite** [baɪt] *vt.* 咬 & *n.* 咬一口；少量的食物 (恆用單數)

- bite, bit [bɪt], bitten [ˈbɪtṇ]
- (1) have a bite of...　　咬一口⋯⋯
  (2) give... a bite　　咬⋯⋯一口
  (3) grab / have a bite to eat
  　　匆匆吃點東西

▶ The little girl tends to bite her nails when she is bored or nervous.
那個小女生無聊或緊張時，往往會咬指甲。

▶ The cake looks delicious; let me have a bite of it.
這蛋糕看起來很好吃，讓我咬一口吧。

▶ Give the cake a bite and tell me if you like it.
吃一口那塊蛋糕然後告訴我你喜不喜歡。

▶ Let's grab a bite to eat after the game.
比賽結束後我們去吃點東西吧。

26 **lamp** [læmp] *n.* 燈

- a table lamp　　檯燈
- light [laɪt] *n.* 燈；光線 ①

▶ I can't read without a table lamp.
沒有檯燈我無法閱讀。

27 **breakfast** [ˈbrɛkfəst] *n.* 早餐 & *vi.* 吃早餐

- eat / have... for breakfast
  早餐吃⋯⋯

▶ Scott always eats peanut butter on toast for breakfast.
史考特早餐總是吃花生醬吐司。

▶ Shall we breakfast on the balcony this morning?
我們今天早上在陽臺上吃早餐好嗎？

lunch [lʌntʃ] *n.* 午餐 & *vi.* 吃午餐
- eat / have... for lunch　　午餐吃⋯⋯

▶ Jack likes to eat vegetarian food for lunch.
傑克午餐喜歡吃蔬食。

▶ We lunched in the hotel's restaurant.
我們在飯店的餐廳吃午餐。

lunchtime [ˈlʌntʃˌtaɪm] *n.* 午餐時間
- at lunchtime　　午餐時

▶ The cafeteria serves sandwiches at lunchtime.
這家自助餐店在午餐時間供應三明治。
＊cafeteria [ˌkæfəˈtɪrɪə] *n.* 自助餐店

dinner [ˈdɪnɚ] *n.* 晚餐
- eat / have... for dinner　　晚餐吃⋯⋯

▶ I don't want to eat pizza for dinner again.
我不想又吃披薩當晚餐了。

1901-1911

1 ticket [ˈtɪkɪt] n. 票；罰單

片 (1) a ticket for...　觀賞……的票
(2) a ticket to + 地方　去某地的票
(3) a speeding / parking ticket
超速 / 違停罰單

▶ Tim has two tickets for the concert. Would you like to go with him?
提姆有 2 張演唱會的票，你要和他一起去嗎？

▶ My husband was upset because he got a ticket for speeding.
我老公不開心，因為他超速被開了一張罰單。

2 nurse [nɜs] n. 護士 & vt. 看護，照顧；餵母乳

衍 (1) nursery [ˈnɜsərɪ] n. 幼兒室 ④
(2) nursing [ˈnɜsɪŋ]
n. 看護（工作）（不可數）
a nursing home　療養院，安養院

▶ The nurse is very nice to her patients.
那位護士對她的病人很好。

▶ Eric has been nursing his elderly sister for over twenty years but has never complained.
艾瑞克照顧他姊姊超過 20 年了，卻從沒有怨言。

▶ We have a private room where you can nurse your baby.
我們有一間私人房間，你可以在那兒餵寶寶母乳。

3 welcome [ˈwɛlkəm] vt. & n. 歡迎 & a. 受歡迎的

片 (1) give sb a (warm) welcome
給某人（熱烈的）歡迎
(2) be welcome to V
歡迎做……；可以隨意做……
(3) You're welcome.
（回應他人道謝時）別客氣。

▶ The host and hostess welcomed us warmly.
男女主人熱情地歡迎我們。

▶ Stephen's friends gave him a warm welcome when he got back from the hospital.
史蒂芬從醫院回來時，他的朋友給予熱烈的歡迎。

▶ You are welcome to come to our house at any time you want.
隨時歡迎你來我們家玩。

4 hungry [ˈhʌŋgrɪ] a. 飢餓的；渴望的

片 be hungry for...　渴望得到……
= be eager for...
衍 hunger [ˈhʌŋgɚ] n. 飢餓 ③
a hunger strike　絕食抗議

▶ If you are hungry, there is some food in the fridge.
你餓的話，冰箱裡有些食物。

▶ Charlie is lonely and hungry for attention.
查理很寂寞，並渴望受到關注。

5 lucky [ˈlʌkɪ] a. 幸運的

片 (1) a lucky charm　幸運符
(2) be lucky to V　很幸運做……

▶ Greg answered the question correctly, but it was a lucky guess.
葛瑞格答對了這道題目，但只是運氣好猜對了而已。

衍 (1) luck [lʌk] *n.* 運氣 ②
   (2) luckily [ˈlʌkəlɪ] *adv.* 幸運地
似 fortunate [ˈfɔrtʃənət] *a.* 幸運的 ④
反 unlucky [ʌnˈlʌkɪ] *a.* 不幸運的

▶ Anita believes that this lucky charm will bring her good luck.
安妮塔相信這個幸運符會為她帶來好運。

▶ Carl is lucky to have a friend like you.
卡爾很幸運有你這樣的朋友。

6 sheep [ʃip] *n.* 綿羊

複 單複數同形
片 a flock of sheep   一群羊
延伸 lamb [læm] *n.* 小羊；羊肉 ②

▶ We saw a flock of sheep grazing on the hillside.
我們看見一群羊在山坡上吃草。
*graze [grez] *vi.* (動物) 吃草
 hillside [ˈhɪlˌsaɪd] *n.* 山坡

7 brave [brev] *a.* 勇敢的

衍 bravery [ˈbrevərɪ] *n.* 勇敢 ③
似 (1) courageous [kəˈredʒəs]
    a. 勇敢的 ④
  (2) fearless [ˈfɪrləs] *a.* 無畏的

▶ Roy knows that a soldier must be brave in battle.
羅伊知道在戰鬥中，一名士兵必須要勇敢。

▶ Be brave, and everything will be fine.
勇敢一點，一切會沒事的。

8 basket [ˈbæskɪt] *n.* 籃子

▶ Mia placed some fruit in a basket.
米雅把一些水果放入籃內。

9 vegetable [ˈvɛdʒətəbl] *n.* 蔬菜

衍 (1) vegetarian [ˌvɛdʒəˈtɛrɪən]
    n. 素食者 ④
  (2) veggie [ˈvɛdʒɪ] *n.* 蔬菜

▶ Eat more vegetables and less meat.
多吃點蔬菜，少吃點肉。

10 rice [raɪs] *n.* 米 (不可數)

片 a grain of rice   一粒米

▶ Most Koreans eat rice daily.
大部分韓國人天天吃米飯。

11 bell [bɛl] *n.* 鈴，鐘；門鈴 (= doorbell [ˈdɔrˌbɛl])

片 a school / church bell
校鐘 / 教堂鐘

▶ When the bell rings, it's time to go to class.
鐘聲響起時，就是該上課的時候。

▶ Nora rushed to answer the door when she heard the bell ring.

= Nora rushed to answer the door when she heard the doorbell ring.
諾拉聽到門鈴響時，衝去應門。

12 taxicab [ˈtæksɪˌkæb] *n.* 計程車 (= taxi [ˈtæksɪ] = cab [kæb])

🅗 hail a taxicab / taxi / cab　攔計程車
▶ Hail a taxicab for the boss right now.
= Hail a taxi for the boss right now.
= Hail a cab for the boss right now.
現在馬上幫老闆攔一部計程車。

13 pie [paɪ] *n.* 派，餡餅

🅗 a piece / slice of pie　一片派
▶ We'd like a piece of apple pie with cream.
我們想要來一片蘋果派上面加奶油。

14 clothes [kloz] *n.* 衣服 (恆用複數)

🅗 (1) wear clothes　穿著衣服
(2) take off clothes　脫衣服
衍 (1) clothing [ˈkloðɪŋ]
n. 衣服 (總稱，不可數) ②
(2) clothe [kloð] *vt.* 給……衣服穿 ③
用法 clothes 視為複數名詞，其後動詞須使用複數動詞。

▶ Dianne likes to make her own clothes.
黛安喜歡自己做衣服。
▶ Josh's clothes are old, and he should buy new ones.
喬許的衣服都舊了，他應該買些新衣服。
▶ The three-year-old girl likes to wear pink clothes.
這名 3 歲的小女孩喜歡穿粉色的衣服。
▶ Hank took off all his clothes and dove into the pool.
漢克脫光衣服跳入泳池中。

shirt [ʃɜt] *n.* 襯衫
似 blouse [blaʊz] *n.* (女用) 襯衫 ③
▶ The shirt fits Rebecca well.
這件襯衫蕾貝卡穿起來很合身。

T-shirt [ˈtiˌʃɜt] *n.* T 恤
▶ Rick really likes the design of this T-shirt.
瑞克很喜歡這件 T 恤的設計。

15 smart [smɑrt] *a.* 聰明的

似 (1) bright [braɪt]
a. 聰明的；靈光的 ①
(2) clever [ˈklɛvɚ] *a.* 聰穎的 ②

▶ The smart child solved the puzzle in two minutes.
這個聰明的小孩只花 2 分鐘就解開謎題了。

stupid [ˈst(j)upɪd] *a.* 愚笨的
似 foolish [ˈfulɪʃ] *a.* 愚蠢的 ②
▶ Danny was so stupid to believe him.
丹尼會相信他的話真是太蠢了。

16 lion [ˈlaɪən] *n.* 獅子

🅗 a lion's den　龍潭虎穴，危險境地
衍 lionhearted [ˈlaɪənˌhɑrtɪd] *a.* 勇敢的
反 lioness [ˈlaɪənəs] *n.* 母獅

▶ On his trip to Africa, George saw many lions.
喬治的非洲之旅看到了許多獅子。
▶ Tim felt like he had entered a lion's den of angry customers.
提姆覺得自己進入了面對憤怒顧客們的危險境地。

tiger [ˋtaɪgɚ] *n.* 老虎
▸ There are not many wild tigers left in the world.
世界上的野生老虎不多了。

17　kiss [kɪs] *vt.* 親吻 & *n.* 吻

複 kisses [ˋkɪsɪz]
片 (1) kiss sb on the lips
親吻某人的雙唇
(2) kiss sb goodbye　和某人吻別
(3) give sb a kiss　吻某人一下
衍 kisser [ˋkɪsɚ] *n.* 接吻的人

▸ The prince kisses the princess on her lips.
王子親吻公主的雙唇。
▸ Mary kissed her boyfriend goodbye before he left.
瑪莉和男友吻別後，男友才離去。
▸ The mother gave her baby a kiss.
媽媽吻了她的小寶寶一下。

18　happy [ˋhæpɪ] *a.* 快樂的；樂意的；滿意的

片 (1) make sb happy　讓某人快樂
(2) be happy (that)...
對……感到快樂
(3) be happy to V
做……很快樂；很樂意做……
(4) be happy about / with...
對……感到滿意
= be satisfied with...
衍 happily [ˋhæpəlɪ] *adv.* 快樂地
似 (1) joyful [ˋdʒɔɪfəl] *a.* 喜悅的 ③
(2) cheerful [ˋtʃɪrfəl] *a.* 愉快的 ③
(3) delighted [dɪˋlaɪtɪd] *a.* 感到高興的
反 unhappy [ˌʌnˋhæpɪ] *a.* 不快樂的

▸ Ronnie is willing to do anything to make his child happy.
羅尼願意做任何能讓孩子快樂的事情。
▸ Elsa is happy that everything's going well.
艾莎為一切都順利進行感到開心。
▸ Carl said he would be happy to help Susan.
卡爾說他很願意幫助蘇珊。
▸ I am happy with my current job.
= I am satisfied with my current job.
我對目前的工作感到很滿意。

glad [glæd]
a. 高興的，愉快的；樂意的

片 (1) be glad (that)...　很高興……
(2) be glad to V
做……很高興；做……很樂意

▸ Vicky was glad that her team won the game.
維琪很高興她的隊伍贏得了比賽。
▸ Eric said he would be glad to give Monica a ride.
艾瑞克說他很樂意載莫妮卡一程。

happiness [ˋhæpɪnəs]
n. 幸福，快樂 (不可數)

似 joy [dʒɔɪ] *n.* 高興 ①

▸ Everyone is eager for happiness in life.
每個人都渴望得到生命中的幸福。

19　sad [sæd] *a.* 難過的

片 (1) a sad movie / story
悲傷的故事 / 電影

▸ The movie was so sad that Brenda cried.
這部電影太悲傷，以致布蘭達哭了。

(2) be sad to V　做⋯⋯令人難過

衍 (1) sadly [ˋsædlɪ] *adv.* 悲傷地

　　(2) sadden [ˋsædn̩] *vt.* 使悲傷

似 sorrowful [ˋsɑrəfəl] *a.* 悲傷的 ⑥

▶ It's really sad to see so much litter on the beach.
看到沙灘上那麼多垃圾真是令人難過。

---

sadness [ˋsædnəs] *n.* 悲傷 (不可數)

似 sorrow [ˋsɑro] *n.* 悲傷 ③

▶ After losing his girlfriend, Tom was trapped in sadness.
在失去了女友後，湯姆便深陷悲傷中。

20　mouse [maʊs] *n.* 老鼠，家鼠；滑鼠

複 mice [maɪs] / mouses

片 a mouse pad　滑鼠墊

用法 mouse 表『老鼠』時，複數形恆為 mice。

▶ There are lots of mice running around the back alley.
有許多老鼠在後巷跑來跑去。

▶ Please click the left mouse button here.
請在這裡點滑鼠的左鍵。

21　soup [sup] *n.* 湯 (不可數)

片 (1) a bowl of soup　一碗湯

　　(2) eat / have soup　喝湯

▶ Eat the soup while it's hot.
趁熱的時候趕快喝湯。

22　loud [laʊd] *a.* 大聲的 & *adv.* 大聲地，吵鬧地 (= loudly)

衍 loudly [ˋlaʊdlɪ] *adv.* 大聲地

反 (1) quiet [ˋkwaɪət] *a.* 安靜的 ①

　　(2) soft [sɔft] *a.* 輕柔的 ②

▶ Don't be too loud. My grandmother is taking a nap.
不要太大聲。我奶奶正在睡午覺。

▶ You'll have to speak louder. I can't hear you.
你得說大聲一點。我聽不見你講話。

23　rope [rop] *n.* 繩子

片 (1) jump / skip rope
跳繩 (rope 之前不加 the)

　　(2) learn / know the ropes
知道訣竅 (ropes 恆用複數)

▶ The children were jumping rope in the park.
這些孩子在公園裡跳繩。

▶ Glen is new to our company; he doesn't know the ropes yet.
葛倫才剛來我們公司，他還沒掌握到訣竅。

24　bat [bæt] *n.* 蝙蝠；球棒 & *vt.* & *vi.* 用球棒打

三 bat, batted [ˋbætɪd], batted

片 a baseball bat　棒球棒

衍 batter [ˋbætɚ] *n.* 打擊手 ⑥

▶ We saw a bat fly through the air.
我們看到有隻蝙蝠飛過天空。

▶ The bat was broken into two halves.
那支球棒斷成兩半。

▶ Randy batted the ball into the right field.
藍迪把球打到右外野。

baseball [ˈbesˌbɔl] *n.* 棒球

▶ Vince's favorite sport to play is baseball.
文斯最喜歡玩的運動是棒球。

---

25 spell [spɛl] *vt. & vi.* 拼(字) & *n.* 咒語

片 cast / put a spell (on sb)
（對某人）施魔咒

衍 spelling [ˈspɛlɪŋ] *n.* 拼字 ②

▶ How do you spell that word?
那個字要怎麼拼？

▶ The wizard cast a spell that turned the prince into a turtle.
巫師下了咒語，把王子變成了烏龜。

---

26 ghost [gost] *n.* 鬼

片 (1) a ghost story 鬼故事
(2) a ghost ship 幽靈船

▶ It is said that this castle is haunted by ghosts.
傳聞說這棟城堡有鬼魂出沒。
＊haunt [hɔnt] *vt.* (鬼魂) 常出沒於

---

27 flower [ˈflauɚ] *n.* 花 & *vi.* 開花

片 (1) a flower garden 花園
(2) a bunch / bouquet of flowers
一束花
＊bouquet [buˈke] *n.* 花束

▶ Grace likes to look at the flowers in her garden.
葛瑞絲喜歡看著花園裡的花朵。

▶ Alan bought a big bouquet of flowers for his wife.
艾倫買了一大束花給他的老婆。

▶ When that plant flowers, it looks quite beautiful.
那株植物開花時會看起來十分漂亮。

---

rose [roz] *n.* 玫瑰花

片 (1) a rose bush 玫瑰花叢
(2) a bunch / bouquet of roses
一束玫瑰花

衍 rosy [ˈrozɪ] *a.* 玫瑰色的

▶ There are rose bushes in my garden.
我的花園內有玫瑰花叢。

▶ David gave his mother a bunch of roses for her birthday.
大衛送媽媽一束玫瑰花慶祝她生日。

---

28 orange [ˈɔrɪndʒ] *n.* 柳橙；橙色 & *a.* 橙色的

片 (1) a slice of orange 一片柳橙
(2) (a glass of) orange juice
（一杯）柳橙汁

延伸 tangerine [ˈtændʒəˌrin] *n.* 橘子 ③

▶ Cindy likes orange juice best.
辛蒂最喜歡柳橙汁了。

▶ We saw Jack at once because he was dressed in orange.
我們馬上就看到傑克了，因為他穿橘色衣服。

▶ The sky turns into a deep orange color when the sun sets.
太陽下山時，天空變成深橘色。

1929

29 meal [mil] *n.* 一餐

(1) a heavy / light meal
　　豐盛 / 簡便的一餐

(2) have / eat a meal　吃飯

(3) serve a meal　　　上 / 供餐

延伸 feast [fist] *n.* 筵席，大餐 ④

▶ Most people have three meals a day.
　大部分的人一天吃 3 餐。

▶ The waiter served our meals soon after he took our orders.
　服務生幫我們點餐不久後就送餐過來了。

172

Unit 20

2001-2005

1　fan [fæn] *n.* 扇子；電扇；迷，粉絲 & *vt.* 搧(風)；激起，煽動

三 fan, fanned [fænd], fanned

片 (1) a fan club　粉絲俱樂部
　 (2) fan the flames (of sth)
　　 (給某事) 火上加油 / 搧風點火

似 stimulate [ˋstɪmjəˌlet] *vt.* 刺激 ⑤

▶ Turn on the fan. It's so hot here.
　把電風扇打開，這裡好熱。

▶ The movie star waved at his fans.
　這位影星向他的粉絲揮手。

▶ Alex is a huge fan of American football.
　艾力克斯是美式橄欖球的大粉絲。

▶ Katie sat in the hot sun, fanning her face.
　凱蒂坐在熱陽下，對著臉搧風。

▶ What Tom said only fanned the flames of Jane's anger.
　湯姆說的話只是給珍的怒氣火上加油。

2　zero [ˋzɪro] *n.* 零

複 zeros / zeroes [ˋzɪroz]

片 (1) from zero　從零開始，從頭開始
　 (2) above / below zero
　　 在零度以上 / 下

▶ Bill got a zero on the test.
　這次考試比爾考了零分。

▶ Your chances of winning are practically zero.
　你獲勝的機會幾乎是零。

▶ It's so cold! The temperature must be below zero.
　天氣真冷！溫度一定是在零度以下。

3　toy [tɔɪ] *n.* 玩具 & *vi.* 玩弄

片 toy with sb/sth
　玩弄某人 (的感情) / 玩弄某事物 (如物
　品、感情等)

▶ The little boy is playing with his toys in the corner.
　那個小男孩在角落裡玩玩具。

▶ You should never toy with other people's feelings.
　你永遠都不應該玩弄別人的感情。

▶ Rosie toyed with her hair as she chatted with the handsome man.
　蘿西和那英俊的男子聊天時，一邊玩弄著自己的頭髮。

4　robot [ˋrobɑt] *n.* 機器人

衍 robotic [roˋbɑtɪk]
　a. 機器人的；呆板的

▶ We need a robot to do this dangerous job.
　我們需要機器人來做這份危險的工作。

5　ant [ænt] *n.* 螞蟻

片 (1) a colony of ants　一窩螞蟻
　 (2) have / get ants in one's pants
　　 (因興奮、不安等) 某人坐不住

▶ There are hundreds of ants crawling on the cake.
　蛋糕上有數百隻螞蟻在爬。

▶ Sit down! Have you got ants in your pants?
坐下！你不能好好坐著嗎？

---

6 pet [pɛt] *n.* 寵物 & *vt.* 撫弄

目 pet, petted [ˋpɛtɪd], petted
片 (1) a pet dog / cat / store
　　寵物狗 / 貓 / 店
　　(2) keep (... as) a pet
　　養 (……當) 寵物

▶ My brother keeps a turtle as a pet.
我弟弟養了一隻烏龜當寵物。
▶ Judy pets her cat as she reads.
茱蒂一邊看書一邊撫弄她的貓。

---

7 ham [hæm] *n.* 火腿

片 (1) a ham sandwich　　火腿三明治
　　(2) ham and eggs　　火腿蛋

▶ Vincent always has ham and eggs for breakfast.
文森早餐總是吃火腿蛋。

---

8 born [bɔrn] *a.* 出生的；天生的

片 (1) be born in + 年分 / 國家
　　於某年分 / 某國家出生
　　(2) be born into + 家庭
　　出生在……的家庭
　　(3) be born to V　注定要做……
　　(4) be born with a silver spoon in one's mouth
　　某人含著金湯匙出生，某人是富裕家庭出身

▶ Barack Obama was born in Hawaii in 1961.
巴拉克·歐巴馬於 1961 年在夏威夷出生。
▶ Chloe was born into an ordinary family.
克蘿伊出生在平凡的家庭。
▶ Jason Mraz is a born singer.
傑森·瑪耶茲是天生的歌手。
▶ Robert was born to be an actor.
羅伯特注定要成為一名演員。
▶ That politician was born with a silver spoon in his mouth.
那名政治人物是含著金湯匙出生的。

---

9 world [wɝld] *n.* 世界，地球 (前面加定冠詞 the)；領域，界

片 travel the world　　環遊世界
似 (1) earth [ɝθ] *n.* 地球 ①
　　(2) globe [glob] *n.* 地球 ④

▶ It is Larry's dream to travel the world.
賴瑞的夢想是環遊世界。
▶ Jackie remains unknown outside of the art world.
潔琪對藝術界以外的事情一無所知。

worldwide [ˋwɝld͵waɪd]
a. 遍及全球的 & *adv.* 遍及全球地
似 (1) global [ˋglobl] *a.* 全球的 ③
　　(2) universal [͵junəˋvɝsl]
　　　 a. 全世界的 ④

▶ *Harry Potter* has attracted worldwide attention.
《哈利波特》吸引了全世界的注意。
▶ More than 10,000 companies worldwide use our products.
全球有超過 1 萬家公司使用我們的產品。

10 frog [frɑg] n. 青蛙

片 have (got) a frog in one's throat
聲音嘶啞

延伸 toad [tod] n. 癩蛤蟆，蟾蜍

▶ Kyle sees many frogs in the pond.
凱爾在池塘裡看到許多青蛙。

▶ Excuse me—I've got a frog in my throat.
抱歉 —— 我的聲音很沙啞。

11 homework [ˈhom,wɝk] n. 家庭作業 (不可數)

片 (1) do homework　做家庭作業

似 (1) assignment [əˈsaɪnmənt]
n. 功課；工作 (可數) ④

(2) schoolwork [ˈskul,wɝk]
n. 課堂作業 (不可數)

▶ Evan has to do a lot of homework every day.
艾凡每天都要做許多家庭作業。

12 juice [dʒus] n. 果汁

衍 juicy [ˈdʒusɪ] a. 多汁的 ③

▶ May I please have a glass of grape juice?
可以給我一杯葡萄汁嗎？

13 lazy [ˈlezɪ] a. 懶惰的；悠閒的

衍 (1) laziness [ˈlezɪnəs]
n. 懶惰 (不可數)

(2) lazily [ˈlezɪlɪ] adv. 懶散地

(3) lazybones [ˈlezɪ,bonz]
n. 懶惰的人 (單複數同形)

▶ I was too lazy to do all those house chores.
我太懶了，所以沒有做那些家事。

▶ Rhonda loves a lazy summer's day.
朗姐喜愛慵懶的夏天。

14 pants [pænts] n. 長褲 (褲管有兩條，故恆用複數) 〔美〕

片 a pair of pants　一條褲子

似 trousers [ˈtrauzɚz] n. 長褲〔英〕

▶ Scott is wearing a pair of dark blue pants and a white shirt.
史考特穿著一條深藍色的褲子跟一件白襯衫。

shorts [ʃɔrts]
n. 短褲 (褲管有兩條，故恆用複數)

片 (1) a pair of shorts　一條短褲

(2) short shorts　熱褲

▶ Hank likes to wear shorts when he's off duty.
漢克沒上班時喜歡穿短褲。

▶ Lily doesn't like to wear short shorts.
莉莉不喜歡穿熱褲。

jeans [dʒinz]
n. 牛仔褲 (褲管有兩條，故恆用複數)

片 a pair of jeans　一條牛仔褲

延伸 denim [ˈdɛnɪm] n. 牛仔布

▶ Rebecca looks great in blue jeans.
蕾貝卡穿藍色牛仔褲很好看。

skirt [skɜt] *n.* 裙子

片 a long / short skirt 長 / 短裙

衍 miniskirt [ˈmɪnɪskɜt] *n.* 迷你裙

▶ Linda wore a long skirt to the party.
琳達穿了一件長裙參加派對。

---

dress [drɛs]
n. 洋裝 & *vt.* & *vi.* (給……) 穿衣服 &
vt. (烹調前) 處理 (魚或肉)

複 dresses [ˈdrɛsɪz]

片 (1) a wedding / an evening dress
婚紗 / 晚禮服
(2) a dress code 衣著規範
(3) dress sb in... 給某人穿……
(4) dress (sb) up (替某人) 盛裝打扮

衍 (1) dressed [drɛst] *a.* 穿著好的
(2) dressing [ˈdrɛsɪŋ] *n.* 沙拉醬 ⑥

似 clothe [kloð] *vt.* 給……穿衣服 ③

▶ The actress looks fabulous in that elegant evening dress.
這名女演員穿那件優雅的晚禮服看起來美極了。

▶ Is there a dress code on the invitation?
邀請函上面有提到衣著規定嗎？

▶ Leona dressed Vincent in a pilot's outfit.
里歐娜給文森穿著飛行員的衣服。

▶ Mike noticed that Joyce always dresses fashionably.
麥克注意到喬伊絲總是穿著時髦。

▶ It's a formal party, so you'll have to dress up.
那是正式的派對，因此你必須盛裝出席。

▶ Would you help me dress the turkey?
你可以幫我處理火雞嗎？

---

15 rainbow [ˈrenˌbo] *n.* 彩虹

衍 bow [bo] *n.* 弓 ①

▶ A beautiful rainbow showed up after the rain.
雨後出現一道美麗的彩虹。

---

16 bug [bʌg] *n.* 小蟲子；(電腦程式、機器的) 毛病 & *vt.* 煩擾；(裝竊聽器 / 裝置以) 竊聽

三 bug, bugged [bʌgd], bugged

衍 ladybug [ˈledɪˌbʌg] *n.* 瓢蟲 ②

似 (1) worm [wɜm] *n.* 蟲 ②
(2) bother [ˈbɑðɚ] *vt.* 煩擾 ②
(3) annoy [əˈnɔɪ] *vt.* 煩擾 ④

▶ The fruit was covered in little black bugs.
水果上爬滿了黑色的小蟲子。

▶ The engineer is trying to fix some bugs in the software.
工程師正在設法解決軟體裡的一些毛病。

▶ Tom kept bugging his sister until she gave him some money.
湯姆不斷煩他姊姊，直到他姊姊給他一點錢才罷休。

▶ I'm afraid the room and the phone have both been bugged.
恐怕這個房間跟電話都被竊聽了。

---

17 kite [kaɪt] *n.* 風箏

片 fly a kite 放風箏

▶ Let's fly a kite this afternoon.
我們今天下午去放風箏吧！

18　kind [kaɪnd] *a.* 和藹的，親切的 & *n.* 種類

片 (1) **It is kind of sb to V**
　　某人做……很親切
　　(2) **be kind to sb**
　　對某人很和藹／親切
　　(3) **kind of**
　　有點 (口語說法為 kinda [ˈkaɪndə])
　　(4) **one of a kind**
　　獨一無二的人／事／物

衍 (1) **kindly** [ˈkaɪndlɪ] *adv.* 親切地
　　(2) **kind-hearted** [ˌkaɪndˈhɑrtɪd]
　　　a. 仁慈的

似 (1) **type** [taɪp] *n.* 類型 ①
　　(2) **sort** [sɔrt] *n.* 種類 ②

反 **unkind** [ʌnˈkaɪnd] *a.* 不仁慈的

▶ It was **very** kind of you to give me a ride.
　你人真好，順道載了我一程。

▶ My father is **always** kind to those less fortunate.
　我爸爸對較不幸的人總是很親切。

▶ What kind of music do you like to listen to?
　你喜歡聽哪一種音樂？

▶ Can I open a window? It's kind of warm in here.
= Can I open a window? It's kinda warm in here.
　我可以打開一扇窗戶嗎？這裡有點熱。

▶ I'll miss Steve when he leaves; he's really one of a kind.
　史蒂夫離開後我會想念他，他獨一無二。

---

kindness [ˈkaɪndnəs]
n. 仁慈 (不可數)

▶ The man treated the poor with love and kindness.
　這位男士以愛與仁慈對待窮人。

19　yummy [ˈjʌmɪ] *a.* 好吃的 (口語)

似 (1) **delicious** [dɪˈlɪʃəs] *a.* 美味的 ②
　　(2) **tasty** [ˈtestɪ] *a.* 美味的 ③

▶ The banana split is really yummy.
　這個香蕉船真好吃。
　＊banana split　香蕉船 (冰淇淋)

20　cellphone [ˈsɛlfon] *n.* 手機〔美〕(= cell phone)

似 (1) **a cellular phone**　手機〔美〕
　　(2) **a mobile phone**　手機〔英〕

▶ My cellphone doesn't work. I need to get it fixed.
　我的手機壞了。我需要把它拿去修理。

---

telephone [ˈtɛləˌfon]
n. 電話 & *vt.* & *vi.* 打電話
(= phone = call)

片 **talk on the telephone**　講電話
= **talk on the phone**

▶ Harry and Ginny are talking on the telephone.
= Harry and Ginny are talking on the phone.
　哈利和金妮正在講電話。

▶ Please telephone the restaurant to tell them we'll be late.
　請打給餐廳，跟他們說我們會晚點到。

21　test [tɛst] *n.* & *vt.* 考試；檢查，檢測

片 (1) **test sb on sth**　測驗某人某事
　　(2) **a blood test**　驗血

▶ Victoria has an English test on Friday.
　維多莉亞星期五有英文考試。

▶ This part will test you on your knowledge of driving rules.
　這個部分將測驗你們對於駕駛規則的了解。

▶ Leo has gone to the hospital for a blood test.
里歐去醫院驗血。

▶ It is an optometrist's job to test your eyesight.
驗光師的工作就是測大家的視力。
＊optometrist [ɑpˈtɑmətrɪst] *n.* 驗光師

grade [gred]
n. 年級；成績 & *vt.* 將⋯⋯分等級

片 (1) be in (the) first / second / third
grade　念 1 / 2 / 3 年級
(2) repeat / skip the grade
留 / 跳級

衍 graded [ˈgredɪd] *a.* 分等級的

▶ When Will was in the first grade, he joined the school soccer team.
威爾念 1 年級的時候加入了學校的足球隊。

▶ Luna gets good grades every semester.
露娜每個學期成績都很好。

▶ Hotels are graded according to their facilities and service.
飯店依照設施與服務分級。

22　mathematics [ˌmæθəˈmætɪks] *n.* 數學 (不可數，常縮寫為 math [mæθ])

片 (1) a mathematics / math teacher
數學老師
(2) a mathematics / math test
數學考試

▶ David showed his talent for mathematics when he was young.
＝ David showed his talent for math when he was young.
大衛年輕時就展現了數學方面的天分。

23　parent [ˈpɛrənt] *n.* 父 / 母親

▶ Michelle's parents are getting a divorce.
米雪兒的父母要離婚了。

son [sʌn] *n.* 兒子
延伸 son-in-law [ˈsʌnɪnˌlɔ] *n.* 女婿

▶ The couple have an only son, named Matthew.
這對夫婦有一位名叫馬修的獨生子。

daughter [ˈdɔtɚ] *n.* 女兒
延伸 daughter-in-law [ˈdɔtɚɪnˌlɔ] *n.* 媳婦

▶ I'd like to introduce you to my daughter, Chloe.
我想把你介紹給我的女兒克蘿伊。

24　write [raɪt] *vt.* & *vi.* 寫 (字、信)

三 write, wrote [rot], written [ˈrɪtn̩]
片 (1) write about...　寫有關⋯⋯
(2) write sth to sb　寫 (信) 給某人
(3) write sth down / write down
sth　寫下某事物
衍 (1) writing [ˈraɪtɪŋ] *n.* 寫作
(2) rewrite [riˈraɪt] *vt.* & *vi.* 重寫

▶ The boy wrote a poem when he was only five.
這名男孩 5 歲時就寫了一首詩。

▶ Jim wrote a love letter to the girl, but she never replied.
吉姆寫了一封情書給那女孩，但她從未回覆。

▶ The teacher asked the students to write about their favorite place.
老師請學生寫他們最喜歡的地方。

▶ Let me write down your address.
讓我寫下你的地址。

writer [ˈraɪtɚ] *n.* 作家
似 author [ˈɔθɚ] *n.* 作者 ②

▶ Ernest Hemingway is my favorite American writer.
厄尼斯特 · 海明威是我最喜歡的美國作家。

25 weather [ˈwɛðɚ] *n.* 天氣 (不可數，指某地短期的氣象型態) & *vt.* & *vi.*
(因長時間風吹日晒而使) 褪色

片 (1) a weather forecast　天氣預報
(2) feel / be under the weather
(感覺) 身體微恙
似 whether [ˈwɛðɚ] *conj.* 是否 ①
比 climate 指『某個地區的氣候』，是
可數名詞，可加冠詞 a 或用複數；
weather 泛指『天氣』，是不可數名詞，
絕對不可以加冠詞 a 或用複數。

▶ We've been having nice weather over the past two weeks.
過去 2 個星期以來，我們這裡的天氣一直都不錯。

▶ It's fine weather today.
今天天氣很好。

▶ The jet lag made me feel under the weather for several days.
時差感讓我不舒服了好幾天。

▶ The outside walls of the house have been weathered by the sun.
房子外面的牆壁因日晒而褪色了。

sunny [ˈsʌnɪ] *a.* 晴朗的
衍 sun [sʌn] *n.* 太陽 ①

▶ We went fishing on a beautiful sunny day.
某個陽光和煦的日子，我們釣魚去了。

rainy [ˈrenɪ] *a.* 下雨的
片 for a rainy day
以備不時之需；未雨綢繆
衍 rain [ren] *n.* 雨 ①

▶ The weather is cold and rainy.
天氣又冷又下雨。

▶ It is wise to set some money aside for a rainy day.
存點錢以備不時之需是明智之舉。

26 file [faɪl] *n.* 文件夾；(電腦) 檔案 & *vt.* 歸檔；提出 (訴訟)

片 (1) keep sth on file　將某物建檔儲存
(2) file a lawsuit (against sb)
(對某人) 提出訴狀

▶ The company's files were in a complete mess.
公司的文件夾亂成一團。

▶ John, would you keep this on file for me?
約翰，你可以幫我把這個建檔儲存嗎？

▶ Please file these documents in that folder.
請把這些文件歸檔在那個卷宗夾內。

▶ Frank filed a lawsuit against the doctor who used illegal drugs.
法蘭克要對那個使用禁藥的醫生提出告訴。

1 today [tə'de] *n. & adv.* (在) 今天；現今

似 (1) present ['prɛzn̩t] *n.* 現在，目前 ①
   (2) nowadays ['nauə,dez]
       adv. 現今 ④

▶ Today is such a beautiful day.
今天天氣真好。

▶ Ben has had a hard time focusing on his work today.
班今天一直無法專心工作。

▶ Never put off until tomorrow what you can do today.
今日事，今日畢。—— 諺語

▶ People of today can contact each other via social media.
現今的人們可以透過社群媒體來聯絡彼此。

▶ Today, thousands of animal species are under threat of extinction.
現今有數千種動物正面臨絕種的威脅。
*extinction [ɪk'stɪŋkʃən] *n.* 絕種

---

yesterday ['jɛstɚ,de]
n. 昨天；往昔 & *adv.* 在昨天

片 the day before yesterday   前天

▶ Yesterday's history test was very difficult.
昨天的歷史測驗很難。

▶ Today's TV dramas are more complex than those of yesterday.
現今的電視劇比過往的還要複雜。

▶ My older sister gave birth to a baby boy yesterday.
我姊姊昨天產下一名男嬰。

---

tomorrow [tə'mɔro]
n. 明天；未來 & *adv.* 在明天

片 (1) the day after tomorrow   後天
   (2) like there is no tomorrow
       好像沒有將來似的

▶ Tomorrow is my best friend's birthday.
明天是我最要好的朋友的生日。

▶ Don't worry about tomorrow—just live in the moment.
不用擔心未來 —— 只管活在當下。

▶ Sam is eating that meal like there is no tomorrow.
山姆好像沒有明天似地狼吞虎嚥吃那頓飯。

▶ The weather forecast said the typhoon would hit the island tomorrow.
氣象預報說明天颱風會侵襲本島。

---

tonight [tə'naɪt] *n. & adv.* (在) 今晚

▶ Our host for tonight's talk show is John Smith.
我們今晚脫口秀節目的主持人是約翰·史密斯。

▶ Let's go shopping at the night market tonight.
我們今晚去逛夜市吧。

2　wonderful [ˈwʌndəfḷ] a. 很棒的

衍 wonder [ˈwʌndə]
　 n. 驚奇；奇蹟 & vt. 想知道 ②

▶ Thank you for this wonderful idea.
　謝謝你這個絕佳的點子。

3　speak [spik] vi. & vt. 說，說話 & vi. 談論

三 speak, spoke [spok], spoken
　[ˈspokṇ]

片 (1) speak to / with sb　　與某人說話
　(2) speak + 語言　　　　說某種語言
　(3) speak about / of...　談論到……
　(4) speak for sb　　　　替某人發言
　(5) speak up (for...)
　　　(替……) 發聲 / 辯護

衍 speaker [ˈspikə] n. 演說者；喇叭 ②

▶ The child began to speak very early.
　這小孩很早就開始會說話。

▶ The professor wants to speak to Larry.
　教授想和賴瑞說話。

▶ The businessmen will speak English at the meeting.
　企業家在會議上將會用英文說話。

▶ The student spoke about his favorite subject.
　這學生談及他最喜愛的科目。

▶ We chose Alex to speak for the group.
　我們選擇艾力克斯來替本組發言。

▶ The politician is speaking up for the rights of migrant workers.
　這名政客替移工的權益發聲。
　＊a migrant [ˈmaɪɡrənt] worker　移工

4　probably [ˈprɑbəblɪ] adv. 很可能，或許

衍 (1) probable [ˈprɑbəbḷ]
　　　a. 很可能的 ③
　(2) probability [ˌprɑbəˈbɪlətɪ]
　　　n. 可能性

▶ We'll probably be there about 30 minutes late.
＝ We'll very likely be there about 30 minutes late.
　我們很可能會晚 30 分鐘到那裡。

5　each [itʃ] a. 每個的 & pron. 每個 & adv. 每個地 (均指兩個或以上中的)

片 each and every
　每一個的 (用於加強語氣)

用法 each 作形容詞時置單數可數名詞前，其後動詞使用單數形動詞；each 作代詞與 of 並用時連接複數名詞，其後動詞亦使用單數形動詞。

▶ A large number of people buy lottery tickets each day.
　每天都有許多人買樂透彩券。

▶ Each and every student should bring his or her own lunch.
　每一個學生都應自備午餐。

▶ Each of you has a job to do.
　你們每個人都有工作要做。

▶ The postcards are on sale for NT$20 each.
　這些明信片特價每張新臺幣 20 元。

both [boθ] a. 兩個的 & pron. 兩個 & adv. 兩個都

▶ There is a long line of trees on both sides of the road.
　在道路的兩側都有一長排的樹。

片 both A and B　A 以及 B

用法 both 作形容詞時置複數名詞前，其後動詞使用複數形動詞；both 作代詞與 of 並用時連接複數名詞，其後動詞亦使用複數形動詞。

▶ Both of my parents sing very well.
我父母兩人都很會唱歌。

▶ Some people like durian, and others like stinky tofu. My mom likes them both.
有些人喜歡榴槤，有些人則喜歡臭豆腐。而我媽兩種都喜歡。

▶ The film has earned praise from both audiences and critics.
這部電影已贏得觀眾以及影評人一致的讚美。

6　hobby [ˋhɑbɪ] n. 嗜好

複 hobbies [ˋhɑbɪz]

似 pastime [ˋpæs͵taɪm] n. 消遣 ⑥

▶ Collecting old records is one of my hobbies.
蒐集舊唱片是我的嗜好之一。

habit [ˋhæbɪt] n. 習慣

片 (1) be in the habit of + V-ing
有……的習慣

(2) break a habit (of + V-ing)
戒掉 (……的) 習慣

▶ Sam is in the habit of listening to music while reading.
山姆有邊看書邊聽音樂的習慣。

▶ You need to break the habit of smoking.
你必須戒掉抽菸的習慣。

7　expensive [ɪkˋspɛnsɪv] a. 昂貴的

似 costly [ˋkɔstlɪ] a. 昂貴的；代價高的 ③

反 inexpensive [͵ɪnɪkˋspɛnsɪv]
a. 便宜的 (但品質不一定差)

▶ That expensive wine tastes delicious with a steak.
那昂貴的酒和牛排一起品嚐起來格外好喝。

cheap [tʃip] a. 便宜的；劣質便宜的 & adv. 便宜地 (口語)

片 not come cheap　不便宜

衍 cheaply [ˋtʃiplɪ] adv. 便宜地

▶ The food in that restaurant is quite cheap.
那間餐廳的食物價格相當便宜。

▶ We made the mistake of staying in a cheap hotel.
我們選擇住在這間廉價劣質的旅館是個錯誤的決定。

▶ An hour of massage doesn't come cheap.
按摩 1 小時的費用可不便宜。

8　million [ˋmɪljən] n. 百萬

片 (1) millions of + 複數名詞
數百萬的 / 數以萬計的……

(2) look like a million dollars
看上去感覺好極了

(3) be one in a million
獨一無二 / 萬中選一的好人

▶ The earthquake left millions of people homeless.
該地震造成數百萬民眾無家可歸。

▶ That house cost Roy five million NT dollars.
那棟房子花了羅伊新臺幣 5 百萬。

▶ That dress suits Kate. She looks like a million dollars.
那件洋裝很適合凱特。她看起來極有魅力。

衍 **millionaire** [ˏmɪljənˋɛr]
n. 百萬富翁 ④

用法 以『數字＋million』表『幾百萬』時，無論前面的數字為多少，million 一律不加 s，例：
one / two / three million
一 / 兩 / 三百萬

延伸 (1) billion [ˋbɪljən] n. 十億 ②
(2) trillion [ˋtrɪljən] n. 兆 ⑥

▸ Thanks so much for your help—you're one in a million.
真的很謝謝你的幫忙 —— 你是絕無僅有的好人。

9　**island** [ˋaɪlənd] n. 島嶼 (s 不發音)

片 **on an island**　在島上

▸ No one lives on that island.
那座島上無人居住。

10　**language** [ˋlæŋgwɪdʒ] n. 語言

片 (1) a foreign language　外語
(2) dirty / body language
　　 髒話 / 肢體語言 (視為不可數名詞)

▸ How many different languages do you speak?
你能說多少種不同的語言？

▸ Do not use dirty language in any situation.
任何情況下都不要說髒話。

11　**tennis** [ˋtɛnɪs] n. 網球運動 (不可數)

片 (1) play tennis　打網球
(2) a tennis player / court / racket
　　 網球選手 / 場 / 拍
(3) tennis shoes　網球鞋

▸ Tom started playing tennis at the age of five.
湯姆 5 歲就開始打網球了。

▸ The tennis player was ranked 8th in the world.
這名網球選手世界排名第 8。

12　**week** [wik] n. 星期，週；工作日 (週一到週五)

衍 (1) weekday [ˋwikˏde]
　　 n. 平日，工作日 (週一到週五) ②
(2) weekly [ˋwiklɪ]
　　 a. 每週的 & adv. 每週地 ③

▸ The museum is open to the public six days a week.
博物館一週開放 6 天給大眾參觀。

▸ Martin worked extra hard during the week so that he could have the weekend off.
馬丁這週工作日特別努力，好能在週末休息。

weekend [ˋwikˏɛnd]
n. 週末 & vi. 度週末

片 (1) on weekends　週末時
(2) on the weekend　這個週末

▸ Most people have to work on weekdays and are off on weekends.
大多數的人平日必須工作，週末則休假。

▸ Gillian's family likes to weekend in the mountains.
吉莉安一家喜歡去山上度週末。

13 topic [ˈtɑpɪk] *n.* (談話或書寫的) 主題

衍 topical [ˈtɑpɪkəl]
a. 熱門話題的；時下關注的

似 subject [ˈsʌbdʒɪkt] *n.* 主題 ①

▶ Have you chosen your topic for the speech?
你選好演講題目了嗎？

14 understand [ˌʌndəˈstænd] *vt. & vi.* 懂，理解，知道

三 understand, understood
[ˌʌndəˈstʊd], understood

衍 understandable [ˌʌndəˈstændəbl]
a. 可理解的

似 (1) know [no] *vt. & vi.* 知道 ①
(2) comprehend [ˌkɑmprɪˈhɛnd]
vt. 了解 ⑤

▶ Dominic's English is so poor that we can hardly understand him.
多明尼克的英文真糟糕，我們幾乎聽不懂他在說什麼。

▶ Do you understand that this must be finished by tomorrow?
你知道這件工作必須在明天以前完成嗎？

15 bedroom [ˈbɛdˌrum] *n.* 臥室

▶ You should tidy up your bedroom every day.
你應該每天將你的臥室收拾乾淨。

kitchen [ˈkɪtʃən] *n.* 廚房

片 everything but the kitchen sink
幾乎所有的東西；過多的東西

衍 kitchenware [ˈkɪtʃənˌwɛr]
n. 廚具 (集合名詞，不可數)

▶ If you can't stand the heat, get out of the kitchen.
你若受不了熱，就離開廚房吧。

▶ Your suitcase is so heavy. You must have packed everything but the kitchen sink.
你的行李箱好重。你一定打包了幾乎所有的東西。

bathroom [ˈbæθˌrum]
n. 浴室；(公共) 廁所〔美〕

片 go to the bathroom　上廁所
= use the bathroom

衍 bath [bæθ] *n.* 沐浴 ①

似 restroom [ˈrɛstˌrum]
n. (公共) 洗手間，廁所 ②

▶ Lucy spent the whole day cleaning the bathroom.
露西花了一整天的時間打掃浴室。

▶ Molly asked the teacher if she could go to the bathroom.
莫莉詢問老師她可不可以去上廁所。

toilet [ˈtɔɪlət] *n.* 馬桶；(公共) 廁所〔英〕

片 flush the toilet　沖馬桶

▶ Be sure to flush the toilet after you use it.
馬桶使用過後務必要沖水。

▶ Excuse me. Is there a toilet near here?
請問一下這附近有廁所嗎？

yard [jɑrd]
n. 院子；碼 (縮寫為 yd 或 yd.)

▶ Shane's father grows many roses in the yard.
夏恩的父親在院子裡種了許多玫瑰。

衍 (1) backyard [ˈbækˌjɑrd] *n.* 後院 ⑤
(2) courtyard [ˈkɔrtˌjɑrd]
    n. 庭院，中庭 ⑥

▶ The boat was fifty yards away.
那艘船在 50 碼外處。

---

16 polite [pəˈlaɪt] *a.* 有禮貌的 ☐

片 (1) be polite to sb　對某人有禮貌
(2) in polite society　在上流社會

▶ One should be polite to one's elders.
對長輩應該要有禮貌。

衍 (1) politely [pəˈlaɪtlɪ] *adv.* 有禮貌地
(2) politeness [pəˈlaɪtnəs]
    n. 禮貌（不可數）

▶ Those who appreciate art or music are respected in polite society.
欣賞藝術或音樂的人在上流社會中受到敬重。

反 impolite [ˌɪmpəˈlaɪt] *a.* 無禮的

---

17 pink [pɪŋk] *n.* 粉紅色 & *a.* 粉紅色的 ☐

▶ I was surprised that Ronald's bedroom was painted pink.
我很訝異羅納德的臥室是漆成粉紅色的。

▶ Mia was wearing a bright pink dress.
米雅穿著一件亮粉色的洋裝。

---

18 lemon [ˈlɛmən] *n.* 檸檬；瑕疵品 ☐

片 (1) a slice of lemon　一片檸檬
(2) lemon juice　檸檬汁

▶ The old man makes a living by selling lemon juice.
這位老先生以賣檸檬汁維生。

衍 lemonade [ˌlɛmənˈed] *n.* 檸檬水 ③

▶ Owen bought an expensive TV, but it was a lemon.
歐文買了一臺很貴的電視機，但它是個瑕疵品。

---

19 large [lɑrdʒ] *a.* 大的 ☐

片 be at large　逍遙法外，尚未被逮捕

衍 (1) largely [ˈlɑrdʒlɪ]
    adv. 大大地；大部分 ④
(2) enlarge [ɪnˈlɑrdʒ]
    vt. 放大（照片）；擴大 ④

似 huge [hjudʒ] *a.* 龐大的 ②

▶ Camels are large animals that can live in the desert.
駱駝是一種能在沙漠生活的大型動物。

▶ Laura wants to play a larger role in the company.
蘿拉想在公司扮演更重要的角色。

▶ The rich old man was murdered half a year ago, and the murderer is still at large.
那位有錢的老先生 6 個月前遭人殺害，而兇手仍逍遙法外。

---

giant [ˈdʒaɪənt] *a.* 巨大的 & *n.* 巨人 ☐

似 gigantic [dʒaɪˈgæntɪk] *a.* 巨大的 ④

▶ The giant building costs lots of money to maintain.
這棟龐大的建築物維修耗費甚鉅。

▶ David killed the nine-foot-tall giant by himself.
大衛單槍匹馬殺了那個 9 尺高的巨人。

20 grass [græs] n. 草

片 (1) a blade / field of grass
一根草 / 一片草地

(2) cut / mow the grass　剪 / 除草

衍 grassy [ˈgræsɪ] a. 長滿草的 ③

似 lawn [lɔn] n. 草皮 ③

▶ The dog is eating grass—he must be sick.
這隻狗在吃草 —— 他一定是生病了。

▶ Phil helps his father cut the grass in the yard on weekends.
週末時菲爾都會幫他父親在院子裡剪草。

21 enjoy [ɪnˈdʒɔɪ] vt. 欣賞，喜歡

片 (1) enjoy + V-ing　喜歡做……
(2) enjoy oneself　玩得愉快

衍 enjoyable [ɪnˈdʒɔɪəbl̩]
a. 令人愉快的 ③

▶ Young children enjoy watching cartoons.
小孩子喜歡看卡通。

▶ Did you enjoy yourself at the party?
你在派對上玩得愉快嗎？

enjoyment [ɪnˈdʒɔɪmənt]
n. 樂趣，享受

似 fun [fʌn] n. 樂趣 ①

▶ Leo likes working on the farm because it gives him enormous enjoyment.
里歐喜歡在田裡工作，因為這帶給他極大的樂趣。
*enormous [ɪˈnɔrməs] a. 極大的；巨大的

22 country [ˈkʌntrɪ] n. 國家 (可數)；鄉間 (不可數)

複 countries [ˈkʌntrɪz]

片 the country　鄉下
= the countryside [ˈkʌntrɪˌsaɪd]

似 (1) nation [ˈneʃən] n. 國家 ②
(2) state [stet] n. 國家；州 ②

▶ How many countries have you visited?
你走訪過幾個國家？

▶ Haley loves visiting the country on weekends.
週末時海莉喜歡到鄉下到處走走。

national [ˈnæʃənl̩]
a. 國家的，國立的；全國的

片 the national anthem　國歌

衍 (1) nation [ˈneʃən] n. 國家 ②
(2) nationality [ˌnæʃənˈælətɪ]
n. 國籍 ④

▶ How many national parks are there in your country?
你們國家有多少座國家公園？

▶ The program was broadcast on a national network.
這個節目在全國聯播網播出。

23 bored [bɔrd] a. 感到無聊 / 厭煩的

片 (1) be bored with...
對……感到無聊 / 厭煩

(2) become / get bored
覺得無聊 / 厭煩

▶ Jack is bored with his current job.
傑克對目前的工作感到厭煩。

▶ If the class is too long, the children may get bored.
如果上課時間太長的話，孩子們可能就會厭煩。

衍 boredom [ˋbɔrdəm]
　　n. 無聊 (不可數) ⑤

反 interested [ˋɪnt(ə)rɪstɪd]
　　a. 感到有趣的 ①

---

boring [ˋbɔrɪŋ] *a.* 令人厭煩的，無趣的

似 dull [dʌl] *a.* 無聊的 ②

反 interesting [ˋɪnt(ə)rɪstɪŋ]
　　a. 有趣的 ①

▸ That book is boring. Josh will choose another one
to read.
那本書很無趣。喬許要找另一本來看。

24　**science** [ˋsaɪəns] *n.* 科學；自然科學

衍 (1) scientific [ˌsaɪənˋtɪfɪk]
　　　a. 科學的 ③
　　(2) scientist [ˋsaɪəntɪst] *n.* 科學家 ③

▸ Science is my least favorite subject in school.
自然科學是我在學校裡最不喜歡的科目。

2201-2205

---

1 arrive [ə'raɪv] *vi.* 到達

- (1) arrive at + 建築物 (如車站、郵局等) 到達……
- (2) arrive in + 大地方 (如城市、國家等) 到達……

arrival [ə'raɪvḷ] *n.* 到達 ②

- ▶ You will get a free pizza if the order doesn't arrive within 30 minutes.
  您點的東西若沒在 30 分鐘內送達,您將可免費獲得一客披薩。
- ▶ Upon arriving at the airport, please claim your luggage.
  一到達機場時,請去提取行李。
- ▶ When Lisa arrived in London, it was 10:15 p.m.
  莉莎在晚上 10 點 15 分抵達倫敦。

---

2 catch [kætʃ] *vt.* 抓住,接住 (移動中的物品);逮住;趕 / 搭乘 (公車、火車、飛機等) & *n.* 接住 (移動中的物品)

- catch, caught [kɔt], caught
- catches ['kætʃɪz]
- (1) catch one's eye 引起某人注意
- (2) catch up (with sb) 趕上 (某人)
- (3) catch (on) fire 著火;失火
- eye-catching ['aɪ,kætʃɪŋ] *a.* 引人注目的

- ▶ Barry dropped his phone but then caught it.
  貝瑞弄掉他的電話但是抓住了。
- ▶ The chocolate cake really caught Lucy's eye.
  巧克力蛋糕吸引了露西的目光。
- ▶ Joe caught a bee in a glass jar.
  喬用玻璃罐逮到了一隻蜜蜂。
- ▶ Every day, Steve catches a bus to work.
  史蒂夫每天搭公車去上班。
- ▶ Ronnie ran to catch up with his big brother.
  羅尼奔跑以追趕上他哥哥。
- ▶ The wood was too wet to catch on fire.
  木頭太溼了,很難起火。
- ▶ Troy made the catch by jumping into the air.
  特洛伊跳到空中接住那顆球。

---

3 although [ɔl'ðo] *conj.* 雖然 (= though)

- ▶ Although Oliver is nice, I don't like him.
- = Oliver is nice, but I don't like him.
  雖然奧利佛人不錯,可是我並不喜歡他。

though [ðo] *conj.* 雖然 (= although) & *adv.* 然而 (= however,通常置於句尾)

although 及 though 作連接詞表『雖然』時,不得再與 but 並用,否則造成雙重連接的錯誤句構。

- ▶ Though the family is poor, they lead a happy life.
- = Although the family is poor, they lead a happy life.
  雖然這家人很窮,但他們的生活很快樂。
- ▶ Joe is fat; he's quick, though.
- = Joe is fat; however, he's quick.
  喬很胖,不過動作卻很敏捷。

Although / Though Jason is not tall, but he plays basketball well. (×)

→ Although / Though Jason is not tall, he plays basketball well. (○)
傑森雖然長得不高，但籃球打得不錯。

---

through [θru]

prep. 經過；透過；自始至終；遍及 & *adv.* 接通 & *a.* 做完的

🔁 (1) put A through to B
把 A 的電話轉接給 B

(2) be through with... 做完……
= be finished with...
= be done with...
= finish...

衍 throughout [θruˈaʊt] *adv.* 遍及 ②

▶ Our car stalled as we were driving through the tunnel.
我們開車經過隧道時，車子拋錨了。
*stall [stɔ] *vi.* (引擎) 熄火

▶ Tom got that job through his father.
湯姆透過他父親得到那份工作。

▶ Those people sang and danced through the night.
那些人徹夜歌舞狂歡。

▶ For a long time, the artist wandered all through the world.
有很長一段時間，那位藝術家在世界各地流浪。

▶ Could you put me through to Andy?
可以幫我把電話轉接給安迪嗎？

▶ I'll call you back right after I'm through with my work.
我做完工作後馬上回電給你。

---

4 traffic [ˈtræfɪk] *n.* 交通 & *vi.* 做非法買賣

🔲 traffic, trafficked [ˈtræfɪkt], trafficked (現在分詞為 trafficking)

🔁 (1) a traffic accident 交通事故
(2) a traffic jam 交通阻塞，塞車
(3) the traffic rules 交通規則
(4) traffic in sth 非法買賣某物

▶ Traffic is always heavy during rush hour.
尖峰時段的交通總是很繁忙。

▶ Harold witnessed a traffic accident on his way to school.
哈洛德上學途中目睹了一場車禍。

▶ I was late for work today because of a traffic jam.
因為塞車，所以我今天上班遲到了。

▶ Both drivers and passengers should always obey the traffic rules.
駕駛和行人始終都應該遵守交通規則。

▶ The man was put in jail for trafficking in drugs.
= The man was put in jail for drug trafficking.
那名男子因非法販賣毒品而入獄。

---

5 restaurant [ˈrɛstərənt] *n.* 餐廳

▶ We often have lunch at a restaurant not far from here.
我們通常在離這兒不遠的餐廳吃午餐。

menu [ˋmɛnju] *n.* 菜單

▶ Can I have the menu, please?
麻煩可以給我一份菜單嗎？

6　serious [ˋsɪrɪəs] *a.* 認真的；嚴肅的；嚴重的

囹 be serious about... 認真看待……
衍 seriousness [ˋsɪrɪəsnəs] *n.* 認真

▶ John is serious about everything he does.
約翰做什麼事都認真看待。

▶ Mandy looks very serious but has a great sense of humor.
曼蒂看似很嚴肅，卻很有幽默感。

▶ The strong earthquake caused serious damage to several buildings in the city.
這起強烈地震對本市幾棟建築物造成嚴重損害。

7　circle [ˋsɝkḷ] *n.* 圓圈 & *vt.* 圈選 & *vi.* 盤旋，繞圈圈

衍 (1) circular [ˋsɝkjələ] *a.* 循環的 ④
　　(2) circulation [ˌsɝkjəˋleʃən] *n.* 循環 ④
似 round [raʊnd] *a.* 圓的 ①

▶ Jill drew five circles on the paper.
吉兒在紙上畫了 5 個圓圈。

▶ Circle the correct answer on your test paper.
在你的試卷上圈選正確的答案。

▶ An eagle is circling above the tree.
有一隻老鷹在這棵樹上方盤旋。

---

square [skwɛr]
n. 正方形；廣場；平方 & *a.* 正方形的

似 plaza [ˋplɑzə] *n.* 廣場
延伸 其他形狀的英文說法：
　　(1) rectangle [ˋrɛktæŋgḷ] *n.* 長方形 ③
　　(2) circle [ˋsɝkḷ] *n.* 圓形 ①
　　(3) triangle [ˋtraɪˌæŋgḷ] *n.* 三角形 ③
　　(4) diamond [ˋdaɪəmənd] *n.* 菱形 ②
　　(5) oval [ˋovḷ] *n.* 橢圓形 ④

▶ The four sides of a square are of the same length.
正方形的四邊等長。

▶ There is a fountain in the middle of the square.
在廣場的中央有一個噴水池。

▶ My apartment is around 100 square meters.
我的公寓大約有 100 平方公尺大。

▶ There's a beautiful square garden in front of the grand palace.
那間壯麗的宮殿前有一座美麗的方形花園。

---

straight [stret] *adv.* 直直地；立刻 & *a.* 直的；坦誠的；連續的 & *n.* 直線跑道

囹 a straight arrow 一板一眼的人
衍 (1) straighten [ˋstretn̩]
　　vi. & *vt.* (使) 變直 ⑤

▶ Wendy went to the salon to have her hair straightened.
溫蒂去美容院把頭髮燙直。

▶ Go straight ahead three blocks, and you'll see the store on your right.
往前直走 3 個街區，你就會看到商店在你的右手邊。

▶ Henry was so tired yesterday that he went straight up to bed.
亨利昨天累到一回家就立刻上床睡覺。

▶ Draw a straight line on the paper.
在紙上畫一條直線。

(2) **straightforward** [ˌstret`fɔrwəd]
a. 坦率的 ⑤

▸ I like to associate with
straightforward people.
我喜歡與坦率的人交往。

▸ John's such a straight arrow. He always follows the
rules.
約翰真是個一板一眼的人。他始終按規則走。

▸ I knew my boyfriend was not completely straight
with me.
我知道我男友沒有對我完全坦誠。

▸ It has rained for two straight months.
= It has rained for two months in a row.
已經連續下雨 2 個月了。

8　couch [kaʊtʃ] *n.* (兩人或三人座的) 長沙發 & *vt.* 表達

複 **couches** [`kaʊtʃɪz]

片 (1) **a couch potato**
　　成天躺在沙發上看電視的人
　　(2) **be couched in...**
　　以……的方式表達

延伸 **armchair** [`ɑrmˌtʃɛr]
n. 單人座沙發；扶手椅

▸ Lucy idled her weekend away, watching TV on the
couch.
露西整個週末就坐在沙發上閒著看電視。
*idle one's time away　虛度時間

▸ Gary becomes a couch potato during holidays.
蓋瑞在放假期間變成了一個成天躺在沙發上看電視的人。

▸ The essay was couched in professional terms.
這篇論文以專業術語寫成。

sofa [`sofə] *n.* 長沙發

▸ Glen fell asleep on the sofa.
葛倫在沙發上睡著了。

9　sleep [slip] *vi.* & *n.* 睡覺 & *n.* 睡眠

三 **sleep, slept** [slɛpt], **slept**

片 (1) **sleep in**　睡懶覺
　　(2) **go to sleep**
　　去睡覺 (sleep 為名詞)
　　= **go to bed**

衍 (1) **asleep** [ə`slip] *a.* 睡著的 ②
　　fall asleep　睡著
　　(2) **sleepy** [`slipɪ] *a.* 想睡的 ②
　　(3) **sleepless** [`slipləs] *a.* 失眠的
　　(4) **oversleep** [`ovəˌslip] *vi.* 睡過頭

▸ Roy was so tired that he slept on the floor.
羅伊累到直接睡在地板上。

▸ Larry likes to sleep in on weekends.
賴瑞週末時喜歡睡懶覺。

▸ Six hours a night is not enough sleep.
每晚睡 6 小時並不足夠。

▸ Gail wanted to go to sleep, but she couldn't.
蓋兒想去睡覺，但無法。

▸ After a good night's sleep, Brenda felt great.
布蘭達一夜好眠，覺得好極了。

10　sick [sɪk] *a.* 生病的；噁心想吐的；厭煩的

片 (1) **feel sick**　身體不適；感到想吐
　　(2) **be sick of...**　對……感到厭煩

▸ Wally didn't go to school because he was sick.
瓦利生病了，所以沒去上學。

衍 sickness [ˈsɪknəs] *n.* 患病（不可數）
似 ill [ɪl] *a.* 生病的 ②

▶ The milk tasted strange and made Betty feel sick.
牛奶嚐起來怪怪的，讓貝蒂想吐。

▶ Tilly was sick of her boring job.
提莉厭倦了她無趣的工作。

sore [sɔr]
a. 酸痛的，刺痛的 & *n.* 酸痛；紅腫

片 (1) (have) a sore throat　喉嚨痛
　　(2) a sight for sore eyes
　　　樂於見到的人 / 事 / 物

衍 sorely [ˈsɔrlɪ] *adv.* 強烈地，疼痛地

▶ My legs were sore after I ran the marathon.
跑完馬拉松之後，我的雙腳酸痛得要命。

▶ I have a sore throat today and cannot speak.
我今天喉嚨痛，沒辦法講話。

▶ To Mr. Smith, seeing his children happily playing when he gets home from work is a sight for sore eyes.
對史密斯先生來說，下班回家看他的孩子開心地玩耍便是人生樂事。

▶ I fell the other day and have got a sore on my right arm.
我前幾天跌倒了，右手臂上有一塊紅腫處。

11　morning [ˈmɔrnɪŋ] *n.* 早晨，上午

片 in the morning　在早晨 / 上午

▶ Tom likes to go jogging early in the morning.
湯姆喜歡一大早去慢跑。

noon [nun] *n.* 中午
片 at noon　正午時分

▶ Rita takes a break at noon every day.
瑞塔每天中午都會休息。

afternoon [ˈæftəˌnun]
n. 下午，午後

片 in the afternoon　在下午 / 午後

▶ Sally enjoys drinking tea in the afternoon sometimes.
莎莉偶爾享受在下午時喝茶。

evening [ˈivnɪŋ] *n.* 傍晚，晚上
片 in the evening　在傍晚 / 晚上

▶ In the evening, George likes to read the newspaper.
喬治喜歡在傍晚時看報紙。

night [naɪt] *n.* 晚上，夜間
片 (1) at night　在晚上
　　(2) in / during the night　在夜裡

▶ Todd heard a loud noise at night and woke up.
陶德在夜裡聽到一聲巨響後醒來。

▶ Francis is having a party on Saturday night.
法蘭西斯將在週六晚上辦派對。

12　basketball [ˈbæskɪtˌbɔl] *n.* 籃球運動

片 play basketball　打籃球

▶ Bobby likes to play basketball with his friends.
巴比喜歡和朋友一起打籃球。

13　choose [tʃuz] *vt.* 選擇

目 choose, chose [tʃoz], chosen [ˈtʃozn̩]

似 (1) pick [pɪk] *vt.* 挑選 ①
　　(2) select [səˈlɛkt] *vt.* 選擇 ②

▶ Choose what you love, and love what you choose.
擇你所愛，愛你所擇。

choice [tʃɔɪs]
n. 選擇 & *a.* (食物) 精選的

片 (1) make a choice　做出選擇
　　(2) have no choice but to V
　　　除了做……之外別無選擇
　　(3) choice steak / beef
　　　精選牛排 / 牛肉

▶ It's hard to make a choice among so many tasty desserts.
這麼多可口的甜點真是令人難以選擇。

▶ You have no choice but to apologize to the public.
你除了向大眾道歉之外別無選擇。

14　main [men] *a.* 主要的 & *n.* (輸送水、煤氣的) 主管道

片 (1) a main point　重點
　　(2) a gas / water main
　　　瓦斯管 / 總水管

衍 mainly [ˈmenlɪ] *adv.* 主要地

似 (1) major [ˈmedʒɚ] *a.* 主要的 ②
　　(2) principal [ˈprɪnsəpl] *a.* 主要的 ②

▶ What are the main points of the professor's speech?
那位教授演講的重點是什麼？

▶ The water main here needs to be fixed.
這裡的總水管需要修繕。

15　picture [ˈpɪktʃɚ] *n.* 圖畫；照片 & *vt.* 想像

片 (1) a picture book
　　　(尤指兒看的) 圖畫書
　　(2) a picture frame　畫框

似 imagine [ɪˈmædʒɪn] *vt. & vi.* 想像 ②

▶ Kelly drew a picture of an elephant.
凱莉畫了一張大象的圖片。

▶ Janis sometimes pictures herself on a nice beach.
珍妮絲有時會想像自己在一片不錯的海灘上。

16　successful [səkˈsɛsfəl] *a.* 成功的

片 be successful in + N/V-ing
　　成功地……

衍 success [səkˈsɛs] *n.* 成功 ②

反 unsuccessful [ˌʌnsəkˈsɛsfəl]
　　a. 失敗的

▶ I was successful in persuading my brother to quit smoking.
我成功說服我哥哥戒菸了。

17　spend [spɛnd] *vt.* 花費 (金錢、時間)

目 spend, spent [spɛnt], spent

▶ Erica spent a lot of money on her trip.
艾瑞卡花了一大筆錢在旅行上。

用法 spend 常以「人」當主詞，用法為：
(1) 人 + spend + 金錢 / 時間 + on...
　　花費金錢 / 時間在……上
(2) 人 + spend + 金錢 / 時間 + V-ing
　　花費金錢 / 時間做……

▶ Donna spends an hour every day studying French.
唐娜每天花 1 小時念法文。

18　terrible [ˈtɛrəbl̩] *a.* 可怕的；極糟的

似 (1) horrible [ˈhɔrəbl̩] *a.* 可怕的 ③
(2) awful [ˈɔfl̩] *a.* 可怕的；極糟的 ③
(3) dreadful [ˈdrɛdfəl] *a.* 可怕的 ⑤

▶ The terrible news shocked all of us.
那可怕的消息震驚了我們所有人。

▶ To tell you the truth, Tim's performance in that play was terrible.
老實說，提姆在那齣舞臺劇裡的表演真是糟透了。

19　best [bɛst] *a.* 最好的 (為 good 的最高級) & *adv.* 最，程度最高地 (為 well 的最高級) & *n.* 最好的人 / 事 / 物 & *vt.* 擊敗，戰勝

片 (1) at best　　最多，充其量
(2) best of all　最棒的是
(3) do / try one's best　盡力
(4) make the best of...　善用……
(5) all the best
　　(用於告別或信末祝福) 祝一切順利

似 (1) beat [bit] *vt.* 打敗，勝過 ②
(2) defeat [dɪˈfit] *vt.* 擊敗 ④

用法 (1) 形容詞 good 的三級變化：good, better, best
(2) 副詞 well 的三級變化：well, better, best

▶ Dennis said it was the best food he had eaten.
丹尼斯說這是他吃過最好吃的食物了。

▶ This dessert is best enjoyed with a cup of tea.
這種甜點最適合搭配一杯茶享用。

▶ Of all the players on the team, Kelly's the best.
在隊上的所有的球員之中，凱莉是最好的。

▶ Ray said the project will take four weeks at best.
雷伊說這項企畫少說也要耗時 4 週。

▶ The job's fun, but best of all the pay's great.
這份工作很好玩，但最棒的是薪水也不錯。

▶ Sandra always tries her best at work.
珊卓拉工作時總是盡自己最大的努力。

▶ Clara makes the best of her free time.
克萊拉善加利用她的空閒時間。

▶ Lana's friends wished her all the best in her marriage.
拉娜的朋友祝福她在婚姻中一切順利。

▶ Jack won the first game but was bested later.
傑克贏了第 1 局，但隨後就被打敗了。

20　secretary [ˈsɛkrəˌtɛrɪ] *n.* 祕書

複 secretaries [ˈsɛkrəˌtɛrɪz]
衍 secret [ˈsikrɪt] *n.* 祕密 ②

▶ My secretary will email you the details later.
稍後我的祕書會用電子郵件將細節寄給你。

21 theater [ˋθiətɚ] *n.* 劇場；電影院〔美〕(= movie theater)；戲劇 (不可數)

衍 **theatrical** [θɪˋætrɪkl] *a.* 戲劇性的

似 **cinema** [ˋsɪnəmə] *n.* 電影院〔英〕③

▶ Last night, I went to the theater to see a new play.
昨晚我到劇場看一齣新話劇。

▶ The theater was packed with moviegoers.
戲院擠滿了看電影的人。
＊moviegoer [ˋmuvɪˏgoɚ] *n.* 看電影的人

▶ My sister is interested in the theater.
我妹妹對戲劇很感興趣。

22 treat [trit] *vt.* 招待；對待；治療 & *n.* 款待，請客；樂事

片 (1) treat sb to sth　招待某人某物
(2) treat sb with...
　　以……的方式對待某人
(3) treat sb/sth with...
　　以……來治療某人 / 某事物
(4) sb's treat　某人請客
(5) Trick or treat.
　　不給糖就搗蛋。(萬聖夜兒童用語)

▶ Pat treated Nancy to dinner last night.
派特昨晚請南西吃飯。

▶ The activity host treated the Nobel Prize winner with respect.
活動的主辦人對這位諾貝爾獎得主很尊敬。

▶ Depression can be treated with medicine or counseling.
憂鬱症可以用藥物或心理諮商來治療。

▶ It's my treat today.
今天我請客。

▶ It's a real treat to go swimming on a hot summer day.
炎熱的夏天去游泳真是一大樂事。

treatment [ˋtritmənt]
n. 對待；治療

▶ Although Kathy was the boss' daughter, she didn't get special treatment.
雖然凱西是老闆的女兒，但她並沒有因此獲得特殊待遇。

▶ Kevin is now receiving treatment for cancer.
凱文現在正接受癌症治療中。

23 somewhere [ˋsʌmˏ(h)wɛr] *adv.* 某處

片 **somewhere else**　別處

▶ Sometimes I want to fly somewhere I have never been before.
有時候我想要飛到某個我沒有去過的地方。

▶ Would you mind going somewhere else to play? I'm working.
你可以到別的地方玩嗎？我在工作。

24 team [tim] *n.* (球) 隊，組 & *vi.* 組隊；合作，聯手

片 **team up (with...)**　(和……) 聯手合作

▶ John is on the school basketball team.
約翰是籃球校隊的一員。

衍 (1) teamwork [ˋtimˌwɝk] *n.* 團隊合作
(2) teammate [ˋtimˌmet] *n.* 隊友

▶ The two companies teamed with each other to develop the product.
這兩家公司組成團隊共同研發這項產品。

▶ Let's team up and get the job done.
我們聯手合作把工作完成吧。

---

member [ˋmɛmbɚ] *n.* 成員
衍 membership [ˋmɛmbɚˌʃɪp] *n.* 會員身分 ②

▶ How many members are there in your family?
你家裡有幾位成員？

Unit 23

2301-2305

1 during [ˈd(j)ʊrɪŋ] *prep.* 在……期間

▶ Wendy ate a lot of popcorn during the movie.
溫蒂在看電影時吃了很多爆米花。

2 medium [ˈmidɪəm] *a.* 中號的，中等的；(牛排) 中等熟度的

延伸 牛排的各種熟度的說法，有下列幾種：
(1) raw [rɔ] *a.* 生的 ③
(2) rare [rɛr] *a.* 一分熟的 ②
(3) medium-rare 三分熟的
(4) medium [ˈmidɪəm] *a.* 五分熟的 ①
(5) medium-well 七分熟的
(6) well-done 全熟的

▶ Please bring me this T-shirt in a medium size.
請給我這件 T 恤的中號尺寸。

▶ My sister is of medium height.
我的妹妹是中等身高。

▶ I'd like my steak medium, thank you.
我要五分熟的牛排，謝謝。

3 together [təˈgɛðɚ] *adv.* 一起

片 (1) get together 相聚
(2) together with... 連同……(一起)
= along with...

反 separately [ˈsɛpərətlɪ]
adv. 分開地，各自地

▶ Are we going together or separately?
我們要一起去還是分開去？

▶ Jerry's family and mine get together to hike every Sunday.
每個星期天，傑瑞家跟我家會相聚去健行。

▶ My parents, together with my grandparents, attended my graduation ceremony.
我父母連同爺爺奶奶一起來參加我的畢典。

4 tooth [tuθ] *n.* (一顆) 牙齒

複 teeth [tiθ]
片 (1) brush one's teeth 刷牙
(2) a wisdom tooth 智齒
衍 (1) toothache [ˈtuθ,ek] *n.* 牙痛 ②
(2) toothbrush [ˈtuθ,brʌʃ]
n. 牙刷 ②

▶ Remember to brush your teeth twice a day.
記得一天要刷 2 次牙。

▶ I'm going to have my wisdom tooth pulled.
我要去拔智齒。

5 change [tʃendʒ] *vt. & vi.* 更換；改變 & *n.* 變更；零錢 (不可數)

片 (1) change A into B 把 A 變成 B
= transform A into B
= turn A into B
(2) keep the change 零錢不用找

▶ The mother changed her baby's diaper in the restroom.
這位媽媽在洗手間替小寶寶換尿布。

▶ The magician changed the mouse into a bird.
魔術師把老鼠變成一隻鳥。

衖 changeable [`tʃendʒəbḷ] a. 多變的

似 (1) alter [`ɔltɚ] vt. & vi. 改變 ⑤
    (2) alteration [,ɔltə`reʃən] n. 改變

▶ Do you think Debbie has changed since she became famous?
你認為黛比自從成名後，是否改變了？

▶ Eddie doesn't like the change of plans.
艾迪不喜歡計畫的變更。

▶ You can keep the change.
零錢不用找了。

---

6 popular [`pɑpjəlɚ] a. 流行的，普及的；受歡迎的

片 (1) popular music　流行樂
    = pop music
    (2) be popular with / among
       受……的歡迎

衖 popularity [,pɑpjə`lærətɪ]
    n. 流行；名望 ④

▶ Our popular culture is heavily influenced by Western countries.
我們的大眾文化受西方國家影響很大。

▶ Peter loves popular music.
彼得喜愛流行樂。

▶ Rap and R&B are popular with young people.
饒舌歌和 R&B 受年輕人的歡迎。

---

7 relative [`rɛlətɪv] a. 相對的 & n. 親戚

片 be relative to...
    與……相應的；與……有關聯

衖 relatively [`rɛlətɪvlɪ] adv. 相對地

似 comparative [kəm`pærətɪv]
    a. 相對的 ⑥

▶ The couple has been living in relative luxury since they won the lottery.
這對夫妻中樂透後，生活就過得相對奢華了。

▶ These facts are relative to the case.
這些事實和本案有關。

▶ Jack finds Amy's relatives hard to get along with.
傑克發現艾咪的親戚不太容易相處。

- -

cousin [`kʌzṇ] n. 表 / 堂兄弟姊妹

▶ Bobby used to play with his two cousins in the backyard.
巴比以前常常跟他的 2 個表弟在後院玩。

---

8 experience [ɪk`spɪrɪəns] n. 經驗 (不可數)；經歷 (可數) & vt. 體驗，經歷

片 work experience　工作經驗

衖 experienced [ɪk`spɪrɪənst]
    a. 有經驗的

似 go through...　經歷……

▶ Those applying for this position should have over three years' work experience.
申請這個職位的人必須有 3 年以上的工作經驗。

▶ I traveled to Italy last year, and it was a great experience.
我去年到義大利旅行，那是個很棒的經歷。

▶ Ted experienced a lot of difficulties during the war.
泰德在戰爭期間經歷了很多困難。

9 **video** [ˋvɪdɪ͵o] *n.* 錄影 (帶) & *a.* 錄影的；電視影像的 & *vt.* 錄影 〔英〕

片 (1) a video camera　攝影機
(2) video games　電動遊戲

衍 videotape [ˋvɪdɪo͵tep] *n.* 錄影帶

似 record [rɪˋkɔrd] *vt.* 錄下 ②

延伸 (1) audio [ˋɔdɪ͵o] *a.* 聲音的 ④
(2) audiovisual [͵ɔdɪoˋvɪʒʊəl]
　　 a. 視聽的
　　 audiovisual education
　　 視聽教育

▶ We stayed at home watching a video last night.
我們昨晚待在家裡看錄影帶。

▶ Many families own a video camera today.
現今很多家庭都擁有一臺攝影機。

▶ The video part of the TV program was clear, but the audio quality was poor.
這個電視節目的影像部分很清楚，但音質卻很差。

▶ Do you mind if I video the whole lecture?
您介意我錄下整場講課嗎？

10 **program** [ˋprogræm] *n.* 節目；(電腦) 程式 & *vt.* 為 (電腦) 設計程式〔美〕

三 program, programed /
programmed [ˋprogræmd],
programed / programmed

片 a TV program　電視節目

衍 programmer [ˋprogræmɚ]
n. 程式設計師

延伸 此單字的英式拼法為 programme
[ˋprogræm]。

▶ What kind of TV programs do you enjoy watching?
你喜歡看哪一種電視節目？

▶ The program wasn't working, so Jason had to restart the computer.
這個程式跑不動，因此傑森得將電腦重新開機。

▶ These computers have been programmed to run the tests once turned on.
這些電腦程式已經被設計成一開機就能跑這些測試。

11 **card** [kɑrd] *n.* 卡片；紙牌

片 (1) a birthday card　生日卡片
(2) a credit card　信用卡
(3) play cards　玩牌

▶ Addison's boyfriend only gave her a card for her birthday.
艾狄森的男友在她生日時只送她一張卡片。

▶ Cherry used her card to buy some clothes.
喬莉用她的卡買了些衣服。

▶ Ronald likes to play cards at night.
羅納德喜歡在晚上玩牌。

12 **pack** [pæk] *vt.* & *vi.* 打包；擠進 & *n.* 包 / 盒 / 副；一群 (狼、狗等犬科動物)

片 (1) pack into...　擠進……
(2) a pack of (playing) cards
　　一副牌
(3) a pack of wolves / wild dogs
　　一群狼 / 野狗

衍 packed [pækt] *a.* 擠滿人的，擁擠的
be packed with...　擠滿……

▶ Make sure you pack a jacket in your suitcase.
別忘了在行李箱裡放進一件夾克。

▶ People packed into the theater to watch the latest movie.
人們擠進這間電影院要來看最新的電影。

▶ Ned bought two packs of playing cards.
奈德買了 2 副紙牌。

反 unpack [ʌn`pæk]
　vt. & vi. 從 (箱) 中取出

▶ A pack of wolves was attacking the sheep.
　一群狼剛正在攻擊這些羊。

......

package [`pækɪdʒ]
n. 組 / 套；包裹 & vt. 打包，包裝

片 a package tour / deal
　整組行程，套裝行程

衍 packaging [`pækɪdʒɪŋ]
　n. 包裝材料 (不可數)

似 parcel [`pɑrsl̩] n. 包裹 ③

▶ This package deal includes transportation, hotels, and meals for a week.
　整組行程包含交通、飯店和一週的餐飲。

▶ A package arrived while you were away.
　你不在的時候有一個包裹送來了。

▶ All our products are sent here to be packaged.
　我們所有的產品都是送來這裡包裝。

---

13 reporter [rɪ`pɔrtɚ] n. 記者

衍 report [rɪ`pɔrt]
　vt. & vi. & n. 報導；報告 ①

似 journalist [`dʒɝnəlɪst]
　n. 新聞工作者，新聞記者 ⑤

▶ The reporter hid a camera inside his jacket.
　那個記者在外套裡面藏了一臺照相機。

---

14 interview [`ɪntɚˌvju] n. & vt. 面試；採訪

片 (1) a job interview　工作面試
　(2) do / conduct an interview (with...)
　　(與……) 進行面試 / 採訪

衍 (1) interviewer [`ɪntɚˌvjuɚ]
　　n. 面試官；採訪者
　(2) interviewee [ˌɪntɚvju`i]
　　n. 被面試者；受訪者

▶ The interviewee was very nervous during the interview.
　面試時，這位面試者非常緊張。

▶ The award-winning director did an interview with six different magazines last month.
　那位得獎導演上個月接受了 6 家不同雜誌社的採訪。

▶ Maria has interviewed several movie directors on her TV show.
　瑪麗亞在她的電視節目上訪問過一些電影導演。

---

15 last [læst] vi. 持續 & a. 最後的；上一次的 & adv. 最後地；上一次地 & n. 最後

片 last but not least
　最後但也同樣重要的

似 (1) continue [kən`tɪn(j)u] vi. 持續 ②
　(2) remain [rɪ`men] vi. 保持 ③
　(3) final [`faɪnl̩] a. 最後的 ②
　(4) previous [`privɪəs] a. 先前的 ③
　(5) end [ɛnd] n. 結束 ①

▶ The meeting lasted for more than two hours.
　這場會議進行了 2 個多小時。

▶ Mark is usually the last student to get to school.
　馬克通常是最後一個到學校的學生。

▶ The last trip Tim took was to America.
　提姆上一次的旅行是去美國。

▶ Joe was last in line to buy tickets.
　喬是買票隊伍中的最後一個。

▶ Freda last talked to her sister a week ago.
　芙蕾達上一次和姊姊講話是一星期以前。

> Ted is tall, strong, and last but not least, smart.
泰德很高、很壯，最後但也同樣重要的是，很聰明。

> The team played hard until the last, but they still lost.
這支隊伍努力奮戰到最後，但仍輸了。

16 hide [haɪd] vt. 把……藏起來 & vi. 藏匿 & n. (用於製作皮革的) 獸皮

- 三 hide, hid [hɪd], hidden [ˈhɪdn̩]
- 片 buffalo / cattle hides　水牛 / 牛皮
- 衍 hideaway [ˈhaɪdəˌwe] n. 藏匿處
- 似 conceal [kənˈsil] vt. 隱藏 ⑤
- 延伸 play hide-and-seek　玩捉迷藏

> Liz hides her diaries on the top shelf of her closet.
麗茲把日記藏在衣櫥的最上層。

> The soldier hid behind a tree until the danger was over.
那名士兵藏匿在一棵樹後面，直到危險過去為止。

> Tina's wearing a pair of buffalo hide shoes.
蒂娜穿著一雙水牛皮製的鞋子。

17 lonely [ˈlonlɪ] a. 孤獨的，寂寞的

- 衍 (1) alone [əˈlon]
  a. 獨自的 & adv. 單獨地 ②
  (2) lone [lon] a. 獨來獨往的 ②

> Eva feels lonely when Patrick is not around.
派翠克不在時伊娃感到很寂寞。

lovely [ˈlʌvlɪ]
a. 漂亮的；很棒的，美好的

- 衍 love [lʌv] n. & vt. 愛 ①
- 似 (1) beautiful [ˈbjutəfl̩] a. 漂亮的 ①
  (2) fine [faɪn] a. 美好的 ①

> What a lovely daughter you have!
你女兒真漂亮！

> We had a lovely time in Rome.
我們在羅馬度過一段美好的時光。

18 dream [drim] n. 夢；夢想 & vi. & vt. 做夢；夢想

- 三 dream, dreamed / dreamt
  [drɛmt], dreamed / dreamt
- 片 (1) have a dream　做夢
  (2) dream about / of + N/V-ing
  夢到……；夢想做……
- 衍 daydream [ˈdeˌdrim]
  n. 白日夢 & vi. 做白日夢
- 延伸 nightmare [ˈnaɪtˌmɛr]
  n. 惡夢；可怕的情景 ④

> Mike had a dream that he was a butterfly.
麥克夢見他是一隻蝴蝶。

> Cindy's dream is to become a famous singer.
辛蒂的夢想是成為一位知名歌手。

> Jasmine always remembers the things that she dreams about.
潔思敏總是記得她所夢見的事情。

> Sammy dreamed his best friend was a monster.
山米夢到他最好的朋友是一隻怪獸。

> Keith dreamed of being rich and having a big house.
凱斯的夢想是變得有錢和有一棟大房子。

19 excellent [ˈɛkslənt] a. 傑出的，出色的

衍 (1) excellence [ˈɛksləns]
   n. 傑出，卓越 (不可數) ③
   (2) excel [ɪkˈsɛl] vi. 突出 ⑥

▶ The brave young man is an excellent soldier.
那位英勇的年輕人是一位傑出的戰士。

20 fool [ful] n. 傻瓜 & vt. 欺騙

片 (1) be no fool　一點都不傻
   (2) fool around　鬼混，無所事事
   = idle around
衍 foolish [ˈfulɪʃ] a. 愚蠢的 ②
似 (1) trick [trɪk] vt. 欺騙 ②
   (2) deceive [dɪˈsiv] vt. 欺騙 ⑤

▶ Only a fool would do such a thing.
只有傻子會做這樣的事。

▶ Phoebe is no fool; she's quite shrewd.
菲比一點都不傻，她很精明。
★shrewd [ʃrud] a. 精明的

▶ Don't be fooled by this advertisement.
別被這個廣告騙了。

▶ Stop fooling around and do something useful.
別再混了，做點有用的事吧。

21 however [hauˈɛvɚ] adv. 然而；無論如何

似 (1) nevertheless [ˌnɛvɚðəˈlɛs]
   adv. 然而 ④
   (2) nonetheless [ˌnʌnðəˈlɛs]
   adv. 但是
用法 however 表『無論如何』時，等於 no matter how，之後先接形容詞或副詞，再接主詞及動詞。

▶ You can come with me. However, you have to pay your own way.
你可以跟我來；不過，你得全程自費。

▶ However good-looking Rudy is, Nora doesn't like him.
= No matter how good-looking Rudy is, Nora doesn't like him.
無論魯迪人多帥，諾拉都不喜歡他。

22 glove [glʌv] n. (一隻) 手套

片 a pair of gloves　一副手套
延伸 (1) fingerless gloves　無指手套
   (2) mitten [ˈmɪtn̩] n. 連指手套

▶ You'd better put on your gloves when doing this job.
做這份工作時最好戴手套。

23 butterfly [ˈbʌtɚˌflaɪ] n. 蝴蝶

複 butterflies [ˈbʌtɚˌflaɪz]
片 have / get butterflies in one's stomach　某人感到很緊張
= feel very nervous
延伸 the butterfly effect
蝴蝶效應，連鎖反應

▶ In winter, millions of butterflies travel to Mexico.
在冬天，有數百萬隻蝴蝶飛至墨西哥。

▶ Nicole had butterflies in her stomach when the teacher called her name.
老師叫到妮可的名字時她緊張死了。

24 **borrow** [`baro] *vt.* (向某人) 借

- **借** borrow sth from sb　向某人借某物
- **比** borrow 與 lend 均有『借』之意，但 borrow 指的是借入，而 lend 是借出東西給別人。

  lend sth to sb　將某物借給某人
  = lend sb sth

- ▶ Can I borrow some money from you? I need to buy a bike.
- = Can you lend some money to me? I need to buy a bike.
- = Can you lend me some money? I need to buy a bike.

  我能向你借一些錢嗎？我需要買輛腳踏車。

25 **already** [ɔl`rɛdɪ] *adv.* 已經

- ▶ Molly has already eaten dinner.
  茉莉已經吃過晚餐了。

26 **corner** [`kɔrnɚ] *n.* 角落

- **借** (1) on the corner　（戶外）轉角處
  (2) in the corner　（室內）角落
  (3) be (just) around the corner
    快要到了
  = be coming soon

- ▶ There is a post office on the corner.
  轉角處有一家郵局。
- ▶ Polly is sitting in the corner, reading.
  波莉正坐在角落裡看書。
- ▶ Christmas is around the corner.
  聖誕節快到了。

27 **early** [`ɝlɪ] *a.* 早的；早期的 & *adv.* 早地；早期地

- **借** (1) in the early morning　一大早
  (2) in early spring / summer /
    January　初春 / 初夏 / 一月初
  (3) in the early + 年代　某年代初期
- **反** late [let] *a.* 晚的 & *adv.* 晚地 ①

- ▶ John said it was too early to know the result.
  約翰說太早，還不知道結果。
- ▶ Bonnie was born in the early 1990s.
  邦妮出生於 1990 年代初。
- ▶ Gordy got up early to finish his homework.
  高迪早起把家庭作業完成。
- ▶ Early in the movie, Mr. Thompson's wife dies.
  電影開始不久，湯普森先生的妻子就去世了。

28 **mine** [maɪn] *vt.* & *vi.* 開採 (礦物) & *n.* 礦；地雷 & *pron.* 我的 (東西)

- **借** a coal / gold mine　煤 / 金礦
- **衍** (1) miner [`maɪnɚ] *n.* 礦工 ④
  (2) mineral [`mɪnərəl]
    n. 礦物 & *a.* 礦物的 ④
  (3) mining [`maɪnɪŋ] *n.* 礦業
  (4) minefield [`maɪn,fild] *n.* 地雷區

- ▶ These men work underground for six hours at a time, mining coal.
  這些人在地底下開採煤礦，一次工作 6 小時。
- ▶ The coal mine on the mountain is depleted.
  那座山上的煤礦已經開採殆盡了。
  *deplete [dɪ`plit] *vt.* 用盡

▶ The soldier was killed when he accidentally stepped on a mine.
那名士兵不小心踩到地雷被炸死了。

▶ The small apartment on the 6th floor is mine.
那間位在 6 樓的小公寓是我的。

29 pick [pɪk] vt. 挑選；摘取 & n. 選擇

用 (1) pick sth out　挑選某物
(2) pick sth up / pick up sth
拾起某物；購買某物
(3) pick sb up / pick up sb
（開車）接某人
(4) pick on sb　找某人麻煩
衍 pickup [ˋpɪkˌʌp] n. 接（人）；取（物）⑤
似 (1) choose [tʃuz] vt. 挑選 ①
(2) select [səˋlɛkt] vt. 挑選 ②
(3) choice [tʃɔɪs] n. 選擇 ①

▶ Pick a color for your bedroom walls.
替你房間的牆選個顏色吧。

▶ Don't pick flowers from the garden.
不要摘花園裡的花。

▶ Pick up the garbage and throw it into the garbage can.
把垃圾撿起來丟到垃圾桶裡。

▶ Lily had to pick up her kids at 4 p.m.
莉莉下午 4 點得去接她的孩子。

▶ Stop picking on me.
不要再找我麻煩了。

▶ My pick for best singer is Ariana Grande.
最佳歌手我選的是亞莉安娜 · 格蘭德。

30 study [ˋstʌdɪ] vi. & vt. 學習，研讀 & n. (專題) 研究；學習 (不可數)

三 study, studied [ˋstʌdɪd], studied
複 studies [ˋstʌdɪz]

▶ Denise is a good student who studies hard.
狄妮絲是個用功念書的好學生。

▶ Martin studies French twice a week.
馬丁一週念 2 次法文。

▶ The study found many bees were dying.
這份研究顯示許多蜜蜂正死去。

▶ Hank was busy and didn't have much time for study.
漢克很忙，沒有太多的時間學習。

31 quarter [ˋkwɔrtɚ] n. 四分之一；一季 (三個月) & vt. 分為四份

用 a quarter of an hour　15 分鐘
衍 quarterly [ˋkwɔrtɚlɪ]
a. 按季的 & adv. 一季一次地 & n. 季刊

▶ A quarter of the population voted for Tony.
有四分之一的人投票給湯尼。

▶ You can easily get there in a quarter of an hour.
你可以很輕易地在 15 分鐘內抵達該地。

▶ The company reaped huge profits in the first quarter of the year.
該公司本年第一季獲利很多。
*reap [rip] vt. 收穫

▶ Tom quartered the sandwiches and gave them to the kids.
湯姆把這些三明治分成四份，然後分給小朋友們。

32 machine [mə`ʃin] *n.* 機器 & *vt.* 用機器製作

片 a washing / vending machine
洗衣機 / 販賣機

衍 (1) machinery [mə`ʃinərɪ]
　　 n. 機器 (集合名詞，不可數) ④
　　(2) mechanic [mə`kænɪk] *n.* 技工 ④
　　(3) mechanical [mə`kænɪkḷ]
　　　 a. 機械的 ④

▶ The machine can make hammers and other tools.
這臺機器可以製作鐵鎚和其他工具。

▶ The workers machined the equipment carefully.
工人們小心地用機器製造設備。

33 wall [wɔl] *n.* 牆壁

衍 wallpaper [`wɔl͵pepɚ] *n.* 壁紙

▶ There was a stone wall around the old city.
舊城被一座石牆圍繞著。

▶ Kathy painted the walls of her daughter's room pink.
凱西把女兒房間的牆壁粉刷成粉色的。

34 hotel [ho`tɛl] *n.* 飯店

片 stay at / in a hotel　住飯店
似 hostel [`hɑstḷ] *n.* 便宜的旅社 ⑥

▶ Charlie stayed at a nice hotel with a big swimming pool.
查理住在一間有大游泳池的優質飯店。

35 knock [nɑk] *vt.* & *vi.* & *n.* 打，撞擊 & *vi.* & *n.* 敲

片 (1) knock... down / knock down...
　　 將……擊倒
　　(2) knock sb out / knock out sb
　　 將某人擊昏
　　(3) knock on / at the door　敲門
　　(4) knock on wood　好險；老天保祐

▶ The boxer knocked his opponent down in the first round.
這位拳擊手在第 1 回合就把對手擊倒了。

▶ Fran knocked her brother out with one punch.
法蘭一拳擊昏她哥哥。

▶ Sam got a nasty knock on the head when he fell down the stairs.
山姆從樓梯上跌下來，頭被重重地撞了一下。

▶ Please knock on the door before entering the room.
進房間之前，請先敲門。

▶ Mom feels much better now. Knock on wood!
媽媽現在好多了。真是老天保祐！

▶ We heard a knock on the door just now.
我們剛才聽到一陣敲門聲。

2401-2409

1 **town** [taʊn] *n.* 城鎮

片 a seaside town　海濱城鎮
- ▶ Brian grew up in a small town in Canada.
  布萊恩在加拿大的一個小鎮長大。
- ▶ In the summer, Carly likes to visit the seaside town.
  卡莉喜歡在夏天時到訪海濱小鎮。

2 **carrot** [ˈkærət] *n.* 胡蘿蔔，紅蘿蔔

延伸 a white radish [ˈrædɪʃ]　白蘿蔔
- ▶ Carrots are rich in vitamin A.
  紅蘿蔔富含維生素 A。

3 **doctor** [ˈdɑktɚ] *n.* 醫生 (= doc [dɑk])

片 go to the doctor　看醫生
用法 doctor 縮寫成 Dr. 時，用於人名前，表稱呼。
　　Dr. Smith　史密斯醫生
- ▶ Susan is a doctor in a large hospital.
  蘇珊是大醫院內的醫生。
- ▶ Renee was sick, so she went to the doctor.
  芮妮生病了，所以她去看醫生。

4 **until** [ənˈtɪl] *conj. & prep.* 直到

片 not until...　直到……才
用法 not until 引導的否定副詞子句置句首時，其後須採倒裝句構。
- ▶ Tony played soccer until he got tired.
  湯尼踢足球踢到累了為止。
- ▶ Helen played video games until almost 2 a.m.
  海倫玩電玩到接近凌晨 2 點。
- ▶ Not until she completed the report did Nancy rest.
  南希直到完成報告後才休息。

5 **medicine** [ˈmɛdəsn̩] *n.* 藥

片 take medicine　吃 / 服藥
衍 (1) medical [ˈmɛdɪkl̩] *a.* 醫療的 ②
　 (2) medication [ˌmɛdɪˈkeʃən]
　　　 n. 藥物 ⑤
- ▶ Remember to take this medicine three times a day.
  記得一天服這個藥 3 次。

6 **comfortable** [ˈkʌmfɚtəbl̩] *a.* 舒適的；自在的

片 feel comfortable with sb
　 與某人在一起感到自在
衍 comfort [ˈkʌmfɚt]
　 n. 舒適 & *vt.* 安慰 ③
反 uncomfortable [ʌnˈkʌmfɚtəbl̩]
　 a. 不舒服的
- ▶ A soft, warm bed is comfortable to lie in.
  柔軟溫暖的床躺起來很舒服。
- ▶ Shy people don't feel comfortable with strangers.
  害羞的人與陌生人在一起時會感覺不自在。

7 wait [wet] *vi.* & *n.* 等，等待

片 (1) wait for sb/sth (to V)
等某人 / 某物（做⋯⋯）

(2) wait to V 等著做⋯⋯

(3) can't wait to V 等不及做⋯⋯

▶ Patty waited for the bus to arrive.
佩蒂在等公車抵達。

▶ Ollie waited in line to buy food.
奧利排隊等候買食物。

▶ Frank couldn't wait to open his present.
法蘭克等不及打開他的禮物。

▶ There is a wait for a table at the restaurant.
那間餐廳的位子要等一下。

8 day [de] *n.* 一天；白天

片 (1) the other day
前幾天（與過去式並用）

(2) some / one day 未來有一天

(3) one day
（過去）有一天（與過去式並用）

(4) day by day 漸漸地，一天一天地

衍 daily [ˈdelɪ] *adv.* 每日 & *a.* 每日的 ②

▶ Joy's favorite day of the week is Saturday.
喬伊一週中最喜歡的一天是星期六。

▶ Carol bought a car the other day.
卡蘿前幾天買了一輛車。

▶ Jamie would like to be rich some day.
傑米未來想要變得有錢。

▶ Tori's English is getting better day by day.
托莉的英文漸漸變得更好了。

▶ During the day, Boris likes to play outside.
白天的時候，包里斯喜歡在外面玩耍。

---

month [mʌnθ] *n.* 月；一個月

衍 monthly [ˈmʌnθlɪ]
a. 每月的 & *adv.* 每月地 & *n.* 月刊 ③

▶ Veronica's birthday is in the month of August.
薇洛妮卡的生日在 8 月。

▶ Karen has been sick for nearly a month.
凱倫生病將近快一個月了。

---

year [jɪr] *n.* 年；年紀；學年，年度

片 the school year 學年

衍 yearly [ˈjɪrlɪ]
a. 每年的 & *adv.* 每年地 ③

▶ Paul has been playing the guitar for 10 years.
保羅彈吉他 10 年了。

▶ Mandy will be 15 years old in June.
曼蒂 6 月時就滿 15 歲了。

▶ When the school year ends, it's summer vacation.
一個學年結束時，暑假就來臨了。

9 apartment [əˈpɑrtmənt] *n.* 公寓〔美〕

似 flat [flæt] *n.* 公寓〔英〕②

▶ Lilly moved into her new apartment last night.
莉莉昨晚搬進她的新公寓。

10 wise [waɪz] *a.* 有智慧的，明智的

片 be wise (of sb) to V
（某人）做……很明智

衍 wisdom [ˈwɪzdəm] *n.* 智慧 ③

▶ I think Susan has made a wise decision to break up with John.
我認為蘇珊和約翰分手是個明智的決定。

▶ It's wise of you to prepare in advance.
你提前做好準備真明智。

11 throat [θrot] *n.* 喉嚨

片 (1) clear one's throat　清喉嚨
(2) have a sore throat　喉嚨痛

▶ The speaker cleared his throat before delivering the speech.
這名講者清了清喉嚨才開始發表演說。

▶ I have to cancel the meeting today because I have a sore throat.
我必須要取消今天的會議，因為我喉嚨痛。

12 salad [ˈsæləd] *n.* (生菜) 沙拉

▶ We ate salad and noodles for dinner last night.
昨晚我們晚餐吃生菜沙拉及麵條。

13 headache [ˈhɛdˌek] *n.* 頭痛；令人頭痛的問題

片 (1) have (got) a headache　頭痛
(2) be a headache for sb
是令某人頭痛的問題

▶ Mike called in sick this morning because he had a headache.
麥可早上因為頭痛請病假。
*call in sick　打電話請病假

▶ Heavy traffic is a common headache for Taipei residents.
交通阻塞是令臺北居民頭痛的共同問題。

14 subject [ˈsʌbdʒɪkt] *n.* 學科；主 / 話題 & *a.* 易受……的 & [səbˈdʒɛkt] *vt.* 使服從

片 (1) be subject to...　易受……的
(2) subject A to B　使 A 受制於 B

衍 subjective [səbˈdʒɛktɪv] *a.* 主觀的 ⑥

似 topic [ˈtɑpɪk] *n.* 主 / 話題 ①

▶ What's your favorite subject at school?
在學校你最愛的科目是什麼？

▶ The subject of today's discussion is COVID-19.
今天討論的主題是新冠肺炎。

▶ I am subject to headaches.
我很容易頭痛。

▶ Prices are subject to change.
價格隨時可能變動。

▶ The principal subjected all the students to strict rules.
校長要求所有的學生服從嚴格的規定。

15　abroad [əˈbrɔd] adv. 在國外；到國外

似 (1) board [bɔrd] vt. 上（船、公車等）②
(2) aboard [əˈbɔrd]
　　prep. & adv. 在（車、船或飛機）上
　　③

▶ Due to COVID-19, people cannot travel abroad these days.
由於新冠肺炎，人們現在都無法出國旅遊。

▶ My dream is to study abroad.
我的夢想是出國念書。

16　museum [mjuˈzɪəm] n. 博物館

延伸 gallery [ˈgælərɪ] n. 畫廊，美術館 ④

▶ The artist's work is on display at the museum now.
這位藝術家的作品正在博物館展覽中。

17　net [nɛt] n. 網子

片 slip through the net　漏網脫逃

衍 network [ˈnɛtwɜk] n. 網路 ②

延伸 the Net　網路
= the internet

▶ The man went fishing with a fishing rod and a net.
這名男子帶了一支釣竿和網子去釣魚。

▶ The cunning robber slipped through the net with ease.
那名狡猾的搶匪輕易地就漏網逃走了。
＊cunning [ˈkʌnɪŋ] a. 狡猾的

18　pleasure [ˈplɛʒɚ] n. 愉快，歡樂

片 (1) take pleasure in + N/V-ing
　　樂於……，以……為樂
(2) for pleasure　消遣，娛樂

衍 (1) please [pliz] vt. 使愉快，使開心 ①
(2) pleasant [ˈplɛznt]
　　a. 令人愉快的 ②

用法 (1) With pleasure.
　　我很樂意。（用於回應請求或邀約）
(2) My pleasure.
　　不客氣。（用於回應道謝）

▶ It's my great pleasure to deliver this speech to you.
能向諸位發表演講是我的榮幸。

▶ Vera takes pleasure in gardening.
薇拉以從事園藝活動為樂。

▶ Rosie went to London for pleasure, not for business.
蘿西是去倫敦玩，不是去出差。

19　lawyer [ˈlɔjɚ] n. 律師

衍 (1) law [lɔ] n. 法律 ②
(2) lawful [ˈlɔfəl] a. 合法的 ④
(3) lawmaker [ˈlɔˌmekɚ]
　　n. 立法者 ⑤

▶ I suggest you consult a lawyer.
我建議你去請教律師。
＊consult [kənˈsʌlt] vt. 請教

20　famous [ˈfeməs] a. 出名的

片 (1) be famous for...　以……聞名
(2) be famous as + 身分
　　以某身分出名

▶ This restaurant is famous for its terrific steaks.
這家餐廳以好吃的牛排聞名。
＊terrific [təˈrɪfɪk] a. 很棒的

衍 fame [fem] *n.* 名聲 ④
fame and wealth 名利

▶ Ginny is famous as an artist.
金妮是一個出名的藝術家。

21 business [`bɪznəs] *n.* 生意 (不可數)；事務 (常用單數)

片 (1) a business trip　出差
(2) be on business　出差
(3) be none of sb's business
不關某人的事
(4) mean business　當一回事

▶ Our business has been prosperous over the past three years.
過去 3 年來，我們的生意蒸蒸日上。

▶ Arthur is currently on business in Japan.
亞瑟目前正在日本出差。

▶ It's none of your business.
不關你的事。

▶ I'm not joking. I mean business.
我可不是在開玩笑。我是認真的。

22 picnic [`pɪknɪk] *n.* 野餐 & *vi.* 去野餐

三 picnic, picnicked [`pɪknɪkt],
picnicked (現在分詞為 picnicking)

片 (1) have a picnic　野餐
(2) go on a picnic　去野餐

▶ Zoe and her family had a picnic in the park.
柔伊和她的家人在公園裡野餐。

▶ Rena didn't go on a picnic because it was raining.
因為下雨，所以芮娜沒去野餐。

▶ Tammy picnicked at the beach on Sunday.
譚美星期天到海邊野餐。

23 future [`fjutʃə] *n.* 未來 & *a.* 未來的

片 (1) in the future　在未來
(2) in the near future
最近的未來，在不久後的未來

延 (1) past [pæst] *n.* 過去 ①
伸 (2) present [`prɛzənt] *n.* 現在 ①

▶ What are you planning to do in the future?
你未來計劃要做什麼？

▶ I'm planning to go on a working holiday in the near future.
我計劃要在不久後去打工度假。

▶ It is our duty to preserve the environment for future generations.
替未來的世代保護環境是我們的責任。
*preserve [prɪ`zɜv] *vt.* 保存；維持

24 convenient [kən`vinjənt] *a.* 方便的

片 (1) be convenient for sb
對某人方便
(2) be convenient to V
做⋯⋯很方便

衍 convenience [kən`vinjəns]
n. 方便；便利設施 ④

▶ Is tomorrow evening convenient for you?
明晚你方便嗎？

▶ It's quite convenient to transfer money via an online bank.
用網路銀行轉帳相當方便。

25 bench [bɛntʃ] *n.* 長椅

複 benches [ˈbɛntʃɪz]

▸ Joan read a newspaper on a bench.
瓊安坐在一張長椅上看報紙。

26 ago [əˈgo] *adv.* 在……以前

片 (a) long time ago　很久以前

▸ Richard and Erin got married five years ago.
理查和艾琳在 5 年前結婚。

▸ Laura moved to England a long time ago.
蘿拉很久以前就搬去英國了。

27 thick [θɪk] *a.* 厚的；茂密的；濃稠的

衍 (1) thickly [ˈθɪklɪ] *adv.* 茂密地
(2) thicken [ˈθɪkən] *vt. & vi.* (使) 變厚

似 dense [dɛns] *a.* 稠密的 ④

▸ The castle walls are 90 cm thick.
這些城牆有 90 公分厚。

▸ A thick forest can support a lot of birds and insects.
茂密的森林可以供許多鳥類及昆蟲生活。

▸ I don't like the soup; it's too thick.
我不喜歡這道湯，太濃稠了。

thin [θɪn]
a. 薄的；瘦的；稀的；稀疏的

片 through thick and thin
無論好壞，在任何情況下

似 (1) slim [slɪm] *a.* 苗條纖細的 ①
(2) skinny [ˈskɪnɪ] *a.* 皮包骨的 ③

反 (1) fat [fæt] *a.* 胖的 ①
(2) chubby [ˈtʃʌbɪ] *a.* 圓胖的 ⑤

▸ The road is covered with a thin layer of ice.
馬路覆蓋著一層薄冰。

▸ That thin, young actress used to be a model.
那位瘦瘦的年輕女演員以前曾是個模特兒。

▸ The sick man could only manage to eat thin broth.
這名生病的男子只能勉強喝一些稀湯。
＊broth [brɑθ] *n.* (常加入蔬菜或米的) 湯

▸ People noticed that Nick's hair was thin on top.
大家注意到尼克頭頂的頭髮很稀疏。

▸ I'll support you through thick and thin.
不論你得意或失意，我都會挺你。

28 invite [ɪnˈvaɪt] *vt.* 邀請；引誘，招致

片 (1) invite sb to + 活動 / 地點
邀請某人去某活動 / 地
(2) invite sb to V　邀某人做……

衍 invitation [ˌɪnvəˈteʃən]
n. 邀請；請帖，邀請卡 ③

似 ask [æsk] *vt.* 邀請；詢問 ①

▸ Our new neighbors invited us to their housewarming party.
我們的新鄰居邀我們去參加他們的喬遷派對。
＊housewarming [ˈhaʊsˌwɔrmɪŋ] *n.* 喬遷派對

▸ The professor was invited to lecture at the meeting.
這位教授應邀到這次會議上演講。

▸ The low security at that store was inviting crime.
那家商店防備不嚴是在引誘犯罪。

29 share [ʃɛr] *vt. & vi.* 分享；分擔 & *n.* 一份

片 share sth with sb
與某人分享 / 分擔某物

▶ Jenny doesn't want to share her toys with her twin sister.
珍妮不願與她的雙胞胎妹妹分享玩具。

▶ There are not enough rooms, so we have to share.
房間不夠多，所以我們必須合住。

▶ Jason didn't give us his share of the bill.
傑森沒給我們他該分擔的那份費用。

30 party [ˋpɑrtɪ] *n.* 派對 & *vi.* 狂歡

複 parties [ˋpɑrtɪz]

三 party, partied [ˋpɑrtɪd], partied

片 (1) a dinner / birthday party
晚宴 / 生日派對

(2) throw / hold a party 舉辦派對

▶ Lauren went to a nice dinner party on Friday night.
蘿倫週五晚上去了一個很棒的晚宴派對。

▶ Hal threw a big party and invited many friends.
海爾舉辦了一場大派對，也邀了很多朋友。

▶ Jeffrey is tired today because he partied last night.
傑佛瑞昨晚去狂歡，所以今天很累。

31 exercise [ˋɛksəˏsaɪz] *n. & vi. & vt.* 運動 & *n.* 練習題 & *vt.* 操練；使用 (權利等)

片 do exercise 做運動

似 work out 運動，鍛鍊身體

▶ Exercise and proper diet are essential for good health.
運動和適當的飲食對健康很重要。

▶ My father exercises every morning at the park.
我爸爸每天早上都在公園運動。

▶ Did you finish the exercises in the chapter?
你做完這一章的練習題了嗎？

▶ Henry exercised his horses twice a day.
亨利一天操練他的馬兒 2 次。

▶ Many fail to exercise their right to vote.
很多人都沒有去行使他們的投票權。

32 modern [ˋmɑdən] *a.* 現代的

衍 modernize [ˋmɑdənˏaɪz]
vt. 使現代化 ⑥

延伸 contemporary [kənˋtɛmpəˏrɛrɪ]
a. 當代的 ⑤

▶ Hazel likes both modern dance and classical ballet.
海瑟喜歡現代舞和古典芭蕾。

33 snow [sno] *n.* 雪 & *vi.* 下雪

衍 (1) snowy [ˋsnoɪ] *a.* 雪的；下雪的 ②
(2) snowflake [ˋsnoˏflek] *n.* 雪花

▶ The snow looked beautiful on the trees.
樹上的雪看起來很漂亮。

▶ In the winter, it snows in many countries.
冬天時，很多國家都會下雪。

---

34 festival [ˈfɛstəvḷ] *n.* 節；節慶

似 (1) holiday [ˈhɑləde] *n.* 節日 ①
  (2) carnival [ˈkɑrnəvḷ] *n.* 嘉年華 ⑤

延伸 the Mid-Autumn Festival / the Moon Festival 中秋節

▶ The music festival is held here every summer.
音樂祭每年夏天都在這裡舉辦。

▶ The Dragon Boat Festival is around the corner.
端午節快到了。

---

35 celebrate [ˈsɛləˌbret] *vt.* 慶祝

衍 (1) celebration [ˌsɛləˈbreʃən]
  n. 慶祝 ④
  (2) celebrity [səˈlɛbrətɪ] *n.* 名人 ⑤

▶ Daniel's coworkers celebrated his promotion with a party.
丹尼爾的同事開派對慶祝他的升遷。

2501-2510

1 button [ˈbʌtn̩] n. 鈕扣；按鈕 & vt. 扣上 (鈕扣)

片 (1) do up a button　扣鈕扣
(2) undo a button　解開鈕扣
(3) press / push a button　按下按鈕
(4) button (up)...　扣上……的鈕扣

▶ Can you undo the buttons on my back?
你可以幫我解開我背後的扣子嗎？

▶ Push that button, and you can withdraw your money.
按下那個按鈕，你就可以領錢了。
*withdraw [wɪðˈdrɔ] vt. 提 (款)

▶ Button up your coat. It's very windy outside.
把外套扣起來。外面風很大。

2 ability [əˈbɪlətɪ] n. 能力

複 abilities [əˈbɪlətɪz]
片 have the ability to V　有能力……
衍 able [ˈebl̩] a. 有能力的 ①

▶ Ants have the ability to carry objects much heavier than themselves.
螞蟻有能力搬動比自己重得多的物體。

3 copy [ˈkɑpɪ] vt. & vi. 仿造；複製 & vt. 模仿 & n. 仿製品；副本；一份 / 本 / 冊 (書報雜誌等)

三 copy, copied [ˈkɑpɪd], copied
複 copies [ˈkɑpɪz]
片 (1) make a copy of...　複印……
(2) a copy of...
　　……的複製品；一份 / 本 / 冊……
衍 (1) copyright [ˈkɑpɪˌraɪt]
　　n. 版權；著作權 ⑤
(2) photocopy [ˈfotəˌkɑpɪ]
　　vt. & vi. 複印 & n. 影本
似 (1) xerox [ˈzɪrɑks] vt. & vi. 影印
(2) imitate [ˈɪməˌtet] vt. 模仿 ④

▶ The company was accused of copying the product of a US manufacturer.
該公司被指控仿造一家美國廠商的產品。

▶ The secretary forgot to copy the document.
= The secretary forgot to make a copy of the document.
那位祕書忘了影印文件。

▶ I used to copy everything my brother did.
我以前會模仿我哥哥做的一切事情。

▶ This is a copy of Rembrandt's painting.
這是林布蘭畫作的臨摹品。

▶ You can get a copy of the magazine in most bookstores.
你可以在大部分的書局買到一本這個雜誌。

4 guy [gaɪ] n. 男子，傢伙；(不分性別的) 大家 (恆用複數)

複 guys [gaɪz]
片 a nice / bad guy　好 / 壞人
似 (1) fellow [ˈfɛlo]
　　n. 男子，傢伙；夥伴 ②
(2) mate [met] n. 老兄，夥伴 [英] ②

▶ I don't like that guy.
我不喜歡那個傢伙。

▶ You guys can take a break now.
你們大家現在可以去休息了。

5 clerk [klɜk] *n.* 店員

▶ The clerk at the drugstore gave me the wrong change.
藥妝店的店員找錯零錢給我。

6 explain [ɪkˋsplen] *vt.* 解釋，說明

用 (1) explain why / how / what...
解釋為何 / 如何 / 什麼……
(2) explain that... 解釋……
(3) explain oneself 解釋自己的行為
衍 explanation [ˌɛkspləˋneʃən]
n. 解釋 ④

▶ After the surgery, the doctor will explain how to take care of your eyes.
手術後，醫生會解釋如何照顧你的眼睛。

▶ The spokesman explained that the delay was a result of bad weather.
發言人解釋誤點是惡劣天氣造成的。

▶ You have three minutes to explain yourself.
你有 3 分鐘可以解釋自己的行為。

7 proud [praʊd] *a.* 自豪的；傲慢的

用 be proud of... 以……為榮
衍 proudly [ˋpraʊdlɪ] *adv.* 驕傲地
反 (1) ashamed [əˋʃemd]
a. 感到可恥的 ④
(2) humble [ˋhʌmbl̩] *a.* 謙虛的 ②

▶ I'm proud of my dad. He takes good care of his family.
我爸很照顧家人，我以他為榮。

▶ The girl is too proud to take others' advice.
這個女孩太傲慢，不願接納別人的建議。

8 online [ˋɑnˌlaɪn] *a.* 網路上的，在線的 & *adv.* 在網路上

反 off-line [ˌɔfˋlaɪn]
a. (網路) 下線的 & *adv.* 下線
(= offline)

▶ Not all online information is correct.
線上資訊並非都是正確的。

▶ Nelly likes to shop online.
納莉喜歡在網路上購物。

9 collect [kəˋlɛkt] *vt.* 收集

衍 (1) collection [kəˋlɛkʃən] *n.* 收藏 ③
(2) collector [kəˋlɛktɚ] *n.* 收集者 ⑤
似 gather [ˋgæðɚ] *vt.* 收集 ②

▶ Bill has been collecting stamps for more than thirty years.
比爾集郵已有 30 多年之久。

▶ The scientist collected lots of data to do the research.
這名科學家收集了大量數據來做研究。

10 hang [hæŋ] *vt.* & *vi.* 懸掛；吊死

三 (1) 表『懸掛』時：
hang, hung [hʌŋ], hung
(2) 表『吊死』時：
hang, hanged [hæŋd], hanged

▶ The painting was hung upside down.
這幅畫被掛顛倒了。

ㅂ hang up (on sb)　掛斷 (某人的) 電話

▶ The criminal was hanged for murdering the old woman.
這名罪犯因謀殺老婦人而被吊死。

▶ Tom hung up on me without saying goodbye.
湯姆沒說再見就掛我電話。

11　teenager [ˋtinˏedʒɚ] *n.* 青少年 (= teen [tin])

衍 (1) teens [tinz] *n.* 十幾歲 ②
　　(2) teenage [ˋtinˏedʒ] *a.* 青少年的 ③

▶ I often made rash decisions when I was a teenager.
我還是青少年時，很常做出輕率的決定。
＊rash [ræʃ] *a.* 輕率的

12　wet [wɛt] *a.* 溼的 & *vt.* 弄溼；尿溼

트 wet, wet / wetted [ˋwɛtɪd], wet / wetted
ㅂ (1) get wet　淋溼
　　(2) wet a / one's bed　尿床
似 (1) humid [ˋhjumɪd] *a.* 溼氣重的 ③
　　(2) moist [mɔɪst] *a.* 潮溼的 ③
　　(3) damp [dæmp] *a.* 潮溼的 ④
反 dry [draɪ] *a.* 乾的 & *vt.* 弄乾 ①

▶ The ground is wet after the rain.
下過雨後地上溼溼的。

▶ Bruce fell into the pond and got wet.
布魯斯跌進池塘裡，全身都溼了。

▶ I wet the cloth and wiped the dining table.
我沾溼抹布後擦拭餐桌。

▶ The five-year-old girl wet her bed last night.
這名 5 歲的小女孩昨晚尿床了。

13　honest [ˋɑnɪst] *a.* 誠實的，坦白的

ㅂ (1) be honest with sb　對某人誠實
　　(2) To be honest, ...　老實說，……
　　＝ Frankly speaking, ...
　　＝ To tell you the truth, ...
衍 honesty [ˋɑnɪstɪ] *n.* 誠實 ③
反 dishonest [dɪsˋɑnɪst] *a.* 不誠實的 ③

▶ You should be honest with your parents.
你應該對父母誠實。

▶ It is not too late to make an honest confession.
現在老實承認還不會太晚。
＊confession [kənˋfɛʃən] *n.* 坦白

▶ To be honest, I don't think Eric is a good guy.
老實說，我覺得艾瑞克不是好人。

14　towel [ˋtaʊəl] *n.* 毛巾 & *vt.* & *vi.* 用毛巾擦乾

ㅂ (1) a paper / hand towel
　　　紙巾 / 擦手巾
　　(2) throw in the towel　認輸
似 tower [ˋtaʊɚ] *n.* 塔 ③

▶ After swimming, dry off with a towel.
游完泳後，用毛巾把身體擦乾。

▶ After three failed attempts, Jack threw in the towel.
傑克歷經 3 次失敗後，決定放棄。

▶ Dean toweled his hair after taking a shower.
狄恩沖澡後用毛巾把頭髮擦乾。

15 **mark** [mɑrk] *n.* 汙點；痕跡；記號 & *vt.* 標示

片 **make a mark on sth**
在某物上做記號

衍 (1) **marker** [`mɑrkɚ]
n. 馬克筆；標誌 ③

(2) **marked** [mɑrkt]
a. 有記號的；顯著的

似 (1) **spot** [spɑt] *n.* 汙點；斑點 ②

(2) **stain** [sten] *n.* 汙點 ⑤

▶ There are some dirty marks on your white dress.
妳的白洋裝上有些髒髒的汙點。

▶ The factory fire left a burn mark on Willy's face.
工廠火災在威利的臉上留下一道燒傷疤痕。

▶ Don't make marks on the pages.
別在頁面上做記號。

▶ The lawyer has marked the pages you need to sign.
律師標示了需要你簽名的頁面。

16 **dictionary** [`dɪkʃən,ɛrɪ] *n.* 字典

複 **dictionaries** [`dɪkʃən,ɛrɪz]

片 (1) **consult a dictionary**　查字典

(2) **look sth up in a dictionary**
在字典上查找某物

延伸 **encyclopedia** [ɪn,saɪklə`pidɪə]
n. 百科全書 ⑥

▶ If you don't know the word, consult the dictionary.
= If you don't know the word, look it up in the dictionary.
你若不懂這個字就查字典。

17 **fail** [fel] *vi.* 失敗 & *vt.* 辜負，有負於；使不及格

片 (1) **fail in one's attempt to V**
某人做……失敗，未能……

(2) **fail to V**　未能……

衍 **failure** [`feljɚ] *n.* 失敗 ②

反 **succeed** [sək`sid] *vi.* 成功 ②

用法 fail 表『辜負』時，以人作受詞。

▶ Lucas failed in his attempt to persuade Willa.
= Lucas failed to persuade Willa.
盧卡斯沒能說服薇拉。

▶ My courage failed me on that important occasion.
在那個重要場合，我卻失去了勇氣。

▶ Mike didn't study hard, and thus failed the test.
邁可沒有認真念書，所以考試不及格。

18 **club** [klʌb] *n.* 社團，俱樂部 & *vt.* 棒擊

三 **club, clubbed** [klʌbd]**, clubbed**

▶ Iris joined the soccer club at school.
艾莉絲加入了學校的足球社。

▶ Jim clubbed the bear, and it ran away.
吉姆用棒子打那隻熊，然後它就逃走了。

19 **wake** [wek] *vt.* & *vi.* 醒來

三 **wake, woke** [wok] **/ waked,**
woken [`wokən] **/ waked**

片 (1) **wake (sb) up**　（把某人叫）醒來

(2) **wake up and smell the coffee**
覺悟，認清事實

▶ Be quiet or you'll wake the baby.
安靜點，不然你會吵醒小寶寶。

▶ Can you wake me up when you leave the house?
你出門時可否把我叫醒？

衍 (1) awake [əˈwek]
　　　vi. 醒來 & *a.* 清醒的 ③
　(2) awaken [əˈwekən] *vt.* 喚醒 ③
　(3) waken [ˈwekən]
　　　vi. 醒來 & *vt.* 喚醒 ④

▸ When do you usually wake up in the morning?
你早上通常幾點醒來？

▸ Wake up and smell the coffee! You won't find a girlfriend by sitting in front of the television all day.
醒醒吧！你整天坐在電視機前面是交不到女朋友的。

20 define [dɪˈfaɪn] *vt.* 下定義，解釋；界定

片 define A as B　將 A 定義為 B
衍 (1) definition [ˌdɛfəˈnɪʃən] *n.* 定義 ③
　(2) definite [ˈdɛfənɪt]
　　　a. 明確的，肯定的 ④
似 explain [ɪkˈsplen] *vt.* & *vi.* 解釋 ①

▸ It is difficult to define the word "love."
要為『愛』這個字去下定義是很困難的。

▸ The dictionary defines this word as a vulgar word.
字典把這個字定義為粗俗不雅的字。
＊vulgar [ˈvʌlgɚ] *a.* 粗俗的

▸ The rules of conduct are clearly defined in the school handbook.
這些行為守則在學校手冊中都有明文規定。

21 tape [tep] *n.* 錄音 / 影帶；膠帶 (不可數) & *vt.* 錄進錄音 / 影帶；用膠帶黏

片 be taped to sth　被貼在某物上
衍 videotape [ˈvɪdɪoˌtep]
　　　n. 錄影帶 & *vt.* 錄成錄影帶
似 cassette [kəˈsɛt] *n.* 卡式錄音帶

▸ Put the tape in the recorder before the speech begins.
演講開始前，把錄音帶放進錄音機裡。

▸ Stick these posters to the wall with tape.
用膠帶把這些海報貼在牆上。

▸ Mom asked me to tape the TV program.
媽媽請我幫她把這檔電視節目錄下來。

▸ The emergency phone numbers are taped to the fridge.
緊急電話號碼貼在冰箱上。

22 expect [ɪkˈspɛkt] *vt.* 預料，預期；等待；要求

片 expect sb to V
　　　預期某人會……；要求某人做……
衍 (1) expectation [ˌɛkspɛkˈteʃən]
　　　n. 期望 ③
　(2) expected [ɪkˈspɛktɪd]
　　　a. 預期要發生的

▸ No one expected Kelly to get married so soon.
大家都沒料到凱莉會這麼快結婚。

▸ I'm expecting a phone call from the doctor to tell me what to do.
我在等醫生打電話來告訴我該做什麼。

▸ Tom expected me to do all the chores myself.
湯姆要求我自己做所有的家務。

23 envelope [ˈɛnvəˌlop] *n.* 信封

▸ What was in the envelope Liam gave you?
連恩給你的那個信封裡裝著什麼？

24　soldier [`soldʒɚ] *n.* 軍人；士兵

> The brave soldier fought in three battles.
> 這個勇敢的軍人參加過 3 次戰役。

25　example [ɪgˋzæmpl] *n.* 例子；典範，榜樣

- (1) for example　舉例來說
  = for instance
  (2) set an example (for sb)
  （為某人）樹立一個榜樣
- instance [ˋɪnstəns] *n.* 例子 ②

> Ethan can play many instruments, for example, piano, violin, and cello.
= Ethan can play many instruments, for instance, piano, violin, and cello.
> 伊森會演奏很多樂器，例如鋼琴、小提琴和大提琴。

> Teachers should set a good example for students.
> 老師應為學生樹立一個好榜樣。

26　uniform [ˋjunəˌfɔrm] *n.* 制服 & *a.* 一致的

- (1) a school uniform　校服
  (2) in uniform　穿著制服

> Belle still looks beautiful in her school uniform.
> 貝兒穿校服看起來仍很美麗。

> Who is that man in uniform?
> 那位穿著制服的男子是誰？

> All the classroom walls were a uniform green.
> 所有教室的牆壁都一致是綠色的。

27　pin [pɪn] *n.* 大頭針，別針；胸針 & *vt.* (用別針) 別住

- pin, pinned [pɪnd], pinned
- pin A to B　將 A 別在 B 上
- brooch [brotʃ] *n.* 胸針
- (1) hairpin [ˋhɛrˌpɪn] *n.* 髮夾
  (2) clothespin [ˋklozˌpɪn] *n.* 衣夾

> My grandmother gave me her antique pin.
> 我的祖母把她的古董胸針給了我。
> *antique [ænˋtik] *a.* 古董的

> The general pinned the medal to my jacket.
> 將軍把獎章別在我的軍常服上。

28　repeat [rɪˋpit] *vt.* & *n.* 重複

- (1) repeatedly [rɪˋpitɪdlɪ]
  adv. 一再地
  (2) repetition [ˌrɛpəˋtɪʃən] *n.* 重複 ④

> Could you please repeat the question?
> 請你再把問題重複一遍好嗎？

> My weekend was a repeat of last weekend. I stayed home and watched movies.
> 我這個週末是上週的翻版。我待在家看電影。

29　drop [drɑp] *vt.* & *vi.* (使) 掉落 & *vi.* 下降 & *n.* 滴；下降

- drop, dropped [drɑpt], dropped

> Be careful. Don't drop the vase.
> 小心。別讓花瓶掉下來。

片 (1) drop by　　　順道來訪
　 (2) drop in on sb　順道探訪某人
　 (3) drop sb a line　給某人寫信
　 (4) a drop of...　　一滴⋯⋯

衍 dropout [ˈdrɑpˌaʊt] *n.* 退學生

似 (1) fall [fɔl] *vi.* & *n.* 落下；下降 ①
　 (2) decrease [dɪˈkris]
　　　 vt. & *vi.* 減少 & [ˈdikris] *n.* 下降，
　　　 減少 ③

▶ Stock prices dropped sharply in Asia yesterday.
　昨天亞洲的股價劇烈下跌。

▶ Ken dropped by to see me this morning.
　肯今早順道來拜訪我。

▶ I dropped in on Stacey on my way home.
　我回家途中順便去看史黛西。

▶ Drop me a line if you can.
　可以的話，寫信給我。

▶ A drop of sweat ran down Harry's forehead.
　一滴汗珠從哈利的額頭流下來。

▶ There was a sudden drop in temperature last night.
　昨晚氣溫驟降。

30　attack [əˈtæk] *vt.* & *n.* 攻擊

片 (1) a personal attack　人身攻擊
　 (2) a terrorist attack　恐攻

▶ A stray dog attacked that little boy yesterday.
　昨天有隻流浪狗攻擊那個小男孩。

▶ You are allowed to disagree with others, but personal attacks will not be tolerated.
　你可以和他人持不同意見，但人身攻擊是不被容許的。
　*tolerate [ˈtɑləˌret] *vt.* 容忍

31　sign [saɪn] *vt.* & *vi.* 簽名 & *n.* 跡象；信號，示意；標示牌

片 (1) sign up for...　報名⋯⋯
　　 = register for...
　 (2) sign a contract　簽約
　 (3) sign language　手語
　 (4) a sign of...　⋯⋯的表現 / 跡象
　 (5) give / make a sign　發出信號

衍 (1) signal [ˈsɪgnl] *n.* 信號 ③
　 (2) signature [ˈsɪgnəˌtʃɚ] *n.* 簽名 ④

▶ Jacob took out his pen to sign the check.
　雅各拿出他的筆來簽支票。

▶ Please sign here.
　請在這裡簽名。

▶ I'm planning to sign up for that course this semester.
　我這學期計劃要修那門課。

▶ The gift was a sign of her love.
　這份禮物是她愛的表現。

▶ Wait until I give the sign.
　等候我發出信號。

▶ The sign reads, "No Smoking."
　這標示牌寫著：『禁止吸菸』。

32　temple [ˈtɛmpl̩] *n.* 寺廟

延伸 (1) church [tʃɝtʃ] *n.* 教堂 ①
　 (2) cathedral [kəˈθidrəl]
　　　 n. 天主教大教堂 ⑤

▶ At the temple, my mother prayed for my grandfather to get well soon.
　我媽媽在寺廟裡祈求爺爺身體早點康復。

33 item [ˈaɪtəm] *n.* 物品

似 (1) thing [θɪŋ] *n.* 東西 ①
(2) object [ˈɑbdʒɪkt] *n.* 物體 ②

▸ None of the items on the table belong to me.
桌上的物品沒有一件是我的。

34 error [ˈɛrɚ] *n.* 錯誤，過失

片 (1) make an error　犯錯
= make a mistake
(2) trial and error　反覆試驗

衍 err [ɛr] *vi.* 犯錯

似 mistake [məˈstek] *n.* 錯誤 ①

▸ Pauline made two grammatical errors in this sentence.
寶琳在這個句子中犯了 2 個文法錯誤。

▸ We learn by trial and error.
我們在嘗試與錯誤中學習。

35 blind [blaɪnd] *a.* 盲的；盲目的 & *n.* 百葉窗（常用複數）& *vt.* 使失明

片 (1) be blind to sth
沒有注意到某事物
(2) turn a blind eye (to sth)
（對某事物）視若無睹

衍 (1) blindness [ˈblaɪndnəs] *n.* 盲目
(2) blinding [ˈblaɪndɪŋ] *a.* 令人眩目的

似 sightless [ˈsaɪtləs] *a.* 看不見的

▸ Audrey was born blind.
奧黛莉天生眼盲。

▸ Blind faith won't do you any good.
盲目的相信對你無益。

▸ Our boss is blind to the current business trends.
我們的老闆看不出來現代商業的趨勢。

▸ The fast pace of city life makes people turn a blind eye to others' feelings.
都市生活的快速步調使大家對他人的感受視若無睹。

▸ Make sure to pull down your blinds at night.
晚上務必要把百葉窗拉下來。

▸ The little girl was blinded in the accident.
那個小女孩在意外中失明了。

36 engineer [ˌɛndʒəˈnɪr] *n.* 工程師 & *vt.* 策劃

片 a computer / mechanical / chemical engineer
電腦 / 機械 / 化學工程師

衍 engineering [ˌɛndʒəˈnɪrɪŋ]
n. 工程（學）（不可數）④

▸ Ezra is a good mechanical engineer.
以斯拉是個優秀的機械工程師。

▸ I'm sure Samantha will engineer the election campaign beautifully.
我相信莎曼珊會把這次選舉活動辦得很漂亮。

37 twice [twaɪs] *adv.* 兩次；兩倍

片 twice a day / week / month
一天 / 週 / 個月 2 次

▸ Annie has only played tennis twice.
安妮只打過 2 次網球。

▸ Nina takes piano lessons twice a week.
妮娜一週上 2 次鋼琴課。

38 string [strɪŋ] n. 線，繩子；一串；(樂器的) 弦

片 (1) a piece of string　一條繩子
(2) a string of pearls / beads
　一串珍珠 / 珠子

似 (1) rope [rop] n. (粗的) 繩索 ①
(2) thread [θrɛd] n. (縫衣服的) 線 ③

▶ I need a piece of string to tie this box.
我需要一條繩子來綁這個箱子。

▶ That rich woman always wears a string of pearls around her neck.
那名貴婦總是在脖子上戴著一串珍珠。

▶ One of the strings broke while Phil was playing the guitar.
菲爾彈吉他時，其中一條弦斷掉了。

39 pipe [paɪp] n. 管子

衍 pipeline [ˋpaɪp͵laɪn]
　n. 管線，輸油管 ⑤

▶ The pipes must be clogged. The sink is full of dirty water.
水管一定是堵住了，水槽裡積滿了汙水。
＊clog [klɑg] vt. 堵塞，塞住

| Level ② |

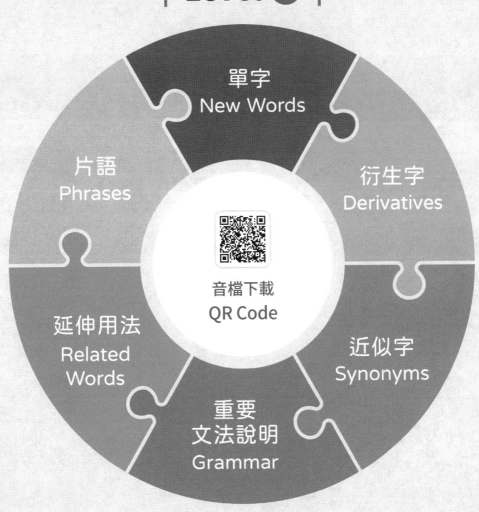

單字
New Words

衍生字
Derivatives

片語
Phrases

音檔下載
QR Code

近似字
Synonyms

延伸用法
Related
Words

重要
文法說明
Grammar

Unit 26

2601-2603

1　provide [prəˈvaɪd] vt. 提供

囝 (1) provide sb with sth
　　提供某人某物
　　= provide sth for sb
　　(2) provide against sth
　　防備 / 預防某事物，為 (防備) 某事物做準備

▶ I'll provide you with everything you need for the mission.
我會提供你這項任務中所需的一切。

▶ I bought a lot of canned food to provide against the coming typhoon.
我買了很多罐頭食物，為即將來襲的颱風做準備。

---

offer [ˈɔfɚ]
vt. 提供 & n. 提議，主動表示

囝 (1) offer sb sth　提供某人某物
　　= offer sth to sb
　　(2) an offer of help　主動提出要幫忙

▶ Thank you for offering me such a great opportunity.
= Thank you for offering such a great opportunity to me.
謝謝你提供我一個這麼好的機會。

▶ Mary accepted their offer of help.
瑪麗接受了他們想幫忙的提議。

---

supply [səˈplaɪ]
vt. 供應 & n. 補給品 (恆用複數)；供給量

冒 supply, supplied [səˈplaɪd], supplied

複 supplies [səˈplaɪz]

囝 (1) supply sb with sth
　　供應某人某物
　　= supply sth to sb
　　(2) a supply of...　……的供應量
　　(3) supply and demand　供需

反 demand [dɪˈmænd]
vt. 要求 & n. 需求 ④

▶ Despite water rationing, the large water tank can supply the residents with the water they need.
儘管有限水，大型水塔仍可為住戶提供用水。
＊rationing [ˈræʃənɪŋ] n. 配給機制 (不可數)

▶ There is a lack of medical supplies in the refugee camp.
這難民營缺乏醫療用品。

▶ In the Middle East, there is a plentiful supply of cheap natural gas.
在中東，廉價天然氣供應充足。
＊plentiful [ˈplɛntɪfəl] a. 充足的

2　company [ˈkʌmpənɪ] n. 公司 (可數)；陪伴 (不可數)

複 companies [ˈkʌmpənɪz]

囝 keep sb company　陪伴某人

衍 accompany [əˈkʌmpənɪ] vt. 陪伴 ④

▶ The company is going out of business soon.
這家公司就要倒閉了。
＊go out of business　倒閉

▶ He kept me company until the bus came.
他陪我直到公車來為止。

3　soft [sɔft] a. 柔軟的；(聲音等) 柔和的

衍 soften [ˈsɔfən] vi. & vt. (使) 柔和 ⑤

反 (1) hard [hɑrd] a. 硬的 ①
　　(2) loud [laʊd] a. 大聲的 ①

▶ This bread is soft and delicious.
這麵包鬆軟好吃。

▶ Nora's voice was so soft that I could hardly hear it.
諾拉的聲音輕柔到我幾乎聽不見。

firm [fɜm] *a.* 堅硬的；堅定的 & *n.* 公司 (= company) & *vi.* 穩定下來 & *adv.* 堅定地

🔑 (1) a firm decision / promise
　　堅決的決定 / 堅定的承諾
　　(2) stand firm　拒不讓步，堅定不移

衍 firmness [ˋfɜmnəs] *n.* 硬度；穩固

▶ I prefer to sleep on a firm bed.
　我比較喜歡睡硬床。

▶ Greg waited until he had more information before making a firm decision.
　葛瑞格等到他掌握了更多資訊後才做出堅決的決定。

▶ I work for a law firm.
　我在一家律師事務所上班。

▶ Housing prices fell during the poor economy, but they have since firmed.
　經濟不景氣時，房價有所下跌，但之後卻穩定了下來。

▶ Despite pressure from management, the employees stood firm in their wage demands.
　儘管有資方的壓力，員工仍然對於工資要求拒不讓步。

4　social [ˋsoʃəl] *a.* 社會的；社交的

🔑 (1) a social issue　社會議題
　　(2) a social life　社交生活
　　(3) a social club　社團

衍 sociology [ˌsoʃɪˋɑlədʒɪ] *n.* 社會學 ⑥

▶ Roger and my father discussed many of today's social issues.
　羅傑和我父親討論了許多當今的社會議題。

▶ That lonely guy doesn't have any social life.
　那孤單的傢伙沒有任何社交生活。

▶ Mark wanted to join a social club to make new friends.
　馬克想加入社團來結交新朋友。

---

society [səˋsaɪətɪ] *n.* 社會

複 societies [səˋsaɪətɪz]

▶ This environmental organization worked hard for the good of society.
　這環保組織為了社會的福祉而努力。

5　figure [ˋfɪgjɚ] *vt.* 認為 & *n.* 數字；身材

🔑 (1) figure (that)...　認為……
　　(2) figure out...
　　　想出……，弄明白……
　　(3) have a fine / good / beautiful figure　身材很好

▶ I never figured Johnny was a talented director.
　我從不認為強尼是位有才華的導演。

▶ We need to figure out a way to fix this problem.
　我們得想出個方法來解決這個問題。

▶ The professional basketball player just signed an eight-figure contract.
　那位職籃選手剛簽下一張價值 8 位數的合約。

▶ That woman has a fine figure.
　那女人身材很好。

6 countryside [ˈkʌntrɪˌsaɪd] n. 鄉間 (不可數)

片 in the countryside　在鄉下
= in the country

衍 country [ˈkʌntrɪ]
　　n. 國家 (可數)；鄉間 (不可數) ①

▶ I enjoy living in the countryside because the air here is fresh.
我喜歡住在鄉下，因為這裡空氣很新鮮。

---

village [ˈvɪlɪdʒ] n. 村莊

衍 villager [ˈvɪlɪdʒɚ] n. 村民

▶ The village was almost destroyed by fire.
這村莊幾乎被大火燒毀了。

---

field [fild]
n. 原 / 田野，牧場；操場；領域

片 (1) in a field　在原 / 田野，在牧場
　　(2) a sports / baseball field
　　　　操場 / 棒球場
　　(3) a field trip　校外教學，實地考察
　　(4) in the field of sth
　　　　在某事物的領域裡

似 (1) area [ˈɛrɪə] n. 範圍 ①
　　(2) aspect [ˈæspɛkt] n. 方面 ④

▶ There are ten cows in the field.
原野上有 10 頭乳牛。

▶ Bobby and his friends played soccer on the large sports field.
巴比和他朋友在這大型運動場上踢足球。

▶ Mrs. Simpson's class took a field trip to a chocolate factory.
辛普森老師班級的校外教學去了一家巧克力工廠。

▶ John is an expert in the field of history.
在歷史學的領域裡約翰是專家。

7 fisherman [ˈfɪʃəmən] n. 漁夫，釣 / 抓魚的人 (= fisher [ˈfɪʃɚ])

複 fishermen [ˈfɪʃəmən]

衍 fishery [ˈfɪʃərɪ] n. 漁場 ⑥

▶ These fishermen were worried about the coming typhoon.
這些漁夫很擔心即將要來的颱風。

---

sailor [ˈselɚ] n. 船員，水手

▶ Those sailors were caught in a violent storm.
那些船員遇到一場猛烈的風暴。

---

sail [sel]
n. 帆 & vi. 航行 & vt. & vi. 駕駛 (船)

片 sail to + 地方　航向某地

▶ The sails of the boat flapped in the strong wind.
這艘船的帆在強風中擺動著。
*flap [flæp] vi. & vt. (使) 飄 / 擺動

▶ As the ship sailed to Europe, it faced heavy waves.
這艘船航向歐洲時遇到了巨浪。

▶ It was a nice day to sail a boat on the lake.
今天在湖泊上開船過得真愉快。

▶ Judy's father taught her how to sail when she was young.
茱蒂年輕時，她父親有教她如何駕船。

8 sock [sɑk] *n.* 短襪

⏃ a pair of socks　一雙襪子

▸ Rex is wearing a pair of yellow socks.
雷克斯穿了一雙黃色襪子。

9 international [ˌɪntɚˋnæʃən̩l] *a.* 國際的

⏃ (1) international trade　國際貿易
(2) the International Date Line
國際換日線

衍 national [ˋnæʃən̩l]
a. 國家的，國立的；全國的 ①

▸ English is an important international language.
英文是個重要的國際語言。

▸ After studying international trade, Max got a good job as a salesman.
麥克斯學了國貿後，就找到了當推銷員這很好的工作。

10 value [ˋvælju] *n.* 價值；重要性；價值觀 (此意恆用複數) & *vt.* 珍惜

⏃ (1) place a high value on sth
非常重視某事物
(2) be of great value
很重要，很有價值
= be valuable

衍 (1) valuable [ˋvæljʊəbl̩]
a. 有價值的；值錢的 ②
(2) valueless [ˋvæljʊləs]
a. 沒有價值的

▸ This building has a value of more than 20 million NT dollars.
這棟建築物價值超過 2,000 萬新臺幣。

▸ Gordon wondered why such a high value was placed on the artwork.
戈登想知道為什麼這藝術品會如此受到重視。

▸ I believe this book will be of great value to both teachers and students.
我相信這本書對老師和學生都很重要。

▸ Herman later learned that his values were different from his girlfriend's.
赫曼後來瞭解到，他的價值觀和他女友的價值觀並不同。

▸ I value / treasure our friendship.
我很珍惜我們的友誼。

11 president [ˋprɛzədənt] *n.* 總統；總裁，董事長

衍 (1) presidential [ˌprɛzəˋdɛnʃəl]
a. 總統的 ⑤
(2) preside [prɪˋzaɪd]
vi. 主持 (會議等) ⑥

preside over a meeting
主持會議
= chair a meeting

▸ The president is planning to visit some diplomatic allies next month.
總統計劃下個月去拜訪一些邦交國家。
＊ally [ˋælaɪ] *n.* 盟友 (複數為 allies)

▸ It is said that Stan Smith will be the new president of this company.
據說史坦・史密斯將成為這家公司的新總裁。

12 regard [rɪˋgɑrd] *vt.* 把……視為 & *n.* 問候 (恆用複數)

⏃ (1) regard A as B　將 A 視為 B
= look on / upon A as B
= think of A as B

▸ We all regard Roger as a hero.
我們都把羅傑視為英雄。

228

Level 2

Unit 26

= see / view A as B

= consider A (to be) B

(2) give A's regards to B
   代 A 向 B 問好

= remember A to B

(3) with / in regard to... 有關……

衍 (1) regarding [rɪˋgɑrdɪŋ]
   prep. 關於 ④

(2) regardless [rɪˋgɑrdləs]
   adv. 不管怎樣 ⑤

▶ Give my best regards to John when you see him.

= Say hello to John for me when you see him.

= Remember me to John when you see him.
   見到約翰時，代我向他問好。

▶ With regard to your request for a refund, we have referred the matter to our general manager.
   關於您請求退款一事，我們已轉請總經理處理。

---

suppose [səˋpoz] *vt.* 想，認為；假定

片 be supposed to V 應該做……

= should + V

衍 (1) supposed [səˋpozd]
   a. 據說的，所謂的

(2) supposedly [səˋpozɪdlɪ]
   adv. 大概，可能 ⑤

▶ It's late, so I suppose you must go home.
   時間很晚了，所以我想你得回家了。

▶ Suppose you are walking on a hot and dusty road.
   假設你正走在一條很熱、塵土又多的路上。

▶ You are not supposed to wear jeans to such a formal meeting.
   在這麼正式的會議上你不該穿牛仔褲的。

---

consider [kənˋsɪdɚ]

vt. 考慮；把……視為

片 (1) consider + V-ing 考慮做……

(2) consider A (to be) + N/adj.
   將……視為……

衍 (1) considerable [kənˋsɪdərəbḷ]
   a. 相當多的 ③

(2) considerate [kənˋsɪdərət]
   a. 體貼的 ⑤

▶ I'm considering taking a trip to Japan.
   我正考慮到日本去旅行。

▶ To my surprise, Judith said she didn't consider Owen (to be) a friend of hers.
   令我很驚訝的是，茱蒂絲說她並沒有把歐文當作是朋友。

▶ In fact, many workers considered the plan (to be) impractical.
   實際上，很多工人認為那計畫很不切實際。

---

consideration [kənˌsɪdəˋreʃən]

n. 考慮

片 take sth into consideration /
   account 考慮 / 顧及到某事物

▶ Further consideration is necessary before we carry out this plan.
   在我們實施這項計畫前，必須再三考慮才行。

▶ Before criticizing Martin, you should take his inexperience into consideration.
   在批評馬丁之前，你必須顧及到他的經驗並不足。

---

thought [θɔt] *n.* 想法

片 (1) at the thought of sth
   一想到某事物

(2) on second thought
   再三考慮後，轉念一想

▶ Kevin felt sad at the thought of his disabled child struggling at school.
   凱文一想到自己的身障孩子在學校掙扎，就感到很難過。

▶ On second thought, maybe we should eat at home.
   再三考慮後，也許我們應該在家吃就好。

13 increase [ɪnˋkris] *vt. & vi. &* [ˋɪnkris] *n.* 增加

片 (an) increase in sth　某事物有增加

似 raise [rez] *vt.* 增加；養育 & *n.* 加薪 ①

反 decrease [dɪˋkris]
vt. & vi. & [ˋdikris] *n.* 減少 ③

▶ The driver increased speed suddenly.
這位駕駛突然加速行駛。

▶ The number of tourists has increased greatly.
遊客的人數已大量增加了。

▶ People were very angry over the recent increase in taxes.
人們對最近的增稅感到很憤怒。

14 escape [əˋskep] *vi. & vt.* 逃脫；躲過 & *n.* 逃脫

片 (1) escape from + 地方　從某處逃脫
　　(2) escape + N/V-ing　躲過……

似 (1) flee [fli] *vi.* 逃走 ④
　　三態為：flee, fled [flɛd], fled
　　(2) avoid [əˋvɔɪd] *vt.* 避開 ②

▶ According to the news, a notorious drug dealer escaped from prison.
據新聞報導，一個惡名昭彰的毒販越獄了。

▶ We were lucky to escape punishment.
= We were lucky to escape being punished.
我們很幸運沒受到處罰。

▶ The media reports of the dangerous prisoner's escape worried the public.
媒體報導有一危險囚犯越獄了，這令大眾憂心忡忡。

15 develop [dɪˋvɛləp] *vi. & vt.* (使) 發展

片 (1) develop into sth
　　發展成為某事物
　　(2) develop a skill　發展 / 培養技能

衍 (1) developed [dɪˋvɛləpt]
　　a. 發達的，先進的
　　(2) developing [dɪˋvɛləpɪŋ]
　　a. 發展中的，開發中的
　　(3) underdeveloped
　　[ˌʌndədɪˋvɛləpt]
　　a. 發展不全的；低度開發的

▶ The mistake was ignored and later developed into a major problem.
這錯誤被忽略，後來就演變成一個大問題。

▶ In this class, you can develop your writing skills.
在這門課裡，你可以提高寫作技巧。

development [dɪˋvɛləpmənt]
n. 發展；(研製) 開發；(事情的) 進展

片 research and development　研發

▶ Economic development is our top priority now.
發展經濟是我們的當務之急。

▶ The development of the medicine took many years.
開發這藥物花了好幾年的時間。

▶ The company's success was due to its investment in research and development.
這公司會成功是因為其在研發方面的投資。

▶ I'll keep you posted on the latest developments.
我會向你通報最新的進展。

16 burn [bɜn] *vt.* 燒毀 & *vi.* 燃燒 & *vi.* & *vt.* 燒焦 & *n.* 燒／灼傷

三 burn, burned [bɜnd] /
burnt [bɜnt], burned / burnt

片 (1) burn... up / burn up...
將 (紙張、文件等) 燒毀

(2) burn... down / burn down...
將 (大樓、房舍) 燒毀

▶ The secretary burned up all the papers before the police came.
那祕書在警方來之前就燒毀了所有的文件。

▶ The fire burned down his house.
大火燒毀了他的房子。

▶ An average candle burns for four hours.
一根蠟燭平均可燃燒 4 小時。

▶ Oh, no! The chocolate cookies have burned. I should have paid more attention to the time.
哦，不！巧克力餅乾燒焦了。我應該更注意一下時間的。

▶ Did you burn the fish?
你把魚煮焦了嗎？

▶ Robert is being treated for terrible burns.
羅伯特因嚴重燙傷正在接受治療中。

17 effect [ɪˋfɛkt] *n.* 效果，影響 & *vt.* 使發生，實現

片 (1) take effect　見效
(2) have a side effect　有副作用
(3) have a(n) + adj. + effect on...
對……有……樣的影響

似 affect [əˋfɛkt] *vt.* 影響 ②

▶ The medicine was starting to take effect.
這藥開始見效了。

▶ The doctor said this drug doesn't have any side effects.
醫生說這藥沒有任何副作用。

▶ Smoking will certainly have a bad effect on your health.
抽菸對你的健康絕對有不良的影響。

▶ The manager knew it would be hard to effect his changes.
經理知道很難實現他的變革。

effective [ɪˋfɛktɪv] *a.* 有效的
反 ineffective [ɪnəˋfɛktɪv] *a.* 無效的

▶ Do you think this medicine is effective?
你認為這藥有效嗎？

18 whenever [(h)wɛnˋɛvɚ] *conj.* 每當 & *adv.* 無論何時

片 whenever possible
盡可能地，有機會就

▶ Whenever I was on stage, my hands couldn't stop shaking.
每當我在臺上時，我手就會抖個不停。

▶ I like to eat vegetarian food whenever possible.
我喜歡有機會就吃素食。

wherever [(h)wɛrˋɛvɚ]
conj. 無論在哪裡 & *adv.* 任何地方

▶ Wherever Joseph hides, this dog can find him.
不論約瑟夫躲在哪裡，這隻狗都找到他。

Level 2　Unit 26

▶ I want to move to Paris, Rome, (or) wherever.
我想搬到巴黎、羅馬，或是其他任何地方。

---

19 bookstore [`bʊk,stɔr ] *n.* 書店 (= bookshop [ `bʊk,ʃɑp]〔英〕)

衍 book [bʊk] *n.* 書 ①

▶ Donald went to a bookstore yesterday and bought a few novels.
唐納德昨天去書店買了幾本小說。

---

20 better [`bɛtɚ] *a.* 更好的 & *adv.* 更好地 & *n.* 更好的事物 / 行為 & *vt.* 提升，改善

H **for better or (for) worse**
不論好壞，不管結果如何

▶ George wants to buy a better car than his current one.
喬治想買一輛比現在更好的車。

▶ Tony was unhappy because his sister did better than him on the final exam.
湯尼很不高興，因為他妹妹期末考考得比他好。

▶ Trevor had a hard life, but he wanted better for his kids.
崔佛的生活過得很艱難，但他想讓他的孩子有更好的生活。

▶ Steve decided to better his job opportunities by getting a master's degree.
史提夫決定去取得碩士學位好來提升自己的工作機會。

▶ Josh knew, for better or worse, he must accept his parents' decision.
喬許知道，無論好壞，他都得接受他父母的決定。

---

worse [wɜs] *a.* 更糟的 & *adv.* 更糟地 & *n.* 更糟的事

H **make matters worse** 使情況更糟

▶ Erica tried to help, but she actually made matters worse.
艾瑞卡試圖幫忙，但她實際上卻把事情弄得更糟。

▶ Larry played tennis worse than usual yesterday because he was tired.
賴瑞昨天打網球打得比平常還差，因為他當時累了。

▶ The typhoon was bad, but Gail had seen worse before.
這次的颱風很厲害，但蓋兒之前還見過更厲害的颱風。

---

worst [wɜst] *a.* 最糟的 & *adv.* 最糟地 & *n.* 最糟的情況

H (1) **worst of all** 最糟的是
(2) **at worst** 在最壞的情況下

▶ Gloria thought the singer was the worst one she had ever heard.
葛蘿莉亞認為這歌手是她聽過唱得最糟的歌手。

▶ Jim was late for school; worst of all, he forgot his books.
吉姆上學遲到了；最糟的是，他忘了帶書。

▶ Eliot knew that, at worst, he would be only 15 minutes late for the meeting.
艾略特知道最壞的情況是他只會開會遲到 15 分鐘。

further [ˋfɝðɚ]
a. 更進一步的，更多的 & *adv.* 更進一步 & *vt.* 增進

囵 **furthermore** [ˋfɝðɚ͵mɔr]
adv. 而且 ④

比 一般來說，further 指的是程度上『更進一步』，farther [ˋfɑrðɚ] 指的是實際空間、距離上『更遠』。

▶ The long-distance runner was exhausted and couldn't go any farther.
該長跑選手已筋疲力盡，沒辦法跑更遠了。

▶ Visit our website for further information.
如需更多資訊請上我們的網站。

▶ Justin said he didn't want to talk about it any further.
賈斯汀說他不想再談這件事了。

▶ To further his English ability, Simon took more classes.
為了進一步提升他的英語能力，西蒙上了更多課程。

---

21 stone [ston] *n.* 石頭 & *vt.* 用石頭砸

片 (1) leave no stone unturned
千方百計，不遺餘力
(2) be a stone's throw from + 地方
在某地方附近

▶ Gordon left no stone unturned in his search for the person who had saved his life.
戈登千方百計地想找出他的救命恩人。

▶ My school is a stone's throw from here.
我學校離這兒只有幾步遠而已。

▶ The protesters were arrested because they stoned the police.
那些抗議人士因向警察扔石頭而被捕。

---

22 suggest [sə(g)ˋdʒɛst] *vt.* 建議；暗示

片 (1) suggest (that) + S + (should) + V... 建議某人 (應該) 做……
(2) suggest (that)... 暗示……

似 **recommend** [͵rɛkəˋmɛnd]
vt. 建議；推薦 ⑤

▶ Frank suggested that we (should) leave early.
法蘭克建議我們早點離開。

▶ Alice's expression suggested that she was getting impatient.
愛麗斯的表情暗示她不耐煩了。

---

23 challenge [ˋtʃæləndʒ] *n.* 挑戰 & *vt.* 向……挑戰

片 (1) face a challenge (of...)
面臨 (……的) 挑戰
(2) meet a challenge (of...)
(成功地) 應對 / 迎接 (……的) 挑戰
= rise to a challenge (of...)
(3) challenge sb to + N/V
挑戰某人……

▶ The politician is facing the biggest challenge of her career.
這位政治人物正面臨她職涯中最大的挑戰。

▶ To our surprise, the little boy met the challenge of taking care of his younger sister.
令我們驚訝的是，那小男孩成功地完成了照顧妹妹的挑戰。

▶ The young chess player challenged the world champion to a game of chess.
這年輕的西洋棋手向世界冠軍挑戰比一回棋賽。

2701-2707

1 pride [praɪd] *n.* 自豪；自尊心；驕傲 & *vt.* 以……為榮

🔲 take pride in...　以……為榮
= pride oneself on...
= be proud of...

衍 prideful [ˈpraɪdfəl] *a.* 自大的

延伸 proud [praʊd]
a. 自豪的；有自尊心的；驕傲的 ①

▶ The father takes pride in his son's excellent performance in school.
= The father prides himself on his son's excellent performance in school.
孩子在學校有優異的表現，這個做父親的引以為榮。

▶ Mary's comments hurt David's pride.
瑪麗的評語傷了大衛的自尊心。

▶ Pride keeps the young man from doing manual labor.
驕傲使這個年輕人不願屈就勞力的工作。
*manual [ˈmænjʊəl] *a.* 體力的

2 govern [ˈgʌvɚn] *vt.* 統治，治理 (= rule [rul])；管理，控制

衍 governor [ˈgʌvɚnɚ] *n.* 州長，省長 ③

似 reign [ren] *vi.* 統治 ⑥

▶ The president has governed that country for the last ten years.
該位總統在過去的 10 年一直統治著那國家。

▶ Many people think we should change the laws that govern charities.
很多人認為我們應該改變管理慈善機構的法律。

government [ˈgʌvɚnmənt]
n. 政府 (可數)；政體 (不可數)

🔲 (1) central / local government
中央 / 地方政府 (皆不可數)
(2) a student government
學生自治會

▶ The central government has promised to cut taxes.
中央政府已承諾要減稅。

▶ Which do you prefer—democratic or communist government?
你比較喜歡哪一種 —— 民主還是共產政體？

3 period [ˈpɪrɪəd] *n.* 一段期間；句點；一節課

🔲 a period of + 時間　一段……時間

衍 (1) periodic [ˌpɪrɪˈɑdɪk] *a.* 週期性的
(2) periodical [ˌpɪrɪˈɑdɪkl] *n.* 期刊

▶ I'm going to stay here for a long period of time.
我將在這裡待上一段很長的時間。

▶ You need to put a period at the end of the sentence.
你需要在句尾加句點。

▶ We have two periods of geography per week.
我們每星期有 2 節地理課。

term [tɝm]
n. 學期；期間；專門用語 & *vt.* 把……稱為

▶ All students are required to hand in a written paper at the end of the term.
所有學生於學期末均須繳交一篇書面報告。

片 (1) at the beginning / end of the term　於學期初 / 末

(2) in the short term / run
短期來看

in the long term / run
從長遠來看

(3) in terms of...
就……而言，從……方面來說

衍 (1) terminal [`tɜmənḷ] *a.* 末期的 ⑤

(2) terminate [`tɜmə‚net] *vt.* 終結

(3) midterm [`mɪd‚tɜm] *n.* 期中考

似 semester [sə`mɛstə] *n.* 學期 ③

▶ I believe the new policy will be beneficial in the long term.
我相信從長遠來看，新政策是有利的。

▶ The article is full of medical terms.
這篇文章有好多醫學專業用語。

▶ In terms of music, I like jazz best.
就音樂而言，我最喜歡爵士樂。

▶ Capital punishment is sometimes termed a "necessary evil."
死刑有時被稱為『必要之惡』。

4　century [`sɛntʃərɪ] *n.* 世紀

片 half a century　半個世紀

延伸 (1) year [jɪr] *n.* 1 年 ①

(2) decade [`dɛked] *n.* 10 年 ③

▶ Many great inventions were made in the 20th century.
許多偉大的發明都是在 20 世紀問世的。

5　accident [`æksədənt] *n.* 意外 (尤指車禍)

片 (1) a car accident　車禍

(2) by accident　無意地，意外地

比 accident 指突發的意外事件，而 incident 則較廣泛，可指突發的意外事件或有人蓄意造成的事件。

▶ David's back was seriously injured in a car accident.
大衛在一場車禍中背部受到重傷。

▶ Jerry hit the woman by accident and apologized to her.
傑瑞不小心撞到了那女子，就向她道歉。

6　result [rɪ`zʌlt] *vi.* 由……引起；導致，造成 & *n.* 結果

片 (1) result from...　起因於……

(2) A result in B　A 導致 B
= A cause B

(3) as a result of...　由於……
= because of...

似 outcome [`aʊt‚kʌm] *n.* 結果 ④

反 cause [kɔz] *n.* 原因 ②

▶ Ben's failure resulted from laziness.
班的失敗起因於懶惰。

▶ The car accident resulted in the death of five people.
這起車禍造成 5 人死亡。

▶ Millions of people died as a result of the pandemic.
數百萬人因該大流行病而死亡。
＊pandemic [pæn`dɛmɪk] *n.* 大流行病

▶ The election results will be announced on May 13th.
選舉結果將於 5 月 13 日宣布。

7　local [`lokḷ] *a.* 當地的，本地的 & *n.* 當地人，本地人

片 a local newspaper / custom
當地的報紙 / 地方風俗

似 regional [`ridʒənḷ] *a.* 地區的 ③

▶ The local market offers a great selection of fruits and vegetables.
本地市場供應種類繁多的蔬果。

▶ The local newspaper wrote about some special customs.
當地報紙寫了一些很特別的習俗。

▶ One of the locals showed me the way to the gas station.
有一個當地人告訴我前往加油站的路。

8 chess [tʃɛs] *n.* 西洋棋 (不可數)

田 play chess　下棋

▶ Jessie is very good at playing chess.
潔西很會下西洋棋。

---

board [bɔrd] *n.* (木頭等製成的) 板子；董事會；伙食 & *vt.* & *vi.* (使) 上 (飛機 / 船 / 車等)

田 (1) a chess board　西洋棋棋盤
　　= a chessboard
　　(2) room and board
　　　伙食及住宿，膳宿

似 (1) aboard [əˋbɔrd]
　　　adv. & *prep.* 在 (飛機 / 船 / 車上) ③
　　(2) abroad [əˋbrɔd] *adv.* 在國外 ①

▶ We need more boards to build the bookshelf.
我們需要更多木板來做這個書架。

▶ Every decision is made by the school board.
每一項決策都由學校董事會決定。

▶ Does the price include room and board?
這價錢包含膳宿在內嗎？

▶ All passengers must board the plane at Gate 77.
所有旅客一律必須於 77 號門登機。

▶ An announcement told passengers it was time to board.
廣播通知乘客現在該登機了。

9 trash [træʃ] *n.* 垃圾 (不可數) 〔美〕 & *vt.* 丟棄

田 a trash can　垃圾桶

似 rubbish [ˋrʌbɪʃ] *n.* 垃圾 〔英〕⑥

用法 trash、garbage、rubbish、litter 皆表『垃圾』，且均為不可數名詞；如表『一件 / 個垃圾』，均須與 a piece of 並用。
　　a trash (✕)
→ a piece of trash (○)　一件 / 個垃圾

▶ The boy picked up a piece of trash and threw it in the trash can.
男孩撿起一個垃圾丟進了垃圾桶裡。

▶ When his smartphone stopped working, Luke trashed it.
當路克的手機壞了，他就把它丟掉了。

---

garbage [ˋgɑrbɪdʒ]
n. 垃圾 (不可數) 〔美〕

▶ Sort out your garbage before dumping it.
倒垃圾前要先將垃圾分類。

▶ Garbage in, garbage out.
垃圾進，垃圾出 / 濫入濫出。—— 諺語，比喻不好的材料就會製作出不好的產品出來

waste [west]
vt. 浪費 & *n.* 浪費；廢棄物

🔑 (1) waste time (in) + V-ing
　　浪費時間做……
(2) a waste of time　浪費時間

▶ Don't waste your time watching TV.
不要浪費時間看電視。

▶ Playing computer games all day is a waste of time.
整天打電腦遊戲很浪費時間。

▶ The disposal of chemical waste is an important issue.
處理化學廢棄物是個很重要的議題。

10　bit [bɪt] *n.* 小塊，小片；少量

🔑 (1) a bit of...　一點點的……
(2) a little bit　一點點
(3) bit by bit　漸漸地

▶ The pasta was so delicious that Susan ate every bit of it.
那義大利麵太美味了，蘇珊吃到一點都不剩。

▶ I need a bit of help with my homework.
我需要有人教一下我功課。

▶ I feel a little bit tired. I think I should go to bed now.
我有點累。我想我該上床睡覺了。

▶ Our project is done bit by bit.
我們的計畫一點一點地完成了。

11　method [ˋmɛθəd] *n.* 方法

似 way [we] *n.* 方法 ①

▶ The method we used earlier to try to get the car started didn't work.
我們先前試著用來發動車子的方法不管用了。

---

approach [əˋprotʃ]
vt. & *vi.* 接近 & *n.* 方法

複 approaches [əˋprotʃɪz]

🔑 (1) be fast approaching　即將來臨
　 = be around the corner
　 = be near at hand
　 = be coming soon
(2) an approach to + N/V-ing
　　……的方法

▶ The dogcatchers approached the dangerous dog with caution.
捕犬員小心翼翼地接近那隻危險的狗。
＊caution [ˋkɔʃən] *n.* 謹慎
　with caution　小心翼翼地

▶ According to the weather forecast, a typhoon is fast approaching.
根據氣象預報，有颱風正快速接近中。

▶ The best approach to learning English is to read English articles out loud and watch English TV programs.
學習英文的最佳途徑是大聲朗誦英文文章和看英文電視節目。

12　necessary [ˋnɛsə͵sɛrɪ] *a.* 必要的

🔑 (1) It is necessary (for sb) to V
　　(某人) 做……是必要的
(2) if necessary　如果必要的話

▶ It is necessary for you to punch in by eight o'clock every morning.
你每天早上一定要在 8 點前打卡上班。
＊punch in　(上班) 打卡

Level 2　Unit 27

衍 necessity [nəˈsɛsətɪ]
   n. 必要 (不可數)；必需品 (可數) ③

---

importance [ɪmˈpɔrtn̩s]
n. 重要 (性)

片 be of great importance 很重要

衍 important [ɪmˈpɔrtn̩t] *a.* 重要的 ①

▸ Our teacher's words are of great importance to us.

= Our teacher's words are very important to us.
   我們老師的話對我們來說很重要。

---

13 control [kənˈtrol] *n. & vt.* 控制

三 control, controlled [kənˈtrold], controlled

片 (1) be under control 在掌控中
   (2) be / go out of control 失控

▸ Don't worry. Everything is under control.
   別擔心。一切都在掌控中。

▸ The whole situation suddenly went out of control.
   整個情況突然失控。

▸ Britney took a deep breath to control the urge to cry.
   布蘭妮深吸一口氣，克制住要大哭的衝動。

---

limit [ˈlɪmɪt]
vt. 限制 & *n.* 限制 (可數)；範圍 (常用複數)

片 (1) limit A to B 將 A 限制於 B
   (2) a speed limit 速限
   (3) within limits 有限度地

衍 (1) limited [ˈlɪmɪtɪd] *a.* 有限的
   (2) limitation [ˌlɪməˈteʃən] *n.* 限制 ④

▸ The doctor told me that I should limit myself to two cups of tea a day.
   醫生告訴我我應該限制自己一天只能喝 2 杯茶。

▸ If you exceed the speed limit, you'll get a ticket.
   你如果超過速限，就會吃上罰單。
   *exceed [ɪkˈsid] *vt.* 超過

▸ I can help you, but within limits.
   我可以幫你，但是有限度的。

---

14 difference [ˈdɪfərəns] *n.* 差別

片 (1) a difference between A and B
   A 和 B 間的差別
   (2) It makes no difference to sb
   對某人來說沒有差別

衍 different [ˈdɪf(ə)rənt] *a.* 不同的 ①

▸ Do you know the difference between a mule and a donkey?
   你知道騾和驢的差別嗎？

▸ It makes no difference to me who wins the presidential election.
   誰贏得總統大選對我來說沒有差別。

---

15 produce [prəˈd(j)us] *vt.* 生產 & [ˈprodus / ˈprɑdus] *n.* 農產品 (不可數)

衍 (1) producer [prəˈd(j)usɚ]
   n. 生產者 ③
   (2) product [ˈprɑdʌkt] *n.* 產品 ③
   (3) productive [prəˈdʌktɪv]
   a. 多產的 ④

▸ This large factory produces furniture.
   這家很大間的工廠生產傢俱。

▸ Henry's farm is famous for its fresh produce.
   亨利的農場素以新鮮的農產品聞名。

production [prəˈdʌkʃən] *n.* 生產
似 **manufacture** [ˌmænjəˈfæktʃɚ]
　n. & vt. (大量) 製造 ④

▶ We need to build two more assembly lines to speed up production.
我們需另外建立 2 條裝配線以加速生產。

16　department [dɪˈpɑrtmənt] *n.* 部門；(大學的) 系

片 a department store　百貨公司

▶ My sister works in the sales department of this company.
我姊姊在這公司的銷售部門工作。

▶ Irene is a professor in the History Department at this university.
艾琳是這所大學歷史系的教授。

▶ Sharon works as a marketing manager in a department store.
雪倫在一間百貨公司擔任行銷經理。

17　attend [əˈtɛnd] *vt. & vi.* 參加，出席 & *vt.* 上 (學等) & *vi.* 照顧

片 attend to sb　照顧某人
衍 (1) attendance [əˈtɛndəns] *n.* 出席 ⑤
　　(2) attendant [əˈtɛndənt] *n.* 隨從 ⑥

▶ All employees are required to attend the meeting.
全體員工一律得去參加該會議。

▶ Brenda invited Jim to her wedding, but he was unable to attend.
布蘭達邀請吉姆來參加她的婚禮，但吉姆無法參加。

▶ George is the first person to attend college in his family.
喬治是他家第一個上大學的人。

▶ Brian hired a caretaker to attend to his father on a 24-hour basis.
布萊恩僱用看護來 24 小時全天候照顧他爸爸。

attention [əˈtɛnʃən]
n. 注意；立正 (姿勢)

片 (1) pay attention to...　注意……
　　(2) stand at / to attention
　　　　立正站好

▶ You should pay attention to the coach.
你該注意聽教練說的話。

▶ We should stand at attention when the national anthem is played.
演奏國歌時，我們應該立正站好。
＊anthem [ˈænθəm] *n.* 國歌

18　describe [dɪˈskraɪb] *vt.* 描述，形容

片 describe sb/sth as + N/adj.
　把某人 / 某物描述成……
似 (1) depict [dɪˈpɪkt] *vt.* 描述 ⑤
　　(2) descriptive [dɪˈskrɪptɪv]
　　　　a. 描述的 ⑤

▶ Can you describe the man who stole your purse?
妳能描述一下偷妳手提包的人的樣子嗎？

▶ Vince described his girlfriend as an intelligent beauty.
文斯把他女友形容為知性美女。

description [dɪˋskrɪpʃən]
n. 描述，形容

片 be beyond description
非筆墨所能形容

▶ The majesty of Jade Mountain is beyond description.
玉山的雄偉非筆墨所能形容。
＊majesty [ˋmædʒəstɪ] *n.* 雄偉

---

19 within [wɪˋðɪn] *prep. & adv.* 在……之內

片 within reach (of...)
（在……）伸手可及的範圍之內

似 inside [ɪnˋsaɪd]
prep. & adv. 在……裡面 ①

▶ Drive within the speed limit, or you'll get a ticket.
要在速限內開車，不然你會被開罰單。

▶ Phil likes to keep a pen within reach to write things down.
菲爾喜歡把筆放在觸手可及的地方，好把事情寫下來。

▶ Since the sign says "Apply within," why don't we just go inside and give it a try?
既然那標語寫著『請入內申請』，我們何不進去試試看呢？

---

20 among [əˋmʌŋ] *prep.* 在……之中

用法 原則上，between 用於『兩者』之間，among 用於『三者以上』之間。

▶ Karen found a picture of her old boyfriend among her photos.
凱倫在她的照片中發現了她以前男友的照片。

---

21 used [just] *a.* 習慣的 & [juzd] 二手的，舊的

片 (1) be used to + N/V-ing
習慣於……
= be accustomed to + N/V-ing
(2) get used to + N/V-ing
變得 / 開始習慣於……
= get accustomed to + N/V-ing

延伸 used to V
過去經常（但現在不再）做……

▶ I used to listen to music when I studied.
我以前讀書時都會聽音樂。

▶ Jack is used to driving to work.
傑克習慣開車去上班。

▶ I can't get used to living in the countryside.
我沒辦法習慣鄉下的生活。

▶ Since Ron doesn't have much money, he just wants to buy a used car.
因為榮恩沒有很多錢，他只想買臺二手車。

---

user [ˋjuzɚ] *n.* 使用者

片 a user manual [ˋmænjʊəl]
使用者手冊

▶ Read the user manual carefully before operating the machine.
操作機器前請詳讀使用者手冊。

22 **such** [sʌtʃ] *a.* 如此 / 這樣的 & *pron.* 這樣的人 / 事物 & *adv.* 例如（用於下列片語中）

(1) such + N + that...
如此的……以致於……

(2) as such 本身

(3) such as... 例如……

▶ It was such an excellent performance.
這真是場精彩絕倫的表演。

▶ Rex is such a good boy that the teachers like him very much.
雷克斯是那麼乖的男孩，所以老師都很喜歡他。

▶ Sam is a friend and should be treated as such.
山姆是朋友，因此就應像朋友般被對待。

▶ Roger has many hobbies, such as hiking and stamp collecting.
羅傑有很多嗜好，例如健行和集郵。

23 **army** [ˈɑrmɪ] *n.* 軍隊（尤指陸軍）；大群

(1) join the army 從軍

(2) an army of... 一大群

▶ My father joined the army when he was eighteen.
我父親 18 歲時從軍。

▶ The mayor was surrounded by an army of reporters.
市長被一大群記者包圍。

military [ˈmɪləˌtɛrɪ]
n. 軍隊（前面加定冠詞 the）& *a.* 軍事的

(1) join the military 從軍

(2) in the military 在軍中

(3) do (one's) military service
服兵役

衍 militant [ˈmɪlətənt] *a.* 好戰的

似 troops [trups] *n.* 軍隊（恆用複數）③

▶ My brother plans to join the military after senior high school.
我弟弟計劃讀完高中後從軍。

▶ Every male in the country has to serve in the military.
這國家的每個男人都必須在軍中服役。

▶ Larry did his military service on a nice island.
賴瑞在一座美麗的島上服兵役。

command [kəˈmænd]
vt. 命令 & *n.* 命令；(語言等) 掌握，精通

(1) at sb's command
聽某人的命令；可運用自如，可支配

(2) have a good command of + 語
言 對某種語言造詣很好

▶ The general commanded the troops to fire on the enemy.
將軍下令部隊向敵軍開火。

▶ The soldiers fired at the enemy at the general's command.
士兵聽將軍的命令向敵人開火。

▶ I'll always be at your command, darling.
親愛的，我將永遠聽候妳的差遣。

▶ Paul has a good command of Spanish.
保羅的西班牙文造詣很不錯。

Level 2 Unit 27

241

obey [o'be] *vt. & vi.* 遵守

片 obey the law　守法
= abide by the law
= comply with the law
= conform to / with the law

衍 (1) obedience [ə'bidɪəns]
　　　n. 服從，順從 ④
　　(2) obedient [ə'bidɪənt] *a.* 服從的 ④

反 disobey [,dɪsə'be] *vt. & vi.* 不服從

▶ Obey the law, or you will be punished.
　要守法，不然你就會受到懲處。

▶ If you don't obey, you'll be in trouble.
　你若不服從，就要倒霉了。

24　border ['bɔrdɚ] *n.* 邊 / 國界 & *vt. & vi.* 與……有共同邊界，與……接壤

片 (1) on the border of A and B
　　　　在 A 和 B 的交界處
　　(2) border on sth　毗鄰某事物旁

▶ My aunt and uncle live on the border of Germany and France.
　我的嬸嬸和叔叔住在德法交界處。

▶ America borders Canada to the north and Mexico to the south.
　美國北與加拿大接壤，南與墨西哥毗鄰。

▶ My house borders on the park, so I have a nice view of the trees.
　我家緊鄰公園，所以我窗前可看見美麗的樹景。

25　super ['supɚ] *a.* 很好的，超級的 (= wonderful ['wʌndɚfəl]) & *adv.* 非常

似 (1) superb [su'pɝb] *a.* 極好的 ⑤
　　(2) extremely [ɪk'strimlɪ]
　　　adv. 非常，極其

▶ Kelly's teacher said that she did a super job on her essay.
　凱莉的老師說她的文章寫得非常好。

▶ Only someone who is super smart would know the answer.
　只有絕頂聰明的人才知道答案。

---

supper ['sʌpɚ]
n. (尤指非正式的) 晚餐

似 dinner ['dɪnɚ] *n.* (正式的) 晚餐 ①

▶ Mother usually makes supper at seven.
　媽媽通常在 7 點做晚飯。

2801-2804

---

1 diet [`daɪət`] *n.* 日常飲食;節食 & *vi.* (為減重而) 節食

- 片 (1) go on a diet　開始節食
- (2) be on a diet　(正在) 節食

▶ Wayne's diet is full of sweet food, so he has gotten fat.
韋恩的日常飲食都是甜食,所以他變胖了。

▶ I've gained weight. I need to go on a diet now.
我胖了,現在該節食了。

▶ I don't want any fried chicken. I'm on a diet.
我不想吃炸雞。我正在節食。

▶ Paula is dieting and has lost a lot of weight.
寶拉正在節食,體重減輕了很多。

---

2 environment [`ɪnˋvaɪrənmənt`] *n.* 環境

- 似 surroundings [`səˋraʊndɪŋz`]
n. 環境,周圍的事物 (恆用複數) ④

▶ We should spare no effort to protect our environment from being polluted.
我們應盡全力保護我們的環境免於汙染。

environmental [`ɪn,vaɪrənˋmɛntḷ`]
a. 環境的

- 片 (1) an environmental issue
環境議題
- (2) environmental protection
環保

- 衍 environmentalist
[`ɪn,vaɪrənˋmɛntḷɪst`] *n.* 環境保護論者

▶ The greenhouse effect is an important environmental issue.
溫室效應是很重要的環境議題。

▶ We should lay emphasis on the importance of environmental protection.
我們應要強調環保的重要性。
＊lay emphasis / stress on...　強調……

---

3 highly [`ˋhaɪlɪ`] *adv.* 極,非常

- 片 think / speak highly of sb
對某人評價很高

▶ David was highly delighted at the news.
大衛聽到這消息高興極了。

▶ The manager thinks very highly of Judith.
經理對茱蒂絲評價很高。

---

4 blank [`blæŋk`] *a.* 空白的 & *n.* 空白處,空格;(頭腦) 一片空白

- 片 (1) leave sth blank　讓某事物留白
- (2) sb's mind is a blank
某人腦中一片空白
- = sb's mind goes blank
- (3) go blank　(電視等) 螢幕空白

▶ Please write here and leave the bottom of the page blank.
請你寫在這裡,這一頁底部留白。

▶ Fill in the blanks first, please.
請先把這些空格填好。

Level 2　Unit 28

243

> My mind was a blank when the teacher asked me the question.
= My mind went blank when the teacher asked me the question.
老師問我問題時,我的腦中一片空白。

> The TV screen went blank again.
電視螢幕又壞了。

---

5 material [məˈtɪrɪəl] *n.* 材 / 原料 (可數);(書 / 電影等的) 資料 / 素材 (不可數) & *a.* 物質的

片 (1) a building material　建材
(2) collect material　蒐集素材
(3) material comforts
物質享受 (恆用複數)

衍 materialism [məˈtɪrɪəlˌɪzəm]
n. 唯物主義

> The company sells building materials such as bricks, tiles, etc.
那家公司販售建材,如磚塊、磁磚等。

> The director is collecting material for his new documentary.
那位導演正為他的新紀錄片蒐集素材。

> Greta is only interested in material comforts.
葛瑞塔只對物質享受有興趣。

---

6 include [ɪnˈklud] *vt.* 包括

衍 including [ɪnˈkludɪŋ] *prep.* 包括 ④
反 exclude [ɪksˈklud] *vt.* 不包括 ⑤

> Service and taxes are included in the room price.
房間價格包括服務費及稅金在內。

---

7 record [ˈrɛkəd] *n.* 唱片;紀錄 & [rɪˈkɔrd] *vt.* 記錄;錄 (音 / 影)

片 (1) set a record　創下紀錄
(2) break the record　打破紀錄
(3) keep a record of...　記錄
= record...

衍 (1) recorder [rɪˈkɔrdə]
n. 錄音 / 影機 ③
(2) recording [rɪˈkɔrdɪŋ]
n. 唱片;錄音帶;錄影帶

> We asked the DJ to play this record.
我們要求 DJ 放這張唱片。

> Not only did Kirk win the race, but he also set a new record.
柯克不僅贏了比賽,也創下了新紀錄。

> He broke the 100-meter dash world record.
他打破了 100 公尺短跑的世界紀錄。

> I keep a record of my expenses every day.
= I record my expenses every day.
我每天都把支出記錄下來。

> Gillian recorded her voice to see how it sounded.
吉莉恩錄下了她的聲音,好知道她聲音聽起來怎麼樣。

---

8 section [ˈsɛkʃən] *n.* 部分 (= part);區域;(報章等的) 版面

片 (1) a non-smoking section
非吸菸區

> Have you finished the final section of the report?
你完成報告的最後一部分了嗎?

(2) a sports / business section
體育 / 商業版

▶ I'd like a seat in the non-smoking section.
我想要非吸菸區的座位。

▶ My sister usually skips the business section of the newspaper since it's not so interesting.
我妹通常會跳過報紙的商業版，因為那一版並不是很有趣。

9 usual [ˈjuʒʊəl] *a.* 通常的，慣例的

片 **as usual** 像往常一樣，照常

衍 **usually** [ˈjuʒʊəlɪ] *adv.* 通常 ①

反 **unusual** [ʌnˈjuʒʊəl]
　a. 不尋常的；非凡的

▶ As usual, Blake was late for work again this morning.
和往常一樣，布萊克今早上班又遲到了。

10 therefore [ˈðɛrˌfɔr] *adv.* 因此

似 (1) **thus** [ðʌs] *adv.* 因此 ②
　(2) **hence** [hɛns] *adv.* 因此 ⑤

▶ Lance didn't study at all; therefore, he failed the test this morning.
蘭斯根本沒有念書，因此他今天早上考不及格。

11 accept [əkˈsɛpt] *vt.* 接受

衍 (1) **acceptable** [əkˈsɛptəbl̩]
　a. 可接受的 ③
　(2) **acceptance** [əkˈsɛptəns]
　n. 接受 ④

▶ I'm glad to accept your invitation.
我很高興接受您的邀請。

refuse [rɪˈfjuz] *vt.* 拒絕

片 **refuse to V** 拒絕做……

衍 **refusal** [rɪˈfjuzl̩] *n.* 拒絕 ④

似 **turn... down** 拒絕……

▶ The mayor refused to answer any questions.
市長拒絕回答任何問題。

reject [rɪˈdʒɛkt] *vt.* 拒絕

衍 **rejection** [rɪˈdʒɛkʃən]
　n. 拒絕；排斥 ④

▶ Gina rejected Derek's offer of help.
吉娜拒絕了德瑞克的好意幫忙。

deny [dɪˈnaɪ] *vt.* 否認；拒絕

三 **deny, denied** [dɪˈnaɪd], **denied**

片 (1) **deny + V-ing** 否認做……
　= **deny that...**
　(2) **There is no denying that...**
　　不可否認……
　(3) **deny sb sth** 拒絕給某人某物
　= **deny sth to sb**

▶ The basketball player denied having ever taken any illegal drugs.
= The basketball player denied that he had ever taken any illegal drugs.
該籃球員否認曾經服用任何禁藥。

▶ There is no denying that honesty is the best policy.
不可否認，誠實至上。

Level 2 Unit 28

 2811-2815

衍 denial [dɪˋnaɪəl] *n.* 否認；拒絕⑤

▶ Father denied me any chance to see Greta.
爸爸拒絕給我任何見葛瑞塔的機會。

12 drama [ˋdrɑmə] *n.* 戲劇；劇情片；戲劇性 (不可數)

衍 dramatic [drəˋmætɪk]
　a. 戲劇的；激動人心的，引人注目的③

▶ What's your favorite Korean TV drama?
你最喜歡的韓劇是哪一部？

▶ I prefer dramas to action movies.
我喜歡劇情片更甚於動作片。

▶ The pop singer's life is full of drama.
那流行歌手的人生充滿戲劇性。

---

stage [stedʒ]

n. 舞臺；階段 & *vt.* 上演；舉辦

片 (1) on stage　　　在舞臺上
　(2) be on the stage　當演員
　　go on the stage　變成演員
　(3) reach a stage　達到一個階段
　(4) stage a strike　發動罷工

▶ Evan was on stage, singing the famous song "You Raise Me Up."
伊凡當時正站在舞臺上，演唱著名的歌曲〈你鼓舞了我〉。

▶ My sister doesn't want to be a doctor; instead, she wants to be on the stage.
我姊姊不想當醫生；她想當演員。

▶ Our project has just reached the final stage.
我們的計畫剛進入最後階段。

▶ The local drama group is going to stage *Hamlet* today.
本地的劇團今天將要上演《哈姆雷特》。

▶ The workers are going to stage a strike next week.
工人下週會發動罷工。

---

character [ˋkærəktɚ]

n. 性格；品格 (不可數)；(書、劇中的) 角色；(中文、日文等的) 文字

片 a man of good / noble / great character
有品德的人，品德高尚的人

衍 (1) characteristic [ˌkærəktəˋrɪstɪk]
　　a. 典型的 & *n.* 特色④
　(2) characterize [ˋkærəktəˌraɪz]
　　vt. 使具有……的特點 (常用被動)⑤

▶ Thomas has a quiet character.
湯瑪斯是個性沉靜的人。

▶ David is a man of great character.
大衛是個品德高尚的人。

▶ There are three main characters in that movie.
那部電影有 3 個主角。

▶ The report was written in Chinese characters.
這報告是用國字寫的。

---

role [rol] *n.* 角色；作用

片 play a(n) + adj. + role / part in...
在……方面扮演……的作用 / 角色

似 part [part] *n.* 部分；角色①

▶ Maria was excited to get a role in a movie.
瑪麗亞很興奮能在電影中扮演一個角色。

▶ Teamwork plays an important role in achieving success.
團結合作是獲取成功很重要的因素。

scene [sin]

n. 景色；(戲劇 / 電影 / 小說等的) 場，景；
(事件的) 現場

劻 (1) at / on the scene (of sth)
   在 (某事件的) 現場
   (2) make a scene
   大吵大鬧以致丟人現眼

衍 (1) scenery ['sinərɪ]
   n. 風景 (不可數) ④
   (2) scenic ['sinɪk] *a.* 風景優美的 ⑥

似 view [vju] *n.* 風景 (可數) ②

▶ The scene from the window was beautiful.
窗外的景色很美。

▶ That was my favorite scene in the play.
那是這齣劇我最喜愛的一場戲。

▶ The police arrived at the scene of the accident.
警方抵達了事故的現場。

▶ Herbert got mad and made a scene in public.
赫伯特生了氣便當眾大吵大鬧丟人現眼。

---

13 spirit ['spɪrɪt] *n.* 精神 (不可數)；鬼魂 (可數)；情緒，心情 (恆用複數)

劻 (1) team spirit   團隊精神
   (2) an evil spirit   邪靈
   (3) be in good / high spirits   心情好
   = be in a good mood
   (4) be in bad / low spirits   心情差
   = be in a bad mood

衍 spiritual ['spɪrɪtʃʊəl] *a.* 精神上的 ④

▶ The coach tried hard to improve the team spirit.
教練很努力要提高團隊精神。

▶ Some people believe in evil spirits.
有些人相信邪靈的存在。

▶ Wendy, you seem to be in high spirits today.
溫蒂，你今天似乎心情很好。

---

14 apply [ə'plaɪ] *vi.* 申請；適用 & *vt.* 運用；塗抹

亘 apply, applied [ə'plaɪd], applied

劻 (1) apply for...   申請 / 應徵……
   (2) apply to...   適用於……
   (3) apply A to B
   把 A 運用到 B；把 A 塗抹在 B 上

衍 (1) application [,æplə'keʃən]
   n. 運 / 應用；申請 ④
   (2) applicant ['æpləkənt] *n.* 申請人 ④

▶ Elmer is applying for admission to that university.
艾爾馬正在申請那間大學的入學許可。

▶ The first half of the questionnaire applies only to graduate students.
這份問卷的前半部只適用於研究生。

▶ Students will learn how to apply this theory to real-life situations.
學生將學習如何將這理論應用於實際生活情境中。

▶ Apply this cream to your wound three times a day.
每天將這藥膏塗在傷口上 3 次。

---

15 education [,ɛdʒə'keʃən] *n.* 教育

衍 (1) educate ['ɛdʒə,ket] *vt.* 教育 ③
   (2) educational [,ɛdʒə'keʃənl]
   a. 教育的 ③

▶ My parents wanted me to have a good education.
我父母要我接受良好的教育。

16 event [ɪˋvɛnt] n. 事件；(比賽) 項目

片 in the event of sth　萬一發生某事
= in the event that...
= in case of sth

▸ Eddy's birthday party is a big event this week.
艾迪的生日派對是本週的大事。

▸ The women's 200-meter freestyle will be the next event.
下一個比賽項目是女子 200 公尺自由式。

▸ I'll back you up in the event of any trouble.
= I'll back you up in the event that there is any trouble.
萬一有麻煩，我一定做你的後盾。

17 personal [ˋpɝsṇḷ] a. 私人的，個人的；親自的

片 (1) personal belongings
隨身私人物品 (恆用複數)
(2) make a personal appearance
親自露面

衍 (1) person [ˋpɝsṇ] n. 人 ①
(2) personnel [ˏpɝsṇˋɛl]
n. 人員，員工 ⑤

▸ My personal belongings on the table were all gone when I returned from the restroom.
我從廁所回來時，我桌上的私人物品全都不見了。

▸ The chairman will make a personal appearance on TV.
主席將親自在電視中露面。

personality [ˏpɝsṇˋælətɪ]
n. 個性；名人

複 personalities [ˏpɝsṇˋælətɪz]
片 a TV personality　電視名人
似 character [ˋkærəktɚ] n. 個性 ②

▸ Lisa has a pleasant personality.
麗莎的個性很好。

▸ Daisy invited many TV personalities to the party.
黛西邀請了許多電視名人來參加這場派對。

private [ˋpraɪvɪt] a. 私人的；私立的

片 (1) private affairs　私事 (恆用複數)
(2) in private　私下地

衍 privacy [ˋpraɪvəsɪ] n. 隱私 ④
反 public [ˋpʌblɪk] a. 公眾的 ①

▸ Yolanda hates when people ask her about her private affairs.
尤蘭達討厭別人問她的私事。

▸ Let's not talk about this in public, but we can talk about it in private.
我們不要在公開場合討論這件事，但我們可以私底下談談。

▸ I graduated from a private high school.
我畢業於一所私立高中。

secret [ˋsikrɪt]
n. 祕密；祕訣 (恆用單數) & a. 祕密的

片 (1) keep sth (a) secret　將某事保密
(2) in secret　祕密地
(3) the secret to / of + N/V-ing
……的祕訣

▸ Don't tell a soul! This secret is just between you and me.
別告訴任何人！這個祕密只有你知我知。

▸ Rick told Ivy to keep his mistake a secret.
瑞克告訴艾薇要對他所犯下的錯誤保密。

▸ The lawyers met in secret in order to keep their discussions private.
律師們祕密會面以讓討論不公開。

▸ The secret to his success is determination.
他成功的祕訣就是決心。

▸ The secret door leads to the place where the old man hid his treasure.
這扇祕門通往當初那個老人埋寶藏的地方。

18　simply [ˈsɪmplɪ] *adv.* 簡單地；完全地，簡直；僅僅（= just = only）

片 to put it simply　簡單地說
= simply put

衍 (1) simple [ˈsɪmpl̩] *a.* 簡單的 ①
(2) simplify [ˈsɪmpləˌfaɪ] *vt.* 簡化 ⑥
(3) simplicity [sɪmˈplɪsətɪ] *n.* 簡單；簡樸 ⑥

▸ To put it simply, Elva is a musical genius.
簡單地說，艾娃是個音樂天才。

▸ Wendy is simply a beautiful lady.
溫蒂實在是一位美女。

▸ Trevor knew he should simply ignore Roy, but he couldn't.
崔佛知道他應該只要不理會羅伊就好，但他卻做不到。

19　create [krɪˈet] *vt.* 創造；造成

衍 (1) creative [krɪˈetɪv] *a.* 有創造力的 ③
(2) creator [krɪˈetə] *n.* 創造者 ③
(3) creation [krɪˈeʃən] *n.* 創作 ④
(4) creativity [ˌkrieˈtɪvətɪ] *n.* 創造力 ④

▸ Gary believes that God created Heaven and Earth.
蓋瑞相信上帝創造了天和地。

▸ Hank's bad behavior created a lot of trouble.
漢克的惡行造成了很多麻煩。

20　beyond [bɪˈjɑnd] *prep. & adv.* 超過；在遠處，更遠

片 (1) be beyond one's control
超過某人能控制的範圍
(2) be beyond description
無法描述，難以形容

▸ The situation is beyond my control.
= The situation is out of my control.
情況超過我能控制的範圍。

▸ Clara's beauty is beyond description.
克萊拉的美非筆墨所能形容。

▸ The company reached its sales goal of $10 million, and beyond.
公司達到了超過 1,000 萬美元的銷售目標。

▸ I could see a vast field of tulips beyond the hill.
我能看到山丘遠處有一大片的鬱金香。

▸ I can throw the ball all the way to the house and even beyond.
我可以把球丟到房子那邊，甚至更遠。

21 brilliant [ˈbrɪlɪənt] *a.* 明亮的；出色的

似 (1) bright [braɪt] *a.* 明亮的 ①
　　(2) excellent [ˈɛkslənt] *a.* 很好的 ③

▶ The light from the sun looked brilliant on the water.
　太陽光在水面上看起來很炫目燦爛。

▶ Josh came up with a brilliant idea to solve the urgent problem.
　喬許想到了個很棒的方法，可解決這緊急的問題。

22 against [əˈgɛnst] *prep.* 違抗，反對；倚，靠

片 be against the law　違法的
反 for [fɔr] *prep.* 贊成 ①

▶ Never do anything against the law.
　千萬別做違法的事。

▶ We decided to put the table against the wall.
　我們決定把桌子靠牆放。

23 blanket [ˈblæŋkɪt] *n.* 毯子 & *vt.* 覆蓋

片 be blanketed with / in sth
　被某物覆蓋
= be covered with / in sth

▶ The mother wrapped the baby in a blanket.
　這母親把嬰兒裹在毯子裡。

▶ In winter, our roof is blanketed / covered in snow.
　冬天時，我們的屋頂都會被雪覆蓋。

24 channel [ˈtʃænl] *n.* 途徑；電視頻道；海峽 & *vt.* 把 (金錢 / 資源 / 情感等) 引入 / 專注於……

片 (1) a channel of communication
　　溝通管道
= a communication channel
　(2) on a channel　在某個電視頻道上
　(3) the English Channel
　　英吉利海峽
　(4) channel A into B
　　把 A 引入 / 專注於 B 上
似 strait [stret] *n.* 海峽 ⑥

▶ The internet has become an important channel of communication.
　網路已成為一個重要的溝通管道。

▶ What channel is the game on?
　那場比賽在哪個頻道播出？

▶ The English Channel separates Britain from France.
　英吉利海峽分隔了英法兩國。

▶ Walter decided to channel his disappointment into trying to improve the report.
　華特決定將他的失望之情轉為試圖改進這份報告。

25 pale [pel] *a.* 蒼 / 灰白的；淡色的

片 turn / go pale　變蒼白

▶ Upon hearing the news that his father passed away last night, Jim went deathly pale.
　吉姆聽到父親昨晚逝世的消息，臉色立即變得一片死白。

▶ Laura is wearing a pale blue skirt today.
　蘿拉今天穿淡藍色的裙子。

26 **cheer** [tʃɪr] *vt.* & *vi.* 喝彩，歡呼 & *n.* 喝彩 / 歡呼聲

片 cheer (sb) up
　　使(某人)振作 / 高興起來

衍 cheerful [ˋtʃɪrfəl]
　　a. 高興的；令人愉快的 ③

▶ William's parents and friends cheered him when he went on stage.
當威廉上臺時，他的父母和朋友都為他歡呼。

▶ When their team scored a goal, the fans cheered.
當他們的球隊進球得分時，球迷們都歡呼了起來。

▶ Cheer up, Kent. Just because your girlfriend has left you, it doesn't mean it's the end of the world.
振作起來，肯特。你女友離你而去並不表示是世界末日。

▶ There was a loud cheer when the star entered the classroom.
當這明星走進教室時，大家都發出了一陣歡呼聲。

27 **similar** [ˋsɪmələ] *a.* 相似的

片 be similar to...　與……相似

衍 similarity [ˌsɪməˋlærətɪ] *n.* 相似 ③

反 different [ˋdɪf(ə)rənt] *a.* 不同的 ①

▶ Your taste in clothes is similar to mine.
你的穿著品味和我很相似。

28 **album** [ˋælbəm] *n.* 專輯；相簿

片 (1) release an album　出專輯
　　(2) a photo album　相簿

▶ This singer is going to release her new album next month.
這歌手下個月會發行她的新專輯。

▶ Don't touch the photo albums on the shelf, or Granddad will get angry.
不要碰架上的相簿，否則爺爺會生氣的。

29 **due** [d(j)u] *a.* 由於；預定的；到期的 & *adv.* 正對著 (某方向) & *n.* 會費 (恆用複數)

片 (1) due / owing to + N/V-ing
　　由於……
　= because of + N/V-ing
　= on account of + N/V-ing
　= as a result of + N/V-ing
　(2) be due to V　預定做……
　= be expected to V

▶ Jim was absent from work yesterday due to illness.
吉姆昨天因生病而沒來上班。

▶ This film is due to be released next Tuesday.
這部電影預定下星期二上映。

▶ The first payment is due on August 31st.
第一筆付款額於 8 月 31 日到期。

▶ The birds were flying due south to escape the winter here.
鳥兒朝正南方飛，以避開這裡的冬天。

▶ As a member of the club, Bill needs to pay dues.
比爾身為此俱樂部的成員，是要繳會費的。

30 influence [ˈɪnfluəns] *n. & vt.* 影響

🔑 have an influence on...
對……有影響

▶ Ms. Brown has a good influence on the students.
布朗老師對學生有正面的影響。

衍 influential [ˌɪnfluˈɛnʃəl]
a. 有影響力的 ④

▶ What you do now will greatly influence your future.
你現在的作為會大大影響你的未來。

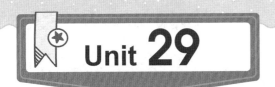

1 surface [ˈsɝfəs] *n.* 表面 & *vi.* 浮出水面

H on / beneath the surface (of sth)
(在某事物的) 表面上 / 下

▶ The surface of the table was covered with dirt.
桌子的表面布滿灰塵。

▶ I could see my feet beneath the surface of the clear water.
我能看見我的腳在清澈的水面下。

▶ Tammy swam the length of the pool and then surfaced.
塔米游完泳池長度後，就浮出了水面。

2 decision [dɪˈsɪʒən] *n.* 決定

H make a decision   做決定
= make up one's mind

衍 (1) decide [dɪˈsaɪd] *vt.* 決定 ①
(2) decisive [dɪˈsaɪsɪv] *a.* 決定性的 ⑥

▶ I'm sorry, but you'll have to make a decision quickly.
很抱歉，但你必須趕快做決定。

3 contain [kənˈten] *vt.* 包含，裝有

衍 container [kənˈtenɚ] *n.* 容器 ④

▶ This photo album contains all of my grandmother's favorite photos.
這本相簿裡裝著所有我奶奶最愛的照片。

4 recent [ˈrisn̩t] *a.* 最近的

▶ Ivy's grades have improved in recent months.
最近幾個月來，艾薇的成績已有進步。

5 organization [ˌɔrgənaɪˈzeʃən] *n.* 組織 (可數)；籌辦 (不可數)

H a non-profit organization
非營利組織

衍 (1) organize [ˈɔrgəˌnaɪz] *vt.* 組織 ③
(2) organizer [ˈɔrgəˌnaɪzɚ] *n.* 籌辦人 ⑥

▶ Greenpeace is a famous non-profit organization.
綠色和平組織是一個有名的非營利組織。

▶ We need volunteers to help with the organization of the event.
我們需要志工幫忙籌辦此次活動。

6 industry [ˈɪndəstrɪ] *n.* 工業 (不可數)；行業 (可數)

複 industries [ˈɪndəstrɪz]

衍 (1) industrial [ɪnˈdʌstrɪəl] *a.* 工業的 ③
(2) industrialize [ɪnˈdʌstrɪəˌlaɪz] *vt.* & *vi.* (使) 工業化 ⑥

▶ Industry in this small country has been developing quickly in recent years.
近年來，這小國工業的發展很迅速。

▶ The fashion industry would be an interesting one to get into.
從事時裝業會很有意思。

7 direct [dəˋrɛkt] *a.* 直達的；直接的 & *adv.* 直達地；直接地 & *vt.* 為……指路；管理，領導

片 direct sb to + 地方
指引 / 告訴某人去某地的路

反 indirect [ˏɪndəˋrɛkt] *a.* 間接的

▶ We took a direct plane to New York.
我們搭乘一班直達紐約的飛機。

▶ The new manager will take direct control of the failing department.
新經理將直接接掌那已顯衰敗的部門。

▶ This train goes direct to London.
這列火車直達倫敦。

▶ James went direct to the president with his report.
詹姆士帶著他的報告直接去找了總裁。

▶ A security guard directed us to the emergency exit.
一名警衛指引我們去緊急出口。

▶ The manager chose Maggie to direct the part-time staff.
經理選擇了瑪姬來管理那些兼職員工。

direction [dəˋrɛkʃən]
n. 方向；指路 (此意恆用複數)；領導，管理 (不可數)

片 (1) in the direction of sth
朝某物的方向

(2) directions to + 地方
去某地的路線

(3) under the direction of sb
在某人的領導 / 管理之下

▶ We were walking in the direction of the park.
我們正朝著公園的方向走去。

▶ Katie asked a local woman for directions to the museum.
凱蒂向一位當地婦女詢問去博物館的路線。

▶ The choral group performed under the direction of the music teacher.
該合唱團在音樂老師的指導下表演。

director [dəˋrɛktə]
n. 董事，經理；導演

▶ Owen was a director of a large software company.
歐文是一家大型軟體公司的董事。

▶ I'm very proud of the Taiwanese director Ang Lee.
我為臺灣導演李安感到很驕傲。

8 complete [kəmˋplit] *vt.* 完成 & *a.* 完全的 (= total)；完整的；完成的

似 (1) finish [ˋfɪnɪʃ] *vt.* & *vi.* 完成 ①
(2) accomplish [əˋkɑmplɪʃ]
vt. 完成 ④

反 incomplete [ˏɪnkəmˋplit]
a. 不完全的

▶ The new undersea tunnel will be completed soon.
那座新的海底隧道很快就會完工。

▶ You need a complete change of diet.
你必須完全改變飲食。

▶ No trip to Taiwan is complete without a visit to the night markets.
沒去過夜市，臺灣之行就不算完整。

▶ Finally, the work on the opera house is complete.
歌劇院的工程終於完成了。

9 realize [ˈrɪəˌlaɪz] *vt.* 瞭解；實現

📙 realize / fulfill a dream　實現夢想
衍 (1) real [ˈrɪəl] *a.* 真實的 ①
　 (2) realization [ˌrɪələˈzeʃən]
　　　 n. 瞭解；實現 ⑥
似 fulfill [fʊlˈfɪl] *vt.* 實現 ④

▶ The boss realized the importance of listening to his employees.
老闆瞭解聆聽員工心聲的重要性。

▶ Roy worked hard to realize his dream.
羅伊努力工作以實現他的夢想。

---

reality [rɪˈælətɪ]
n. 現實 (情況) (不可數)；事實 (可數)

複 realities [rɪˈælətɪz]
📙 in reality　事實上
= in fact / practice

▶ Ken told me he couldn't tell the difference between fantasy and reality when he was sick.
肯告訴我他生病時無法分辨幻想與現實。

▶ That dream has become a reality.
那個夢想成真了。

▶ Stan sometimes complained about his wife, but in reality, he loved her dearly.
史坦有時會抱怨他的太太，但事實上，他非常愛她。

---

10 base [bes] *n.* 底部，基部 (= bottom [ˈbɑtəm])；(軍事) 基地；(棒球) 壘 &
　　　 vt. 以……為基礎

📙 (1) an air base　空軍基地
　 (2) first base　(棒球) 一壘
　 (3) base A on / upon B
　　　 A 根據 B 為基礎
　 (4) be based on...　以……為依據
衍 (1) basement [ˈbesmənt]
　　　 n. 地下室 ③
　 (2) baseball [ˈbesˌbɔl] *n.* 棒球 ①

▶ The dessert has a delicious, crunchy base.
這甜點底部的口感鬆脆可口。

▶ The air base is located in the southern part of the island.
該空軍基地位於本島的南端。

▶ The batter hit the ball and ran to first base.
打擊者擊中球後跑到一壘。

▶ The director based the movie on a true story.
導演根據一個真實的故事拍這部片子。

▶ The movie was based on a true story.
這部電影是根據一個真實故事所拍攝的。

---

basis [ˈbesɪs] *n.* 根據，基礎
複 bases [ˈbesiz]
📙 on the basis of...　根據……

▶ What's the basis for the theory?
該理論的基礎為何？

▶ On the basis of what Alex said, I think he's innocent.
根據艾力克斯的說詞，我認為他是無辜的。

---

basic [ˈbesɪk] *a.* 基本的
似 fundamental [ˌfʌndəˈmɛntl̩]
　　 a. 基礎的 ④

▶ Basic computer skills are required for this job.
這份工作須具備基本的電腦技巧。

2910-2913

basics [`besɪks]

n. 基本內容 / 原則；基本需求，必需品 (皆恆用複數)

🔷 **get back to basics**
開始注重基礎面，回到根本

▶ To take that course, you need to understand the basics of chemistry.
要上這門課程，你得要懂化學的基本內容。

▶ Every parent must provide their child with at least the basics.
每個父母都必須至少為其子女提供基本需求。

▶ After focusing on too many trivial things, the company decided to get back to basics.
此公司在聚焦於太多瑣碎的事情之後，決定要開始注重基礎面。

---

source [sɔrs]

n. 來源；消息來源，消息人士；(文章中引文的) 出處

▶ Reading is a wonderful source of pleasure.
閱讀是很棒的快樂泉源。

▶ The love of money is the source of all evil.
貪財是一切罪惡的來源。—— 諺語

▶ Sources close to the mayor say that she will run for president.
市長身邊的消息人士說她將角逐總統大位。

---

origin [`ɔrədʒən]

n. 起源；出身 (皆常用複數)

🔷 (1) original [ə`rɪdʒənḷ]
　　a. 起初的 & *n.* 原作 ③
　(2) originality [ə,rɪdʒə`nælətɪ]
　　n. 原創性 ⑤
　(3) originate [ə`rɪdʒə,net]
　　vi. 源於 (與介詞 in 或 from 並用) ⑥

▶ There are many English words of Latin origin.
英文有許多字源自拉丁文。

▶ Terry tried to hide his humble origins.
泰瑞試圖隱瞞他卑微的出身。

---

11 peace [pis] *n.* (交戰等後的) 和平；平靜 (皆不可數)

🔷 **live in peace with sb**
與某人和睦共處

▶ Many common people in that war-torn country longed for peace.
在那飽受戰爭蹂躪的國家，很多平民百姓都渴望和平。

▶ Zora loves the peace of the countryside.
卓拉喜歡鄉間的平靜。

▶ Jerry told me he could no longer live in peace with his wife.
傑瑞告訴我，他再也不能和他老婆和平共處了。

---

peaceful [`pisfəl] *a.* 和平的；平靜的

▶ We want our kids to grow up in a peaceful world.
我們想要我們的孩子在和平的世界裡長大。

▶ We spent a peaceful night at home.
我們在家度過了一個平靜的夜晚。

12 single [ˈsɪŋgl̩] *a.* 單身的；單一的 & *vt.* 挑選 & *n.* 單身者（常用複數）

片 single... out　挑選出……

衍 singular [ˈsɪŋgjələ˞]
a. 單數的；奇特的 & *n.* (文法) 單數(形)
④

延伸 (1) married [ˈmærɪd] *a.* 已婚的
(2) divorced [dəˈvɔrst] *a.* 離婚的
(3) separated [ˈsɛpəˌretɪd] *a.* 分居的

▶ Wendy has decided to remain single for the rest of her life.
溫蒂已經決定此後終生單身。

▶ There was not a single cookie left in the box.
盒子裡一塊餅乾也沒剩。

▶ Who do you think will be singled out as the best athlete of the year?
你認為誰會被選為年度最佳運動員？

▶ This party is for singles only.
這派對只限單身人士參加。

double [ˈdʌbl̩]
a. 雙倍的 & *vt.* 使加倍 & *n.* 極相似的人 & *adv.* 雙 / 加倍地

片 double pay　雙倍薪水

▶ I'll give you double pay for working overtime.
你加班我會付你雙倍薪水。

▶ The boss was surprised when the new employee asked him to double his salary.
這位新進員工要求將薪資加倍時，老闆吃了一驚。

▶ Sam is the double of his father.
山姆是他父親的翻版。

▶ I have been charged double for this item.
這商品我被收了雙倍的價錢。

13 natural [ˈnætʃərəl] *a.* 大自然的；自然的；輕鬆自如的，不做作的

片 (1) It is natural (for sb) to V
（某人）做……是很自然的
(2) be / act natural
（行為）自然一點

衍 (1) nature [ˈnetʃə˞] *n.* 大自然 ①
(2) naturalist [ˈnætʃərəlɪst]
n. (文學等) 自然主義者

反 (1) unnatural [ʌnˈnætʃərəl]
a. 不自然的
(2) artificial [ˌɑrtəˈfɪʃəl] *a.* 人工的 ④
(3) man-made [ˌmænˈmed]
a. 人造的

▶ We enjoyed the natural beauty of the Grand Canyon.
我們欣賞著大峽谷的自然美景。

▶ It's natural for you to feel upset in this situation.
你在這種情況下會感到不開心是很自然的。

▶ Try to relax and be natural. Grandma doesn't know the truth yet.
試著放鬆一點並保持自然。奶奶還不知道真相。

▶ The actor has a natural way of speaking on stage.
這位演員在臺上的說話方式自然不做作。

14 clever [ˈklɛvɚ] a. 聰明的；絕妙的

似 (1) smart [smɑrt] a. 聰明的 ①
　　(2) bright [braɪt] a. 聰明的 ①

反 stupid [ˈst(j)upɪd] a. 愚笨的 ①

▸ Sally is such a clever girl.
　莎莉是個如此聰明的女孩。

▸ What a clever idea it is!
　這真是個妙計！

15 mask [mæsk] n. 面具；口罩 & vt. 遮蔽，蓋住

片 (1) a gas mask　防毒面具
　　(2) wear a (face) mask　戴口罩

▸ The police in gas masks tear-gassed the protestors.
　戴著防毒面具的警察用催淚瓦斯驅散抗議者。
　＊tear-gas [ˈtɪrˌɡæs] vt. 用催淚瓦斯攻擊

▸ Always wear a face mask when you are sweeping the floor.
　你掃地的時候，一定要戴口罩。

▸ Larry is good at masking his feelings.
　賴瑞很會掩飾自己的情感。

16 likely [ˈlaɪklɪ] a. 有可能的 & adv. 可能

片 (1) It is likely that...　可能……
　　＝ S + be likely to V
　　(2) (That's) a likely story!
　　　說得倒像是真的一樣！／聽起來像
　　　真的一樣！
　　(3) most / very likely　極有可能

衍 likelihood [ˈlaɪklɪˌhʊd] n. 可能性 ⑤

反 unlikely [ʌnˈlaɪklɪ] a. 不大可能的

▸ It is likely that John and Lulu will get married.
＝ John and Lulu are likely to get married.
　約翰和露露可能會結婚。

▸ You're late because your dog is sick? That's a likely story!
　你遲到是因為你的狗生病了？說得倒像是真的一樣！

▸ Most likely, Sam will lose all his money.
　極有可能山姆會輸光全部的錢。

17 actual [ˈæktʃʊəl] a. 真實的，確實的

▸ This is the actual sword that was used in the film.
　這是那部電影中真正用的劍。

true [tru]
a. 真實的；忠實的，忠誠的 (＝ loyal) &
adv. 準確地 & vt. 擺正，弄直 / 平

片 (1) come true　(夢想) 實現
　　(2) be true to sb　對某人忠實
　　＝ be faithful to sb

▸ Because of hard work, Bradley's dream finally came true.
　由於努力，布萊德利的夢想終於實現了。

▸ You should be true to your wife.
　你應對太太忠實。

▸ I couldn't believe that the ball flew straight and true to the goal.
　我真不敢相信球會精準地直飛向球門。

▸ Make sure you true the edges of the boxes carefully.
　確保你有仔細地把盒子的邊緣對齊好。

truth [truθ]

n. 事實（前面加定冠詞 the）；真理

片 (1) to tell (you) the truth　老實說
　(2) in truth　事實上

衍 truthful [ˈtruθḷ] *a.* 誠實的 ③

▶ Robert doesn't dare to tell his wife the truth.
羅伯特不敢告訴他太太事實真相。

▶ To tell the truth, I don't like Albert.
老實說，我不喜歡亞伯特。

▶ Kyle acted calm, but in truth, he was very worried.
凱爾表現得很冷靜，但事實上，他很擔心。

false [fɔls] *a.* 不實的；假的

片 a false name　假名

▶ Circle "F" if the statement is false.
如果敘述是錯的，請圈『F』。

▶ Tim gave a false name to a police officer.
提姆跟警官虛報假名。

18　lack [læk] *n. & vt.* 缺乏

片 (1) a lack of...　缺乏……
　(2) for lack of...　因為欠缺……

▶ We can't go on with the project for lack of money.
我們因為欠缺資金，所以計畫無法進行下去。

▶ This soup lacks salt. Maybe you should add some.
這碗湯沒加鹽，也許你應該加一點。

19　empty [ˈɛmptɪ] *a.* 空的 & *vt.* 使變空 & *vi.* 注入（海／湖／河等）

三 empty, emptied [ˈɛmptɪd], emptied

片 empty into...　注入……

反 full [fʊl] *a.* 滿的 ①

▶ The classroom was empty, with no teacher or children in sight.
這教室裡空無一人，都沒看到老師和小孩。

▶ I was shocked to find that my room had been emptied by thieves.
我看到竊賊把房間洗劫一空，嚇了一跳。

▶ The Mississippi River empties into the Gulf of Mexico.
密西西比河注入墨西哥灣。
＊gulf [gʌlf] *n.* 海灣

20　lift [lɪft] *vt.* 舉起；解除 & *n.* 舉，抬

片 lift a ban on...　解除對……的禁令

▶ That box is too heavy to lift.
那箱子太重而提不動。

▶ Some restaurants want to lift the ban on smoking.
有些餐廳希望可以解除禁菸令。

▶ With a lift of his glass, Gary toasted the newly married couple.
蓋瑞舉起玻璃杯，向這對新婚夫婦敬酒。

2921-2925

21 fashion [ˈfæʃən] *n.* 流行；方式 & *vt.* 塑造

(1) be in fashion　流行
(2) be / go out of fashion　退流行
(3) in a(n) + adj. + fashion
　　以……的方式
(4) fashion A out of B　用 B 塑造出 A

衍 fashionable [ˈfæʃənəbl̩]
　　a. 流行的，時髦的 ③

▶ Miniskirts used to be in fashion, but they're out of fashion now.
　迷你裙以前很流行，但現在退燒了。

▶ Austin always does things in that fashion.
　奧斯汀總是以那種方式行事。

▶ The old man fashioned a pipe out of clay.
　這老人用陶土捏出一根菸管。

---

style [staɪl] *n.* 風格，作風；潮流 & *vt.* 設計，把……設計得吸引人

(1) in style　流行
(2) in fine / great style　風光地

衍 stylish [ˈstaɪlɪʃ] *a.* 時髦的，流行的 ⑥

▶ Mr. Smith's Western style of management did not work well in Asia.
　史密斯先生西式的管理風格在亞洲並不是那麼有效。

▶ These kinds of jeans are no longer in style.
　這些款式的牛仔褲已不流行了。

▶ The tennis player won the championship in fine style.
　該網球選手風光地贏得了冠軍。

▶ Connie's hair has been styled to suit the shape of her face.
　康妮的髮型被設計成符合她臉型的樣子。

---

22 detail [ˈditel] *n.* 細節 & *vt.* 詳細描述 / 討論

in detail　詳細地
= at length

衍 detailed [ˈdiˌteld / dɪˈteld] *a.* 詳細的

▶ I haven't had time to review the plan in detail yet.
　我還沒有時間詳細審閱這計畫。

▶ The manager wanted a report detailing the pros and cons of our products.
　經理要一份詳細說明我們產品優缺點的報告。

---

23 equal [ˈikwəl] *a.* 平等的 & *vt.* 等於；匹敵 & *n.* (能力、地位等) 同樣 / 相當的人

(1) be equal in...
　　在……方面是相同的
(2) A be equal to B
　　A 等於 B；A 和 B 相同
= A equal B
(3) have no equal
　　沒有勢均力敵的對手，出類拔萃

衍 (1) equality [ɪˈkwɑlətɪ]
　　n. 平等，同等 ④
(2) equalize [ˈikwəlˌaɪz] *vt.* 使平等 ⑥
(3) equivalent [ɪˈkwɪvələnt]
　　a. 相對等的 ⑤

▶ The two people were equal in ability.
　這 2 人在能力方面相當。

▶ Four plus four is equal to eight.
= Four plus four equals eight.
　4 加 4 等於 8。

▶ I equal Andrew in strength.
　我和安德魯的力氣不相上下。

▶ When it comes to singing, Kent has no equal.
= When it comes to singing, Kent is second to none.
　說到唱歌，肯特沒有勢均力敵的對手。

(4) equation [ɪˈkweʃən] *n.* 等式 ⑤

反 unequal [ʌnˈikwəl] *a.* 不平等的

24 **manage** [ˈmænɪdʒ] *vt.* 經營，管理；成功做到……

片 manage to V　成功做到……

▶ Erin managed the hotel while her father was ill.
艾琳父親生病時，飯店是由艾琳經營的。

▶ Jamie managed to contact the busy manager in that company.
傑米成功聯絡到了那家公司業務很繁忙的經理了。

manager [ˈmænədʒɚ] *n.* 經理

片 (1) a general manager　　總經理
　　(2) an assistant manager　副理

▶ The general manager fired two employees for stealing.
總經理將 2 位偷竊的員工開除了。

management [ˈmænɪdʒmənt]
n. 經營，管理；資方，管理階層

▶ The management of the factory was a tough job.
管理這家工廠是個艱難的工作。

▶ The union decided to go on strike after management refused to give way.
資方拒絕讓步後，工會決定罷工。

25 **prize** [praɪz] *n.* 獎金 / 品 & *vt.* 珍 / 重視

片 win a prize　贏得獎金 / 品

似 (1) price [praɪs] *n.* 價格 ①
　　(2) value [ˈvælju] *vt.* 珍惜 ②
　　(3) cherish [ˈtʃɛrɪʃ] *vt.* 珍惜 / 愛 ④

▶ Dolly won a big prize for her science experiment.
朵莉所做的科學實驗為她贏得了大獎。

▶ I prize the watch my girlfriend gave me for my birthday.
我珍惜生日時女友送我的手錶。

Level 2

Unit 29

3001-3008

1 artist [ˈɑrtɪst] *n.* 藝術家；藝術表演者，藝人

- a street artist 街頭藝人
- (1) art [ɑrt] *n.* 藝術 ①
  (2) artistic [ɑrˈtɪstɪk] *a.* 藝術的 ④

▶ Paul Cézanne is one of the famous nineteenth-century artists.
保羅‧塞尚是 19 世紀著名的藝術家之一。

▶ That street artist attracted a large crowd of visitors.
那位街頭藝人吸引了一大群的遊客。

2 failure [ˈfeljɚ] *n.* 失敗 (不可數)；失敗的人 / 事 (可數)

- (1) a complete failure
  徹底失敗的人 / 事
  (2) a power failure 停電
- fail [fel] *vi.* & *vt.* 失敗；(使) 不及格 ①
- success [səkˈsɛs] *n.* 成功 ②

▶ Failure is the mother of success.
失敗為成功之母。── 諺語

▶ The party turned out to be a complete failure.
這次派對辦得完全失敗。

▶ There was a power failure throughout the whole city.
整個城市都停電了。

3 occur [əˈkɝ] *vi.* 發生 (= happen = take place)；突然想到

- occur, occurred [əˈkɝd], occurred
- It occurs to sb that...
  某人突然想起……
- = It strikes sb that...
- occurrence [əˈkɝəns]
  n. 發生 (不可數)；事件 (可數) ⑥

▶ The serious car accident occurred because of the taxi driver's carelessness.
會發生那起嚴重車禍是因為那計程車司機很粗心大意。

▶ It occurred to me that it's Randy's birthday tomorrow.
我突然想到明天是藍迪的生日。

4 charge [tʃɑrdʒ] *vt.* & *vi.* 收費；充電 & *vt.* 控訴 & *n.* 收費；控訴；負責

- (1) charge sb + 費用 (+ for sth)
  向某人索取 (某物的) 費用
  (2) charge for sth 某事物要收費
  (3) charge sb with sth
  指控某人犯了某項罪名
  (4) free of charge 免費
  (5) on a charge of sth
  被控某項罪名
  (6) take charge of sth
  負責 (管理) 某事物

▶ The company charged me NT$500 for fixing the television.
那家公司向我索取新臺幣 500 元的電視修理費。

▶ Stores in this country all charge for plastic bags.
此國商店的塑膠袋都要收費。

▶ Did you charge the battery for the digital camera?
數位相機的電池你充電了嗎？

▶ Your cellphone went dead. You should let your battery charge.
你手機沒電了。你電池應該要充電了。

▶ The police charged the man with robbery.
警方以強盜罪起訴該名男子。

衍 rechargeable [riˋtʃɑrdʒəbḷ]
a. (蓄電池) 可再充電的

▶ Do you think rechargeable batteries work well?
你覺得充電電池好用嗎？

▶ The booklet is free of charge.
這本小冊子是免費的。

▶ Luke was arrested on a charge of car theft.
路克因被控偷車罪而被捕。

▶ Who takes charge of this department?
誰負責這個部門？

---

5 **entire** [ɪnˋtaɪr] a. 整個 / 全部的 ☐

似 (1) all [ɔl] a. 所有的 ①
(2) whole [hol] a. 全體的 ②

▶ The entire staff in that company were against the new policy.
那家公司的全體員工一致反對那項新政策。

---

6 **manner** [ˋmænɚ] n. 方法；態度；禮貌 (恆用複數) ☐

片 in a(n) + adj. + manner
以……的方式

衍 (1) well-mannered [ˏwɛlˋmænɚd]
a. 有禮貌的
(2) ill-mannered [ˏɪlˋmænɚd]
a. 態度惡劣的

似 (1) way [we] n. 方法 ①
(2) attitude [ˋætət(j)ud] n. 態度 ③

▶ The little girl answered her teacher's question in a confident manner.
小女孩很有自信地回答了老師的問題。

▶ Jill has changed her manner toward Michael.
吉兒已經改變了她對邁可的態度。

▶ Why don't the couple sitting at the table over there teach their children good manners?
坐那桌的夫妻怎麼不教他們的小孩要懂禮貌呢？

---

7 **range** [rendʒ] vi. (在一定幅度內) 變動 & n. 範圍 ☐

片 range from A to B 從 A 到 B

▶ The singer has many fans, ranging from children to grandparents.
這名歌手有許多粉絲，從小孩子到爺爺奶奶都有。

▶ The price range of the product is from US$40 to US$400.
這種產品的價格範圍從 40 美元到 400 美元不等。

---

8 **quality** [ˋkwɑlətɪ] n. 品質 (不可數)；特徵 / 性 (可數) ☐

複 qualities [ˋkwɑlətɪz]
片 be of high / low quality 品質好 / 差
似 qualify [ˋkwɑləfaɪ] vt. 使合格 ⑤

▶ That shirt is of high quality, and the price is reasonable.
那件襯衫品質很好，價格又合理。

▶ What do you think is the most important quality of a good teacher? 你認為好老師最重要的特質是什麼？

---

quantity [ˋkwɑntətɪ] n. 量 ☐

複 quantities [ˋkwɑntətɪz]

片 a large / small quantity of + 複數
可數名詞 / 不可數名詞
大 / 少量的……

▶ We need a large quantity of time and money to get this job done.
我們需要大量的時間及金錢才能完成這件工作。

Level 2 Unit 30

延 a large / small number of + 複數可數名詞　大 / 少量的……

amount [əˋmaʊnt] *n.* 量 & *vi.* 總計
片 (1) a large / small amount of + 不可數名詞　大量 / 少量的……
(2) amount to...　總計……

▶ Asians eat a large amount of rice every year.
亞洲人每年吃掉大量的米。
▶ Our total purchases amounted to $2,000 today.
我們今天購買的東西總計 2,000 美元。

9　**relation** [rɪˋleʃən] *n.* (人、團體之間的) 關係 / 往來 (恆用複數)；(兩物之間的) 關係

片 (1) relations between A and B
A 和 B (指人或團體) 之間的關係
(2) a relation between A and B
A 和 B (指事物) 之間的關係
衍 (1) relative [ˋrɛlətɪv]
n. 親戚 & *a.* 相關的 ①
(2) relate [rɪˋlet] *vt.* 使有關聯 ②
似 correlation [ˏkɔrəˋleʃən]
n. 相互關係，相關性 ⑤

▶ In recent months, relations between Calvin and his wife have been worsening.
近幾個月來，卡文和他太太的關係日益惡化。
▶ I think there is a relation between media violence and crime.
我認為媒體暴力與犯罪之間是有關係的。

relationship [rɪˋleʃənˏʃɪp]
n. (人、團體之間的) 關係 / 往來；(兩物之間的) 關係；戀愛關係

片 (1) a relationship between A and
B　A 和 B 之間的關係
(2) be in a relationship
有穩定交往的對象

▶ The relationship between this powerful country and some Arab countries deepened.
該強國與一些阿拉伯國家之間的關係加深了。
▶ According to the study, there is a relationship between healthy diets and weight loss.
據研究，健康飲食和減重彼此之間是有關係的。
▶ Cathy is in a relationship. Didn't you know that?
凱西有穩定交往的對象了。難道你不知道嗎？

10　**central** [ˋsɛntrəl] *a.* 中央的

衍 center [ˋsɛntɚ] *n.* 中心 ①
反 marginal [ˋmɑrdʒənl] *a.* 邊緣的 ⑥
延 middle [ˋmɪdl] *a.* 中間的 ①

▶ The park is in the central part of the city.
那座公園位於市中心。

11　**support** [səˋport] *vt.* 支持；供養 & *n.* 支持 (不可數)

片 (1) support sb in + N/V-ing
支持某人……
(2) support sb by + N/V-ing
靠……來撫養某人
(3) public support　大眾支持

▶ My father has always supported me in whatever I want to do.
不論我想做什麼，我父親總是支持我。
▶ Duke supports his family by working as a food delivery man.
杜克靠做食物外送員來養家。

衍 (1) supporter [səˋpɔrtɚ]
　　　n. 支持者；擁護者
　　(2) supportive [səˋpɔrtɪv] a. 支持的

▶ The policy never gained much public support.
這項政策從未得到大眾的大力支持。

12　model [ˋmɑdl̩] n. 模特兒；模型；模範 & vt. 使模仿

片 (1) a fashion model　　時裝模特兒
　　(2) a role model　　　模範，表率
　　(3) A be modeled after B　A 仿照 B
　　(4) model oneself after sb
　　　仿效某人，以某人為榜樣

▶ Mary is a famous fashion model.
瑪麗是知名的時裝模特兒。

▶ My little brother collects a lot of model planes.
我弟弟蒐集了很多模型飛機。

▶ Peter is our role model in many ways.
在許多方面，彼得堪稱我們的表率。

▶ This TV show is modeled after one from South Korea.
此電視節目是仿照韓國一個電視節目。

▶ I'll model myself after my father and become an English teacher.
我要以父親為榜樣，當個英文老師。

---

pattern [ˋpætɚn]
n. 模式，方式；圖案，花樣 & vt. 仿造，
使模仿

片 (1) a weather pattern　　天氣型態
　　(2) A be patterned after B　A 仿照 B
　　(3) pattern oneself after sb
　　　仿效某人，以某人為榜樣

▶ The weather patterns in this area have remained the same for the past 10 years.
該區的天氣型態在過去 10 年內都維持不變。

▶ My brother would never wear clothes with floral patterns.
我哥絕對不會穿有花朵圖案的衣服。

▶ Sally's wedding dress is patterned after the one her grandmother wore.
莎莉的婚紗是仿照她奶奶曾穿的婚紗所設計的。

▶ I'll pattern myself after my mother and become a French teacher.
我要以母親為榜樣，當個法文老師。

13　northern [ˋnɔrðɚn] a. 北方的 (字首可大寫)

衍 north [nɔrθ] n. 北方 & a. 北方的 ①

▶ The northern part of this country is very beautiful.
這國家的北部很美麗。

---

southern [ˋsʌðɚn]
a. 南方的 (字首可大寫)

衍 south [sauθ] n. 南方 & a. 南方的 ①

▶ My grandparents live in southern Taiwan.
我祖父母住在臺灣南部。

---

eastern [ˋistɚn]
a. 東方的 (字首可大寫)

衍 east [ist] n. 東方 & a. 東方的 ①

▶ Eastern countries play a more and more important role in the world economy.
東方國家在世界經濟中扮演越來越重要的角色。

western [ˈwɛstən]
a. 西方的 & *n.* (美國) 西部片 / 小說等 (字首可大寫)

衍 west [wɛst] *n.* 西方 & *a.* 西方的 ①

▶ James Joyce is one of the major Western writers.
詹姆士‧喬哀斯是西方很重要的作家之一。

▶ *Dances with Wolves* is an award-winning western.
《與狼共舞》是一部獲獎的西部片。

cowboy [ˈkaʊˌbɔɪ] *n.* 牛仔

衍 cow [kaʊ] *n.* 母牛 ①

▶ Ken used to work as a cowboy on a ranch in Texas.
肯以前曾在德州的大牧場做過牛仔。

---

14 opinion [əˈpɪnjən] *n.* 意見

片 in one's opinion　依某人之見

▶ In my opinion, students should not be allowed to bring cellphones to school.
依我之見，不應允許學生帶手機到學校。

---

view [vju] *n.* 觀點；視野，景色 & *vt.* 將……看成，看待；(觀) 看

片 (1) in one's view　依某人之見
　= from one's point of view
　= from one's viewpoint
　(2) in view of sth
　　因為某事物，考慮到某事物
　(3) view A as B　將 A 視為 B
　= regard A as B

衍 (1) viewer [ˈvjuɚ] *n.* (電視) 觀眾 ⑤
　(2) viewpoint [ˈvjuˌpɔɪnt] *n.* 觀點 ⑤

▶ In my view, this policy is impractical.
= From my point of view, this policy is impractical.
= From my viewpoint, this policy is impractical.
依我之見，這政策並不切實際。

▶ That room has great views over the sea.
那房間的視野很棒，可以俯瞰海景。

▶ In view of Kyle's great performance, the manager decided to give him a raise.
因為凱爾優異的表現，經理決定給他加薪。

▶ I always view Thanksgiving as a time for family togetherness.
我一向視感恩節為家人親近的時刻。
＊togetherness [təˈgɛðɚnəs] *n.* 親密無間

▶ A large number of tourists come to view this famous statue every day.
每天都有大量的遊客來參觀這座著名的雕像。

---

15 rather [ˈræðɚ] *adv.* 相當，頗；寧願

片 would rather V than V
寧願……而不願……

似 (1) quite [kwaɪt] *adv.* 相當，頗 ①
　(2) fairly [ˈfɛrlɪ] *adv.* 相當地 ③

▶ It's rather hot today.
今天相當熱。

▶ Since it's raining, I would rather stay at home than go out.
因為外面在下雨，我寧願待在家裡也不要出門。

---

16 growth [groθ] *n.* 成長，生長

衍 grow [gro] *vi.* 生長 ①
反 decline [dɪˈklaɪn] *n.* & *vi.* 衰退 ⑤

▶ There has been a steady growth in Amber's business over the past 10 years.
過去 10 年來，安柏的事業一直穩定成長。

17 repair [rɪˈpɛr] vt. & n. 修理

片 (1) have sth repaired　把某物送修
　 (2) be in need of repair　需要修理
　 (3) be beyond repair　不能修理
　 (4) be under repair　在修理中

衍 repairman [rɪˈpɛrˌmæn] n. 修理工

似 (1) fix [fɪks] vt. 修理②
　 (2) mend [mɛnd] vt. 修理③

▶ My car broke down yesterday, so I'm going to have it repaired today.
我的車子昨天拋錨了，因此我今天要把它拿去送修。

▶ The truck is badly in need of repair.
這輛卡車極需修理。

▶ The car is beyond repair. You should buy a new one.
那輛車不能修理了。你該買新車了。

▶ The bridge is under repair. Please take a detour.
橋正在維修中。請繞道行駛。
＊detour [ˈditʊr] n. & vi. 繞道

18 whom [hum] pron. 誰 (用作疑問代名詞，who 的受詞)；誰 (用作關係代名詞，who 的受詞)

衍 who [hu]
pron. 誰 (用作疑問代名詞)；……的 (用作關係代名詞)①

▶ Whom will the people of this country choose to be president?
這國家的人民將選擇誰擔任總統呢？

▶ Hank didn't know whom he should talk to about his problem.
漢克不知道他應該和誰談談自己的問題。

19 remove [rɪˈmuv] vt. 移開，除去

片 remove A from B　將 A 從 B 中除去

衍 removal [rɪˈmuvl̩] n. 移開；除去⑤

▶ I removed a coffee stain from the shirt with a special cleanser.
我用一種特別的清潔劑把襯衫上的咖啡漬去掉了。
＊cleanser [ˈklɛnzɚ] n. 清潔劑

20 arrival [əˈraɪvl̩] n. 到達，抵達；問世

片 upon / on (one's) arrival
在 (某人) 到達時

衍 arrive [əˈraɪv] vi. 到達①
arrive at / in + 地方　抵達某地

反 departure [dɪˈpɑrtʃɚ] n. 離開④

▶ Upon his arrival at the station, David rushed to the hospital to see his grandfather.
＝ As soon as he arrived at the station, David rushed to the hospital to see his grandfather.
大衛一到車站，就趕往醫院去看他爺爺。

▶ Our lives have greatly changed since the arrival of the mobile phone.
自從手機問世後，我們的生活便大大的改變了。

21 rent [rɛnt] vt. & vi. 租借 & vt. 出租，租給 & n. 租金

片 (1) rent sth from sb (for + 金額)
(以若干金額) 向某人租某物

▶ I rent an apartment from Mr. Wang for NT$6,000 a month.
我向王先生租了一間公寓，每月新臺幣 6,000 元。

(2) rent sth (out) to sb
將某物租給某人

(3) for rent （以供）出租

衍 rental [ˈrɛntl̩] n. 出租；租金 ⑤

▶ Becky was still considering buying or renting an apartment in this city.
貝琪還在考慮要在這城市買還是租公寓。

▶ Mr. Brown makes ends meet by renting rooms (out) to students.
布朗先生把房間租給學生，以維持收支平衡。
＊make ends meet　使收支平衡

▶ How much is your monthly rent for your apartment?
你每月公寓租金是多少錢？

▶ That rich landlord has five apartments for rent.
那個有錢的房東有 5 棟公寓要出租。

22　nerve [nɜv] n. 神經 (可數)；膽量，勇氣 (不可數)

片 (1) have the nerve to V
有勇氣做……
＝ have the courage / guts to V

(2) get on sb's nerves　讓某人心煩

似 (1) courage [ˈkɝɪdʒ] n. 勇氣，膽量 ②

(2) guts [gʌts]
n. 勇氣，膽量 (恆用複數)

▶ The doctor said the nerves in Richard's wrist were damaged.
醫生說理查德手腕的神經已受損。

▶ Arthur doesn't have the nerve to apologize to Bonnie for what he said.
亞瑟沒有勇氣為他說的話向邦妮道歉。

▶ My dad's nagging really gets on my nerves.
老爸一直嘮叨實在讓我很心煩。

---

nervous [ˈnɝvəs] a. 神經的；緊張的

片 a nervous system　神經系統

▶ The illness is due to a disorder of the nervous system.
這疾病是因為神經系統出了問題。

▶ Allison was quite nervous when delivering a speech at the university yesterday.
艾莉森昨天在大學演講時相當緊張。

23　blood [blʌd] n. 血

片 a blood type　血型

衍 (1) bloody [ˈblʌdɪ] a. 血腥的 ③

(2) bleed [blid] vi. 流血 ③

▶ Help! A man is losing a lot of blood here.
救命啊！有人在這裡流好多血。

▶ Blood is thicker than water.
血濃於水。—— 諺語

▶ I don't know what my blood type is.
我不知道我的血型是什麼。

---

bone [bon] n. 骨頭

衍 bony [ˈbonɪ]
a. (魚) 多刺的；瘦骨如柴的

▶ This fish is bony.
這種魚的刺很多。

▶ I broke a bone in my foot when I jumped off the tree.
我從樹上跳下來時，把腿上的一根骨頭摔斷了。

24 **particular** [pəˈtɪkjələ] *a.* 特別的；挑剔的

片 (1) in particular   特別地，尤其地
(2) be particular about...
    對……很挑剔 / 講究
= be picky / choosy about...

▶ You should pay particular attention to spelling.
你應該特別注意拼字。

▶ It was a good movie—I liked the last scene in particular.
這部電影很精彩 —— 我特別喜歡最後一幕。

▶ The little boy is very particular about the food he eats.
那小男孩對他吃的食物很挑剔。

---

especially [əˈspɛʃəlɪ]
(= particularly [pəˈtɪkjələlɪ])
adv. 特別地；專門地

衍 special [ˈspɛʃəl] *a.* 特別的；專門的 ①

▶ Everyone in our class studies very hard, especially Ashley.
我們班上每個人都很用功，尤其是艾希莉。

▶ This program is especially designed for the elderly.
這程式是特地為老年人所設計的。

25 **unless** [ʌnˈlɛs] *conj.* 除非

▶ Unless you make a reservation today, you won't get a table at that restaurant this weekend.

= If you don't make a reservation today, you won't get a table at that restaurant this weekend.
除非今天去訂位，要不然這週末在那家餐廳你不會有位子坐的。

26 **conversation** [ˌkɑnvəˈseʃən] *n.* 對話

片 (1) have a conversation with sb
    和某人交談
(2) strike up a conversation with sb
    與某人開始攀談起來

衍 converse [kənˈvɝs] *vi.* 交談 ④

▶ Matt was eager to have a conversation with the pretty girl.
麥特非常想和那漂亮的女孩聊天。

▶ You can strike up a conversation with people by talking about the weather.
你可以從談論天氣與人開始攀談起來。

---

dialogue [ˈdaɪəˌlɔɡ] *n.* 對話

衍 monologue [ˈmɑnḷˌɔɡ]
n. 獨白 (= monolog)

▶ Simply reading the dialogue is not enough. You should act it out.
光唸對話是沒用的。你應該把它演示出來才對。

27 **shy** [ʃaɪ] *a.* 害羞的

似 (1) timid [ˈtɪmɪd] *a.* 羞怯的 ④
(2) cowardly [ˈkaʊədlɪ] *a.* 膽小的 ⑥

反 bold [bold] *a.* 大膽的 ③

▶ The little girl is too shy to talk to anyone.
那小女孩太害羞了，因此沒辦法跟任何人交談。

28 **emphasize** [ˈɛmfəˌsaɪz] *vt.* 強調，重視

衍 emphasis [ˈɛmfəsɪs] *n.* 強調，重視 ④

似 stress [strɛs] *vt.* 強調 ②

▸ The study emphasizes the importance of a balanced diet.
這份研究強調均衡飲食的重要性。

1　triangle [ˈtraɪˌæŋgl̩] *n.* 三角形

㊗ triangular [traɪˈæŋgjələ]
　　a. 三角形的

▶ The child is learning to draw a triangle.
　這小朋友正在學畫三角形。

2　shut [ʃʌt] *vt.* & *vi.* 關閉 & *a.* 關上的

㊢ 三態同形

㊍ (1) shut up　住口，閉嘴
　　(2) shut down
　　　　關門大吉，倒閉，歇業
　　= close down

㊒ close [kloz] *vt.* & *vi.* 關閉；歇業 ①

▶ Shut the window before you leave.
　離開前把窗戶關起來。

▶ This door won't shut. Why is that?
　這扇門關不起來。怎麼會這樣？

▶ Shut up! I couldn't hear what the teacher was talking about.
　住口！我聽不到老師在說什麼。

▶ It's a pity that this grocery store is going to shut down.
　很可惜這家雜貨店要關門大吉了。

▶ Julie thought the window was open, but it was shut.
　茱莉以為窗戶是開著的，但卻是關上的。

3　wallet [ˈwɑlɪt] *n.* 皮夾子，錢包

㊂ purse [pɝs]
　　n. (女用) 手提包 (= handbag) ③

▶ Dad gave me a leather wallet for my birthday.
　老爸送我皮夾子當生日禮物。

4　addition [əˈdɪʃən] *n.* 添加；加法

㊍ in addition to + N/V-ing
　　除了……之外還
　　= besides + N/V-ing

㊂ (1) subtraction [səbˈtrækʃən] *n.* 減法
　　(2) multiplication [ˌmʌltəpləˈkeʃən]
　　　　n. 乘法
　　(3) division [dəˈvɪʒən] *n.* 除法 ②

▶ The addition of the spice to the soup makes it taste better.
　在湯中添加這種香料會讓它更美味。

▶ Mom, my teacher told me we would learn addition first.
　媽媽，我老師說我們會先學加法。

▶ In addition to attending school during the day, Sandy goes to work at night.
　珊蒂除了白天上學之外，晚上還要工作。

5　express [ɪkˈsprɛs] *vt.* 表達 (思想 / 感情等) & *a.* 快遞的，快速的 & *n.* 特快列車，直達公車；快遞 (服務) & *adv.* 用快遞

㊐ expresses [ɪkˈsprɛsɪz]

㊍ (1) express oneself
　　　　表達自己的想法 / 感受
　　(2) express mail　快遞
　　(3) by express　用快遞

▶ He can express himself fluently in English.
　他能用流利的英文表達自己的意思。

衍 **expressive** [ɪkˈsprɛsɪv] *a.* 表達的 ③

▶ I'll send the package by express mail.
我會用快遞寄送這份包裹。

▶ We took the first express to Tainan.
我們搭乘到臺南的頭班快車。

▶ The manager said we had to send this mail by express.
經理說這封信我們必須寄快遞。

▶ It cost more to send the package express.
用快遞寄包裹的費用更高。

expression [ɪkˈsprɛʃən]
n. 表達；表情；(詞) 語，措詞

▶ Laughter is an expression of happiness.
笑是一種快樂的表現。

▶ Taylor had an expression of anger on his face.
泰勒神情很憤怒。

▶ My grandmother knew many funny old expressions in French.
我祖母知道許多古怪的法文古老用語。

phrase [frez]
n. 詞組，片語；慣用語，警句 & *vt.* 用語言表達，敘述

▶ Amy learned many new English phrases in her class yesterday.
艾咪昨天在課堂上學了很多新的英文片語。

▶ "Have a nice day" is a common phrase.
『祝你有美好的一天』是一個常見的慣用語。

▶ Jenny phrased her words very carefully.
珍妮措辭嚴謹。

6　loss [lɔs] *n.* 失去；損失；去世

片 (1) loss of...　遺失……；……過世
　(2) a great loss to sb
　　　對某人來說是一大損失
　(3) be at a loss
　　　茫然不知所措，不知如何是好

衍 (1) lose [luz] *vt.* 遺失 ①
　(2) lost [lɔst] *a.* 遺失的；迷路的
　(3) loser [ˈluzɚ] *n.* 輸家 ③

▶ You should report the loss of your luggage to the police.
你遺失了行李應該要去報警才是。

▶ Mr. Wang's death was a great loss to our company.
王先生去世是我們公司的一大損失。

▶ Toby has been very down since the loss of his pet dog.
托比自從愛犬過世後，心情就一直很沮喪。

▶ I'm at a loss as to what I should do.
我很迷惘，不知該怎麼做。

gain [gen]
vt. 獲 / 贏得；增加 & *n.* 利益，獲得；增加

片 (1) gain weight　增重
　　= put on weight

▶ The candidate gained over 80% of the vote.
那候選人得到超過 80% 的選票。

▶ It's not polite to ask someone whether he or she has gained weight.
問某人是否變胖了是不禮貌的。

(2) **personal gain** 私利

👥 (1) **get** [gɛt] *vt.* 獲得 ①
　　(2) **obtain** [əbˋten] *vt.* 獲得 ④
　　(3) **increase** [ɪnˋkris]
　　　　 vt. & vi. & [ˋɪnkris] *n.* 增加 ②

▶ Roger claimed that he had never done anything for personal gain.　羅傑宣稱從未做過任何事來獲取私利。

▶ No pain, no gain.　沒有耕耘就沒有收穫。——諺語

▶ An unhealthy diet might result in weight gain.
不健康的飲食可能會導致體重增加。

---

7 **couple** [ˋkʌpḷ] *n.* 兩 / 幾個；(一對) 夫婦 / 情侶 & *vt.* 結合 (= combine [kəmˋbaɪn]) (常用被動)

🔑 (1) **a couple of...** 一對 / 幾個……
　　(2) **A be coupled with B** A 加上 B

▶ I'll invite a couple of friends over.
我會邀請幾個朋友過來。

▶ Steve, I think the young couple next door is very kind.
史提夫，我覺得隔壁那對年輕夫婦很友善。

▶ Water shortage coupled with a power failure last weekend made us feel quite miserable.
上週末缺水加上停電，讓我們感到十分痛苦。

---

partner [ˋpɑrtnɚ]
n. 搭檔；(生意上的) 合夥人；配偶

🔑 (1) **a dancing partner** 舞伴
　　(2) **a trading partner** 貿易夥伴

衍 **partnership** [ˋpɑrtnɚˏʃɪp]
　　 n. 合夥關係 ④

👥 (1) **companion** [kəmˋpænjən]
　　　 n. 同伴 ④
　　(2) **associate** [əˋsoʃɪət]
　　　 n. (生意) 夥伴 ④

▶ The man talking with Megan is my dancing partner.
和梅根說話的那個人是我的舞伴。

▶ Germany is one of our major trading partners in Europe.
德國是我們在歐洲主要貿易夥伴國之一。

▶ Is it true that Julie's partner is a German?
茱莉的老公是德國人，是真的嗎？

---

wedding [ˋwɛdɪŋ] *n.* 婚禮

衍 **wed** [wɛd] *vt. & vi.* (與……) 結婚 ③

延伸 **newlywed** [ˋn(j)ulɪˏwɛd]
　　 n. 新婚的人 (常用複數)

▶ The wedding is to be held in the middle of June.
婚禮預定在 6 月中旬舉行。

---

marriage [ˋmærɪdʒ] *n.* 婚姻

▶ Unfortunately, their marriage ended in divorce.
不幸地，他們的婚姻以離婚收場。

---

marry [ˋmærɪ] *vt. & vi.* 結婚，嫁，娶

三 marry, married [ˋmærɪd], married

🔑 **marry sb** 與某人結婚
　= get married to sb

▶ Do you know when Linda will marry Sam?
= Do you know when Linda will get married to Sam?
你知道琳達何時會和山姆結婚嗎？

 3107-3110

衍 **married** [ˈmærɪd] *a.* 結 / 已婚的 ①
be married　已婚的

▶ Rita is married with 3 children.
麗塔已婚，有 3 個孩子。

---

match [mætʃ]

n. 比賽〔英〕（= game〔美〕）；火柴；(實力相當的) 對手；相配的人 / 物 & *vt.* 比得上；使競賽 & *vt.* & *vi.* (與……) 相配

複 **matches** [ˈmætʃɪz]

片 (1) strike a match　點火柴
(2) be no match for...
不是……的對手，敵不過……
(3) match A against B　使 A 對決 B
= A be matched against B

衍 (1) matchless [ˈmætʃləs]
a. 無人能及的
(2) matchmaker [ˈmætʃˌmekɚ]
n. 媒人

▶ Who won the tennis match?
誰贏了這場網球比賽？

▶ Simon struck a match and lit a fire.
賽門點了火柴，升起了火。

▶ Although Rick runs fast, he is no match for Jim.
雖然瑞克跑很快，但他不是吉姆的對手。

▶ My sister and Toby are a good match.
我姊姊和托比是天生絕配。

▶ When it comes to singing, no one matches / rivals / equals Willy.
= When it comes to singing, Willy is unmatched / unrivaled / unequaled.
說到唱歌，威利無以倫比。

▶ Peter will be matched against Paul in the men's tennis semifinal next week.
下星期的男網準決賽將由彼得對決保羅。

▶ Your dress matches your shoes perfectly.
= Your dress and shoes match perfectly.
你的洋裝很搭你的鞋子。

8　**meaning** [ˈminɪŋ] *n.* 意思；含義；意義，重要性

片 meaning behind...　……背後的含義
衍 (1) mean [min] *vt.* 表示……的意思 ①
(2) meaningful [ˈminɪŋfl]
a. 有意義的 ③
(3) meaningless [ˈminɪŋləs]
a. 無意義的

▶ What's the meaning of this word?
= What do you mean by this word?
這個字是什麼意思？

▶ Not many people understand the meaning behind his words.
不是很多人了解隱藏在他話背後的含意。

▶ I'm still searching for the meaning of life.
我還在找尋人生的意義。

---

means [minz] *n.* 方法

複 單複數同形

片 (1) by means of...　藉由……
(2) by no means　絕 (對) 不 (會)
= not... by any means

▶ LINE is a useful means of communication.
LINE 是一種很好用的通訊方法。

▶ Thoughts are usually expressed by means of language.
思想通常經由語言來表達。

▸ I am by no means happy to see Michael.
= I am not happy to see Michael by any means.
看到邁可我絕對不會覺得高興。

9　form [fɔrm] n. 表格；形狀；形式 & vt. 形成

🏠 (1) fill in / out a form 　　填表格
　　(2) an application form 　　申請表
　　(3) in the form of...
　　　　是 / 以⋯⋯的形狀

衍 (1) formal [`fɔrml̩] a. 正式的 ②
　　(2) formation [fɔr`meʃən]
　　　　n. 形成；編 / 列隊 ④
　　　　in formation 　　編 / 列隊

▸ Fill out the application form, and then wait in line.
填妥申請表格，然後排隊等候。

▸ The table in the corner of the kitchen is in the form of a triangle.
在廚房角落的那張桌子是三角形的。

▸ Nowadays, email is a common form of communication.
現今，電子郵件是很常見的通訊形式。

▸ We formed a circle and danced around the campfire.
我們圍成一個圓圈，繞著營火跳舞。

---

former [`fɔrmɚ]
a. 之前的 & pron. 前者 (此意前面加定冠詞 the)

▸ The former president died of cancer last week.
前任總統上星期因癌症過世了。

▸ Thomas and Ned are good friends. The former has a talent for music, and the latter is good at painting.
湯瑪斯跟奈德是好友。前者很有音樂天分，而後者則工於繪畫。

---

latter [`lætɚ]
a. 後者的 & pron. 後者 (此意前面加定冠詞 the)

▸ The resume of the latter interviewee was quite impressive.
後一位面試者的履歷令人印象相當深刻。
＊resume [`rɛzə͵me] n. 履歷，簡歷

▸ Leo and Kyle are both my friends. The former is a teacher, while the latter is a soldier.
李歐和凱爾都是我的朋友。前者是老師，而後者則是軍人。

10　distant [`dɪstənt] a. (距離 / 時間等) 遙遠的；遠房 / 親的

🏠 in the not too distant future
在不久的將來

▸ Gina plans to study abroad in the not too distant future.
吉娜計劃在不久的將來要出國留學。

▸ The two boys are distant relatives of mine.
這 2 個男孩是我的遠房親戚。

---

distance [`dɪstəns] n. 距離
🏠 (1) distance between A and B
A 和 B 之間的距離

▸ The distance between John's home and school was not far.
約翰的家和學校之間距離並不遠。

(2) in the distance 在遙遠的地方

(3) keep sb at a distance
與某人保持距離

(4) be within walking distance of...
距離……走幾步路就到了

▶ I see a girl in the distance.
我看到遠處有個女孩。

▶ He is a liar. Keep him at a distance.
他是個騙子，跟他保持距離。

▶ The castle is within walking distance of the hotel.
那座城堡就在從飯店步行即可到達的距離內。

---

11 gather [ˈɡæðɚ] *vt.* 蒐集 & *vi.* 聚集

衍 gathering [ˈɡæðərɪŋ]
n. 集會 (可數) ⑤

似 collect [kəˈlɛkt] *vt.* 收集；蒐藏 ①

▶ We need to gather information about the situation before taking action.
我們採取行動之前，得先蒐集相關情況的資訊。

▶ A lot of students are gathering there for a big anti-war rally.
很多學生正聚集在那裡準備參加一場大型的反戰集會活動。

---

12 respect [rɪˈspɛkt] *n.* 尊敬；方面 & *vt.* 尊敬；尊重

片 (1) show(one's) respect for...
向……表 (某人的) 敬意

(2) hold sb in great / high respect
很尊敬某人

= hold sb in great / high regard

(3) in many / some respects
在很多 / 一些方面

in this respect 在這個方面

(4) respect A for B
因 B 而非常尊敬 / 敬佩 A

衍 (1) respectable [rɪˈspɛktəbl]
a. 值得尊敬的 ④

(2) respectful [rɪˈspɛktfl]
a. 滿懷敬意的 ④

▶ Students should show their respect for their teachers.
學生應該尊敬老師。

▶ We hold Bill in great respect for all the good deeds he has done.
比爾做的種種善行，使我們非常尊敬他。

▶ This essay is similar to mine in many respects.
這篇短文在很多方面和我的很類似。

▶ I respect him for his bravery.
因為他的勇敢，所以我很尊敬他。

▶ We should respect other people's feelings.
我們應尊重他人的感受。

---

13 trade [tred] *n.* 貿易，買賣 (不可數) & *vi.* & *vt.* 做買賣 / 生意 & *vt.* 交換

片 (1) trade in... 做……的買賣
(2) trade with sb 和某人做買賣
(3) trade sth with sb
和某人交換某物
(4) trade A for B 以 A 交換 B

衍 (1) trader [ˈtredɚ] *n.* 商人 ③
(2) trademark [ˈtred,mɑrk]
n. 商標 ⑥

▶ This country banned the trade in rare animals many years ago.
這國家多年前就已禁止買賣稀有動物了。

▶ Our company has been trading with this French company for several years.
我們公司已和這家法國公司做生意做好幾年了。

▶ Flora traded bracelets with her friend Sarah.
芙蘿拉和朋友莎拉交換手鐲。

▶ Jim traded his favorite comic book for his brother's new toy car.
吉姆用他最喜歡的漫畫書和弟弟換新的玩具車。

commercial [kə'mɝʃəl]
a. 商業的 & *n.* (廣播 / 電視的) 廣告

☐ a commercial success
商業上的成功

▶ Some of the commercial laws have been amended.
商業法有部分已有所修訂。

▶ The company's new product was a commercial success.
該公司的新產品取得了商業上的成功。

▶ I don't watch much TV because the commercials drive me crazy.
我很少看電視因為廣告會令我抓狂。

businessman ['bɪznəs,mæn]
n. 商人

複 businessmen ['bɪznəs,mɛn]
反 businesswoman
['bɪznəs,wumən]
n. 女商人 (複數為 businesswomen
['bɪznəs,wɪmən])

▶ My father is a successful businessman.
我父親是一名成功的商人。

14 difficulty ['dɪfə,kʌltɪ] *n.* 困難

☐ have difficulty (in) + V-ing
在做……方面有困難
= have trouble + V-ing
衍 difficult ['dɪfə,kʌlt] *a.* 困難的 ①

▶ Do you have any difficulty understanding spoken Chinese?
你聽口語中文有困難嗎？

15 enemy ['ɛnəmɪ] *n.* 敵人

複 enemies ['ɛnəmɪz]
反 friend [frɛnd] *n.* 朋友 ①

▶ Laziness is your own worst enemy.
懶惰是你最大的敵人。

16 sample ['sæmpl] *vt.* 抽樣檢查 / 研究 / 詢問；試吃 & *n.* 樣品 & *a.* 作為例子的

似 (1) test [tɛst] *vt.* 檢驗 & *n.* 測驗 ①
(2) specimen ['spɛsəmən]
n. 樣本 / 品 ⑤
延伸 random sampling　隨機抽樣

▶ 23% of students sampled said they slept less than six hours a day.
23% 的受訪學生表示他們每天的睡眠時間不到 6 小時。

▶ You are welcome to sample any of the ice cream.
我們歡迎您試吃任何一種冰淇淋。

▶ The supermarket gives customers samples of food every day.
此超市每天都給客人提供試吃。

Level 2　Unit 31

▶ In this booklet, you'll see some sample questions and answers.
在這手冊裡，你會看到一些示範例題和答案。

17 toast [tost] *n.* 烤麵包片 (不可數)；敬酒 (可數) & *vt.* 向……敬酒

(1) a slice / piece of toast
一片烤麵包片

(2) make / propose a toast to sb
向某人敬酒

(3) toast A with B　用 B 來向 A 敬酒

▶ I had two slices of toast for breakfast this morning.
我今早吃了 2 片烤麵包片當早餐。

▶ I made a toast to Paul and his beautiful bride at the wedding reception.
在婚宴上，我向保羅跟他美麗的新娘子敬酒。

▶ We toasted the guests with wine.
我們以紅酒向來賓敬酒。

cereal [ˈsɪrɪəl]
n. (拌以牛奶等作早餐的) 穀類食品，麥片；穀類作物

▶ My favorite breakfast is cereal and milk.
我最喜愛的早餐是麥片加牛奶。

▶ The cereal crops in this area suffered because of a serious disease.
這地區的穀物因一種很嚴重的疾病而無法正常生長。

cream [krim]
n. (鮮) 奶油；護膚霜；藥膏；精華 & *a.* 奶油色的，米色的

(1) ice cream　冰淇淋

(2) face / sun cream　面霜 / 防晒乳

(3) be the cream of the crop
是最棒的，是最頂尖的
= be the very best

▶ Would you like cream and sugar in your coffee?
請問您的咖啡要加奶精和糖嗎？

▶ Linda puts on face cream before she goes to bed.
琳達在睡覺前都會塗面霜。

▶ Apply the cream to the sore area.
將藥膏塗抹在酸痛的部位。

▶ These students excel in math. In fact, they are the cream of the crop.
這些學生數學棒得不得了。事實上，他們是最頂尖的。

▶ Bess looked pretty in her cream dress and shoes.
貝絲身穿米色的洋裝和鞋子看起來很漂亮。

pudding [ˈpʊdɪŋ] *n.* 布丁

▶ This restaurant makes the most delicious pudding in the whole world.
這家餐廳的布丁是全世界最好吃的。

18 whole [hol] *a.* 整個的 & *n.* 全部

(1) the whole of...　整個……

(2) on the whole　大體上說
= in general

▶ Tell me the whole story.
把整個故事都告訴我。

▶ The whole of my weekend was spent on cleaning the apartment that I had just moved into.
我整個週末都在打掃我剛搬進來的公寓。

▸ On the whole, girls in Asia are shyer than boys.
一般而言，亞洲女孩子比男孩子害羞。

19 **weigh** [we] *vt.* 秤重量；重達……；衡量，仔細考慮

▸ I weigh myself right after I wake up in the morning.
我早上一醒來就量體重。

▸ A: How much do you weigh?
= What's your weight?
B: I weigh 120 pounds.
A：你多重？
B：我重 120 磅。

▸ We weighed the options before we made a decision.
我們先衡量了這些選擇，再做出決定。

Level 2 Unit 31

weight [wet] *n.* 重量，體重

🔑 (1) in weight　　　重量上
(2) put on weight　增重
= gain weight
(3) lose weight　瘦下來

衍 (1) heavyweight [ˈhɛvɪˌwet]
　　n. 重量級拳擊手
(2) lightweight [ˈlaɪtˌwet]
　　n. 輕量級拳擊手

▸ The fan was about ten pounds in weight.
這臺風扇重量大約是 10 磅。

▸ I put on some weight during the vacation, so I need to go on a diet now.
我放假時變胖了，所以現在需要開始節食。

▸ Jamie has lost a lot of weight recently.
傑米最近瘦了很多。

20 **degree** [dɪˈgri] *n.* 程度，等級；學位；度

🔑 (1) to some degree　在某種程度上
= to a (certain) degree
to a large degree　很大程度上
(2) by degrees　漸漸地
= little by little
(3) a PhD degree　博士學位
(4) 0 degrees　0 度 (*非 0 degree)

▸ I think George is right to some degree.
我認為喬治在某種程度上是對的。

▸ Under Mr. Wang's guidance, my English is getting better by degrees.
在王老師的指導下，我的英文正逐漸進步中。

▸ Bill is working hard to get his PhD degree.
比爾正努力攻讀他的博士學位。

▸ It's 0 degrees Celsius today.
今天氣溫攝氏 0 度。

21 **trick** [trɪk] *vt.* 欺騙 & *n.* 惡作劇；竅門；把戲

🔑 (1) trick sb into + V-ing
　　欺騙某人去做……
(2) play a trick on... 戲 / 捉弄……
(3) do the trick　使某事成功

▸ Anna tricked Tim into carrying drugs for her.
安娜欺騙提姆替她攜帶毒品。

衍 tricky [ˈtrɪkɪ] *a.* 狡猾的 ③

似 (1) cheat [tʃit] *vt.* & *vi.* 欺騙 ②
　 (2) deceive [dɪˈsiv] *vt.* 欺騙 ⑤

▶ Billy was playing tricks on his little brother.
比利在戲弄他弟弟。

▶ The soup tastes a bit plain, but maybe a little more pepper will do the trick.
這湯喝起來有點無味，但也許再加一點胡椒就會很美味了。

▶ You can't teach an old dog new tricks.
老狗學不會新把戲。── 諺語

22 wound [wund] *vt.* 使受傷 & *n.* 傷口（可數）

片 rub salt into the wound
在傷口上灑鹽，雪上加霜

似 (1) hurt [hɝt] *vt.* 傷害 ①
　 (2) damage [ˈdæmɪdʒ] *vt.* 傷害 ②
　 (3) harm [hɑrm] *vt.* 傷害 ③

▶ The soldier was seriously wounded in the battle.
這名士兵在作戰時受到重傷。

▶ Time heals all wounds.
時間會癒合所有的傷痛。── 諺語

▶ Susan is already crying. Why do you still want to rub salt into the wound?
蘇珊已經在哭了。你為什麼還要在她傷口上灑鹽呢？

23 confident [ˈkɑnfədənt] *a.* 有信心的

片 be confident of... 對……有信心

衍 (1) confidence [ˈkɑnfədəns]
　　 n. 信心 ④
　 (2) confidential [ˌkɑnfəˈdɛnʃəl]
　　 a. 機密的 ⑤

▶ The ruling party was confident of winning the upcoming election.
執政黨有信心贏得即將到來的選舉。

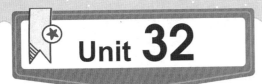

Level 2 Unit 32

1 **discuss** [dɪ'skʌs] *vt.* 討論

片 discuss sth with sb
和某人討論某事

▶ The professor discussed the case with us.
教授和我們討論這個案例。

discussion [dɪ'skʌʃən] *n.* 討論

片 be under discussion　在討論中

▶ After a lengthy discussion, the board denied Andy's request.
經過漫長的討論後，董事會駁回安迪的請求。

▶ The plan is still under discussion.
這計畫還在討論中。

2 **hardly** ['hɑrdlɪ] *adv.* 幾乎不

衍 hard [hɑrd] *a.* 困難的；費力的 &
adv. 努力地；大量地 ①

似 (1) barely ['bɛrlɪ] *adv.* 幾乎沒有 ③
(2) scarcely ['skɛrslɪ] *adv.* 幾乎不 ④

▶ Don't marry Paul just yet because you hardly know him.
現在還不要嫁給保羅，因為妳幾乎不了解他。

seldom ['sɛldəm] *adv.* 不常，鮮少

似 rarely ['rɛrlɪ] *adv.* 很少，難得

▶ My grandfather's eyesight is not good, so he seldom reads newspapers.
我爺爺的視力不佳，所以他很少看報紙。

3 **waiter** ['wetɚ] *n.* 男服務生

反 waitress ['wetrəs] *n.* 女服務生 ②

▶ A waiter came to take my order.
一位服務生過來幫我點餐。

customer ['kʌstəmɚ]
n. (尤指商店的) 顧客

片 a regular customer　老主顧，常客

似 client ['klaɪənt]
n. (向某公司請求專業服務的) 客戶；
訴訟委託人 ③

▶ Because of its advertisement, the new store attracted many customers.
這家新開的店因為有做廣告而吸引了很多顧客。

bill [bɪl] *n.* 帳單；紙鈔；法案；(鳥)喙
& *vt.* 給……開立 / 寄送帳單

片 (1) pay a bill　付帳
　 = foot a bill
(2) bill sb for sth
　　給某人開……的帳單

延伸 coin [kɔɪn] *n.* 硬幣 ②

▶ In Western countries, the father of the bride traditionally foots the bill for the wedding.
在西方國家，傳統上婚禮是由新娘的父親付帳。

▶ I need five 100-dollar bills.
我需要 5 張 100 元的鈔票。

▶ Congress passed the new bill to help endangered animals.
國會通過這項幫助瀕危動物的新法案。

▶ A woodpecker has a strong bill.
啄木鳥的喙很硬。

▶ The garage billed William for the repairs to his car.
修車廠給威廉開立修車的帳單。

---

4 **none** [nʌn] *pron.* 無一人／物 & *adv.* 一點也不……

句 (1) none of + 複數可數名詞
沒有一個……（＊ 做主詞時，其後接單、複數動詞皆可）

(2) none the + 比較級
一點也不……

用法 none 單獨當主詞時，動詞常用單數。

▶ None is able to complete this task.
= No one is able to complete this task.
沒人能完成這任務。

▶ Ryan wanted to borrow money from me, but I told him I had none.
萊恩想向我借錢，但我告訴他我沒錢。
＊此處的 none 等於 no money。

▶ None of my friends sings well.
我朋友沒一個唱歌唱得好。

▶ Brandon did practice the piano, but he seemed none the better for it.
布蘭登確實有練鋼琴，但他似乎絲毫沒有因為這樣而彈得比較好。

---

neither [ˋniðɚ／ˋnaɪðɚ]
adv. 也不 & *pron.* 兩者皆不 & *a.* 兩者都不的 & *conj.* 既不（與連接詞 nor 並用）

句 (1) neither of + 複數可數名詞
……兩者皆不（＊ 做主詞時，其後接單、複數動詞皆可）

(2) neither... nor... 既不……也不……
（＊連接對等的單字或片語；若連接主詞時，動詞按第 2 個主詞作變化。）

衍 either [ˋiðɚ／ˋaɪðɚ] *adv.* 也（用於否定句）& *pron.*（兩者中的）任一個 & *a.*（兩者中）任一個的 & *conj.* 或者 ①

用法 neither 單獨當主詞時，動詞常用單數。

▶ Greg isn't hungry right now and neither is Fred.
葛瑞格現在並不餓，弗瑞德也不餓。

▶ Neither of the two boys was absent.
這 2 個男孩都沒缺席。

▶ Neither boy is foolish.
2 個男孩都不笨。

▶ Danny is neither friendly nor generous.
丹尼既不友善也不慷慨。

▶ Neither you nor I am wrong.
你沒錯，我也沒錯。

---

5 **musical** [ˋmjuzɪkḷ] *a.* 音樂的 & *n.* 音樂劇

衍 music [ˋmjuzɪk] *n.* 音樂 ①
延伸 opera [ˋɑp(ə)rə] *n.* 歌劇 ④

▶ Ashley has a musical talent.
艾希莉有音樂天賦。

▶ This film was adapted from a Broadway musical.
這電影改編自一齣百老匯音樂劇。

musician [mjuˈzɪʃən]
n. 音樂家，樂師

▸ Mozart's father himself was a talented musician and composer.
莫札特的父親本身就是個才華洋溢的音樂家兼作曲家。

---

6 **fix** [fɪks] *vt.* 修理；使固定；準備 (食物 / 飲料) & *n.* 解決方案 / 措施

複 fixes [ˈfɪksɪz]
衍 fixed [fɪkst] *a.* 固定的
似 repair [rɪˈpɛr] *vt.* 修理 ②

▸ Do you know how to fix the copier?
你知道如何修理這部影印機嗎？

▸ My dad tried to fix the mirror to the wall.
我爸設法要把那面鏡子固定在牆上。

▸ It's time to fix / make / prepare dinner now.
現在該準備晚飯了。

▸ Rudy's suggestion isn't a fix; something else must be done.
魯迪的建議並不是個能解決問題的辦法；我們得做些別的事才行。

---

7 **design** [dɪˈzaɪn] *n.* 設計 (過程)；設計 (樣式) & *vt.* 設計；打算

片 be designed for... 為……所設立的
似 designate [ˈdɛzɪɡˌnet]
vt. 指定，劃定 (用途)

▸ The building project is still in the design stage.
此建築工程仍處於設計的階段。

▸ The design of this building is very stylish and unique.
這棟建築物的設計非常時尚又獨特。

▸ This bridge was designed by a Japanese architect.
這座橋是一位日本建築師設計的。

▸ This course is designed for students who know little about English.
本課程是為對英語所知不多的學生所設立的。

---

8 **affair** [əˈfɛr] *n.* 事務 / 情；私通 (皆可數)

片 have an affair with sb
與某人有婚外情

▸ While in college, I majored in international affairs.
大學時我主修國際事務。

▸ Rumor has it that Andrew is having an affair with his secretary.
謠傳安德魯和他的祕書有婚外情。

---

9 **wealth** [wɛlθ] *n.* 財富，富裕 (不可數)；大量，豐富 (恆用單數)

片 (1) personal wealth 個人財富
(2) a wealth of + 可數 / 不可數名詞
大量的 / 許多的 (有用或很好的東西)
= a lot of + 可數 / 不可數名詞
= lots of + 可數 / 不可數名詞

▸ According to the news, the pop singer's personal wealth is about US$80 million.
據報導，這流行歌手的個人財富約為 8 千萬美元。

Level 2 Unit 32

▶ The writer likes to travel because he believes it can provide him with a wealth of material for his writing.
這位作家喜歡旅行，因為他相信旅行可提供他很多寫作的素材。

riches [ˈrɪtʃɪz] *n.* 財富 (恆用複數)

片 go from rags to riches　由貧轉富
＊rags [rægz] *n.* 破爛的衣服 (恆用複數)

衍 rich [rɪtʃ] *a.* 有錢的 ①

▶ The lottery winner went from rags to riches overnight.
那樂透獎得主一夕之間由貧轉富。

---

10 **succeed** [səkˈsid] *vi.* 成功，達到目的 & *vi.* & *vt.* 繼承 / 位

片 (1) succeed in + N/V-ing　成功……
(2) succeed sb as sth
繼承某人擔任某職位

衍 (1) succeeding [səkˈsidɪŋ]
a. 繼起的，隨後的
(2) successor [səkˈsɛsɚ] *n.* 繼任者 ⑤
(3) succession [səkˈsɛʃən]
n. 連續；繼承 ⑥
(4) successive [səkˈsɛsɪv] *a.* 連續的 ⑥

反 fail [fel] *vi.* & *n.* 失敗 ①
without fail　必定

▶ You'll never succeed without hard work.
你不努力就絕不會成功。

▶ Adam succeeded in borrowing a large amount of money from the bank.
亞當順利從銀行借了一大筆錢。

▶ The young prince succeeded his father as king.
年輕的王子繼承他的父親，當上了國王。

---

success [səkˈsɛs]
n. 成功 (不可數)；成功的人 / 事 (可數)

複 successes [səkˈsɛsɪz]

反 failure [ˈfeljɚ]
n. 失敗 (不可數)；失敗的人 / 事 (可數)
②

▶ Stephen was quite excited at the success of his latest movie.
史蒂芬對他最新的電影很成功感到相當興奮。

▶ The party last night was quite a success.
昨晚的派對辦得很成功。

---

11 **poet** [ˈpoɪt] *n.* 詩人

衍 poetic [poˈɛtɪk]
a. 富有詩意的；詩 (歌) 的 ⑤

▶ Shakespeare is a famous English poet and playwright.
莎士比亞是知名的英國詩人兼劇作家。

---

poem [ˈpoɪm] *n.* 詩 (可數)

▶ I enjoy reading poems about nature.
我喜歡讀有關大自然的詩。

---

poetry [ˈpoɪtrɪ]
n. 詩 (集合名詞，不可數)

▶ Annie read some of her poetry to the students.
＝ Annie read some of her poems to the students.
安妮唸了一些她寫的詩給學生聽。

12 project [ˈprɑdʒɛkt] n. 計畫 & [prəˈdʒɛkt] vt. 預計，規 / 計劃；投射 / 放映 (影 / 圖片等)

片 (1) be projected to V　預計做……
 (2) project A onto B
　　 把 A 投射 / 放映到 B

衍 (1) projector [prəˈdʒɛktə] n. 投影機
 (2) projection [prəˈdʒɛkʃən]
　　 n. 投射，投影 ⑤

▶ I believe this new project will make a profit by the end of the year.
我相信這新計畫年底以前會獲利。

▶ The game is projected to take place at the new gym.
這場比賽預計在新體育館舉行。

▶ Julie projected the map onto the wall.
茱莉把地圖投射到牆上。

13 scare [skɛr] vt. & vi. (使) 驚恐 (= frighten [ˈfraɪtn̩]) & n. 驚恐

片 give sb a scare　嚇某人一跳
衍 scary [ˈskɛrɪ] a. 恐怖的 ③
延伸 scarecrow [ˈskɛr͵kro] n. 稻草人

▶ Don't scare me. I'm a coward.
別嚇我。我是個膽小鬼。

▶ Irene doesn't scare easily: She didn't even blink when she saw a flying cockroach.
艾琳不容易害怕：她看到蟑螂在飛時，眼睛甚至都沒有眨一下。

▶ When Melvin passed out, he gave us a scare.
馬文昏倒的時候，嚇了我們一跳。

scared [skɛrd] a. 感到害怕的
片 be scared of...　害怕……
似 afraid [əˈfred] a. 害怕的 ①

▶ When I was very young, I was scared of dogs.
我小的時候很怕狗。

14 receive [rɪˈsiv] vt. 收到；接待，迎接

衍 (1) receiver [rɪˈsivə]
　　 n. 話筒；收件者，受領人 ③
 (2) reception [rɪˈsɛpʃən]
　　 n. 接待，歡迎；歡迎會；服務臺，
　　 櫃檯 ④
 (3) receptionist [rɪˈsɛpʃənɪst]
　　 n. 接待員；櫃檯服務人員

▶ Did you receive the email that I sent you?
我寄給你的電子郵件收到了嗎？

▶ Luke received his guests as they arrived at the dinner party.
客人來到晚宴時，路克去迎接他們。

return [rɪˈtɜn]
vi. 返回，回到 & vt. 歸還；回應 / 報 &
n. 返回；歸還；回應 / 報

片 (1) return to / from + 地方
　　 回來某地 / 從某地回來
 (2) return A to B　把 A 還給 B

▶ When will you return to Taiwan?
你什麼時候會回臺灣？

▶ You should return the book to the library by Friday.
你要在星期五以前把這本書還給圖書館。

▶ My mom told me that when someone helped me, I also had to return the favor.
我媽告訴我，當有人幫助我時，我也必須回報。

Level 2　Unit 32

(3) return the favor 回報，禮尚往來
(4) sb's return to / from + 地方
　　某人回來某地 / 某人從某地回來
(5) in return for... 以回報……
(6) many happy returns (of the day)
　　祝 (你) 長命百歲 / 祝 (你) 生日快樂

▶ No one knows the date of Owen's return from France.
沒人知道歐文從法國回來的日期。

▶ All the old man wanted was the safe return of his expensive violin.
那老人只想要他那昂貴的小提琴平安歸來。

▶ I gave Martin a watch in return for his help.
我給馬丁一隻手錶以回報他的幫忙。

▶ On Mandy's birthday, Tom wished her many happy returns.
在曼蒂生日當天，湯姆祝她長命百歲。

---

15 schedule [ˈskɛdʒʊl] *vt.* 安排，計劃 & *n.* 日程 / 計畫表

(1) be scheduled to V 預定做……
(2) on schedule 按照進度
　　ahead of schedule 進度超前
　　behind schedule 進度落後

▶ The mayor is scheduled to make a speech on TV tomorrow.
市長預定明天會在電視上發表演說。

▶ I'm glad that we finished the work ahead of schedule.
真高興我們提前完工。

---

16 shine [ʃaɪn] *vi.* 發亮，照耀 & *vt.* 擦亮 & *n.* 光亮

shine 的三態有兩種：
照耀：shine, shone [ʃon], shone
擦亮：shine, shined, shined
shiny [ˈʃaɪnɪ] *a.* 發亮的，有光澤的 ③

▶ The sun shone brightly in the sky yesterday.
昨天艷陽高照。

▶ I just had my shoes shined.
我才請人擦過我的鞋。

▶ Kelly's hair lost its shine after she dyed her hair.
凱莉染頭髮後，頭髮就失去了光澤。

---

17 conclude [kənˈklud] *vt.* 作結論 & *vi.* & *vt.* (以……) 結束 (演講 / 文章等)

(1) conclude that... 斷 / 論定……
(2) conclude A with B
　　以 B 來結束 A
= end A with B
= wind up A with B
conclusion [kənˈkluʒən]
n. 結果；結論 ③

▶ The police concluded that the accident was caused by the driver's carelessness.
警方的結論是這次意外是那駕駛粗心大意所造成的。

▶ Cathy concluded by thanking everyone for listening to her speech.
演說的最後，凱西感謝大家來聽她的演講。

▶ The professor concluded his lecture with a good joke.
= The professor ended his lecture with a good joke.
= The professor wound up his lecture with a good joke.
教授課堂結束前講了一個很好笑的笑話。

18 concern [kənˈsɝn] *vt.* 使擔心；涉及到，關於 & *n.* 關心，掛念

衍 **concerned** [kənˈsɝnd]
　　a. 有關的；擔心的
　　be concerned about...　擔心……
= **be worried about...**

▶ More and more parents are concerned about school violence.
越來越多的家長擔心校園暴力的問題。

似 **worry** [ˈwɝɪ] *vt.* 使擔心 & *n.* 擔心 ①

▶ Because of the accident, the safety of the MRT concerns many people in this country.
因為這意外，捷運的安全引起許多國人的關切。

▶ The email concerns important information, so it must be read.
此電子郵件涉及到很重要的資訊，因此必須閱讀。

▶ Your health is my concern, Dad.
老爸，我很擔心你的健康。

19 restroom [ˈrɛstˌrum] *n.* 公共廁所

似 **bathroom** [ˈbæθˌrum]
　　n. 公共廁所；浴室 ①

▶ Excuse me. I need to go to the restroom now.
不好意思，我現在得去一下洗手間。

soap [sop]
n. 肥皂 & *vt.* 用肥皂擦洗，在……上面抹肥皂

片 (1) **a bar of soap**　一塊肥皂
　= **a cake of soap**
　(2) **a soap opera**　肥皂/連續劇

▶ Wash your hands thoroughly with soap and water.
用肥皂和水徹底清洗你的雙手。

▶ Remember that we've also got to buy three bars of soap.
記住我們還得買 3 塊肥皂。

▶ Sharon enjoys watching soap operas from Korea and Japan.
雪倫喜歡看韓國和日本的肥皂劇。

▶ Before eating the meal, Gary soaped his hands well and washed them.
用餐前，蓋瑞用肥皂塗抹雙手，然後洗乾淨。

wash [wɑʃ]
vt. 清洗；沖走 & *n.* 洗濯（常用單數）

片 (1) **wash sth away**　沖走某物
　(2) **a good wash**　徹底洗一洗

延伸 (1) **dishwasher** [ˈdɪʃˌwɑʃɚ] *n.* 洗碗機
　　(2) **a washing machine**　洗衣機

▶ Wash your hands thoroughly before you eat dinner.
晚餐前把手徹底洗乾淨。

▶ My car was washed away by the flood.
我的車被洪水沖走了。

▶ My sneakers need a good wash.
我的球鞋需要好好洗一洗了。

20 continue [kənˈtɪnju] *vi.* & *vt.* 繼續

片 **continue + V-ing**　繼續做……
= **continue to V**
= **go on + V-ing**

衍 (1) **continuous** [kənˈtɪnjuəs]
　　　a. 連續不斷的 ④
　　(2) **continuity** [ˌkɑntəˈn(j)uətɪ]
　　　n. 連貫性（不可數）⑥

▶ Despite the blackout, the baseball game continued.
儘管停電了，棒球比賽依舊繼續進行。

▶ Although it started to rain, Dennis continued jogging.
= Although it started to rain, Dennis continued to jog.
雖然開始下雨了，丹尼斯還是繼續在慢跑。

21 cause [kɔz] vt. 引起；導致 & n. 原因；理由 (= reason)

⚑ cause sb to V　致使某人做……
= make sb + V

▶ Ron's carelessness caused the accident.
榮恩的粗心大意釀成了這起意外。

▶ The sad movie caused me to cry.
= The sad movie made me cry.
那部傷感的電影讓我哭了出來。

▶ What was the cause of the explosion?
那起爆炸的原因是什麼？

▶ The concert was terrific—I had no cause for complaint.
音樂會精彩極了 —— 我沒有理由可以抱怨。

factor [ˈfæktɚ] n. 因素
⚑ a factor in sth　某事物的因素

▶ Arrogance was a major factor in Nathan's failure.
傲慢自大是納森失敗的主因。
*arrogance [ˈærəgəns] n. 傲慢

22 excuse [ɪkˈskjuz] vt. 原諒；使免除 & [ɪkˈskjus] n. 藉口

⚑ (1) excuse sb for + N/V-ing
因……原諒某人

(2) excuse sb from + N/V-ing
准許某人不需……

(3) excuse me
打擾一下；對不起；不好意思，借過

(4) make an excuse for + N/V-ing
就……來找藉口

⿰ forgive [fɚˈgɪv] vt. 原諒 ②

▶ Please excuse me for not coming to the wedding last week.
我上星期沒有去參加婚禮，請見諒。

▶ Can I be excused from doing the chores today?
我今天可以不做這些雜務嗎？

▶ Excuse me, does this train go south or north?
打擾一下，請問這列火車是往南還是往北的？

▶ Oh! Excuse me. I didn't know this pen was yours.
喔！對不起。我不知道這支筆是你的。

▶ Excuse me, I need to get off at this station.
不好意思借過一下，我得在這站下車。

▶ Harry made a poor excuse for being late to work.
哈利為他上班遲到找了一個很差勁的藉口。

pardon [ˈpardn̩]
vt. 原諒；赦免 & n. 赦免

⚑ (1) pardon me
打擾一下；不好意思，對不起；請再說一遍

(2) receive a pardon　得到赦免

▶ Pardon me, but may I ask you a question?
打擾一下，請問我能問你個問題嗎？

▶ Pardon me. I think I accidentally stepped on your foot.
不好意思。我想我不小心踩到你的腳了。

▶ Pardon me? It's too noisy here. Would you say it louder?
請再說一遍好嗎？這裡太吵了。你能說大聲點嗎？

▶ To our surprise, the president pardoned several criminals.
令我們吃驚的是，總統赦免了幾個罪犯。

▶ Because he received a pardon, the prisoner was not killed.
因為這囚犯得到了赦免，所以他並沒有被處決。

---

23 flag [flæg] *n.* 旗（子）

片 a national flag　國旗

延伸 banner [ˋbænɚ] *n.* 橫幅，標語 ⑤

▶ During the parade, many of the onlookers waved national flags.
遊行期間，許多圍觀的民眾都揮舞著國旗。
＊onlooker [ˋɑn͵lʊkɚ] *n.* 圍觀者

---

24 candle [ˋkændl̩] *n.* 蠟燭

延伸 a candle-lit dinner　燭光晚餐

▶ Make a wish and blow out the candles.
許個願，然後把蠟燭吹熄。

---

lantern [ˋlæntɚn] *n.* 燈籠

片 Lantern Festival　元宵節

延伸 jack-o'-lantern [͵dʒækəˋlæntɚn] *n.* 南瓜燈

▶ The Lantern Festival falls on the 15th day of the first lunar month.
元宵節是在農曆 1 月 15 日。

3301-3306

---

1 **shock** [ʃɑk] *vt.* 震驚 & *n.* 震驚；觸電 (= electric [ɪˈlɛktrɪk] shock)

(1) shock sb that...
讓某人震驚的是……
= shock sb to V

(2) It was a shock to find / discover that...
發現……是很令人震驚的

(3) come as a shock
突如其來令人震驚

(4) get a shock　觸電

▸ It shocked us that Abby was going to marry a man she hardly knew.
= It shocked us to learn that Abby was going to marry a man she hardly knew.
讓我們震驚的是，艾比要嫁給一個她幾乎不認識的人。

▸ It was a shock to find that my car had been stolen.
我發現車子被偷時非常震驚。

▸ The news that Thomas would resign came as a shock.
湯瑪斯要辭職的消息突如其來令人震驚。

▸ Don't touch the switch with your wet hands. You might get a shock.
不要用濕的手碰開關。你可能會觸電。

---

2 **nail** [nel] *n.* 指甲，腳趾甲；釘子 & *vt.* 將……釘住

(1) drive / hammer a nail into...
把釘子釘進……

(2) nail A to B　把 A 釘在 B 上

(3) the final nail in the coffin of sb/sth
某人 / 事最後致命的一擊
= the final nail in sb's/sth's coffin

▸ The girl painted her nails pink.
那女孩把指甲塗成粉紅色。

▸ Brad's hand got hurt when he tried to drive the nail into the wall.
布萊德試著要把釘子釘進牆壁時，把手弄傷了。

▸ The argument over money was the final nail in the coffin of Sam's marriage.
為錢爭吵是導致山姆婚姻失敗的最後一擊。

▸ Joe nailed the doorplate to the wall.
喬把標示牌釘在牆上。

---

3 **strike** [straɪk] *n.* 打，擊；罷工 & *vt.* 打，擊；突然想起 & *vi.* 罷工

strike, struck [strʌk], struck / stricken [ˈstrɪkən]

(1) a lightning strike　雷擊

(2) go on strike　罷工

(3) It strikes sb that...
某人突然想起……

(4) strike for sth
為爭取某事物而罷工

striking [ˈstraɪkɪŋ]
a. 醒目的，明顯的 ⑤

▸ The house was hit by lightning strikes.
這房子遭到雷擊。

▸ The factory workers went on strike for better pay and working conditions.
該工廠工人罷工，要求加薪及改善工作環境。

▸ Karen was so angry that she struck Ralph on the face.
凱倫很生氣，往雷夫臉上打了一拳。

▸ It struck me that it's Norman's birthday today.
我突然想起今天是諾曼的生日。

▸ The workers are striking for a raise.
這些工人正在罷工要求加薪。

4　crow [kro] n. 烏鴉

** 片 crow's feet**　魚尾紋 (恆用複數)

▸ There were four crows sitting in a tree.
有 4 隻烏鴉棲息在樹上。

▸ Crow's feet are the fine lines around the eyes.
魚尾紋就是眼睛周圍的小細紋。

---

dove [dʌv]
n. 白鴿；(政治上的) 溫和派人士，鴿派

ㄈ hawk [hɔk]
n. 鷹；(政治上的) 鷹派人物，主戰分子 ④

▸ Doves are often seen as a symbol of peace.
鴿子常被視為是和平的象徵。

▸ Compared to the other candidates, Mr. Wilson is a dove.
和其他候選人相比，威爾遜先生是屬於溫和派人士。

---

eagle [ˈigl] n. 老鷹 (體型比 hawk 大)

▸ Eagles have longer and broader wings than other birds.
老鷹的翅膀比其他鳥類更長更寬。

---

rooster [ˈrustɚ]
n. 公雞 (= cock [kɑk])

用法 cock 在俚語中是表『男性生殖器』，故較常用 rooster 表『公雞』。

▸ Roosters usually crow in the early morning.
公雞通常一大早就會啼叫。
*crow [kro] vi. (公雞) 啼叫

---

goose [gus] n. 鵝
複 geese [gis]
片 goose bumps　雞皮疙瘩 (恆用複數)

▸ A goose is like a duck but is larger.
鵝長得像鴨子，但體型較大。

▸ The scary movie gave Rita goose bumps.
這恐怖電影讓麗塔起了雞皮疙瘩。

5　energy [ˈɛnɚdʒɪ] n. 精力；體力；能源

片 solar / nuclear energy
太陽能 / 核能

衍 energetic [ˌɛnɚˈdʒɛtɪk]
a. 精力旺盛的 ③

▸ Eric has more energy than his younger brother.
艾瑞克比他弟弟有活力。

▸ It takes a lot of energy to move the piano.
要移動這架鋼琴需要花很大的力氣。

▸ As oil supplies are decreasing, many countries have been trying other forms of energy.
由於原油的供應量減少，很多國家正試著用其他種能源。

▸ Solar energy is known as a kind of clean energy.
太陽能被稱為一種乾淨的能源。

6　compare [kəmˈpɛr] vt. & vi. 比較 & vt. 把……比作 & vi. (可與……) 匹敵

片 (1) compare A with / to B
比較 A 與 B

▸ It's interesting to compare Western customs with Taiwanese ones.
比較西方與臺灣的習俗相當有趣。

(2) compare with / to... 比較……
(3) compare A to B 把 A 比喻為 B
(4) A doesn't compare with B
A 比不上 B，A 和 B 不能相比

衍 (1) comparison [kəm`pærəsn]
　　 n. 比較 ③
(2) comparable [`kɑmpərəbl]
　　 a. 可匹敵的 ⑤
(3) comparative [kəm`pærətɪv]
　　 a. 比較的，相對 (而言) 的 ⑥

▶ Compared with my plain boxed meal, Becky's seemed like a great delicacy.
和我很普通的便當相比，貝琪的便當看起來是山珍海味。

▶ Life is often compared to a long journey.
人生常被比喻為一段漫長的旅程。

▶ Store-bought cookies don't compare with handmade cookies.
商店賣的餅乾比不上手工餅乾。

7　depend [dɪ`pɛnd] *vi.* 依賴 (= rely)；視……而定

片 depend on...
依賴…… (= rely on...)；取決於……

衍 (1) dependent [dɪ`pɛndənt]
　　 a. 依賴的 ④
　　 be dependent on... 依賴……
(2) dependence [dɪ`pɛndəns]
　　 n. 依賴
(3) dependable [dɪ`pɛndəbl]
　　 a. 可靠的

▶ You shouldn't depend on your parents for everything.
你不應該凡事都依賴你父母。

▶ Usually, students' scores depend on how hard they study.
通常學生的分數是取決於他們多用功。

---

independent [ˌɪndɪ`pɛndənt]
a. 獨立的

片 be independent of...
脫離……而獨 / 自立

▶ Because he wanted to be independent of his parents, Danny moved out and lived on his own.
因為丹尼想要不依賴雙親生活，所以他從家裡搬出來一個人住。

---

independence [ˌɪndɪ`pɛndəns]
n. 獨立

片 have financial independence
經濟能獨立

▶ In my mother's view, it's important for women to have financial independence.
我母親認為女性經濟能獨立是很重要的。

8　shoot [ʃut] *vi.* & *vt.* 射擊；拍攝 (電影) & *n.* 嫩芽，幼苗

三 shoot, shot [ʃɑt], shot
片 (1) be shot to death 被射殺身亡
(2) shoot a movie 拍電影

▶ Aim at the target before you shoot.
瞄準好了再射擊。

▶ In the movie, the bad guy was shot to death.
電影中這個壞蛋被射殺身亡。

▶ The director said we would start shooting in a minute.
導演說我們馬上會開始拍攝。

> That movie studio is currently shooting a movie in my hometown.
> 那家製片廠現在正在我的老家拍電影。

> Karen was happy to see new green shoots in her garden.
> 凱倫很高興在她花園裡看到了新的綠芽。

shot [ʃɑt] *n.* 注射；射擊，開火；嘗試

🔑 (1) have a shot　打針，注射
 (2) take a shot at sb/sth
  向某人 / 物射擊 / 開火
 (3) have a shot at + N/V-ing
  試著……
 (4) give it a shot / try　試試看
 (5) a big shot　大人物
🔖 shotgun [ʃɑtˏgʌn] *n.* 獵槍

> Infants younger than 6 months old can't have a flu shot.
> 不足 6 個月大的嬰兒不能注射流感疫苗。

> The man took a shot at the deer.
> 那男子向那隻鹿射擊。

> Ted'll have a shot at painting the house by himself.
> 泰德要試試看自己粉刷房屋。

> I know the job is difficult, but at least you should give it a shot.
> 我知道這個工作很難，但至少你應該試試看。

> Ken's father is a big shot in the film industry.
> 肯的父親是電影圈的大人物。

9　**childhood** [ˋtʃaɪldˏhʊd] *n.* 童年時期

🔑 in one's childhood　某人小時候

> Andrew was quite naughty in his childhood.
> 安德魯小時候很調皮。
> *naughty [ˋnɔtɪ] *a.* 調皮的

---

youth [juθ]
n. 青年時期 (不可數)；(尤指惹麻煩的)
年輕男子 (可數)；(統稱) 年輕人 (集合名詞)

🔑 (1) in one's youth　某人年輕時
  = when one was / is young
 (2) the youth　(統稱) 年輕人
 (3) the youth of today
  現在的年輕人
🔖 (1) young [jʌŋ] *a.* 年輕的 ①
 (2) youngster [ˋjʌŋstɚ]
  n. 年輕人 (可數) ③

📘 youth 為『(統稱) 年輕人』之意時，其後可接『單數動詞』或『複數動詞』。

> In his youth, Mark dreamed of becoming a fighter pilot.
> 馬克年輕時，曾夢想成為戰鬥機飛行員。

> It seems that more and more youths have tattoos on their bodies.
> 似乎越來越多年輕人身上都有刺青。

> The youth of today are more inclined to surf the internet than read a book.
> 現在的年輕人比較喜歡上網勝過閱讀。

Level 2

Unit 33

teens [tinz] *n.* 青少年時期 (恆用複數)
用 in one's teens　某人青少年的時候
衍 teen [tin] *n.* 青少年 (= teenager) &
a. 青少年的 (= teenage)
似 adolescence [ˏædəˈlɛsn̩s]
n. 青春期 (不可數) ⑥

▶ I was reckless in my teens.
我青少年時期非常魯莽。

adult [ˈædʌlt / əˈdʌlt]
n. 成年人 & *a.* 成年的；成熟的
似 grown-up [ˏɡronˈʌp]
n. 成年人 & *a.* 成年的；成熟的
反 childish [ˈtʃaɪldɪʃ] *a.* 幼稚的 ②

▶ You are no longer a child. You are an adult.
你已經不再是小孩子了。你現在是成年人了。
▶ An adult brown bear can weigh more than 650 kilograms.
成年棕熊的體重可超過 650 公斤。
▶ We should deal with this problem in an adult way.
我們應該以成熟的方式來處理這個問題。

elder [ˈɛldɚ]
n. 年長者，長輩 & *a.* (兩者中) 較年長的
用 one's elder brother / sister
　某人的哥哥 / 姊姊
= one's older brother / sister
衍 elderly [ˈɛldɚlɪ] *a.* 年長的 ③

▶ Only the elders in the tribe know the history.
只有族裡的長者知道這段歷史。
▶ Who is your elder / older brother?
你哥哥是哪一位？

10　region [ˈridʒən] *n.* 區域

衍 regional [ˈridʒənl̩] *a.* 地區的 ③
似 (1) area [ˈɛrɪə] *n.* 地區 ①
　(2) district [ˈdɪstrɪkt]
　　n. 地區；行政區 ④

▶ The government is going to send troops to maintain peace in this region.
政府將派軍隊來維持這地區的和平。

11　claim [klem] *vt.* 宣稱；索取 (錢)；領取；奪取 (生命) & *n.* 說法，聲稱

用 (1) claim that...　聲稱……
　= claim to V
　(2) claim a / sb's life
　　奪走 (某人的) 性命
　(3) a claim that...　……的說法
　(4) lay claim to sth　聲稱擁有某物
衍 (1) proclaim [prəˈklem] *vt.* 宣告 ⑤
　(2) acclaim [əˈklem]
　　vt. 稱讚 (= praise) ⑥

▶ The report claimed that three hostages had been killed.
該報導聲稱有 3 名人質已經遇害。
▶ Connie should claim her money back because the painting is a fake.
康妮應該把錢要回來，因為這幅畫是贗品。
▶ Go over there to claim your luggage.
到那邊去領取你的行李。

▸ The flood claimed twenty lives.
這場洪水奪走了 20 條人命。

▸ The mayor rejected the claim that he had received bribes.
市長否認了他收賄的這種說法。

▸ Three tribes lay claim to this land.
有 3 個部落聲稱擁有這片土地。

12　forward [ˈfɔrwəd] *a.* 向前的 & *vt.* 轉寄 (信件) & *n.* 前鋒

🅗 forward a letter / an email to sb
將信 / 電子郵件轉寄給某人

▸ I think Cindy is sitting in the forward part of the upper deck.
我想辛蒂正坐在上層甲板的前面。

▸ Please forward these emails to Harry.
請將這些電子郵件轉寄給哈利。

▸ The forward kicked the ball and scored a goal.
那前鋒踢球,並進了一球。

---

forward(s) [ˈfɔrwəd(z)] *adv.* 向前

▸ The soldiers are moving forward steadily.
士兵們正以穩定的速度前進中。

---

backward [ˈbækwəd]
a. 向後的;落後的

🅗 without a backward glance
頭也不回地 (表示很高興離開某地)

▸ Chuck left the company without a backward glance.
查克頭也不回地就離開了公司。

▸ That village is poor and backward.
那座村落既貧窮又落後。

---

backward(s) [ˈbækwəd(z)]
adv. 向後

▸ A good football player has to be able to run backwards fast as well.
優秀的橄欖球員向後跑也必須跑得很快。

---

toward(s) [təˈwɔrd(z)]
prep. 朝向;對於

▸ Paul walked towards Wendy and gave her a warm kiss.
保羅走向溫蒂給她一個熱吻。

▸ I hope Andrew can change his attitude towards his mother.
我希望安德魯可以改變對他母親的態度。

13　duty [ˈd(j)utɪ] *n.* 責任

🅟 duties [ˈd(j)utɪz]

🅗 (1) It is sb's duty to V
　　做……是某人的責任

　　(2) on duty　上 / 值班

🅓 dutiful [ˈd(j)utɪfəl] *a.* 盡責的

▸ It's my duty to walk the dog after dinner.
晚餐後遛狗是我的責任。

▸ Dad is on duty today, so he won't be back for dinner.
今天爸爸值班,所以不會回來吃晚飯。

14 wonder [ˈwʌndɚ] vt. & vi. 想知道 & n. 驚奇；奇觀，奇事

(1) wonder + 疑問詞 (when, what, how, where 等) 引導的名詞子句
想知道……

(2) wonder about...
想知道有關……

(3) work / do wonders 有奇效

(4) no wonder 難怪

衍 wonderful [ˈwʌndɚfəl] a. 很棒的 ①

▶ I wonder what my friends got me for my birthday.
我很想知道我朋友買給我什麼生日禮物。

▶ I was wondering about the proper way to respond to my boss' message.
我想知道如何恰當地回應老闆的訊息。

▶ Carl had a look of wonder on his face at that moment.
那一刻卡爾臉上帶著驚訝的表情。

▶ Aspirin works wonders for a headache.
阿斯匹靈對治療頭痛很有效。

▶ No wonder the remote doesn't work. The batteries are dead.
難怪遙控器不能用。電池沒電了。

15 self [sɛlf] n. 自身，自我

▶ Jenny is trying to find her true self.
珍妮正設法找到真正的自我。

selfish [ˈsɛlfɪʃ] a. 自私的

▶ A selfish guy is hard to get along with.
自私的傢伙很難相處。

16 condition [kənˈdɪʃən] n. 狀況；條件 & vt. (經歷或環境) 影響，使習慣於

(1) be in good / excellent condition
情況很好

be in poor condition 情況不佳

(2) on (the) condition that...
條件是……

= only if...

▶ The second-hand car is still in excellent condition.
這輛二手車的車況仍相當不錯。

▶ I can lend you the money on the condition that you pay it back on time.
你若準時還錢，我就借給你。

▶ Many people have been conditioned to believe that men should not cry.
很多人已經習慣地認為男人不應該哭。

17 instead [ɪnˈstɛd] adv. 作為替代，反而

instead of... 取代……；而非……
= rather than...

▶ Rick doesn't want a cake. Instead, he wants a pizza.
瑞克不想要蛋糕，而是想要披薩。

▶ Instead of chicken, I'd like to have fish for dinner.
我晚餐不想吃雞肉而想吃魚肉。

▶ Some say that happiness, instead of working hard, is the key to success.

= Some say that happiness, rather than working hard, is the key to success.
有人說快樂，而非努力，才是成功的祕訣。

18 **perfect** [ˈpɝfɛkt] *a.* 完美的；完全的 & *n.* (文法) 完成式 & [pəˈfɛkt] *vt.* 使完美，改善

片 the perfect (tense)　完成式

似 (1) flawless [ˈflɔləs] *a.* 完美的
　　(2) faultless [ˈfɔltləs] *a.* 無缺點的

反 imperfect [ɪmˈpɝfɛkt] *a.* 有瑕疵的

▶ The weather is perfect for outdoor activities.
這是適合戶外活動的好天氣。

▶ I'm a perfect stranger around here.
我對這附近完全陌生。

▶ Please make a sentence using the present perfect tense.
請用現在完成式造句。

▶ Raymond perfected his French by living in Paris for years.
雷蒙透過在巴黎居住多年來精進自己的法語。

ideal [aɪˈdɪəl] *a.* 理想的 & *n.* 理想

衍 (1) idealism [aɪˈdɪəlˌɪzm]
　　 n. 理想主義
　　(2) idealistic [aɪˌdɪəlˈɪstɪk]
　　 a. 理想主義的
　　(3) idealist [aɪˈdɪəlɪst] *n.* 理想主義者

似 goal [gol] *n.* 目標 ②

▶ The boss thinks Debbie is an ideal employee.
老闆認為黛比是個理想的員工。

▶ The politician urged people to live up to the country's democratic ideals.
這位政治家呼籲人們要實現這國家的民主理想。

19 **sense** [sɛns] *n.* 感覺 (五感官之一)；意識 (感)，觀念；含意，意義 & *vt.* 察覺 / 意識到

片 (1) a sense of hearing / smell / taste　聽 / 嗅 / 味覺
　　(2) a sense of humor / responsibility　幽默 / 責任感
　　(3) in a sense　從某種意義來說
　　(4) make sense　合理，說得通
　　(5) sense (that)...　察覺 / 意識到……

▶ Blind people usually have a good sense of hearing.
盲人通常有敏銳的聽覺。

▶ My father has a good sense of humor.
我爸爸很有幽默感。

▶ Ken knew his brother was right in a sense.
肯知道他哥哥從某種意義上來說是對的。

▶ What Sean says doesn't make sense.
尚恩說的話沒道理。

▶ Candice sensed something was wrong.
坎蒂絲察覺到有些不對勁。

sensitive [ˈsɛnsətɪv]
a. 敏感的，易被冒犯的

片 be sensitive to / about sth
　　對某事物很敏感，很容易因某事物而被冒犯

衍 (1) sensitivity [ˌsɛnsəˈtɪvətɪ]
　　 n. 敏感，易被冒犯；靈敏度 ⑤

▶ Fred is sensitive to others' remarks.
弗瑞德對別人的話很敏感。

▶ Don't mention Donald's missing dog—he's very sensitive about that.
不要提到唐納德走失的狗 —— 他對那件事非常敏感。

(2) sensible [ˈsɛnsəbl̩]
　　a. 明智的；(鞋子等) 耐用的 ③
(3) sensation [sɛnˈseʃən]
　　n. 感覺；引起轟動的人 / 事件等 ⑤
(4) sensory [ˈsɛnsərɪ]
　　a. 感覺的，知覺的
反 insensitive [ɪnˈsɛnsətɪv] *a.* 遲鈍的

20　author [ˈɔθɚ] *n.* (某本書或文章的) 作者 & *vt.* 創作，撰寫

似 writer [ˈraɪtɚ] *n.* 作家 ①

▶ The author of the novel is very famous in this country.
　這小說的作者在這國家很有名。

▶ Charles Dickens authored many famous novels and short stories.
　查爾斯・狄更斯寫了許多著名的小說和短篇故事。

21　human [ˈhjumən] *n.* 人類 (= human being) (可數) & *a.* 人類的；人性的

片 human nature　人性
衍 (1) humanity [hjuˈmænətɪ]
　　n. (統稱) 人 (不可數)；人性 ④
(2) humane [hjuˈmen] *a.* 人道的
似 (1) mankind [mænˈkaɪnd]
　　n. 人類 (不可數) ③
(2) humankind [ˈhjumənˌkaɪnd]
　　n. 人類 (不可數) ③

▶ In 1969, humans first walked on the moon.
　1969 年，人類首次登陸月球。

▶ Do you know what the biggest organ in the human body is?
　你知道人體中最大的器官是什麼嗎？

▶ It is human nature to want to win.
　想贏是人的天性。

▶ To err is human, to forgive divine.
　犯錯是人性，寬恕乃是神性。—— 諺語
　*divine [dəˈvaɪn] *a.* 神聖的

---

individual [ˌɪndəˈvɪdʒuəl]
a. 個別的，個人的 & *n.* 個人，個體

衍 (1) individualism
　　[ˌɪndəˈvɪdʒuəlˌɪzəm] *n.* 個人主義
(2) individuality [ˌɪndəˌvɪdʒuˈælətɪ]
　　n. 個性，獨特性

▶ Ms. Smith couldn't give the students individual attention because the class was too large.
　由於這班級太大，史密斯老師無法個別去照料學生。

▶ The students discussed the rights of the individual versus the rights of the group.
　學生討論比較個人權益和團體權益。
　*versus [ˈvɜsəs] *prep.* 與……相比

22　hall [hɔl] *n.* (房子等的) 門廳；(大樓裡的) 走廊，通道；大廳，禮堂

片 (1) a lecture hall　演講廳
(2) a city hall　市政府大樓
　　City Hall　市政府 (不可數)

▶ Once you enter a Japanese person's house, you usually have to take off your shoes in the hall.
　一旦你進入日本人的房子，你通常必須要在門廳脫鞋。

衍 hallway [ˋhɔlˏwe]
n. (房子等的) 門廳；(大樓裡的) 走廊，通道 ③

▶ There are many rooms on both sides of the hall.
走廊兩邊有許多房間。

▶ The famous novelist will give a speech in the lecture hall.
這位知名的小說家將在演講廳演講。

▶ Many people gathered in front of the city hall to protest against the mayor's rude comment.
許多人聚集在市政府大樓前，抗議市長的粗魯言論。

1 **pizza** [ˋpitsə] *n.* 披薩

用法 a pizza　一整塊披薩
　　 a piece of pizza　一小片披薩

▶ I'd like to have a piece of pizza for lunch.
我想吃一小片披薩當中餐。

2 **delicious** [dɪˋlɪʃəs] *a.* 好吃的

似 yummy [ˋjʌmɪ] *a.* 好吃的 (口語)

▶ These fries are so delicious.
這些薯條太好吃了。

3 **balloon** [bəˋlun] *n.* 氣球

片 a hot-air balloon　熱氣球

▶ These balloons will be used for decoration.
這些氣球將用來做裝飾。

▶ There is a hot-air balloon festival in Taitung every year.
臺東每年都有熱氣球節。

4 **press** [prɛs] *vt.* & *vi.* 按，(擠) 壓；按 (按鈕等) & *vt.* 熨平；竭力勸說，催促 & *n.* 新聞界，記者 (集合名詞，不可數)

片 (1) press sb to V
竭力勸說某人做……，逼某人做……

(2) the press + 單數動詞〔美〕
新聞界，記者
= the press + 單 / 複數動詞〔英〕

(3) freedom of the press　新聞自由

(4) hold / give a press conference
開記者會
= hold / give a news conference

似 push [puʃ] *vt.* 推動 & *n.* 推 ①

▶ Hannah pressed her hands together in excitement.
漢娜激動地把雙手握在一起。

▶ The doctor pressed on Kyle's chest to check his heartbeat.
醫生按著凱爾的胸口來檢查他的心跳。

▶ Press this button to start the engine.
按這按鈕來啟動引擎。

▶ Press here to close the elevator doors.
按這裡來關閉電梯門。

▶ My dad always presses his own shirts.
我老爸一向自己燙襯衫。

▶ Don't press me to do anything against my will.
不要逼我做任何違反我意願的事。

▶ The press was waiting to interview the royal couple.
記者正等著採訪這對皇室夫妻。

▶ Freedom of the press is important to modern society.
新聞自由對現代社會很重要。

▶ The president is holding a press conference this afternoon.
總統今天下午將開記者會。

pressure [ˈprɛʃɚ]

n. 壓力；壓迫 & *vt.* 強迫，迫使

- 片 (1) under pressure
  處於 (工作等) 壓力之下
- (2) peer pressure　　同儕壓力
- (3) blood pressure　　血壓
- (4) a pressure cooker　壓力鍋
- (5) pressure sb into + V-ing
  強迫某人做……
  = pressure sb to V

▶ Some people do very well under pressure.
有些人在壓力下會表現得非常好。

▶ Running puts pressure on your knees.
跑步會對膝蓋造成壓迫。

▶ Jenny never gives in to peer pressure.
珍妮從不屈服於同儕的壓力。

▶ Eating too much salt can increase your blood pressure.
吃太多鹽會使血壓升高。

▶ It seemed that the salesman pressured Gordon into buying the car.
= It seemed that the salesman pressured Gordon to buy the car.
那推銷員似乎向戈登施壓，要他買那輛車。

---

stress [strɛs] *n.* 精神壓力；強調 &

vt. 緊張，焦慮；強調

- 片 (1) under stress　有 (精神) 壓力下
- (2) lay / put / place stress on...
  強調……
  = lay / put / place emphasis on...
  = stress / emphasize...
- (3) stress sb out
  使某人壓力過大 / 焦慮不安
- (4) stress the importance of...
  強調……的重要性

- 衍 stressful [ˈstrɛsfəl]
  a. 緊張的，壓力重的

- 似 emphasis [ˈɛmfəsɪs] *n.* 強調 ④

▶ Whenever Elaine is under stress, she has a headache.
每當伊蓮有壓力時，她就會頭痛。

▶ Mr. Johnson lays stress on the importance of punctuality.
強森先生強調守時的重要性。
＊punctuality [ˌpʌŋktʃʊˈæləti] *n.* 守時

▶ Work and housework stress Maggie out.
工作和家事讓瑪姬喘不過氣來。

▶ My mother always stresses the importance of honesty.
我母親總是強調誠實的重要性。

---

5 **post** [post] *vt.* 張貼，公布；郵寄〔英〕(= mail〔美〕) & *vt.* & *vi.* (在網站上) 發 / 公布 & *n.* 郵政〔英〕(= mail〔美〕)；郵件〔英〕(不可數)(= mail〔美〕)；職位 & *adv.* 快速地 (過時用法)

- 片 (1) post sth to sb　把某物郵寄給某人
- (2) keep sb posted on...
  隨時將……的最新消息告知某人
- (3) a post office　　郵局
- (4) by post　　　以郵寄的方式
- 衍 (1) postage [ˈpostɪdʒ] *n.* 郵資 ④
- (2) postal [ˈpostl] *a.* 郵政的
- (3) postman [ˈpostmən] *n.* 郵差〔英〕
  (= mailman [ˈmel͵mæn]〔美〕)

▶ Your grades have been posted on the wall.
你們的成績已經貼在牆上了。

▶ Can you post this letter to Mr. White?
你可以把這封信寄給懷特先生嗎？

▶ The internet celebrity has posted a video on YouTube again.
這網紅又在 YouTube 上發布了一個影片。

▶ Warren only posts on Instagram once in a while.
華倫只會偶爾在 Instagram 上發文。

▶ Keep me posted on the progress of the project.
請隨時告知我這個計畫的進展。

▶ Excuse me. Would you please tell me where the post office is?
不好意思，您能告訴我郵局在哪裡嗎？

▶ It is better to send these documents by post.
這些文件最好用郵寄的。

▶ It is illegal to open other people's post.
拆他人信件是非法的。

▶ I am interested in the post of sales manager.
我對業務經理這個職位感興趣。

▶ "Please come post," said the character in the old novel.
這本舊小說中的角色說：『請快點過來。』

---

postcard [`post,kɑrd] *n.* 明信片

▶ Tony sent me a postcard from Switzerland.
湯尼從瑞士寄了張明信片給我。

---

stamp [stæmp]
n. 郵票；印記，印章 & *vt.* 蓋章；貼郵票
& *vt.* & *vi.* 跺 (腳)

🔢 (1) collect stamps　　集郵
　　　stamp collecting　集郵
　　(2) stamp one's foot　跺腳

▶ I have been collecting stamps since childhood.
我從小就開始集郵。

▶ Stamp collecting is my hobby.
集郵是我的嗜好。

▶ This stamp in my passport shows I've been to Russia.
我護照上的這印記表示我去過俄羅斯。

▶ The document is only official after you stamp it.
這份文件只有在你蓋章之後才正式生效。

▶ Please stamp these letters and mail them by Friday.
請將這些信件貼上郵票並於星期五前寄出。

▶ Henry stamped his foot in anger when he heard the bad news.
亨利聽到這壞消息後氣得跺腳。

▶ After arguing with his girlfriend, Terence stamped out of the classroom.
泰倫斯和女友吵架後，就跺著腳走出了教室。

---

address [`ædrɛs / ə`drɛs]
n. 地址；網址；電子郵件地址；演說 &
[ə`drɛs] *vt.* 對……發表演說；寄給……

複 addresses [`ædrɛsɪz / ə`drɛsɪz]

🔢 (1) a web / website address　網址
　　(2) an email address　電子郵件地址

▶ Please write down your address and phone number.
請把您的地址跟電話號碼寫下來。

▶ This is the web address of our company: www.ivy.com.tw.
這是我們公司的網址：www.ivy.com.tw。

▶ Do you know what Nora's email address is?
你知道諾拉的電子郵件地址嗎？

(3) an address book　通訊錄

(4) deliver / give an address
　　發表演說

(5) be addressed to sb　寄給某人

延伸 (1) receiver [rɪˋsivɚ] *n.* 收件人 ③

(2) sender [ˋsɛndɚ] *n.* 寄件人

(3) addressee [͵ædrɛˋsi] *n.* 收信人

▸ Edwin looked up a contact in his address book.
愛德溫在他的通訊錄裡搜尋了某位聯絡人。

▸ The President delivered an inaugural address yesterday.
總統於昨日發表就職演說。
＊inaugural [ɪnˋɔgjərəl] *a.* 就職 / 任的

▸ The mayor is going to address the conference.
市長將對大會發表演說。

▸ This letter was addressed to me.
這封信是寄給我的。

6　pain [pen] *n.* (肉體上的) 疼痛；(心理上的) 痛苦 & *vt.* 使痛苦

片 (1) feel a pain in sth
　　感到某部位一陣劇痛

(2) cause (sb) pain
　　讓 (某人) 內心很痛苦

(3) take (great) pains to V
　　煞費苦心 / 小心翼翼地做……，努
　　力試著做……

(4) It pains sb to V
　　要某人做……是很痛苦的

衍 (1) painkiller [ˋpen͵kɪlɚ] *n.* 止痛藥

(2) painstaking [ˋpenz͵tekɪŋ]
　　a. (調查等) 十分小心的，極其仔細
　　的

▸ Thomas felt a sharp pain in his stomach.
湯瑪斯感到胃一陣劇痛。

▸ What Monica's boyfriend told her caused her great pain.
莫妮卡男友說的話使她很痛苦。

▸ We took great pains to keep the party a secret.
我們煞費苦心地保密這派對一事。

▸ It pained Hank to think of his father in hospital.
漢克想到他父親在醫院，就覺得很痛苦。

---

painful [ˋpenfəl] *a.* 痛苦的

反 (1) unpainful [ʌnˋpenfəl]
　　a. 不痛的〔英〕

(2) painless [ˋpenləs] *a.* 無痛的

▸ A painful experience will make you stronger and wiser.
痛苦的經驗能使你更堅強，也更有智慧。

7　ending [ˋɛndɪŋ] *n.* (故事等的) 結局

片 a happy ending　快樂的結局

衍 end [ɛnd] *vt.* & *vi.* (使) 結束 ①

▸ I love romantic movies with happy endings.
我喜歡有快樂結局的浪漫電影。

---

final [ˋfaɪnl̩]
a. 最後的；(決定) 不可改的 &
n. 期末考；決賽

片 a final examination　期末考

▸ Terry is busy preparing for the final examinations.
＝ Terry is busy preparing for the finals.
泰瑞正忙著準備期末考。

▸ The CEO's decision is final.
執行長的決定不可更改。

▸ We lost to the home team in the finals.
我們在決賽中輸給地主隊。

beginner [bɪ'gɪnə] *n.* 初學者，新人
衍 begin [bɪ'gɪn] *vt. & vi.* 開始 ①

▶ This book is for beginners, not for advanced readers.
本書適合初學者，並不適合進階讀者。

8　war [wɔr] *n.* 戰爭

衍 (1) warrior ['wɔrɪə]
　　n. (舊時的) 武士 ⑤
　　(2) pre-war [ˌpri'wɔr] *a.* 戰前的
　　(3) postwar ['post,wɔr] *a.* 戰後的
反 peace [pis] *n.* 和平 ②

▶ It was a war between science and religion.
那是一場科學與宗教之間的戰爭。

battle ['bætl] *n.* 戰役 & *vi.* 搏鬥，奮戰
片 battle against...　與……搏鬥
似 fight [faɪt] *n. & vi.* 戰鬥 ①
比 war 指全面的『戰爭』，而 battle 指在戰爭中一場一場的『戰役』。

▶ The battle took at least 200 lives.
這場戰役奪走了至少 200 條性命。

▶ Steve is battling bravely against lung cancer.
史提夫正勇敢地與肺癌搏鬥。

conflict ['kɑnflɪkt] *n.* 衝突 & [kən'flɪkt] *vi.* 衝突，相抵觸
片 A conflict with B
　　A 和 B 衝突 / 相抵觸
似 quarrel ['kwɔrəl] *n. & vi.* 爭吵 ④
　　quarrel with sb over sth
　　與某人因某事而爭吵

▶ The conflict between the two countries lasted nearly twenty years.
這 2 國之間的衝突延續了將近 20 年。

▶ The results of the experiment conflict with Dr. Johnson's theory.
實驗的結果與強森博士的理論相抵觸。

danger ['dendʒə] *n.* 危險
片 be in danger of + N/V-ing
　　有……的危險
衍 dangerous ['dendʒərəs] *a.* 危險的 ①

▶ Polar bears are in danger of extinction.
北極熊有絕種的危險。
＊extinction [ɪk'stɪŋkʃən] *n.* 絕種，滅絕

fear [fɪr] *n. & vt.* 懼怕
片 (1) overcome one's fear
　　克服某人的恐懼
　　(2) for fear of + N/V-ing
　　以免 / 免得 / 唯恐……
　　= for fear that...
衍 (1) fearful ['fɪrfəl]
　　a. 害怕的；可怕的 ③
　　(2) fearsome ['fɪrsəm] *a.* 可怕的
　　(3) fearless ['fɪrləs] *a.* 無懼的

▶ The young soldier tried to overcome his fear.
這名年輕的士兵試圖克服他的恐懼。

▶ The boy didn't even try for fear of failing.
= The boy didn't even try for fear that he might fail.
這男孩唯恐失敗，甚至連試一試都不敢。

▶ My little sister fears snakes.
我妹妹怕蛇。

9 hole [hol] *n.* 洞

- 片 (1) dig a hole　挖洞
-    (2) a black hole　黑洞

▶ Before planting the tree, we'll have to dig a hole.
要種樹前我們得先挖個洞。

▶ Not even light can escape from a black hole.
連光都逃不出黑洞。

10 prefer [prɪˋfɝ] *vt.* 比較喜歡

- 三 prefer, preferred [prɪˋfɝd], preferred
- 片 (1) prefer A to B　喜歡 A 甚於 B
-    (2) prefer to V rather than + V
     喜歡做……甚於做……
- 衍 preference [ˋprɛfərəns] *n.* 偏好 ⑤

▶ Which would you prefer, tea or coffee?
你比較喜歡哪種，茶或咖啡？

▶ Eric prefers jazz to classical music.
艾瑞克喜歡爵士樂甚於古典樂。

▶ I prefer to go to the movies rather than watch TV.
我喜歡看電影甚於看電視。

11 disease [dɪˋziz] *n.* 疾病

- 似 illness [ˋɪlnəs] *n.* 疾病

▶ Mosquitoes spread diseases such as dengue fever.
蚊子會傳染像登革熱這樣的疾病。
*dengue [ˋdɛŋgɪ] *n.* 登革熱 (= dengue fever)

stomachache [ˋstʌməkˌek]
n. 胃／腹痛 (= stomach ache)
- 衍 stomach [ˋstʌmək] *n.* 胃 ③

▶ After eating at the restaurant, Claire had a stomachache.
克萊兒在餐廳吃完飯後，胃就痛了起來。

cancer [ˋkænsɚ] *n.* 癌症

▶ Shane has been diagnosed with stomach cancer.
夏恩已經被診斷出有胃癌。

flu [flu]
n. 流行性感冒 (= influenza [ˌɪnfluˋɛnzə])
- 片 have / get / catch (the) flu
     得到流感
- 延伸 have / get / catch a cold
     得到一般感冒

▶ I had the flu and couldn't go to work for a week.
我得了流感，一個星期都不能去上班。

fever [ˋfivɚ] *n.* 發燒
- 片 have a (high) fever　發 (高) 燒

▶ I had a high fever that made me feel very uncomfortable.
我發高燒，覺得很不舒服。

12 patient [ˋpeʃənt] *a.* 有耐心的 & *n.* 病患

- 片 be patient with sb　對某人很有耐心
- 衍 patience [ˋpeʃəns] *n.* 耐心 ③

▶ Teachers must be patient with slower students.
老師對學習較慢的學生必須要有耐心。

▶ This hospital has too many patients and doesn't have enough nurses.
這家醫院病人太多而護士不足。

ill [ɪl] *a.* 生病的 & *adv.* 惡劣地 & *n.* 問 / 難題（常用複數）

片 (1) fall ill　生病了
(2) speak ill of sb　說某人的壞話

似 sick [sɪk] *a.* 有病的；噁心的 ①

▶ Trevor fell ill and asked for sick leave this morning.
崔佛生病了，他今天早上請病假。

▶ It's immoral to speak ill of the dead.
說死者的壞話是不道德的。

▶ The politician promised to cure the country's ills.
這政治家承諾要解決這國家的問題。

medical [ˈmɛdɪkl] *a.* 醫療 / 學的

片 medical school　醫學院

衍 medicine [ˈmɛdəsn̩] *n.* 藥；醫學 ①

▶ It's important that you have a medical checkup once a year.
每年做一次醫療檢查是很重要的。

▶ Sadie is hoping to attend medical school.
莎蒂希望能上醫學院。

cure [kjʊr] *vt.* 治癒 & *n.* 治療方法

片 a cure for sth　治療某疾病的方法

似 heal [hil] *vt.* & *vi.* 治癒 ③

▶ The doctor tried every way he could to cure the patient, but in vain.
醫生竭盡所能地治療那病人，結果卻是徒勞一場。

▶ The scientists have found a cure for the rare disease.
科學家們已經找到了治療這罕見疾病的方法。

recover [rɪˈkʌvɚ]
vi. & *vt.* 恢復；重新找到 / 拿回

片 (1) recover from...
從……恢復過來 / 復元
= get over...
= recuperate from...
(2) recover one's heath　恢復健康

似 (1) recuperate [rɪˈk(j)upəˌret]
vi. 恢 / 康復（與介詞 from 並用）
(2) retrieve [rɪˈtriv] *vt.* 取 / 找回 ⑥

▶ It took me a long time to recover from the shock.
= It took me a long time to get over the shock.
我花了很長的時間才從驚嚇中回復過來。

▶ Tony recovered his health.
湯尼恢復了他的健康。

▶ Melinda was so happy that the police recovered her stolen wallet.
梅琳達好高興警方找回了她被偷走的皮夾。

13 examine [ɪgˈzæmən] *vt.* 檢查；考試

片 examine sb in / on sth　考某人某事

▶ Examine the car carefully before you buy it.
要買下那部車以前，你得仔細地檢查一遍。

▶ Our teacher will examine us in English tomorrow morning.
明天早上我們老師會考我們英文。

examination [ɪgˌzæməˈneʃən]
n. 檢查；考試 (= exam [ɪgˈzæm]，比 test 還正式)

☐ (1) have a physical examination
做體檢
= have a physical checkup
(2) a final examination / exam
期末考

似 test [tɛst] *n.* 測驗，考試 ①

▶ Eliot had a physical examination and found that he had high blood pressure.
艾略特做了體檢，發現他有高血壓。

▶ Harold did quite well on the final examination.
哈洛德期末考考得很好。

---

quiz [kwɪz] *n.* 小考

複 quizzes [ˈkwɪzɪz]

☐ a pop quiz　隨堂小考

▶ Ms. Miller is going to give us a quiz tomorrow.
米勒老師明天要給我們小考。

▶ I hope we won't have any pop quizzes in math class tomorrow.
我希望我們明天數學課不會有隨堂小考。

---

cheat [tʃit]
vt. 欺騙 & *vi.* 作弊；對……不忠 & *n.* 作弊的人，騙子

☐ (1) cheat sb (out) of sth
騙取某人某物
(2) cheat on sb　對某人不忠

▶ Don't try to cheat people.
別試圖騙人。

▶ Melvin cheated me (out) of all my money.
馬文騙走了我所有的錢。

▶ I never cheat on exams.
我考試從不作弊。

▶ Rex cheated on his wife, so she left him.
雷克斯對妻子不忠，所以他妻子離開了他。

▶ This school does not tolerate cheats.
這所學校不能容忍作弊的人。

14　barber [ˈbɑrbɚ] *n.* (修剪男性頭髮的) 理髮師

衍 barbershop [ˈbɑrbɚˌʃɑp] *n.* 理髮店

▶ I asked the barber to cut my hair shorter.
我請理髮師把我的頭髮剪短一些。

---

haircut [ˈhɛrˌkʌt] *n.* 理髮

☐ have / get a haircut　剪頭髮

▶ When was the last time you had a haircut?
你上次理髮是什麼時候？

15　eve [iv] *n.* 前夕

☐ (1) on the eve of...　在……的前夕
(2) on New Year's Eve
在新年前夕，在跨年夜那天，在除夕那天
on Christmas Eve　在平安夜那天

▶ On the eve of her wedding, Julia changed her mind and ran away with her high school sweetheart.
結婚前夕，茱莉亞改變了心意跟高中時代的情人跑了。

▶ Many shops close early on New Year's Eve.
很多商店在新年前夕提早關門。

Level 2　Unit 34

midnight [ˈmɪdˌnaɪt] *n.* 半夜

片 at midnight 在半夜

比 midday [ˈmɪdˌde] *n.* 正午
　 at midday 正午時分

▸ An earthquake happened at midnight last night.
昨晚半夜有地震。

16　ahead [əˈhɛd] *adv.* 在前面

片 (1) ahead of... 在……的前面
　 (2) go ahead 開始吧

衍 head [hɛd] *n.* 頭 ①

▸ Nathan stared straight ahead.
納森直直瞪著前方。

▸ There's a truck ahead of us. Be careful when driving.
我們前面有一輛卡車。開車時要小心。

▸ Go ahead; we are all ears.
開始說吧！我們正洗耳恭聽。
*be all ears　洗耳恭聽

Unit 35

3501-3504

1　mirror [ˈmɪrɚ] n. 鏡子 & vt. 反映

🔑 (1) look in / into a mirror　照鏡子
(2) a rearview / side mirror
後視鏡 / (車兩側其中一面的) 後視鏡

▶ Roy looked in the mirror and found that he looked terrible.
羅伊照鏡子，發現自己臉色很差。

▶ Calvin glanced in his car's rearview mirror.
凱文匆匆看了一下他車子的後視鏡。

▶ The wrinkles on Stan's face mirrored the difficult years he had been through.
史坦臉上的皺紋反映出他所歷經的艱辛歲月。
＊wrinkle [ˈrɪŋkl̩] n. 皺紋

2　prince [prɪns] n. 王子

🔑 Prince Charming　白馬王子
反 princess [ˈprɪnsəs] n. 公主 ②

▶ Prince Charles is the eldest son of Queen Elizabeth II.
查爾斯王子是英國女王伊莉莎白二世的長子。

▶ Iris is still waiting for her Prince Charming to appear.
艾莉絲還在等待她的白馬王子出現。

3　spread [sprɛd] vi. 蔓延，散播 & vt. 攤開；塗抹 & vt. & vi. 伸展 & n. 蔓延，散播

三 三態同形
🔑 (1) spread like wildfire
迅速地傳開來
＊wildfire [ˈwaɪld͵faɪr] n. 野火
(2) spread sth (out)
把某物攤開來；把身體某部位伸展開來
(3) spread A on B　把 A 塗抹在 B 上
＝ spread B with A
衍 widespread [͵waɪdˈsprɛd]
a. 普遍的，廣泛的 ⑤

▶ The rumor spread like wildfire.
謠言很快就蔓延開來。

▶ Roger spread the map out on the table and pointed out where we were.
羅傑將地圖攤在桌上，指出我們的所在地。

▶ Kelly spread peanut butter on the toast.
＝ Kelly spread the toast with peanut butter.
凱莉把花生醬塗在烤麵包片上。

▶ After playing with his cellphone for a while, Victor spread his arms out.
玩了一會兒手機後，維克多張開伸展他的雙臂。

▶ The spread of the disease left the whole city in a state of panic.
此疾病蔓延使整座城市陷入一片恐慌。
＊panic [ˈpænɪk] n. 恐慌

4　foolish [ˈfulɪʃ] a. 愚蠢的

衍 fool [ful] n. 傻瓜 ①

▶ How did Ricky come up with such a foolish idea?
瑞奇怎麼想出這麼蠢的點子？

3504-3509

silly [ˈsɪlɪ] *a.* 愚蠢的
▶ Don't play that silly game again, Adam.
別再玩那個愚蠢的遊戲了，亞當。

5　desert [ˈdɛzɚt] *n.* 沙漠 & [dɪˈzɝt] *vt.* 丟 / 拋棄

似 (1) dessert [dɪˈzɝt] *n.* (餐後) 甜點 ③
(2) abandon [əˈbændən] *vt.* 丟棄 ④

▶ It's impossible for you to cross the desert alone.
你一個人要穿越沙漠是不可能的。
▶ Those who desert their pets on the street are really heartless.
把寵物丟棄在街上的人真的很無情。
＊heartless [ˈhɑrtləs] *a.* 無情的

---

sand [sænd]
n. 沙粒 & *vt.* (用砂紙) 磨光 / 打磨

片 (1) a grain of sand　一粒沙
(2) bury / have one's head in the sand　持鴕鳥心態

▶ Maggie and Tom played in the sand on the beach.
瑪姬與湯姆在海灘玩沙。
▶ The president must stop burying his head in the sand.
總裁必須擺脫自己的鴕鳥心態。
▶ You should sand the wood to make it smooth.
你應該用砂紙打磨木頭以使其光滑。

---

camel [ˈkæml̩] *n.* 駱駝
似 the ship of the desert
沙漠之舟 (指『駱駝』)

▶ Camels are large animals that can live in the desert.
駱駝是一種能在沙漠生活的大型動物。

6　cockroach [ˈkɑkˌrotʃ] *n.* 蟑螂 (= roach [rotʃ])

複 cockroaches [ˈkɑkˌrotʃɪz]

▶ Are you afraid of cockroaches?
你怕蟑螂嗎？

---

spider [ˈspaɪdɚ] *n.* 蜘蛛

▶ Doris screamed when she saw a spider.
朵莉絲看到蜘蛛時嚇得大叫。
＊scream [skrim] *vi.* & *vt.* 尖叫

---

worm [wɝm]
n. (蠕) 蟲 & *vi.* & *vt.* 艱難地移動，蜷縮著身子走

片 worm (one's way) through...
擠過……，艱難地移動 / 蜷縮著身子穿過……

衍 (1) earthworm [ˈɝθˌwɝm] *n.* 蚯蚓
(2) silkworm [ˈsɪlkˌwɝm] *n.* 蠶

▶ I found there was a worm in the apple.
我發現蘋果裡有隻蟲。
▶ The dog wormed under the fence and into the neighbor's garden.
那隻狗在籬笆下蜷縮著身子走，鑽進了鄰居的花園。
＊fence [fɛns] *n.* 籬笆
▶ The little girl wormed her way through the crowd to the stage.
那小女孩擠過人群，到了舞臺前。

7 liquid [ˈlɪkwɪd] n. 液體 & a. 液體的

似 fluid [ˈfluɪd]
　　n. 液體 & a. (設計等) 流暢優美的 ⑤

反 solid [ˈsɑlɪd] n. 固體 & a. 固體的 ③

延伸 (1) gas [gæs] n. 氣體 ③
　　(2) gaseous [ˈgæsɪəs] a. 氣體的

▶ The ice turned into a liquid soon after it was taken out of the freezer.
冰塊從冷凍庫拿出來後很快就融成液體了。
*freezer [ˈfrizɚ] n. 冷凍庫

▶ Brenda prefers to use liquid soap.
布蘭達更喜歡用液態皂。

---

boil [bɔɪl] vt. & vi. (使) 沸騰 & n. 沸騰

片 (1) boil down to...　　歸結為……
　　(2) bring sth to a boil　把某液體燒開

似 bubble [ˈbʌbl̩]
　　vi. 冒泡，沸騰 & n. 氣泡 ③

▶ We boiled some water to make tea for the guests.
我們燒了些開水來泡茶招待客人。

▶ The water is boiling.
水沸騰了。

▶ What Sean has just said may boil down to this: He has a crush on you.
尚恩剛才說的話可以歸結成這一點：他迷上妳了。
*have a crush on sb　迷戀上某人

▶ You should bring the soup to a boil.
你應該把湯煮沸。

---

8 castle [ˈkæsl̩] n. 城堡

片 castles in the air
　　幾乎不可能實現的事情 / 計畫

衍 sandcastle [ˈsændˌkæsl̩] n. 沙堡

▶ The current owner of this castle is an oil tycoon.
這城堡現在的主人是個石油大王。
*tycoon [taɪˈkun] n. 企業大亨

▶ My little brother is a dreamer. He always talks about castles in the air.
我老弟是個不切實際的人。他老愛說些幾乎不可能實現的事情。

---

dragon [ˈdrægən] n. 龍

▶ This TV drama is full of fire-breathing dragons.
這部電視劇常會看到很多噴火龍。

---

9 chalk [tʃɔk] n. 粉筆 (不可數) & vt. 用粉筆寫 / 畫

片 a piece of chalk　一根粉筆

用法 a chalk (×)
→ a piece of chalk (○)　一根粉筆

▶ The little boy drew a picture on the blackboard with a piece of chalk.
小男孩用一根粉筆在黑板上畫圖。

▶ The teacher chalked the new words in this unit on the blackboard.
老師在黑板上用粉筆寫了這個單元的新字。

Level 2　Unit 35

blackboard [ˈblæk,bɔrd]
n. 黑板 (= chalkboard [ˈtʃɔk,bɔrd])

▶ These days, many teachers use a whiteboard, not a blackboard.
現在很多老師是使用白板，而不是黑板。 ☐

10 notebook [ˈnot,bʊk] *n.* 筆記本 ☐

▶ Take out your notebook and write the sentences down.
把你們的筆記本拿出來，把這些句子抄下來。

workbook [ˈwɜk,bʊk]
n. (學生的) 練習本

▶ Mrs. Franks told the students to finish page 29 in their workbooks.
弗蘭克斯老師告訴學生要完成練習本的第 29 頁。 ☐

textbook [ˈtɛkst,bʊk] *n.* 課本
延伸 a reference book 參考 / 工具書

▶ Ryan was reading an English textbook in the classroom.
萊恩當時正在教室內看英文課本。 ☐

text [tɛkst]
n. (書籍等) 文字部分 (不可數)；原文 (不可數)；(行動電話等) 簡訊
(= text message)
片 the text of... ……的原文
延伸 (1) article [ˈɑrtɪkḷ] *n.* 文章 ②
(2) script [skrɪpt] *n.* 劇本，廣播稿 ⑤

▶ This magazine contains too much text.
這本雜誌的文字太多了。 ☐

▶ The full text of the speech is on our website.
這演講的全文就在我們的網站上。

▶ Amy likes to call rather than send a text.
艾咪喜歡打電話，而不是傳簡訊。

pupil [ˈpjupḷ]
n. 學生；學徒，弟子；瞳孔
似 student [ˈst(j)udṇt] *n.* 學生 ①
反 master [ˈmæstɚ] *n.* 師父 ②
延伸 principal [ˈprɪnsəpḷ]
n. 校長 & *a.* 主要的 ②

▶ Natasha is one of my most prized pupils.
娜塔莎是我最重視的學生之一。 ☐

▶ William was one of this famous painter's pupils.
威廉是此著名畫家的學徒之一。

▶ The pupils enlarge when there is no light.
沒有光的時候，瞳孔會放大。

11 active [ˈæktɪv] *a.* 忙碌活躍的，精力充沛的；積極主動的 ☐

片 (1) lead an active life
過著很忙碌活躍的生活
(2) be active in + N/V-ing
積極參與……
衍 (1) act [ækt] *n.* 行為；法案 &
vi. 行為，表現 & *vt.* & *vi.* 扮演 ①
(2) action [ˈækʃən] *n.* 行動；動作 ①
反 passive [ˈpæsɪv] *a.* 被動的 ④

▶ Although my grandmother is 80 years old, she remains healthy and leads an active life.
雖然我的奶奶已經 80 歲了，但她仍然很健康，過著很忙碌活躍的生活。

▶ Jimmy has been active in helping to raise money for charity.
吉米一直都很積極主動幫忙慈善機構募款。

activity [æk'tɪvətɪ] *n.* 活動

複 **activities** [æk'tɪvətɪz]

片 (1) an outdoor activity　戶外活動
　　*outdoor ['aut,dɔr] *a.* 戶外的
　　(2) an extracurricular activity
　　課外活動
　　*extracurricular
　　[,ɛkstrəkə'rɪkjələ] *a.* 課外的

▶ Cycling is George's favorite outdoor activity.
騎腳踏車是喬治最喜歡的戶外活動。

▶ Gina enjoys many extracurricular activities such as tennis.
吉娜喜歡很多課外活動,例如網球。

12　task [tæsk] *n.* 任務,工作 & *vt.* 給……分配任務,派給……(工作)

片 (1) take sb to task for + V-ing
　　責罵某人做了……
　　(2) be tasked with + V-ing
　　被指派去做……

▶ Our first task is to gather all the information we need.
我們的首要工作就是蒐集一切所需的資料。
　*information [,ɪnfə'meʃən] *n.* 資料

▶ My boss took me to task for being late again.
我又遲到了,老闆為此而責備了我。

▶ Brian was tasked with checking the whole book for errors.
布萊恩被指派去檢查整本書是否有錯誤。

13　message ['mɛsɪdʒ] *n.* 訊息

片 (1) leave a message　留言
　　(2) take a message
　　幫忙傳話 (給某人)

衍 messenger ['mɛsəndʒə]
　n. 使者,信差 ④

▶ Fred left a message and said he would be late for the meeting.
弗瑞德留言說他開會會遲到。

▶ I'm sorry; Greg is out at the moment. Can I take a message?
很抱歉,葛瑞格現在不在。我可以幫忙傳話嗎?

14　spot [spɑt] *n.* 斑點;地點;汙漬 & *vt.* 認出,注意到

三 spot, spotted ['spɑtɪd], spotted
片 on the spot　立刻,當場
衍 spotted ['spɑtɪd] *a.* 有斑點的

▶ Ella was wearing a yellow dress with green spots.
艾拉穿了一件有綠色斑點的黃色洋裝。

▶ This is my favorite spot for sunbathing.
這是我最喜歡做日光浴的地方。
　*sunbathe ['sʌn,beð] *vi.* 做日光浴

▶ The murderer was caught on the spot by the police.
凶手當場被警方逮到。
　*murderer ['mɝdərə] *n.* 凶手

▶ How did you get that spot on your shirt?
你襯衫上那塊汙漬是怎麼來的?

▶ I easily spotted Gail in the crowd because of her red hat.
人群中,我輕易地就從那頂紅帽認出了蓋兒來。

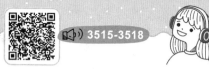
15 travel [ˈtrævl̩] *vi.* & *vt.* & *n.* 旅行

用 (1) travel (around) the world
環遊世界

(2) space travel 太空旅行

似 (1) trip [trɪp] *n.* 旅行 ①

(2) journey [ˈdʒɜnɪ] *vi.* & *n.* 旅行 ③

▶ My dream is to travel (around) the world.
我的夢想是環遊世界。

▶ Do you know how much space travel costs?
你知道太空旅行要花多少錢嗎？

---

tour [tʊr]
n. 旅行，觀光；巡迴演出 / 活動等 &
vt. & *vi.* 旅遊，觀光 & *vt.* 做巡迴演出

用 (1) go on a tour 遊覽

(2) on tour 巡迴演出 / 活動等

衍 (1) tourist [ˈtʊrɪst] *n.* 觀光客 ③

(2) tourism [ˈtʊrɪzəm]
n. 觀光事業，旅遊業 ③

▶ Mike went on a world tour last year.
邁可去年去環遊世界。

▶ The Korean band is on tour in Taipei.
這韓國樂團正在臺北巡迴演出。

▶ Bill is touring France this summer.
比爾今年夏天將到法國旅遊。

▶ I spent my last vacation touring in Spain.
我最近一次度假是去西班牙玩。

▶ The ballet performance is going to tour 15 cities around the world.
這芭蕾舞表演將在世界 15 個城市巡迴演出。
＊ballet [bæˈle] *n.* 芭蕾
performance [pəˈfɔrməns] *n.* 表演

---

guide [gaɪd]
n. 嚮導；指引；指南，手冊；旅遊指南
(＝ guidebook [ˈgaɪd͵bʊk]) & *vt.* 帶……
參觀；指導

用 (1) a tour guide 導遊

(2) a guide dog 導盲犬
＝ a seeing-eye dog

(3) a guide to... ……的指南 / 手冊

(4) a travel guide to...
有關……的旅遊指南

(5) guide sb around + 地方
帶某人參觀某處

衍 guidance [ˈgaɪdəns] *n.* 指導 ③

▶ Jeff used to work as a tour guide.
傑夫以前做過導遊。

▶ Let instinct be your guide.
讓直覺指引你吧！
＊instinct [ˈɪnstɪŋkt] *n.* 直覺

▶ Molly is being trained as a guide dog.
莫莉正在受訓成為導盲犬。
＊train A as B 把 A 訓練成 B
＝A be trained as B

▶ Maybe we should buy Emma this book: *A Guide to Vegan Dishes*.
也許我們應該買這本《純素菜肴指南》的書給艾瑪。

▶ I want to buy a travel guide to Italy before I set off.
出發前我想買本義大利的旅遊指南。

▶ My friend guided me around this famous museum.
我朋友帶我參觀了這個著名的博物館。

▶ I don't know much about the work, so you'll have to guide me.
這工作我不太熟，因此你得指導我。

16 introduce [ˌɪntrəˈd(j)us] *vt.* 介紹；引進，推出 (產品等)

🔢 introduce A to B
把 A 介紹給 B，向 B 介紹 A

衍 introductory [ˌɪntrəˈdʌktərɪ]
a. 介紹的

▶ The chairman introduced the speaker to the audience.
主席向聽眾介紹這位演講者。
*audience [ˈɔdɪəns] *n.* 聽眾，觀眾

▶ The company introduced a new product recently.
這家公司最近推出了一項新產品。

---

introduction [ˌɪntrəˈdʌkʃən]
n. 介紹；引進，推出 (產品等)；(書) 序，引言

🔢 a letter of introduction　介紹信

▶ After introductions were through, we started the meeting.
介紹完畢後，我們便開會了。

▶ I'd like to ask Mr. Smith to write me a letter of introduction.
我想請史密斯先生幫我寫一封介紹信。

▶ Doctor Beck encouraged the introduction of new medical treatments.
貝克醫生鼓勵引進新的醫療方法。

▶ Before reading a book, you can usually get its main idea in the introduction.
在你讀一本書之前，通常可以在引言中了解到這本書的主旨。

---

17 arrange [əˈrendʒ] *vt.* 排列，布置 & *vi.* & *vt.* 安排，籌劃

🔢 arrange for sth to V　安排某物做……

延伸 flower arranging　插花 (技藝)
▶ My mother takes a flower arranging class every Wednesday.
我媽媽每週三上插花課。

▶ Books on the shelf were arranged alphabetically.
架上的書是依字母順序排列。

▶ I'll arrange for a car to pick you up at the airport.
我會安排一臺車去機場接你的。

▶ I'll arrange a picnic, so don't forget to come.
我會安排野餐的，所以別忘了要來哦。

---

arrangement [əˈrendʒmənt]
n. 排列，布置；安排，籌畫 (此意常用複數)

🔢 make arrangements for...
為……做安排

▶ Greta didn't like the arrangement of furniture in the room.
葛瑞塔不喜歡房間裡傢俱的擺設。

▶ Have you made any arrangements for the meeting?
你有為那會議做安排了嗎？

---

18 contact [ˈkɑntækt] *n.* 聯繫；接觸，碰到 & *vt.* 聯繫

🔢 (1) get in contact with sb
去聯絡某人

(2) keep in contact with sb
與某人保持聯絡

▶ Try to get in contact with Kate as soon as you get into town.
你一進城就設法和凱特聯絡。

(3) lose contact with sb
與某人失去聯繫

(4) come into contact with...
接觸到……，碰到……

(5) make eye contact with sb
與某人有眼神的接觸

▶ No matter where you go, you should keep in contact with me.
不論你到哪裡，都要和我保持聯絡。

▶ I lost contact with Natalie after she moved to another city.
娜塔麗搬到別座城市後，我跟她便失去了聯繫。

▶ Because Jerry is a waiter, he comes into contact with people from all walks of life every day.
因為傑瑞是服務生，他每天都能接觸到各行各業的人。
*from all walks of life 來自各行各業

▶ You should make eye contact with your audience when giving a speech.
你演講時應該要跟觀眾有眼神接觸。

▶ Contact me at qvcservice@qvc.com if you have any problems.
如果您有任何問題，就用 qvcservice@qvc.com 這電子郵件地址和我聯繫。

19 dentist [ˈdɛntɪst] n. 牙醫

衍 dental [ˈdɛntḷ] a. 牙科的 ⑥
a dental clinic 牙科診所

▶ I need to go to see the dentist because I have a toothache.
因為我牙痛，我得去看牙醫。

toothache [ˈtuθˌek] n. 牙痛

片 have (a) toothache 牙痛

延伸 a decayed tooth 蛀牙
*decayed [dɪˈked] a. 蛀爛的

▶ Bill had a toothache this morning.
比爾今早牙痛。

toothbrush [ˈtuθˌbrʌʃ] n. 牙刷

衍 toothpaste [ˈtuθˌpest] n. 牙膏 (不可數)

▶ I need to buy a new toothbrush.
我需要買一支新牙刷。

brush [brʌʃ] n. 刷子 & vt. 刷

衍 hairbrush [ˈhɛrˌbrʌʃ] n. 梳子

▶ Joseph bought new brushes before he started painting his house.
約瑟夫在開始粉刷房子之前買了新刷子。

▶ Bill is in the bathroom brushing his teeth.
比爾正在浴室刷牙。

20 feeling [ˈfilɪŋ] n. 知覺；感覺

片 have / get the feeling that...
覺得 / 預感……

▶ Rick gradually lost feeling in his feet.
瑞克的雙腳逐漸失去知覺。

衍 **feel** [fil] *vi.* & *vt.* 感覺 & *n.* 觸覺 ①

▶ I have the feeling that he'll come.
我覺得他會來。

21 **fireman** [ˈfaɪrmən] *n.* 男消防員

複 firemen [ˈfaɪrmən]

反 firewoman [ˈfaɪrˌwʊmən]
n. 女消防員 (複數為 firewomen
[ˈfaɪrˌwɪmɪn]) ②

▶ Two firemen were injured while fighting the fire in the building.
2 名消防員在那棟大樓裡試圖滅火時受傷了。

1 leaf [lif] *n.* 葉子；一頁 & *vi.* 翻閱

複 leaves [livz]

片 (1) turn over a new leaf
改過自新，重新做人

(2) take a leaf out of sb's book
效法某人，以某人為榜樣

(3) leaf through...　翻閱……
= browse through...

▶ In the fall, most leaves turn brown, orange, and gold.
秋天時，樹葉大多會變成棕色、橙色還有金色。

▶ This is an old book—be careful turning the leaves.
這是一本舊書 —— 要小心翻頁。

▶ The criminal claims he has turned over a new leaf.
那罪犯聲稱他已改過自新了。

▶ You should take a leaf out of Elmer's book and study harder!
你應該要效法艾爾馬，要更用功讀書！

▶ The girl was leafing through the magazine in the coffee shop.
這女孩在咖啡店裡正在翻閱雜誌。

2 umbrella [ʌm'brɛlə] *n.* 雨傘

延伸 parasol ['pærə,sɔl] *n.* 陽傘

▶ It looks like rain. You'd better carry an umbrella.
看起來要下雨的樣子。你最好帶把傘。

raincoat ['ren,kot] *n.* 雨衣

延伸 a rain boot　雨靴 / 鞋 (常用複數)
= a rubber boot

▶ Put on your raincoat. It's raining outside.
把雨衣穿上。外面正在下雨。

3 beer [bɪr] *n.* 啤酒

片 (1) draft beer　生啤酒，桶裝啤酒〔美〕
= draught beer〔英〕

(2) bottled / canned beer
瓶 / 罐裝啤酒

▶ What's better than a glass of ice-cold beer on a hot summer day?
在炙熱的夏天，還有什麼會比一杯冰涼的啤酒更好的呢？

▶ David prefers draft beer to bottled ones.
與瓶裝啤酒相比，大衛更喜歡生啤酒。

wine [waɪn] *n.* 葡萄酒 (不可數)

片 (1) a bottle / drop of wine
一瓶 / 滴葡萄酒

(2) red / white wine　紅 / 白酒

▶ After the wedding, we drank wine and danced the night away.
婚禮後，我們徹夜跳舞喝酒。
＊dance the night away　徹 / 整夜跳舞

▶ I asked Ken to buy two bottles of wine for me.
我請肯幫我買 2 瓶葡萄酒。

▶ Shall we have some red wine with dinner?
我們晚餐時喝點紅酒好嗎？

cola [ˈkolə] *n.* 碳酸類飲料，可樂飲料
圆 **Coke** [kok] *n.* (廠牌名) 可口可樂
(= **Coca-Cola** [ˌkokəˈkolə]) ②

▶ Debbie doesn't like cola because she hates drinks with too much sugar.
黛比不喜歡碳酸類飲料，因為她討厭含糖過多的飲料。

---

soda [ˈsodə] *n.* 汽水

▶ Brenda ordered an apple pie and an orange soda.
布蘭達點了一個蘋果派和一杯柳橙汽水。

---

4 **hamburger** [ˈhæmbɝɡɚ] *n.* 漢堡，漢堡牛肉餅 (= **burger** [ˈbɝɡɚ])

▶ Jenny cooked some hamburgers and hot dogs on the barbecue.
珍妮在烤肉架上烤了一些漢堡牛肉餅和熱狗。

---

sandwich [ˈsæn(d)wɪtʃ]
n. 三明治 & *vt.* 將……夾在中間

▶ Luke's mother made him a chicken sandwich for lunch.
路克的媽媽為他做了一個雞肉三明治當午餐。

▶ Owen sandwiched the bad news between two bits of good news.
歐文把壞消息夾在兩個好消息中間。

---

fries [fraɪz]
n. 薯條 (恆用複數) (= **French fries**)

▶ Lydia ordered fries and ate them quickly.
莉迪亞點了薯條，然後迅速地吃完。

---

fry [fraɪ]
vt. & *vi.* 油煎或炸 & *n.* 油炸物，炒 / 煎出來的菜餚 (恆用單數)

目 **fry, fried** [fraɪd], **fried**

▶ Cover the onions with flour and fry them till they turn golden.
把洋蔥裹上麵粉，並把它們油炸至金黃色為止。
＊**onion** [ˈʌnjən] *n.* 洋蔥

▶ I love the smell of sweet potato frying.
我喜歡番薯在炸的味道。

▶ Ashley prefers to eat salad, rather than a fry, in the early morning.
一大早艾希莉喜歡吃沙拉，而不是吃油炸的食物。

---

ketchup [ˈkɛtʃəp]
n. 番茄醬 (不可數) 〔美〕〔英〕
(= **tomato ketchup** 〔美〕〔英〕
= **catsup** [ˈkætsəp] 〔美〕)

▶ Can you pass me the ketchup, please?
麻煩把番茄醬遞給我好嗎？

---

5 **beauty** [ˈbjutɪ] *n.* 美 (不可數)；美人 (可數)

複 **beauties** [ˈbjutɪz]

▶ Beauty is only skin deep.
美麗只不過是一層皮 / 美麗是膚淺的。—— 諺語

3605-3608

日 (1) a beauty shop　美容／髮店
= a beauty parlor
　　*parlor [ˋpɑrlɚ] n. 店舖
(2) beauty sleep　美容覺
衍 (1) beautiful [ˋbjutəfl] a. 美麗的 ①
(2) beautify [ˋbjutəˏfaɪ] vt. 美化 ⑥

▶ Beauty is in the eye of the beholder.
情人眼裡出西施。——諺語
▶ Nina is going to a beauty shop to have her nails done.
妮娜要去美髮店做指甲。
▶ I especially need my beauty sleep on weekends.
我週末特別需要睡美容覺。
▶ It is said that Mrs. Brown was a beauty when she was young.
據說布朗太太年輕時是個美人。

---

handsome [ˋhænsəm]
a. 英俊的（= good-looking）；數量可觀的

▶ Stan is the most handsome boy I have ever seen. ☐
史坦是我見過最帥的男生。
▶ Connie earns a handsome salary at the law firm.
康妮在律師事務所的薪水很可觀。

---

ugly [ˋʌglɪ] a. 醜的
日 an ugly duckling　醜小鴨
反 pretty [ˋprɪtɪ]
　　a. 漂亮的（= beautiful）①

▶ Though the man is very ugly, he has a kind heart. ☐
那人雖醜，卻有顆善良的心。
▶ Rachel was an ugly duckling, but look how pretty she is now!
瑞秋以前是隻醜小鴨，但你看她現在多漂亮！

6　excite [ɪkˋsaɪt] vt. 使興奮；激起 ☐

衍 (1) excited [ɪkˋsaɪtɪd]
　　　a. 感到興奮的 ①
(2) exciting [ɪkˋsaɪtɪŋ]
　　　a. 令人興奮的 ①
似 (1) thrill [θrɪl] vt. & vi. (使) 興奮 ⑤
(2) arouse [əˋraʊz] vt. 激起 ⑤

▶ The magic show excited all the children.
這場魔術表演使所有的孩子都看得好興奮。
▶ The news of the attack excited anger and fear among the people.
這次攻擊的消息激起大家的憤怒和恐懼。

---

excitement [ɪkˋsaɪtmənt]
n. 興奮 (不可數)；令人興奮的事 (可數)

用法 凡 表 情 緒 的 名 詞 如 excitement、sorrow（難過、悲傷）、delight（愉快）、joy（高興）、disappointment（失望）、satisfaction（滿意）等，均可與介詞 to 並用，形成下列介詞片語：
to one's + 情緒名詞　令某人……的是

▶ To my disappointment, Tim didn't show up as he had promised.
令我失望的是，提姆並未如約出現。

▶ Much to my excitement, my girlfriend has accepted my proposal. ☐
令我大感興奮的是，我女友已接受了我的求婚。
▶ The excitements I experienced on my trip to Bangkok last week are truly unforgettable.
上星期我到曼谷一遊，在那裡所經歷的種種刺激實在令人難忘。

7　lend [lɛnd] *vt.* 借給

目 lend, lent [lɛnt] , lent
片 (1) lend sth to sb　借某物給某人
　　= lend sb sth
　　(2) lend / give sb a helping hand
　　　幫助某人
似 borrow [ˋbaro] *vt.* 借入 ①

▸ Kate is unwilling to lend money to me.
= Kate is unwilling to lend me money.
　凱特不太願意借錢給我。

▸ This extra money should lend you a helping hand.
　這筆額外的錢應該可以幫到你。

---

debt [dɛt] *n.* 負債
片 (1) get / run / fall into debt
　　　開始負債
　　(2) be in debt (to sb)　欠 (某人) 債
　　(3) be up to one's neck in debt
　　　債台高築
　　(4) pay off a / one's debt　償還債務

▸ Nancy got into debt because of her university fees.
　南希因為大學學費而負債累累。

▸ The company is in debt to the bank.
　那家公司欠銀行債務。

▸ The gambler is up to his neck in debt.
　這名賭徒債台高築。

▸ I wish I earned enough to pay off my debts.
　我希望我的收入足以償還債務。

8　sport [spɔrt] *n.* 運動 & *vt.* 引人注目地穿戴

衍 sports [spɔrts] *a.* 運動的，運動相關的
　a sports car　　跑車
　a sports drink　運動飲料
▸ After my workout, I prefer to take water, rather than a sports drink.
　運動完後，我比較喜歡喝水，而不是喝運動飲料。

▸ I like to play all kinds of sports, especially volleyball.
　我喜歡玩各種運動，尤其是排球。
　*volleyball [ˋvalɪˏbɔl] *n.* 排球

▸ Rose walked into the room, sporting a brand-new designer hat.
　蘿絲走進房間，戴著一頂全新的名牌帽子。

---

football [ˋfʊtˏbɔl]
n. 美式橄欖球〔美〕(= American football〔英〕) ; 足球〔英〕

片 play football
　打美式橄欖球〔美〕; 踢足球〔英〕
似 rugby [ˋrʌgbɪ] *n.* 英式橄欖球〔英〕

▸ Did you see the football game last night?
　你有看昨晚的美式橄欖球比賽了嗎？

▸ My boyfriend is crazy about football.
　我男友是足球迷。

---

soccer [ˋsakɚ] *n.* 足球〔美〕
片 play soccer　踢足球

▸ I used to play soccer every day after school.
　以前我每天放學就去踢足球。

---

badminton [ˋbædmɪntən]
n. 羽毛球

片 play badminton　打羽毛球

▸ Candy sprained her ankle while playing badminton.
　康蒂打羽毛球時扭傷了腳踝。

Level 2　Unit 36

延伸 (1) racket [ˈrækɪt] n. 球拍
(2) birdie [ˈbɝdɪ] n. 羽毛球〔美〕
= shuttlecock [ˈʃʌtlˌkɑk]〔英〕

9 wool [wʊl] n. 羊毛 (不可數)

似 wood [wʊd] n. 木頭 ②

▶ A pure wool shirt can keep you very warm.
純羊毛襯衫非常保暖。

10 pan [pæn] n. 平底鍋

片 a flash in the pan　曇花一現

▶ Nora heated up the soup in a pan.
諾拉把平底鍋裡的湯加熱。

▶ Kelly's success proved she was not just a flash in the pan.
凱莉的成功證明她不只是曇花一現。

teapot [ˈtiˌpɑt] n. 茶壺

片 a tempest in a teapot　小題大作
衍 pot [pɑt]
　n. 茶壺;咖啡壺;(裝果醬等的) 罐 ①

▶ Polly put two tea bags and hot water into the teapot.
波莉在茶壺加了 2 個茶包和熱水。

▶ Your fight with Mark was just a tempest in a teapot.
你和馬克吵架只是小題大作而已。

refrigerator [rɪˈfrɪdʒəˌretɚ]
n. 冰箱 (= fridge [frɪdʒ])

片 a fridge magnet　冰箱磁鐵

▶ Remember to put all the food in the refrigerator, or it will go bad.
記得把所有食物放進冰箱,不然會壞掉。
＊go bad　壞掉的,不新鮮的

▶ Tammy likes to buy a fridge magnet wherever she goes.
塔米無論到哪裡都喜歡買個冰箱磁鐵。

11 bark [bɑrk] vi. 吠 & n. 吠 (聲);樹皮

片 (1) bark at...　對……吠叫
(2) bark up the wrong tree
　找錯方法 / 原因
(3) give a bark　吠
(4) sb's bark is worse than sb's
　bite　刀子口豆腐心
衍 barking [ˈbɑrkɪŋ] a. 瘋狂的〔英〕

▶ The dog kept barking at us.
那隻狗一直對我們亂吠。

▶ Don't come to me for advice. I know nothing about this topic. You're barking up the wrong tree.
別來問我的意見。我對這主題一點也不懂。你找錯人了。

▶ Monica's dog gave a noisy bark when he saw the stranger.
莫妮卡的狗看到那陌生人時發出了嘈雜的吠聲。

▶ Although Trevor easily loses his temper, his bark is worse than his bite.
雖然崔佛很容易發脾氣,但他是刀子口豆腐心。

▶ Some bark can be used to make clothes.
有些樹皮可用來做衣服。

---

12 listener [ˈlɪsn̩ɚ] *n.* (電臺廣播的) 聽眾；傾聽者

比 a listener　　一個聽眾
　　an audience　　一群聽眾

▶ This radio program appeals to many young listeners.
這電臺節目吸引了很多年輕的聽眾。

▶ Being a good listener helps establish friendship.
做個好的傾聽者有助於建立友誼。

---

speaker [ˈspikɚ]
n. 演說者；講(某種)語言的人；音響喇叭；
(議會 / 立法機構等的) 議長 (此意前面加
定冠詞 the，字首大寫)

片 a native speaker of + 語言
　　說某語言的母語人士
= a native + 語言 + speaker

衍 (1) speak [spik] *vi.* 說話 ①
　　(2) loudspeaker [ˈlaʊdˌspikɚ]
　　　　n. 廣播喇叭，擴音器 ⑥

延伸 reader [ˈridɚ] *n.* 讀者；愛讀書的人
▶ Grace is an avid / a great reader.
She can read six to nine books per
month.
葛瑞絲是個很喜歡閱讀的人。她每個月
能讀 6 至 9 本的書。
＊avid [ˈævɪd] *a.* 熱衷的

▶ The speaker seemed a little nervous.
那演說者似乎有點緊張。

▶ Is Josh a native speaker of English?
= Is Josh a native English speaker?
喬許是英語母語人士嗎？

▶ My computer's speakers aren't working.
我電腦的喇叭故障了。

▶ It is the Speaker's job to keep order.
維持秩序是議長的工作。

---

speech [spitʃ]
n. 演講；口語；說話 (能力)

片 (1) make / give / deliver a speech
　　　on...　　就……發表演講
　　(2) in speech　用口語的方式，用言語
　　(3) freedom of speech　言論自由
　　(4) a part of speech
　　　　詞性 (複數為 parts of speech)

▶ Martha made a speech on Taiwanese opera.
瑪莎就臺灣歌仔戲這一主題來演講。
＊opera [ˈɑpərə] *n.* 歌劇

▶ The little boy couldn't express himself well in speech.
那小男孩無法用言語清楚地表達自己。

▶ We have freedom of speech in this country.
在這國家我們有言論自由。

▶ The part of speech of this word is a verb.
這個字的詞性是動詞。

---

13 skill [skɪl] *n.* 技巧，技能

片 (1) with skill　很有技巧地
　　(2) skill at / in + N/V-ing
　　　　……的技能

▶ Sam plays the piano with great skill.
山姆彈鋼琴的技巧非常好。

Level 2　Unit 36

衍 skillful [ˈskɪlfəl] *a.* 熟練的 ③

似 expertise [ˌɛkspɚˈtiz]
　　n. 專門技術／知識 ⑤

▶ I envy Cindy's skill in painting!
我好羨慕辛蒂的畫功！
＊envy [ˈɛnvɪ] *vt.* 羨慕

---

skilled [skɪld] *a.* 熟練的，有技術的

片 be skilled at / in + N/V-ing
　　擅長某事，具有某種技術

反 unskilled [ʌnˈskɪld]
　　a. 不熟練的，無技能的；無需技能的，
　　非技術性的

▶ David asked his uncle whether
there were any unskilled jobs in
his company.
大衛問他叔叔他公司裡是否有非技術性
的工作。

▶ It took Louis four years to train to become a
skilled engineer.
路易斯花了 4 年的時間才成為一名熟練的工程師。

▶ Kenny is skilled in negotiating.
肯尼很擅長談判。

---

14 favor [ˈfevɚ] *n.* 贊同，支持；幫助，恩惠 & *vt.* 贊同；賜／給予

片 (1) win (sb's) favor
　　得到 (某人的) 支持，博得 (某人的)
　　好感
　(2) be in favor of sth　贊成某事
　　＝ favor sth
　(3) do sb a favor　幫某人忙
　(4) ask sb (for) a favor　請某人幫忙
　(5) favor A over B
　　贊同 A 而不贊同 B，喜歡 A 勝於 B
　(6) favor sb with sth
　　賜／給予某人某事物

衍 favorable [ˈfevərəbl]
　　a. 贊同的；有利的 ④

▶ Lance did all he could to win Jill's favor.
蘭斯盡全力要博得吉兒的好感。

▶ The manager was in favor of the proposal.
＝ The manager favored the proposal.
經理贊成這提案。

▶ Could you do me a favor and open the window?
可以幫我開窗戶嗎？

▶ I hate asking people for favors.
我不喜歡請別人幫忙。

▶ I favor Heather's plan over the other.
我贊成海瑟的計畫，不贊成另一個計畫。

▶ The university didn't favor me with a quick reply.
那間大學並沒有馬上給我回覆。

---

favorite [ˈfevərɪt]
a. 最喜愛的 & *n.* 最喜愛的人／物

▶ That's my favorite color.
那是我最喜愛的顏色。

▶ The song was one of Kelly's favorites.
這首歌是凱莉的最愛之一。

---

15 spoon [spun] *n.* 湯匙

衍 spoonful [ˈspunˌful] *n.* 一匙的量
　　a spoonful of...　一匙／勺的……

▶ I need a spoon to eat my soup.
我需要一根湯匙來喝湯。

▶ Add a spoonful of sugar to the mixture.
在這混合物中加入一勺糖。

16　purple [ˋpɝpl] *a.* 紫色的 & *n.* 紫色

片 (1) be / turn purple in the face
　　　氣得臉色發青
　= be / turn purple with rage
　(2) dress in purple　穿紫色的衣服

▶ Cassie likes to wear purple clothes.
凱西喜歡穿紫色的衣服。

▶ A man just cut in line, and Eric soon turned purple in the face.
有個人剛插隊，艾瑞克很快就氣得臉色發青。

▶ Kevin is a strange guy who likes to dress in purple.
凱文是個奇怪的傢伙，他喜歡穿紫色的衣服。

17　vacation [veˋkeʃən] *n.* 假期〔美〕(= holiday [ˋhɑləˏde] 〔英〕) &
vi. 度假〔美〕(= holiday [ˋhɑləˏde] 〔英〕)

片 (1) go on vacation　去度假
　(2) be on vacation　度假中

似 vocation [voˋkeʃən] *n.* 職業 ⑥

▶ Kayla will go on vacation next week.
凱拉下星期會去度假。

▶ I'll be on vacation in Paris next month.
下個月我將在巴黎度假。

▶ My family vacationed in Europe that summer.
那年夏天我們全家在歐洲度假。

---

backpack [ˋbækˏpæk]
n. (登山、長途旅行用的) 背包〔美〕
(= pack [pæk]〔美〕= rucksack
[ˋrʌkˏsæk]〔英〕) & *vi.* 背包旅行

衍 backpacker [ˋbækˏpækɚ] *n.* 背包客

▶ The two backpackers asked a local woman to give them directions to a tourist attraction.
這 2 個背包客請當地一名婦女告訴他們怎麼去某個旅遊景點。

▶ Can you carry the snacks in your backpack?
你可以把零食放在你的背包嗎？

▶ Tanya is backpacking around Asia this year.
坦雅今年在亞洲各地當背包客旅行。

18　puppy [ˋpʌpɪ] *n.* 小狗 (= pup [pʌp])

複 puppies [ˋpʌpɪz]
片 puppy love　兩小無猜的戀 / 感情

▶ I picked up a puppy on my way home.
我回家途中撿到了一隻小狗。

▶ Fred and Dora are young—it's just a case of puppy love.
弗瑞德和朵拉還年輕 —— 這只是他們兩小無猜的感情。

19 beat [bit] *vt.* 毆打；擊敗 & *vi.* 跳動 & *n.* (心臟) 跳動聲；敲打聲；節拍

目 beat, beat, beaten [`bitn]

片 (1) beat sb up　毆打某人

(2) (It) beats me.
　　考倒我了。/ 我不知道。

(3) dance to the beat of...
　　跟著……的拍子跳舞

衍 heartbeat [`hart,bit] *n.* 心跳

▶ A bully beat Johnny up at school.
在學校有個惡霸毆打強尼。
＊bully [`bulɪ] *n.* 惡霸，以大欺小者

▶ We beat that team (by) 97-95.
我們以 97 比 95 的比數打敗那支隊伍。

▶ A: How long will it take to finish the job?
B: (It) beats me.
A：這工作需要多久才能做完？
B：這可考倒我了。

▶ Hearing Clara's voice made my heart beat fast.
聽到克萊拉的聲音讓我心跳加速。

▶ The nurse told me my grandfather had a heart rate of 60 beats per minute.
護士告訴我，我爺爺的心跳為每分鐘跳 60 下。

▶ The beat of the raindrops on the roof is very noisy.
屋頂上的雨滴敲打聲很吵。
＊raindrop [`ren,drap] *n.* 雨滴

▶ Everyone danced to the beat of the music.
大家都跟著這音樂的拍子跳舞。

Unit 37

3701-3703

---

1 fee [fi] *n.* 服務費，費用

☐ a monthly membership fee
會員月費

似 fare [fɛr] *n.* 交通費 ③
a bus fare   公車費
a taxi fare   計程車費

▶ You have to pay a monthly membership fee to use this fitness center.
使用這家健身中心得先付會員月費。

---

2 luck [lʌk] *n.* 好運，幸運

☐ (1) by luck   只是運氣好
(2) be in luck   很幸運，運氣很好
(3) good luck to sb 祝某人好運

衍 lucky [ˋlʌkɪ] *a.* 幸運的 ①

▶ It was only by luck that we avoided the accident.
我們避免了這次意外只是運氣好而已。

▶ You're in luck—we have one room still available.
你很幸運 —— 我們還有一個空房間。

▶ Good luck to you in your new job.
祝你的新工作順利。

---

fate [fet] *n.* 命運

衍 destiny [ˋdɛstənɪ] *n.* 命運 ⑤

▶ The board is going to have a meeting that will decide the fate of the company and its 500 employees.
董事會即將召開會議，決定這間公司及其 500 名員工的命運。

---

3 guard [gɑrd] *n.* 警衛；警戒 (不可數) & *vt.* 守衛，保護

☐ (1) be on guard   守衛
= stand guard
(2) guard against... 防止……

衍 (1) guardian [ˋgɑrdɪən]
n. 守護者；監護人 ④
(2) bodyguard [ˋbɑdɪˏgɑrd]
n. 保鏢 ⑤

▶ The guard stopped us from going inside.
警衛不讓我們進去。

▶ George was on guard at the front gate last night.
喬治昨晚在大門口守衛。

▶ Bill kept a dog to guard his house.
比爾養了一隻狗看家。

▶ Guard against pickpockets when you are shopping in the mall.
在商場購物時，要謹防扒手。

---

protect [prəˋtɛkt] *vt. & vi.* 保護，防禦

☐ protect sb from / against... 保護
某人免受……的傷害

衍 protection [prəˋtɛkʃən]
n. 保護物；保護 ③

似 defend [dɪˋfɛnd] *vt.* 防衛 ④

▶ While riding a scooter, you should wear a helmet because it'll protect your head.
你騎機車時應該要戴安全帽，因為安全帽可以保護頭部。

▶ Albert tried to protect his family from the gangsters.
亞伯特試著保護家人免受歹徒的傷害。
*gangster [ˋgæŋstɚ] *n.* 歹徒

protective [prəˈtɛktɪv] *a.* 保護的

🔑 be protective of sb
保護某人，對某人呵護備至

▶ A boxer can easily be hurt if he doesn't wear protective gear.
拳擊手要是不穿護具很容易就會受傷。
＊gear [gɪr] *n.* 裝備 (集合名詞，不可數)

▶ Some parents are too protective of their children.
有些父母過於保護他們的小孩。

---

4 **satisfy** [ˈsætɪsˌfaɪ] *vt.* 使滿足；符合 (要求、條件)

▤ satisfy, satisfied [ˈsætɪsˌfaɪd], satisfied

🔑 satisfy / meet a requirement
符合要求

衍 (1) satisfying [ˈsætɪsˌfaɪɪŋ]
a. 令人愉悅 / 滿足的

(2) satisfied [ˈsætɪsˌfaɪd]
a. 感到滿意的

(3) satisfactory [ˌsætɪsˈfæktərɪ]
a. 令人滿意的 ③

(4) satisfaction [ˌsætɪsˈfækʃən]
n. 滿足，滿意 ④

反 dissatisfy [dɪsˈsætɪsˌfaɪ]
vt. 使不滿意

▶ That meal didn't satisfy me at all.
那頓飯一點都沒讓我吃飽。

▶ The teacher we just interviewed seems to satisfy all requirements.
＝ The teacher we just interviewed seems to meet all requirements.
我們剛剛面試的那位老師似乎符合所有的要求。

---

5 **owner** [ˈonɚ] *n.* 所有者

衍 (1) own [on]
vt. 擁有 & *a.* 自己的 & *vi.* 承認 ①
own up to + V-ing 承認做……

(2) ownership [ˈonɚˌʃɪp] *n.* 所有權 ③

▶ I am the owner of this land.
我是這塊地的所有人。

---

6 **shelf** [ʃɛlf] *n.* (櫥櫃的或固定在牆上的) 架子

複 shelves [ʃɛlvz]

片 (1) clear a / one's shelf
把 (某人的) 架子清空

(2) be left on the shelf 乏人問津

(3) a shelf life (食品的) 保存期 (限)

▶ Don't forget to clear your shelf when you move out.
你搬走時別忘了把你架子清空。

▶ That philosophy book has been left on the shelf for years.
那本哲學書乏人問津，已經放在架上好幾年了。

▶ This kind of cookie usually has a shelf life of six months.
這種餅乾的保存期通常是 6 個月。

drawer [ˈdrɔɚ] *n.* 抽屜

▸ The scissors are placed in the top drawer.
剪刀放在最上面的抽屜裡。

目 a top / bottom drawer
最上 / 下面的抽屜

衍 draw [drɔ] *vt.* 拉 ①

---

7 drug [drʌg] *n.* 藥 (物)；毒品 & *vt.* 下藥 (以使昏迷)

目 drug, drugged [drʌgd], drugged

▸ The drug is efficient in getting rid of a cold.
這個藥治療感冒很有效。

目 (1) take drugs 吃藥；吸毒
(2) drug trafficking 毒品買賣

▸ Andy has been taking drugs for high blood pressure for almost a year.
安迪已經吃高血壓的藥將近有一年了。

衍 drugstore [ˈdrʌgˌstor] *n.* 藥妝店 ③

▸ Never take drugs, or you'll be sorry for the rest of your life.
絕對不要吸毒，否則你會後悔一輩子。

▸ Drug trafficking is illegal in almost every country.
幾乎在每一個國家毒品交易都是非法的。

▸ Be careful! The juice might be drugged.
小心！這果汁可能被下藥。

---

8 cash [kæʃ] *n.* 現金 & *vt.* & *vi.* 兌現

目 (1) in cash 用現金
(2) cash out... ……換成現金

▸ How much cash do you have with you?
你身上有多少現金？

衍 cashier [kæˈʃɪr] *n.* 出納員 ⑥

▸ Candy still prefers to pay in cash.
坎蒂仍然喜歡付現。

▸ Can you cash this check for me?
能麻煩您將這張支票兌現嗎？

▸ Robert cashed out his stocks and made a large profit.
羅伯特把他的股票兌現而獲得了巨額利潤。

---

coin [kɔɪn] *n.* 硬幣 & *vt.* 發明 (新字詞)

目 (1) spin a coin
旋轉硬幣 (用於猜測哪一面朝上)

▸ The beggar said, "Can you spare me a few coins?"
那乞丐說：『你能施捨我幾個硬幣嗎？』

(2) toss a coin 擲硬幣決定

▸ I'll spin the coin, and you say "heads" or "tails."
我來旋轉硬幣，然後你說『正面』或『反面』。

(3) be two sides of the same coin
是 (同) 一件事情 / 一個問題的兩面

▸ Let's toss a coin to see who has to clean the kitchen.
讓我們擲硬幣來決定誰必須打掃廚房。

= be different / opposite sides of the same coin

▸ Success and failure are actually two sides of the same coin.
成功和失敗實際上是同一件事情的兩面。

(4) the other side of the coin
從另一方面來說，事情的另一面

延伸 bill [bɪl] *n.* 鈔票；帳單 ②
pay / foot a bill　付帳

▶ The work is easy, but the other side of the coin is it's low-paid.
這工作很輕鬆，但從另一方面來說工資卻很低。

▶ The writer likes to coin new words in his novels.
這位作家喜歡在他的小說裡發明新字詞。

9　stranger [ˋstrendʒɚ] *n.* 陌生人

片 (1) Hello, stranger!
　　（用於稱呼熟人）你好，稀客！
(2) be no stranger to sth
　　對某事物毫不陌生

衍 strange [strendʒ] *a.* 奇怪的 ①

▶ Don't talk to strangers.
別和陌生人談話。

▶ Hello, stranger! Long time no see!
你好，稀客！好久不見！

▶ Lucy is no stranger to tennis.
露西對網球毫不陌生。

10　brain [bren] *n.* (頭) 腦；智力；極聰明的人

片 (1) rack one's brains　絞盡腦汁
　　＝ beat one's brains
(2) use one's brain
　　用某人的腦子，動動某人的腦子
(3) a brain drain　人才外流

衍 brainpower [ˋbren͵pauɚ] *n.* 腦/智力

似 (1) intelligence [ɪnˋtɛlədʒəns]
　　n. 智力 ④
(2) intellect [ˋɪntḷ͵ɛkt] *n.* 智力 ⑥

▶ Calvin's brain was damaged in the car accident.
凱文的腦部在該起車禍中受了傷。

▶ Andrew racked his brains, trying to remember Becky's phone number.
安德魯絞盡腦汁想記起貝琪的電話號碼。

▶ Use your brain, Darren. Don't just ask me to give you the answer directly.
用你的大腦，達倫。不要只要求我直接給你答案。

▶ A brain drain is a problem for many poor countries.
人才外流是許多貧困國家的問題。

tongue [tʌŋ] *n.* 舌頭

片 (1) a mother / native tongue　母語
(2) a slip of the tongue
　　口誤，不小心講錯

▶ The coffee was so hot that I burned my tongue.
咖啡太燙了，我舌頭都被燙到了。

▶ Derek's mother tongue is French, not English.
德瑞克的母語是法文，不是英文。

▶ Sorry, it must have been a slip of the tongue. I meant tomorrow, not today.
抱歉，可能是我不小心講錯了，我是指明天，不是今天。

11　climate [ˋklaɪmɪt] *n.* 氣候 (指某地長期的氣象型態)

片 climate change　氣候變遷
衍 climatic [klaɪˋmætɪk] *a.* 氣候的

▶ The climate on this island is generally very nice in autumn.
一般來說，這島上秋天的氣候非常舒適宜人。

似 (1) climax [ˈklaɪˌmæks]
　　vi. 達到最高峰 & n. 頂點；最精彩的部分 ⑥
　(2) weather [ˈwɛðə]
　　n. 天氣 (指某地短期的氣象型態) ①

▶ Many countries are working together to combat climate change.
多國正在共同努力對付氣候變遷。

---

cloudy [ˈklaʊdɪ] a. 多雲的，陰的

衍 cloud [klaʊd] n. 雲 ①

似 overcast [ˈovəˌkæst]
　　a. 陰天的，多雲的

▶ It's cloudy today. I'd better bring an umbrella.
今天是陰天。我最好還是帶把傘。

---

snowy [ˈsnoɪ] a. 下雪的

衍 snow [sno] n. 雪 ①

▶ Dennis came to see me on a snowy night.
丹尼斯在一個下雪的夜晚來看我。

---

windy [ˈwɪndɪ] a. 多風的

衍 wind [wɪnd] n. 風 ①

▶ It's too windy for a picnic.
風太大了，不適合野餐。

12　hike [haɪk] n. & vi. 健行，遠足

片 (1) go on a hike　去健行 / 遠足
　　= go hiking
　(2) hike up...　快速拉起……
　　= quickly raise...

衍 (1) hiker [ˈhaɪkə] n. 健行 / 遠足的人
　(2) hiking [ˈhaɪkɪŋ] n. 健行，遠足

似 walk [wɔk] n. & vi. & vt. 走 ①

▶ We went on a hike to Sun Moon Lake last weekend.
我們上週末健行到日月潭。

▶ I go hiking simply because I enjoy the lush countryside.
我健行純粹是因為我很喜歡綠意盎然的鄉間景色。
＊lush [lʌʃ] a. 綠意盎然的

▶ I hiked up my pants to wade across the river.
我把褲管拉起好涉水過這條河。

13　pleasant [ˈplɛznt] a. 令人愉快的 (多指天氣)；親切友好的

衍 (1) please [pliz] vi. & vt. (使) 快樂 ①
　(2) pleasure [ˈplɛʒə] n. 愉快，開心 ①

似 agreeable [əˈgriəbl] a. 宜人的 ④

反 unpleasant [ʌnˈplɛznt]
　　a. 令人不愉快的

▶ The weather today is really pleasant—not too cold nor too hot.
今天的天氣極舒適 —— 不會太冷也不會太熱。

▶ Ray is a very pleasant guy.
雷是一個很親切友好的人。

---

anger [ˈæŋgə] n. 憤怒 & vt. 激怒

片 (1) be filled with anger　滿腔怒火
　(2) to one's anger　令某人生氣的是

▶ Danny is filled with anger because his girlfriend lied to him.
丹尼怒火中燒，因為他女友對他說謊。

▶ To my anger, John didn't show up as he had promised.
令我生氣的是，約翰並未如約出現。

▶ The politician's comments angered the public.
這政治家的言論激怒了大眾。

14 **fit** [fɪt] *vt.* & *vi.* 適合 & *a.* 健康的；合適的 & *n.* 合適 / 身 & *adv.* 充滿，非常

三 三態同形

用 (1) stay / keep fit　保持健康
　= stay healthy
　(2) be fit to V　適合做……
　(3) be fit to burst with sth
　　……極了，充滿 (……情緒) 的

▶ These pants no longer fit me. They're too tight.
這條褲子不再合我身。它太緊了。

▶ My feet are killing me because these shoes don't fit.
我的腳痛死了，因為這雙鞋不合腳。

▶ To stay fit, you should exercise every day.
要保持健康，就應該每天運動。

▶ Mr. Li said the man was not fit to marry his daughter.
李先生說這個男人不適合和他女兒結婚。

▶ The pants were a perfect fit.
這件褲子很合身。

▶ Linda was fit to burst with excitement.
琳達興奮極了。

---

suit [sut]
n. 西裝，套裝 (= business suit)；
訴訟 (= lawsuit [ˈlɔ͵sut]) & *vt.* 適合

用 file / bring a suit against sb
　對某人提出訴訟

似 suite [swit] *n.* 套房 ⑤

▶ You look very handsome in that black business suit.
你穿上那套黑色西裝看起來很帥。

▶ The writer filed a suit against the company because it violated his intellectual rights.
那作家對該公司提起訴訟，因為該公司侵犯了他的智慧財產權。

▶ Brenda is quite active, so the job as a secretary doesn't suit her.
布蘭達很好動，因此祕書這工作並不適合她。

---

suitable [ˈsutəbḷ] *a.* 適當的

用 (1) a suitable place to V
　　適合做……的地方
　(2) be suitable for...　適合……

反 unsuitable [ʌnˈsutəbḷ] *a.* 不適當的

▶ This village is a suitable place to retire.
這村莊是個很適合退休的地方。

▶ I'm afraid this novel is not suitable for your children.
恐怕這本小說並不適合你的孩子閱讀。

---

15 **magazine** [͵mægəˈzin] *n.* 雜誌

用 (1) a fashion / computer / travel magazine　時尚 / 電腦 / 旅遊雜誌
　(2) subscribe to a magazine
　　訂雜誌

▶ Rick is a writer for a fashion magazine.
瑞克是某時尚雜誌的撰稿人。

▶ Subscribe to the magazine today and get a special discount!
今天訂閱這份雜誌就有特別優惠喔！

16　whale [(h)wel] *n.* 鯨魚

㗊 go whale watching　去賞鯨

▶ Scientists have been studying these whales for many years.
科學家研究這些鯨魚多年。

▶ We went whale watching in Iceland.
我們去冰島賞鯨。

shark [ʃɑrk] *n.* 鯊魚

㗊 (1) shark finning
割鰭棄身，割取鯊魚

(2) a loan shark　放高利貸的人

▶ The scuba diver got attacked by a shark and was rushed to the hospital.
該潛水員受到鯊魚攻擊，被緊急送醫。

▶ Most countries have banned shark finning.
大多數國家都已禁止割取鯊魚這行為。

▶ You should never borrow money from a loan shark.
你應該永遠都不要向放高利貸的人借錢。

turtle [ˈtɝtl̩] *n.* 海龜

㗊 tortoise [ˈtɔrtəs] *n.* 陸龜 ④

▶ My younger sister was surprised the turtle beat the rabbit in the race.
我妹妹很驚訝烏龜賽跑贏了兔子。

17　ocean [ˈoʃən] *n.* 海洋

㗊 a drop in the ocean　滄海一粟〔英〕
= a drop in the bucket〔美〕

▶ Many beautiful and wonderful creatures live in the ocean.
海洋裡棲息著許多美麗又奇妙的生物。

▶ To Eric's anger, the government's contribution was dismissed as a drop in the ocean.
令艾瑞克生氣的是，政府的捐款被視為滄海一粟。

swim [swɪm] *vi.* & *vt.* & *n.* 游泳

目 swim, swam [swæm], swum
[swʌm]

㗊 (1) swim with the tide
順應潮流，隨波逐流

(2) swim against the tide
不順應潮流

(3) sink or swim
自生自滅，載浮載沉

(4) go for a swim　去游泳

▶ Teddy wants to learn how to swim.
泰迪想學游泳。

▶ Melody swam the River Eden.
美樂蒂游過了伊登河。

▶ Just swim with the tide and vote for the proposal.
就順應潮流投票支持這提案吧。

▶ Julie will never agree—she always swims against the tide.
茱莉永遠不會同意 —— 她總是不順應潮流。

▶ Harry complained that we left him to sink or swim.
哈利抱怨我們任他自生自滅。

▶ Charlie went for a swim in the ocean in the morning.
查理早上去海裡游泳。

swimsuit [ˈswɪmsut] *n.* 游泳衣

▶ Gordon lost weight, so he had to buy a new swimsuit.
戈登變瘦了，所以他得買件新泳衣。

---

surf [sɜf] *vi.* 衝浪 & *vt.* 上網
🅗 surf the Net / net　上網
= surf / browse the internet

▶ I learned how to surf while I was on vacation in Hawaii.
我在夏威夷度假時學會了衝浪。

▶ Nancy spends her free time surfing the Net.
南西的休閒時間都用來上網。

18　seafood [ˈsiˌfud] *n.* 海鮮 (不可數)

衍 sea [si] *n.* 海 (洋) ①

▶ George likes some seafood, such as salmon.
喬治喜歡一些如鮭魚等的海鮮。

19　runner [ˈrʌnɚ] *n.* 跑者

🅗 a drug runner　毒品販子
衍 (1) run [rʌn] *vi.* 跑 ①
　(2) runner-up [ˌrʌnɚˈʌp]
　　n. 第 2 名，亞軍

▶ Andy is an excellent marathon runner.
安迪是位很優秀的馬拉松跑者。

▶ James is playing the role of a drug runner in his latest movie.
詹姆士在他最新的電影裡是扮演一個毒品販子。

---

jog [dʒɑg] *vi.* & *n.* 慢跑
🅗 go jogging　去慢跑
= go for a jog

▶ I go jogging along the riverbank every morning.
我每天早上沿著河岸慢跑。

▶ My uncle goes for a one-hour jog every day.
我叔叔每天慢跑 1 個小時。

20　cloth [klɔθ] *n.* 布 (料) (不可數)；(用於某特定用途的) 布 (可數)

🅗 a piece of cloth　一塊布料
衍 (1) clothes [klo(ð)z]
　　n. 衣服 (恆用複數) ①
　(2) clothe [kloð]
　　vt. 給……衣服穿 (= dress) ③

▶ The tailor used two pieces of silk cloth to make that suit.
裁縫師傅用了 2 塊絲布料做那套西裝。

▶ Clean your glasses with a cloth.
找塊拭布把你的眼鏡擦一擦吧。

---

clothing [ˈkloðɪŋ]
n. 衣服 (集合名詞，不可數)

🅗 (1) an article / item of clothing
　　一件衣服
　= a piece of clothing
　(2) a wolf in sheep's clothing
　　披著羊皮的狼

▶ Everyone needs food, clothing, and shelter.
每個人都需要食物、衣服和棲身之所。

▶ Ken packed only a few articles of clothing and left home.
肯只打包了幾件衣物就離開家了。

▶ Don't trust Marie—she's a wolf in sheep's clothing.
不要相信瑪麗 —— 她是個披著羊皮的狼。

sweater [ˈswɛtɚ] *n.* 毛衣

似 sweat [swɛt] *n.* 汗 & *vi.* 出汗 ③

▶ You'd better put on a sweater because it's getting cold outside.

你最好穿件毛衣，因為外面變冷了。

21　spelling [ˈspɛlɪŋ] *n.* 拼字／寫能力 (不可數)；拼法 (可數)

片 a spelling bee　拼字比賽

衍 spell [spɛl] *vi.* & *vt.* 拼寫 ①

▶ You should pay more attention to your spelling and grammar.

你應該多留意你的拼字及文法。

▶ I can never remember the correct spelling of "conscientious."

我永遠不記得 "conscientious" 這個字的正確拼法。

▶ Connie is taking part in a spelling bee next Monday.

康妮下週一將參加英文拼字比賽。

Unit 38

3801-3804

1 flight [flaɪt] n. 班機

片 (1) a flight attendant 空服員
(2) a flight crew 全體機組人員
(3) a flight deck / path
飛機駕駛艙 / 飛機航線
(4) take flight 逃跑

▶ The flight is scheduled to leave at 1:30 p.m.
這班機預定下午 1 點半起飛。

▶ The flight attendant is so pretty and friendly.
那位空服員人好漂亮又好親切。

▶ The flight crew boarded the plane before the passengers.
機組人員比乘客先登機。

▶ As soon as the security alarm went off, the bank robber took flight.
安全警報一響，銀行劫匪就逃走了。

---

aircraft [ˋɛr͵kræft]
n. 飛機，飛行器 (單複數同形)

似 airline [ˋɛr͵laɪn] n. 航空公司 ③
用法 (1) an aircraft 一架飛機
= an airplane
(2) two aircraft 兩架飛機
= two airplanes

▶ There are three aircraft in the sky.
空中有 3 架飛機。

2 search [sɜtʃ] vt. & vi. & n. 搜尋

片 (1) search A for B 在 A 中找 B
(2) search for... 搜尋 / 尋找……
(3) go in search of...
去搜尋 / 尋找……

▶ Mick searched the living room for his missing keys.
米克在客廳找他遺失的鑰匙。

▶ The police have been searching for the missing child for nearly two weeks.
警方尋找那名失蹤兒童已經將近 2 星期了。

▶ Sean went in search of a good doctor to treat his father's illness.
尚恩到處去尋找能治療父親疾病的良醫。

---

seek [sik] vt. 尋找；設法
三 seek, sought [sɔt] , sought
片 seek to V 設法做……

▶ The government is seeking new ways to fight against crime.
= The government is looking for new ways to fight against crime.
政府正在尋找新的方法來打擊犯罪。

▶ Many countries are seeking to stop global warming.
很多國家正在設法阻止全球暖化。

chase [tʃes]

vt. & vi. 追趕；追求 (女孩子) & *n.* 追逐

片 chase (after) sb
追趕某人；追求某人

似 pursue [pəˈsu] *vt.* 追趕；追求 ④

▶ The cat chased the mouse around the room.
= The cat ran after the mouse around the room.
貓把老鼠追得滿房間跑。

▶ I saw two policemen chasing after a man on my way home.
我回家路上看到 2 個警察在追 1 個人。

▶ John wasted a lot of time chasing (after) girls.
約翰浪費很多時間在追求女孩子。

▶ Have you heard the news about a high-speed car chase in that area?
你有聽到那個地區有飛車追逐的新聞嗎？

---

3 **emotion** [ɪˈmoʃən] *n.* 情感，感性 (不可數)；情緒 (喜、怒、哀、樂等) (可數)

片 with emotion
感情激動地，帶著強烈的情感

衍 emotional [ɪˈmoʃənḷ]
a. 感情激動的；情緒的 ③

似 (1) passion [ˈpæʃən] *n.* 熱情 ③
(2) feelings [ˈfilɪŋz] *n.* 感情

▶ Sue read the poem with great emotion.
蘇感情非常激動地唸這首詩。

▶ Sarah is a quiet person; she often hides her emotions.
莎拉的話不多，她經常隱藏自己的情緒。

---

4 **playground** [ˈpleˌgraʊnd] *n.* (學校) 操場，(公園) 遊樂場

片 (1) a school playground　學校操場
(2) in a playground
在 (學校) 操場，在 (公園) 遊樂場

▶ Some children are running in the school playground.
有一些孩子正在學校操場上奔跑。

---

swing [swɪŋ]

n. 鞦韆；擺動 & *vi. & vt.* 擺動

三 swing, swung [swʌŋ] , swung

片 (1) play on a swing　盪鞦韆
(2) be in full swing
如火如荼地進行中
(3) get into the swing of things / it
進入狀態，開始積極投入

▶ Some children are playing on the swings in the park.
公園裡有一些小朋友在盪鞦韆。

▶ The anti-corruption movement is now in full swing.
反貪汙運動目前正如火如荼地進行中。
*corruption [kəˈrʌpʃən] *n.* 貪汙，腐敗

▶ Melinda is a newcomer, so she hasn't got into the swing of things yet.
梅琳達是新人，所以她還沒有進入狀態。

▶ I see palm trees swinging in the wind.
我看到棕櫚樹在風中搖曳。

▶ The little boy sat on the chair, swinging his legs and eating some cookies.
小男孩坐在椅子上，擺動著雙腿吃著一些餅乾。

slide [slaɪd] *n.* 溜滑梯 & *vi.* & *vt.*
(使) 滑動 & *vi.* (價錢、數字等) 下跌 / 滑

🔺 slide, slid [slɪd], slid

🔶 (1) go down a slide　玩溜滑梯
　(2) let sth slide
　　　對於某事鬆懈了，放任某事惡化
🔷 (1) landslide [`lænd,slaɪd]
　　　n. 山崩 ⑥
　(2) mudslide [`mʌd,slaɪd] *n.* 土石流

▶ Many kids were lining up to go down the slide.
　許多孩子在排隊要玩溜滑梯。

▶ I see some kids sliding on the ice.
　我看到一些小孩在冰上溜來溜去。

▶ Steve slid the Post-it into my pocket.
　史提夫把那張便利紙塞進了我的口袋。

▶ The New Taiwan dollar slid a little yesterday, but it rose today.
　新臺幣昨天小幅下跌，但今天卻上漲。

▶ Maggie exercised regularly, but it seems that she's let it slide recently.
　瑪姬曾經常運動，但最近她似乎鬆懈了。

---

seesaw [`si,sɔ] *n.* 蹺蹺板
(= teeter-totter [,titɚ`tɑtɚ] 〔美〕)

🔶 play on a seesaw　玩蹺蹺板

▶ Some children are playing on a seesaw.
　有一些小朋友正在玩蹺蹺板。

5　sweep [swip] *vt.* 打掃 & *vi.* 襲捲 & *n.* 打掃

🔺 sweep, swept [swɛpt], swept
🔶 (1) sweep the board　大獲全勝
　(2) sweep across / through + 地方
　　　襲捲某地方
　(3) give + 地方 + a quick sweep
　　　快速打掃某地方
🔷 sweeper [`swipɚ] *n.* 清潔工；清掃機

▶ Sweep the floor before mopping it.
　先掃地板，然後再拖地。

▶ Director Lee's film swept the board at last night's movie awards ceremony.
　李導演的電影在昨晚的電影頒獎典禮上大獲全勝。

▶ A storm swept through the small town last night.
　昨晚暴風雨襲捲了那座小鎮。

▶ Sid gave the living room a quick sweep.
　席德快速打掃了一下客廳。

---

mop [mɑp] *n.* 拖把 & *vt.* 用拖把拖
🔶 mop a floor　拖地板

▶ Use the mop in the corner to clean the floor.
　用角落那支拖把把地板拖乾淨。

▶ The floor is dusty. Can you help me mop it?
　地板有很多灰塵。你可以幫我拖一下嗎？

6　score [skɔr] *n.* 分數；20 個 (左右)；真相 & *vt.* & *vi.* 評分；得分

🔻 score 的意思為『20 個 (左右)』時，
　其單複數同形。
🔶 (1) know the score　知道真相
　　　= know the truth
　(2) score high / low on a test / an exam　考試考高 / 低分

▶ I got a score of ninety-five on the English test.
　這次的英文考試我考了 95 分。

▶ Two score years ago, Stan's parents moved to this city.
　40 年前，史坦的父母搬到了這城市。

▶ Ask Taylor. He knows the score.
　去問泰勒。他知道真相。

> The contest is scored by some experts and teachers.
這項競賽是由一些專家跟老師評分的。

> It is said that Mr. Smith will score the writing tests.
據說史密斯老師會評分寫作的考試。

> The soccer player scored the goal that won the game.
那足球員進球得分而贏了比賽。

> George scored high on the geography test.
喬治的地理考試得了高分。

7　tear [tɪr] *n.* 眼淚 & [tɛr] *n.* 裂縫 & *vt.* & *vi.* (被) 撕開

🔢 tear, tore [tor], torn [torn]

📖 (1) in tears　哭
　　(2) tear... to pieces　把……撕成碎片
　　(3) tear... up　　將 (紙張等) 撕碎
　　(4) tear down...　將 (建築物等) 拆除

> Nancy was in tears while watching the movie.
南希看這部電影時淚流滿面。

> There was a tear in the curtain.
窗簾上有個裂口。

> Toby tore the letter to pieces.
托比將那封信撕成碎片。

> Julia tore the letter up and threw it away.
茱莉亞把這封信撕碎丟掉。

> The company tore down the old building and built a new one.
此公司拆除該舊建物，蓋了一棟新的。

8　painting [ˋpentɪŋ] *n.* 畫畫 (不可數)；畫作 (尤指水彩畫、油畫等) (可數)

📖 an oil / watercolor painting
油畫 / 水彩畫

衍 paint [pent] *vt.* 繪畫 ①

延伸 watercolor [ˋwɑtɚ͵kʌlɚ] *n.* 水彩畫

> Patty enjoys painting more than dancing.
派蒂喜歡畫畫甚於跳舞。

> The oil painting on the wall is beautiful.
牆上的油畫很美。

---

drawing [ˋdrɔɪŋ]
n. 畫畫 (不可數)；素描，圖畫 (可數)

📖 go back to the drawing board
(失敗後) 從頭開始
　　*a drawing board　繪 / 製圖板

衍 draw [drɔ] *vt.* 畫畫 ①

> My sister has a passion for drawing.
我妹妹熱愛畫畫。

> I hung a drawing of the Eiffel Tower on the wall in the living room.
我掛了一幅艾菲爾鐵塔的圖在客廳牆上。

> We have to go back to the drawing board because the previous attempt failed.
我們必須從頭開始，因為前一次的嘗試失敗了。

---

crayon [ˋkreən] *n.* 蠟筆

延伸 pastel [pæsˋtɛl] *n.* 粉蠟筆

> The child is using a few crayons to draw a picture.
這孩子正用幾支蠟筆在畫圖。

9 novel [ˈnɑvl̩] *n.* 小說 & *a.* 新奇的

衍 (1) novelist [ˈnɑvlɪst] *n.* 小說家 ③
　 (2) novelty [ˈnɑvl̩tɪ] *n.* 新奇

似 unusual [ʌnˈjuʒʊəl]
　 a. 與眾不同的；不尋常的

▶ That novel George wrote soon turned out to be a bestseller.
喬治寫的那本小說很快就成了暢銷書。

▶ John came up with a novel idea.
約翰想出了一個很新穎的點子。

10 motorcycle [ˈmotɚˌsaɪkl̩] *n.* 機車（250 c.c. 以上）(= motorbike [ˈmotɚˌbaɪk])

▶ Ken goes to work by motorcycle every day.
肯每天騎機車上班。

scooter [ˈskutɚ]
n. (小型) 機車 (介於 50c.c. 到 250 c.c. 之間)；滑板車

▶ Hank doesn't have a car, but he rides a scooter.
漢克沒有車，但他有騎機車。

▶ Little Lucy loves to ride her scooter on the sidewalk.
小露西喜歡在人行道上騎滑板車。

engine [ˈɛndʒən] *n.* 引擎；火車頭

似 locomotive [ˌlokəˈmotɪv] *n.* 火車頭

▶ My car wouldn't move because there was something wrong with the engine.
我的車動不了，因為引擎有毛病了。

tire [taɪr]
vt. & *vi.* (使) 疲倦 & *n.* 輪胎 (= tyre〔英〕)

片 (1) tire of + N/V-ing　厭倦……
　 (2) have a flat tire　(車子) 爆胎

衍 tiresome [ˈtaɪrsəm] *a.* 令人厭煩的 ⑥

▶ The long walk tired the children.
長時間步行讓孩子們累壞了。

▶ The pop singer soon tired of singing the same songs all day long.
這位流行歌手很快就厭倦了整天唱同樣的歌。

▶ I have a flat tire, and I need to get the car repaired.
我車子爆胎了，我需要將它送修。

11 noodle [ˈnudl̩] *n.* 麵條 (常用複數)

延伸 spaghetti [spəˈgɛtɪ]
　 n. 義大利麵條 (不可數) ③

▶ Molly usually has noodles or rice for lunch.
茉莉午餐通常吃麵或飯。

12 treasure [ˈtrɛʒɚ] *n.* 寶藏 & *vt.* 珍惜

片 a treasure chest　寶箱

▶ The museum has many art treasures.
這間博物館有許多藝術寶藏。

▶ Megan found a treasure chest buried in her garden.
梅根發現有一個寶箱埋在她花園裡。

▶ Troy treasured the books that his grandfather had passed down to him.
特洛依很珍惜那些祖父遺留給他的書。

diamond [ˈdaɪmənd] *n.* 鑽石
延伸 (1) gem [dʒɛm] *n.* 寶石
　　 (2) ruby [ˈrubɪ] *n.* 紅寶石

▶ Some people say that diamonds are a woman's best friend.
有些人說鑽石是女人的最愛。

---

necklace [ˈnɛkləs] *n.* 項鍊
延伸 pendant [ˈpɛndənt] *n.* 有垂飾的項鍊

▶ Mr. Brown gave his wife a necklace on her 45th birthday.
布朗先生在他太太 45 歲生日那天，送給了她一條項鍊。

---

earring [ˈɪrˌrɪŋ] *n.* 耳環
片 a pair of earrings　一副耳環

▶ I bought my girlfriend a pair of earrings on my trip.
我旅途中買了一副耳環給我女友。

---

13 powerful [ˈpaʊɚfəl] *a.* 強壯的；強大的；有權勢的；令人折服的

衍 power [ˈpaʊɚ]
　 n. 力量；權力；電力①

似 strong [strɔŋ] *a.* 強壯的①

反 powerless [ˈpaʊɚləs] *a.* 無力的

▶ Mr. Wu was a powerful man who could lift a motorcycle off the ground.
吳先生孔武有力，能把機車舉離地面。

▶ The powerful storm did a lot of damage to the village.
這場強大的暴風雨對那村莊造成了很大的損害。
*do damage to...　對⋯⋯造成損害

▶ That woman is one of the most powerful people in American politics.
那個女子是美國政壇最有權勢的人之一。

▶ The principal made a powerful speech yesterday morning.
校長昨天早上發表了一場令人折服的演說。

---

14 prove [pruv] *vt.* 證明；(結果) 是

片 (1) prove to sb that...
　　 向某人證明⋯⋯
　 (2) prove to be...　結果證明是⋯⋯
衍 proof [pruf] *n.* 證據③

▶ I will prove to you that what I said was true.
我會向你證明我所說的話是真的。

▶ Wesley proved to be an ideal husband.
結果證明衛斯理是一位理想的老公。

---

15 generous [ˈdʒɛnərəs] *a.* 慷慨的；寬宏大量的

片 (1) be generous to sb
　　 對某人很慷慨
　 (2) It is generous of sb to V
　　 某人很寬宏大量做⋯⋯
衍 generosity [ˌdʒɛnəˈrɑsətɪ] *n.* 慷慨④
反 stingy [ˈstɪndʒɪ] *a.* 吝嗇的④

▶ Paul is not rich, but he is generous to beggars.
保羅不富有，但他仍對乞丐慷慨解囊。

▶ It is generous of Peggy to ignore my careless mistake.
佩姬很寬宏大量，不計較我的無心之過。

16 calm [kɑm] *a.* 鎮定的 & *vt.* & *vi.* (使) 鎮定 & *n.* 平靜

片 (1) stay calm 保持鎮定 / 冷靜
(2) calm (sb) down
使 (某人) 冷靜下來
(3) the calm before the storm
暴風雨前的寧靜

衍 calmness [ˈkɑmnəs] *n.* 平靜

反 (1) nervous [ˈnɝvəs] *a.* 緊張的 ②
(2) stormy [ˈstɔrmɪ] *a.* 狂暴的 ③

▶ Whatever happens, you must stay calm.
無論發生什麼事，你一定要保持鎮定。

▶ The policeman tried to calm the angry crowd.
那名員警試圖要使憤怒的群眾鎮定下來。

▶ Calm down, honey. There's no need to worry.
親愛的，冷靜下來。沒什麼好擔心的。

▶ It's just the calm before the storm. You'd better be prepared.
這只是暴風雨前的寧靜。你最好有心理準備。

17 earthquake [ˈɝθ͵kwek] *n.* 地震 (= quake [kwek])

▶ The great earthquake caused serious damage to the area.
這場大地震造成該區損失慘重。

18 calendar [ˈkæləndɚ] *n.* 日曆

片 a solar / lunar calendar 陽 / 陰曆

▶ Look at the calendar and tell me what day it is today.
看一下日曆告訴我今天星期幾。

▶ The Gregorian calendar is an example of a solar calendar.
格列高里曆是陽曆的一個例子。

weekday [ˈwik͵de] *n.* 平日，工作日

衍 (1) week [wik] *n.* 一星期 ①
(2) weekend [ˈwik͵ɛnd] *n.* 週末 ①
(3) weekly [ˈwiklɪ]
a. 每週一次的 & *adv.* 每週一次地 ③

▶ This store is open from 9 a.m. to 9 p.m. on weekdays.
這家店平日從早上 9 點開到晚上 9 點。

daily [ˈdelɪ]
n. 日報 & *a.* 每日的 & *adv.* 每天

複 dailies [ˈdelɪz]

片 on a daily basis 每天
= every day

▶ *The New York Times* is one of the biggest dailies in the United States.
《紐約時報》是美國最大的日報之一。

▶ You should exercise on a daily basis.
你每天都應運動。

▶ Jill phones her mother daily.
吉兒每天都打電話給她媽媽。

diary [ˈdaɪərɪ] *n.* 日記
複 diaries [ˈdaɪərɪz]

▶ We found a diary in my grandmother's attic.
我們在奶奶的閣樓找到了一本日記。

| 用法 | write a diary (×) |
| → keep a diary (○)　寫日記 |

▶ I started keeping a diary at age 15.
　我 15 歲便開始寫日記。

journal [ˈdʒɝnl̩] *n.* 日誌，日記；期刊

用法 write a journal (×)
→ keep a journal (○)　寫日誌／記

▶ Judy's latest research results were published in this scientific journal.
　茱蒂最新的研究結果刊登在這本科學期刊上。

▶ Cindy kept a journal of her travels in France.
　辛蒂把她在法國的遊歷寫成了日誌。

19　glue [glu] *n.* 膠水 & *vt.* 黏貼

片 (1) glue A to / onto B　把 A 黏到 B 上
　(2) be glued to sth
　　目不轉睛地看某物

▶ Can I borrow your glue to stick this stamp onto the envelope?
　我能借你的膠水把這郵票貼在信封上嗎？

▶ Thomas glued eggshells onto the paper in the art class yesterday.
　昨天上美術課時湯瑪斯把蛋殼黏在紙上。

▶ My son's eyes are glued to the computer screen all day long.
　我兒子的眼睛整天都盯著電腦螢幕看。

---

paste [pest]
vt. (用漿糊) 黏貼 & *n.* 漿糊 (不可數)

衍 toothpaste [ˈtuθ͵pest] *n.* 牙膏
　a tube of toothpaste　一條牙膏

▶ Milly pasted a picture of her favorite singer in her scrapbook.
　蜜莉在剪貼簿上貼了一張她最喜歡的歌手的照片。

▶ I need some paste and a pair of scissors to make a card.
　我需要一些漿糊和一把剪刀來做卡片。

---

stick [stɪk]
vi. & *vt.* 刺，扎；黏住 & *n.* 棍子

三 stick, stuck [stʌk], stuck

片 (1) stick to sth
　　黏住某事物；堅守某事物
　(2) stick together
　　黏在一起；團結一致
　(3) stick around　別走開，留下

衍 sticky [ˈstɪkɪ] *a.* 黏的 ③

▶ The rusty nail stuck in the runner's foot.
　那跑者的腳上扎了一根生鏽的釘子。
　*rusty [ˈrʌstɪ] *a.* 生鏽的

▶ Be careful not to stick the needle in your finger.
　小心不要讓針扎到手指。

▶ The toffee stuck to the roof of Tony's mouth.
　太妃糖黏在湯尼的上顎上。
　*toffee [ˈtɑfɪ] *n.* 太妃糖

▶ The pages of the book stuck together.
　這本書的內頁黏在一起了。

▶ Martin stuck a stamp on the postcard.
　馬丁在明信片上貼了張郵票。

▶ Stick to the rules, or you'll be punished.
　堅守這些規定，否則你會受到懲罰。

▶ Tom and Jerry stuck together in the war.
湯姆與傑利在戰爭當中同甘共苦。

▶ Stick around—some friends are coming for a party soon.
別走開 —— 有些朋友很快就要來開派對了。

▶ The boy played with a stick he found on the ground.
這男孩玩著一支他在地上撿到的棍子。

20　alone [əˋlon] *a.* 單獨的；僅僅，只有 (此意置於名詞之後) & *adv.* 單獨地

片 (1) leave / let sb alone　不要管某人
(2) let alone...
　　更別提說……，更不用說……(用於否定句之後)

衍 lonely [ˋlonlɪ] *a.* 寂寞的 ①

似 (1) along [əˋlɔŋ] *prep.* 沿著 ①
(2) only [ˋonlɪ] *a.* 唯一的 ①
(3) solely [ˋsolɪ] *adv.* 單獨地，唯一地

▶ Andrew was alone at home yesterday.
安德魯昨天一個人在家。

▶ Leave me alone.
別管我。

▶ The service fee alone is 30 dollars.
單單服務費就 30 元了。

▶ Do you like living alone?
你喜歡獨居嗎？

▶ Polly can't sing, let alone dance.
波莉不會唱歌，更別提跳舞了。

---

1 **thirsty** [ˈθɝstɪ] *a.* 口渴的

衍 thirst [θɝst] *n.* 口渴；渴望 ③
thirst after / for sth　渴望某事物

▶ I felt thirsty after jogging for almost two hours.
慢跑了將近 2 小時後我覺得很渴。

---

2 **trust** [trʌst] *vt. & vi. & n.* 信任

片 (1) trust sb with sth
把某物交託給某人

(2) trust in...　　信任……
(3) have trust in...　信任……
(4) mutual trust　　互信
(5) a lack of trust　缺乏信任

衍 trustee [trʌˈsti]
n. (財產) 受託人，託管人 ⑥

似 believe [bəˈliv]
vt. 相信 & *vi.* 信仰 (此意與介詞 in 並
用) ①

▶ If you keep on telling lies, no one will trust you.
如果你繼續撒謊，沒人會相信你。

▶ I would trust Nathan with my life.
我可把我的性命交給納森。

▶ Do you trust in God?
你信任主嗎？

▶ Since Sam has lied to me, I have no trust in him.
因為山姆對我說過謊，我一點也不相信他。

▶ Our relations with this country are based on mutual trust.
我們與這國家的關係是建立在互信的基礎上。
＊relations [rɪˈleʃənz]
n. (人與人之間或團體之間的) 關係 (恆用複數)

▶ It was the lack of trust that broke up Ken and Juliet's marriage.
正是因為缺乏信任而使肯和茱麗葉的婚姻破裂了。

---

3 **neighbor** [ˈnebɚ] *n.* 鄰居

衍 (1) neighborhood [ˈnebɚˌhʊd]
n. 鄰近地區 ③

(2) neighborly [ˈnebɚlɪ] *a.* 親切的

▶ I baked a cake for Lucy and her husband as a neighborly gesture.
我烤了塊蛋糕給露西和她老公，以示友好。
＊gesture [ˈdʒɛstʃɚ] *n.* 表示

▶ I'm lucky that all my neighbors are friendly.
很幸運地，我所有的鄰居都很友善。

---

4 **wild** [waɪld] *a.* 野生的；狂野的 & *n.* 自然 / 野生環境；偏遠地區 (此意恆用複數) & *adv.* 野生地；不受控制地

片 (1) go wild
變得興奮異常不受控制；暴跳如雷

(2) be wild about...　瘋狂喜愛……
＝ be crazy / mad about...

▶ Global warming is threatening the survival of wild animals.
全球暖化正威脅到野生動物的生存。

(3) in the wild　在自然／野生環境中
(4) in the wilds (of + 地方)
　　在某地的偏遠地區
(5) grow wild　野生生長
(6) run wild　(行為等) 不受控制

衍 (1) wilderness [`wɪldə·nəs] n. 荒野 ⑤
(2) wildlife [`waɪld,laɪf]
　　n. 野生動植物 (集合名詞，不可數)
　　⑤

▶ The girl's wild dancing attracted everyone's attention at the party.
這女孩狂野的舞姿引起派對上所有人的注意。

▶ The children went wild when their parents were away.
爸媽不在時，這些小朋友便變得興奮異常不受控制。

▶ When Greg said what he'd done, his dad went wild.
當葛瑞格說出他做了什麼事時，他的父親暴跳如雷。

▶ My grandfather is wild about gardening.
我爺爺很熱衷園藝。

▶ The organization will release the tiger back into the wild tomorrow.
該組織明天會將老虎野放。
＊release [rɪ`lis] vt. 釋放

▶ I'd love to see elephants in the wild.
我很想看到野生的大象。

▶ Gillian now lives in the wilds of Vietnam.
吉莉恩現在住在越南的偏遠地區。

▶ Why did you let these plants grow wild?
你為什麼任由這些植物放任生長？

▶ Rudy always lets his children run wild.
魯迪總是放縱他的孩子。

5　highway [`haɪ,we] n. 公路

片 (1) on a highway　在公路上
(2) a highway patrol　公路巡邏隊

衍 (1) freeway [`frɪ,we] n. 高速公路 ⑥
(2) expressway [ɪk`sprɛs,we]
　　n. 高速公路

▶ You should take the expressway—it's quicker.
你應該走高速公路 —— 那樣會更快。

(3) superhighway [,supə·`haɪ,we]
　　n. (超級) 高速公路

▶ There was a car accident on the highway this morning.
今天上午公路發生了一起車禍。

▶ Bruce was pulled over by the highway patrol.
布魯斯被公路巡邏隊攔住。

---

speed [spid]
n. 速度 & vi. & vt. (使) 快速前行

三 speed, sped [spɛd] / speeded,
sped / speeded

▶ Our car was traveling at high speed.
我們的車子正高速行駛。

▶ The car was traveling at a speed of 90 mph.
這輛車以每小時 90 英里的速度行駛。
＊mph　每小時行駛英里數 (為 miles per hour 的縮寫)

▶ The car sped down the road.
這車沿著馬路疾駛而去。

片 (1) at high / great speed　以高速
(2) at a speed of...　以⋯⋯的速度
(3) speed up　加速

▶ Speed up, or we'll be late.
快一點，否則我們會遲到。

▶ The taxi sped the old lady to the hospital.
計程車載老太太飛速到醫院。

6　fox [fɑks] n. 狐狸

複 foxes [ˈfɑksɪz]

衍 foxy [ˈfɑksɪ] a. 狡猾的（= cunning
[ˈkʌnɪŋ]）；迷人 / 性感的

▶ To our surprise, a foxy woman
entered the bar and said hi to Kevin.
令我們驚訝的是，一個很性感的女人走
進了酒吧，然後跟凱文打招呼。

▶ Foxes are considered very clever and cunning.
狐狸被視為聰明又狡猾。

---

wolf [wʊlf] n. 野狼

複 wolves [wʊlvz]

▶ Have you heard of the story "The Wolf and the
Seven Young Goats"?
你有聽過《大野狼與 7 隻小羊》的故事嗎？

---

giraffe [dʒɪˈræf] n. 長頸鹿

▶ Do you know why the giraffe has a long, black
tongue?
你知道為什麼長頸鹿的舌頭又長又黑嗎？

---

zebra [ˈzibrə] n. 斑馬

▶ Each zebra has its own pattern of stripes.
每一隻斑馬都有自己獨特的條紋。
＊stripe [straɪp] n. 條紋

---

deer [dɪr] n. 鹿

複 deer / deers

衍 reindeer [ˈrɛndɪr]
n. 馴鹿（複數為 reindeer 或 reindeers）

▶ Rudolph is Santa's most famous
reindeer.
魯道夫是聖誕老人最著名的馴鹿。
＊Santa [ˈsæntə] n. 聖誕老人

▶ The hikers saw two deer in the woods.
這些登山客在樹林裡見到兩隻鹿。

---

goat [got] n. 山羊

比 sheep [ʃip] n. 綿羊（單複數同形）

▶ Have you ever eaten goat's cheese?
你有吃過羊起司嗎？

---

hippopotamus [ˌhɪpəˈpɑtəməs]
n. 河馬（= hippo [ˈhɪpo]）

複 hippopotamuses
[ˌhɪpəˈpɑtəməsɪz] / hippos

▶ The hippopotamus is one of the most dangerous
animals in Africa.
河馬是非洲最危險的動物之一。

panda [ˈpændə] *n.* 熊貓

▶ Many people went to the zoo to see the baby panda.
許多人到動物園去看熊貓寶寶。

---

ape [ep] *n.* 人猿 & *vt.* 模仿

似 mimic [ˈmɪmɪk] *vt.* 模仿 ⑥

比 (1) monkey [ˈmʌŋkɪ] *n.* 猴子 ①

(2) chimpanzee [ˌtʃɪmpænˈzi] *n.* 黑猩猩 (比大猩猩小很多) ⑥

(3) gorilla [gəˈrɪlə] *n.* 大猩猩 ⑥

▶ Gorillas are the largest apes.
大猩猩是體型最大的猿類。

▶ John aped the way the teacher talked, and that made us laugh so loudly.
約翰模仿老師講話的樣子，讓我們笑得超大聲的。

---

7 **grape** [grep] *n.* 葡萄

衍 grapefruit [ˈgrepˌfrut] *n.* 葡萄柚 ⑥

延伸 wine [waɪn] *n.* 葡萄酒 ②

▶ This kind of wine is made from special grapes.
這種酒是用特別的葡萄製成的。

---

strawberry [ˈstrɔˌbɛrɪ] *n.* 草莓

複 strawberries [ˈstrɔˌbɛrɪz]

衍 (1) berry [ˈbɛrɪ] *n.* 莓果，漿果 ③

(2) blueberry [ˈbluˌbɛrɪ] *n.* 藍莓

(3) blackberry [ˈblækˌbɛrɪ] *n.* 黑莓

(4) cranberry [ˈkrænˌbɛrɪ] *n.* 蔓越莓，小紅莓

(5) mulberry [ˈmʌlˌbɛrɪ] *n.* 桑椹

(6) raspberry [ˈræzˌbɛrɪ] *n.* 覆盆子

▶ Strawberries are in season now.
草莓現在正值產季。
＊be in season　正值產季

---

papaya [pəˈpaɪə] *n.* 木瓜

用法 a papaya　一條木瓜
a slice / piece of papaya　一片木瓜

▶ It is said that eating papayas can help cure some minor health problems.
據說吃木瓜可以幫忙治療一些輕微的身體不適。

---

peach [pitʃ] *n.* 桃子

複 peaches [ˈpitʃɪz]

▶ The peach is sweet and juicy.
這桃子又甜又多汁。
＊juicy [ˈdʒusɪ] *a.* 多汁的

---

pear [pɛr] *n.* 梨

▶ Can you tell the difference between a pear and an avocado?
你可以分辨梨與酪梨的不同嗎？
＊avocado [ˌævəˈkɑdo] *n.* 酪梨

---

guava [ˈgwavə] *n.* 芭樂，番石榴

▶ My grandfather prefers red guavas to regular ones.
我爺爺喜歡紅芭樂甚於一般的芭樂。

mango [ˈmæŋgo] *n.* 芒果
複 mangos / mangoes [ˈmæŋgoz]

▶ Are mangos in season this time of year?
芒果現在是盛產季嗎？

watermelon [ˈwɑtɚˌmɛlən]
n. 西瓜
衍 melon [ˈmɛlən] *n.* 甜瓜 ③

▶ Watermelons can be red or yellow inside, and both are very juicy.
西瓜裡面可能是紅的或黃的，兩種都很多汁。

---

8 dancer [ˈdænsɚ] *n.* 舞者

衍 dance [dæns]
vi. & vt. 跳 (舞) & *n.* 跳舞；舞蹈，舞步；舞曲 ①

▶ Wendy takes dancing classes every day and wants to be a dancer.
溫蒂每天上跳舞課，她想成為一名舞者。

step [stɛp] *vi.* 跨步，踩，踏 &
n. 步 (伐)；步驟；措施；舞步

三 step, stepped [stɛpt], stepped

用 (1) step into... 步入……
(2) watch / mind one's step
小心某人的腳步
(3) step by step 逐步地
(4) take a step 採取措施 / 行動
(5) be out of step
舞步不協調，步伐錯亂

▶ Everyone quieted down when the teacher stepped into the classroom.
老師步入教室時，每個人都安靜了下來。

▶ Watch your step. The floor is wet.
小心你的腳步。地板是溼的。

▶ Can you show me how to do it step by step?
你可以逐步教我要怎麼做嗎？

▶ The problem will get worse if you don't take steps to deal with it.
如果你不採取行動處理的話，問題會變得更嚴重。

▶ My wife's a good dancer, but I'm always out of step.
我太太很會跳舞，但我的舞步總是不協調。

---

9 ink [ɪŋk] *n.* 墨水 (不可數) & *vt.* 簽訂 / 署 〔美〕

用法 write... with ink (×)
→ write... in ink (○) 用墨水寫……

▶ Write your name in blue ink.
用藍墨水寫下你的名字。

▶ We have inked a new deal with that international company.
我們已與那家國際公司簽訂了新協議。

---

10 policeman [pəˈlismən] *n.* 男警察 (= cop [kɑp])

複 policemen [pəˈlismən]
衍 police [pəˈlis] *n.* 警方 (集合名詞) ①
反 policewoman [pəˈlisˌwʊmən]
n. 女警 (複數為 policewomen
[pəˈlisˌwɪmən])

▶ A policeman asked me to pull over.
有個警察要我把車靠邊停。

11 hunt [hʌnt] *vt. & vi. & n.* 打獵；尋找

片 (1) go on a hunt　打獵
(2) hunt for...　尋找……
(3) a hunt for...　尋找……

衍 hunting [ˋhʌntɪŋ] *n.* 打獵

似 search [sɝtʃ] *vt. & vi. & n.* 尋找 ②

▶ Mike hunted a goat and a deer yesterday.
麥可昨天獵了一頭山羊和一頭鹿。

▶ Have you ever hunted before?
你之前有打獵過嗎？

▶ Ron didn't like the idea of going on a hunt.
榮恩不喜歡打獵。

▶ The police hunted the bank robber throughout the city.
警察在全市搜捕那銀行搶匪。
*robber [ˋrɑbɚ] *n.* 搶匪

▶ Tom has been hunting for a good job since last June.
自去年 6 月開始，湯姆就一直在找一份好工作。

▶ The hunt for the missing child was not successful.
尋找這名失蹤孩童的行動並未成功。

hunter [ˋhʌntɚ] *n.* 獵人

▶ Primitive man had to be a good hunter to survive.
原始人必須是個打獵高手才能存活下來。
*primitive [ˋprɪmətɪv] *a.* 原始的

12 bake [bek] *vt.* 烘焙

片 a bake sale　烘焙義賣活動

衍 baker [ˋbekɚ] *n.* 麵包 / 糕點師

▶ My mother is baking a birthday cake for me.
我媽媽正在為我烤生日蛋糕。

▶ Our school is having a bake sale tomorrow.
我們學校明天有烘焙義賣活動。

bakery [ˋbekərɪ]
n. 麵包店 (= bakeshop)

複 bakeries [ˋbekərɪz]

▶ I bought an apple pie at the bakery.
我在這間麵包店買了蘋果派。

bun [bʌn] *n.* 小圓麵包 (可數)

片 a hamburger bun　做漢堡用的麵包

似 bin [bɪn] *n.* 垃圾箱 〔英〕④

▶ We need to buy a dozen hamburger buns.
我們需要買一打做漢堡用的麵包。

jam [dʒæm] *n.* 果醬；交通堵塞；困境
& vt. & vi. (使) 塞滿

三 jam, jammed [dʒæmd], jammed

片 (1) a traffic jam　塞車
be stuck in a traffic jam
遇到塞車

▶ I prefer to have jam, rather than butter, on my toast.
我比較喜歡抹果醬在烤麵包片上，而不是抹奶油。

▶ I was late because I was stuck in a traffic jam.
我因為遇到塞車所以遲到了。

▶ Ray's in a jam, and he needs my help.
雷有困難，他需要我幫忙。

(2) be in a jam 遇到困難

▶ The shopping mall was jammed with hundreds of people.
這大購物中心擠滿了數百人。

▶ Hundreds of people jammed into the department store.
數百人湧入這家百貨公司。

---

13 barbecue [ˋbɑrbɪkju] *n.* 烤肉聚會 (可數) ; 烤肉架 (可數) ; 烤出來的食物 (不可數) & *vt.* 烤 (肉等) (縮寫為 BBQ [ˋbɑrbɪkju])

H have a barbecue
烤肉，有個烤肉聚會

▶ We had a barbecue on the beach last Sunday.
上星期天我們在海邊烤肉。

▶ Brandon put another sausage on the barbecue.
布蘭登再放一條香腸到烤肉架上。

▶ This restaurant serves delicious barbecue.
這家餐廳供應美味的燒烤食物。

▶ We barbecued corn and bell peppers.
我們烤了玉米和甜椒。
＊pepper [ˋpɛpɚ]
n. 甜椒 (＝ bell pepper) (可數) ; 胡椒粉 (不可數)

---

steak [stek] *n.* 牛排

▶ The waitress asked Ralph, "How would you like your steak done?"
女服務生問雷夫：『你的牛排要幾分熟？』

▶ I'd like my steak well done / medium / rare.
我的牛排要全熟 / 5 分熟 / 1 分熟。

---

pork [pɔrk] *n.* 豬肉 (不可數)

▶ Muslims don't eat pork. So don't recommend this dish to Lena.
回教徒不吃豬肉。所以不要推薦這道菜給莉娜。
＊recommend [͵rɛkəˋmɛnd] *vt.* 推薦

---

lamb [læm]
n. 小 / 羔羊 (可數) ; 羔羊肉 (不可數) & *vi.* 生小羊

H (1) a lamb chop 小羊排
(2) like a lamb to the slaughter
如同待宰羔羊

比 mutton [ˋmʌtn̩] *n.* 羊肉 (不可數)

▶ The lamb was lost and cried for its mother.
小羊迷路了，哭著找媽媽。

▶ The restaurant is famous for its lamb chops.
這家餐廳的小羊排很有名。

▶ When Ron was on the operating table, he felt he was like a lamb to the slaughter.
榮恩在手術臺上時，他認為自己像一隻待宰的羔羊。

▶ Those sheep will be lambing soon.
這些羊很快就要生小羊了。

▶ Betsy loves to eat mutton with mint sauce.

貝琪喜歡沾薄荷醬來吃羊肉。

＊mint [mɪnt] n. 薄荷

用法 lamb 的 b 不發音

---

14 forest [ˈfɔrɪst] n. 森林

片 (1) a forest fire　森林火災
(2) a rain forest　雨林
= a rainforest

▶ Thankfully, the forest fire has been brought under control.

謝天謝地，森林火災已受到控制。

▶ This rain forest is home to billions of creatures.

這片雨林是很多生物的家園。

＊creature [ˈkritʃɚ] n. 生物

---

wood [wʊd]

n. 木頭 (不可數)；樹林，森林

(= woods)

片 in the wood / woods　在樹 / 森林裡

衍 (1) wooden [ˈwʊdn̩]
　　a. 木製的；呆板的 ②
(2) woody [ˈwʊdɪ] a. 很多樹木的

▶ This area of the countryside is quite woody.

這鄉村的這個區域有很多樹木。

▶ The desk is made of hard wood.

這張書桌是硬木製的。

▶ Several hikers got lost in the woods.

有幾名健行的人在這森林裡迷路了。

---

15 comb [kom] n. 梳子 & vt. 梳髮

延伸 hairpin [ˈhɛrˌpɪn] n. 髮夾

▶ George always carries a comb in his pocket.

喬治總是會在口袋裡放把梳子。

▶ Did you not have time to comb your hair?

你沒時間梳頭髮嗎？

---

16 hurry [ˈhɝɪ] vt. 催促 & vi. & n. 匆忙

三 hurry, hurried [ˈhɝɪd], hurried

片 (1) hurry up　快一點
(2) in a hurry / rush　匆忙
= in haste
(3) be in a hurry to V
　　匆匆忙忙地做……

▶ The father hurried his son to finish his homework.

那位父親催促他兒子把作業寫完。

▶ You'll need to hurry if you want to catch the train.

你如果想趕上火車就必須快一點。

似 (1) rush [rʌʃ]
   n. 衝 & *vi.* & *vt.* 衝；匆促行動 ③

(2) hasten [ˈhesn̩]
   vt. 催促 & *vi.* 急忙，趕快 ④

(3) haste [hest] *n.* 匆忙，急促 ④

▸ Hurry up, or you'll miss the bus.
  快一點，不然你會趕不上公車的。

▸ You're likely to make mistakes if you do things in such a hurry.

= You're likely to make mistakes if you do things in such a rush.

= You're likely to make mistakes if you do things in such haste.
  做事如果這麼匆促，是很可能會出錯的。

▸ Emily should not be in a hurry to get married.
  艾蜜莉不應該倉促成婚。

4001-4005

---

1 wing [wɪŋ] *n.* 翅膀；側廳；派系 & *vt.* 即興做……

片 (1) take wing　飛走
(2) take A under B's wing
　B 對 A 呵護有加
(3) be on the right / left wing of...
　屬於……的右 / 左派
(4) wing it　即興發揮 / 行事

衍 winged [wɪŋd] *a.* 有翅膀的

▶ I like to eat chicken wings.
　我喜歡吃雞翅膀。

▶ The bird took wing before the hunter shot.
　獵人開槍前，那隻鳥早飛走了。

▶ The editor took Bonnie under his wing and taught her how to edit a book.
　編輯對邦妮呵護有加，還教她如何編輯一本書。

▶ Our office is in the east wing of the building.
　我們的辦公室位於這棟大樓東邊的側廳。

▶ Bruce is on the left wing of this political party.
　布魯斯屬於這政黨的左派。

▶ The manager suddenly asked me to make a short speech in the meeting this afternoon. I guess I'll have to wing it, then.
　經理突然要我在下午的會議上做個簡短的演說。看來到時我只好即興發揮了。

---

2 combine [kəmˋbaɪn] *vt.* & *vi.* (使) 結合 & [ˋkɑm͵baɪn] *n.* 聯盟；聯合收割機
(= combine harvester)

片 (1) combine A with B
　將 A 與 B 結合
(2) combine against...
　聯合對抗……

▶ Maybe we should combine the plan with Jeff's idea.
　也許我們應該將這計畫與傑夫的想法結合起來。

▶ The three tribes combined against the invaders.
　這 3 個部落聯合起來對抗入侵者。

▶ Those media companies have formed a combine.
　這些媒體公司組成了一個聯盟。

▶ With the help of the combine, harvesting became more efficient.
　在聯合收割機的幫助下，收割作物變得更有效率。

---

mix [mɪks] *vt.* & *vi.* (使) 混合 & *vi.* 打交道，結交 & *n.* 混合

片 (1) mix A with B　將 A 與 B 混合
(2) mix with sb
　和某人打交道，和某人結交
(3) a mix of A and B　混合 A 和 B

▶ Mix the flour with more water to make a soft dough.
　把麵粉混合更多的水，這樣就可做出柔軟的麵團了。
　*dough [do] *n.* 生麵團

▶ After you add oil and sugar into the bowl, make sure you mix well.
　在碗中加入油和糖之後，一定要攪拌均勻。

▶ Becky is always friendly. No wonder she can mix well with everyone.
　貝琪總是很友善。難怪她能和大家打成一片。

> Chuck thinks life is a mix of misery and sadness.
查克認為人生是摻雜了痛苦與悲傷。
*misery [ˈmɪzərɪ] *n.* 痛苦

mixture [ˈmɪkstʃɚ] *n.* 混和；混和物
片 a mixture of A and B 混合 A 和 B

> Taipei city is a mixture of the old and the new.
臺北是一個新舊混雜的城市。

> After you stir the mixture, pour it into a pan and fry until it turns golden brown.
攪拌混合物後，將其倒入平底鍋中煎至金黃色。

3　deaf [dɛf] *a.* 耳聾的，失聰的；充耳不聞的

片 turn a deaf ear to...
　　對……充耳不聞
衍 deafness [ˈdɛfnəs] *n.* 聾

> Although Beethoven became deaf later in his life, he still wrote great music.
儘管貝多芬晚年失聰，但他仍創作出偉大的音樂作品。

> The protestors turned a deaf ear to the policemen's warning.
抗議者對警察的警告充耳不聞。

4　gentle [ˈdʒɛntl̩] *a.* 溫柔的；柔和的

似 (1) soft [sɔft] *a.* 柔軟的；輕柔的 ②
　　(2) tender [ˈtɛndɚ] *a.* 溫柔的 ③
　　(3) mild [maɪld] *a.* 溫和的 ④
反 rough [rʌf] *a.* 粗糙的；粗暴的 ③

> We told the child to be gentle while playing with the kitten.
我們告訴孩子和小貓玩時要溫柔一點。

> Connie's singing voice is like a gentle breeze.
康妮的歌聲就像一陣柔和的微風。

gentleman [ˈdʒɛntl̩mən]
n. 紳士，彬彬有禮的人；(對人禮貌的稱呼) 先生

複 gentlemen [ˈdʒɛntl̩mən]

> A gentleman never forgets his table manners.
紳士決不會忘記他的餐桌禮儀。
*table manners　餐桌禮儀 (恆用複數)

> Evan, show this gentleman to the meeting room.
伊凡，帶這位先生到會議室去。

lady [ˈledɪ] *n.* 淑女，女士
複 ladies [ˈledɪz]
片 (1) a ladies' room　女用洗手間
　　(2) a first lady　第一夫人

> That lady over there is my mother.
那邊那位女士是我媽媽。

> Dorothy has just gone to the ladies' room.
桃樂西剛剛去了洗手間。

> The president and first lady are going to visit the UK next week.
總統和第一夫人下週將造訪英國。

5　nephew [ˈnɛfju] *n.* 姪兒；外甥

> My sister's son is my nephew.
我姊姊的兒子是我的外甥。

niece [nis] *n.* 姪女；外甥女

▶ My little niece is only five years old.
我的小姪女只有 5 歲。

6 mug [mʌg] *n.* 馬克杯，大杯子

▶ Please give us two mugs of cocoa.
請給我們 2 大杯熱可可。

7 pumpkin [ˈpʌmpkɪn] *n.* 南瓜

▶ Pumpkins can be used to make jack-o'-lanterns for Halloween.
南瓜可以用來做萬聖節的南瓜燈。
*jack-o'-lantern [ˌdʒækəˈlæntɚn] *n.* 南瓜燈

yam [jæm]
n. 番薯（＝ sweet potato）〔美〕；山藥

▶ You can get a bowl of yam porridge for NT$15.
你可以用新臺幣 15 元買到一碗番薯稀飯。
*porridge [ˈpɔrɪdʒ] *n.* 麥片粥

▶ Inside a yam, it may be white, yellow, pink, or purple.
山藥裡面的顏色有可能是白、黃、粉紅或紫色。

corn [kɔrn] *n.* 玉米（不可數）

▶ At the barbecue, we ate meat, corn, and salad.
在烤肉聚會上，我們吃了肉、玉米和沙拉。

cabbage [ˈkæbɪdʒ]
n. 高麗菜；植物人（貶義）〔英〕

🈂 Chinese cabbage　大白菜
＝ bok choy [ˈbɑkˈtʃɔɪ]

🈁 (1) vegetable [ˈvɛdʒətəbl̩]
　　n. 植物人（貶義）；蔬菜 ①
　(2) a persistent vegetative state
　　持續性植物狀態，（俗稱）植物人（縮寫為 PVS）
　*persistent [pɚˈsɪstənt] *a.* 持續的
　vegetative [ˈvɛdʒəˌtetɪv] *a.* 植物人的

▶ Mother grows some cabbages in the garden.
媽媽在菜園裡種了些高麗菜。

▶ Cindy is cooking some Chinese cabbage.
辛蒂正在煮一些大白菜。

▶ It is not acceptable to call someone who suffers from PVS a "cabbage."
把患有持續性植物狀態的人叫成『植物人』是不可被接受的。

garlic [ˈɡɑrlɪk] *n.* 蒜頭（不可數）
🈂 garlic bread　大蒜麵包

▶ Garlic is often used in Taiwanese dishes.
臺菜經常會用到大蒜。

▶ Maria loves eating garlic bread with ham.
瑪麗亞喜歡吃有火腿的大蒜麵包。

nut [nʌt] *n.* 堅果；螺帽；瘋子，怪人
🈂 a betel [ˈbitl̩] nut　檳榔

▶ Dad likes to eat nuts when watching TV.
老爸看電視的時候喜歡吃堅果。

衍 nuts [nʌts] *a.* 發瘋的，愚蠢的
　go nuts　氣瘋，大發雷霆
= go crazy / bananas
▶ Frank went nuts when his girlfriend decided to leave him.
法蘭克的女友決定離他而去時，法蘭克氣瘋了。

延伸 (1) walnut [ˋwɔlnət] *n.* 胡桃 ⑥
(2) cashew [ˋkæʃu]
　　n. 腰果（= cashew nut）

▶ Chewing betel nuts can be bad for your health.
嚼檳榔對健康有害。
▶ A nut on the wheel came loose. Would you help me tighten it?
車輪的一顆螺帽鬆掉了。你可以幫我把它鎖緊嗎？
▶ Tim is a nut; you should be wary of him.
提姆是個怪人，你要小心提防他。
＊wary [ˋwɛrɪ] *a.* 小心的
　be wary of...　小心提防⋯⋯

8　soybean [ˋsɔɪ͵bin] *n.* 大豆〔美〕（= soya bean [ˋsɔɪə͵bin]〔英〕）

延伸 (1) soy sauce　醬油〔美〕
= soya sauce〔英〕
(2) soy milk　豆漿〔美〕
= soya milk〔英〕

▶ Soybeans are used to make a wide variety of products, such as tofu.
大豆被用來製成各式各樣的產品，例如豆腐。

tofu [ˋtofu]
n. 豆腐（= bean curd [kɝd]）

▶ Tofu is a very healthy source of protein.
豆腐是非常健康的蛋白質來源。

9　mood [mud] *n.* 心情

片 (1) be in the mood to V　有意做⋯⋯
= be in the mood for sth
(2) be in a good / high mood
　　心情很好
　　be in bad / low spirits　心情不好

衍 moody [ˋmudɪ]
a. 喜怒無常的，心情不穩的 ⑥

▶ I'm not in the mood to go to the movies with you. Just leave me alone.
我沒有心情跟你去看電影。不管我就行了。
▶ Don't talk to Eric—he's in a bad mood.
不要和艾瑞克說話 —— 他心情不好。

10　skin [skɪn] *n.* 皮膚

片 (1) be / get soaked to the skin
　　溼透
= be / get wet to the skin
(2) have (a) thin / thick skin
　　臉皮很薄 / 厚

▶ Polly has such beautiful olive skin.
波莉擁有如此美麗的橄欖色肌膚。
▶ Because of the sudden heavy rain, Rebecca got soaked to the skin.
因為突如其來的大雨，蕾貝嘉渾身都溼透了。
▶ Be careful what you say—Willy has a very thin skin.
小心你說的話 —— 威利的臉皮很薄。

tissue [ˋtɪʃu]
n. 面紙（可數）；（動植物的）組織（不可數）

▶ Can you give me a tissue? I need to blow my nose.
可以跟你拿張衛生紙嗎？我要擤鼻涕。
＊blow one's nose　擤鼻涕

Level 2　Unit 40

🈳 toilet tissue　衛生紙 (不可數)
= toilet paper
　a roll of toilet tissue / paper
　一卷衛生紙
　a piece of toilet tissue / paper
　一張衛生紙

▶ The scientist took some leaf tissue from the plant for further examination.
科學家擷取了該植物的一些葉片組織以供進一步檢驗。

11　seem [sim] vi. 似乎，看起來

🈳 (1) seem + adj. / N　似乎……
　(2) seem like sb/sth
　　看起來是某人 / 某事物
　(3) seem to V　　似乎做……
　(4) It seems that...　似乎……
🈳 appear [əˋpɪr] vi. 似乎 ①

▶ Mother seems angry. Don't you think?
媽媽好像很生氣。你不覺得嗎？

▶ Your uncle seems (like) a nice guy.
你的舅舅看起來是個好人。

▶ Nobody seemed to know the truth.
似乎沒有人知道事實真相。

▶ It seems that Dana won't go to the party.
看來黛娜不會去參加派對了。

12　mention [ˋmɛnʃən] vt. & n. 提及

🈳 (1) mention A to B　向 B 提到 A
　(2) mention that...　提到……
　(3) not to mention sth
　　更不用說某事物
　= not to mention the fact that...
　= to say nothing of...
　= not to speak of...
　(4) make no mention of sth
　　未提及某事物

▶ We have mentioned the idea to the boss.
我們有向老闆提過這個想法了。

▶ Alex mentioned that he is going to France next week.
艾力克斯提到他下週要去法國。

▶ Daphne is good at playing the guitar and the violin, not to mention the piano.
達芙妮擅長演奏吉他和小提琴，鋼琴就更不用說了。

▶ The hotel is in a poor location, not to mention the fact that it's too expensive.
這飯店位置不好，更不用說太貴了。

▶ In public, the pop singer made no mention of his private life.
公眾場合上，那位流行歌手不會提到他的私生活。

13　dryer [ˋdraɪɚ] n. 烘乾機，吹風機 (= drier)

🈳 a hair dryer　吹風機
= a hairdryer
🈳 dry [draɪ] a. 乾燥的；枯燥無味的 & vt. & vi. (使) 乾燥 ①

▶ Now that we have a dryer, we don't have to worry about rainy days anymore.
我們既然有了烘乾機，就不用再擔心下雨天了。

▶ Do you know where the hair dryer is?
你知道吹風機在哪裡嗎？

14 **internet** [ˈɪntɚˌnɛt] *n.* 網路（範圍是全世界）（字首可大寫）

团 surf the internet / Internet　上網
= surf the net / Net

▶ Ricky was surfing the internet instead of doing homework.
瑞奇正在上網，而不是在寫作業。

---

network [ˈnɛtˌwɝk]
n. 網狀系統；電腦網路（範圍較 internet 小）& *vt.* 使（電腦）連上（數個電腦的）網路 & *vi.* 建立人脈

团 network with sb　和某人打交道

衍 net [nɛt] *n.* 網（狀物）①

似 system [ˈsɪstəm] *n.* 系統②

▶ Traveling by train is fast and comfortable in this country because of its efficient rail network.
因為這國家的鐵路網很有效率，坐火車旅遊既快速又舒適。

▶ Robert will connect your computer to the network.
羅伯特會把你的電腦連接上網路。
＊connect [kəˈnɛkt] *vt.* & *vi.* （使）連接
　connect A to B　把 A 連接到 B

▶ Ask Stephen whether he has networked the computers to the server.
問史蒂芬他有沒有把電腦連接到伺服器了。

▶ Annie attends those events to network with lots of different people.
安妮參加那些活動是為了和許多不同的人來打交道。

---

screen [skrin]
n. 螢幕；屏風，隔板 & *vt.* 篩選

团 a screen door　紗門

▶ The words on the screen are too small. Can you enlarge them a little bit?
螢幕的字太小了。你能不能稍微放大一點？

▶ Nurse Mandy pulled a screen around the hospital bed.
曼蒂護士在病床周圍拉起了屏風。

▶ Don't forget to close the screen door!
別忘了關上紗門！

▶ The club strictly screens all their candidates.
那家俱樂部嚴格篩選所有的申請人。
＊candidate [ˈkændədet] *n.* 申請人，候選人

---

15 **load** [lod] *n.* 負載量 & *vt.* & *vi.* 裝載

团 load A with B　用 B 裝滿 A
= A be loaded with B

衍 (1) overload [ˌovɚˈlod]
　　 vt. 使超過負荷 & [ˈovɚˌlod]
　　 n. 超過負荷

　　 (2) workload [ˈwɝkˌlod] *n.* 工作量

▶ I had a heavy workload this month.
這個月我的工作量很重。

▶ The truck's load was over the limit allowed on the bridge.
這輛卡車的負載量超出橋的載重限制。

▶ The van is loaded with groceries.
這臺小貨車載滿了食品雜貨。
＊groceries [ˈgrosɚɪz] *n.* 食品雜貨（恆用複數）

▶ We haven't finished loading. It might take a while.
我們還沒完成裝貨。可能會需要花一點時間。

Level 2

Unit 40

upload [ʌpˋlod] *vt.* (電腦) 上傳

► It takes a while to upload these images to my blog.
把這些圖片上傳到我的部落格要花一點時間。

download [ˋdaʊnˌlod]
vt. (電腦) 下載

► First, download these files and save them on the hard disk.
首先，下載這些檔案並將它們存在硬碟裡。

---

16 print [prɪnt] *n.* 印刷；痕跡 (指腳印或指紋等) & *vt.* & *vi.* 印刷；用印刷體書寫 & *vt.* (用電腦) 列印

片 (1) be in print　仍在印行 / 出版
　= be published
　(2) be out of print　停印，絕版
　(3) print... out
　　(用電腦) 把……列印出來

似 (1) footprint [ˋfʊtˌprɪnt] *n.* 腳印
　(2) fingerprint [ˋfɪŋɡɚˌprɪnt]
　　n. 指紋

► Dora's latest novel will soon be in print.
朵拉最新的小說很快就要出版了。

► The book is now out of print.
這本書現在絕版了。

► The officer found the suspect's prints on a mug at the crime scene.
警官在犯罪現場的一個馬克杯上發現了嫌疑犯的指紋。

► The magazine prints more than 100,000 copies every month.
該雜誌每月印行超過 10 萬份。

► The document is printing right now.
正在印那份文件。

► Print your name at the bottom of the paper.
請在文件下方用印刷體簽名。

► Do not sign your name; please print in block letters.
不要簽你的名字；請書寫正體大寫字母。
＊block letters　正體大寫字母 (恆用複數)

► Could you help me print this out?
你可以幫我把這列印出來嗎？

printer [ˋprɪntɚ] *n.* 印表機

衍 (1) printery [ˋprɪntərɪ] *n.* 印刷工廠
　(2) printing [ˋprɪntɪŋ]
　　n. 印刷 (不可數)

► Would you please add paper to the printer?
可以麻煩你幫印表機加紙嗎？

---

17 hero [ˋhɪro] *n.* 英雄；男主角；偶像

衍 heroic [hɪˋroɪk] *a.* 英勇的；壯烈的 ⑥
似 idol [ˋaɪdḷ] *n.* 偶像 ④
反 heroine [ˋhɛroˌɪn]
　n. 女英雄；女主角；(女) 偶像 ②

► The old man was a war hero.
這位老伯曾是一名戰地英雄。

► The hero of the story finally marries the princess.
小說中的男主角終於與公主結婚了。

► This actor has been my hero since I was little.
打從我小時候開始，這演員就一直是我的偶像。

18 safety [ˈseftɪ] n. 安全

片	for safety's sake　為了安全起見
衍	safe [sef] a. 安全的 ①
似	security [sɪˈkjʊrətɪ] n. 安全 ③
反	danger [ˈdendʒɚ] n. 危險 ②

▶ For safety's sake, children should avoid going out alone at night.
為了安全起見，小孩子應避免晚上獨自外出。

19 café [kæˈfe] n. 咖啡店／館 (= cafe)

| 似 | a coffee shop　咖啡店 |

▶ I had a good time chatting with my friend Dan at the café around the corner.
我和我的朋友丹在街角那家咖啡廳聊得很開心。

snack [snæk]
n. 點心，零食 & vi. 吃點心

| 延伸 | refreshments [rɪˈfrɛʃmənts] n. (會議或宴會時所供應的) 茶點 (恆用複數) ⑥ |

▶ After class, we ate some snacks.
下課後我們吃了一些點心。

▶ Jamie cannot snack between meals because she's on a diet.
潔咪不能在餐與餐之間吃點心，因為她在節食。

biscuit [ˈbɪskɪt]
n. 甜餅乾〔英〕(= cookie [ˈkʊkɪ]〔美〕)；比司吉 (麵包)〔美〕

| 延伸 | cracker [ˈkrækɚ] n. (常配起司一起吃的) 薄脆餅乾 ⑥ |

▶ My grandma made wonderful biscuits.
我祖母做的甜餅乾很好吃。

▶ Biscuits and gravy is a popular dish in the southern US.
比司吉佐肉汁是美國南部一道很受歡迎的菜餚。

cocoa [ˈkoko]
n. 可可粉 (= cocoa powder)；可可飲料

| 似 | chocolate [ˈtʃɑklət] n. 巧克力 ① |

▶ Add two teaspoons of cocoa to the cake mixture.
在蛋糕糊中加入 2 茶匙可可粉。

▶ Please give me a mug of hot cocoa.
請給我一杯熱可可。

20 salty [ˈsɔltɪ] a. 鹹的

衍	salt [sɔlt] n. 鹽 ①
延伸	(1) sweet [swit] a. 甜的 ①
	(2) hot [hɑt] a. 辣的 ①
	(3) spicy [ˈspaɪsɪ] a. 辛辣的；加很多香料的 ⑤
	(4) sour [saʊr] a. 酸的 ②

▶ The soup is too salty to eat.
湯太鹹了，沒辦法喝。

21 beg [bɛg] vi. & vt. 懇求；行乞

| 三 | beg, begged [bɛgd], begged |
| 片 | (1) beg for sth　懇求某事物；乞討某物 |

▶ Sam got down on his knees and begged for forgiveness.
山姆跪下來請求原諒。

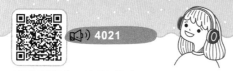

(2) beg sb to V　懇求某人做……

(3) beg sth from sb　向某人乞討某物

衍 beggar [ˋbɛgɚ] *n.* 乞丐 ④

▶ The thief begged me to forgive him for stealing my bike.

那個賊偷了我的腳踏車，懇求我原諒他。

▶ A homeless man is begging for food in front of the church.

一個流浪漢在教堂前乞討食物。

▶ The once successful businessman now begs food from strangers.

那曾經成功的商人現在向陌生人乞討食物。

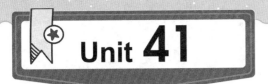

1 silver [ˈsɪlvɚ] *n.* 銀 & *a.* 銀製的；銀色的

(1) a silver coin 銀幣
(2) silver hair 銀髮
(3) be born with a silver spoon in one's mouth
某人生來就命好，某人是富裕家庭出身，某人含著金湯匙出生

▶ My grandmother's necklace is made of silver.
我祖母的項鍊是銀製的。

▶ Paul likes to collect different kinds of silver coins.
保羅喜歡收集不同的銀幣。

▶ The man with silver hair over there is Kelly's grandfather.
那邊有位一頭銀髮的男士是凱莉的爺爺。

▶ The politician was born with a silver spoon in his mouth.
這個政治人物生來就命好。

gold [gold]
n. 黃金 & *a.* 黃金製的；金色的

(1) pure gold 純金
(2) have a heart of gold 心地很善良
(3) a gold coin 金幣
(4) a gold ring 金戒指

▶ The watch is made of pure gold.
這支錶是純金打造的。

▶ Mother Teresa had a heart of gold.
德雷莎修女的心地很善良。

▶ Owen was surprised that there were so many gold coins in the box.
歐文驚訝地發現盒子裡竟然有這麼多金幣。

▶ Juliet received a gold ring as her birthday present.
茱麗葉收到了一枚金戒指作為生日禮物。

▶ The basketball players wore gold jackets.
那些籃球員穿金色夾克。

golden [ˈgoldn̩]
a. 黃金製的；金色的；極好的，有發展前途的

a golden opportunity
大好 / 絕佳機會

▶ My grandmother asked me whether I had seen her golden necklace.
我奶奶問我有沒有看到她的金項鍊。

▶ Sarah has beautiful golden hair.
莎拉有一頭美麗的金髮。

▶ You should take up this golden opportunity.
你應要把握這大好機會。

wooden [ˈwʊdn̩] *a.* 木頭的；呆板的

(1) wood [wʊd]
n. 木頭；樹林，森林 ②
in the wood / woods
在樹 / 森林裡
(2) woody [ˈwʊdɪ] *a.* 很多樹木的

▶ That wooden table has a very long history.
那張木桌子有很悠久的歷史。

▶ The actor's performance in the movie was wooden.
這演員在那部電影的演出很呆板。

2 silent [ˈsaɪlənt] *a.* 安／寂靜的；沉默的

H keep / stay silent 保持沉默

似 quiet [ˈkwaɪət] *a.* 安靜的 ①

▶ The school is usually silent on Sundays.
學校星期天的時候通常很安靜。

▶ No matter what your uncle asks, just keep silent.
不管你叔叔問什麼，保持沉默就好了。

silence [ˈsaɪləns]
n. 安／寂靜；沉默 & *vt.* 使沉默

H in silence 靜靜地 (做某事)

▶ The silence in the room made me very nervous.
房間裡鴉雀無聲，讓我很緊張。

▶ Every night, we eat together in silence.
每晚，我們都靜靜地一起吃飯。

▶ The sad news silenced all the children.
這悲傷的消息使所有的孩子都安靜了下來。

3 plain [plen] *n.* 平原 & *a.* 樸素的 (= simple)

似 prairie [ˈprɛrɪ] *n.* 大草原

▶ Most of the city is built on the plain.
這城市大部分建在平原上。

▶ Karen always wears plain clothes to work.
凱倫去上班總是穿著樸素。

average [ˈæv(ə)rɪdʒ]
a. 平均的；普通的，一般的 & *n.* 平均 &
vt. 平均為

H (1) an average of + 數字
平均為若干……

(2) on average 平均而言

▶ The average age of my students is fifteen.
我的學生平均年齡是 15 歲。

▶ Don't ask difficult questions. They're just students of average intelligence.
不要問很難的問題。他們只是智力一般的學生。

▶ The workaholic works an average of 16 hours a day.
= The workaholic works 16 hours a day on average.
這個工作狂每天平均工作 16 小時。

▶ On average, we work five hours overtime each week.
平均而言，我們一星期加班 5 小時。

▶ That rich man averages ten vacations a year.
那個富翁平均每年有 10 個假期。

general [ˈdʒɛnərəl]
a. 大致的；一般的，普遍的 & *n.* 將軍

H in general 一般而言
= generally speaking
= by and large
= for the most part
= on the whole

▶ After reading the report, you will have a general idea of the project.
讀完這份報告後，你會對這計畫有個大略的概念。

▶ In general, I spend most of my weekends with my family.
一般來說，我週末大部分是和家人一起度過的。

▶ Douglas MacArthur was considered a great general.
道格拉斯·麥克阿瑟被認為是位偉大的將軍。

folk [fok] *n.* 人們；雙親(此意恆用複數)

用法 folk 當『人們』之意時，本身即為複數，也可寫成 folks。

▶ The folk(s) in this part of the country are generally farmers and factory workers.
此國這一帶的居民多半是農民和工廠勞工。

▶ My folks are coming to see me today.
我爸媽今天會來看我。

4　host [host] *n.* 男主人 & *vt.* 主辦

片 play host to...　主辦……
反 hostess [`hostɪs] *n.* 女主人 ②

▶ A good host always makes his guests feel at home.
好的主人總是讓客人有賓至如歸的感覺。

▶ Which country played host to the Olympic Games last time?

= Which country hosted the Olympic Games last time?
上次奧運是哪個國家主辦的？

guest [gɛst]
n. 客人；特別來賓，特邀嘉賓

片 a special guest　(節目的)特別來賓

▶ How many guests are coming to the party?
有多少位客人會來參加這派對？

▶ Tom Cruise appeared on the show as a special guest.
湯姆·克魯斯作為特別來賓出現在這節目中。

5　bother [`baðɚ] *vi.* 費心 & *vt.* 打擾；使煩惱 & *n.* 造成煩惱的人 / 事 / 物

片 (1) not bother to V
不願意 / 懶得做……
(2) bother sb with sth
用某事去打擾 / 煩某人
(3) It bothers sb that...
讓某人感到煩惱的是……
= It bothers sb to V
衍 bothersome [`baðɚsəm]
a. 令人討厭的；麻煩的
似 brother [`brʌðɚ]
n. 兄，弟；兄弟，同胞 ①

▶ Andy didn't bother to call Mr. Grey.
安迪不願意打電話給葛雷先生。

▶ Am I bothering you?
我打擾到您了嗎？

▶ Don't bother me with such silly questions again!
別再用這種愚蠢的問題來煩我。

▶ It bothered Milly that her boyfriend was going to study abroad.
蜜莉的男朋友要出國留學，這讓她很煩惱。

▶ John is such a bother.
約翰真是個麻煩。

6　royal [`rɔɪəl] *a.* 皇家的

片 (1) the royal family　王室
(2) the royal road to sth
很容易達成某事物
似 (1) loyal [`lɔɪəl] *a.* 忠心的 ④
(2) noble [`nobḷ]
a. 高貴的；貴族的 ④

▶ The president will visit the royal family this weekend.
總統將於本週末拜訪王室。

▶ There is no royal road to learning.
學無坦途。—— 諺語

7 chemical [ˈkɛmɪkl̩] n. 化學 (製) 品 (可數) & a. 化學的

衍 (1) chemistry [ˈkɛmɪstrɪ] n. 化學 ④
(2) chemist [ˈkɛmɪst] n. 化學家 ⑥

▶ Medicines are mostly chemicals.
藥物大多是化學製品。

▶ The chemical industry is highly developed in Germany.
德國有高度發展的化學工業。

8 pillow [ˈpɪlo] n. 枕頭

片 pillow talk （情人間的）枕邊細語
衍 pillowcase [ˈpɪloˌkes] n. 枕頭套

▶ Stanley sleeps with a soft pillow under his head.
史丹利睡覺時頭底下都會墊一個軟的枕頭。

▶ The couple enjoyed some pillow talk before falling asleep. 這對夫妻在入睡前很喜歡先枕邊細語一下。

pajamas [pəˈdʒɑməz]
n. 睡衣 (恆用複數)
（= pyjamas [pəˈdʒɑməz]〔英〕）

片 a pair of pajamas 一套睡衣

用法 pajamas 含上衣及褲子，故恆用複數。

▶ My pajamas are made of cotton.
我的睡衣是棉質的。

9 primary [ˈpraɪˌmɛrɪ] a. 主要的，首要的；初級教育的

片 (1) primary education 初等教育
(2) a primary school 小學
(3) a primary color 基本色，原色
似 (1) main [men] a. 主要的 ①
(2) fundamental [ˌfʌndəˈmɛntl̩]
a. 主要的；根本的 ④

▶ Trevor's primary reason for going to the party was to meet girls.
崔佛去參加派對的主要原因是要去認識女孩子。

▶ Many people believe in the importance of primary education. 許多人深信初等教育的重要。

▶ Many primary school students in this country exercise less than 2 hours a week.
很多這國家的小學生每週運動不到 2 個小時。

▶ Blue is my favorite primary color.
藍色是我最喜歡的基本色。

secondary [ˈsɛkənˌdɛrɪ]
a. 次要的；(學校) 中等教育的

片 (1) be secondary to...
（重要性）次於……
(2) secondary education 中等教育
(3) a secondary school 中學
衍 second [ˈsɛkənd] a. 第二的 ①
延伸 higher education 高等教育

▶ In Warren's view, wealth is secondary to health.
華倫認為財富的重要性次於健康。

▶ After several years of secondary education, Frank decided to work to support his family.
接受幾年的中等教育後，法蘭克決定要工作來養家。

▶ Martha teaches geography at a secondary school.
瑪莎在一所中學教地理。

major [ˈmedʒɚ]
a. 主要的，重要的 & *vi.* 主修 & *n.* 主修科目

🄷 major in... 　主修……
= choose... as one's major

▶ Vincent played a major role in the play.
文森在這齣戲中扮演一個重要的角色。

▶ I majored in accounting in college.
= I chose accounting as my major in college.
我大學主修會計。

---

minor [ˈmaɪnɚ]
a. 不重要的；輕微的 & *vi.* 輔修 & *n.* 輔修科目

🄷 minor in... 　輔修……
= choose... as one's minor

▶ Melvin got his start in a minor role in a TV series.
馬文先是在電視連續劇裡演小角色起家的。

▶ Sue suffered only minor injuries in the fall.
蘇跌倒時只受到輕傷。

▶ Patrick minored in French.
= Patrick chose French as his minor.
派翠克輔修法文。

---

minority [məˈnɔrətɪ / maɪˈnɔrətɪ]
n. 少數；少數民族 / 群體

🄬 minorities [məˈnɔrətɪz / maɪˈnɔrətɪz]
🄷 a minority of... 　少部分的……

▶ Only a minority of the voters approved of the tax increase.
只有少數選民贊成加稅。

▶ This organization aims to help women and minorities.
此組織旨在幫助婦女和少數民族。

10　divide [dɪˈvaɪd] *vt.* & *vi.* (使) 劃分 / 分開；除以 & *n.* 分歧

🄷 (1) divide sth into...　把某物分成……
　 (2) divide into...　　　分成……
　 (3) divide A by B　　　A 除以 B

▶ Divide the pizza into eight slices, please.
請把披薩分成 8 片。

▶ These books divide into three categories.
這些書分成 3 個種類。

▶ If you divide 8 by 4, you get 2.
8 除以 4 得 2。

▶ There is a political divide between the two families.
這 2 個家庭之間在政治方面的看法分歧。

---

division [dɪˈvɪʒən]
n. 劃分；分歧；除法；部門

🄷 make a division of sth into...
　 把某事物分成……

🄵 department [dɪˈpɑrtmənt] *n.* 部門 ②

▶ We can make a broad division of this artist's works into "realistic" and "impressionistic."
我們可以把這位藝術家的作品大致分為『寫實』和『印象派』。

▶ Those strong arguments have resulted in divisions in the team.
那些激烈的爭辯已造成了團隊分裂。

▶ My little brother learned division in his math class today.
我弟弟今天數學課學了除法。

▶ Who is in charge of this division?
誰負責這個部門？

11 discover [dɪsˈkʌvɚ] *vt.* 發現

延伸 (1) find out... 發現……
(2) invent [ɪnˈvɛnt] *vt.* 發明 ③

▶ The scientists have discovered a cure for the terrible disease.
科學家們已經發現了可治療此可怕疾病的方法了。

discovery [dɪsˈkʌvərɪ]
n. 發現；被發現的事物

複 discoveries [dɪsˈkʌvərɪz]
片 make a discovery 有所發現
似 invention [ɪnˈvɛnʃən]
    n. 發明；發明物 ④

▶ The scientist made a great discovery while he was doing the experiments.
這位科學家在做實驗時有了重大發現。

▶ Pompeii was seen as one of the most important discoveries in history.
龐貝城被視為歷史上最重要的發現之一。

12 curious [ˈkjʊrɪəs] *a.* 好奇的；古怪的，不尋常的

片 (1) be curious about...
    對……感到好奇
(2) It is curious that...
    ……真奇怪，……真不尋常

衍 curiosity [ˌkjʊrɪˈɑsətɪ] *n.* 好奇心 ④
似 (1) strange [strendʒ] *a.* 奇怪的 ①
(2) unusual [ʌnˈjuʒʊəl] *a.* 不尋常的

▶ Scientists have always been curious about outer space.
科學家對於外太空始終充滿好奇。

▶ It was curious that my talkative brother was so quiet today.
我那很愛說話的弟弟今天這麼安靜真的很奇怪。

13 railroad [ˈrelˌrod] *n.* 鐵路〔美〕(= railway [ˈrelˌwe]〔英〕)

片 a railroad station 火車站〔美〕
= a railway station〔英〕
= a train station
衍 rail [rel] *n.* 鐵路交通系統；鐵軌 ⑤

▶ I'll see you at the railroad station at 8 a.m. tomorrow.
我們明天早上 8 點在火車站見。

platform [ˈplætˌfɔrm]
n. 講臺，舞臺；(鐵路等的) 月臺

似 (1) rostrum [ˈrɑstrəm] *n.* 演講臺
(2) stage [stedʒ] *n.* 舞臺 ②

▶ Ella stepped up onto the platform and sang a beautiful song. 艾拉走上舞臺，唱了一首優美的歌曲。

▶ Wait for me on Platform C. I'll be there in a minute.
在 C 月臺等我，我馬上就到。

14 display [dɪˈsple] *vt.* 展示 & *n.* 陳列，展示；表演

片 (1) be on display 陳列展示
= be on exhibition
(2) a fireworks display 煙火秀
似 (1) show [ʃo] *vt.* 顯示；陳列 ①
(2) demonstrate [ˈdɛmənˌstret]
    vt. 展示 ④
(3) exhibit [ɪgˈzɪbɪt] *vt.* 展示，陳列 ④

▶ The toys displayed in the window attracted the attention of every child that passed by.
櫥窗內展示的玩具吸引了每個路過的小孩的目光。

▶ Picasso's paintings are now on display at the museum.
目前畢卡索的畫作正在該博物館陳列展示。

▶ Did you see the fireworks display on New Year's Eve?
你有看跨年夜的煙火秀嗎？

15 **male** [mel] *n.* 男 / 雄性 & *a.* 男 / 雄性的

🗂 male chauvinism [ˈʃovəˌnɪzəm]
大男人主義

似 (1) masculine [ˈmæskjəlɪn]
　　a. 男性的 ⑤

　(2) manly [ˈmænlɪ] *a.* 有男子氣概的

▶ In many societies, males are expected to support their families once they get married.
許多社會期望男性結婚後就要能養家活口。

▶ The male peacock is much more beautiful than the female one.
雄孔雀比雌孔雀更漂亮。
＊peacock [ˈpikɑk] *n.* 孔雀

▶ The woman accused Roger of male chauvinism.
那名女人指責羅傑有大男人主義。
＊accuse [əˈkjuz] *vt.* 指控

female [ˈfimel]
n. 女 / 雌性 & *a.* 女 / 雌性的

似 (1) womanly [ˈwʊmənlɪ]
　　a. 有女人味的

　(2) feminine [ˈfɛmənɪn]
　　a. 女性 (化) 的 ⑥

▶ Females are getting more and more powerful in modern society.
在現代社會中，女性越來越有權力。

▶ The female bear will protect her offspring at all costs.
母熊會不計一切來保護自己的小寶寶。
＊offspring [ˈɔfˌsprɪŋ] *a.* (動物的) 幼獸 (單複數同形)

sex [sɛks] *n.* 性別；性

▶ What is the sex of your new puppy?
你新小狗的性別是什麼？

▶ The topic of sex is seldom discussed between Asian parents and their children.
亞洲的父母很少和他們的孩子討論『性』這個話題。

16 **slip** [slɪp] *vi.* 滑倒；溜走；下降 & *vt.* 遺忘 & *n.* 過失；紙條

☰ slip, slipped [slɪpt], slipped

🗂 (1) slip by / away　(時間) 流逝

　(2) sth slip one's mind / memory
　　某人忘了某事物

　(3) a slip of paper　一張紙條

衍 slippery [ˈslɪpərɪ] *a.* 滑的；狡滑的 ③

▶ Norman slipped and fell on the muddy road.
諾曼在泥濘的道路上滑了一跤。

▶ Melvin tried to catch the fluttering bill, but it slipped out of his hand.
馬文試圖抓住飛舞的紙鈔，但它卻從手中溜走了。

▶ As time slipped by, I thought less and less about my ex-boyfriend.
隨著時間流逝，我越來越少想前男友了。

▶ Oil prices have slipped in recent weeks.
最近幾週油價一直在下跌。

▶ The girl's name just slipped my mind.
我忘了那女孩的名字。

▶ The whole plan will fail with the slightest slip.
任何一點小過失都會讓計畫全盤失敗。

▶ Lulu wrote down her phone number on a slip of paper and gave it to me.
露露把她的電話號碼寫在一張紙條上給我。

slipper [ˈslɪpɚ] *n.* 拖鞋
居 a pair of slippers 　一雙拖鞋

▶ Please don't walk around with your slippers on.
請不要穿著拖鞋四處走。

smooth [smuð]
a. 平滑的；順利的 & *vt.* & *vi.* (使) 平坦
居 smooth out...
　把 (衣服或紙張等的皺褶) 用平
反 rough [rʌf] *a.* 粗糙的 ③

▶ The lady looks all the more beautiful because of her smooth skin.
這位女士滑嫩的皮膚讓她看起來更美。

▶ All the people in that country hope for a smooth transition of power after the election.
該國所有人民都希望選舉後新政府的權力交接能夠順利進行。

▶ Brandy smoothed her hair with her hand.
布蘭蒂用手順了順頭髮。

▶ Allison stood up and smoothed out her skirt.
愛麗森起身把裙子弄平。

17 bend [bɛnd] *vt.* & *vi.* 折彎 & *vt.* 扭曲 (事實) & *vi.* 俯身 & *n.* (道路等的) 轉彎處

目 bend, bent [bɛnt], bent
居 (1) bend the truth 　扭曲事實真相
　 (2) bend down 　彎腰
　 (3) be bent on + V-ing 　下決心做……
衍 bendy [ˈbɛndɪ] *a.* 多彎道的

▶ The strong man can bend a steel rod with one hand.
那個大力士可以用單手折彎鋼條。

▶ Tim bent the truth to protect his girlfriend.
提姆為了保護他女友而扭曲事實真相。

▶ Mandy bent down to kiss her daughter goodbye.
曼蒂俯身和女兒吻別。

▶ The mayor is bent on improving the cultural level of the citizens.
市長下決心要提高市民的文化水準。

▶ Be careful! There's a sharp bend ahead.
小心！前方有個急轉彎。

18 rare [rɛr] *a.* 稀有的；罕見的，不常發生的；(肉) 一分熟的，嫩的

居 It is rare (for sb/sth) to V
　(某人 / 物) 做……是很罕見的
衍 rareness [ˈrɛrnəs] *n.* 稀罕，珍貴
似 (1) scarce [skɛrs] *a.* 稀有的 ③
　 (2) unusual [ʌnˈjuʒʊəl] *a.* 不尋常的
反 (1) common [ˈkɑmən] *a.* 常見的 ①
　 (2) general [ˈdʒɛnərəl] *a.* 一般的 ②

▶ The number of rare wild birds is decreasing.
稀有野生鳥類的數量正在減少。

▶ Tom is a bookworm; it is rare for him to go to a movie.
湯姆是個書呆子，很少去看電影。

▶ I always order my steak rare.
我每次都點一分熟的牛排。

19 **rude** [rud] *a.* 無禮的，粗魯的

> ▶ I don't like Jim because of his rude manners.
> 我不喜歡吉姆，因為他很無禮。

naughty [ˋnɔtɪ] *a.* 頑皮的

似 mischievous [ˋmɪstʃəvəs]
a. 調皮的 ⑥

> ▶ I was a naughty boy at school.
> 我念書時很頑皮。

20 **effort** [ˋɛfət] *n.* 氣力，精力；努力試著要……

片 (1) with effort   很費 / 吃力
     without effort   毫不費力
(2) make an effort to V
     努力試著要做……
(3) in an effort to V
     為了試著要做……
(4) make every effort to V
     盡全力做……

衍 effortless [ˋɛfətləs] *a.* 不費力的

比 affect [əˋfɛkt] *vt.* 影響 ②

> ▶ Hank carried a refrigerator up seven flights of stairs without much effort.
> 漢克沒費多少力氣就把冰箱搬上 7 層樓。

> ▶ Kent made an effort to please his girlfriend.
> 肯特努力試著要討好女友。

> ▶ The president called an urgent meeting in an effort to handle the sudden spread of the disease.
> 總統召開了緊急會議，以處理這疾病突然蔓延開來的問題。

> ▶ Herbert made every effort to get to the church on time.
> 赫伯特盡一切努力要準時趕到教堂。

Level 2

Unit 41

Unit 42

  4201-4208

1　strict [strɪkt] *a.* 嚴格的，嚴厲的

🔁 (1) be strict with sb　對某人很嚴厲
　　(2) be strict about sth　很講究某事

🔂 strictness [ˋstrɪktnəs] *n.* 嚴格

🔄 (1) harsh [hɑrʃ] *a.* 嚴厲的 ④
　　(2) serious [ˋsɪrɪəs]
　　　　a. 嚴肅的，認真的；嚴重的 ①

▶ Those trucks have a strict weight limit on their loads.
　那些卡車有嚴格的載重限制。

▶ The teacher is strict with every student he teaches.
　這位老師對他教的學生都很嚴厲。

▶ My company is strict about efficiency.
　我的公司很講究效率。

2　crowd [kraʊd] *n.* 一群人 & *vt.* 擠滿 & *vi.* 聚集

🔁 (1) a crowd of...　一群……
　　(2) crowd around...
　　　　聚集在……周圍

🔂 crowded [ˋkraʊdɪd] *a.* 擁擠的
　　be crowded with...　擠滿了……
　　= be full of...

▶ There was a large crowd of elders in the park.
　公園裡有一大群年長者。

▶ A lot of factory workers crowded the seafood restaurant.
　許多工廠工人坐滿了這家海鮮餐廳。

▶ The students crowded around their teacher.
　那些學生圍聚在他們老師的身旁。

3　wheel [(h)wil] *n.* (汽車) 方向盤；輪子

🔁 (1) behind the wheel　開車
　　= driving
　　(2) four-wheel drive　四輪傳動

🔂 wheelchair [ˋ(h)wil,tʃɛr] *n.* 輪椅 ⑤

▶ I get nervous whenever my wife is behind the wheel.
　每當我太太開車時，我都很緊張。

▶ Dad bought a four-wheel drive jeep last week.
　爸爸上星期買了一輛四輪傳動的吉普車。

4　latest [ˋletɪst] *a.* 最新的，最近的

🔂 (1) late [let] *a.* 遲到的 & *adv.* 遲到地 ①
　　(2) later [ˋletɚ]
　　　　adv. 較晚地，較遲地 ①
　　(3) lately [ˋletlɪ] *adv.* 最近 ③

▶ That song is from this artist's latest album.
　那首歌取自這位歌手的最新專輯。

delay [dɪˋle]
vt. & *vi.* & *n.* (使) 延誤 / 延期

🔁 (1) delay + N/V-ing　延誤 / 期……
　　(2) a delay in + N/V-ing
　　　　……延誤 / 期

🔄 postpone [postˋpon] *vt.* 延期 ③

▶ Don't delay paying the bill.
　不要延誤繳帳單的時間。

▶ The release date of the movie is delayed until the end of this month.
　這部電影的上映日期延到本月月底。

▶ We're trying to figure out what caused the delay in payment.
　我們正在努力找出導致付款延遲的原因。

5　thief [θif] *n.* 小偷

複 thieves [θivz]

延伸 (1) steal [stil] *vt.* 偷竊 ③
(2) robber [ˈrɑbɚ] *n.* 強盜 ④

▶ The thief was caught at last.
小偷最後被抓到了。

6　income [ˈɪnˌkʌm] *n.* 收入

片 (1) have a high / large income
收入高
have a low / small income
收入低
(2) income tax　（個人）所得稅

似 outcome [ˈaʊtˌkʌm] *n.* 結果 ④

▶ Plumbers in that country have high incomes.
那個國家的水電工收入很高。
*plumber [ˈplʌmɚ] *n.* 水電工，水管工人

---

earn [ɝn] *vt. & vi.* 賺得；贏得

片 earn a living　維生
= make a living

衍 earnings [ˈɝnɪŋz] *n.* 收入（恆用複數）

▶ The famous singer once earned a living by singing in nightclubs.
這位著名歌手曾在夜總會唱歌謀生。

▶ Bill's honesty earned him a lot of respect.
比爾的誠實使他深受敬重。

7　nod [nɑd] *vt. & vi. & n.* 點頭

三 nod, nodded [ˈnɑdɪd], nodded
片 (1) nod / shake one's head
某人點 / 搖頭
(2) give sb a nod of
encouragement / agreement
對某人點頭以示鼓勵 / 同意

▶ Mrs. Wilson nodded her head to show that she agreed.
= Mrs. Wilson nodded to show that she agreed.
魏爾遜夫人點頭表示同意。

▶ Greta's father gave her a nod of encouragement, and she began to sing.
葛瑞塔的父親對她點了點頭以示鼓勵，然後葛瑞塔便開始唱歌。

8　hip [hɪp] *n.* 臀部，屁股（常用複數）

似 (1) bottom [ˈbɑtəm] *n.* 臀部 ①
(2) butt [bʌt] *n.* 臀部

▶ Generally, women have rounder hips than men.
一般來說，女人的臀部比男人要來得圓。

---

waist [west] *n.* 腰（部）

▶ Those jeans are too tight around your waist.
那條牛仔褲的腰身對你來說太緊了。

---

lap [læp] *n.* （人坐著時的）大腿部

片 on sb's lap　在某人的大腿上

▶ When I was young, I liked to sit on my grandfather's lap as he told stories.
小時候我喜歡坐在爺爺的大腿上聽他說故事。

ankle [ˈæŋkl̩] *n.* 腳踝

片 twist one's ankle 扭傷腳踝

似 angle [ˈæŋgl̩] *n.* 角度；觀點 ②

▶ The child twisted his ankle and was sent to the hospital.
這孩子扭傷腳踝後被送往醫院。

eyebrow [ˈaɪˌbraʊ]
n. 眉毛 (常用複數) (= brow [braʊ])

▶ The principal has peculiar-looking eyebrows.
校長的眉毛長得很奇特。
*peculiar [pɪˈkjuljə] *a.* 奇怪的

9 **gymnasium** [dʒɪmˈnezɪəm] *n.* (有屋頂的) 體育館，健身房 (= gym [dʒɪm])

▶ We often go to the gym to work out.
我們常到健身房去鍛鍊身體。
*work out 鍛鍊，健身 (= exercise)

10 **shame** [ʃem] *n.* 可惜，遺憾；羞愧 & *vt.* 使感到羞愧

片 (1) It is a shame that... 真可惜……
= It is a pity that...
= It is too bad that...
(2) shame on sb
某人應該感到羞愧，某人真不像話

衍 (1) ashamed [əˈʃemd]
a. 感到可恥的 ④
(2) shameful [ˈʃemfəl] *a.* 可恥的 ④
(3) shameless [ˈʃemləs]
a. 無恥的，厚顏的

似 pity [ˈpɪtɪ] *n.* 遺憾 ③

▶ It is a shame that you didn't show up at the party last night. We all had a wonderful time there, you know.
真遺憾昨晚的派對你沒到場。你知道嗎？我們大家都玩得很開心呢。

▶ Shame on you, Kevin. You didn't even pass the simple test.
凱文，羞羞臉。這很簡單的考試你都沒過。

▶ What Adam did shamed his family.
亞當的所作所為使他的家人蒙羞。

11 **sour** [saʊr] *a.* (味道) 酸的

片 (1) turn / go sour 變酸
(2) sour grapes 酸葡萄心理

反 sweet [swit] *a.* 甜的 ①

▶ This milk has turned sour.
牛奶變酸了。

▶ Alice said Mark's job isn't that great, but that's just sour grapes.
艾麗絲說馬克的工作沒那麼好，但那只是酸葡萄心理。

12 **technology** [tɛkˈnɑlədʒɪ] *n.* 科技

複 technologies [tɛkˈnɑlədʒɪz]

▶ Perhaps we have put too much faith in the power of technology.
或許我們太過相信科技的力量了。

Level 2

Unit 42

13 sheet [ʃit] *n.* 一張 (紙)；床單

厈 (1) a sheet of paper　一張紙
= a piece of paper
(2) change the sheets　更換床單

▶ I need a sheet of paper to write answers on.
我需要一張紙來寫答案。

▶ We asked the housekeeper to change the sheets every other day.
我們要求管家每隔一天更換床單。

14 chain [tʃen] *n.* 錬子；連鎖店 & *vt.* 用鐵錬鎖住

厈 be chained to...　被鎖／栓在……
衍 chain-smoker [ˋtʃenˏsmokɚ]
n. 癮君子，老菸槍

▶ Jim is a chain-smoker. He smokes one cigarette right after another.
吉姆是個癮君子。他菸一根接著一根抽。

延伸 link [lɪŋk]
n. (鏈的) 環節，圈 & *vt.* 連接 ②

▶ Bill wears a gold chain around his neck.
比爾的脖子上掛了條金錬子。

▶ The ice cream parlor around the corner is part of a 10-location chain in this city.
附近的那家冰淇淋店是本市有 10 家店面的連鎖店的其中一家。
＊parlor [ˋpɑrlɚ] *n.* 店

▶ The dog is chained to the tree.
狗被用錬子拴在那棵樹。

15 image [ˋɪmɪdʒ] *n.* 形象；意象；影像，圖像

衍 (1) self-image [ˏsɛlfˋɪmɪdʒ]
n. 自我形象
(2) imagination [ɪˏmædʒəˋneʃən]
n. 想像力 ③
(3) imaginative [ɪˋmædʒəˏnetɪv]
a. 有想像力的 ④
(4) imaginary [ɪˋmædʒəˏnɛrɪ]
a. 想像出來的，虛構的 ④

▶ The aim of this activity is to improve the public image of the politician.
這個活動的目的就是要改善這位政治人物的公眾形象。

▶ You can find images of spring everywhere in the poem.
你在這首詩裡到處可以看到春天的意象。

▶ The images of people at war make me feel uncomfortable.
那些處於戰爭時期人們的圖像讓我感到很不舒服。

imagine [ɪˋmædʒən] *vt.* 想像

▶ Children often imagine monsters hiding under their beds.
小孩常會幻想怪物躲在他們床下。

▶ I can't imagine what will happen if you don't show up and offer your help.
要是你沒現身幫忙，我無法想像會發生什麼事。

16 separate [ˋsɛpəˏret] *vt.* & *vi.* (使事物) 分開；(使人) 分開／散 & [ˋsɛpərət] *a.* 分開的

厈 separate A from B　把 A 與 B 分開來
= A be／got separated from B

▶ The woman separated the two fighting dogs.
這名婦女把這 2 隻正在打架的狗分開。

衍 **separated** [ˈsɛpəˌretɪd] *a.* 分居的
似 **divide** [dəˈvaɪd] *vt. & vi.* (使) 分開 ②

▸ Mother separated the good eggs from the bad ones.
母親把好蛋和壞蛋區分開來。

▸ I got separated from my friends in the big crowd.
我和我的朋友在廣大的人群中被隔開了。

▸ Melody and Stan separated at the corner.
美樂蒂和史坦兩人在這轉角處分開了。

▸ The hotel and the restaurant are under separate management.
旅館和餐廳是分開經營的。

---

17 **metal** [ˈmɛtl̩] *n.* 金屬 & *a.* 堅強的

似 (1) **medal** [ˈmɛdl̩] *n.* 獎章 ③
(2) **mental** [ˈmɛntl̩] *a.* 心理的 ③

▸ These bars are made of a solid metal.
這些欄杆是用一種很堅固的金屬所製成。

▸ Kate is so metal; it seems she could overcome any difficulties.
凱特好堅強；她似乎可以克服任何困難。

---

steel [stil] *n.* 鋼鐵 & *vt.* 準備應付……

片 (1) **stainless steel** 不鏽鋼
(2) **steel oneself for / against sth**
準備應付某 (不好的) 事

▸ That knife is made of stainless steel.
那把刀是不鏽鋼製的。

▸ Kelly steeled herself for the bad news Robin was going to tell her.
凱莉為羅賓要告訴她的壞消息做好了準備。

---

iron [ˈaɪɚn]
n. 熨斗 (可數)；鐵 (不可數) & *vt.* 用熨斗燙
& *a.* 強硬堅定的

▸ Someone left the iron on all day.
有人把熨斗整天開著沒關。

▸ These artworks are made of iron.
這些藝術品是鐵製的。

▸ Strike while the iron is hot.
打鐵趁熱。—— 諺語

▸ Would you please iron my shirt? I have an important meeting this morning.
能不能請你幫我熨襯衫？我今天早上有個重要的會要開。

▸ Lydia has such an iron will that I think her dream will come true soon.
莉迪亞有著鋼鐵般的意志，所以我認為她的夢想很快就會實現的。

---

18 **narrow** [ˈnæro] *vi. & vt.* (使) 變窄 & *a.* 狹窄的；勉強的

片 (1) **narrow sth down (to...)**
將某事物縮減至……

▸ The wide road narrowed as we entered the city's center.
我們進入市中心後，這條大馬路逐漸變窄。

(2) win by a narrow margin
以些微差距獲勝

(3) have a narrow escape (from...)
(從……) 死裡逃生

🈺 narrow-minded [ˌnæroˋmaɪndɪd]
a. 心胸狹窄的

▶ The police narrowed the choices down to five sites after some adjustments.
調整過後，警方已把選擇範圍縮小到 5 個地點。
*adjustment [əˋdʒʌstmənt] *n.* 調整

▶ The car was unable to drive through the narrow alley.
車子沒辦法通過那條窄巷。

▶ That basketball team only won by a narrow margin.
那支籃球隊僅以些微差距獲勝。

▶ Kevin had a narrow escape from the house fire.
凱文從那場民宅火災中死裡逃生。

19　stretch [strɛtʃ] *vt. & vi.* 伸展；(使) 拉長 / 緊 & *vt.* 伸出 / 長 & *n.* 一段時間

🈺 (1) stretch one's legs
（站起來走動以）活動一下筋骨

(2) stretch out one's hand / foot to V 伸出某人的手 / 腳來做……

(3) at a stretch　持續地

▶ After sitting for a long time in the car, I got out to stretch my legs.
在車內久坐之後，我下車活動一下筋骨。

▶ Be sure to stretch before exercising.
運動前一定要先做伸展。

▶ Tina stretched the rubber band so hard that it broke quickly.
蒂娜很用力拉緊橡皮筋，結果它很快就斷了。

▶ Jerry stretched out his hands to take the award.
傑瑞伸出雙手領取獎品。

▶ You have to stand for 6 hours at a stretch for this job.
這個工作需要連續站 6 小時。

20　vote [vot] *vt. & vi. & n.* 投票

🈺 (1) vote sb sth
投票給某人讓其擔任某職務

(2) vote for...
投票給……，投票贊成……

(3) vote against...　投票反對……

(4) have / take a vote on...
針對……進行投票

▶ We voted Mr. Wilson our mayor.
我們票選魏爾遜先生當我們的市長。

▶ Who did you vote for in the last legislative election?
上次的立委選舉你投票給誰？

▶ All the villagers voted against the construction of the nuclear power plant.
所有村民一致投票反對興建核電廠。

▶ We'll take a vote on this issue.
我們將針對這個議題投票表決。

21　culture [ˋkʌltʃɚ] *n.* 文化

🈺 (1) culture shock　文化衝擊

(2) pop culture　流行 / 大眾文化

▶ This little town is rich in culture.
這個小鎮有豐富的文化。

▶ Students who are studying abroad may experience culture shock at one time or another.
到國外念書的學生有時會體驗到文化衝擊。

cultural [ˈkʌltʃərəl] *a.* 文化的

▶ The argument was caused by cultural differences. ☐
這場爭執是由於文化差異所引起的。

---

22 valley [ˈvælɪ] *n.* 山谷 ☐

似 canyon [ˈkænjən] *n.* 峽谷 ③

▶ Below the mountain is a beautiful valley full of lovely flowers.
山下有座美麗的山谷，山谷裡面開滿了嬌媚的花朵。

---

peak [pik]
n. 山頂；最高點 & *vi.* 達到頂峰，達到最大值

用 (1) at sth's peak　在某事的最高點
　　(2) reach a peak　達到巔峰
　　　　reach sth's peak
　　　　達到某事物的巔峰
　　(3) peak at...　達到……

似 summit [ˈsʌmɪt] *n.* 山頂 ③

▶ The young man climbed to the peak of the mountain in record time. ☐
這位年輕人以破紀錄的時間攀上山峰。

▶ Sam's business was at its peak when he was in his mid-40s.
山姆在 45 歲左右時事業到達巔峰。

▶ Traffic in Taipei reaches its peak at about 8 a.m.
臺北的交通大約在早上 8 點達到巔峰。

▶ The temperature in this area may peak at thirty seven degrees Celsius tomorrow.
明天這地區的溫度可能會達到攝氏 37 度。

---

23 expert [ˈɛkspɜt] *n.* 專家 & *a.* 熟練的 ☐

用 be expert on / in / at + N/V-ing
　　對……很熟練
＝ be experienced in + N/V-ing

衍 expertise [ˌɛkspɚˈtiz] *n.* 專業知識 ⑤

▶ After three years of special training, Amy has become an expert in this field.
經過 3 年特訓，艾咪已成為這一領域的專家。

▶ David is expert in teaching English.
大衛對教英文很有經驗。

---

24 struggle [ˈstrʌgl̩] *n.* 奮 / 努力；難事 & *vi.* 奮 / 努力 ☐

用 (1) a struggle for / against...
　　努力爭取 / 對抗……
　　(2) struggle to V　奮 / 努力做
　　(3) struggle for / against...
　　努力爭取 / 對抗……

▶ The small nation's struggle for independence finally bore fruit two years ago.
這個小國為了獨立所做的努力終於在 2 年前有了成果。

▶ Climbing up the mountain was a struggle, but I'm glad I finally reached the summit.
爬山真是件難事，但我很高興我最後終於攻頂了。

▶ There are many families struggling to survive on low incomes.
有許多家庭靠著微薄的收入努力過活。

> The puppy was struggling for breath because its collar was too tight.

那隻小狗因為項圈太緊而呼吸困難。

---

25 entrance [ˈɛntrəns] *n.* 入口 (可數)；進入許可，進入權 (不可數)

月 entrance to + 地方　某地的進入權

衍 (1) enter [ˈɛntɚ] *vt.* & *vi.* 進入 ①
(2) entry [ˈɛntrɪ] *n.* 進入 ③

> The guard stood near the bank entrance.
> 這名警衛站在銀行入口附近。

> Improperly dressed people will be denied entrance to the restaurant.
> 衣冠不整的人不得進入那家餐廳。
> *improperly [ɪmˈprɑpɚlɪ] *adv.* 不適當地

---

exit [ˈɛksɪt / ˈɛgzɪt]
n. 出口 & *vt.* 離開 & *vi.* 從……離開

月 (1) an emergency exit
緊急逃生出口
(2) exit from / through / by...
從……出去

似 leave [liv] *vt.* & *vi.* 離開 ①

> Knowing where the emergency exits are in a building can save your life.
> 知道緊急逃生出口在大樓何處可以救你一命。

> Penny exited the classroom in a fury.
> 佩妮氣沖沖地走出教室。
> *fury [ˈfjʊrɪ] *n.* 暴怒
> in a fury　盛怒之下

> Ladies and gentlemen, when the show is over, please exit through the rear door.
> 各位女士先生，節目表演完了之後，請由後門離開。

---

26 absent [ˈæbsn̩t] *a.* 缺席的；缺乏的 & *vt.* 缺席

月 (1) be absent from...
自……缺席；缺乏……
(2) absent oneself (from + 地方)
某人沒有出現 (在某地方)

衍 absent-minded [ˌæbsn̩tˈmaɪndɪd]
a. 心不在焉的

反 present [ˈprɛzn̩t] *a.* 出席的 ①

> Sally was absent from work today.
> 莎莉今天曠工。

> Love is absent from Ted's marriage.
> 泰德的婚姻中沒有愛。

> Sam absented himself from school today.
> 山姆今天曠課。

---

absence [ˈæbsn̩s] *n.* 缺席；缺乏

月 in the absence of... 沒有……
= without...

反 (1) presence [ˈprɛzn̩s] *n.* 出席 ③
(2) attendance [əˈtɛndəns] *n.* 出席 ⑤

> Tell me the reason for your absence.
> 告訴我你缺席的原因。

> In the absence of evidence, we couldn't prove the man's guilty.
> 我們缺乏證據，無法證明該男子有罪。

---

27 current [ˈkɝənt] *a.* 當前的 & *n.* 水流，氣流

月 (1) an ocean current 洋流
(2) against a current 逆流

> Have you bought this dictionary's current edition?
> 你買了這字典的最新版本了嗎？

▶ Strong ocean currents often cause rapid and high waves.

強勁的洋流時常引起快速又很高的浪潮。

▶ Learning things is like sailing a boat against the current; it either advances or retreats.

學如逆水行舟，不進則退。

＊retreat [rɪ'trit] *vi.* 撤退

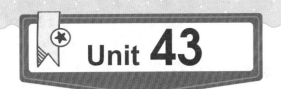

1 **storm** [stɔrm] *n.* 暴風雨 & *vi.* & *vt.* 怒罵

🅗 storm at sb　怒罵某人

▸ A storm is headed this way.
一場暴風雨正直撲這裡而來。

▸ Peter stormed at John because of his terrible attitude.
彼得因為約翰的態度不好而怒斥他。

thunder [ˋθʌndɚ] *n.* 雷聲 & *vi.* 打雷

衍 (1) thunderstorm [ˋθʌndɚˏstɔrm]
n. 雷雨

(2) thunderbolt [ˋθʌndɚˏbolt]
n. 雷電

延伸 lightning [ˋlaɪtnɪŋ] *n.* 閃電 ③

▸ The thunder scared the dog.
雷聲把狗嚇了一跳。

▸ It started to pour after it thundered several times.
打了幾聲雷後就下起了傾盆大雨。

typhoon [taɪˋfun]
n. 颱風 (發生於西太平洋沿岸的風暴)

延伸 (1) hurricane [ˋhɝɪˏken]
n. 颶風 (發生於北大西洋沿岸的風暴) ④

(2) cyclone [ˋsaɪklon]
n. 氣旋，旋風 (發生於南太平洋和印度洋沿岸的風暴)

＊以上 3 字其實皆指『颱風』，只是在不同的地區有不同的名稱。

▸ The typhoon came and did a lot of damage to this area.
颱風來襲，對該區造成很大的損害。

fog [fɑg]
n. 霧 & *vi.* & *vt.* 起霧，被霧籠罩

≡ fog, fogged [fɑgd], fogged

🅗 fog up　(玻璃、鏡片等) 起霧

衍 foggy [ˋfɑgɪ] *a.* 多霧的 ③

▸ I couldn't see anything in front of me because of the heavy fog.
我看不到前方的任何東西，因為霧太大了。

▸ My glasses fogged up as soon as I walked out the door.
我一走出門外，眼鏡馬上起霧。

2 **temperature** [ˋtɛmp(ə)rətʃɚ] *n.* 溫度；體溫

🅗 (1) at a(n) + adj. + temperature
在……樣的溫度下

(2) take sb's temperature
量某人的體溫

▸ The laboratory must be kept at a steady temperature.
這間實驗室必須保持恆溫。

▸ The nurse took sally's temperature and gave her a shot.
護士量完莎莉的體溫後，為她打了一針。

＊give sb a shot　為某人打針

Level 2　Unit 43

381

3 bar [bɑr] *n.* 酒吧，吧臺；棒；條 & *vt.* 禁止；妨礙 (通行)

三 bar, barred [bɑrd], barred
片 (1) a chocolate bar　巧克力 (棒)
(2) bar sb from + N/V-ing
禁止某人……
(3) bar sb's way / path
擋住某人的路

▶ We went to a bar for beer and snacks after work.
下班後我們到一間酒吧去喝啤酒、吃點心。

▶ The grocery store owner gave little Katy a chocolate bar.
這家雜貨店的老闆給小凱蒂一條巧克力棒。

▶ The authorities barred Jackson from entering the country.
當局禁止傑克森入境。

▶ I tried to go back inside, but Ross barred my way.
我試著要進入屋內，但是羅斯擋住了我的路。

4 chopstick [ˈtʃɑpˌstɪk] *n.* 筷子 (常用複數)

片 a pair of chopsticks　一雙筷子

▶ Many foreigners feel it's difficult to eat with chopsticks.
許多外國人認為用筷子吃東西很難。

5 coal [kol] *n.* 煤 (炭)

延伸 (1) gasoline [ˈgæsəˌlin] *n.* 汽油〔美〕③
= gas [gæs]〔美〕
= petrol [ˈpɛtrəl]〔英〕
(2) petroleum [pəˈtroliəm]
n. 石油 (可提煉汽油、柴油或煤油)
⑥

▶ Coal is no longer used to fuel trains in many countries.
許多國家不再用煤炭來當火車燃料了。

6 victory [ˈvɪktərɪ] *n.* 勝利

複 victories [ˈvɪktərɪz]
片 declare (a) victory　宣告勝利
衍 victorious [vɪkˈtorɪəs] *a.* 勝利的
反 defeat [dɪˈfit]
vt. 擊敗 & *n.* 戰敗，失敗 ④

▶ The candidate declared a victory soon after the election.
選舉一結束，這位候選人就宣告勝利。

7 memory [ˈmɛmərɪ] *n.* 記憶力；回憶

複 memories [ˈmɛmərɪz]
片 (1) have a good / bad memory
記憶力很好 / 差
(2) in memory of sb
以 / 為記念某人
衍 (1) memorable [ˈmɛmərəbl̩]
a. 難忘的 ④

▶ My sister has a good memory.
我姊姊的記憶力很好。

▶ My grandfather told me his childhood memories.
我爺爺告訴我他的兒時回憶。

▶ The local government built the park in memory of the soldiers who died in the war.
當地政府建了這座公園，以記念那些在戰爭中陣亡的士兵。

(2) memorize [ˈmɛməˌraɪz]
　　vt. 背熟 ④

(3) memorial [məˈmorɪəl]
　　n. 紀念碑／物 ④

8　forgive [fəˈgɪv] *vt.* & *vi.* 原諒

目 forgive, forgave [fəˈgev], forgiven
　[fəˈgɪvṇ]
片 (1) forgive sb for + N/V-ing
　　　原諒某人……
　(2) forgive and forget　不念舊惡
衍 (1) forgiving [fəˈgɪvɪŋ] *a.* 寬容的
　(2) forgiveness [fəˈgɪvnəs] *n.* 寬恕

▶ I couldn't forgive Tom for lying to me.
　我不能原諒湯姆欺騙我。

▶ The old lady prayed: "God, would you please tell me how to forgive and forget?"
　老太太祈禱道：『上帝啊，您能告訴我如何能夠不念舊惡嗎？』

9　universe [ˈjunəˌvɝs] *n.* 宇宙 (前面加定冠詞 the)

片 in the universe　在宇宙中
似 space [spes] *n.* (外) 太空 ①

▶ I believe somewhere in the universe there are aliens.
　我相信宇宙某處有外星人存在。
　*alien [ˈelɪən] *n.* 外星人；外國人

---

university [ˌjunəˈvɝsətɪ] *n.* 大學
複 universities [ˌjunəˈvɝsətɪz]
片 (1) a university student　大學生
　　= a college student
　(2) the university of one's choice
　　　某人理想中的大學

▶ Aaron was admitted to the university of his choice.
　亞倫獲准進入他理想中的大學。

---

college [ˈkɑlɪdʒ]
n. 大學；(大學的) 學／分院
片 go to college / university　念大學

▶ Peter started going to college at age 15.
　彼得 15 歲就開始念大學了。

▶ Do you know Harry attended the College of Arts and Sciences at this university?
　你知道哈利曾在這所大學的文理學院念書嗎？

10　official [əˈfɪʃəl] *a.* 官方的，正式的 & *n.* (高層) 官員；主管

衍 (1) office [ˈɔfɪs] *n.* 辦公室 ①
　(2) officer [ˈɔfɪsɚ]
　　　n. 軍官；警官；長官 ①

▶ The official explanation of the event is not convincing.　該事件的官方解釋沒有說服力。
　*convincing [kənˈvɪnsɪŋ] *a.* 有說服力的

▶ The company made an official announcement that they didn't bribe the policemen.
　該公司發表正式聲明，表示他們並未行賄那些警察。

▶ The bill was strongly opposed by the officials.
　這項法案遭到官員們強烈反對。

formal [`ˈfɔrml`] *a.* 正式的
☐ on a formal occasion　在正式場合中

▶ Jack looks very serious on formal occasions.
傑克在正式場合中看起來很嚴肅。

11　promise [`ˈprɑməs`] *vt. & vi.* 承諾，答應 & *n.* 承諾，諾言

☐ (1) promise to V　承諾做……
　= make a promise to V
　(2) promise (sb) that...
　　承諾／答應（某人）……
　(3) keep / break a promise
　　守／背信

衍 **promising** [`ˈprɑməsɪŋ`]
　a. 有為的，有前途的 ④

▶ Grandma promised to teach me how to bake a cake.
= Grandma made a promise to teach me how to bake a cake.
奶奶承諾要教我烤蛋糕。

▶ Luke promised Gina that he would quit smoking.
路克向吉娜保證他會戒菸。

▶ A: Honey, I'm sorry. I can't go to the beach with you tomorrow.
　B: But you promised!
　A：親愛的，對不起，我明天不能和你一起去海灘了。
　B：可是你答應過的！

▶ I don't trust my boyfriend anymore because he keeps breaking his promises.
我不再信任我男友，因為他一直不守信用。

12　appearance [`əˈpɪrəns`] *n.* 出現，露面；外表

☐ make an appearance　出現
衍 **appear** [`əˈpɪr`] *vi.* 出現 ①
　= show up

▶ The thieves were surprised by the appearance of the police.
警方的出現讓那些小偷嚇了一跳。

▶ I'm quite tired, but I'll make an appearance at the party.
我很累，但我會去派對露面一下。

▶ The two women looked very much alike in appearance.
這 2 名女子在外貌上非常相像。

---

disappear [`ˌdɪsəˈpɪr`] *vi.* 消失
☐ disappear from...　從……消失
衍 **disappearance** [`ˌdɪsəˈpɪrəns`] *n.* 消失
似 **vanish** [`ˈvænɪʃ`] *vi.* 消失 ③

▶ The necklace seemed to have magically disappeared from the safe.
那條項鍊似乎神奇地從保險箱中消失了。

13　indeed [`ɪnˈdid`] *adv.* 確實，的確

似 (1) **really** [`ˈrɪəlɪ`]
　　adv. 確實，的確；真正地 ①
　(2) **truly** [`ˈtrulɪ`] *adv.* 確實；真正地

▶ A friend in need is a friend indeed.
困境中的朋友才是真正的朋友／患難見真情。—— 諺語

14 admit [əd`mɪt] vt. 准許……進入；准許……加入；承認

目 admit, admitted [əd`mɪtɪd], admitted

用 (1) admit sb to / into...
准許某人進 / 加入……
= sb be admitted to / into...
(2) admit (to) + V-ing 承認做……

衍 (1) admission [əd`mɪʃən]
n. 准許加入；入 (學)；入場費；承認 ④
(2) admittance [əd`mɪtəns]
n. (常指實際或實體的) 進入 (非『抽象的』進入)

似 confess [kən`fɛs] vt. & vi. 承認 ④

反 deny [dɪ`naɪ] vt. 否認 ②

▶ Children are not admitted to the theater without an adult.
小朋友沒有大人帶是不能進入那間劇院的。

▶ Only five percent of the applicants are admitted to the university.
只有 5% 的申請者獲准進入該所大學。

▶ Jake admitted stealing the money from the cash register.
傑克承認偷了收銀機裡的錢。
＊cash register [`kæʃ ˏrɛdʒɪstɚ] n. 收銀機

▶ The politician admitted to taking bribes.
那位政客坦承受賄。

15 courage [`kɝɪdʒ] n. 勇氣

用 pluck up the courage
某人鼓起勇氣

衍 courageous [kə`redʒəs]
a. 勇敢的 ④

似 bravery [`brevərɪ] n. 勇氣 ③

▶ I plucked up the courage and asked Alice to marry me.
我鼓起勇氣向艾莉絲求婚。

encourage [ɪn`kɝɪdʒ]
vt. 鼓勵；助長，促進

用 encourage sb to V 鼓勵某人做……

反 discourage [dɪs`kɝɪdʒ]
vt. 使氣餒；勸阻 ④

▶ The teacher encouraged us to try again.
老師鼓勵我們再試一次。

▶ Giving someone too much help will encourage his or her dependence.
給某人太多幫助會助長其依賴性。

encouragement [ɪn`kɝɪdʒmənt]
n. 鼓勵；助長，促進

反 discouragement [dɪs`kɝɪdʒmənt]
n. 沮喪；阻止 ④

▶ I owe my success to your encouragement.
我的成功要歸因於你的鼓勵。

▶ The target of this plan is the encouragement of economic growth.
該計畫的目標是促進經濟成長。

16 ordinary [`ɔrdnˏɛrɪ] a. 平常的，普通的

似 (1) common [`kɑmən] a. 常見的 ①
(2) usual [`juʒʊəl] a. 平常的 ②

反 extraordinary [ɪk`strɔrdnˏɛrɪ]
a. 非凡的 ⑤

▶ I just want to live an ordinary life.
我只想過普通的人生。

▶ I thought it was a very ordinary novel.
我還以為那是一本很普通的小說。

Level 2 Unit 43

17 measure [ˈmɛʒɚ] *vt.* 測量;衡/估量;尺寸(或數量等)為……& *n.* 度量單位;衡量標準 ☐

片 measure up to sb's expectations
　符合/達到某人的期望
= live up to sb's expectations
= meet sb's expectations

▶ Help me measure the length of this table.
　幫我量桌子的長度。

▶ We can't measure a writer's success in terms of book sales.
　我們不能以書籍銷售數字來衡量一個作家的成就。

▶ This room measures 30 square meters.
　這個房間的大小為 30 平方公尺。

▶ Without hard work, you can't measure up to your parents' expectations.
　你若不努力就不能達到你父母的期望。

▶ A yard is a measure of length.
　碼是一種長度的度量單位。

▶ Age is not an accurate measure of maturity.
　年齡並非衡量成熟度的精確標準。

measurement [ˈmɛʒɚmənt]
n. 測量;(量出來的) 尺寸/大小等

片 take measurements of...
　測量……(的尺寸/大小等)

▶ The professor said, "Objective measurement is very important in any experiment." ☐
　教授說：『客觀的測量在任何實驗中都非常重要。』

▶ Jenny is taking measurements of the bed to see if it will fit in her room.
　珍妮在量這張床,看看是否擺得進她房間。

18 length [lɛŋθ] *n.* 長度 ☐

片 (1) ... in length　長為……
　(2) at length　詳細地
　= in detail

衍 (1) long [lɔŋ]
　　a. 長的 & *adv.* 長時間地 ①
　(2) lengthen [ˈlɛŋθən]
　　vt. & *vi.* 使變長,加長 ④
　(3) lengthy [ˈlɛŋθɪ] *a.* 冗長的 ⑥

▶ This river is two kilometers in length.
= This river is two kilometers long.
　這條河長 2 公里。

▶ Tell me at length what happened.
　詳細告訴我發生了什麼事。

width [wɪdθ] *n.* 寬度

片 ... in width　寬為……

衍 (1) wide [waɪd]
　　a. 寬闊的;寬的 & *adv.* 很大地 ①
　(2) widen [ˈwaɪdn̩]
　　vt. & *vi.* (使) 變寬 ③

▶ The river is 120 feet in width. ☐
= The river is 120 feet wide.
　這條河寬 120 英尺。

depth [dɛpθ]

n. 深度；(海洋或陸地的) 深處 (此意恆用複數)

片 (1) ... in depth　深 (度) 為……
(2) a man of great depth
很有深度的人
(3) be out of one's depth
能力不及，無法了解

衍 (1) deep [dip]
a. 深的；深沉的 & *adv.* 深地 ①
(2) deepen [ˈdipən]
vt. & *vi.* (使) 變深 ③

▶ This lake reaches about 210 meters in depth.
這個湖泊深約 210 公尺。

▶ The ring Emma threw sank into the depths of the sea.
艾瑪扔出去的戒指沉到了海底深處。

▶ Tom's friends call him a man of great depth.
湯姆的朋友說他這個人很有深度。

▶ Ken told me he was out of his depth in Ms. Smith's class.
肯告訴我他認為史密斯老師的課太難了。

---

19 upper [ˈʌpɚ] *a.* 上方的，較高的

片 (1) an upper arm　上臂
(2) upper management
上層管理階級
(3) get / have the upper hand
占上風

▶ The motorcyclist's upper arms were badly injured in the accident.
這名摩托車騎士的上臂在這起意外中嚴重受傷。

▶ The upper management has the power and responsibility to make important decisions.
上層管理階級有做重要決策的權力和責任。

▶ In her relationship with Ray, Judy is always the one who has the upper hand.
在茱蒂和雷的交往關係裡，茱蒂總是占上風的一方。

---

lower [ˈloɚ]
a. 下方的，底部的 & *vt.* 降低

▶ My lower back hurts. Could I just take a rest?
我的下背疼痛。我可以休息一下嗎？

▶ Mary's friends felt that she was lowering her standards when she agreed to marry Peter.
瑪麗同意嫁給彼得時，她的朋友認為她在降低標準。

---

20 rapid [ˈræpɪd] *a.* 迅速的

似 (1) fast [fæst] *a.* 快速的 ①
(2) speedy [ˈspidɪ] *a.* 快速的

▶ John's rapid advancement in the company has been because of his hard work.
約翰在公司內可快速升遷是由於他很努力工作。

---

21 positive [ˈpɑzətɪv] *a.* 確信的，有把握的；積極正面的；(化驗 / 檢驗等結果) 陽性的 & *n.* 優點，好處

片 (1) be positive that...　確信 / 定……
= be sure that...

▶ Are you positive that Jerry is right?
= Are you sure that Jerry is right?
你確定傑瑞是對的嗎？

(2) test positive for...
……的化驗 / 檢驗 (等) 結果為陽性

似 (1) sure [ʃʊr] *a.* 確定的 ①
(2) confident [ˈkɑnfədənt]
a. 確信的 ②

反 unsure [ˌʌnˈʃʊr] *a.* 沒把握的

▶ Try to be more positive. Everything is going to be OK.
設法積極正面一點。一切都會沒事的。

▶ Derek tested positive for COVID-19.
德瑞克冠狀病毒的檢驗結果為陽性。

▶ The positives of this job include good employee welfare.
這份工作的好處包括有很好的員工福利。

---

negative [ˈnɛɡətɪv]
a. 否定的，拒絕的；消極負面的；
(化驗 / 檢驗等結果) 陰性的 & *n.* 缺點

片 test negative for...
……的檢驗 / 檢驗 (等) 結果為陰性

▶ I thought that Peter would give me a negative answer, but he surprised me by agreeing to come.
我以為彼得會給我否定的答案，但他出乎我意料地答應要來。

▶ I don't like Bonnie since she always has a negative attitude to everything.
我不喜歡邦妮，因為她對任何事都是消極負面的態度。

▶ Fortunately, my friend tested negative for COVID-19.
幸好我朋友冠狀病毒的檢驗結果為陰性。

▶ The only negative of this apartment is that it's a little far from the MRT station.
這間公寓唯一的缺點是離捷運站有點遠。

---

22 disagree [ˌdɪsəˈɡri] *vi.* 不同意

片 disagree with sb　與某人意見相左
似 dissent [dɪˈsɛnt] *vi.* 不同意 ⑥
反 (1) agree [əˈɡri] *vt.* & *vi.* 同意 ①
(2) consent [kənˈsɛnt] *vi.* 同意 ⑤

▶ If you disagree with me, please tell me.
如果你不同意我的話，請告訴我。

---

disagreement [ˌdɪsəˈɡrimənt]
n. 意見不一，分歧

片 be in disagreement about / over...
對於……意見分歧
= have a disagreement about / over...

▶ We are in disagreement about what to do.
對於要做什麼我們意見分歧。

▶ The two friends had a sharp disagreement over money.
這兩個朋友在金錢上有嚴重的分歧。

---

23 dial [ˈdaɪəl] *n.* (設備等的) 調節 / 控制器 & *vt.* 撥 / 按 (電話號碼)

片 dial a number　撥電話號碼

▶ Dan, help me turn the dial to 180 degrees.
丹，幫我把調節器調到 180 度。

▶ Dial this number in case you need help.
如果需要幫忙的話，就撥這個號碼。

24 instruction [ɪnˋstrʌkʃən] *n.* 教／指導（不可數）；指示（常用複數）；（機器等）使用說明（常用複數）

🄷 follow (sb's) instructions
遵從某人的指示

衍 (1) instruct [ɪnˋstrʌkt]
vt. 教導；指示 ④

(2) instructor [ɪnˋstrʌktɚ]
n. 教練；大學講師 ④

▶ This church offers English instruction to immigrants.
這間教堂為移民提供英語指導。

▶ Follow my instructions carefully, or you're likely to make mistakes.
小心地遵從我的指示，否則你可能會犯錯。

▶ Read the instructions carefully before operating the machine.
仔細看完說明書後再操作機器。

25 wire [waɪr] *n.* 電線；金屬絲 & *vt.* 接電線

🄷 a telephone wire　電話線

衍 (1) wiring [ˋwaɪrɪŋ] *n.* 線路系統

(2) wired [waɪrd] *a.* 有連上網路的

▶ Closer examination showed that these telephone wires had been cut.
進一步檢查顯示這些電話線都被人切斷了。

▶ This wire is made of copper.
這條金屬絲是銅製的。

▶ The whole house needs to be wired.
整棟房子都需要安裝線路。

4401-4406

---

1 standard [ˈstændəd] *n.* 標準，水準 & *a.* 標準的

🔑 (1) a high / low living standard
高 / 低生活水準

(2) be up to standard 達到標準

▸ The airline has very strict safety standards.
該航空公司採取很嚴格的安全標準。

▸ That country has a very high living standard.
那國有很高的生活水準。

▸ Howard's work is not up to standard.
霍華的工作未達到標準。

▸ Try to speak standard English.
試著說標準的英文。

---

2 damage [ˈdæmɪdʒ] *n.* & *vt.* 破壞，損壞 (名詞為不可數)

🔑 do / cause damage to sb/sth
對某人 / 事物造成損害

= do / cause harm to sb/sth

衍 damaging [ˈdæmɪdʒɪŋ] *a.* 有害的

似 harm [hɑrm] *n.* & *vt.* 傷害 ③

反 benefit [ˈbɛnəfɪt]
n. 利益 & *vt.* 有益於 ③

▸ Taking drugs does damage to one's body and mind.
= Taking drugs does harm to one's body and mind.
吸毒有害身心。

▸ The car was totally damaged in a traffic accident.
這輛車在一起交通事故中全毀了。

---

3 article [ˈɑrtɪkl̩] *n.* (報章雜誌的) 文章；一件物品 (如衣物、傢俱等)

🔑 an article of clothing / furniture
一件衣服 / 傢俱

= a piece of clothing / furniture

似 object [ˈɑbdʒɪkt / ˈɑbdʒɛkt]
n. 物品 ②

▸ Have you read the article about climate change in the newspaper?
你看了報上那篇關於氣候變遷的文章了嗎？

▸ Paul bought several articles of furniture recently.
保羅最近買了幾件傢俱。

·····

essay [ˈɛse]
n. (學生就某課程所寫的) 論說文，短文；
論文，專文 (皆與介詞 on 或 about 並用)

▸ Ms. Jones asked us to write an essay on any Victorian novel.
瓊斯老師讓我們寫一篇關於任何一本維多利亞時期小說的短文。

▸ I'm planning to write an essay on global warming.
我正計劃要寫一篇有關全球暖化的論文。

---

4 deliver [dɪˈlɪvɚ] *vt.* & *vi.* 遞送，投遞 & *vt.* 發表 (演講)；生產，分娩；拯救

🔑 (1) deliver a speech / report
發表演講 / 報告

(2) deliver sb from sth
拯救某人脫離某事

▸ The letter won't be delivered if you don't stick a stamp on the envelope.
如果不在信封上貼郵票，這封信就無法送達。

衍 **deliverance** [dɪ`lɪvərəns]
　　n. 拯救，救出 (不可數)

似 **send** [sɛnd] *vt.* 寄 ①

▶ The president of the company delivers a speech to all employees every Monday morning.
每週一早上公司總裁都會對全體員工發表演講。

▶ Tina's going to deliver her second baby tonight.
蒂娜今晚就要生第 2 胎了。

▶ Years of hard work has finally delivered Sam from poverty.
山姆多年的努力使他終於能擺脫貧窮。

---

delivery [dɪ`lɪvərɪ] *n.* 遞送

複 **deliveries** [dɪ`lɪvərɪz]

片 (1) pay on delivery 　貨到付款
　　(2) take / accept delivery of sth
　　　　收到某物

▶ There is no mail delivery on Sundays.
星期天郵差不送信。

▶ I haven't paid yet; I need to pay on delivery.
我還沒付款；我需要貨到付款。

▶ Helen's neighbor took delivery of the package for her.
海倫的鄰居幫她代收包裹。

5　worth [wɝθ] *a.* 值 (若干金額) 的；值得 (做) 的 & *n.* 值 (若干金額或時間)；價值，重要性

片 (1) be worth + N/V-ing 　值得……
　　(2) worth one's salt 　　稱職的
　　(3) 金額's / 時間's + worth of sth
　　　　價值若干金額的某事物 / 需花費若
　　　　干時間的某事物
　　　　*若金額為阿拉伯數字，則不加『'』。

衍 (1) worthy [`wɝðɪ] *a.* 值得的 ⑤
　　(2) worthwhile [ˏwɝθ`(h)waɪl]
　　　　a. 值得 (做) 的 ⑤

▶ The painting is worth five million dollars.
這幅畫值 5 百萬美元。

▶ The record is worth listening to again and again.
這張唱片值得一聽再聽。

▶ Any worker worth his or her salt knows the importance of punctuality.
任何一個稱職的員工都知道守時的重要。
*punctuality [ˏpʌŋktʃʊ`ælətɪ] *n.* 守時

▶ If you're lucky, you could get one thousand dollars' worth of coupons.
= If you're lucky, you could get $1,000 worth of coupons.
幸運的話，可以獲得價值 1,000 元的禮券。
*coupon [`kupɑn / `kjupɑn] *n.* 禮券

▶ This is a book of real worth.
這是一本真正有價值的書。

6　willing [`wɪlɪŋ] *a.* 願意的，情願的；自動自發的

片 be willing to V 　願意做……

衍 will [wɪl] *n.* 意願 ①

反 unwilling [ʌn`wɪlɪŋ] *a.* 不願意的

▶ Sally is willing to help her mother with the chores.
莎莉願意幫母親做家事。

▶ Diana and Gordon are both willing workers.
戴安娜和戈登都是很自動自發的員工。

7 **advance** [əd'væns] *vt.* 促進 & *vi.* 前進，行進 & *n.* 進步；預付款

片 (1) make an advance 進步
(2) give sb an advance
給某人預付款
(3) an advance on sth
關於某物的預付款
(4) in advance 事先，預先
= beforehand [br'for,hænd]
衍 advanced [əd'vænst]
a. 先進的；進階的；年紀大的 ③

▶ The government has put a lot of effort to advance research on computer science.
政府花了很多心力促進電腦科學的研究。

▶ The officer told the soldiers to advance.
那名軍官下令士兵前進。

▶ We have not made great advances in the fight against AIDS.
我們在對抗愛滋病方面，並沒有很大的進步。

▶ The boss gave me an advance on my next month's salary.
老闆讓我預支下個月的薪水。

▶ Sean booked the hotel six months in advance.
尚恩提前 6 個月訂飯店。

8 **brief** [brif] *a.* 短暫的；(某事物) 簡短的，簡潔的；(某人) 簡明扼要的 & *n.* 概要 & *vt.* 向……簡單說明

片 (1) a news brief 新聞摘要 / 簡報
(2) in brief 簡而言之
= in short
(3) brief sb on sth
就某事向某人做簡報
衍 briefcase ['brif,kes] *n.* 公事包 ⑤
似 short [ʃɔrt] *a.* 短的 ①

▶ Greg took a brief look at the newspaper before going to work.
葛瑞格在上班前迅速瀏覽了一下報紙。

▶ The teacher asked us to write a brief summary of this article.
老師要求我們寫這篇文章的簡短摘要。

▶ I know we're all in a hurry, so I'll be brief.
我知道我們的時間很趕，所以我會長話短說。

▶ There's only a four-paragraph news brief on the event in the newspaper.
這份報紙上關於那事件的新聞摘要只有 4 段。

▶ In brief, it's a job worth doing.
簡言之，這份工作值得做。

▶ The commander briefed those soldiers on the nature of their mission.
指揮官向那些士兵就此次任務的性質做了簡單的說明。

9 **cartoon** [kɑr'tun] *n.* (報紙等的) 漫畫；(電視等的) 卡通片 & *vt.* 為……畫漫畫

▶ Hank likes the political cartoons in the newspaper because they're really funny.
漢克喜歡報上的政治漫畫，因為它們真的很有趣。

▶ I like to watch cartoons on TV.
我喜歡看電視卡通節目。

▶ Mac cartooned the politician for the newspaper.
麥克幫報社畫該政客的漫畫。

comic [ˈkɑmɪk] *a.* 喜劇的；滑稽的 &
n. 漫畫書 (= a comic book)

片 a comic strip　連環漫畫

似 funny [ˈfʌnɪ] *a.* 滑稽的 ①

▶ This comic writer has a talent for describing common events in a humorous way.
這位喜劇作家有用幽默的方式來呈現平凡事件的天分。

▶ Jimmy delighted us all by singing a comic song.
吉米唱了一首很滑稽的歌，逗得大家都很開心。

▶ Tim was punished for reading comics in class.
提姆上課時看漫畫書而遭到懲罰。

Level 2　Unit 44

10　building [ˈbɪldɪŋ] *n.* 建築物，大樓

衍 build [bɪld] *vt.* 興建 ①

▶ This building has been here for more than 40 years.
這棟大樓屋齡已有 40 多年了。

roof [ruf] *n.* 屋頂 & *vt.* 給……蓋屋頂

複 roofs [rufs]

片 (1) under sb's roof
住在某人的家裡
(2) be roofed with sth
用某物來做屋頂

▶ We need to get someone to fix the roof as soon as possible.
我們得盡快找人來修理屋頂。

▶ When you're under my roof, you follow my rules.
你住我家時，就要遵守我的規定。

▶ The shed is roofed with bamboo.
這棚屋的屋頂是用竹子做的。

ceiling [ˈsilɪŋ] *n.* 天花板

片 hit the ceiling / roof
大發雷霆，勃然大怒

延伸 dome [dom] *n.* 圓屋頂 ⑤

▶ The ceiling was painted white.
天花板被粉刷成白色。

▶ Upon hearing that John had been kicked out of school, his father hit the ceiling.
約翰的父親一聽到他被學校開除就勃然大怒。

balcony [ˈbælkənɪ]
n. 陽臺；(劇場的) 包廂

複 balconies [ˈbælkənɪz]

延伸 porch [pɔrtʃ] *n.* 走廊 ⑤

▶ I planted some flowers on the balcony.
我在陽臺上種了一些花。

▶ The balcony on the fifth floor has a good view of the entire stage.
5 樓的包廂有極佳的視野可以看到整個舞臺。

11　upset [ʌpˈsɛt] *a.* 難過的，沮喪的 & *vt.* 使難過 & *n.* 爆冷門；難過，沮喪

三 三態同形

似 unhappy [ʌnˈhæpɪ] *a.* 不悅的

▶ We were all upset when we heard the news.
我們得知這個消息時都很難過。

▶ It upset Mary to have lost the race to her brother.
瑪麗賽跑輸給弟弟，令她很難過。

▶ In a huge upset, Gary's team beat the former champions.
蓋瑞的隊伍打敗前次的冠軍，真是大爆冷門。

▶ Dana's marriage problems were causing her great upset.
黛娜的婚姻問題使她很難過。

12 valuable [ˈvæljuəbl̩] a. 值錢的，貴重的；有價值的，有用的

衍 (1) value [ˈvælju] n. 價值 & vt. 評價②
(2) invaluable [ɪnˈvæljuəbl̩]
　 a. 無價的⑥

似 (1) expensive [ɪkˈspɛnsɪv]
　 a. 昂貴的①
(2) precious [ˈprɛʃəs] a. 貴重的③
(3) priceless [ˈpraɪsləs] a. 無價的⑥
　 (= invaluable)
(4) useful [ˈjusfəl] a. 有用的①
(5) helpful [ˈhɛlpfl̩] a. 有用的①

反 valueless [ˈvæljuləs] a. 沒有價值的

▶ Gold is considered more valuable than silver.
一般認為黃金比白銀來得值錢。

▶ I'd like to thank you for your valuable advice.
我很感謝你寶貴的意見。

13 custom [ˈkʌstəm] n. 習俗；(個人的) 習慣

片 as be one's custom　是某人的習慣
衍 (1) customs [ˈkʌstəmz]
　 n. 海關 (恆用複數)⑤
(2) customary [ˈkʌstəmˌɛrɪ]
　 a. 依據風俗的；依慣例的⑥

▶ It is a Chinese custom for adults to give red envelopes to children during Chinese New Year.
大人過年給小孩紅包是華人的習俗。

▶ Judy had breakfast in bed, as was her custom.
茱蒂在床上吃早餐，這是她的習慣。

14 per [pɝ] prep. 每……(年、人、公里等)

似 (1) each [itʃ]
　 a. 各自的 & pron. 每個 & adv. 各自地①
(2) every [ˈɛvrɪ] a. 每一①

▶ The scenic spot attracts about 3 million visitors per year.
此旅遊景點每年吸引大約 3 百萬名觀光客。

15 goal [gol] n. 目標

片 achieve a goal　達成目標

▶ Maria achieved a goal of getting a master's degree.
瑪麗亞達成了取得碩士學位的目標。

aim [em]
vt. & vi. (使) 瞄準；打算 & n. 瞄準；目標

▶ Tom aimed the stone at the thief.
湯姆把石頭瞄準小偷。

(1) aim A at B 把 A 瞄準 B
(2) aim at... 瞄準……
(3) aim to V 打算做……
(4) take aim at... 瞄準……
aimless [ˋemləs] *a.* 沒目標的

▶ Although Ivan was aiming at the bird, he hit the tree.
艾凡雖然瞄準的是那隻鳥，卻打到了樹。

▶ Richard aims to retire before he is fifty.
理查打算在 50 歲前退休。
＊retire [rɪˋtaɪr] *vi.* 退休

▶ That policeman took aim at the killer and shot him to death.
那警察瞄準了殺手並射殺了他。

▶ My aim in life is to be a doctor and help the poor.
我人生的目標是當醫生來幫助窮人。

---

purpose [ˋpɝpəs] *n.* 目的
(1) for the purpose of + V-ing
為了做……
(2) on purpose
故意地（= purposely）
(3) to no purpose 徒勞無功
= in vain
= to / of no avail

▶ Jenny went to Austria for the purpose of studying music.
珍妮為了學音樂便到奧地利去了。

▶ I can't believe Sarah hurt me on purpose.
我不敢相信莎拉會故意傷害我。

▶ I tried to ask Ned to quit smoking, but to no purpose.
我設法要奈德戒菸，卻徒勞無功。

---

target [ˋtɑrgɪt]
n. (想要實現的) 目標；靶子 & *vt.* 以……為目標
be targeted at... 以……為目標

▶ Our target this month is to produce at least four thousand cars.
我們本月的目標是要生產至少 4,000 輛車子。

▶ Frank missed the target and hit the wall.
法蘭克沒打中靶子而是打到了牆上。

▶ This new store is targeted at wealthy customers.
這家新開的店是以有錢的客戶為目標。

---

focus [ˋfokəs]
vt. & *vi.* (使) 集中 & *n.* 焦點
focuses [ˋfokəsɪz] / **foci** [ˋfo͵saɪ]
(1) focus A on B 把 A 聚焦在 B 上
(2) focus (one's attention) on...
(某人) 把注意力集中在……
= concentrate (one's attention) on...
(3) the focus of attention
眾所矚目的焦點
attention [əˋtɛnʃən] *n.* 注意 ②

▶ Be quiet! I'm trying to focus my mind on this paper.
安靜點！我正設法集中心思在這份論文上。

▶ I am so tired that I cannot focus on anything today.
我今天累死了，做什麼事都沒有辦法集中注意力。

▶ Diana's beauty made her the focus of attention at the party tonight.
黛安娜的美貌讓她在今晚的宴會成為眾所矚目的焦點。

16 **data** [ˋdetə] *n.* 資料 (複數形)

衍 **database** [ˋdetə͵bes] *n.* 資料庫 ③

用法 (1) data 的單數形為 datum [ˋdetəm]
(2) data 常被視為不可數名詞，其後動詞用單數形，但於正式寫作中常用複數形動詞。

▶ A lot of scientific data have been proven wrong upon further research.
經過進一步的研究後，很多科學資料已被證實有誤。

17 **chapter** [ˋtʃæptɚ] *n.* 章，回，篇；一段時期；分會

延伸 (1) article [ˋɑrtɪk!] *n.* 文章 ②
(2) section [ˋsɛkʃən] *n.* 節 ②
(3) paragraph [ˋpærə͵græf] *n.* 段落 ④

▶ The last chapter of the book was quite exciting.
這本書的最後一章相當精彩。

▶ That was a chapter of my life I'd rather not discuss.
我那段人生是我不願討論的。

▶ The local chapter of the Lions Club meets every Tuesday.
獅子會本地分會每週二會聚一次。

unit [ˋjunɪt] *n.* 單位

衍 (1) unite [juˋnaɪt]
vt. 使聯合 & *vi.* 團結 ③
(2) unity [ˋjunətɪ]
n. 一致；團結 (不可數) ③

▶ The basic unit of modern society is the family.
現代社會的基本單位是家庭。

▶ The light year is a unit of distance.
光年是距離的單位。

chart [tʃɑrt]
n. 圖表；排行榜 (此意常用複數)

片 a bar / pie / line / flow chart
長條 / 圓餅 / 曲線 / 流程圖

似 graph [græf]
n. (直線或曲線表示的) 圖表 ④

▶ According to the bar chart, the sales for this book have gone up.
根據此長條圖，這本書的銷量已增加。

▶ Ed Sheeran is number one in the charts again.
紅髮艾德再度登上排行榜冠軍。

18 **judge** [dʒʌdʒ] *vt.* 審判；裁判；判斷 & *n.* 法官；裁判

片 (1) judge A by / from B
根據 B 來判斷 A
(2) a good / bad judge of sth
很會 / 很不會判斷某事物

衍 (1) judicial [dʒuˋdɪʃəl] *a.* 司法的 ⑤
(2) judgmental [dʒʌdʒˋmɛnt!]
a. 武斷的

▶ The court wouldn't judge the case until all the evidence was collected.
法庭要等到所有證據蒐齊後才會審判該案。

▶ Is Sue going to judge the singing contest again?
蘇將再次擔任這次歌唱比賽的裁判嗎？

▶ We should judge a man by his deeds rather than by his words.
我們應根據一個人的所為，而非他的所言，來評斷他。

▶ Do not judge a book by its cover.
勿憑書皮評斷一本書 / 勿以貌取人。── 諺語

► The judge ordered us to remain silent.
法官命令我們保持肅靜。

► I'm not a very good judge of character.
我不太會判斷別人的人品。

judgment [ˈdʒʌdʒmənt]
n. 判決；判斷力；看法，意見
(= judgement〔英〕)

🅷 in sb's judgment　依某人判斷

► The judgment was against the victim.
這次判決對受害者不利。

► Don't ask me anymore. I trust your judgment.
不要再問我了。我相信你的判斷力。

► In my judgment, Hank is a very good actor.
依我看來，漢克是一個非常好的演員。

justice [ˈdʒʌstɪs]
n. 公道，正義；司法審判

🅷 (1) a sense of justice　正義感
(2) do sb/sth justice
為某人 / 事說公道話；公平對待某
人 / 合理處理某事
= do justice to sb/sth
(3) bring sb to justice
將某人繩之以法

衍 (1) just [dʒʌst] *a.* 公平的 ①
(2) justify [ˈdʒʌstəˌfaɪ]
vt. 證明……是合理的；使合理化 ⑤

► A good judge should have a sense of justice.
好法官應有正義感。

► To do Eliot justice, we must admit that he meant no harm.
為艾略特說句公道話，我們必須承認他無意傷害任何人。

► Sheila's playing didn't do Beethoven's music justice.
席拉的演奏未能呈現貝多芬音樂的原貌。

► The murderer must be arrested and brought to justice.
必須逮捕那兇手並將其繩之以法。

law [lɔ]
n. 法律 (體系) (不可數，前面常加定冠詞 the)；法則，定律

🅷 (1) obey / observe the law　守法
(2) break the law　犯法
(3) the laws of nature　自然法則

衍 (1) lawyer [ˈlɔjɚ] *n.* 律師 ①
(2) lawful [ˈlɔfəl]
a. 合法的，正當的 ④
(3) lawmaker [ˈlɔˌmekɚ]
n. 立法者 ⑤
(4) lawsuit [ˈlɔˌsut] *n.* 訴訟 ⑤

► Everybody is equal before the law.
法律之前人人平等。

► You must obey the law, or you will be punished.
你必須守法，不然會被處罰。

► Rebecca would never dream of breaking the law.
蕾貝嘉從沒想過要犯法。

► Human beings should follow the laws of nature.
人類應遵守自然法則。

legal [ˈligl] *a.* 與法律相關的；合法的
🅷 It is legal (for sb) to V
(某人) 做……是合法的

► Henry went to the lawyer for legal help.
亨利去找律師尋求法律上的協助。

Level 2　Unit 44

反 **illegal** [ɪˋligl] *a.* 非法的

▶ Is it legal for children to buy betel nuts in Taiwan?
在臺灣，兒童買檳榔合法嗎？
＊betel nut [ˋbitl ͵nʌt] *n.* 檳榔

---

fair [fɛr] *a.* 公平的；相當多的 & *adv.*
遵守規定地 & *n.* 露天遊樂場（＝ carnival
[ˋkɑrnəvl]）；(某類商品的) 展銷會

片 (1) **fair enough**　這說得過去，有道理
　　(2) **by fair means or foul**　不擇手段
　　(3) **play fair**　按規則比賽 / 競爭
　　(4) **a book / craft fair**
　　　　畫展 / 手工藝展銷會

衍 (1) **fairly** [ˋfɛrlɪ] *adv.* 相當地，蠻 ③
　　(2) **fairness** [ˋfɛrnəs] *n.* 公正；公平

▶ It's not fair for you to speak ill of Jill, especially when she's your best friend.
你說吉兒壞話很不公平，尤其她還是你最好的朋友。

▶ A: I'll do the dishes, and you'll mop the floor.
B: Fair enough.
A：我洗碗，你拖地。
B：這說得過去。

▶ Linda has fair knowledge of Chinese kung fu.
琳達懂得不少中國功夫。

▶ The coach wants the team to win by fair means or foul.
教練想要隊伍不擇手段贏得勝利。

▶ Ricky didn't play fair in the game.
瑞奇沒有按規則比賽。

▶ The children enjoyed all the rides at the fair very much.
這些小朋友很喜歡露天遊樂園的所有遊樂裝置。

▶ Sally bought a handmade vase at the craft fair.
莎莉在手工藝展銷會買了一個手工花瓶。

19　anywhere [ˋɛnɪ͵(h)wɛr] *adv.* 任何地方 (＝ anyplace [ˋɛnɪ͵ples])

似 **somewhere** [ˋsʌm͵(h)wɛr]
　　adv. 某處 ①

▶ Stop asking. I didn't go anywhere last night.
別問了。我昨晚哪兒也沒去。

---

anytime [ˋɛnɪ͵taɪm] *adv.* 任何時候

▶ Call me anytime. I'm always home.
隨時打給我。我都在家。

---

anyway [ˋɛnɪ͵we]
adv. 無論如何，還是，仍然

似 **anyhow** [ˋɛnɪ͵haʊ] *adv.* 無論如何 ③

▶ It was raining, but Mary went out anyway.
那時候在下雨，但瑪麗還是出門了。

20　alike [əˋlaɪk] *a.* 相似的 & *adv.* 相似地；同樣地

片 **A and B alike**　A 以及 B
＝ **both A and B**

似 (1) **similar** [ˋsɪmələ] *a.* 相像的 ②
　　(2) **identical** [aɪˋdɛntɪkl] *a.* 同樣的 ④

▶ The twins look so much alike that only their mother can tell them apart.
這對雙胞胎長得太相像了，只有他們的母親分辨得出來。

▶ The teacher treated his students alike.
這位老師對待他的學生都一視同仁。

▶ The strike is harmful to management and labor alike.
這場罷工對勞資雙方都同樣造成損失。

alive [əˈlaɪv] *a.* 活著的

🄗 (1) be alive with...　充滿……
(2) be alive to sth　意識到某事

▶ The police found two people alive at the scene of the car accident.
警方在車禍現場發現 2 名生還者。

▶ The ocean is alive with all kinds of salt water creatures.
海洋裡充滿著各式各樣的鹽水生物。

▶ The little girl wasn't alive to the danger.
那小女孩並未意識到危險。

4501-4506

1 debate [dɪˋbet] *n.* & *vt.* & *vi.* 辯論

﹝片﹞ debate about / over...
針對……來辯論

﹝衍﹞ debatable [dɪˋbetəbḷ]
a. 可爭論的，未定論的

﹝似﹞ (1) argument [ˋɑrgjəmənt] *n.* 爭論 ②
(2) dispute [dɪˋspjut / ˋdɪspjut]
n. & [dɪˋspjut] *vt.* 爭執 ④

▶ After lengthy debate, the committee finally reached a conclusion. 經過冗長的爭論，委員會終於得出結論。

▶ Daisy and I debated whether abortion should be made legal. 黛西和我為墮胎是否應該合法化而辯論。
＊abortion [əˋbɔrʃən] *n.* 墮胎

▶ Danny and Brandon debated over who was to blame for the mistake.
丹尼和布蘭登針對誰該為這個錯誤負責而辯論。

argue [ˋɑrgju] *vi.* 爭執，爭論

﹝片﹞ (1) argue about / over... 爭論……
(2) argue with sb 與某人爭論

▶ Will you kids stop arguing about whose toy that is?
你們這些孩子不要再爭吵那個玩具是誰的了，好嗎？

▶ Don't argue with me, son. Just do as you are told.
別和我爭論，兒子。只要照我說的去做就好。

argument [ˋɑrgjəmənt] *n.* 爭論

﹝片﹞ have an argument with sb about / over sth
為了某事物和某人爭論

▶ Allen was having an argument with his wife about their children.
亞倫正為了孩子們的事和太太起爭執。

2 title [ˋtaɪtḷ] *n.* 頭銜；標題 & *vt.* 為……加上標題

﹝衍﹞ entitle [ɪnˋtaɪtḷ] *vt.* 給……命名 ⑤

▶ Lauren's official title is Public Relations Director.
蘿倫的正式頭銜是公共關係部主任。

▶ What's the title of the play we're going to see tomorrow?
我們明天要看的那場戲戲名是什麼？

▶ This famous writer titled her latest novel *Sunrise*.
這位名作家為她的最新小說起名為《日出》。

3 mate [met] *n.* (動物的) 配偶；配偶，情人 & *vt.* & *vi.* (使) 交配

﹝片﹞ mate A with / to B 使 A 和 B 交配

﹝似﹞ (1) partner [ˋpɑrtnɚ]
n. 配偶，情人 ②
(2) spouse [spaʊs] *n.* 配偶 ⑤
(3) lover [ˋlʌvɚ] *n.* 情人 ③

▶ Female black widow spiders eat their mates.
雌的黑寡婦蜘蛛會吃掉牠們的配偶。

▶ Rita told me Taylor was her ideal mate.
麗塔告訴我泰勒是她的理想伴侶。

▶ Charlie mated his male donkey with a female one.
查理讓他的公驢和一匹母驢交配。

▶ Many animals mate in spring.
很多動物在春天交配。

classmate [ˈklæsˌmet] *n.* 同班同學

衍 class [klæs] *n.* 班級；課 ①

▶ Linda asked a classmate whether she could borrow his pen.
琳達問同學說她是否可以借支筆。

---

friendship [ˈfrɛndʃɪp] *n.* 友誼

衍 (1) friend [frɛnd] *n.* 朋友 ①
　　(2) friendly [ˈfrɛndlɪ] *a.* 友善的 ①

▶ Sam will treasure / cherish / value your friendship forever.
= Sam will hold your friendship dear forever.
山姆會永遠珍惜你的友誼。
＊hold... dear　非常在意……

4　shell [ʃɛl] *n.* 貝殼，(海洋生物的) 殼

片 bring sb out of sb's shell
使某人不再害羞

似 seashell [ˈsiˌʃɛl] *n.* (海) 貝殼

▶ We collected shells at the beach.
我們在海邊收集貝殼。

▶ Dancing has brought Tammy out of her shell.
跳舞讓泰咪變得不再害羞。

5　puzzle [ˈpʌzl̩] *n.* (遊戲的) 謎；難以理解的事，謎 & *vt.* & *vi.* (使) 困惑

片 (1) a crossword puzzle　填字遊戲
　　(2) puzzle over sth　苦思某事

衍 (1) puzzled [ˈpʌzl̩d] *a.* 困惑的
　　(2) puzzling [ˈpʌzlɪŋ] *a.* 令人困惑的
　　(3) puzzlement [ˈpʌzlmənt] *n.* 迷惑 (不可數)

似 (1) mystery [ˈmɪstərɪ]
　　　n. 謎團；神祕 ③
　　(2) confusion [kənˈfjuʒən]
　　　n. 困惑；雜亂 ④

▶ It took Eric four hours to solve the crossword puzzle.
艾瑞克花了 4 小時才解開這個字謎遊戲。

▶ How pyramids were built is still a puzzle.
金字塔是如何建造的仍是個謎。

▶ This question puzzles me a lot. Maybe I should ask the teacher.
這問題讓我很困惑。或許我該去問老師。

▶ Jim has been puzzling over the math question for two days.
這數學問題讓吉姆苦思了 2 天。

6　pose [poz] *n.* 姿勢 & *vt.* 造成 & *vi.* 擺姿勢 (好讓人拍照或繪畫)

片 (1) in a(n) + adj. + pose
　　　以……的姿勢
　　(2) pose a threat to...
　　　對……造成威脅
　　(3) pose for a photo / picture
　　　擺好姿勢拍照

衍 poser [ˈpozɚ] *n.* 裝模作樣的人；難題

▶ The model sat in a sexy pose.
那個模特兒用性感的姿勢坐著。

▶ Global warming is posing a threat to human survival.
全球暖化正對人類生存構成威脅。

▶ The couple posed for wedding photographs.
這對情侶擺好姿勢要拍婚紗照。

---

position [pəˈzɪʃən] *n.* 位置；姿勢；地位；立場；職務 & *vt.* 放置

片 (1) in a(n) + adj. + position
　　　地處……的位置；以……的姿勢

▶ Our hotel is in a superb position overlooking the sea.
本飯店地處絕佳位置，可俯瞰海景。

(2) hold a high position　位居要職
(3) in sb's position　處在某人的情況
(4) be in a position to V
　　有立場／資格做……
　　be in no position to V
　　沒立場／資格做……

▶ Just relax and sit in a comfortable position.
只需放鬆並舒服地坐著。

▶ My cousin holds a high position in the government.
我表哥在政府位居要職。

▶ What would you do if you were in my position?
假如你處在我的情況下會怎麼做？

▶ You're in no position to criticize others. You are at fault, too.

= You're not entitled to criticize others. You are at fault, too.
你沒有資格批評他人。你也有錯。

▶ This position pays a lot of money, but the work is hard.
這個職務待遇不錯，不過工作挺辛苦的。

▶ Position these tomato plants on the right-hand side of the balcony.
將這些番茄植物放在陽臺的右側。

7　sidewalk [`ˈsaɪdˌwɔk ] n. 人行道〔美〕(= pavement [ `ˈpevmənt]〔英〕)

衍 side [saɪd] n. 面，邊；一方，觀點 ①
延伸 (1) tunnel [`ˈtʌnḷ] n. 隧道 ③
(2) underpass [`ˈʌndɚˌpæs]
　　n. 地下道 ⑥
(3) overpass [`ˈovɚˌpæs] n. 天橋

▶ An artist is drawing on the sidewalk.
一位畫家正在人行道上作畫。

---

subway [`ˈsʌbˌwe]
n. 地鐵〔美〕(= underground
[`ˈʌndɚˌgraʊnd ]〔英〕= metro [ `ˈmɛtro])
延伸 MRT　大眾捷運系統 (為 Mass Rapid Transit 的縮寫)

▶ Shane takes the subway to work every day.
夏恩每天都搭地鐵上班。

8　whisper [`ˈ(h)wɪspɚ] vt. & vi. & n. 低／耳語

片 (1) whisper sth in sb's ear
　　在某人耳邊悄悄說某事
(2) whisper in / into sb's ear
　　在某人耳邊說悄悄話
(3) in a whisper　悄悄／小聲說
　 = in whispers
衍 whispering [`ˈ(h)wɪspərɪŋ]
　　n. 流言；呢喃

▶ Look! Natasha is whispering something in Taylor's ear again.
瞧！娜塔莎又在對泰勒說悄悄話了。

▶ The little girl whispered in my ear, but I didn't really hear her.
那小女孩在我耳邊說悄悄話，但我其實沒聽到她說的話。

▶ Jason and Linda were talking in a whisper. They're not speaking ill of me, are they?
傑森和琳達在小聲交談。他們不是在說我壞話，是吧？

9　china [`ˋtʃaɪnə`] *n.* 瓷器 (集合名詞，不可數)

片 **like a bull in a china shop**
是個莽撞的人，是個笨手笨腳的人

似 (1) **China** [`ˋtʃaɪnə`] *n.* 中國
(2) **pottery** [`ˋpɑtərɪ`]
　　n. 陶器 (集合名詞，不可數) ③
(3) **ceramics** [`səˋræmɪks`]
　　n. 陶瓷製品 (恆用複數)

▶ Please be careful not to break any china.
請小心不要打破瓷器。

▶ I don't want to invite Trevor to my party because he'll act like a bull in a china shop.
我不想邀請崔佛來我的派對，因為他會很莽撞。

10　rat [`ræt`] *n.* (大) 老鼠

片 **smell a rat**
覺得很可疑，察覺事有蹊蹺

似 **mouse** [`maʊs`]
　　n. 老鼠 (複數為 mice [`maɪs`]) ①

▶ Martha screamed as she saw a rat in the kitchen.
瑪莎看到廚房有老鼠就尖叫了起來。

▶ My husband has been coming home very late recently—I smell a rat!
我老公最近很晚才回家 —— 我覺得很可疑！

11　evil [`ˋivḷ`] *a.* 邪惡的；(氣味) 難聞的 & *n.* 邪惡

似 (1) **devil** [`ˋdɛvḷ`] *n.* 惡魔 ③
(2) **wicked** [`ˋwɪkɪd`] *a.* 邪惡的 ③
(3) **malicious** [`məˋlɪʃəs`] *a.* 惡意的

▶ Dragons are thought to be evil creatures in the West.
龍在西方世界裡被視為邪惡的生物。

▶ My American friend doesn't like stinky tofu because he thinks it gives off an evil smell.
我的美國朋友不喜歡臭豆腐，因為他認為臭豆腐的味道很難聞。

▶ The love of money is the root of all evil.
錢是萬惡之源。—— 諺語

12　found [`faʊnd`] *vt.* 建立，創辦

三 **found, founded** [`ˋfaʊndɪd`],
　　founded

比 **find** [`faɪnd`] *vt.* 發現 ①
　　三態為：find, found, found

▶ The United Nations was founded in 1945.
聯合國創立於西元 1945 年。

13　nearby [ˌ`nɪrˋbaɪ`] *a.* 附近的 & *adv.* 在附近

衍 (1) **near** [`nɪr`] *a.* 近的 & *adv.* 接近 & *prep.* 在……附近 ①
(2) **nearness** [`ˋnɪrnəs`] *n.* 接近

▶ We went swimming at the beach and stayed at a nearby hotel.
我們去海邊游泳，並在附近一家旅館過夜。

▶ Unfortunately, we had a flat tire, and there was no garage nearby.
很不幸我們的車爆胎了，且附近也沒有修車廠。

nearly [ˈnɪrlɪ] *adv.* 幾乎

似 almost [ˈɔlˌmost] *adv.* 幾乎 ①

▶ Mike was nearly hit by a car when he ran across the street toward the school bus.
麥克跑向對街的校車時差一點被車撞到。

14　ancient [ˈenʃənt] *a.* 古代的

反 modern [ˈmadən] *a.* 現代的 ①

▶ The custom is derived from an ancient story.
這習俗源自於古代的一個故事。

15　insist [ɪnˈsɪst] *vt. & vi.* 堅決要求；堅決認為，堅稱

片 (1) insist that + S + (should) + V
堅持要求……

insist that...　堅稱……

(2) insist on + N/V-ing
堅決要求……；堅稱……

衍 insistence [ɪnˈsɪstəns] *n.* 堅持 ⑥

▶ Dad insists that I (should) go on a diet.
老爸堅持要我減肥。

▶ The teacher insisted on having weekly tests as scheduled.
這位老師堅持要如期舉行週考。

▶ Andy insists that I am wrong.
安迪堅決認為我錯了。

▶ The boy insisted on his innocence and said he didn't steal the money.
那男孩堅稱自己是清白的，說他並沒有偷錢。

16　tradition [trəˈdɪʃən] *n.* 傳統

片 by tradition　按傳統

似 (1) custom [ˈkʌstəm]
n. 習俗，傳統 ②

(2) convention [kənˈvɛnʃən]
n. 傳統 ④

▶ By tradition, we eat rice dumplings on the Dragon Boat Festival.
按傳統，我們端午節會吃粽子。

---

traditional [trəˈdɪʃənl] *a.* 傳統的

似 classic [ˈklæsɪk] *a.* 傳統的；經典的 ②

▶ Zack prefers the traditional music of his homeland to Western music.
查克喜歡家鄉的傳統音樂甚於西洋音樂。

---

historical [hɪsˈtɔrɪkl]
a. 與歷史有關的

衍 historic [hɪsˈtɔrɪk]
a. 歷史上著名 / 重要的 ③

▶ Emma doesn't enjoy historical novels; she likes modern short stories instead.
艾瑪不喜歡歷史小說，她倒喜歡現代短篇小說。

17　regular [ˈrɛgjələ] *a.* 經常發生的；規律 / 固定的；普通 / 一般的 & *n.* 老顧客，常客

片 (1) on a regular basis　定期
(2) regular as clockwork　準時
＊clockwork [ˈklɑkˌwɝk]
n. (時鐘等的) 發條裝置

▶ Joyce is one of our store's regular customers.
喬伊絲是我們店裡的常客之一。

▶ John doesn't have a regular job.
約翰沒有固定的工作。

反 **irregular** [ɪˋrɛgjələ]
  a. 不定期的；不規則的

▶ Peggy visits her grandmother on a regular basis.
  佩琪定期探望她的祖母。

▶ My sister's boyfriend phones her at 8 p.m. every day, regular as clockwork.
  我姊姊的男朋友每天晚上 8 點打電話給她，非常準時。

▶ Tommy looks like a regular guy, but in fact, he is a billionaire.
  湯米看起來像普通人，但事實上他是個億萬富豪。
  ＊billionaire [ˌbɪljəˋnɛr] *n.* 億萬富翁

▶ The bartender offered the regulars free drinks on New Year's Eve.
  調酒師在跨年夜提供常客免費的飲料。

---

18 broad [brɔd] *a.* 寬闊的

衍 (1) **broaden** [ˋbrɔdn̩]
    vi. & vt. (使) 變寬 ⑥
  (2) **breadth** [brɛdθ] *n.* 寬度 ⑥
似 (1) **abroad** [əˋbrɔd] *adv.* 在國外 ①
  (2) **wide** [waɪd] *a.* 寬的；廣泛的 ①

▶ Sam is six feet tall with broad shoulders.
  山姆身高 6 英尺，有著寬闊的肩膀。

---

19 belief [bəˋlif] *n.* 相信；信仰；信念，堅定的看法

片 (1) **a belief in...** 相信 (有) ……
  (2) **It is sb's belief that...**
    某人相信……
衍 **believe** [bəˋliv] *vt.* 相信 ①
反 **disbelief** [ˌdɪsbəˋlif] *n.* 懷疑 ⑥

▶ Small children often have a belief in Santa Claus.
  小孩子通常都相信有聖誕老公公。
  ＊Santa (Claus) 聖誕老人

▶ Randy doesn't eat any meat or seafood because of his religious beliefs.
  由於藍迪的宗教信仰，他並不吃任何肉類或海鮮。

▶ It is my belief that Kate will succeed in the near future.
  我相信不久的將來凱特會成功。

---

20 reply [rɪˋplaɪ] *n. & vt. & vi.* 回答 / 覆

三 **reply, replied** [rɪˋplaɪd], **replied**
複 **replies** [rɪˋplaɪz]
片 (1) **in reply to sth** 回答 / 覆某事物
  (2) **reply to sth** 回答 / 覆某事物
  (3) **reply that...** 回答 / 覆……

▶ Oliver wrote a brief message in reply to his customer's email.
  奧利佛寫了一封簡訊來回覆他客戶的電子郵件。

▶ When the manager asked Ray whether he had finished the work, he replied, "Not yet."
  當經理問雷他工作做完了沒，他回答：『還沒。』

▶ Have you replied to Alan's letter yet?
  你回艾倫的信了沒？

21 **responsible** [rɪˈspɑnsəbḷ] *a.* 應負責的；負責可靠的

- be responsible for + N/V-ing
  負責……，為……負責
  = have responsibility for + N/V-ing
- responsibility [rɪˌspɑnsəˈbɪlətɪ]
  n. 責任 ③

- ▶ Adults are responsible for their actions.
  成年人要為自己的行為負責。
- ▶ Wendy is a responsible young woman.
  溫蒂是個負責任的女青年。

22 **object** [ˈɑbdʒɛkt] *n.* 物體；目標 & [əbˈdʒɛkt] *vi.* 反對

- (1) an object of sth　某事物的目標
  (2) object to + N/V-ing　反對……
  = oppose + N/V-ing
  = be opposed to + N/V-ing
- (1) objection [əbˈdʒɛkʃən] *n.* 反對 ④
  (2) objective [əbˈdʒɛktɪv]
  　　a. 客觀的 ④
- UFO　幽浮
  （為 unidentified flying object 的縮寫）

- ▶ Did you see the strange flying object in the sky?
  你看到空中那個奇怪的飛行物體了嗎？
- ▶ The object of this class is to teach students how to write a poem.
  本課程的目標就是要教導學生如何寫詩。
- ▶ Henry objects to what you just said.
  亨利反對你剛才說的話。

23 **handle** [ˈhændḷ] *n.* 把手，柄 & *vt.* 處理；搬動

- (1) a door handle　　　門把
  (2) handle a problem　處理問題
  = deal / cope with a problem

- ▶ Dad quietly turned the door handle to see if my little brother was studying in his room.
  爸爸悄悄轉動門把，看看我弟弟是不是在房間裡讀書。
- ▶ Kelly handled the emergency calmly and quickly.
  凱莉冷靜快速地處理這起緊急事件。
- ▶ The marked boxes must be handled with care.
  那些做了記號的箱子搬動時要小心。

24 **crisis** [ˈkraɪsɪs] *n.* 危機

- crises [ˈkraɪsiz]
- (1) handle a crisis　處理危機
  = deal with a crisis
  = solve / resolve a crisis
  (2) a financial crisis　金融危機

- ▶ The government handled the financial crisis quite well.
  這次金融危機政府處置得相當不錯。

25 **pound** [paʊnd] *n.* 英鎊（貨幣單位，縮寫為 £)(= pound sterling)；磅（重量單位，縮寫為 lb) & *vt.* & *vi.* 猛擊，連續重擊

- pound A on / against B
  用 A 猛擊 B，用 A 連續重擊 B

- ▶ This cellphone is only 30 pounds.
  = This cellphone is only £30.
  這支手機僅售 30 英鎊。

用法 pound sterling 之複數為 pounds sterling；lb 之複數為 lb / lbs。

▶ The box weighs 10 pounds.
= The box weighs 10 lbs.
這箱子重達 10 磅。

▶ An ounce of prevention is worth a pound of cure.
一盎司的預防等於一磅的治療 / 預防勝於治療。── 諺語

▶ Andrew suddenly pounded his fist on the table and scared all of us.
安德魯突然用拳頭猛擊桌子，嚇到了我們所有的人。

▶ Two policemen were pounding at my neighbor's door.
兩個警察正在不停地大力敲我鄰居的門。

26 leadership [ˈlidɚʃɪp] n. 領導（地位）；領導能力（皆不可數）

片 under sb's leadership
在某人的領導下

衍 (1) lead [lid] vt. 帶領 ①
(2) leader [ˈlidɚ] n. 領袖 ①

▶ Jenny believes things will get better under the new manager's leadership.
珍妮相信在新任經理的領導下，情況將會有所改善。

▶ Patrick was known for his courage and leadership.
派翠克以他的勇氣和領導能力聞名。

27 solve [sɑlv] vt. 解決；解（題）

片 solve a problem   解決問題
= resolve a problem

似 resolve [rɪˈzɑlv] vt. 解決 ④

▶ Money alone cannot solve all your problems.
光靠錢不能解決你所有的問題。

▶ Matthew is not good at solving math problems.
馬修不太擅長解數學題。

solution [səˈluʃən]
n. 解決辦法；答案；溶液

片 a solution to sth
某事物的解決辦法；某事物的答案

▶ The solution to the conflict between the two nations has yet to be found.
該兩國間衝突的解決之道仍有待探求。

▶ The solutions to the puzzles are at the back of the book.
= The answers to the puzzles are at the back of the book.
這些謎語的答案在書的最後面。

▶ Whenever I have a sore throat, my mom asks me to clean my throat with a salt solution.
每當我喉嚨痛時，我媽都要我用鹽水清潔我的喉嚨。

28 impressive [ɪmˈprɛsɪv] a. 令人印象深刻的，壯觀的

似 imposing [ɪmˈpozɪŋ] a. 壯觀的 ⑥

▶ Tiffany found the pianist's performance most impressive.
蒂芬妮覺得這位鋼琴家的演奏最令人印象深刻。

29 require [rɪˈkwaɪr] vt. 要求；需要

(1) require that S + (should) + V
要求……

(2) be required to V 被要求
做……，必須要做……

(3) require + V-ing 需要做……

required [rɪˈkwaɪrd] a. 必須的

▶ Karl's parents required that he clean his own room.
卡爾的父母要求他打掃自己的房間。

▶ Everyone is required to wear a uniform to the ceremony.
每個人都必須穿制服參加典禮。

▶ The machine required fixing.
這臺機器需要修理。

requirement [rɪˈkwaɪrmənt]
n. 要求，必要條件

meet a requirement 達到要求

▶ It's hard for Michael to meet the requirements of the job.
對麥可而言，符合這工作的需求很難。

Level 2 Unit 46

---

1 **instant** [`ɪnstənt`] *n.* 頃刻 & *a.* 立即的 (= immediate [ɪˋmidɪət])；即食 / 溶的

用 (1) for an instant
那一瞬間，有那麼一會兒

(2) in an instant 　馬上，立刻，瞬間

(3) instant noodles / coffee / soup
泡麵 / 即溶咖啡 / 即溶湯品

▶ As Jason heard the gunshots, for an instant he froze and his mind went blank.
傑森聽到槍聲時，一瞬間僵住了，腦子也一片空白。

▶ Kelly said she would pick me up in an instant.
凱莉說她會馬上來接我。

▶ Henry received an instant response from the company.
亨利收到了那家公司的立即回覆。

▶ Don't eat instant noodles too often, as they're not good for your heath.
不要太常吃泡麵，因為它們對你的健康並不好。

---

instance [`ɪnstəns`] *n.* 例子

用 for instance / example 　舉例來說

▶ Sandra has a lot of work to do. For instance, she has to clean the kitchen.
珊卓有很多工作要做。比如說，她必須打掃廚房。

---

sudden [`sʌdn̩`]
a. 突然的 & *n.* 突然發生的事

用 all of a sudden 　突然間
= suddenly

似 abrupt [əˋbrʌpt] *a.* 突然的 ⑤

▶ There was a sudden change in the weather.
天氣突然起了變化。

▶ All of a sudden, a loud noise outside our window disturbed our sleep.
突然窗外一聲巨響，打斷了我們的睡眠。

---

2 **furniture** [`fɝnɪtʃɚ`] *n.* 傢俱 (集合名詞，不可數)

用法 a furniture (✗)
a lot of furnitures (✗)
→ a piece of furniture (○) 　一件傢俱
a lot of furniture (○) 　許多傢俱

▶ This piece of furniture Paul bought last week is said to have a long history.
保羅上星期買的這件傢俱據說歷史悠久。

---

curtain [`kɝtn̩`]
n. 窗簾；(舞臺上的) 布幕 & *vt.* 給……裝窗簾

用 (1) draw / close / pull the curtains
拉上窗簾
draw back the curtains
拉開窗簾
= open the curtains

(2) curtain off sth 　用簾子遮住某物

▶ Can I draw the curtains? The sun is too bright.
我可以拉上窗簾嗎？太陽太大了。

▶ Katie drew back the curtains to reveal a sunny day outside.
凱蒂拉開窗簾，露出外面的晴天。

▶ Katie started to sing after the curtain opened.
舞臺上的布幕拉開後，凱蒂就開始唱歌。

▶ Donald curtained the windows of the building so that no one could see inside.
唐諾給這棟建物的窗戶裝上了窗簾，這樣就沒有人可以看到裡面了。

似 drapes [dreps]
　　n. 窗簾，帷幕 (恆用複數)

▸ The nurse curtained off Nathan's bed completely and then cleaned and dressed his wound.
護士將納森的床的周圍完全拉上窗簾，然後清洗包紮他的傷口。
＊dress [drɛs] *vt.* 包紮處理 (傷口)

mat [mæt] *n.* 墊子
衍 doormat [ˋdɔrˏmæt] *n.* 門前的地墊

▸ Mom put a mat in front of the door.
媽媽在門口擺了一張墊子。

3　following [ˋfɑloɪŋ] *prep.* 在……之後 & *n.* 接下來的人 / 事 / 物 & *a.* 接著的

用 (1) The following is + 單數可數名詞
　　　以下是……
　　(2) The following are + 複數可數名詞
　　　以下是……

衍 (1) follow [ˋfɑlo] *vt.* 跟隨；遵從；理解 (＝ understand)；在……之後發生 ①
　　(2) follower [ˋfɑloɚ]
　　　n. 追隨者；擁護者 ③

反 previous [ˋprivɪəs] *a.* 之前的 ③

▸ Following the film, there will be an interview with the director.
電影結束之後，將會對導演進行訪談。

▸ The following is a list of common errors found in student compositions.
以下是在學生作文中常發現的錯誤列表。

▸ The following are the winners of this game: Mike, Sue, and Jeff.
以下是這場比賽的優勝者：麥克、蘇和傑夫。

▸ Steve arrived on Thursday and left the following day.
史提夫星期四抵達，隔天就離開了。

4　praise [prez] *n.* & *vt.* 讚美

用 (1) in praise of...　讚美……
　　(2) praise... for +N/V-ing
　　　因……讚美……

反 (1) criticism [ˋkrɪtəˏsɪzəm] *n.* 批評 ④
　　(2) criticize [ˋkrɪtɪˏsaɪz]
　　　vt. & *vi.* 批評 ④

▸ Daniel gave a speech in praise of the success of the new products.
丹尼爾發表演講，稱讚新產品很成功。

▸ The teacher praised the little boy for his courage.
老師讚許這小男孩很有勇氣。

5　cancel [ˋkænsl̩] *vt.* 取消

衍 cancellation [ˏkænsl̩ˋeʃən] *n.* 取消
似 call... off　取消 / 中止……

▸ We canceled the meeting because of the typhoon.
我們因颱風天而取消了會議。

6　asleep [əˋslip] *a.* 睡著的

用 fall asleep　睡著
衍 sleep [slip] *vi.* 睡覺 ①
反 awake [əˋwek] *a.* 醒著的 ③

▸ The guard fell asleep while he was on duty last night.
守衛昨晚值班時睡著了。

sleepy [ˈslipɪ] *a.* 想睡的
🔠 be / feel sleepy　覺得很睏，想睡覺

▸ Wesley felt sleepy after finishing all that work.
把所有的工作做完後衛斯理覺得很睏。

---

7 **dot** [dɑt] *n.* 小點 & *vt.* 布滿，散布

📖 dot, dotted [ˈdɑtɪd], dotted
🔠 (1) on the dot　準時
　　(2) be dotted with...
　　　　布滿著……，有很多……
📎 spot [spɑt] *n.* (斑) 點 ②

▸ We watched the balloon flying away until it became a dot.
我們看著氣球飛走，直到它變成一個小點為止。

▸ It's nine o'clock on the dot.
= It's nine o'clock sharp.
= It's nine o'clock exactly.
現在是 9 點整。

▸ The night sky was dotted with shining stars.
夜空布滿著閃爍的星星。

---

8 **alarm** [əˈlɑrm] *vt.* 使恐慌，使擔心 & *n.* 警報器；鬧鐘

🔠 (1) set off an alarm　觸動警報器
　　(2) a fire alarm　火災警報器
　　(3) an alarm (clock)　鬧鐘
📎 frighten [ˈfraɪtṇ] *vt.* 使害怕 ③

▸ I didn't want to alarm our grandmother so I didn't tell her that my mother was sick.
我不想驚動我外婆，所以我沒有告訴她我母親生病了。

▸ The guards said they still had no idea what set off the fire alarm in this building.
守衛說他們仍不知道是什麼觸動了這座大樓的火災警報器。

▸ The alarm clock went off at seven.
鬧鐘在 7 點鐘響起。

---

9 **childish** [ˈtʃaɪldɪʃ] *a.* 幼稚的 (貶義)

🔀 (1) child [tʃaɪld] *n.* 小孩 ①
　　(2) childlike [ˈtʃaɪld͵laɪk] *a.* 純真的
📎 immature [͵ɪməˈtʃʊr] *a.* 不成熟的

▸ Your childish behavior is not suitable for a working environment.
就一個工作環境而言，你這樣幼稚的行為很不恰當。

---

mature [məˈtʃʊr] *a.* 成熟的 & *vi.* 成熟

🔀 (1) maturity [məˈtʃʊrətɪ]
　　　n. 成熟 (不可數) ④
　　　reach maturity　達到成熟期
　　(2) premature [͵priməˈtʃʊr]
　　　a. 不成熟的；過早的 ⑤
　　　a premature baby　早產兒

▸ You're already a mature adult, so you should make a decision by yourself.
你已經是一個成熟的大人了，所以你應該自己做決定。

▸ Girls usually mature earlier than boys.
女孩子通常比男孩子早熟。

10 improve [ɪmˈpruv] vt. & vi. 改善

衍 improved [ɪmˈpruvd]
　　a. 已改善的，有改進的

似 better [ˈbɛtɚ] vt. 改善 ②

▶ Tom would like to improve his English speaking ability.
湯姆想要增進自己英語口說的能力。

▶ As you can see, your father's health has improved a lot.
正如你所見，你父親的健康已改善了很多。

---

improvement [ɪmˈpruvmənt]
n. 改善

片 an improvement in...
　　……方面有改善

▶ There has been a great improvement in Debbie's writing skills.
黛比的寫作技巧已有了顯著的改善。

---

progress [ˈprɑɡrɛs]
n. 進步；前進 (皆不可數) & [prəˈɡrɛs]
vi. 進步；逐漸進行

片 make progress　進步；前進

衍 progressive [prəˈɡrɛsɪv] a. 進步的 ⑤

似 advance [ədˈvæns] vi. 前進，行進 &
　　vt. 促進 & n. 進步；預付款 ②

▶ My daughter has made great progress in tennis.
我女兒的網球大有進步。

▶ It was hard for us to make progress because of the heavy snow.
因為下大雪，我們很難前進。

▶ Under Bill's expert guidance, the soccer team progressed very well.
在比爾專業的指導下，足球隊進步得很快。

▶ Repair work has progressed slower than expected.
維修工作進行得較預期慢。

---

11 doubt [daʊt] n. & vt. 懷疑

片 (1) without (a) doubt　無疑地
　　(2) doubt that...　懷疑……
　　(3) doubt whether / if...
　　　　懷疑……是否……

衍 (1) doubtful [ˈdaʊtfəl] a. 懷疑的 ③
　　(2) undoubtedly [ʌnˈdaʊtɪdlɪ]
　　　　adv. 無庸置疑地 ⑤
　　(3) doubtless [ˈdaʊtləs]
　　　　adv. 毫無疑問

反 (1) believe [bəˈliv] vt. 相信 ①
　　(2) trust [trʌst] vt. 信任 ②

▶ Phil is without a doubt a man you can trust.
毫無疑問菲爾是一個你可以信任的人。

▶ I doubt that this team will win.
我懷疑這支球隊是否會贏。

▶ Annie really doubts whether the complaint will make a difference.
安妮真的很懷疑申訴會不會有用。

---

12 ease [iz] n. 舒適；容易 (皆不可數) & vt. & vi. (使) 減緩 / 降低

片 (1) live a life of ease
　　過著安逸的生活

▶ My grandfather retired and is living a life of ease.
我爺爺退休了，現在生活過得很安樂。

(2) at ease　　感到自在
　　ill at ease　感到不自在
(3) with ease　輕鬆地
= easily

▶ I don't want Kenny to be my partner. I never feel at ease with him.

我不想讓肯尼成為我的搭檔。和他在一起我從不會感到自在過。

▶ Thanks to our teamwork, we finished the work with ease.

多虧大夥的團隊合作，我們輕鬆地完成了工作。
＊teamwork [ˋtim,wɝk] n. 合作

▶ The doctor said the medicine would ease the pain.

醫生說這藥能減輕疼痛。

▶ After Rex took the medicine, his stomach pain eased a little bit.

雷克斯吃了藥之後，胃痛稍微緩解了一些。

13　aid [ed] *vt.* & *n.* 幫助　☐

片 (1) aid sb in + N/V-ing
　　協助某人……
　= assist sb in + N/V-ing
　= help sb (to) V
　(2) come / go to sb's aid　幫助某人
衍 aide [ed] *n.* 助手 / 理
似 (1) help [hɛlp] *vt.* & *vi.* & *n.* 幫助 ①
　(2) assistance [əˋsɪstəns] *n.* 幫助 ④

▶ Wendy aided her husband in managing the company.

溫蒂協助她先生管理這家公司。

▶ We all came to Luke's aid when we knew that he was in trouble.

我們得知路克有難時，大家都來幫他一把。

14　review [rɪˋvju] *vt.* & *vi.* 複習 & *vt.* 評論 & *n.* 複習；評論　☐

片 (1) review for a test / an exam
　　為考試來複習
　= do review for a test / an exam
　(2) have a(n) + adj. + review
　　有……的評論
　= receive a(n) + adj. + review
衍 (1) reviewer [rɪˋvjuɚ] *n.* 評論家
　(2) preview [ˋpri,vju]
　　n. 試映，預演 / 展 & *vt.* 預先觀看為
　　(書 / 電影等) 寫報導、預評等 ⑥

▶ Review the first five lessons before the exam.

= Go over the first five lessons before the exam.

考試前要複習前 5 課。

▶ I have to review for the math exam tomorrow.

= I have to do the review for the math exam tomorrow.

我得為明天的數學考試進行複習才行。

▶ The famous writer's latest novel was reviewed in this weekly magazine.

這週刊有評論這位著名作家最新的小說。

▶ This book has had mixed reviews.

這本書的評論褒貶不一。

15　exist [ɪgˋzɪst] *vi.* 存在　☐

▶ Do you really think that ghosts exist?

你真的相信鬼存在嗎？

existence [ɪɡˈzɪstəns] *n.* 存在

🔗 (1) come into existence
　　誕生，問世
　　= come into being
　　(2) in existence　現存

▶ Our ancestors had to struggle for existence.
我們的祖先不得不為生存而奮鬥。

▶ Tell me exactly when the first radio came into existence.
告訴我第一臺收音機到底是何時問世的。

▶ This is the oldest building in existence in our town.
這是我們鎮上現存最古老的建築物。

16　upon [əˈpɑn] *prep.* 在……之上；一……(就……)；馬上來臨

🔗 upon / on + N/V-ing　一……(就……)
似 on [ɑn] *prep.* 在……之上；關於 ①

▶ There is a dictionary upon the desk.
書桌上有一本字典。

▶ Upon seeing his teacher, Mark ran away.
= As soon as he saw his teacher, Mark ran away.
馬克一見到他老師便拔腿就跑。

▶ Christmas is almost upon us.
聖誕節快到了。

17　serve [sɝv] *vt.* 服務 & *vt.* & *vi.* 供應 (餐點)

衍 (1) server [ˈsɝvɚ]
　　n. 服務生；伺服器 ⑤
　　(2) service [ˈsɝvɪs] *n.* 服務 ①

▶ I'm afraid Leo is busy serving the customers right now. Can I take a message?
恐怕李歐現在正忙著服務客人。我可以幫您留言嗎？

▶ A waitress will serve your food in just a few minutes.
過幾分鐘就會有女服務生過來為您上菜了。

▶ You sprinkle some sesame on it, and I'll serve.
你在上面灑點芝麻，我來上菜。

---

servant [ˈsɝvənt] *n.* 僕人

🔗 a civil servant　公務員
似 maid [med] *n.* 女傭 ③

▶ The rich man has many servants but no friends.
那位有錢人有很多僕人，卻沒有朋友。

▶ A civil servant is someone who works for a government department.
公務員指的是在政府部門工作的人。

---

master [ˈmæstɚ]
vt. 精通 & *n.* 主人；大師

🔗 (1) be sb's own master
　　某人自己做主
　　(2) a master of...　擅長……的大師
　　(3) a master's degree　碩士學位

▶ To master English, you have to study it on a daily basis.
要想精通英文，你就必須每天讀英文。

▶ Doug wanted to be his own master. Thus, he decided to start his own business last year.
道格想要能夠自己做主。所以他去年決定自己創業。

▶ Chopin was a master of piano music.
蕭邦是鋼琴音樂大師。

衍 masterpiece [ˈmæstəˌpis] *n.* 傑作 ⑤
似 (1) owner [ˈonə] *n.* 主人，所有人 ②
   (2) guru [ˈguru]
      n. (某一領域的) 專家，大師

▶ Brenda has a master's degree in history.
布蘭達有歷史學的碩士學位。

---

18 **rocky** [ˈrɑkɪ] *a.* 岩石的，多岩石的；不穩定的，困難重重的

片 a rocky road
困難重重的路程，艱辛的路程
衍 rock [rɑk]
  vt. & vi. (使) 搖晃 & *n.* 石頭 ①

▶ The Gobi Desert has vast rocky areas.
戈壁沙漠有廣大的岩石區。

▶ According to the news, experts predict a rocky road ahead for the global economy.
據報導，專家預測全球經濟前景不穩定。
＊predict [prɪˈdɪkt] *vt.* 預測
  global [ˈglobḷ] *a.* 全球的
  economy [ɪˈkɑnəmɪ] *n.* 經濟

---

19 **population** [ˌpɑpjəˈleʃən] *n.* 人口，全體人民

片 (1) have a population of + 數字
    擁有若干人口
  (2) a small / large population
    人口稀少 / 眾多
衍 populate [ˈpɑpjəˌlet]
  vt. (大批地) 居住於 ⑥

▶ Taiwan has a population of about 23 million.
臺灣的人口約 2,300 萬人。

▶ New Zealand has a small population, while Taiwan has a large population.
紐西蘭人口稀少，而臺灣人口眾多。

---

20 **settle** [ˈsɛtḷ] *vt.* 解決 (糾紛等)；決定，安排好 & *vi.* 安頓，定居

片 (1) settle a dispute   解決糾紛
  (2) settle down   安定 / 頓下來
衍 settler [ˈsɛtlə] *n.* 開拓者，殖民者 ④

▶ Lawyers are hired to settle disputes between the two companies.
2 家公司之間有爭執時就委請律師來解決糾紛。

▶ The place for the party hasn't been settled yet.
派對的地點還沒決定好。

▶ Henry didn't get married and settle down until he was 42 years old.
亨利直到 42 歲才結婚安定下來。

---

settlement [ˈsɛtḷmənt]
n. 解決 (糾紛等)；定居點 / 地

▶ We hope there will be a peaceful settlement of the Middle East conflict.
我們希望中東地區的衝突能有和平的解決方法。

▶ The whites wanted to build new settlements on this island.
白人想在這島上建立新的定居點。

4621-4626

21 whatever [(h)wɑt'ɛvɚ] *pron.* 任何東西 (= everything / anything that)；
不管怎樣 (= no matter what) & *a.* 任何的，全部的

- ▶ Bess believes whatever you say.
- = Bess believes everything that you say.
  貝絲相信你所說的任何話。

- ▶ Whatever happens, my parents will back me up.
- = No matter what happens, my parents will back me up.
  不論發生什麼事，我父母都會支持我。

- ▶ If you can't come for whatever reason, please let us know as soon as possible.
  如果你因任何原因不能來，請盡快通知我們。

whoever [hu'ɛvɚ]
pron. 任何一人，無論什麼人
(= anyone who)

- ▶ A $1,000 reward will be offered to whoever finds the painting.
  任何人尋獲這幅畫，將可獲得 1,000 美元的酬金。

22 exact [ɪg'zækt] *a.* 精確的

- 片 to be exact　精確地說
- 似 accurate ['ækjərət] *a.* 精確的 ③

- ▶ We still don't know the exact cause of the fire.
  我們仍不知道火災發生的確切原因。

- ▶ Dennis is in his late thirties—thirty-eight to be exact.
  丹尼斯現在快 40 歲了 —— 精確地說是 38 歲。

23 mass [mæs] *n.* 團，塊；大量；一般大 / 民眾 (此意恆用複數，前面加定冠詞 the) & *a.* 一般大 / 民眾的

- 複 masses ['mæsɪz]
- 片 (1) a mass of...
  一塊 / 團……；大量的……
  (2) mass media
  大眾傳播媒體 (複數形)
- 衍 massive ['mæsɪv] *a.* 大量的 ⑤

- ▶ A huge mass of earth shifted during the landslide.
  一個大土塊在山崩中移位了。

- ▶ Greg has to work on a mass of data.
  葛瑞格有一堆的資料要處理。

- ▶ This kind of performance won't appeal to the masses.
  這種表演不會吸引到一般大眾的。

- ▶ The mass media includes newspapers, magazines, radio, television, films, etc.
  大眾傳播媒體包括報紙、雜誌、廣播、電視、電影等等。

24 avoid [ə'vɔɪd] *vt.* 避免；避開

- 片 avoid + N/V-ing　避免……
- 衍 (1) avoidable [ə'vɔɪdəbl̩] *a.* 可避免的
  (2) avoidance [ə'vɔɪdəns] *n.* 逃避

- ▶ Avoid cutting in while people are talking.
  人家在講話時，要避免插嘴。

- ▶ Unless you avoid the city center, it will take you hours to get there.
  除非你避開市中心，否則得花上好幾個小時才能到那裡。

 416

25 select [səˋlɛkt] *vt.* 選拔，挑選 & *a.* 精選的，優等的

田 (1) select A as B　把A選為B
= A be selected as B
(2) select A for B
挑選A給B，為B挑選A

衍 selective [səˋlɛktɪv] *a.* 嚴格篩選的

似 (1) choose [tʃuz] *vt. & vi.* 選擇 ①
(2) pick [pɪk] *vt.* 挑選 ①

▶ Who has been selected as the class leader?
誰被選為班長呢？

▶ Parents should select safe toys for their children.
家長應該為小孩挑選安全的玩具。

▶ Only a few select members are invited, and you are one of them.
只有一些經過精挑細選的會員在獲邀之列，而你就是其中之一。

---

selection [səˋlɛkʃən]
n. 選拔，挑選；可供挑選的東西

田 (1) make a selection
挑選意中人選，挑選中意的事物

(2) a wide selection of...
很多可供挑選的……

▶ The manager will make a final selection by Friday.
經理將在週五之前做出最終選擇。

▶ The store has a wide selection of clothes.
那家店有各式衣服可供選擇。

26 propose [prəˋpoz] *vt.* 提議，建議 & *vi.* 求婚

田 (1) propose that S + (should) + V
提議……

(2) propose to sb　向某人求婚

衍 (1) proposal [prəˋpozl̩]
n. 建議，提案；求婚 ④

(2) proposition [ˌprɑpəˋzɪʃən]
n. (常指商業上的) 提議；主張

似 suggest [səˋdʒɛst] *vt.* 建議 ②

▶ We proposed that the concert be held indoors.
我們提議把演唱會辦在室內。

▶ Duke proposed to Betty last night.
杜克昨晚向貝蒂求婚了。

1 survive [sə`vaɪv] vt. & vi. 倖存，留存；比 (某人) 活得久

片 survive sb by + 歲數
比某人多活若干年

衍 survivor [sə`vaɪvə]
n. 生還者，獲救者 ③

▶ Only a few people survived the flood.
這次洪水只有一些人生還。

▶ After the war, only a few historical buildings survived.
戰後，只有少數歷史建築倖存下來。

▶ Charlie's wife survived him by ten years.
查理的老婆比他多活 10 年。

survival [sə`vaɪvl] *n.* 倖存；生存
片 a chance of survival　生存機會

▶ The boy needs immediate medical treatment if he is to have any chance of survival.
如果那小男孩要活命的話，就得立即進行治療。

▶ Global warming is threatening the survival of wildlife.
全球暖化正威脅野生動植物的生存。
*wildlife [`waɪld,laɪf] *n.* 野生動植物 (集合名詞，不可數)

2 contract [`kɑntrækt] n. 合 / 契約 & [kən`trækt] vt. & vi. (使) 縮短 & vt. 感染

片 sign a contract with sb
和某人簽訂合 / 契約

衍 contractor [`kɑntræktə] *n.* 承包商 ⑤

似 agreement [ə`grimənt] *n.* 契約 ①

▶ The singer has signed a five-year contract with the record company.
這位歌手和唱片公司簽了 5 年的合約。

▶ In English, "is not" often contracts to "isn't."
英文的 is not 常縮寫成 isn't。

▶ Nearly half of the adult population there has contracted malaria.
那一帶有近半數的成年人感染了瘧疾。
*malaria [mə`lɛrɪə] *n.* 瘧疾

3 edition [ɪ`dɪʃən] n. 版本；版次，一次印刷量

片 a paperback / hardback edition
平 / 精裝本

▶ Do you know where I can buy the paperback edition of this novel?
你知道我可以在哪裡買到這本小說的平裝本嗎？

▶ This is the first edition of this book.
這是這本書的第 1 版。

4 identity [aɪ`dɛntətɪ] n. 身分

片 an identity card　身分證
= an ID card

衍 identification [aɪ,dɛntəfə`keʃən]
n. 身分證明 (文件) (縮寫為 ID)；辨認
(皆不可數) ④

▶ We still have no clue as to the identity of the murderer.
關於凶手的身分我們仍然毫無線索。

5 grand [grænd] a. 雄偉的，壯麗的；重要的

似 magnificent [mæg`nɪfəsənt]
　　a. 壯麗的 ④

▶ Susan took a picture in front of the grand palace.
　蘇珊在那座雄偉的宮殿前拍了張照片。

▶ Our team won the grand prize in the competition.
　我們的團隊在比賽中贏得了大獎。

6 gardener [`gardnɚ] n. 園丁

衍 garden [`gardṇ] n. 花園①

▶ Perhaps you should hire a gardener to take care of these flowers.
　或許你該僱用一位園丁來照顧這些花。

soil [sɔɪl] n. 土壤 & vt. 弄髒，汙損
似 earth [ɝθ] n. 土壤①

▶ The soil here is very fertile.
　這裡的土壤很肥沃。

▶ I soiled my shirt while eating a sandwich.
　我吃三明治的時候把我的襯衫弄髒了。

7 system [`sɪstəm] n. 系統；制度

片 (1) a computer system　電腦系統
　　(2) an educational / education
　　　　system　教育制度
似 structure [`strʌktʃɚ]
　　n. 結構；體系③

▶ Our company wants to improve our computer system.
　我們公司想改善我們的電腦系統。

▶ Few parents are in favor of the recent changes in the education system.
　贊成最近教育制度改革的家長寥寥可數。

8 thus [ðʌs] adv. 因此

似 (1) therefore [`ðɛr͵for] adv. 因此②
　　(2) hence [hɛns] adv. 因此⑤

▶ The contract will end next week, and thus we'll have to sign a new one.
　合約將於下週到期，因此我們必須簽署一份新的。

9 employ [ɪm`plɔɪ] vt. 僱用；運用

似 (1) hire [haɪr] vt. 僱用③
　　(2) apply [ə`plaɪ] vt. 運用②

▶ This company employs twenty-five people.
　這家公司僱用了 25 個人。

▶ I will employ the new technique I learned to fix this TV.
　我將會用我學到的新技術來修理這臺電視機。

employment [ɪm`plɔɪmənt]
n. 僱用；就業，在職；工作；運用(皆不可數)
片 be in employment　在職中
反 unemployment [͵ʌnɪm`plɔɪmənt]
　　n. 失業(不可數)⑤

▶ The employment of children under 18 is forbidden in this country.
　該國禁止僱用 18 歲以下的孩童。

▶ During the course of Amber's employment as manager, the company made large profits.
　在安柏擔任經理的期間，公司獲得了巨額利潤。

> It is hard for many college graduates to find employment this year.
> 今年很多大學畢業生找工作都很困難。

> Is Eric still in employment?
> 艾瑞克仍在職嗎？

> The employment of certain policies can be controversial.
> 運用某些政策可能會備受爭議。
> *controversial [ˌkɑntrəˈvɝʃəl] a. 引起爭論的

employee [ˌɪmplɔɪˈi] n. 員工
似 worker [ˈwɝkɚ] n. 員工；勞工 ①

> All employees are covered under the insurance plan.
> 這項保險計畫涵蓋了所有的員工。

employer [ɪmˈplɔɪɚ] n. 僱主，老闆

> Barbie worked for the same employer for most of her life.
> 芭比一輩子大部分都是替同個老闆工作。

10 electric [ɪˈlɛktrɪk] a. 電的

片 (1) get an electric shock　被電到
(2) an electric appliance　電器
　= an electrical appliance
(3) an electric light / car / blanket
　電燈 / 電動車 / 電熱毯

> Bob got an electric shock from the wire.
> 鮑伯被電線電到了。

> Life wouldn't be so comfortable without such electric appliances as refrigerators and TV sets.
> 若沒有電視和電冰箱等電器，生活是不會那麼舒適的。

electrical [ɪˈlɛktrɪkḷ] a. 電的

> Lightning is an electrical phenomenon.
> 閃電是一種電的現象。
> *phenomenon [fəˈnɑməˌnɑn] n. 現象

11 tale [tel] n. 故事，傳說

片 (1) a fairy tale　童話故事
(2) a tall tale　荒誕不經的故事

> I loved fairy tales when I was little.
> 我小時候很喜歡童話故事。

> I don't believe the tall tale that Billy just told me.
> 我才不相信比利剛剛告訴我那荒誕不經的故事。

12 till [tɪl] conj. & prep. 直到……為止 (= until)

片 not + V... till / until...
直到……才……

用法 till 與 until 用法相同，但 till 較常用於口語中。

> Mark didn't go to bed till his wife came back home.
> 直到老婆回家後，馬克才上床睡覺。

> Hong Kong was a British colony till 1997.
> 香港在 1997 年之前都是英國的殖民地。

13 edge [εdʒ] *n.* 邊緣；刀鋒 & *vt.* 給……加上邊

片 (1) be on the edge of...
在……的邊緣；快要……
(2) be on edge　很緊張
= be nervous
(3) be edged with / in...
四周都有……

▶ Phoebe put some lace around the edge of the gift box.
菲碧在禮物盒的邊緣黏上蕾絲。
*lace [les] *n.* 蕾絲
▶ My father sharpened the edge of the knife before he cut the meat.
我父親切那塊肉之前先將刀鋒磨利。
▶ The company is on the edge of bankruptcy.
該公司快要破產了。
*bankruptcy [ˋbæŋkrəptsɪ] *n.* 破產
▶ The players were on edge before the game.
賽前球員們都很緊張。
▶ The square was edged with flowers and trees.
那座廣場四周都種了花朵與樹木。

14 lone [lon] *a.* 單獨的，獨自的

似 (1) lonely [ˋlonlɪ] *a.* 孤獨的 ①
(2) alone [əˋlon]
a. 孤獨的 & *adv.* 孤獨地 ②

▶ Lone women are advised not to walk down that dark lane at night.
建議女性獨自一人不要在夜晚走那條暗巷。

15 typical [ˋtɪpɪk]] *a.* 典型的；特有的，一向如此的

片 (1) be typical of...　是……的典型
(2) It is typical of sb to V
某人一向都做……
衍 type [taɪp] *n.* 形式，類型 ①

▶ It was a typical summer morning, and I was eating the delicious cereal.
那是個典型的夏日早晨，而我正在吃美味的麥片。
▶ This sunny weather is typical of the Mediterranean climate.
這種有陽光的天氣是典型的地中海型氣候。
▶ It is typical of Ken to be late for school.
肯上學一向都遲到。

16 somewhat [ˋsʌmˌ(h)wat] *adv.* 有點；稍微

似 slightly [ˋslaɪtlɪ] *adv.* 約略，稍微

▶ After working all day, I was somewhat tired.
工作了一天後，我有點累了。

17 proper [ˋprapɚ] *a.* 合宜的，適當的；得體的

似 (1) suitable [ˋsutəbl]] *a.* 適合的 ②
(2) adequate [ˋædəkwət]
a. 適當的 ④

▶ I couldn't think of the proper words to say.
我想不出有什麼適當的話可說。
▶ Obviously, the team lacks proper training.
顯然這支球隊缺乏適當的訓練。

▶ It is not proper to arrive late for a dinner party.
參加晚宴遲到是不得體的。

---

18 pop [pɑp] *n.* 流行音樂 (= popular music) & *a.* 流行音樂的 & *vt.* & *vi.* (使) 發出爆裂聲 & *vi.* (突然) 出現

目 pop, popped [pɑpt], popped
片 (1) pop up　(突然) 出現
(2) sth pop into sb's mind / head
　　某人突然想到某事物
衍 popcorn [ˋpɑpˌkɔrn] *n.* 爆米花 ①

▶ Leo likes all kinds of music—pop, jazz, soul, rock, etc.
李歐喜歡各種音樂 —— 流行樂、爵士樂、靈魂樂、搖滾樂等。

▶ I enjoy pop music, while my sister loves classical music.
我喜歡流行樂，我姊姊則喜歡古典樂。

▶ I won't play the game since I don't like to pop balloons.
我不要玩這個遊戲，因為我不喜歡把氣球弄破。

▶ The balloon Diana held suddenly popped and gave her a fright.
黛安娜拿的氣球突然爆破，嚇了她一大跳。

▶ I didn't invite Frank, but he just popped up at the party.
我沒有邀請法蘭克來，但他卻突然出現在派對裡。

▶ A good idea just popped into my mind.
我剛剛突然想到一個好點子。

---

19 complex [kəmˋplɛks] *a.* 複雜的 & [ˋkɑmplɛks] *n.* 綜合大樓，建築群大樓

複 complexes [ˋkɑmplɛksɪz]
片 an apartment complex
公寓大樓，公寓住宅區
衍 complexity [kəmˋplɛksətɪ]
　　n. 複雜性 ⑤
似 complicated [ˋkɑmpləˌketɪd]
　　a. 複雜的
▶ The philosophical question is too complicated for these children to understand.
這個哲學問題對這群孩子來說太複雜了，他們很難理解。
反 simple [ˋsɪmpl] *a.* 簡單的 ①

▶ This is such a complex problem that we can't come up with a quick solution to it.
這是一個很複雜的問題，我們還無法很快地想出一個解決方案。

▶ Max told me that Judith lives in this expensive apartment complex.
麥克斯告訴我茱蒂絲住在這個昂貴的公寓大樓裡。

---

20 rub [rʌb] *vt.* & *vi.* & *n.* 摩擦，揉搓

目 rub, rubbed [rʌbd], rubbed
片 (1) rub one's eyes　揉眼睛
(2) give... a rub　擦……，揉搓……

▶ The woman rubbed her hands together to warm them up.
這個婦人摩擦雙手，好讓手溫暖起來。

▶ During the pandemic, you are advised not to rub your eyes, especially if you haven't washed your hands.

疫情期間，建議不要揉眼睛，特別是如果你沒有洗手的話。

＊pandemic [pænˈdɛmɪk] *n.* 大規模流行病

▶ Jeff gave his elbow a quick rub after hitting it against the desk.

傑夫手肘撞到桌子後，他快速地搓揉一下他的手肘。

rubber [ˈrʌbɚ]

n. 橡膠 (不可數)；橡皮擦 (可數)〔英〕

(＝ eraser〔美〕)

🔠 a rubber band　橡皮筋〔美〕

＝ an elastic band〔英〕

▶ The soles of the shoes are made of rubber.

這鞋子的鞋底是橡膠做的。

▶ Tina put a rubber band around the pens.

蒂娜用橡皮筋套住這些筆。

▶ Could I borrow your rubber? I forgot to bring mine.

我可以向你借橡皮擦嗎？我忘了帶我的。

21　salesperson [ˈselzˌpɝsn̩] *n.* 推銷員，業務員

衍 (1) salesman [ˈselzmən]

n. 男業務員 (複數為 salesmen [ˈselzmən]) ②

(2) saleswoman [ˈselzˌwʊmən]

n. 女業務員 (複數為 saleswomen [ˈselzˌwɪmən]) ②

▶ The salesperson made a fortune by selling used cars.

這名業務員靠販售中古車發了財。

22　feature [ˈfitʃɚ] *n.* 特徵，特色 & *vt.* 以……為特色；主打 (特色、功能等)

似 (1) characteristic [ˌkærəktəˈrɪstɪk]

n. 特色；特點 ④

(2) trait [tret] *n.* 特徵；特性 ⑤

▶ What are the features of your new smartphone?

你的新手機有什麼特色？

▶ This book features the beauty of nature.

＝ This book highlights the beauty of nature.

這本書以大自然的美為主題。

▶ The singer's new album features a song written by a famous Japanese songwriter.

這位歌手的新專輯主打一首知名日本作曲家所寫的歌。

23　huge [hjudʒ] *a.* 巨大的

似 (1) big [bɪg] *a.* 大的 ①

(2) large [lardʒ] *a.* 大的 ①

▶ Andy owns a huge house in the center of the city.

安迪在市中心擁有一棟大房子。

tiny [ˈtaɪnɪ] *a.* 微 / 極小的

似 little [ˈlɪtl̩] *a.* 小的 ①

▶ The tiny little baby cried for milk.

小嬰兒哭著要喝奶。

Level 2　Unit 47

24 obvious [`ˋɑbvɪəs`] *a.* 明顯的

似 (1) evident [`ˋɛvədənt`] *a.* 明顯的 ④
(2) apparent [`əˋpærənt`] *a.* 明顯的 ④

▸ There has been no obvious improvement in the patient's condition.
這位病人的情況一直沒有明顯的改善。

25 possibility [`͵pɑsəˋbɪlətɪ`] *n.* 可能性

衍 possible [`ˋpɑsəbḷ`] *a.* 可能的 ①

▸ People in that country were worried about the possibility of another terrorist attack.
那一國人民擔心可能會發生另一起恐怖攻擊。

26 blame [blem] *vt. & n.* 責怪／備

片 (1) blame A for B 把 B 怪罪在 A 身上
= blame B on A
(2) be to blame for sth
應對某事負責
(3) get the blame for sth
因某事而受到責備

▸ Don't blame me for your misery.
= Don't blame your misery on me.
不要把你的痛苦怪罪到我身上。
＊misery [`ˋmɪzərɪ`] *n.* 痛苦

▸ The authorities concerned believe that more than one person is to blame for the fire.
有關當局認為要為這場火災負責的人不只 1 個。

▸ Jason felt upset to get the blame for the mistake.
傑森因為那個錯誤而被責備覺得很難過。

27 throughout [θruˋaut] *prep.* 遍及……；在整個……期間 & *adv.* 處處；自始至終

似 during [`ˋd(j)urɪŋ`]
prep. 在整個……期間 ①

▸ People throughout the country are against war.
全國人民都反對戰爭。

▸ Those kids were all excited throughout the performance.
那群孩子在整個表演過程中全都興奮不已。

▸ Jill's room was painted green throughout.
吉兒的房間全被漆成綠色。

▸ Despite the criticism, the writer's family supported her throughout.
儘管那位作家遭受批評，其家人自始至終都支持她。

28 respond [rɪˋspɑnd] *vt. & vi.* 回答 & *vi.* 反應

片 (1) respond that... 回答／應為……
(2) respond to sth
回答／應某事；對某事做出反應
(3) respond with sth 以某方式回應

▸ The host asked the singer how she came up with the song, and she responded that it all just came out naturally.
主持人問那位歌手她是怎麼想出這首歌的，她回答說這一切都是自然而然寫出來的。

衍 (1) response [rɪˈspɑns]
　　n. 回應，回答；反應 ③
　(2) respondent [rɪˈspɑndənt]
　　n. 應答者，答覆者 ⑤

似 (1) answer [ˈænsɚ] *vt. & vi.* 回答 ①
　(2) reply [rɪˈplaɪ]
　　vi. & n. 回覆；回應 ②

▸ I asked Katie a math question and she responded to it quickly.
我問凱蒂一個數學問題，她很快便回答我。

▸ The patient responded well to the new medicine.
病人對新藥的反應良好。

▸ The teacher responded with a smile when the students waved at her.
當學生們向那位老師揮手時，她報以微笑。

29　attempt [əˈtɛmpt] *n. & vt.* 企圖，嘗試　☐

片 (1) make an attempt to V
　　企圖 / 試著做……
　= attempt to V
　(2) in an attempt to V　　試圖做……
　= in order to V

▸ I made an attempt to warn Peter of the dangers of the task, but he just wouldn't listen.
= I attempted to warn Peter of the dangers of the task, but he just wouldn't listen.
我試著警告彼得該任務的危險性，但他根本聽不進去。
＊warn [wɔrn] *vt. & vi.* 警告
　warn sb of sth　警告某人某事

▸ In an attempt to beat the traffic, many people hit the road earlier.
為了避免交通擁擠，許多人提早上路。
＊beat [bit] *vt.* 避免
　hit the road　出發

30　operate [ˈɑpəˌret] *vi.* 運轉；動手術 & *vt.* 操作　☐

片 operate on...　為 / 替……動手術
　= perform an operation on...
衍 (1) operation [ˌɑpəˈreʃən]
　　n. 操作；手術；運轉 ③
　(2) operational [ˌɑpəˈreʃənl̩]
　　a. 操作上的 ⑤

▸ This machinery operates night and day.
這個機械裝置日夜運轉。
＊night and day　夜以繼日
＝day and night

▸ The doctors decided to operate on the man who just had a serious car accident.
醫生決定要替那剛發生嚴重車禍的男子動手術。

▸ It takes practice to operate this machine.
要操作這部機器需要練習才行。

---

operator [ˈɑpəˌretɚ]
n. 操作人員；接線生，總機

片 a machine / computer operator
　機械 / 電腦操作員

▸ All the machine operators in our factory are well-trained.
我們工廠所有的機器操作人員都經過良好的訓練。

▸ Operator, please connect me to Mr. Wilson.
總機，麻煩幫我接威爾遜先生。
＊connect [kəˈnɛkt] *vt.* 為……接通（電話）

31 poison [`pɔɪzn̩] n. 毒藥 & vt. 使中毒

衍 (1) poisonous [`pɔɪznəs] a. 有毒的 ④

(2) poisoning [`pɔɪznɪŋ] n. 中毒
food poisoning　食物中毒

▸ It seems that Henry suffers food poisoning.
亨利似乎是食物中毒了。

▸ In the movie, the servant tried to kill herself by swallowing poison.
這部電影裡,那僕人試圖服毒自殺。

▸ The workers tried to poison the rats in the city's sewers.
那些工人試圖放藥毒死城市下水道的老鼠。
＊sewer [`suɚ] n. 下水道

4801-4803

---

1 state [stet] *vt.* (正式的) 陳述，聲明 & *n.* 狀態，情況；國家；(美國等國家的) 州，邦

🅗 in a(n) + adj. + state
　　處於……的狀態

衍 statesman [ˈstetsmən] *n.* 政治家 ⑥

▸ The driver stated the facts clearly.
該名駕駛人清楚地陳述了事實。

▸ My grandpa's health is in a good state.
我爺爺的健康狀況良好。

▸ Some European states are willing to help the refugees from that country.
一些歐洲國家願意幫助來自那一國的難民。

▸ Which state of the United States do you live in?
你住在美國的哪一州？

statement [ˈstetmənt]
n. (正式地) 聲明，陳述

🅗 make a statement (to sb)
(向 / 對某人) 發表聲明

▸ I'd like to make a statement to all of you.
本人想向諸位發表一份聲明。

---

2 chief [tʃif] *a.* 主要的，最重要的 & *n.* 負責人，首領

🅗 (1) an editor in chief
　　總編輯 (複數為 editors in chief)
　= an editor-in-chief
　(2) a commander in chief
　　總司令 (複數為 commanders in chief)
　= a commander-in-chief

似 (1) main [men]
　　a. 主要的，最重要的 ①
　(2) major [ˈmedʒɚ]
　　a. 主要的，重大的 ②
　(3) primary [ˈpraɪˌmɛrɪ]
　　a. 首 / 主要的 ②

▸ The chief reason for holding this meeting is to talk about the business trip.
舉行這個會議的主要原因是要討論這趟出差。

▸ Mr. Wilson is the chief of our department.
威爾遜先生是我們部門的主管。

▸ The editor in chief of this magazine is responsible for the quality and the schedule of the magazine.
這本雜誌的總編輯負責雜誌的品質和進度。

▸ When the commander in chief walked into the hall, all the people became quiet.
當總司令走進禮堂時，所有人都安靜了下來。

---

3 appreciate [əˈpriʃɪˌet] *vt.* 感激；欣賞 & *vi.* (貨幣) 升值

🅗 appreciate + N/V-ing　感激……
= be thankful for sth
= be grateful for sth
衍 appreciative [əˈpriʃətɪv] *a.* 感激的

▸ I really appreciate this opportunity to speak to you.
= I really appreciate having this opportunity to speak to you.
我很感激能有機會跟諸位說幾句話。

反 depreciate [dɪ`priʃɪˌet]
　　vt. 輕視，小看 *vt.* & *vi.* (使) 貶值

▶ I really appreciate your help.
= I'm thankful for your help.
= I'm grateful for your help.
　我很感激你的幫忙。

▶ John's abilities were not fully appreciated by his employer.
　約翰的能力並未受到僱主充分賞識。

▶ The US dollar keeps depreciating, while the Euro keeps appreciating.
　美元持續貶值，而歐元則持續升值。
　*Euro [`jʊro] *n.* 歐元

4　cycle [`saɪkl̩] *n.* 循環 & *vi.* 騎 (腳踏車)　☐

衍 recycle [ri`saɪkl̩] *vt.* 回收再利用 ④
似 bike [baɪk] *vi.* 騎 (腳踏車) ①

▶ The cycle of the seasons is not obvious in Taiwan.
　在臺灣，四季的循環並不明顯。

▶ By cycling to and from work every day, I not only save money, but I get a chance to exercise.
　我每天騎腳踏車上下班，這樣做我不僅省錢，也有機會運動。

5　downstairs [ˌdaʊn`stɛrz] *adv.* 往 / 在樓下 & *a.* 樓下的 & *n.* 樓下 (此意前面加定冠詞 the)　☐

片 go downstairs　下樓
衍 stairs [stɛrz] *n.* 樓梯 (恆用複數) ①

▶ Benny just went downstairs to get something to eat.
　班尼剛剛下樓去找東西吃。

▶ My downstairs neighbor is very sensitive to sound.
　我樓下的鄰居對聲音很敏感。

▶ The downstairs is undergoing renovation.
　樓下正在整修中。

---

upstairs [ˌʌp`stɛrz]
adv. 往 / 在樓上 & *a.* 樓上的 & *n.* 樓上 (此意前面加定冠詞 the)

片 go upstairs　上樓

▶ Could you go upstairs to answer the phone?
　你可以上樓去接電話嗎？

▶ The upstairs window was left open.
　樓上的窗戶沒關。

▶ Melvin is going to rent the upstairs.
　馬文會租樓上。

6　membership [`mɛmbɚˌʃɪp] *n.* 會員身分 / 資格　☐

片 a membership fee　會費
衍 member [`mɛmbɚ] *n.* 成員 ①

▶ The membership fee at the golf club is $50,000 per year.
　這間高爾夫球俱樂部的會費是 1 年 5 萬美金。

7 **tone** [ton] *n.* 語氣，口吻；音調

☐ in a(n) + adj. + tone
以……的語氣 / 口吻

▸ I like Haley because she always talks in a gentle tone.
我喜歡海莉，因為她總是用溫和的語氣說話。

▸ The guitar has a clean and beautiful tone.
這把吉他的音色純淨美妙。

8 **motion** [`moʃən] *n.* (物體的) 移動

☐ in motion　移動中

▸ Don't get on the train when it's in motion.
火車開動了就不要上車。

9 **balance** [`bæləns] *n.* 平衡；(銀行帳戶的) 餘額 *vt. & vi.* (使) 平衡 & *vt.* 權衡，斟酌

☐ (1) keep / lose one's balance
某人保持 / 失去平衡
(2) strike a balance between A and B　在 A 與 B 之間維持平衡
(3) a bank balance
帳戶 / 戶頭餘額
(4) balance A on B　把 A 平衡在 B 上
(5) balance A against B
對 A 和 B 兩者作出權衡

衍 balanced [`bælənst] *a.* 各方兼顧的

反 imbalance [ɪm`bæləns] *n.* 失衡

▸ This yoga pose is so hard; I could hardly keep my balance.
這個瑜伽姿勢太難了；我幾乎無法保持平衡。

▸ To lead a happy life, you should strike a balance between work and play.
你若想有個愉快的生活，就應在工作及遊樂之間保持平衡。

▸ Tim is nearly broke. His bank balance is only NT$50.
提姆幾乎已身無分文了。他戶頭餘額只剩新臺幣 50 元。
*broke [brok] *a.* 身無分文的 (= penniless [`pɛnɪləs])

▸ Can you balance an egg on the floor?
你會立蛋在地板上嗎？

▸ It's not easy to balance when you learn to ride a bike for the first time.
第一次學騎腳踏車要保持平衡不是件易事。

▸ You should balance the advantages against the disadvantages before moving to the countryside.
你搬到鄉下前應先權衡利弊。

10 **affect** [ə`fɛkt] *vt.* 影響；(疾病) 侵襲；感動，震撼；假裝

衍 (1) affection [ə`fɛkʃən] *n.* 喜愛 ⑤
(2) affectionate [ə`fɛkʃənət]
a. 深情的 ⑥

似 effect [ɪ`fɛkt] *n.* 影響，結果 ②

▸ The bad weather affected everyone's mood.
惡劣的天氣影響了每個人的心情。

▸ This disease mainly affects children under 3.
這種疾病主要是 3 歲以下的小孩容易得到。

▸ The little boy's miserable life affected us so much that we decided to adopt him.
那個小男孩的可憐身世深深觸動了我們，因此我們決定收養他。

▶ Although Dad affected indifference, he was actually very angry.

雖然老爸裝作若無其事，但他其實很生氣。

＊indifference [ɪnˋdɪfərəns] *n.* 漠不關心，冷淡

11　force [fɔrs] *n.* 武力，暴力；力 & *vt.* 強迫；擠進，強行通過

🔑 (1) force sb to V　強迫某人做……

　(2) force one's way through...

　　強行穿過……，衝過……

衍 forceful [ˋfɔrsfəl] *a.* 強有力的

▶ Under no circumstances should you resort to force.

不管任何情況你都不應該訴諸暴力。

▶ The force of the wind was so strong that it almost knocked me over.

風力之強勁幾乎把我整個人都吹倒了。

▶ Don't force me to do anything I don't want to do.

不要強迫我做任何我不想做的事。

▶ The policeman forced his way through the crowd to run after the thief.

警察強行穿過人群以追趕小偷。

12　snail [snel] *n.* 蝸牛

🔑 at a snail's pace　非常緩慢地

似 nail [nel] *n.* 指甲，腳趾甲 ②

▶ Due to heavy traffic, everyone was driving at a snail's pace.

由於交通壅塞，車輛都行駛得非常緩慢。

---

ladybug [ˋledɪˌbʌg] *n.* 瓢蟲

衍 bug [bʌg] *n.* 小蟲子 ①

▶ The little girl looked at the ladybug on the leaf with curiosity.

小女孩好奇地看著葉子上的瓢蟲。

＊curiosity [ˌkjʊrɪˋɑsətɪ] *n.* 好奇心

13　click [klɪk] *vt.* & *vi.* (使) 發出短促又響亮的聲音，(使) 發出卡嗒聲；按 (滑鼠) & *n.* 短促又響亮的聲音，卡嗒聲；按 (滑鼠)

🔑 (1) click one's heels

　　某人喀的一聲併攏腳跟

　(2) click shut　卡嗒一聲關上

　(3) click on sth　(用滑鼠) 點擊某物

　(4) the click of a mouse　點擊滑鼠
　　(比喻某事可透過電腦很快地達成)

▶ The soldier clicked his heels and saluted the general.

這位士兵喀的一聲併攏腳跟向將軍行禮。

＊salute [səˋlut] *vt.* 向……敬禮

▶ Alone at home, the little boy was so afraid that he screamed when a door suddenly clicked shut.

小男孩獨自在家非常害怕，所以當門突然卡嗒一聲關上時，他尖叫出聲。

▶ Just click this link and you can download the file.

只要點擊此連結，你就可以下載那檔案了。

▶ Just click on the icon twice, and the file will open.

只需用滑鼠點 2 下這個圖示，檔案就會開啟。

＊icon [ˋaɪkɑn] *n.* (電腦) 圖示

▶ Turn the dial until you hear a little click.
轉動這個調節器，直到你聽到喀的一聲。

▶ You can get almost any information you want with the click of a mouse.
你幾乎可以透過點擊滑鼠來得到任何你想要的資訊。

---

14 religion [rɪˈlɪdʒən] *n.* 宗教 (信仰)

片 freedom of religion 宗教信仰自由

▶ Freedom of religion is a fundamental human right.
宗教信仰自由是一項基本人權。

---

heaven [ˈhɛvən] *n.* 天堂

似 paradise [ˈpærəˌdaɪs] *n.* 天堂 ③

用法 此字前面不加 the。

▶ Some Christians believe that they will go to heaven after they die.
一些基督徒相信他們死後會上天堂。

▶ Heaven's vengeance is slow but sure.
天堂的復仇是緩慢的，但卻是必然的 / 不是不報，時機未到。—— 諺語
*vengeance [ˈvɛndʒəns] *n.* 報仇

---

soul [sol] *n.* 靈魂；人

片 (1) a soul mate　心靈伴侶
　(2) not a soul in sight
　　半個人都沒看到

▶ The victim's family said their prayers for the soul of the dead.
被害者的家屬祈禱著，以告慰往生者的在天之靈。

▶ Erin and her husband are soul mates for each other.
愛倫和她的丈夫是彼此的心靈伴侶。

▶ There was not a soul in sight when I got there.
我到那裡時，半個人影都沒看到。

---

priest [prist] *n.* 神父，牧師

似 (1) minister [ˈmɪnəstɚ] *n.* 牧師 ④
　(2) pastor [ˈpæstɚ] *n.* 牧師

▶ The convict confessed all his sins to the priest before the execution.
這名囚犯在被處決之前向神父懺悔了他所有的罪。
*convict [ˈkɑnvɪkt] *n.* 囚犯
　confess [kənˈfɛs] *vt.* 懺悔；承認 (錯誤等)
　sin [sɪn] *n.* 罪

---

15 pray [pre] *vt.* & *vi.* 祈禱 / 求

片 (1) pray that...　祈禱 / 求……
　(2) pray to God for sth
　　祈求上帝給予某事物

▶ Kent prayed that his grandfather would recover soon.
肯特祈禱他的爺爺能早日康復。

▶ The woman's husband was seriously ill, so she prayed to God for help.
那位婦人的丈夫病重，所以她祈求上帝幫助。

---

prayer [prɛr] *n.* 祈禱，禱告；(祈) 禱文

▶ Heidi found peace in prayer.
海蒂在祈禱中找到了平靜。

片 (1) in prayer　　在祈禱／禱告
　　(2) say a prayer　禱告

▶ Lucy says her prayers before going to bed every night.
露西每晚睡前都會禱告。

16　saw [sɔ] vt. & vi. 鋸 & n. 鋸子

三 saw, sawed [sɔd], sawn [sɔn] /
sawed

片 saw through...　鋸斷……

比 see [si] vi. & vt. 看見 ①
　三態為：see, saw, seen [sin]

▶ The workers sawed the table in half.
那些工人把桌子鋸成兩半。

▶ Be careful. You don't want to saw through your fingers.
小心。你不會想鋸斷你的手指的。

▶ I need an electric chain saw to cut the trees down.
我需要一把電鋸來鋸樹。

17　policy [ˈpɑləsɪ] n. 政策

複 policies [ˈpɑləsɪz]

▶ Honesty is the best policy.
誠實為上策。—— 諺語

18　bathe [beð] vi. 洗澡 & vt. 浸泡；幫……沐浴；使沉浸於／籠罩在……

片 be bathed in...　沉浸／籠罩在……

衍 bath [bæθ] n. 洗澡 ①

▶ Do you know why many Westerners like to bathe in the morning, rather than in the evening?
你知道為什麼很多西方人喜歡早上洗澡而不是晚上洗澡嗎？

▶ The boy bathed his feet in the cold river water.
小男孩把雙腳浸泡在沁涼的河水中。

▶ The baby smiled brightly when her mother bathed her.
小寶寶的媽媽幫她洗澡時，她笑得很燦爛。

▶ The church was bathed in golden sunlight.
教堂浸浴在金色的陽光下。

19　tax [tæks] n. 稅金 & vt. 向……課稅

片 (1) an import tax　　進口稅
　　an export tax　　出口稅
　　(2) a tax on...　有關……的稅

▶ Many people think that the import tax on foreign goods is unreasonably high.
很多人認為舶來品的進口稅高到不合理。

▶ All the goods should be taxed before they're sold.
所有的貨品皆須課稅後才能出售。

20　account [əˈkaʊnt] n. 帳戶；報導，描述 & vi. 說明，解釋

片 (1) open an account　開立帳戶
　　(2) on account of...　因為……
　　= because of...
　　= due to...
　　= owing to...

▶ I'd like to open a savings account at the bank.
我想在銀行開一個儲蓄帳戶。

▶ I read an account of the plane crash in the newspaper.
我在報紙上讀到一篇有關墜機事件的報導。

(3) take... into account
　　考慮到……
　= take... into consideration
(4) account for sth　說明某事
　= explain sth

衍 accountable [əˋkauntəbḷ]
　a. 應負責的 ⑥

▶ Larry failed the exam on account of laziness.
賴瑞因懶惰而沒通過考試。

▶ Before asking Bob to handle this huge mission, you should take his physical condition into account.
你要鮑伯處理此一艱鉅的任務之前，應要先考慮他的身體狀況。

▶ Hard work accounts for Daisy's success.
努力是黛西成功的原因。

---

password [ˋpæswɚd] *n.* 密碼

片 enter a password　輸入密碼

似 code [kod] *n.* 代碼，密碼 ④

▶ You need to enter the password to withdraw money.
你得輸入密碼才能領錢。

21　**billion** [ˋbɪljən] *n.* 10 億

片 billions of + 複數可數名詞
　非常多的……

衍 billionaire [ˏbɪljəˋnɛr] *n.* 億萬富翁

▶ The company had a debt of nearly one billion NT dollars after it went bankrupt.
那間公司破產後負債近 10 億新臺幣。

▶ The government spent billions of dollars to build a subway system.
該政府花了大筆的錢建造地鐵系統。

22　**arrow** [ˋæro] *n.* 箭；箭頭 (符號)

片 shoot an arrow at...　用箭射……

▶ The hunter shot an arrow at the deer but missed it.
獵人把箭射向那隻鹿卻沒射中。

▶ Follow the red arrows to the meeting room.
跟著紅色的箭頭到會議室去。

23　**liberal** [ˋlɪbərəl] *a.* 自由的，開放 / 明的；肆意的，大量的

片 be liberal (with sth)
　(在某事物方面) 很肆意，有大量的 (某事物)

衍 liberty [ˋlɪbɚtɪ] *n.* 自由 ③

反 conservative [kənˋsɝvətɪv]
　a. 保守的 ④

▶ Nowadays, teenagers seem to take a more liberal attitude toward sex.
現在的青少年似乎對性的態度比較開放。

▶ Norman was criticized for being too liberal with the company's money.
諾曼被批評花公司的錢太隨便。

---

freedom [ˋfridəm] *n.* 自由

片 freedom of speech / religion
　言論 / 宗教自由
　freedom of the press　新聞自由

衍 free [fri] *a.* 自由的 ①

▶ Without freedom, I would rather die.
不自由毋寧死。

▶ People in this country enjoy freedom of the press, so there are various kinds of news media.
這個國家的人民享有新聞自由，因此有各種不同的新聞媒體。

24 sort [sɔrt] *n.* 種類 & *vt.* 把……分類

片 (1) a sort / type / kind of...
一種……

all sorts / types / kinds of...
各式各樣的……

(2) sort out... 清理……

▶ This is a sort of music that can make you relax.
這是種能讓你放鬆的音樂。

▶ The little boy was excited to see all sorts of animals in the zoo.
小男孩在動物園看到各式各樣的動物非常興奮。

▶ The manager asked us to sort these documents.
經理要我們分類這些文件。

▶ Wendy helped her mom sort out the garbage.
溫蒂幫她媽媽清理垃圾。

25 clap [klæp] *vt.* & *vi.* 拍手，鼓掌 & *n.* 突然很大聲的聲音

目 clap, clapped [klæpt], clapped
片 (1) clap (one's hand)
(某人) 拍手鼓掌

(2) a clap of... 一聲很大聲的……

似 applaud [əˋplɔd] *vt.* & *vi.* 鼓掌 ⑥

▶ We all clapped (our hands) at the end of the speech.
演講結束時，我們都拍手鼓掌。

▶ The little girl cried loudly because a clap of thunder scared her.
小女孩因為一聲雷鳴而嚇得大哭了起來。

26 court [kɔrt] *n.* 法庭；(籃球、網球等的) 球場 & *vt.* 奉承，討好 & *vt.* & *vi.* 追求

片 (1) take sb to court 控告某人
(2) a basketball / tennis court
籃 / 網球場

▶ I'll take you to court if you do not issue a public apology.
如果你不公開道歉，我會告你。

▶ Mandy and Selene are having a friendly game on the tennis court.
蔓蒂和賽琳正在網球場打友誼賽。

▶ Some of Pat's colleagues started to court him after he was promoted.
派特的幾個同事在他升遷後開始向他獻殷勤。

▶ Tom has been courting Susan for six years.
湯姆追求蘇珊 6 年了。

trial [ˋtraɪəl]
n. 審判；試用 / 驗；麻煩人物 / 事物

片 (1) be on trial for... 因……而受審
(2) by / through trial and error
反覆試驗，嘗試錯誤
(3) be a trial (to / for sb)
(對某人來說) 是個麻煩

▶ Edward was on trial for murder.
愛德華因涉及謀殺而受審。

▶ The trial version of the software is limited to one month.
本試用版軟體的使用期限為 1 個月。

▶ The scientists finally succeeded through trial and error.
那些科學家在反覆試驗後終於成功了。

▶ Richard is a real trial to the teachers.
理查德對老師來說真是一個麻煩人物。

27　maintain [menˋten] vt. 保持；維修保養；堅稱

片 maintain that...　堅稱……

衍 maintenance [ˋmentənəns]
　n. 保持；維修保養 ⑤

▶ Our team maintained the lead until the end.
　我們的隊伍一直到終場都保持領先。

▶ Such a large yard is hard to maintain.
　這麼大的院子很難維護。

▶ The man maintained that he didn't steal the woman's purse.
　男子堅稱他沒有偷那位婦人的手提包。

28　indicate [ˋɪndəˌket] vt. 顯示，表明

片 indicate that...　顯示 / 表明……

衍 indication [ˌɪndəˋkeʃən]
　n. 顯示，表明 ④

▶ The survey of women in six Asian countries indicates that Korean women are the least satisfied with their looks.
　那項針對亞洲 6 國女性的調查顯示，韓國女性對外貌的滿意度最低。

29　internal [ɪnˋtɝnḷ] a. 內部的

似 inner [ˋɪnɚ] a. 內部的；內心的 ③

反 external [ɪksˋtɝnḷ] a. 外部的 ⑤

▶ The inspectors decided to examine the corpse's internal organs.
　這些探員決定開驗這具屍體的內臟。
　*corpse [kɔrps] n. 屍體

30　lay [le] vt. 放置 (= place)；產 (卵)

三 lay, laid [led], laid
　(現在分詞為 laying)

片 lay an egg　下蛋

比 (1) lie [laɪ] vi. 說謊 ①
　三態為：lie, lied, lied (現在分詞為 lying)

(2) lie [laɪ] vi. 躺 ①
　三態為：lie, lay, lain[len] (現在分詞為 lying)

▶ Please don't lay anything on the table.
　桌上請不要放任何東西。

▶ The hen just laid an egg.
　那隻母雞剛剛下蛋了。

4901-4905

1 **track** [træk] *n.* 小徑;(火車的)軌道;跑道;田徑運動 (= track and field);歌 / 樂曲 & *vt.* 追蹤;留下(泥巴等)痕跡於……

(1) be on the right track
走向正道,做法得當

(2) keep track of...
隨時掌握……,持續追蹤……
lose track of...　失去……的蹤跡

(3) track down...　追蹤查 / 到……

▸ This track leads to a wooden hut.
這條小徑通向一棟小木屋。

▸ The workmen are repairing the train track.
工人們在維修火車軌道。

▸ Randy used to be a gangster, but he's on the right track now.
藍迪曾混過幫派,但他現在回到正軌了。

▸ It's hard to keep track of all my old friends; in fact, I've lost contact with most of them.
和所有的老友保持聯繫很困難,事實上,我已經和他們大部分的人失聯了。

▸ The cars must do 100 laps of the race track.
這些車必須繞比賽跑道 100 圈。

▸ Although Paul is not good at math or English, he always does well in track and field.
雖然保羅不擅長數學和英文,但他在田徑運動方面的表現總是很出色。

▸ That's my favorite track on the album.
那是我這張專輯最愛的曲子。

▸ These dogs are used to track those who have escaped from jail.
這些狗被用來追蹤越獄的人。

▸ The police finally tracked down the place where the robbers were hiding.
警方終於找到了那些搶匪的藏身處。

▸ The cat tracked mud all over the kitchen floor.
這隻貓在整個廚房地板留下泥巴的痕跡。

path [pæθ] *n.* 小徑,小路;途徑
a path to success / freedom
(前往)成功 / 自由之路

▸ We walked down the path that led to the village.
我們沿著通往村莊的小路走下去。

▸ Believing in yourself is the first step on the path to success.
相信自己是前往成功途徑的第一步。

lane [len] *n.* 巷子 / 道;車道

▸ Walk down the lane and you'll see my house.
沿著這條巷子走下去,你就會看到我家。

▸ Cars are not allowed to drive in the bike lane.
車子不能行駛在自行車道上。

2 nation [ˈneʃən] n. 國家

片 the United Nations 聯合國

衍 (1) national [ˈnæʃənl]
a. 國家的；國立的 ①

(2) international [ˌɪntɚˈnæʃənl]
a. 國際的 ②

(3) nationality [ˌnæʃəˈnælɪtɪ]
n. 國籍；民族 ④

(4) nationalism [ˈnæʃənlˌɪzəm]
n. 國家 / 民族主義 ⑥

似 country [ˈkʌntrɪ] n. 國家 ①

▶ This nation only has a small population.
這個國家僅有少數人口。

▶ The purpose of the United Nations is to maintain international peace.
聯合國的宗旨是維繫國際和平。

---

domestic [dəˈmɛstɪk]
a. 國內的；家庭的

衍 domesticate [dəˈmɛstəˌket]
vt. 馴養

反 foreign [ˈfɔrɪn] a. 外國的 ①

▶ Ralph prefers domestic products to imported ones.
與進口產品相比，雷夫更喜歡國產品。

▶ I have many domestic chores to do on weekends.
週末時我有許多家事要做。
*chore [tʃɔr] n. 雜務，瑣事

---

3 appetite [ˈæpəˌtaɪt] n. 胃口；強烈欲望，渴望

片 (1) give sb a good appetite
讓某人胃口很好

(2) have an appetite for sth
很渴望某物

= have a liking for sth

= have a passion for sth

= enjoy sth

衍 appetizer [ˈæpəˌtaɪzɚ] n. 開胃菜

▶ Regular exercise gives us a good appetite.
規律的運動會讓我們的胃口很好。

▶ My son has a great appetite for basketball.
我兒子很愛打籃球。

---

4 grain [gren] n. 穀粒，穀 (物)；細粒

片 take sth with a grain of salt
對某事採保留態度，對某事半信半疑

用法 任何粒狀物皆可與 grain 並用：
(1) a grain of salt 一粒鹽
(2) a grain of sand 一粒沙
(3) a grain of sugar 一粒砂糖

▶ Last year's grain harvest was the worst since 1995.
去年的穀物收成是自 1995 年以來最差的一次。

▶ Chris is a liar, so you'd better take his story with a grain of salt.
克里斯是個騙子，所以你最好對他的說詞採取保留的態度。

---

5 instrument [ˈɪnstrəmənt] n. 樂器 (= musical [ˈmjuzɪkl] instrument)；器械 / 具

似 tool [tul] n. 工具 ①

▶ How many musical instruments can you play?
你會彈奏幾種樂器？

▶ A scale is a common instrument in science.
磅秤是科學中常用的工具。

---

6 fault [fɔlt] *n.* 過失 (不可數)；缺點 & *vt.* 挑出毛病

片 (1) be at fault　有過錯
= be wrong
(2) find fault with...
對……吹毛求疵

似 (1) mistake [məˋstek] *n.* 錯誤 ①
(2) defect [ˋdifɛkt]
n. 缺點；生理缺陷 ⑥

▶ No one was at fault in the accident.
這次的意外誰都沒有錯。

▶ Laziness is definitely Ray's biggest fault.
懶惰肯定是雷最大的缺點。

▶ I don't like Owen because he tends to find fault with everything I do.
我不喜歡歐文，因為他總是對我做的每件事吹毛求疵。

▶ It's hard to fault Oliver's performance.
要從奧利佛的表現中挑毛病很難。

---

7 trap [træp] *n.* 陷阱；圈套，騙局，詭計 & *vt.* 設陷阱捕捉

三 trap, trapped [træpt], trapped
片 (1) be / get caught in a trap
落入了陷阱中，困在陷阱中
(2) fall into the trap of + V-ing
上了當去做……，掉入圈套去做……
(3) be trapped　被困住，受困
= be stuck
衍 mousetrap [ˋmaʊs͵træp] *n.* 捕鼠器

▶ A lion was caught in the hunter's trap.
一頭獅子困在獵人的陷阱中。

▶ Don't fall into the trap of buying more than you need.
別掉入圈套去買你不需要的東西。

▶ The reporter asked the natives how they trap animals.
記者問當地人他們是如何設陷阱捕捉動物的。

▶ Many people were trapped in the building when a fire broke out.
失火時，很多人被困在大樓裡。

---

8 altogether [͵ɔltəˋgɛðɚ] *adv.* 總共；完全地

似 totally [ˋtotḷɪ] *adv.* 完全地
= completely [kəmˋplitlɪ]

▶ There are 18 people in the meeting altogether.
這次會議共有 18 人參加。

▶ You ought to kick the bad habit altogether.
你應該徹底戒除這個壞習慣。

---

9 flat [flæt] *a.* 平的；無趣的；不景氣的；(輪胎) 洩了氣的 & *n.* 公寓 〔英〕(= apartment 〔美〕)；平底鞋 (此意恆用複數) & *adv.* 平直地，水平地

片 have a flat tire　爆胎
似 (1) level [ˋlɛvl] *a.* 水平的 ①
(2) even [ˋivən] *a.* 平的；均等的 ①

▶ People used to believe the earth was flat.
人們曾一度相信地球是平的。

▶ The party was totally flat, so we decided to leave.
那派對很無趣，所以我們決定離開。

▶ Sales have been flat for months.
已經好幾個月業績不振了。

▶ We had a flat tire on our way to work this morning.
今天早上去上班的途中，我們的車爆胎了。

▶ The young couple lives in a small flat.
那對年輕夫妻住在一間小公寓。

▶ Katie prefers wearing flats rather than heels.
凱蒂比較喜歡穿平底鞋而不是高跟鞋。

▶ Geoff laid the blanket out flat.
傑夫把毯子平放。

dull [dʌl] *a.* 枯燥乏味的；(刀等) 鈍的 (= blunt [blʌnt])；愚笨的 & *vt.* 使變遲鈍

囫 (1) boring [ˋborɪŋ]
　　a. 乏味的，無聊的 ①
　(2) stupid [ˋst(j)upɪd] *a.* 愚蠢的 ①

囵 (1) interesting [ˋɪnt(ə)rɪstɪŋ]
　　a. 有趣的 ①
　(2) sharp [ʃɑrp] *a.* 尖銳的；精明的 ①

▶ The guest's speech was pretty dull.
那位來賓的演說相當枯燥乏味。

▶ This knife is so dull that it is useless for slicing bread.
這把刀很鈍，沒辦法拿來切麵包。

▶ All work and no play makes Jack a dull boy.
只知工作不玩耍，聰明孩子也變傻。── 諺語

▶ Drinking heavily every day dulls Rick's mind.
每天大量飲酒使瑞克的頭腦變得遲鈍。

10　hop [hɑp] *vi.* (單腳) 跳躍；(鳥獸等) 蹦跳；快速去 / 跳 & *n.* (單腳) 跳躍

冒 hop, hopped [hɑpt], hopped

囫 (1) jump [dʒʌmp] *vi.* & *n.* 跳躍 ①
　(2) spring [sprɪŋ] *vi.* 跳 & *n.* 春天 ①

▶ The little boy was hopping along the river bank and singing the tune his grandma taught him.
小男孩正沿著河岸跳來跳去，唱著奶奶教他的旋律。

▶ There is a little bird hopping on the ground there.
那裡有一隻小鳥在地面上跳躍著。

▶ Hop in! I can give you a ride home.
快上車！我可以載你回家。

▶ What Billy did was more of a hop than a jump.
比利做的不過是單腳跳而已，還稱不上是真的跳躍。

11　birth [bɝθ] *n.* 出生

囼 (1) give birth to...　　生下……
　(2) at birth　　　　　　出生時
　(3) a place of birth　　出生地
　(4) American / Canadian / French /... by birth
　　生於美國 / 加拿大 / 法國等

衍 born [bɔrn] *a.* 出生的 ①

▶ Nancy gave birth to a baby boy last night.
南西昨晚產下一名男嬰。

▶ My sister's son weighed 3,000 grams at birth.
我妹妹的兒子出生時重達 3 千公克。

▶ Is your place of birth on your passport?
你護照上有寫出生地嗎？

▶ George is Canadian by birth.
= George was born in Canada.
喬治生於加拿大。

12 function [ˈfʌŋkʃən] n. 功能，職責 & vi. 運作

冎 function as...
行使……的職責，有……的作用

衍 functional [ˈfʌŋkʃən!] a. 實用的 ④

▶ I think one of the functions of art is healing.
我認為藝術的功用之一是療癒。

▶ The computer stopped functioning after the power failure.
停電之後，電腦就停止運作了。

▶ Rick is an accountant and also functions as a dance teacher.
瑞克是會計師，同時也是名舞蹈老師。

▶ The basement also functions as a gym.
地下室也可當健身房使用。

13 cage [kedʒ] n. 籠子 & vt. 把……關進籠子 (通常使用被動)

衍 caged [kedʒd] a. 關在籠子裡的

▶ The bird in the cage is a parrot.
籠子裡的鳥是鸚鵡。

▶ The snake was caged by the firemen.
那條蛇被消防隊員關到籠子裡。

14 capital [ˈkæpət!] n. 大寫字母 (= capital letter)；首都；資本 (不可數) & a. 大寫字母的

冎 capital punishment　死刑
衍 (1) capitalist [ˈkæpətlɪst]
　　a. 資本主義的 & n. 資本主義者；資本家 ④
(2) capitalism [ˈkæpətl͵ɪzəm]
　　n. 資本主義 (不可數) ④
(3) capitalize [ˈkæpətl͵aɪz]
　　vt. 將……大寫；給……提供資金

▶ A proper noun begins with a capital.
= A proper noun begins with a capital letter.
專有名詞要以大寫字母為首。

▶ Washington, D.C., is the capital of the United States.
華府是美國首都。

▶ We need more capital to run this restaurant.
我們需要更多的資本來經營這家餐廳。

▶ Capital punishment is a controversial issue in many countries.
在很多國家死刑是個爭議性很高的議題。

15 port [pɔrt] n. 港口

冎 a port city　港都
= a harbor city
似 harbor [ˈhɑrbɚ] n. 港口 ③

▶ The port is capable of receiving large ships.
這個港口可以停泊大噸位的船隻。

▶ Hamburg is a famous port city in Germany.
漢堡是德國有名的港都。

coast [kost] n. 海岸
冎 (1) on the coast　在海 / 沿岸

▶ The east coast of Taiwan is full of beautiful views.
臺灣東海岸盡是美景。

(2) off the coast　在海岸外
(3) from coast to coast
　　從此岸到彼岸，全國各地

▶ We have a vacation home on the coast.
　我們在海邊有間度假屋。

▶ The accident just happened off the coast.
　這起意外就發生在海岸不遠處。

▶ Sam is riding his bicycle across Ireland from coast to coast.
　山姆騎腳踏車遊歷愛爾蘭各地。

---

shore [ʃɔr] *n.* 岸（邊），濱，畔

H on shore　在岸上
　off shore　在（海／湖等）岸外

衍 (1) offshore [ˌɔfˋʃɔr]
　　　a. 離岸的，海上的 ⑥
　(2) onshore [ˋɑnˌʃɔr] *a.* 陸上的

▶ We started swimming back to the shore at the sight of a shark.
　一看見鯊魚的蹤跡，我們便開始游回岸邊。

▶ The crew of the ship are all on shore now.
　全體船員現在都在岸上了。

16　**needle** [ˋnidl̩] *n.* 針

H a needle and thread　針線
　thread [θrɛd] *n.* (縫衣服的) 線

延伸 **pin** [pɪn] *n.* 大頭針；胸針；別針 ①

▶ You need a needle and thread to sew.
　你需要有針線才能縫紉。

17　**swallow** [ˋswɑlo] *vt. & vi.* 吞嚥 & *vt.* 相信 & *n.* 吞嚥；一次吞食之物；燕子

H (1) swallow one's pride
　　　某人忍氣吞聲
　(2) a bitter pill to swallow
　　　難以接受的事
　(3) be hard to swallow
　　　令人難以相信／接受
　(4) in / with one swallow
　　　一口吞下
　(5) take a swallow of...
　　　吞／喝一口……

▶ Robert swallowed many mouthfuls of food in a short time.　羅伯特在短時間內吞下很多口的食物。

▶ The clerk swallowed his pride and continued to explain the problem to the rude customer.
　店員忍氣吞聲，繼續向那位沒禮貌的客人解釋該問題。

▶ The fact that Leo is no longer a superstar is a bitter pill to swallow.
　里歐很難接受不再是當紅巨星的事實。

▶ Tina's throat hurts when she swallows.
　蒂娜吞嚥時會喉嚨痛。

▶ The truth may be hard to swallow.
　真相可能讓人難以接受。

▶ Joyce drank the bitter herbal medicine in one swallow.
　喬伊絲一口氣喝下了那很苦的草藥水。

▶ Jack took a swallow of water and began the speech.
　傑克喝一口水，然後開始演講。

▶ One swallow doesn't make a summer.
　孤燕不成夏／一事成功並不代表萬事大吉。── 諺語，喻不要高興得太早

4918-4923

18 being [ˈbiɪŋ] *n.* 存在；生命，生物

片 (1) come into being　開始存在
= come into existence
(2) a human (being)　人類

▶ Impressionism came into being in the 1860s.
印象派從 1860 年代起就出現了。

▶ Some people still doubt that human beings evolved from apes.
有些人仍不相信人類是由人猿演化而來。
*evolve [ɪˈvɑlv] *vi.* 進化
evolve from...　從……進化而成

19 gram [græm] *n.* (重量單位) 公克 (縮寫為 g)

▶ One thousand grams equals one kilogram.
1 千公克等於 1 公斤。

kilogram [ˈkɪləˌgræm]
n. (重量單位) 公斤 (= kilo [ˈkilo])
(縮寫為 kg)

用法 2 kilograms　2 公斤
= 2 kilos
= 2 kg

▶ That heavy bag probably weighs about 50 kilograms.
那個沉甸甸的袋子大概有 50 公斤。

20 mile [maɪl] *n.* (長度單位) 英里 (約等於 1.6 公里)

片 see for miles　看得很遠
衍 milestone [ˈmaɪlˌston] *n.* 里程碑 ⑤

▶ The movie theater is two miles away.
電影院離這裡 2 英里遠。

▶ On a clear day, you can see for miles from this mountaintop.
天空萬里無雲時，你可以從這山頂看得很遠。

meter [ˈmitɚ]
n. (長度單位) 公尺 (縮寫為 m)；計，儀，表

片 a water / an electricity meter
水 / 電表

用法 10 meters　10 公尺
= 10 m

▶ When it comes to the 100-meter race, my friend Kathy is second to none.
說到百米賽跑，沒人可以跑贏我朋友凱西。
*be second to none　是最棒的
= be the best

▶ Where is the water meter for this apartment?
這棟公寓的水表在哪裡？

centimeter [ˈsɛntəˌmitɚ]
n. (長度單位) 公分 (縮寫為 cm)

用法 10 centimeters　10 公分
= 10 cm

▶ An inch equals 2.54 centimeters.
一英寸等於 2.54 公分。

442

21 terrorist [ˈtɛrərɪst] n. 恐怖分子 & a. 恐怖分子的

片 (1) a terrorist attack　　恐怖攻擊
(2) a terrorist threat　　恐怖威脅
(3) a terrorist organization
　　恐怖組織

衍 (1) terrible [ˈtɛrəbl̩]
　　a. 可怕的；糟糕的 ①
(2) terror [ˈtɛrɚ]
　　n. 恐懼；可怕的人／物 ④
(3) terrify [ˈtɛrəˌfaɪ] vt. 使恐懼 ⑤

▶ The terrorist was captured at the border.
這名恐怖分子在邊境被捕。

▶ There has been a series of terrorist attacks in that country.
那國家已連續發生一連串的恐怖攻擊事件了。

▶ The number of terrorist threats has increased recently.
最近恐怖威脅的次數已加增。

▶ The president will not deal with a terrorist organization.
總統不會和恐怖組織打交道。

terrorism [ˈtɛrəˌrɪzm̩] n. 恐怖主義

片 (1) an act of terrorism
　　恐怖主義活動
(2) fight (against) terrorism
　　打擊恐怖主義

▶ Terrorism is designed to create fear.
恐怖主義是為製造恐懼而產生的。

▶ These latest acts of terrorism have ended the peace talks.
最近的恐怖主義活動已讓和平會談停止。

▶ Several of our allies have joined with us to fight (against) terrorism.
我們好幾位盟友已加入我們一起來打擊恐怖主義。

22 available [əˈveləbl̩] a. 可用的，可得到的；(人) 有空的

片 be available for...
　　可用來……，可以……

衍 availability [əˌveləˈbɪlətɪ]
　　n. 可得性；能出席

似 free [fri] a. 有空的 ①

▶ The church is available for weddings Monday through Saturday.
那間教堂星期一到星期六可用來舉行婚禮。

▶ Tickets are still available at the entrance.
入口處仍有售票。

▶ Are you available now?
= Are you free now?
= Do you have time now?
你現在有空嗎？

23 nor [nɔr] conj. 也不 (常與 neither 並用)

片 neither A nor B　　既不是 A 也不是 B

似 or [ɔr／ɚ] conj. 或者 ①

用法 以 neither A nor B 連接主詞時，動詞按最接近的主詞作變化。

▶ A: I have never been to Iceland.
　B: Nor have I.
　A：我從沒去過冰島。
　B：我也沒有。

▶ Neither my father nor I am tall.
我爸爸不高，我也不高。

24 participate [paɾˈtɪsəˌpet] *vi.* 參加

片 participate in... 參加……
= take part in...

衍 (1) participation [paɾˌtɪsəˈpeʃən]
　　n. 參加 / 與 ④
　(2) participant [paɾˈtɪsəpənt]
　　n. 參加者 ⑤

▸ Linda participated in the speech contest and came in third.
琳達參加演講比賽得了第 3 名。

---

25 behave [bɪˈhev] *vi.* 守規矩；表現

片 (1) behave (oneself) 守規矩
　(2) behave well / badly
　　表現很好 / 差

衍 behavior [bɪˈhevjɚ]
　n. 行為 (不可數) ④

▸ Mother told us to behave ourselves while she was away.
媽媽告訴我們她不在時我們要好好守規矩。

▸ Alice behaves well only when her father is around.
愛麗絲只有在她爸爸在的時候,她才會表現得很乖巧。

---

punish [ˈpʌnɪʃ] *vt.* 懲罰

片 punish sb for + N/V-ing
　因……處罰某人

▸ I punished my daughter for smoking.
我女兒抽菸,因此我處罰她。

---

punishment [ˈpʌnɪʃmənt] *n.* 懲罰

片 receive (a) punishment for +
　N/V-ing 會因為……而受到處罰

似 penalty [ˈpɛnḷtɪ] *n.* 懲罰 ④

▸ You will receive severe punishment for breaking the law.
你犯法就會受到嚴厲的懲罰。

---

26 fellow [ˈfɛlo] *n.* (男)人;同伴;(大學裡有領獎學金的) 研究生 & *a.* 同伴的

似 (1) person [ˈpɝsṇ] *n.* 人 ①
　(2) man [mæn] *n.* 男人 ①
　(3) guy [gaɪ] *n.* 男人 ①

▸ Zach seems like a friendly fellow, doesn't he?
查克看起來是個很和善的人,不是嗎?

▸ Sue often missed her fellows in the dance club.
蘇常想念她在舞蹈社的同伴。

▸ Victor is a research fellow at Harvard University.
維特是哈佛大學領有獎學金的研究生。

▸ This is Michael, a fellow salesman at my company.
這位是邁可,他是我公司的業務同仁。

---

27 symbol [ˈsɪmbḷ] *n.* 象徵;符號

片 (1) be a symbol of... 是……的象徵
　(2) a symbol for... ……的符號

衍 (1) symbolic [sɪmˈbɑlɪk] *a.* 象徵的 ⑤
　(2) symbolize [ˈsɪmbḷˌaɪz]
　　vt. 象徵 ⑥

▸ A cross is the symbol of Christianity.
十字架是基督教的象徵。
＊Christianity [ˌkrɪstʃɪˈænətɪ] *n.* 基督教

▸ The symbol for calcium is Ca.
鈣的符號是 Ca。

28 greet [grit] *vt.* 問候，迎接；對……做出回應

片 (1) greet sb with sth
以……來迎接某人

(2) be greeted with...　以……來回應

衍 greeting [ˈgritɪŋ] *n.* 招呼，問候；祝
賀詞，問候語 (此意恆用複數形) ④

▶ Rebecca greeted everyone at the party.
蕾貝嘉問候每個來參加派對的人。

▶ The hostess warmly greeted me with a hug.
女主人給了我一個擁抱，親切地迎接我。

▶ George's ideas were greeted with anger.
喬治的想法引起憤怒。

Level 2

Unit 49

Unit 50

1 melody [ˋmɛlədɪ] *n.* 旋律，曲調

衍 melodious [məˋlodɪəs]
　a. 旋律優美的

似 (1) tune [t(j)un] *n.* 旋律，曲調 ③
　(2) song [sɔŋ] *n.* 歌曲 ①

▶ I like that song because of its beautiful melody.
　我喜歡那首歌是因為它優美的旋律。

2 burden [ˋbɝdn̩] *n.* 重物，負荷；負擔 & *vt.* 使煩惱

片 (1) shoulder / bear / carry the
　burden of + V-ing
　負起做⋯⋯的重擔，負責做⋯⋯
　(2) place a burden on sb
　讓某人背負重擔
　(3) burden sb with sth
　用某事物來煩某人

似 load [lod]
　n. 負重，負荷 & *vt.* & *vi.* 裝載 ②

▶ The old horse looked sad under its heavy burden.
　老馬馱著重物看起來很哀傷。

▶ Ever since his father passed away, Stanley has shouldered the burden of raising his family.
　史丹利的父親過世後，他就負起養家的重擔。

▶ Tom's illness placed a huge burden on his parents.
　湯姆生病讓他的雙親背負沉重的負擔。

▶ I don't want to burden you with these matters; I can take care of them myself.
　我不想讓這些事造成你的負擔；我自己可以處理。

3 gradual [ˋgrædʒuəl] *a.* 逐漸的；平緩的

反 (1) sudden [ˋsʌdn̩] *a.* 突然的 ②
　(2) steep [stip] *a.* 陡峭的 ③

▶ After Taylor exercised twice a week and ate less, there was a gradual change in his body.
　泰勒每週運動 2 次並少吃後，他的身體逐漸出現了變化。

▶ A gradual slope leads to the castle's main entrance.
　這緩坡會通往城堡的主要入口。

4 classic [ˋklæsɪk] *a.* 經典的，優秀的；典型的；典雅的 & *n.* 經典之作；古典文學名著
　（此意恆用複數，前面加定冠詞 the）

似 typical [ˋtɪpɪkl̩] *a.* 典型的 ②

▶ This novel is considered a classic work of science fiction.
　這本小說被認為是科幻小說的經典之作。

▶ The soccer team's winning goal was classic.
　這支足球隊致勝進的那一球真是漂亮。

▶ Teddy was suffering from the classic symptoms of the illness.
　泰迪患有該疾病的典型症狀。

▶ Eileen's mother prefers classic furniture designs.
　艾琳的母親偏好典雅的傢俱設計。

▶ Ingmar Bergman's films are true classics.
英格瑪・柏格曼的電影是真正的經典名作。

▶ Eric likes to spend some time reading the classics.
艾瑞克喜歡花時間閱讀古典文學作品。

classical [ˈklæsɪkl̩]
a. (音樂) 古典的；傳統的

🔤 classical music　古典樂

🔄 traditional [trəˈdɪʃənl̩] *a.* 傳統的 ②

▶ Do you like to listen to classical music?
你喜歡聽古典樂嗎？

▶ I prefer modern ballet to classical ballet because the former makes my body feel free.
與古典芭蕾相比，我更喜歡現代芭蕾，因為現代芭蕾讓我的身體感到很自由。

5　beard [bɪrd] *n.* 下巴及兩耳下方的鬍鬚

🔤 (1) wear / have a beard　有鬍子
　(2) grow a beard　留鬍子
　(2) shave (off) a beard
　　剃某人的鬍子

🔄 bear [bɛr] *n.* 熊 ①

🔄 mustache [ˈmʌstæʃ]
　n. 八字鬍，小鬍子〔美〕
　（= moustache〔英〕）⑥

▶ My grandfather wears a bushy beard.
我的爺爺有很濃密的鬍子。

▶ My brother told me he wanted to grow his beard, but I said he would look ugly that way.
我哥哥告訴我說他想留鬍子，但我說那樣他會很醜。

▶ David shaves off his beard every morning.
大衛每天早上剃鬍子。

6　link [lɪŋk] *vt.* 使有 (實體) 連結；使相關聯 & *n.* 關聯；(網際網路的) 連結

🔤 (1) link A to / with B
　　將 A 與 B 有 (實體) 連結；使 A 與 B
　　有相關性
　= A be linked to / with B
　(2) a link between A and B
　　A 和 B (之間) 有相關性

🔄 (1) connect [kəˈnɛkt]
　　vt. & vi. (使) 連結 ③
　(2) associate [əˈsoʃɪˌet]
　　vt. 使有關聯 ④
　(3) hyperlink [ˈhaɪpəˌlɪŋk]
　　n. 超連結

▶ The bridge links the island to the mainland.
這座橋連接這個小島到大陸。

▶ Researchers say lung cancer is linked to smoking.
研究者指出肺癌與抽菸有關。

▶ There's a strong link between diet and obesity.
飲食與肥胖間有強烈的關聯。
*obesity [oˈbisətɪ] *n.* 肥胖 (症)

▶ Just click on this link, and you can see the pdf.
只需點這個連結，你就可以看到 pdf 檔。

---

connection [kəˈnɛkʃən]
n. 關係，關聯；(實體) 連接；(電線等的)
接頭，連接部分

🔤 (1) have a connection with...
　　和……有關係

▶ Do you have any connection with the Mafia?
你和黑手黨有什麼關係嗎？

▶ The man was questioned in connection with a robbery.
這男子因與搶案有關聯而被審問。

(2) **in connection with...**
與……有關

▶ I think something is wrong with the Wi-Fi connection.
我認為無線網路的連接有問題。

似 (1) **association** [ə͵sosɪˈeʃən]
n. 關聯；協會 ④

▶ Ted fixed the loose connection, and now the copy machine works fine.
泰德修好鬆動的接頭了，現在影印機能用了。

(2) **bond** [band] *n.* 關係 & *vi.* & *vt.* (與某人) 建立關係 ④

---

relate [rɪˈlet] *vt.* 使相關；敘述 & *vi.* 和……有關；理解

▶ Spanish and French are related to Latin.
西班牙文及法文與拉丁文有淵源。

片 (1) **relate A to B**　找到 A 與 B 有關
= A is related to B

▶ Grandfather related a story to us yesterday.
爺爺昨天跟我們說了一個故事。

(2) **relate sth to sb**
向某人敘述某事物

▶ That news relates to the problem we were just discussing.
那則新聞和我們剛才討論的問題有關。

(3) **relate to sb/sth**
和某人 / 事物有關

(4) **relate to sb**
理解某人，與某人產生共鳴

▶ Dean can relate to the main character in the movie because he also had a difficult childhood.
狄恩可以與電影中的主角產生共鳴，因為他的童年也過得很艱辛。

衍 (1) **relation** [rɪˈleʃən]
n. 關係；親戚 ②

(2) **relationship** [rɪˈleʃənʃɪp]
n. 關係 ②

---

joint [dʒɔɪnt] *a.* 共有的，聯合的 & *n.* 關節；結合處，連接點

▶ The young couple opened a joint account for convenience's sake.
這對年輕夫婦為了方便起見開了個共同戶頭。

片 **a joint venture**　合資企業

▶ It is said that our company wants to start a joint venture with a German company.
據說我們公司想和一家德國公司合資。

衍 **join** [dʒɔɪn] *vt.* 連接 & *vi.* & *vt.* 參加 & *n.* 接頭，接合處 ①

反 **individual** [͵ɪndəˈvɪdʒʊəl]
a. 個人的 ②

▶ Toby can't run anymore because his knee joint was injured in a race.
托比的膝關節在某次賽跑中受傷因此不再跑步了。

▶ The joints in the bridge are starting to wear away.
這座橋梁的結合處開始磨損了。

---

7 **tube** [t(j)ub] *n.* (裝牙膏等的) 軟管 / 金屬管等；管子；電視〔美〕(此意前面加定冠詞 the)

片 (1) **a tube of...**　一條……
(2) **watch the tube**　看電視
= watch TV

▶ Can you buy a new tube of toothpaste?
你可以買條新的牙膏嗎？

▶ Water will come out of this tube and flow into the pond.
水會從這條管子流出，再流進小池裡。

▶ Stop watching the tube.
不要看電視了。

8 burst [bɝst] *vt. & vi.* (使) 爆破 / 炸 & *n.* 爆破 / 炸，噴；(感情) 爆發

三 三態同形

片 (1) burst out crying / laughing
　　　突然大哭 / 笑
　　= burst into tears / laughter
　(2) a burst of laughter　突然大笑

▶ The little boy used a needle to burst the balloon.
　小男孩用一根針刺破氣球。

▶ Melissa burst out crying when she heard about the accident.
= Melissa burst into tears when she heard about the accident.
　梅莉莎聽到關於這個意外的消息就大哭了起來。

▶ We could hear the bomb burst in the distance.
　我們可以聽到遠處炸彈爆炸的聲響。

▶ Do you know what caused the burst of water?
　你知道造成水噴出來的原因嗎？

▶ Tommy gave a loud burst of laughter when he heard my joke.
　湯米聽到我講的笑話就放聲大笑。

9 forth [fɔrθ] *adv.* 向前 (走)，向外 (走)

片 (1) back and forth　前後來回
　(2) put forth...　提出⋯⋯
　(3) and so forth　等等，諸如此類
　　= and so on
　　= and the like
　　= etc

▶ Joseph stepped forth, inviting his girlfriend to dance with him.
　喬瑟夫往前走，邀請他女友一起跳支舞。

▶ Henry walked back and forth, looking very impatient.
　亨利前後來回地走著，看來很不耐煩。

▶ I put forth my ideas at the meeting, and to my great joy, my boss accepted all of them.
　我在開會時提出了我的看法，而令我很高興的是，老闆全部接受了。

▶ In the library, there are many novels, magazines, periodicals, and so forth.
　圖書館裡有很多小說、雜誌和期刊等等。

10 gun [gʌn] *n.* 槍 & *vt.* 開槍射擊

三 gun, gunned [gʌnd], gunned

片 (1) aim one's gun at...
　　　某人將槍瞄準⋯⋯
　(2) gun sb down　開槍將某人射倒

▶ The policeman aimed his gun at the bad guy.
　警察把槍瞄準那個壞蛋。

▶ The robber was gunned down as he tried to run away.
　那名搶匪在企圖逃跑時遭開槍射倒。

11 crime [kraɪm] *n.* 犯罪案件，罪行 (可數)；犯罪行為 / 活動 (不可數)；愚蠢的作法

片 commit a crime　犯罪

衍 criminal [ˋkrɪmən!]
　n. 罪犯 & *a.* 犯罪的 ③

▶ The man was put in jail for committing two crimes.
　這名男子犯了 2 條罪而入獄了。

似 (1) **evil** [`ɪvḷ] *n.* 罪惡 & *a.* 邪惡的 ②
(2) **sin** [sɪn]
　　n. 惡行；(宗教或良心上的) 罪惡 ③

▶ The politician thought hiring more police officers would help prevent crime in our city.
那政治家認為僱用更多的員警可幫助預防本市的犯罪活動。

▶ It's a crime to waste so much money.
浪費這麼多錢真是愚蠢。

---

prison [`prɪzṇ] *n.* 監獄
片 (1) **in prison**　坐牢
(2) **put sb in prison**　把某人關進監獄
衍 **imprison** [ɪm`prɪzṇ] *vt.* 監禁 ⑥
似 **jail** [dʒel] *vt.* 監禁 & *n.* 監獄 ③

▶ That prison has about two hundred convicts.
那所監獄有大約 200 名囚犯。

▶ Andy spent a lot of time in prison.
安迪坐了很長時間的牢。

▶ The police should put the bad guy in prison.
警察應該把那壞人關進監獄。

---

prisoner [`prɪzṇɚ] *n.* 囚犯
似 **convict** [`kɑnvɪkt] *n.* 囚犯 ⑤

▶ The prisoner was punished for trying to escape.
該囚犯因企圖逃獄而被懲罰。

12　switch [swɪtʃ] *n.* 開關；突然轉換 & *vt.* 打開或關閉 (電器等的開關)；調換

片 (1) **switch / turn... on**　打開……
= **switch / turn on...**
　　switch / turn... off　關掉……
= **switch / turn off...**
(2) **switch A for B**　用 B 來代替 A

▶ The machine's switch was broken, so it couldn't work.
這臺機器的開關故障了，所以機器無法運作。

▶ Renee's new job is a complete switch from her old one.
蕾妮的新工作與她的舊工作完全不同。

▶ When Tim got home, he switched on the TV.
提姆一到家就打開電視。

▶ Sandra switched the batteries in the toy for new ones.
珊卓拉把玩具內的電池換新的。

13　advice [əd`vaɪs] *n.* 勸告，忠告，建議 (不可數)

片 (1) **a piece of advice**　一個建議
(2) **give sb advice**　給某人建議
衍 (1) **advise** [əd`vaɪz]
　　vt. & *vi.* 勸告，忠告 ③
(2) **adviser** [əd`vaɪzɚ]
　　n. 顧問 (= advisor) ③
(3) **advisory** [əd`vaɪzərɪ]
　　a. 提供意見的 ⑥
似 (1) **suggestion** [sə`dʒɛstʃən]
　　n. 建議 ④
(2) **recommendation**
　　[ˌrɛkəmɛn`deʃən] *n.* 建議 ⑤

▶ Can you give me a piece of advice?
= Can you give me a suggestion?
你可以給我一個建議嗎？

14 lid [lɪd] *n.* 蓋子

衍 eyelid [ˈaɪˌlɪd] *n.* 眼皮 ⑥

▶ Could you help me open the lid of the trash can?
你可以幫我把垃圾桶蓋打開嗎？

15 congratulations [kənˌgrætʃəˈleʃənz] *n.* 恭喜 (恆用複數)

用 (1) congratulations on... 恭喜……
(2) give A B's congratulations
代 B 向 A 道賀

衍 congratulate [kənˈgrætʃəˌlet]
vt. 道賀，慶賀 ④

▶ Congratulations on your success!
恭喜你成功了！

▶ I've heard Peter has passed the exam. Give him my congratulations.
聽說彼得已經通過考試了。請代我向他道賀。

16 aloud [əˈlaʊd] *adv.* 大聲地

衍 loud [laʊd] *a.* 大聲的 & *adv.* 大聲地 ①
似 out loud 大聲地

▶ Please read it aloud. I can't hear you.
= Please read it out loud. I can't hear you.
請大聲唸。我聽不到你的聲音。

17 plus [plʌs] *prep.* (算數) 加；以及 & *n.* 加號 (= plus sign)；好處 & *a.* (數字) 正值的；高於……的

似 positive [ˈpɑzətɪv]
a. (數字) 正值的；確信的 ②

延伸 算術題：2 − 1 = 1
英文說法：Two minus one equals one.
算術題：2 × 2 = 4
英文說法：Two times two equals four.
算術題：4 ÷ 2 = 2
英文說法：Four divided by two equals two.

▶ Six plus six is / equals twelve.
6 加 6 等於 12。

▶ Bruce owns five restaurants, plus a movie theater.
= Bruce owns five restaurants as well as a movie theater.
布魯斯有 5 家餐廳，還有 1 家電影院。

▶ Click on the plus sign icon, and you can add a new contact in your smartphone.
點那個加號圖標，這樣你就可以在你的智慧型手機裡加入新的聯絡人了。

▶ Some knowledge of Japanese is a definite plus in this job. 懂些日文對做這項工作絕對是個優勢。

▶ This container is subjected to temperatures of minus twenty degrees and plus ninety degrees.
這容器可以承受負 20 度到正 90 度。

▶ Jerry got an A plus on his English paper.
傑瑞的英文報告拿了 A 加。

extra [ˈɛkstrə]
n. 另外付點錢就可額外得到的東西，加購品 & *a.* 額外的 & *adv.* 額外地

▶ The pan comes with some nice extras, such as these mugs.
平底鍋有附一些不錯的加購品，比如這些杯子。

▶ We need an extra two hours to complete the work.
我們需要額外 2 個小時才能完成這工作。

片 an extra + 數字　額外若干……
= an additional + 數字

似 (1) additional [əˋdɪʃənḷ] a. 額外的 ③
(2) spare [spɛr] a. 多餘的，備用的 ④
(3) surplus [ˋsɝpləs] a. 多餘的 ⑤

▶ The restaurant charges extra if we bring our own drinks.
如果我們自己帶飲料，那家餐廳會額外收費。

18　humble [ˋhʌmbḷ] a. (地位) 卑微的，清寒的；謙遜的

衍 humbleness [ˋhʌmbḷnəs]
n. (地位) 卑微；謙遜

似 modest [ˋmɑdɪst] a. 謙虛的 ④

▶ Barbara was born into a humble family.
芭芭拉出生在一個清寒的家庭。

▶ Though Jackson is very famous, he is humble.
雖然傑克森很有名，他為人卻很謙虛。

19　expense [ɪkˋspɛns] n. 花錢；代價

片 (1) be worth the expense
值得花錢
(2) at sb's expense　花某人的錢
(3) at the expense of sth
以某事物為代價，放棄某事物

衍 (1) expensive [ɪkˋspɛnsɪv]
a. 昂貴的 ①
(2) expenditure [ɪkˋspɛndətʃɚ]
n. (政府或個人的) 開支 / 銷 ⑥

▶ Nick thinks buying a bigger car is worth the expense.
尼克認為值得花錢買臺大一點的車。

▶ We took a trip to Spain at my mom's expense.
我們花我媽媽的錢去西班牙旅行。

▶ Some taxi drivers often drive fast at the expense of safety.
一些計程車司機經常不顧安全在開快車。

20　angle [ˋæŋgḷ] n. 角度；觀點

片 (1) a right angle　直角
(2) from a different angle /
perspective　從另一個角度來看
＊perspective [pɚˋspɛktɪv]
n. 看法，觀點

似 angel [ˋendʒḷ] n. 天使 ③

▶ The interior angles of a square are right angles.
正方形的內角是直角。

▶ From a different angle, divorce might be the best solution to your problems.
從另一個角度來看，離婚也許是解決你們問題的最佳途徑。

21　branch [bræntʃ] n. 分部，分公司；樹枝 & vi. 分岔

片 (1) open a branch
成立分部 / 分公司
(2) branch off from...
從……岔開 / 分岔
(3) branch out　涉足 (新工作)

▶ Simon is planning to open a branch in Bangkok next month.
賽門計劃下個月在曼谷成立一家分公司。

▶ We tied two ropes to the tree branch to make a swing.
我們將 2 條繩子綁在樹枝上做成鞦韆。

▶ Aaron drove down a street that branched off from the main road.

艾倫行駛在一條從主要道路分支出來的街道上。

▶ Don't be afraid to branch out and try something new.

別害怕涉足新工作，要試試新事物。

---

brand [brænd] *n.* 商標，牌子

(1) brand new　　全新的
(2) a brand name　品牌名稱

▶ That brand of soap is my favorite.

那個牌子的肥皂是我的最愛。

▶ Sean's brand new car was stolen two days after he bought it.

尚恩的新車買了 2 天後就被偷了。

▶ Ken wanted to start his own business and asked me to give him advice on the brand name.

肯想自己創業，請我給他有關品牌名稱的建議。

22　principal [ˋprɪnsəpḷ] *a.* 最主 / 重要的，首要的 & *n.* (中小學) 校長

(1) headteacher [ˏhɛd ˋtitʃɚ]
　　n. 校長〔英〕
(2) headmaster [ˋhɛdˏmæstɚ]
　　n. 男校長〔英〕

▶ Rita's principal reason for dancing is to improve her health.

麗塔跳舞的主要原因是為了改善她的健康。

▶ The principal blamed the naughty student.

校長責備這個頑皮的學生。

---

principle [ˋprɪnsəpḷ]

n. 原則，原理；道德原則，行為準則

(1) in principle　原則上，基本上
(2) a man of principle
　　有道德準則的人

▶ I agree with you in principle; it is your method that I disagree with.

原則上我同意你；我不同意的是你的方法。

▶ You can trust Ned. He's a man of principle.

你可以信任奈德，他是個有道德準則的人。

23　ignore [ɪgˋnɔr] *vt.* 忽 / 無視；裝做沒看見，不理會

(1) ignorance [ˋɪgnərəns] *n.* 無知 ④
(2) ignorant [ˋɪgnərənt]
　　a. 無知的；不知道的 ④

▶ That fool ignores all warnings from his parents.

那個傻瓜無視他父母給他的種種警告。

▶ I was angry because Lisa kept ignoring me.

我很生氣，因為麗莎一直不理我。

24　organ [ˋɔrgən] *n.* 器官；管風琴 (= pipe organ)；機構

an organ donor　器官捐贈者
(1) organic [ɔrˋgænɪk] *a.* 有機的 ③
(2) organism [ˋɔrgənɪzəm]
　　n. 有機物 ⑤

▶ Would you like to be an organ donor?

你想成為器官捐贈者嗎？

▶ Calvin played us a tune on the pipe organ.

克爾文用風琴為我們彈奏了一首曲子。

> Parliament is the major organ of the government in the UK.
> 在英國，議會是主要的政府機構。

liver [ˈlɪvɚ] *n.* 肝 (臟)

延伸 **hepatitis** [ˌhɛpəˈtaɪtəs] *n.* 肝炎
hepatitis A / B / C　A / B / C 型肝炎

> Drinking heavily will do a lot of damage to your liver.
> 飲酒過量會對肝臟造成很大的傷害。

cell [sɛl]
n. 細胞；單間牢房；手機 (= cellphone [ˈsɛlfɑn] = cellular [ˈsɛljəlɚ] phone)

> The life span of skin cells is quite short—about two to three weeks.
> 皮膚細胞的壽命很短 —— 大約 2 到 3 週。
> The local jail only has two or three cells.
> 本地監獄只有 2 或 3 間牢房。
> Is that your new cell?
> 那是你的新手機嗎？

25　lens [lɛnz] *n.* 鏡片，鏡頭

複 **lenses** [ˈlɛnzɪz]
片 (1) a contact (lens)　隱形眼鏡鏡片
a pair of contact lenses
一副隱形眼鏡
(2) a camera lens　相機鏡頭

> Disposable contact lenses are rather popular among young people.　拋棄式隱形眼鏡很受年輕人歡迎。
> Tony looked through the camera lens as his girlfriend posed for photographs in the park.
> 湯尼透過相機鏡頭看他女友在公園裡擺姿勢拍照。

26　keeper [ˈkipɚ] *n.* 保管 / 看守人；(動物園) 飼養 / 保育員

片 a lighthouse keeper
燈塔看守人 / 管理員
衍 (1) housekeeper [ˈhaʊsˌkipɚ]
n. 管家 ③
(2) goalkeeper [ˈgolˌkipɚ]
n. 守門員 ⑥

> Robert has been a lighthouse keeper for more than 30 years.
> 羅伯特擔任燈塔看守人已有 30 多年了。
> The kid wants to be a zoo keeper in the future.
> 這小孩將來想當動物園的保育員。

shopkeeper [ˈʃɑpˌkipɚ]
n. 店主 (= storekeeper)

> Jerry is a shopkeeper who sells puzzles and games.
> 傑瑞是賣智力遊戲玩具的店長。

27　stream [strim] *n.* 溪流；流量 & *vi.* 流動 & *vt.* & *vi.* 在線收聽或收看

片 stream down...　流下……
衍 (1) mainstream [ˈmenˌstrim]
a. (思想等) 主流的 ⑤
(2) streamline [ˈstrimˌlaɪn]
vt. 使成流線型
(3) livestream [ˈlaɪvˌstrim]
vt. & *vi.* 線上直播

> The water in this stream is so clear that I can see fish in it.
> 這條小溪的水真清澈，我都可看到裡面有魚。
> The news reported an endless stream of traffic on the highway.
> 新聞報導高速公路車量川流不息。

似 (1) **creek** [krik] *n.* 小溪 ⑤
(2) **brook** [brʊk] *n.* 小溪流 ⑥

▶ As soon as Mabel heard the bad news, tears streamed down her face.
梅寶一聽到這個惡耗，眼淚便流下來了。

▶ Jay is streaming the latest episode of his favorite show.
傑正在線上收看他最愛看的節目的最新一集。

flow [flo] *n.* & *vi.* 流動

▶ During rush hour, the traffic flow is very slow in this region.
尖峰時段這區域的車流非常慢。

▶ The river flows gently into the sea.
那條河緩緩流入大海。

Notes

A

ability	214	agreement	99	anytime	398
able	81	ahead	308	anyway	398
about	40	aid	413	anywhere	398
above	91	aim	394	apartment	207
abroad	209	air	74	ape	348
absence	379	aircraft	336	appear	65
absent	379	airplane	74	appearance	384
accept	245	airport	74	appetite	437
accident	235	alarm	411	apple	22
account	432	album	251	apply	247
across	76	alike	398	appreciate	427
act	66	alive	399	approach	237
action	66	all	47	area	57
active	312	allow	88	argue	400
activity	313	almost	72	argument	400
actor	66	alone	344	arm	5
actress	66	along	88	army	241
actual	258	aloud	451	arrange	315
add	71	already	203	arrangement	315
addition	271	also	5	arrival	267
address	302	although	188	arrive	188
admit	385	altogether	438	arrow	433
adult	294	always	131	art	81
advance	392	am	156	article	390
advice	450	among	240	artist	262
affair	283	amount	264	as	87
affect	429	ancient	404	ask	47
afraid	144	anger	331	asleep	410
afternoon	192	angle	452	attack	220
again	35	angry	155	attempt	425
against	250	animal	108	attend	239
age	73	ankle	374	attention	239
ago	211	another	44	aunt	31
agree	99	answer	107	author	298
agreement	99	ant	173	available	443

索引

average	364	battle	304	big	21
avoid	416	beach	133	bill	281
B		bean	19	billion	433
baby	9	bear	59	bird	35
back	48	beard	447	birth	439
backpack	325	beat	326	biscuit	361
backward	295	beautiful	137	bit	237
backward(s)	295	beauty	319	bite	165
bad	7	because	38	black	136
badminton	321	become	47	blackboard	312
bag	2	bed	12	blame	424
bake	350	bedroom	184	blank	243
bakery	350	bee	23	blanket	250
balance	429	beef	146	blind	221
balcony	393	beer	318	block	121
ball	125	beg	361	blood	268
balloon	300	begin	52	blow	145
banana	23	beginner	304	blue	36
band	137	behave	444	board	236
bank	128	behind	86	boat	18
bar	382	being	442	body	10
barbecue	351	belief	405	boil	311
barber	307	believe	66	bone	268
bark	322	bell	167	book	4
base	255	belong	121	bookstore	232
baseball	171	below	92	border	242
basic	255	belt	20	bored	186
basics	256	bench	211	boring	187
basis	255	bend	370	born	174
basket	167	beside	145	borrow	203
basketball	192	best	194	boss	17
bat	170	better	232	both	181
bath	161	between	44	bother	365
bathe	432	beyond	249	bottle	157
bathroom	184	bicycle	23	bottom	105

bow	157	**C**		cent	102
bowl	159	cabbage	356	center	75
box	34	café	361	centimeter	442
boy	1	cage	440	central	264
brain	330	cake	2	century	235
branch	452	calendar	342	cereal	278
brand	453	call	50	certain	84
brave	167	calm	342	chain	375
bread	156	camel	310	chair	24
break	82	camera	155	chalk	311
breakfast	165	camp	131	challenge	233
bridge	126	can	38	chance	100
brief	392	cancel	410	change	197
bright	129	cancer	305	channel	250
brilliant	250	candle	289	chapter	396
bring	55	cap	143	character	246
broad	405	capital	440	charge	262
brother	30	car	24	chart	396
brown	157	card	199	chase	337
brush	316	care	119	cheap	182
bug	176	careful	120	cheat	307
build	78	careless	120	check	129
building	393	carrot	206	cheer	251
bun	350	carry	67	cheese	16
burden	446	cartoon	392	chemical	366
burn	231	case	55	chess	236
burst	449	cash	329	chicken	8
bus	24	castle	311	chief	427
business	210	cat	21	child	79
businessman	277	catch	188	childhood	293
busy	27	cause	288	childish	411
butter	16	ceiling	393	china	403
butterfly	202	celebrate	213	chocolate	139
button	214	cell	454	choice	193
buy	7	cellphone	177	choose	193

索 引

chopstick	382	collect	215	copy	214
church	69	college	383	corn	356
circle	190	color	36	corner	203
city	3	comb	352	correct	154
claim	294	combine	354	cost	79
clap	434	come	31	couch	191
class	76	comfortable	206	count	135
classic	446	comic	393	country	186
classical	447	command	241	countryside	227
classmate	401	commercial	277	couple	273
clean	142	common	91	courage	385
clear	90	company	225	course	51
clearly	91	compare	291	court	434
clerk	215	complete	254	cousin	198
clever	258	complex	422	cover	91
click	430	computer	33	cow	12
climate	330	concern	287	cowboy	266
climb	151	conclude	286	coworker	45
clock	32	condition	296	crayon	339
close	5	confident	280	crazy	19
cloth	334	conflict	304	cream	278
clothes	168	congratulations	451	create	249
clothing	334	connection	447	crime	449
cloud	135	consider	229	crisis	406
cloudy	331	consideration	229	cross	77
club	217	contact	315	crow	291
coal	382	contain	253	crowd	372
coast	440	continue	287	cry	9
coat	154	contract	418	cultural	378
cockroach	310	control	238	culture	377
cocoa	361	convenient	210	cup	26
coffee	157	conversation	269	cure	306
coin	329	cook	152	curious	368
cola	319	cookie	113	current	379
cold	13	cool	138	curtain	409

custom	394	deny	245	discussion	281
customer	281	department	239	disease	305
cut	81	depend	292	dish	159
cute	27	depth	387	display	368
cycle	428	describe	239	distance	275
D		description	240	distant	275
daily	342	desert	310	divide	367
damage	390	design	283	division	367
dance	10	desk	24	doctor	206
dancer	349	detail	260	dog	21
danger	304	develop	230	doll	19
dangerous	143	development	230	dollar	102
dark	107	dial	388	domestic	437
data	396	dialogue	269	door	26
date	112	diamond	341	dot	411
daughter	178	diary	342	double	257
day	207	dictionary	217	doubt	412
dead	75	die	75	dove	291
deaf	355	diet	243	download	360
deal	111	difference	238	downstairs	428
dear	160	different	70	dozen	135
death	75	difficult	97	dragon	311
debate	400	difficulty	277	drama	246
debt	321	dig	160	draw	83
decide	86	dinner	165	drawer	329
decision	253	direct	254	drawing	339
deep	122	direction	254	dream	201
deer	347	director	254	dress	176
define	218	dirty	163	drink	46
degree	279	disagree	388	drive	93
delay	372	disagreement	388	driver	93
delicious	300	disappear	384	drop	219
deliver	390	discover	368	drug	329
delivery	391	discovery	368	drum	164
dentist	316	discuss	281	dry	138

索引

dryer	358	emphasize	270	examination	307
duck	7	employ	419	examine	306
due	251	employee	420	example	219
dull	439	employer	420	excellent	202
during	197	employment	419	except	94
duty	295	empty	259	excite	320
E		encourage	385	excited	131
each	181	encouragement	385	excitement	320
eagle	291	end	52	exciting	131
ear	6	ending	303	excuse	288
early	203	enemy	277	exercise	212
earn	373	energy	291	exist	413
earring	341	engine	340	existence	414
earth	98	engineer	221	exit	379
earthquake	342	enjoy	186	expect	218
ease	412	enjoyment	186	expense	452
east	102	enough	8	expensive	182
eastern	265	enter	84	experience	198
easy	110	entire	263	expert	378
eat	46	entrance	379	explain	215
edge	421	envelope	218	express	271
edition	418	environment	243	expression	272
education	247	environmental	243	extra	451
effect	231	equal	260	eye	6
effective	231	eraser	22	eyebrow	374
effort	371	error	221	**F**	
egg	27	escape	230	face	4
either	94	especially	269	fact	54
elder	294	essay	390	factor	288
electric	420	eve	307	factory	144
electrical	420	even	41	fail	217
elephant	12	evening	192	failure	262
else	32	event	248	fair	398
email	155	evil	403	fall	78
emotion	337	exact	416	false	259

family	30	finger	11	fork	137
famous	209	finish	110	form	275
fan	173	fire	94	formal	384
far	74	fireman	317	former	275
farm	109	firm	226	forth	449
farmer	109	first	150	forward	295
fashion	260	fish	161	forward(s)	295
fast	118	fisherman	227	found	403
fat	155	fit	332	fox	347
fate	327	fix	283	free	78
father	30	flag	289	freedom	433
fault	438	flat	438	fresh	127
favor	324	flight	336	friend	96
favorite	324	floor	98	friendly	96
fear	304	flow	455	friendship	401
feature	423	flower	171	fries	319
fee	327	flu	305	frog	175
feed	121	fly	128	front	48
feel	52	focus	395	fruit	22
feeling	316	fog	381	fry	319
fellow	444	folk	365	full	81
female	369	follow	53	fully	81
festival	213	following	410	fun	156
fever	305	food	31	function	440
few	140	fool	202	funny	156
field	227	foolish	309	furniture	409
fight	101	foot	11	further	233
figure	226	football	321	future	210
file	179	for	38	**G**	
fill	92	force	430	gain	272
film	15	foreign	107	game	8
final	303	foreigner	108	garbage	236
finally	91	forest	352	garden	128
find	41	forget	80	gardener	419
fine	104	forgive	383	garlic	356

索
引

索　引

gate	26	grape	348	hardly	281
gather	276	grass	186	hat	143
general	364	gray	136	hate	144
generous	341	great	46	head	3
gentle	355	green	37	headache	208
gentleman	355	greet	445	health	120
get	28	ground	80	healthy	120
ghost	171	group	55	hear	62
giant	185	grow	71	heart	92
gift	152	growth	266	heat	108
giraffe	347	guard	327	heaven	431
girl	1	guava	348	heavy	116
give	40	guess	142	height	140
glad	169	guest	365	help	116
glass	139	guide	314	helpful	117
glasses	139	guitar	164	hen	27
glove	202	gun	449	hero	360
glue	343	guy	214	hide	201
go	1	gymnasium	374	high	14
goal	394	**H**		highly	243
goat	347	habit	182	highway	346
god	162	hair	110	hike	331
goddess	162	haircut	307	hill	119
gold	363	half	78	hip	373
golden	363	hall	298	hippopotamus	347
goose	291	ham	174	historical	404
govern	234	hamburger	319	history	76
government	234	hand	11	hit	117
grade	178	handle	406	hobby	182
gradual	446	handsome	320	hold	54
grain	437	hang	215	hole	305
gram	442	happen	72	holiday	159
grand	419	happiness	169	home	112
grandfather	30	happy	169	homework	175
grandmother	30	hard	17	honest	216

honey	24	impressive	407	island	183
hop	439	improve	412	item	221
hope	97	improvement	412	**J**	
horse	123	inch	126	jacket	154
hospital	114	include	244	jam	350
host	365	income	373	jeans	175
hot	13	incorrect	154	job	71
hotel	205	increase	230	jog	334
hour	32	indeed	384	join	103
house	49	independence	292	joint	448
housewife	49	independent	292	joke	164
how	45	indicate	435	journal	343
however	202	individual	298	joy	152
huge	423	industry	253	judge	396
human	298	influence	252	judgment	397
humble	452	ink	349	juice	175
hundred	34	insect	27	jump	143
hungry	166	inside	125	just	43
hunt	350	insist	404	justice	397
hunter	350	instance	409	**K**	
hurry	352	instant	409	keep	54
hurt	164	instead	296	keeper	454
husband	79	instruction	389	ketchup	319
I		instrument	437	key	133
ice	159	interest	62	kick	161
idea	114	interested	62	kid	9
ideal	297	interesting	62	kill	104
identity	418	internal	435	kilogram	442
ignore	453	international	228	kind	177
ill	306	internet	359	kindness	177
image	375	interview	200	king	121
imagine	375	introduce	315	kiss	169
importance	238	introduction	315	kitchen	184
important	16	invite	211	kite	176
impossible	64	iron	376	knee	6

索 引

knife	137	left	86	lone	421
knock	205	leg	6	lonely	201
know	148	legal	397	long	2
knowledge	148	lemon	185	look	124
L		lend	321	lose	73
lack	259	length	386	loss	272
lady	355	lens	454	lot	99
ladybug	430	less	83	loud	170
lake	142	lesson	146	love	21
lamb	351	let	57	lovely	201
lamp	165	letter	20	low	14
land	82	level	80	lower	387
landing	82	liberal	433	luck	327
lane	436	library	4	lucky	166
language	183	lid	451	lunch	165
lantern	289	lie	88	lunchtime	165
lap	373	life	43	**M**	
large	185	lift	259	machine	205
last	200	light	135	mad	155
late	131	like	42	magazine	332
later	90	likely	258	magic	147
latest	372	limit	238	mail	154
latter	275	line	56	main	193
laugh	9	link	447	maintain	435
law	397	lion	168	major	367
lawyer	209	lip	125	make	17
lay	435	liquid	311	male	369
lazy	175	list	102	man	1
lead	67	listen	62	manage	261
leader	67	listener	323	management	261
leadership	407	little	139	manager	261
leaf	318	live	43	mango	349
learn	76	liver	454	manner	263
least	48	load	359	map	163
leave	50	local	235	mark	217

market	98	meter	442	move	58
marriage	273	method	237	movement	58
married	109	middle	134	movie	15
marry	273	midnight	308	Mr. / mister	148
mask	258	mile	442	Mrs.	148
mass	416	military	241	Ms.	148
master	414	milk	15	mud	163
mat	410	million	182	mug	356
match	274	mind	66	museum	209
mate	400	mine	203	music	164
material	244	minor	367	musical	282
mathematics	178	minority	367	musician	283
matter	65	minute	32	**N**	
mature	411	mirror	309	nail	290
maybe	69	miss	124	name	64
meal	172	mistake	147	narrow	376
mean	63	mix	354	nation	437
meaning	274	mixture	355	national	186
means	274	model	265	natural	257
measure	386	modern	212	nature	93
measurement	386	moment	73	naughty	371
meat	146	money	35	near	75
medical	306	monkey	108	nearby	403
medicine	206	month	207	nearly	404
medium	197	mood	357	necessary	237
meet	65	moon	19	neck	127
meeting	65	mop	338	necklace	341
melody	446	morning	192	need	60
member	196	most	48	needle	441
membership	428	mother	30	negative	388
memory	382	motion	429	neighbor	345
mention	358	motorcycle	340	neither	282
menu	190	mountain	119	nephew	355
message	313	mouse	170	nerve	268
metal	376	mouth	125	nervous	268

net	209	offer	225	panda	348
network	359	office	72	pants	175
never	132	officer	72	papaya	348
new	27	official	383	paper	132
news	119	often	132	pardon	288
newspaper	119	oil	128	parent	178
next	25	old	26	park	122
nice	32	once	61	parking	122
niece	356	online	215	part	51
night	192	only	23	participate	444
nod	373	open	4	particular	269
noise	153	operate	425	partner	273
noisy	153	operator	425	party	212
none	282	opinion	266	pass	70
noodle	340	orange	171	password	433
noon	192	order	61	past	120
nor	443	ordinary	385	paste	343
north	102	organ	453	path	436
northern	265	organization	253	patient	305
nose	6	origin	256	pattern	265
note	98	outside	125	pay	68
notebook	312	own	43	payment	68
notice	133	owner	328	peace	256
novel	340	**P**		peaceful	256
now	28	pack	199	peach	348
number	53	package	200	peak	378
nurse	166	page	116	pear	348
nut	356	pain	303	pen	22
O		painful	303	pencil	22
obey	242	paint	127	people	69
object	406	painting	339	per	394
obvious	424	pair	134	perfect	297
occur	262	pajamas	366	perhaps	69
ocean	333	pale	250	period	234
o'clock	32	pan	322	person	69

personal	248	poem	284	prepare	96
personality	248	poet	284	present	152
pet	174	poetry	284	president	228
photograph	155	point	56	press	300
phrase	272	poison	426	pressure	301
piano	164	police	112	pretty	137
pick	204	policeman	349	price	103
picnic	210	policy	432	pride	234
picture	193	polite	185	priest	431
pie	168	pond	142	primary	366
piece	92	pool	115	prince	309
pig	10	poor	111	principal	453
pillow	366	pop	422	principle	453
pin	219	popcorn	159	print	360
pink	185	popular	198	printer	360
pipe	222	population	415	prison	450
pizza	300	pork	351	prisoner	450
place	36	port	440	private	248
plain	364	pose	401	prize	261
plan	114	position	401	probably	181
planet	141	positive	387	problem	54
plant	107	possibility	424	produce	238
plate	160	possible	64	production	239
platform	368	post	301	program	199
play	69	postcard	302	progress	412
player	70	pot	106	project	285
playground	337	potato	163	promise	384
pleasant	331	pound	406	proper	421
please	122	power	64	propose	417
pleased	122	powerful	341	protect	327
pleasing	122	practice	111	protective	328
pleasure	209	praise	410	proud	215
plus	451	pray	431	prove	341
pm	156	prayer	431	provide	225
pocket	146	prefer	305	public	73

pudding	278	rat	403	requirement	408
pull	109	rather	266	respect	276
pumpkin	356	reach	67	respond	424
punish	444	read	96	responsible	406
punishment	444	ready	104	rest	101
pupil	312	real	77	restaurant	189
puppy	325	reality	255	restroom	287
purple	325	realize	255	result	235
purpose	395	really	77	return	285
push	109	reason	16	review	413
put	55	receive	285	rice	167
puzzle	401	recent	253	rich	133

Q

		record	244	riches	284
quality	263	recover	306	ride	116
quantity	263	red	37	right	85
quarter	204	refrigerator	322	ring	153
queen	121	refuse	245	rise	89
question	54	regard	228	river	99
quick	119	region	294	road	33
quiet	135	regular	404	robot	173
quite	83	reject	245	rock	126
quiz	307	relate	448	rocky	415

R

		relation	264	role	246
rabbit	12	relationship	264	roll	130
race	120	relative	198	roof	393
radio	114	religion	431	room	62
railroad	368	remember	80	rooster	291
rain	25	remove	267	root	151
rainbow	176	rent	267	rope	170
raincoat	318	repair	267	rose	171
rainy	179	repeat	219	round	160
raise	89	reply	405	row	145
range	263	report	93	royal	365
rapid	387	reporter	200	rub	422
rare	370	require	408	rubber	423

rude	371	seafood	334	shame	374
rule	103	search	336	shape	117
ruler	104	season	123	share	212
run	60	seat	144	shark	333
runner	334	second	150	sharp	130
S		secondary	366	sheep	167
sad	169	secret	248	sheet	375
sadness	170	secretary	194	shelf	328
safe	143	section	244	shell	401
safety	361	see	95	shine	286
sail	227	seed	147	ship	18
sailor	227	seek	336	shirt	168
salad	208	seem	358	shock	290
sale	110	seesaw	338	shoe	12
salesperson	423	seldom	281	shoot	292
salt	147	select	417	shop	117
salty	361	selection	417	shopkeeper	454
same	113	self	296	shore	441
sample	277	selfish	296	short	3
sand	310	sell	7	shorts	175
sandwich	319	send	154	shot	293
satisfy	328	sense	297	shoulder	127
save	108	sensitive	297	shout	137
saw	432	sentence	153	show	49
say	23	separate	375	shower	161
scare	285	serious	190	shut	271
scared	285	servant	414	shy	269
scene	247	serve	414	sick	191
schedule	286	service	64	side	57
school	50	set	63	sidewalk	402
science	187	settle	415	sight	126
scooter	340	settlement	415	sign	220
score	338	several	63	silence	364
screen	359	sex	369	silent	364
sea	18	shake	127	silly	310

471

silver	363	soap	287	spell	171
similar	251	soccer	321	spelling	335
simple	97	social	226	spend	193
simply	249	society	226	spider	310
since	59	sock	228	spirit	247
sing	140	soda	319	spoon	324
singer	140	sofa	191	sport	321
single	257	soft	225	spot	313
sir	162	soil	419	spread	309
sister	30	soldier	219	spring	105
sit	59	solution	407	square	190
size	105	solve	407	stage	246
skill	323	sometimes	132	stair	162
skilled	324	somewhat	421	stamp	302
skin	357	somewhere	195	stand	59
skirt	176	son	178	standard	390
sky	18	song	140	star	34
sleep	191	soon	89	start	52
sleepy	411	sore	192	state	427
slide	338	sorry	46	statement	427
slim	156	sort	434	station	99
slip	369	soul	431	stay	94
slipper	370	sound	85	steak	351
slow	118	soup	170	steel	376
small	21	sour	374	step	349
smart	168	source	256	stick	343
smell	159	south	102	still	44
smile	8	southern	265	stomachache	305
smoke	162	soybean	357	stone	233
smooth	370	space	95	stop	14
snack	361	speak	181	store	117
snail	430	speaker	323	storm	381
snake	155	special	79	story	17
snow	212	speech	323	straight	190
snowy	331	speed	346	strange	133

stranger	330	surf	334	tear	339
strawberry	348	surface	253	technology	374
stream	454	surprise	134	teenager	216
street	33	surprised	134	teens	294
stress	301	surprising	134	telephone	177
stretch	377	survival	418	television	31
strict	372	survive	418	tell	47
strike	290	swallow	441	temperature	381
string	222	sweater	335	temple	220
strong	90	sweep	338	tennis	183
struggle	378	sweet	144	term	234
student	33	swim	333	terrible	194
study	204	swimsuit	334	terrorism	443
stupid	168	swing	337	terrorist	443
style	260	switch	450	test	177
subject	208	symbol	444	text	312
subway	402	system	419	textbook	312
succeed	284	**T**		thank	46
success	284	table	24	theater	195
successful	193	tail	162	then	40
such	241	take	39	therefore	245
sudden	409	tale	420	thick	211
sugar	147	talk	113	thief	373
suggest	233	tall	140	thin	211
suit	332	tape	218	thing	35
suitable	332	target	395	think	42
sun	19	task	313	third	151
sunny	179	taste	138	thirsty	345
super	242	tax	432	though	188
supermarket	148	taxicab	168	thought	229
supper	242	tea	12	thousand	34
supply	225	teach	33	throat	208
support	264	teacher	33	through	189
suppose	229	team	195	throughout	424
sure	88	teapot	322	throw	100

索引

thunder	381	tour	314	type	149
thus	419	toward(s)	295	typhoon	381
ticket	166	towel	216	typical	421
tidy	142	town	206	**U**	
tie	145	toy	173	ugly	320
tiger	169	track	436	umbrella	318
till	420	trade	276	unable	81
time	39	tradition	404	uncertain	84
tiny	423	traditional	404	uncle	30
tip	96	traffic	189	understand	184
tire	340	train	108	uniform	219
tired	157	training	109	unit	396
tiring	157	trap	438	universe	383
tissue	357	trash	236	university	383
title	400	travel	314	unless	269
toast	278	treasure	340	until	206
today	180	treat	195	upload	360
toe	12	treatment	195	upon	414
tofu	357	tree	23	upper	387
together	197	trial	434	upset	393
toilet	184	triangle	271	upstairs	428
tomato	163	trick	279	use	42
tomorrow	180	trip	112	used	240
tone	429	trouble	100	useful	42
tongue	330	truck	113	useless	42
tonight	180	true	258	user	240
tool	143	truly	84	usual	245
tooth	197	trust	345	usually	132
toothache	316	truth	259	**V**	
toothbrush	316	try	57	vacation	325
top	105	T-shirt	168	valley	378
topic	184	tube	448	valuable	394
total	118	turn	53	value	228
totally	118	turtle	333	vegetable	167
touch	124	twice	221	victory	382

video	199	weight	279	woman	1
view	266	welcome	166	wonder	296
village	227	well	45	wonderful	181
violin	164	west	103	wood	352
visit	148	western	266	wooden	363
visitor	149	wet	216	wool	322
voice	85	whale	333	word	153
vote	377	whatever	416	work	45

W

		wheel	372	workbook	312
waist	373	whenever	231	worker	45
wait	207	wherever	231	world	174
waiter	281	whether	71	worldwide	174
wake	217	while	51	worm	310
walk	83	whisper	402	worry	130
wall	205	white	136	worse	232
wallet	271	whoever	416	worst	232
want	13	whole	278	worth	391
war	304	whom	267	wound	280
warm	138	wide	109	write	178
wash	287	width	386	writer	179
waste	237	wife	79	wrong	86

Y

watch	95	wild	345		
water	57	will	38	yam	356
watermelon	349	willing	391	yard	184
wave	123	win	72	year	207
way	41	wind	129	yellow	37
weak	90	window	26	yesterday	180
wealth	283	windy	331	yet	72
wear	101	wine	318	young	26
weather	179	wing	354	youth	293
wedding	273	wire	389	yummy	177

Z

week	183	wise	208		
weekday	342	wish	97	zebra	347
weekend	183	within	240	zero	173
weigh	279	wolf	347	zoo	108

索引

Cardinal Numbers　基數

① **one** [wʌn] 一
② **two** [tu] 二
③ **three** [θri] 三
④ **four** [fɔr] 四
⑤ **five** [faɪv] 五
⑥ **six** [sɪks] 六
⑦ **seven** [ˋsɛvən] 七
⑧ **eight** [et] 八
⑨ **nine** [naɪn] 九
⑩ **ten** [tɛn] 十
⑪ **eleven** [ɪˋlɛvən] 十一
⑫ **twelve** [twɛlv] 十二
⑬ **thirteen** [θɝˋtin] 十三
⑭ **fourteen** [fɔrˋtin] 十四
⑮ **fifteen** [fɪfˋtin] 十五
⑯ **sixteen** [sɪksˋtin] 十六
⑰ **seventeen** [ˌsɛvənˋtin] 十七
⑱ **eighteen** [eˋtin] 十八
⑲ **nineteen** [naɪnˋtin] 十九
⑳ **twenty** [ˋtwɛntɪ] 二十
㉑ **twenty-one** [ˋtwɛntɪˌwʌn] 二十一

㉒ **twenty-two** [ˋtwɛntɪˌtu] 二十二
㉓ **twenty-three** [ˋtwɛntɪˌθri] 二十三
㉔ **twenty-four** [ˋtwɛntɪˌfɔr] 二十四
㉕ **twenty-five** [ˋtwɛntɪˌfaɪv] 二十五
㉖ **thirty** [ˋθɝtɪ] 三十
㉗ **thirty-one** [ˋθɝtɪˌwʌn] 三十一
㉘ **thirty-two** [ˋθɝtɪˌtu] 三十二
㉙ **thirty-three** [ˋθɝtɪˌθri] 三十三
㉚ **thirty-four** [ˋθɝtɪˌfɔr] 三十四
㉛ **forty** [ˋfɔrtɪ] 四十
㉜ **fifty** [ˋfɪftɪ] 五十
㉝ **sixty** [ˋsɪkstɪ] 六十
㉞ **seventy** [ˋsɛvəntɪ] 七十
㉟ **eighty** [ˋetɪ] 八十
㊱ **ninety** [ˋnaɪntɪ] 九十
㊲ **one hundred** [wʌn ˋhʌndrəd] 一百
㊳ **one thousand** [wʌn ˋθauzn̩d] 一千
㊴ **one million** [wʌn ˋmɪljən] 一百萬
㊵ **one billion** [wʌn ˋbɪljən] 十億

Ordinal Numbers　序數

① **first** [fɝst] 第一
② **second** [ˋsɛkənd] 第二
③ **third** [θɝd] 第三
④ **fourth** [fɔrθ] 第四
⑤ **fifth** [fɪfθ] 第五
⑥ **sixth** [sɪksθ] 第六
⑦ **seventh** [ˋsɛvənθ] 第七
⑧ **eighth** [eθ] 第八

⑨ **ninth** [naɪnθ] 第九
⑩ **tenth** [tɛnθ] 第十
⑪ **eleventh** [ɪˋlɛvənθ] 第十一
⑫ **twelfth** [twɛlfθ] 第十二
⑬ **thirteenth** [θɝˋtinθ] 第十三
⑭ **fourteenth** [fɔrˋtinθ] 第十四
⑮ **fifteenth** [fɪfˋtinθ] 第十五
⑯ **sixteenth** [sɪksˋtinθ] 第十六

⑰ **seventeenth** [ˌsɛvənˈtinθ] 第十七

⑱ **eighteenth** [eˈtinθ] 第十八

⑲ **nineteenth** [naɪnˈtinθ] 第十九

⑳ **twentieth** [ˈtwɛntɪɪθ] 第二十

㉑ **twenty-first** [ˈtwɛntɪˌfɜst]
第二十一

㉒ **twenty-second** [ˈtwɛntɪˌsɛkənd]
第二十二

㉓ **twenty-third** [ˈtwɛntɪˌθɜd]
第二十三

㉔ **twenty-fourth** [ˈtwɛntɪˌforθ]
第二十四

㉕ **twenty-fifth** [ˈtwɛntɪˌfɪfθ]
第二十五

㉖ **thirtieth** [ˈθɜtɪɪθ] 第三十

㉗ **fortieth** [ˈfɔrtɪɪθ] 第四十

㉘ **fiftieth** [ˈfɪftɪɪθ] 第五十

㉙ **sixtieth** [ˈsɪkstɪɪθ] 第六十

㉚ **seventieth** [ˈsɛvəntɪɪθ] 第七十

㉛ **eightieth** [ˈetɪɪθ] 第八十

㉜ **ninetieth** [ˈnaɪntɪɪθ] 第九十

㉝ **hundredth** [ˈhʌndrədθ] 第一百

㉞ **thousandth** [ˈθauzṇdθ] 第一千

㉟ **millionth** [ˈmɪljənθ] 第一百萬

㊱ **billionth** [ˈbɪljənθ] 第十億

☐ Days of the Week 一星期

❶ **Monday** [ˈmʌnde] / **Mon.** 星期一

❷ **Tuesday** [ˈtjuzde] / **Tue.** 星期二

❸ **Wednesday** [ˈwɛnzde] / **Wed.**
星期三

❹ **Thursday** [ˈθɜzde] / **Thu.** 星期四

❺ **Friday** [ˈfraɪde] / **Fri.** 星期五

❻ **Saturday** [ˈsætɚde] / **Sat.** 星期六

❼ **Sunday** [ˈsʌnde] / **Sun.** 星期日

☐ Months 月份

❶ **January** [ˈdʒænjʊˌɛrɪ] / **Jan.**
一月

❷ **February** [ˈfɛbruˌɛrɪ] / **Feb.**
二月

❸ **March** [mɑrtʃ] / **Mar.** 三月

❹ **April** [ˈeprəl] / **Apr.** 四月

❺ **May** [me] 五月

❻ **June** [dʒun] / **Jun.** 六月

❼ **July** [dʒuˈlaɪ] / **Jul.** 七月

❽ **August** [ˈɔgəst] / **Aug.** 八月

❾ **September** [sɛpˈtɛmbɚ] / **Sep.**
九月

❿ **October** [ɑkˈtobɚ] / **Oct.** 十月

⓫ **November** [noˈvɛmbɚ] / **Nov.**
十一月

⓬ **December** [dɪˈsɛmbɚ] / **Dec.**
十二月

Seasons　季節

❶ spring [ˋsprɪŋ] 春天
❷ summer [ˋsʌmɚ] 夏天
❸ autumn [ˋɔtəm] / fall [fɔl] 秋天
❹ winter [ˋwɪntɚ] 冬天

Countries and Areas　國家與地區

❶ Argentina [͵ɑrdʒənˋtinə] 阿根廷
❷ Australia [ɔˋstrelɪə] 澳洲
❸ Brazil [brəˋzɪl] 巴西
❹ Canada [ˋkænədə] 加拿大
❺ China [ˋtʃaɪnə] 中國
❻ France [fræns] 法國
❼ Germany [ˋdʒɝmənɪ] 德國
❽ India [ˋɪndɪə] 印度
❾ Indonesia [͵ɪndoˋniʒə] 印尼
❿ Italy [ˋɪtəli] 義大利
⓫ Japan [dʒəˋpæn] 日本
⓬ Malaysia [məˋleʒə] 馬來西亞
⓭ Mexico [ˋmɛksɪ͵ko] 墨西哥
⓮ (the) Philippines [(ðə) ˋfɪlə͵pinz] 菲律賓
⓯ Republic of China [rɪˋpʌblɪk əv ˋtʃaɪnə] 中華民國

⓰ Russia [ˋrʌʃə] 俄羅斯
⓱ Saudi Arabia [͵saʊdɪ əˋrebɪə] 沙烏地阿拉伯
⓲ Singapore [ˋsɪŋgə͵por] 新加坡
⓳ South Africa [͵saʊθ ˋæfrɪkə] 南非
⓴ South Korea [͵saʊθ koˋrɪə] 南韓
㉑ Spain [spen] 西班牙
㉒ Taiwan [͵taɪˋwan] 臺灣
㉓ Thailand [ˋtaɪlənd] 泰國
㉔ Turkey [ˋtɝkɪ] 土耳其
㉕ (the) United Kingdom [(ðə) juˋnaɪtɪd ˋkɪŋdəm] 英國
㉖ (the) United States [(ðə) juˋnaɪtɪd ˋstets] 美國
㉗ Vietnam [͵vjɛtˋnæm] 越南

Continents　大陸；洲

❶ Africa [ˋæfrɪkə] 非洲
❷ Antarctica [ænˋtɑrktɪkə] 南極洲
❸ Asia [ˋeʒə] 亞洲
❹ Australia [ɔˋstrelɪə] 澳洲
❺ Europe [ˋjʊrəp] 歐洲
❻ North America [͵nɔrθ əˋmɛrɪkə] 北美洲
❼ South America [͵saʊθ əˋmɛrɪkə] 南美洲

☐ The Principal Oceans of the World　世界主要海洋

❶ **(the) Arctic Ocean**
[(ði) ˈɑrktɪk ˈoʃən] 北極海

❷ **(the) Atlantic Ocean**
[(ði) ətˈlæntɪk ˈoʃən] 大西洋

❸ **(the) Indian Ocean**
[(ði) ˈɪndɪən ˈoʃən] 印度洋

❹ **(the) Pacific Ocean**
[(ðə) pəˈsɪfɪk ˈoʃən] 太平洋

☐ Religions　宗教

❶ **Buddhism** [ˈbudɪzəm] /
Buddhist [ˈbudɪst] 佛教 / 佛教的；
佛教徒

❷ **Catholicism** [kəˈθɑləˌsɪzəm] /
Catholic [ˈkæθəlɪk] 天主教 /
天主教的；天主教徒

❸ **Christianity** [ˌkrɪstʃɪˈænətɪ] /
Christian [ˈkrɪstʃən] 基督教 /
基督教的；基督徒

❹ **Eastern Orthodoxy**
[ˈistən ˈɔrθəˌdɑksɪ] /
Eastern Orthodox
[ˈistən ˈɔrθəˌdɑks] 東正教 / 東正教的

❺ **Hinduism** [ˈhɪnduˌɪzəm] /
Hindu [ˈhɪndu] 印度教 / 印度教的；
印度教徒

❻ **Islam** [ˈɪsləm] / **Muslim**
[ˈmʌzˌlɪm / ˈmuzˌlɪm] 伊斯蘭教，回教 /
回教的；回教徒

❼ **Judaism** [ˈdʒudɪˌɪzəm] /
Jewish [ˈdʒuɪʃ] 猶太教 / 猶太教的；
猶太人

❽ **Taoism** [ˈtauˌɪzəm] / **Taoist**
[ˈtauɪst] 道教 / 道教的；道教徒

☐ Parts of Speech　詞性

❶ **adjective** [ˈædʒɪktɪv] / *adj.* 形容詞

❷ **adverb** [ˈædvɚb] / *adv.* 副詞

❸ **article** [ˈɑrtɪkḷ] / *art.* 冠詞

❹ **auxiliary** [ɔgˈzɪljərɪ] / *aux.* 助動詞

❺ **conjunction** [kənˈdʒʌŋkʃən] /
conj. 連接詞

❻ **noun** [naun] / *n.* 名詞

❼ **preposition** [ˌprɛpəˈzɪʃən] / *prep.*
介詞

❽ **pronoun** [ˈpronaun] / *pron.* 代名詞

❾ **verb** [vɝb] / *v.* 動詞

國家圖書館出版品預行編目（CIP）資料

英文字彙王：基礎單字 2000 Levels 1 & 2
／賴世雄作. -- 初版. -- 臺北市：
常春藤有聲出版股份有限公司, 2022.01
面；　公分.--（英文字彙王系列；E62）
ISBN 978-626-95430-2-1（平裝）
1. 英語　2. 詞彙
805.12　　　　　　　　　　110020678

英文字彙王系列【E62】
英文字彙王：基礎單字 2000 Levels 1 & 2

總 編 審	賴世雄
終　　審	李　端
執行編輯	許嘉華
編輯小組	常春藤中外編輯群
設計組長	王玥琦
封面設計	胡毓芸
排版設計	王穎緁・林桂旭
錄　　音	劉書吟
播音老師	Tom Brink・Terri Pebsworth
法律顧問	北辰著作權事務所蕭雄淋律師
出 版 者	常春藤數位出版股份有限公司
地　　址	臺北市忠孝西路一段 33 號 5 樓
電　　話	(02) 2331-7600
傳　　真	(02) 2381-0918
網　　址	www.ivy.com.tw
電子信箱	service@ivy.com.tw
郵政劃撥	50463568
戶　　名	常春藤數位出版股份有限公司
定　　價	350 元

100009 臺北市忠孝西路一段 33 號 5 樓

常春藤有聲出版股份有限公司　行政組　啟

常春藤　www.ivy.com.tw
愛上英語的第一站

常春藤 英語集團

讀者問卷【E62】
英文字彙王：基礎單字 2000 Levels 1 & 2

感謝您購買本書！為使我們對讀者的服務能夠更加完善，請您詳細填寫本問卷各欄後，寄回本公司或傳真至（02）2381-0918，或掃描 QR Code 填寫線上問卷，我們將於收到後七個工作天內贈送「常春藤網路書城熊贈點 50 點（一點 = 一元，使用期限 90 天）」給您（每書每人限贈一次），也懇請您繼續支持。若有任何疑問，請儘速與客服人員聯絡，客服電話：（02）2331-7600 分機 11～13，謝謝您！

線上填寫
免郵寄最環保

姓　　名：＿＿＿＿＿＿＿　性別：＿＿＿　生日：＿＿＿年＿＿月＿＿日

聯絡電話：＿＿＿＿＿＿＿　E-mail：＿＿＿＿＿＿＿＿＿＿＿＿＿

聯絡地址：□□□□□□
＿＿＿＿＿＿＿＿＿＿＿＿＿＿＿＿＿＿＿＿＿＿＿＿＿

教育程度：□國小　□國中　□高中　□大專／大學　□研究所含以上

職　　業：**1** □學生

　　　　　2 社會人士：□工　□商　□服務業　□軍警公職　□教職　□其他＿＿＿＿

1 您從何處得知本書：□書店　□常春藤網路書城　□FB／IG／Line@ 社群平臺推薦
□學校購買　□親友推薦　□常春藤雜誌　□其他＿＿＿＿＿＿＿＿＿＿＿

2 您購得本書的管道：□書店　□常春藤網路書城　□博客來　□其他＿＿＿＿＿＿

3 最滿意本書的特點依序是（限定三項）：□字詞解析　□編排方式　□印刷　□音檔朗讀
□封面　□售價　□信任品牌　□其他＿＿＿＿＿＿＿＿＿＿＿＿＿＿

4 您對本書建議改進的三點依序是：□無（都很滿意）□字詞解析　□編排方式　□印刷
□音檔朗讀　□封面　□售價　□其他＿＿＿＿＿＿＿＿＿＿＿＿

原因：＿＿＿＿＿＿＿＿＿＿＿＿＿＿＿＿＿＿＿＿＿＿＿＿＿＿＿＿＿

對本書的其他建議：＿＿＿＿＿＿＿＿＿＿＿＿＿＿＿＿＿＿＿＿＿＿＿

5 希望我們出版哪些主題的書籍：＿＿＿＿＿＿＿＿＿＿＿＿＿＿＿＿＿＿

6 若您發現本書誤植的部分，請告知在：書籍第＿＿＿＿＿頁，第＿＿＿＿行

有錯誤的部分是：＿＿＿＿＿＿＿＿＿＿＿＿＿＿＿＿＿＿＿＿＿＿＿＿

7 對我們的其他建議：＿＿＿＿＿＿＿＿＿＿＿＿＿＿＿＿＿＿＿＿＿＿

感謝您寶貴的意見，您的支持是我們的動力！　常春藤網路書城 www.